Dick Francis has written forty-one international best-sellers and is widely acclaimed as one of the world's finest thriller writers. His awards include the Crime Writers' Association's Cartier Diamond Dagger for his outstanding contribution to the crime genre, and an honorary Doctorate of Humane Letters from Tufts University of Boston. In 1996 Dick Francis was made a Mystery Writers of America Grand Master for a lifetime's achievement and in 2000 he received a CBE in the Queen's Birthday Honours list.

Dick Francis Omnibus Four

ENQUIRY
RAT RACE
SMOKESCREEN

PAN BOOKS

Enquiry first published 1969 by Michael Joseph Ltd
and published by Pan Books in 1971
Rat Race first published 1970 by Michael Joseph Ltd
and published by Pan Books in 1972
Smokescreen first published 1972 by Michael Joseph Ltd
and published by Pan Books in 1974

This omnibus edition published 2000 by Pan Books
an imprint of Pan Macmillan Ltd
Pan Macmillan, 20 New Wharf Road, London N1 9RR
Basingstoke and Oxford
Associated companies throughout the world
www.panmacmillan.com

ISBN 0 330 48484 2

579864

A CIP catalogue record for this book is available from
the British Library.

Phototypeset by Intype London Ltd
Printed and bound in Great Britain by
Mackays of Chatham plc, Chatham, Kent

ENQUIRY

PART ONE

FEBRUARY

CHAPTER ONE

Yesterday I lost my licence.

To a professional steeplechase jockey, losing his licence and being warned off Newmarket Heath is like being chucked off the medical register, only more so.

Barred from race riding, barred from racecourses. Barred, moreover, from racing stables. Which poses me quite a problem, as I live in one.

No livelihood and maybe no home.

Last night was a right so-and-so, and I prefer to forget those grisly sleepless hours. Shock and bewilderment, the feeling that it couldn't have happened, it was all a mistake ... this lasted until after midnight. And at least the disbelieving stage had had some built-in comfort. The full thudding realization which followed had none at all. My life was lying around like the untidy bits of a smashed teacup, and I was altogether out of glue and rivets.

This morning I got up and percolated some coffee and looked out of the window at the lads bustling around in the yard and mounting and cloppeting away up the road to the Downs, and I got my first real taste of being an outcast.

Fred didn't bellow up at my window as he usually did, 'Going to stay there all day, then?'

This time, I was.

None of the lads looked up ... they more or less kept their eyes studiously right down. They were quiet, too. Dead quiet. I watched Bouncing Bernie heave his ten stone seven on to the gelding I'd been riding lately, and there was something apologetic about the way he lowered his fat bum into the saddle.

And he, too, kept his eyes down.

Tomorrow, I guessed, they'd be themselves again. Tomorrow they'd be curious and ask questions. I understood that they weren't despising me. They were sympathetic. Probably too sympathetic for their own comfort. And embarrassed: that too. And instinctively delicate about looking too soon at the face of total disaster.

When they'd gone I drank my coffee slowly and wondered what to do next. A nasty, very nasty, feeling of emptiness and loss.

The papers had been stuck as usual through my letterbox. I wondered what the boy had thought, knowing what he was delivering. I shrugged. Might as well read what they'd said, the Goddamned pressmen, God bless them.

The *Sporting Life*, short on news, had given us the headlines and the full treatment.

'Cranfield and Hughes Disqualified.'

There was a picture of Cranfield at the top of the page, and halfway down one of me, all smiles, taken the day I won the Hennessy Gold Cup. Some little sub-editor letting his irony loose, I thought sourly, and printing the most cheerful picture he could dig out of the files.

The close-printed inches north and south of my happy face were unrelieved gloom.

' "The Stewards said they were not satisfied with my explanation," Cranfield said. "They have withdrawn my licence. I have no further comment to make." '

Hughes, it was reported, had said almost exactly the same. Hughes, if I remembered correctly, had in fact said nothing whatsoever. Hughes had been too stunned to put one word collectedly after another, and if he had said anything at all it would have been unprintable.

I didn't read all of it. I'd read it all before, about the other people. For 'Cranfield and Hughes' one could substitute any other trainer and jockey who had been warned off. The newspaper reports on these occasions were always the same; totally uninformed. As a racing Enquiry was a private trial the ruling authorities were not obliged to open the proceedings to the public or

7

the Press, and as they were not obliged to, they never did. In fact like many another inward-looking concern they seemed to be permanently engaged in trying to stop too many people from finding out what was really going on.

The *Daily Witness* was equally fog-bound, except that Daddy Leeman had suffered his usual rush of purple prose to the head. According to him:

'Kelly Hughes, until now a leading contender for this season's jump-jockeys' crown, and fifth on the list last year, was sentenced to an indefinite suspension of his licence. Hughes, thirty, left the hearing ten minutes after Cranfield. Looking pale and grim, he confirmed that he had lost his licence, and added "I have no further comment." '

They had remarkable ears, those pressmen.

I put down the paper with a sigh and went into the bedroom to exchange my dressing-gown for trousers and a jersey, and after that I made my bed, and after that I sat on it, staring into space. I had nothing else to do. I had nothing to do for as far ahead as the eye could see. Unfortunately I also had nothing to think about except the Enquiry.

Put baldly, I had lost my licence for losing a race. More precisely, I had ridden a red-hot favourite into second place in the Lemonfizz Crystal Cup at Oxford in the last week of January, and the winner had been an unconsidered outsider. This would have been merely unfortunate, had it not been that both horses were trained by Dexter Cranfield.

The finishing order at the winning post had been greeted with roars of disgust from the stands, and I had been booed all the way to the unsaddling enclosure. Dexter Cranfield had looked worried more than delighted to have taken first and second places in one of the season's big sponsored steeplechases, and the Stewards of the meeting had called us both in to explain. They were not, they announced, satisfied with the explanations. They would refer the matter to the Disciplinary Committee of the Jockey Club.

The Disciplinary Committee, two weeks later, were equally sceptical that the freak result had been an accident. Deliberate fraud on the betting public, they said. Disgraceful, dishonest, disgusting, they said. Racing must keep its good name clean. Not the first time that either of you have been suspected. Severe penalties must be inflicted, as a deterrent to others.

Off, they said. Warned off. And good riddance.

It wouldn't have happened in America, I thought in depression. There, all runners from one stable, or one owner, for that matter, were covered by a bet on any of them. So if the stable's outsider won instead of its favourite, the backers still collected their money. High time the same system crossed the Atlantic. Correction, more than high time; long, long overdue.

The truth of the matter was that Squelch, my red-hot favourite, had been drying under me all the way up the straight, and it was in the miracle class that I'd finished as close as second, and not fifth or sixth. If he hadn't carried so many people's shirts, in fact, I wouldn't have exhausted him as I had. That it had been Cranfield's other runner Cherry Pie who had passed me ten yards from the finish was just the worst sort of luck.

Armed by innocence, and with reason to believe that even if the Oxford Stewards had been swayed by the crowd's hostile reception, the Disciplinary Committee were going to consider the matter in an atmosphere of cool common-sense, I had gone to the Enquiry without a twinge of apprehension.

The atmosphere was cool, all right. Glacial. Their own common-sense was taken for granted by the Stewards. They didn't appear to think that either Cranfield or I had any.

The first faint indication that the sky was about to fall came when they read out a list of nine previous races in which I had ridden a beaten favourite for Cranfield. In six of them, another of Cranfield's runners had won. Cranfield had also had other runners in the other three.

'That means,' said Lord Gowery, 'that this case

before us is by no means the first. It has happened again and again. These results seem to have been unnoticed in the past, but this time you have clearly overstepped the mark.'

I must have stood there looking stupid with my mouth falling open in astonishment, and the trouble was that they obviously thought I was astonished at how much they had dug up to prove my guilt.

'Some of those races were years ago,' I protested. 'Six or seven, some of them.'

'What difference does that make?' asked Lord Gowery. 'They happened.'

'That sort of thing happens to every trainer now and then,' Cranfield said hotly. 'You must know it does.'

Lord Gowery gave him an emotionless stare. It stirred some primeval reaction in my glands, and I could feel the ripple of goose pimples up my spine. He really believes, I thought wildly, he really believes us guilty. It was only then that I realized we had to make a fight of it; and it was already far too late.

I said to Cranfield, 'We should have had that lawyer,' and he gave me an almost frightened glance of agreement.

Shortly before the Lemonfizz the Jockey Club had finally thrown an old autocratic tradition out of the twentieth century and agreed that people in danger of losing their livelihood could be legally represented at their trials, if they wished. The concession was so new

11

that there was no accepted custom to be guided by. One or two people had been acquitted with lawyers' help who would presumably have been acquitted anyway; and if an accused person engaged a lawyer to defend him, he had in all cases to pay the fees himself. The Jockey Club did not award costs to anyone they accused, whether or not they managed to prove themselves innocent.

At first Cranfield had agreed with me that we should find a lawyer, though both of us had been annoyed at having to shell out. Then Cranfield had by chance met at a party the newly elected Disciplinary Steward who was a friend of his, and had reported to me afterwards, 'There's no need for us to go to the expense of a lawyer. Monty Midgely told me in confidence that the Disciplinary Committee think the Oxford Stewards were off their heads reporting us, that he knows the Lemonfizz result was just one of those things, and not to worry, the Enquiry will only be a formality. Ten minutes or so, and it will be over.'

That assurance had been good enough for both of us. We hadn't even seen any cause for alarm when three or four days later Colonel Sir Montague Midgely had turned yellow with jaundice and taken to his bed, and it had been announced that one of the Committee, Lord Gowery, would deputize for him in any Enquiries which might be held in the next few weeks.

Monty Midgely's liver had a lot to answer for. Whatever he had intended, it now seemed all too appallingly clear that Gowery didn't agree.

The Enquiry was held in a large lavishly furnished room in the Portman Square headquarters of the Jockey Club. Four Stewards sat in comfortable armchairs along one side of a polished table with a pile of papers in front of each of them, and a shorthand writer was stationed at a smaller table a little to their right. When Cranfield and I went into the room the shorthand writer was fussing with a tape-recorder, unwinding a lead from the machine which stood on his own table and trailing it across the floor towards the Stewards. He set up a microphone on a stand in front of Lord Gowery, switched it on, blew into it a couple of times, went back to his machine, flicked a few switches, and announced that everything was in order.

Behind the Stewards, across a few yards of plushy dark red carpet, were several more armchairs. Their occupants included the three Stewards who had been unconvinced at Oxford, the Clerk of the Course, the Handicapper who had allotted the Lemonfizz weights, and a pair of Stipendiary Stewards, officials paid by the Jockey Club and acting at meetings as an odd mixture of messenger boys for the Stewards and the industry's private police. It was they who, if they thought there had been an infringement of the rules, brought it to the notice of the Stewards of the meeting concerned, and advised them to hold an Enquiry.

As in any other job, some Stipendiaries were reasonable men and some were not. The Stipe who had been acting at Oxford on Lemonfizz day was notoriously the most difficult of them all.

Cranfield and I were to sit facing the Stewards' table, but several feet from it. For us, too, there were the same luxurious armchairs. Very civilized. Not a hatchet in sight. We sat down, and Cranfield casually crossed his legs, looking confident and relaxed.

We were far from soul-mates, Cranfield and I. He had inherited a fortune from his father, an ex-soap manufacturer who had somehow failed to acquire a coveted peerage in spite of donating madly to every fashionable cause in sight, and the combination of wealth and disappointed social ambition had turned Cranfield *fils* into a roaring snob. To him, since he employed me, I was a servant; and he didn't know how to treat servants.

He was, however, a pretty good trainer. Better still, he had rich friends who could afford good horses. I had ridden for him semi-regularly for nearly eight years, and although at first I had resented his snobbish little ways, I had eventually grown up enough to find them amusing. We operated strictly as a business team, even after all that time. Not a flicker of friendship. He would have been outraged at the very idea, and I didn't like him enough to think it a pity.

He was twenty years older than me, a tallish, thin Anglo-Saxon type with thin fine mousy hair, greyish-blue eyes with short fair lashes, a well-developed straight nose, and aggressively perfect teeth. His bone structure was of the type acceptable to the social circle in which he tried to move, but the lines his outlook on life had etched in his skin were a warning to anyone looking for tolerance or generosity. Cranfield was mean-minded by habit and open handed only to those who could lug him upwards. In all his dealings with those he considered his inferiors he left behind a turbulent wake of dislike and resentment. He was charming to his friends, polite in public to his wife, and his three teenage children echoed his delusions of superiority with pitiful faithfulness.

Cranfield had remarked to me some days before the Enquiry that the Oxford Stewards were all good chaps and that two of them had personally apologized to him for having to send the case on to the Disciplinary Committee. I nodded without answering. Cranfield must have known as well as I did that all three of the Oxford Stewards had been elected for social reasons only; that one of them couldn't read a number board at five paces, that another had inherited his late uncle's string of racehorses but not his expert knowledge, and that the third had been heard to ask his trainer which

15

his own horse was, during the course of a race. Not one of the three could read a race at anything approaching the standard of a racecourse commentator. Good chaps they might well be, but as judges, frightening.

'We will show the film of the race,' Lord Gowery said.

They showed it, projecting from the back of the room on to a screen on the wall behind Cranfield and me. We turned our armchairs round to watch it. The Stipendiary Steward from Oxford, a fat pompous bully, stood by the screen, pointing out Squelch with a long baton.

'This is the horse in question,' he said, as the horses lined up for the start. I reflected mildly that if the Stewards knew their job they would have seen the film several times already, and would know which was Squelch without needing to have him pointed out.

The Stipe more or less indicated Squelch all the way round. It was an unremarkable race, run to a well-tried pattern: hold back at the start, letting someone else make the pace; ease forwards to fourth place and settle there for two miles or more; move smoothly to the front coming towards the second last fence, and press on home regardless. If the horse liked that sort of race, and if he were good enough, he would win.

Squelch hated to be ridden any other way. Squelch was, on his day, good enough. It just hadn't been his day.

The film showed Squelch taking the lead coming into the second last fence. He rolled a bit on landing, a sure sign of tiredness. I'd had to pick him up and urge him into the last, and it was obvious on the film. Away from the last, towards the winning post, he'd floundered about beneath me, and if I hadn't been ruthless he'd have slowed to a trot. Cherry Pie, at the finish, came up surprisingly fast and passed him as if he'd been standing still.

The film flicked off abruptly and someone put the lights on again. I thought that the film was conclusive and that that would be the end of it.

'You didn't use your whip,' Lord Gowery said accusingly.

'No, sir,' I agreed. 'Squelch shies away from the whip. He has to be ridden with the hands.'

'You were making no effort to ride him out.'

'Indeed I was, sir. He was dead tired, you can see on the film.'

'All I can see on the film is that you were making absolutely no effort to win. You were sitting there with your arms still, making no effort whatsoever.'

I stared at him. 'Squelch isn't an easy horse to ride, sir. He'll always do his best but only if he isn't upset. He has to be ridden quietly. He stops if he's hit. He'll only respond to being squeezed, and to small flicks on the reins, and to his jockey's voice.'

17

'That's quite right,' said Cranfield piously. 'I always give Hughes orders not to treat the horse roughly.'

As if he hadn't heard a word, Lord Gowery said, 'Hughes didn't pick up his whip.'

He looked enquiringly at the two Stewards flanking him, as if to collect their opinions. The one on his left, a youngish man who had ridden as an amateur, nodded non-committally. The other one was asleep.

I suspected Gowery kicked him under the table. He woke up with a jerk, said, 'Eh? Yes, definitely,' and eyed me suspiciously.

It's a farce, I thought incredulously. The whole thing's a bloody farce.

Gowery nodded, satisfied. 'Hughes never picked up his whip.'

The fat bullying Stipe was oozing smugness. 'I am sure you will find this next film relevant, sir.'

'Quite,' agreed Gowery. 'Show it now.'

'Which film is this?' Cranfield enquired.

Gowery said, 'This film shows Squelch winning at Reading on January 3rd.'

Cranfield reflected. 'I was not at Reading on that day.'

'No,' agreed Gowery. 'We understand you went to the Worcester meeting instead.' He made it sound suspicious instead of perfectly normal. Cranfield had run a hot young hurdler at Worcester and had wanted to see how he shaped. Squelch, the established star, needed no supervision.

The lights went out again. The Stipe used his baton to point out Kelly Hughes riding a race in Squelch's distinctive colours of black and white chevrons and a black cap. Not at all the same sort of race as the Lemon-fizz Crystal Cup. I'd gone to the front early to give myself a clear view of the fences, pulled back to about third place for a breather at midway, and forced to the front again only after the last fence, swinging my whip energetically down the horse's shoulder and urging him vigorously with my arms.

The film stopped, the lights went on, and there was a heavy accusing silence. Cranfield turned towards me, frowning.

'You will agree,' said Gowery ironically, 'that you used your whip, Hughes.'

'Yes, sir,' I said. 'Which race did you say that was?'

'The last race at Reading,' he said irritably. 'Don't pretend you don't know.'

'I agree that the film you've just shown was the last race at Reading, sir. But Squelch didn't run in the last race at Reading. The horse in that film was Wanderlust. He belongs to Mr Kessel, like Squelch does, so the colours are the same, and both horses are by the same sire, which accounts for them looking similar, but the horse you've just shown is Wanderlust. Who does, as you saw, respond well if you wave a whip at him.'

19

There was dead silence. It was Cranfield who broke it, clearing his throat.

'Hughes is quite right. That is Wanderlust.'

He hadn't realized it, I thought in amusement, until I'd pointed it out. It's all too easy for people to believe what they're told.

There was a certain amount of hurried whispering going on. I didn't help them. They could sort it out for themselves.

Eventually Lord Gowery said, 'Has anyone got a form book?' and an official near the door went out to fetch one. Gowery opened it and took a long look at the Reading results.

'It seems,' he said heavily, 'that we have the wrong film. Squelch ran in the sixth race at Reading, which is of course usually the last. However, it now appears that on that day there were seven races, the Novice Chase having been divided and run in two halves, at the beginning and end of the day. Wanderlust won the *seventh* race. A perfectly understandable mix-up, I am afraid.'

I didn't think I would help my cause by saying that I thought it a disgraceful mix-up, if not criminal.

'Could we now, sir,' I asked politely, 'see the right film? The one that Squelch won.'

Lord Gowery cleared his throat. 'I don't, er, think we have it here. However,' he recovered fast, 'we don't need it. It is immaterial. We are not considering the Reading result, but that at Oxford.'

I gasped. I was truly astounded. 'But sir, if you watch Squelch's race, you will see that I rode him at Reading exactly as I did at Oxford, without using the whip.'

'That is beside the point, Hughes, because Squelch may not have needed the whip at Reading, but at Oxford he did.'

'Sir, it *is* the point,' I protested. 'I rode Squelch at Oxford in exactly the same manner as when he won at Reading, only at Oxford he tired.'

Lord Gowery absolutely ignored this. Instead he looked left and right to his Stewards alongside and remarked, 'We must waste no more time. We have three or four witnesses to call before lunch.'

The sleepy eldest Steward nodded and looked at his watch. The younger one nodded and avoided meeting my eyes. I knew him quite well from his amateur jockey days, and had often ridden against him. We had all been pleased when he had been made a Steward, because he knew at first hand the sort of odd circumstances which cropped up in racing to make a fool of the brightest, and we had thought that he would always put forward or explain our point of view. From his downcast semi-apologetic face I now gathered that we had hoped too much. He had not so far contributed one single word to the proceedings, and he looked, though it seemed extraordinary, intimidated.

As plain Andrew Tring he had been lighthearted, amusing, and almost reckless over fences. His recently inherited baronetcy and his even more recently acquired Stewardship seemed on the present showing to have hammered him into the ground.

Of Lord Plimborne, the elderly sleepyhead, I knew very little except his name. He seemed to be in his seventies and there was a faint tremble about many of his movements as if old age were shaking at his foundations and would soon have him down. He had not, I thought, clearly heard or understood more than a quarter of what had been said.

An Enquiry was usually conducted by three Stewards, but on this day there were four. The fourth, who sat on the left of Andrew Tring, was not, as far as I knew, even on the Disciplinary Committee, let alone a Disciplinary Steward. But he had in front of him a pile of notes as large if not larger than the others, and he was following every word with sharp hot eyes. Exactly where his involvement lay I couldn't work out, but there was no doubt that Wykeham, second Baron Ferth, cared about the outcome.

He alone of the four seemed really disturbed that they should have shown the wrong film, and he said quietly but forcefully enough for it to carry across to Cranfield and me, 'I did advise against showing the Reading race, if you remember.'

Gowery gave him an icelance of a look which would have slaughtered thinner-skinned men, but against Ferth's inner furnace it melted impotently.

'You agreed to say nothing,' Gowery said in the same piercing undertone. 'I would be obliged if you would keep to that.'

Cranfield had stirred beside me in astonishment, and now, thinking about it on the following day, the venomous little exchange seemed even more incredible. What, I now wondered, had Ferth been doing there, where he didn't really belong and was clearly not appreciated.

The telephone bell broke up my thoughts. I went into the sitting-room to answer it and found it was a jockey colleague ringing up to commiserate. He himself, he reminded me, had had his licence suspended for a while three or four years back, and he knew how I must be feeling.

'It's good of you, Jim, to take the trouble.'

'No trouble, mate. Stick together, and all that. How did it go?'

'Lousy,' I said. 'They didn't listen to a word either Cranfield or I said. They'd made up their minds we were guilty before we ever went there.'

Jim Enders laughed. 'I'm not surprised. You know what happened to me?'

'No. What?'

'Well, when they gave me my licence back, they'd called the Enquiry for the Tuesday, see, and then for some reason they had to postpone it until the Thursday afternoon. So along I went on Thursday afternoon and they hummed and hahed and warned me as to my future conduct and kept me in suspense for a bit before they said I could have my licence back. Well, I thought I might as well collect a Racing Calendar and take it home with me, to keep abreast of the times and all that, so, anyway, I collected my Racing Calendar which is published at twelve o'clock on Thursdays, twelve o'clock mind you, and I opened it, and what is the first thing I see but the notice saying my licence has been restored. So how about *that*? They'd published the result of that meeting two hours before it had even begun.'

'I don't believe it,' I said.

'Quite true,' he said. 'Mind you, that time they were giving my licence back, not taking it away. But even so, it shows they'd made up their minds. I've always wondered why they bothered to hold that second Enquiry at all. Waste of everyone's time, mate.'

'It's incredible,' I said. But I did believe him: which before my own Enquiry I would not have done.

'When are they giving you your licence back?' Jim asked.

'They didn't say.'

'Didn't they tell you when you could apply?'

'No.'

Jim shoved one very rude word down the wires. 'And that's another thing, mate, you want to pick your moment right when you *do* apply.'

'How do you mean?'

'When I applied for mine, on the dot of when they told me I could, they said the only Steward who had authority to give it back had gone on a cruise to Madeira and I would have to wait until he turned up again.'

CHAPTER TWO

When the horses came back from second exercise at midday my cousin Tony stomped up the stairs and trod muck and straw into my carpet. It was his stable, not Cranfield's, that I lived in. He had thirty boxes, thirty-two horses, one house, one wife, four children, and an overdraft. Ten more boxes were being built, the fifth child was four months off, and the overdraft was turning puce. I lived alone in the flat over the yard and rode everything which came along.

All very normal. And, in the three years since we had moved in, increasingly successful. My suspension meant that Tony and the owners were going to have to find another jockey.

He flopped down gloomily in a green velvet armchair.

'You all right?'

'Yes,' I said.

'Give me a drink, for God's sake.'

I poured half a cupful of J and B into a chunky tumbler.

'Ice?'

'As it is.'

I handed him the glass and he made inroads. Restoration began to take place.

Our mothers had been Welsh girls, sisters. Mine had married a local boy, so that I had come out wholly Celt, shortish, dark, compact. My aunt had hightailed off with a six-foot-four languid blond giant from Wyoming who had endowed Tony with most of his physique and double his brain. Out of USAAF uniform, Tony's father had reverted to ranch-hand, not ranch owner, as he had led his in-laws to believe, and he'd considered it more important for his only child to get to ride well than to acquire any of that there fancy book learning.

Tony therefore played truant for years with enthusiasm, and had never regretted it. I met him for the first time when he was twenty-five, when his Pa's heart had packed up and he had escorted his sincerely weeping Mum back to Wales. In the seven years since then he had acquired with some speed an English wife, a semi-English accent, an unimpassioned knowledge of English racing, a job as assistant trainer, and a stable of his own. And also, somewhere along the way, an unquenchable English thirst. For Scotch.

He said, looking down at the diminished drink, 'What are you going to do?'

27

'I don't know, exactly.'

'Will you go back home?'

'Not to live,' I said. 'I've come too far.'

He raised his head a little and looked round the room, smiling. Plain white walls, thick brown carpet, velvet chairs in two or three greens, antique furniture, pink and orange striped curtains, heavy and rich. 'I'll say you have,' he agreed. 'A big long way from Coedlant Farm, boyo.'

'No farther than your prairie.'

He shook his head. 'I still have grass roots. You've pulled yours up.'

Penetrating fellow, Tony. An extraordinary mixture of raw intelligence and straws in the hair. He was right; I'd shaken the straws out of mine. We got on very well.

'I want to talk to someone who has been to a recent Enquiry,' I said, abruptly.

'You want to just put it behind you and forget it,' he advised. 'No percentage in comparing hysterectomies.'

I laughed, which was truly something in the circumstances. 'Not on a pain for pain basis,' I explained. 'It's just that I want to know if what happened yesterday was ... well, unusual. The procedure, that is. The form of the thing. Quite apart from the fact that most of the evidence was rigged.'

'Is that what you were mumbling about on the way home? Those few words you uttered in a wilderness of silence?'

'Those,' I said, 'were mostly "they didn't believe a word we said".'

'So who rigged what?'

'That's the question.'

He held out his empty glass and I poured some more into it.

'Are you serious?'

'Yes. Starting from point A, which is that I rode Squelch to win, we arrive at point B, which is that the Stewards are convinced I didn't. Along the way were three or four little birdies all twittering their heads off and lying in their bloody teeth.'

'I detect,' he said, 'that something is stirring in yesterday's ruins.'

'What ruins?'

'You.'

'Oh.'

'You should drink more,' he said. 'Make an effort. Start now.'

'I'll think about it.'

'Do that.' He wallowed to his feet. 'Time for lunch. Time to go back to the little nestlings with their mouths wide open for worms.'

'Is it worms, today?'

'God knows. Poppy said to come, if you want.'

I shook my head.

'You must eat,' he protested.

'Yes.'

He looked at me consideringly. 'I guess,' he said, 'that you'll manage.' He put down his empty glass. 'We're here, you know, if you want anything. Company. Food. Dancing girls. Trifles like that.'

I nodded my thanks, and he clomped away down the stairs. He hadn't mentioned his horses, their races, or the other jockeys he would have to engage. He hadn't said that my staying in the flat would be an embarrassment to him.

I didn't know what to do about that. The flat was my home. My only home. Designed, converted, furnished by me. I liked it, and didn't want to leave.

I wandered into the bedroom.

A double bed, but pillows for one.

On the dressing chest, in a silver frame, a photograph of Rosalind. We had been married for two years when she went to spend a routine weekend with her parents. I'd been busy riding five races at Market Rasen on the Saturday, and a policeman had come into the weighing-room at the end of the afternoon and told me unemotionally that my father-in-law had set off with his wife and mine to visit friends and had misjudged his overtaking distance in heavy rain and had driven head on into a lorry and killed all three of them instantly.

It was four years since it had happened. Quite often I could no longer remember her voice. Other times she seemed to be in the next room. I had loved her passionately, but she no longer hurt. Four years was a long time.

I wished she had been there, with her tempestuous nature and fierce loyalty, so that I could have told her about the Enquiry, and shared the wretchedness, and been comforted.

That Enquiry . . .

Gowery's first witness had been the jockey who had finished third in the Lemonfizz, two or three lengths behind Squelch. About twenty, round faced and immature, Master Charlie West was a boy with a lot of natural talent but too little self-discipline. He had a great opinion of himself, and was in danger of throwing away his future through an apparent belief that rules only applied to everyone else.

The grandeur of Portman Square and the trappings of the Enquiry seemed to have subdued him. He came into the room nervously and stood where he was told, at one end of the Stewards' table: on their left, and to our right. He looked down at the table and raised his eyes only once or twice during his whole testimony. He didn't look across to Cranfield and me at all.

Gowery asked him if he remembered the race.

'Yes, sir.' It was a low mumble, barely audible.

'Speak up,' said Gowery irritably.

The shorthand writer came across from his table and moved the microphone so that it was nearer Charlie West. Charlie West cleared his throat.

31

'What happened during the race?'

'Well, sir . . . Shall I start from the beginning, sir?'

'There's no need for unnecessary detail, West,' Gowery said impatiently. 'Just tell us what happened on the far side of the course on the second circuit.'

'I see, sir. Well . . . Kelly, that is, I mean, Hughes, sir . . . Hughes . . . Well . . . Like . . .'

'West, come to the point.' Gowery's voice would have left a lazer standing. A heavy flush showed in patches on Charlie West's neck. He swallowed.

'Round the far side, sir, where the stands go out of sight, like, for a few seconds, well, there, sir . . . Hughes gives this hefty pull back on the reins, sir . . .'

'And what did he say, West?'

'He said, sir, "OK. Brakes on, chaps." Sir.'

Gowery said meaningfully, though everyone had heard the first time and a pin would have crashed on the Wilton, 'Repeat that, please, West.'

'Hughes, sir, said, "OK. Brakes on, chaps." '

'And what did you take him to mean by that, West?'

'Well sir, that he wasn't trying, like. He always says that when he's pulling one back and not trying.'

'*Always?*'

'Well, something like that, sir.'

There was a considerable silence.

Gowery said formally, 'Mr Cranfield . . . Hughes . . . You may ask this witness questions, if you wish.'

I got slowly to my feet.

'Are you seriously saying,' I asked bitterly, 'that at any time during the Lemonfizz Cup I pulled Squelch back and said "OK. Brakes on, chaps"?'

He nodded. He had begun to sweat.

'Please answer aloud,' I said.

'Yes. You said it.'

'I did not.'

'I heard you.'

'You couldn't have done.'

'I heard you.'

I was silent. I simply had no idea what to say next. It was too like a playground exchange: you did, I didn't, you did, I didn't . . .

I sat down. All the Stewards and all the officials ranked behind them were looking at me. I could see that all, to a man, believed West.

'Hughes, are you in the habit of using this phrase?' Gowery's voice was dry acid.

'No, sir.'

'Have you *ever* used it?'

'Not in the Lemonfizz Cup, sir.'

'I said, Hughes, have you *ever* used it?'

To lie or not to lie . . . 'Yes, sir, I have used it, once or twice. But not on Squelch in the Lemonfizz Cup.'

'It is sufficient that you said it at all, Hughes. We will draw our own conclusions as to *when* you said it.'

He shuffled one paper to the bottom of his pack and picked up another. Consulting it with the unseeing

33

token glance of those who know their subject by heart, he continued, 'And now, West, tell us what Hughes did after he had said these words.'

'Sir, he pulled his horse back, sir.'

'How do you know this?' The question was a formality. He asked with the tone of one already aware of the answer.

'I was just beside Hughes, sir, when he said that about brakes. Then he sort of hunched his shoulders, sir, and give a pull, sir, and, well, then he was behind me, having dropped out, like.'

Cranfield said angrily. 'But he finished in front of you.'

'Yes, sir.' Charlie West flicked his eyes upwards to Lord Gowery, and spoke only to him. 'My old horse couldn't act on the going, sir, and Hughes came past me again going into the second last, like.'

'And how did Squelch jump that fence?'

'Easy, sir. Met it just right. Stood back proper, sir.'

'Hughes maintains that Squelch was extremely tired at that point.'

Charlie West left a small pause. Finally he said, 'I don't know about that, sir, I thought as how Squelch would win, myself, sir. I still think as how he ought to have won, sir, being the horse he is, sir.'

Gowery glanced left and right, to make sure that his colleagues had taken the point. 'From your position during the last stages of the race, West, could you see

34

whether or not Hughes was making every effort to win?'

'Well, he didn't look like it, sir, which was surprising, like.'

'Surprising?'

'Yes, sir. See, Hughes is such an artist at it, sir.'

'An artist at what?'

'Well, at riding what looks from the stands one hell of a finish, sir, while all the time he's smothering it like mad.'

'Hughes is in the habit of not riding to win?'

Charlie West worked it out. 'Yes, sir.'

.'Thank you, West,' Lord Gowery said with insincere politeness. 'You may go and sit over there at the back of the room.'

Charlie West made a rabbit's scurry towards the row of chairs reserved for those who had finished giving evidence. Cranfield turned fiercely to me and said, 'Why didn't you deny it more vehemently, for God's sake? Why the hell didn't you insist he was making the whole thing up?'

'Do you think they'd believe me?'

He looked uneasily at the accusing ranks opposite, and found his answer in their inplacable stares. All the same, he stood up and did his best.

'Lord Gowery, the film of the Lemonfizz Cup does not bear out West's accusation. At no point does Hughes pull back his horse.'

35

I lifted my hand too late to stop him. Gowery's and Lord Ferth's intent faces both registered satisfaction. They knew as well as I did that what West had said was borne out on the film. Sensing that Squelch was going to run out of steam, I'd given him a short breather a mile from home, and this normal everyday little act was now wide open to misinterpretation.

Cranfield looked down at me, surprised by my reaction.

'I gave him a breather,' I said apologetically. 'It shows.'

He sat down heavily, frowning in worry.

Gowery was saying to an official, 'Show in Mr Newtonnards,' as if Cranfield hadn't spoken. There was a pause before Mr Newtonnards, whoever he was, materialized. Lord Gowery was looking slightly over his left shoulder, towards the door, giving me the benefit of his patrician profile. I realized with almost a sense of shock that I knew nothing about him as a person, and that he most probably knew nothing about me. He had been, to me, a figure of authority with a capital A. I hadn't questioned his right to rule over me. I had assumed naïvely that he would do so with integrity, wisdom, and justice.

So much for illusions. He was leading his witnesses in a way that would make the Old Bailey reel. He heard truth in Charlie West's lies and lies in my truth.

36

He was prosecutor as well as judge, and was only admitting evidence if it fitted his case.

He was dispersing the accepting awe I had held him in like candyfloss in a thunderstorm, and I could feel an unforgiving cynicism growing in its stead. Also I was ashamed of my former state of trust. With the sort of education I'd had, I ought to have known better.

Mr Newtonnards emerged from the waiting-room and made his way to the witnesses' end of the Stewards' table, sporting a red rosebud in his lapel and carrying a large blue ledger. Unlike Charlie West he was confident, not nervous. Seeing that everyone else was seated he looked around for a chair for himself, and not finding one, asked.

After a fractional pause Gowery nodded, and the official-of-all-work near the door pushed one forwards. Mr Newtonnards deposited into it his well-cared-for pearl-grey-suited bulk.

'Who is he?' I said to Cranfield. Cranfield shook his head and didn't answer, but he knew, because his air of worry had if anything deepened.

Andrew Tring flipped through his pile of papers, found what he was looking for, and drew it out. Lord Plimborne had his eyes shut again. I was beginning to expect that: and in any case I could see that it didn't matter, since the power lay somewhere between Gowery and Ferth, and Andy Tring and Plimborne were so much window-dressing.

Lord Gowery too picked up a paper, and again I had the impression that he knew its contents by heart.

'Mr Newtonnards?'

'Yes, my lord.' He had a faint cockney accent overlaid by years of cigars and champagne. Mid-fifties, I guessed; no fool, knew the world, and had friends in show business. Not too far out: Mr Newtonnards, it transpired, was a bookmaker.

Gowery said, 'Mr Newtonnards, will you be so good as to tell about a certain bet you struck on the afternoon of the Lemonfizz Cup?'

'Yes, my lord. I was standing on my pitch in Tattersall's when this customer come up and asked me for five tenners on Cherry Pie.' He stopped there, as if that was all he thought necessary.

Gowery did some prompting. 'Please describe this man, and also tell us what you did about his request.'

'Describe him? Let's see, then. He was nothing special. A biggish man in a fawn coat, wearing a brown trilby and carrying race glasses over his shoulder. Middle-aged, I suppose. Perhaps he had a moustache. Can't remember, really.'

The description fitted half the men on the racecourse.

'He asked me what price I'd give him about Cherry Pie,' Newtonnards went on. 'I didn't have any price chalked on my board, seeing Cherry Pie was such an outsider. I offered him tens, but he said it wasn't enough, and he looked like moving off down the line. Well...' Newtonnards waved an expressive pudgy hand '... business wasn't too brisk, so I offered him a hundred to six. Couldn't say fairer than that now, could I, seeing as there were only eight runners in the race? Worst decision I made in a long time.' Gloom mixed with stoicism settled on his well-covered features.

'So when Cherry Pie won, you paid out?'

'That's right. He put down fifty smackers I paid him nine hundred.'

'Nine hundred pounds?'

'That's right, my lord,' Newtonnards confirmed easily, 'nine hundred pounds.'

'And we may see the record of this bet?'

'Certainly.' He opened the big blue ledger at a marked page. 'On the left, my lord, just over halfway down. Marked with a red cross. Nine hundred and fifty, ticket number nine seven two.'

The ledger was passed along the Stewards' table. Plimborne woke up for the occasion and all four of them peered at the page. The ledger returned to Newtonnards, who shut it and let it lie in front of him.

'Wasn't that a very large bet on an outsider?' Gowery asked.

'Yes it was, my lord. But then, there are a lot of mugs about. Except, of course, that once in a while they go and win.'

'So you had no qualms about risking such a large amount?'

'Not really, my lord. Not with Squelch in the race. And anyway, I laid a bit of it off. A quarter of it, in fact, at thirty-three. So my actual losses were in the region of four hundred and eighty-seven pounds ten. Then I took three hundred and two-ten on Squelch and the others, which left a net loss on the race of one eight five.'

Cranfield and I received a glare in which every unit of the one eight five rankled.

Gowery said, 'We are not enquiring into how much you lost, Mr Newtonnards, but into the identity of the client who won nine hundred pounds on Cherry Pie.'

I shivered. If West could lie, so could others.

'As I said in my statement, my lord, I don't know his name. When he came up to me I thought I knew him from somewhere, but you see a lot of folks in my game, so I didn't think much of it. You know. So it wasn't until after I paid him off. After the last race, in fact. Not until I was driving home. Then it came to me, and I went spare, I can tell you.'

'Please explain more clearly,' Gowery said patiently. The patience of a cat at a mousehole. Anticipation making the waiting sweet.

'It wasn't him, so much, as who I saw him talking to. Standing by the parade ring rails before the first race. Don't know why I should remember it, but I do.'

'And who did you see this client talking to?'

'Him.' He jerked his head in our direction. 'Mr Cranfield.'

Cranfield was immediately on his feet.

'Are you suggesting that I advised this client of yours to back Cherry Pie?' His voice shook with indignation.

'No, Mr Cranfield,' said Gowery like the North Wind, 'the suggestion is that the client was acting on your behalf and that it was you yourself that backed Cherry Pie.'

'That's an absolute lie.'

His hot denial fell on a lot of cold ears.

'Where is this mysterious man?' he demanded. 'This unidentified, unidentifiable nobody? How can you possibly trump up such a story and present it as serious evidence? It is ridiculous. Utterly, utterly ridiculous.'

'The bet was struck,' Gowery said plonkingly, pointing to the ledger.

'And I saw you talking to the client,' confirmed Newtonnards.

Cranfield's fury left him gasping for words, and in the end he too sat down again, finding like me nothing to say that could dent the preconceptions ranged against us.

'Mr Newtonnards,' I said, 'would you know this client again?'

He hesitated only a fraction. 'Yes, I would.'

'Have you seen him at the races since Lemonfizz day?'

'No. I haven't.'

'If you see him again, will you point him out to Lord Gowery?'

'If Lord Gowery's at the races.' Several of the back ranks of officials smiled at this, but Newtonnards, to give him his due, did not.

I couldn't think of anything else to ask him, and I knew I had made no headway at all. It was infuriating. By our own choice we had thrust ourselves back into the bad old days when people accused at racing trials were not allowed a legal defendant. If they didn't know how to defend themselves: if they didn't know what sort of questions to ask or in what form to ask them, that was just too bad. Just their hard luck. But this wasn't hard luck. This was our own stupid fault. A lawyer would have been able to rip Newtonnards' testimony to bits, but neither Cranfield nor I knew how.

Cranfield tried. He was back on his feet.

'Far from backing Cherry Pie, I backed Squelch. You can check up with my own bookmaker.'

Gowery simply didn't reply. Cranfield repeated it.

Gowery said, 'Yes, yes. No doubt you did. It is quite beside the point.'

Cranfield sat down again with his mouth hanging open. I knew exactly how he felt. Not so much banging the head against a brick wall as being actively attacked by a cliff.

They waved Newtonnards away and he ambled easily off to take his place beside Charlie West. What he had said stayed behind him, stuck fast in the officials' minds. Not one of them had asked for corroboration. Not one had suggested that there might have been a loophole in identity. The belief was written plain on their faces: if someone had backed Cherry Pie to win nine hundred pounds, it must have been Cranfield.

Gowery hadn't finished. With a calm satisfaction he picked up another paper and said, 'Mr Cranfield, I have here an affidavit from a Mrs Joan Jones, who handled the five-pound selling window on the Totalizator in the paddock on Lemonfizz Cup day, that she sold ten win-only tickets for horse number eight to a man in a fawn raincoat, middle-aged, wearing a trilby. I also have here a similar testimony from a Mr Leonard Roberts, who was paying out at the five-pound window in the same building, on the same occasion. Both of these Tote employees remember the client well, as these were almost the only five-pound tickets sold on Cherry Pie, and certainly the only large block. The Tote paid out to this man more than eleven hundred pounds in cash. Mr Roberts advised him not to carry so much on his person, but the man declined to take his advice.'

There was another accusing silence. Cranfield looked totally nonplussed and came up with nothing to say.

superiority. 'Trainers are often caught out, as you know, when one of their horses suddenly develops his true form. Well, I thought Cherry Pie might just be one of those. So I backed him, on the off chance.'

Some off chance. Fifty pounds with Newtonnards and fifty pounds on the Tote. Gross profit, two thousand.

'How much did you have on Squelch?'

'Two hundred and fifty.'

'Whew,' I said. 'Was that your usual sort of bet?'

'He was odds on . . . I suppose a hundred is my most usual bet.'

I had come to the key question, and I wasn't sure I wanted to ask it, let alone have to judge whether the answer was true. However . . .

'Why,' I said matter-of-factly, 'didn't you back Cherry Pie with your own usual bookmaker?'

He answered without effort, 'Because I didn't want Kessel knowing I'd backed Cherry Pie, if he won instead of Squelch. Kessel's a funny man, he takes everything personally, he'd as like as not have whisked Squelch away . . .' He trailed off, remembering afresh that Squelch was indeed being whisked.

'Why should Kessel have known?'

'Eh? Oh, because he bets with my bookmaker too, and the pair of them are as thick as thieves.'

Fair enough.

This time, I tried for him. 'Sir, did this man back any other horses in the race, on the Tote? Did he back all, or two or three or four, and just hit the jackpot by accident?'

'There was no accident about this, Hughes.'

'But did he, in fact, back any other horses?'

Dead silence.

'Surely you asked?' I said reasonably.

Whether anyone had asked or not, Gowery didn't know. All he knew was what was on the affidavit. He gave me a stony stare, and said, 'No one puts fifty pounds on an outsider without good grounds for believing it will win.'

'But sir . . .'

'However,' he said, 'we will find out.' He wrote a note on the bottom of one of the affidavits. 'It seems to me extremely unlikely. But we will have the question asked.'

There was no suggestion that he would wait for the answer before giving his judgement. And in fact he did not.

CHAPTER THREE

I wandered aimlessly round the flat, lost and restless. Reheated the coffee. Drank it. Tried to write to my parents, and gave it up after half a page. Tried to make some sort of decision about my future, and couldn't.

Felt too battered. Too pulped. Too crushed.

Yet I had done nothing.

Nothing.

Late afternoon. The lads were bustling round the yard setting the horses fair for the night, and whistling and calling to each other as usual. I kept away from the windows and eventually went back to the bedroom and lay down on the bed. The day began to fade. The dusk closed in.

After Newtonnards they had called Tommy Timpson, who had ridden Cherry Pie.

Tommy Timpson 'did his two' for Cranfield and rode such of the stable's second strings as Cranfield cared to give him. Cranfield rang the changes on three jockeys: me, Chris Smith (at present taking his time over a fractured skull) and Tommy. Tommy got the crumbs and deserved better. Like many trainers, Cranfield couldn't spot talent when it was under his nose, and it wasn't until several small local trainers had asked for his services that Cranfield woke up to the fact that he had a useful emerging rider in his own yard.

Raw, nineteen years old, a stutterer, Tommy was at his worst at the Enquiry. He looked as scared as a two-year-old colt at his first starting gate, and although he couldn't help being jittery it was worse than useless for Cranfield and me.

Lord Gowery made no attempt to put him at ease but simply asked questions and let him get on with the answers as best he could.

'What orders did Mr Cranfield give you before the race? How did he tell you to ride Cherry Pie? Did he instruct you to ride to win?'

Tommy stuttered and stumbled and said Mr Cranfield had told him to keep just behind Squelch all the way round and try to pass him after the last fence.

Cranfield said indignantly, 'That's what he *did*. Not what I told him to do.'

Gowery listened, turned his head to Tommy, and said again, 'Will you tell us what instructions Mr Cranfield gave you *before* the race? Please think carefully.'

Tommy swallowed, gave Cranfield an agonized glance, and tried again. 'M ... M ... M ... Mr Cranfield s ... s ... said to take my p ... p ... pace from S ...

S ... Squelch and s ... s ... stay with him as long as I c ... c ... could.'

'And did he tell you to win?'

'He s ... s ... said of course g ... go ... go on and w ... w ... win if you c ... c ... can, sir.'

These were impeccable instructions. Only the most suspicious or biased mind could have read any villainy into them. If these Stewards' minds were not suspicious and biased, snow would fall in the Sahara.

'Did you hear Mr Cranfield giving Hughes instructions as to how he should ride Squelch?'

'N ... No, sir. M ... Mr Cranfield did ... didn't g ... give Hughes any orders at all, sir.'

'Why not?'

Tommy ducked it and said he didn't know. Cranfield remarked furiously that Hughes had ridden the horse twenty times and knew what was needed.

'Or you had discussed it with him privately, beforehand?'

Cranfield had no explosive answer to that because of course we *had* discussed it beforehand. In general terms. In an assessment of the opposition. As a matter of general strategy.

'I discussed the race with him, yes. But I gave him no specific orders.'

'So according to you,' Lord Gowery said, 'you intended both of your jockeys to try to win?'

'Yes. I did. My horses are always doing their best.'

Gowery shook his head. 'Your statement is not borne out by the facts.'

'Are you calling me a liar?' Cranfield demanded.

Gowery didn't answer. But yes, he was.

They shooed a willing Tommy Timpson away and Cranfield went on simmering at boiling point beside me. For myself, I was growing cold, and no amount of central heating could stop it. I thought we must now have heard everything, but I was wrong. They had saved the worst until last, building up the pyramid of damning statements until they could put the final cap on it and stand back and admire their four-square struc-ture, their solid, unanswerable edifice of guilt.

The worst, at first, had looked so harmless. A quiet slender man in his early thirties, endowed with an utterly forgettable face. After twenty-four hours I couldn't recall his features or remember his voice, and yet I couldn't think about him without shaking with sick impotent fury.

His name was David Oakley. His business, enquiry agent. His address, Birmingham.

He stood without fidgeting at the end of the Stew-ards' table holding a spiral-bound notebook which he consulted continually, and from beginning to end not a shade of emotion affected his face or his behaviour or even his eyes.

'Acting upon instructions, I paid a visit to the flat of Kelly Hughes, jockey, of Corrie House training stables,

48

Corrie, Berkshire, two days after the Lemonfizz Crystal Cup.'

I sat up with a jerk and opened my mouth to deny it, but before I could say a word he went smoothly on.

'Mr Hughes was not there, but the door was open, so I went in to wait for him. While I was there I made certain observations.' He paused.

Cranfield said to me, 'What is all this about?'

'I don't know. I've never seen him before.'

Gowery steamrollered on. 'You found certain objects.'

'Yes, my lord.'

Gowery sorted out three large envelopes, and passed one each to Tring and Plimborne. Ferth was before them. He had removed the contents from a similar envelope as soon as Oakley had appeared, and was now, I saw, watching me with what I took to be contempt.

The envelopes each held a photograph.

Oakley said, 'The photograph is of objects I found on a chest of drawers in Hughes' bedroom.'

Andy Tring looked, looked again, and raised a horrified face, meeting my eyes accidentally and for the first and only time. He glanced away hurriedly, embarrassed and disgusted.

'I want to see that photograph,' I said hoarsely.

'Certainly.' Lord Gowery turned his copy round and

pushed it across the table. I got up, walked the three dividing steps, and looked down at it.

For several seconds I couldn't take it in, and when I did, I was breathless with disbelief. The photograph had been taken from above the dressing chest, and was sparkling clear. There was the edge of the silver frame and half of Rosalind's face, and from under the frame, as if it had been used as a paperweight, protruded a sheet of paper dated the day after the Lemon-fizz Cup. There were three words written on it, and two initials.

As agreed. Thanks. D.C.

Slanted across the bottom of the paper, and spread out like a pack of cards, were a large number of ten-pound notes.

I looked up, and met Lord Gowery's eyes, and almost flinched away from the utter certainty I read there.

'It's a fake,' I said. My voice sounded odd. 'It's a complete fake.'

'What is it?' Cranfield said from behind me, and in his voice too everyone could hear the awareness of disaster.

I picked up the photograph and took it across to him, and I couldn't feel my feet on the carpet. When he had grasped what it meant he stood up slowly and in a low biting voice said formally, 'My lords, if you believe this, you will believe anything.'

It had not the slightest effect.

Gowery said merely, 'That is your handwriting, I believe.'

Cranfield shook his head. 'I didn't write it.'

'Please be so good as to write those exact words on this sheet of paper.' Gowery pushed a plain piece of paper across the table, and after a second Cranfield went across and wrote on it. Everyone knew that the two samples would look the same, and they did. Gowery passed the sheet of paper significantly to the other Stewards, and they all compared and nodded.

'It's a fake,' I said again. 'I never had a letter like that.'

Gowery ignored me. To Oakley he said, 'Please tell us where you found the money.'

Oakley unnecessarily consulted his notebook. 'The money was folded inside this note, fastened with a rubber band, and both were tucked behind the photo of Hughes's girlfriend, which you see in the picture.'

'It's not true,' I said. I might as well not have bothered. No one listened.

'You counted the money, I believe?'

'Yes, my lord. There was five hundred pounds.'

'There was no money,' I protested. Useless. 'And anyway,' I added desperately, 'why would I take five hundred for losing the race when I would get about as much as that for winning?'

I thought for a moment that I might have scored a hit. Might have made them pause. A pipe dream. There was an answer to that, too.

'We understand from Mr Kessel, Squelch's owner,' Gowery said flatly, 'that he pays you ten per cent of the winning stake money through official channels by cheque. This means that all presents received by you from Mr Kessel are taxed; and we understand that as you pay a high rate of tax your ten per cent from Mr Kessel would have in effect amounted to half, or less than half, of five hundred pounds.'

They seemed to have enquired into my affairs down to the last penny. Dug around in all directions. Certainly I had never tried to hide anything, but this behind-my-back tin-opening made me feel naked. Also, revolted. Also, finally, hopeless. And it wasn't until then that I realized I had been subconsciously clinging to a fairytale faith that it would all finally come all right, that because I was telling the truth I was bound to be believed in the end.

I stared across at Lord Gowery, and he looked briefly back. His face was expressionless, his manner entirely calm. He had reached his conclusions and nothing could overthrow them.

Lord Ferth, beside him, was less bolted down, but a great deal of his earlier heat seemed to have evaporated. The power he had generated no longer troubled Gowery at all, and all I could interpret from his expression was some kind of resigned acceptance.

There was little left to be said. Lord Gowery briefly summed up the evidence against us. The list of former races. The non-use of the whip. The testimony of Charlie West. The bets struck on Cherry Pie. The riding orders given in private. The photographic proof of a pay off from Cranfield to Hughes.

'There can be no doubt that this was a most flagrant fraud on the racing public . . . No alternative but to suspend your licences . . . And you, Dexter Cranfield, and you, Kelly Hughes, will be warned off Newmarket Heath until further notice.'

Cranfield, pale and shaking, said, 'I protest that this has not been a fair hearing. Neither Hughes nor I are guilty. The sentence is outrageous.'

No response from Lord Gowery. Lord Ferth, however, spoke for the second time in the proceedings.

'Hughes?'

'I rode Squelch to win,' I said. 'The witnesses were lying.'

Gowery shook his head impatiently. 'The Enquiry is closed. You may go.'

Cranfield and I both hesitated, still unable to accept that that was all. But the official near the door opened it, and all the ranks opposite began to talk quietly to each other and ignore us, and in the end we walked out. Stiff legged. Feeling as if my head were a floating football and my body a chunk of ice. Unreal.

There were several people in the waiting-room outside, but I didn't see them clearly. Cranfield, tight lipped, strode away from me, straight across the room and out of the far door, shaking off a hand or two laid on his sleeve. Dazed, I started to follow him, but was less purposeful, and was effectively stopped by a large man who planted himself in my way.

I looked at him vaguely. Mr Kessel. The owner of Squelch.

'Well?' he said challengingly.

'They didn't believe us. We've both been warned off.'

He hissed a sharp breath out between his teeth. 'After what I've been hearing, I'm not surprised. And I'll tell you this, Hughes, even if you get your licence back, you won't be riding for me again.'

I looked at him blankly and didn't answer. It seemed a small thing after what had already happened. He had been talking to the witnesses, in the waiting-room. They would convince anyone, it seemed. Some owners were unpredictable anyway, even in normal times. One day they had all the faith in the world in their jockey, and the next day, none at all. Faith with slender foundations. Mr Kessel had forgotten all the races I had won for him because of the one I had lost.

I turned blindly away from his hostility and found a

54

more welcome hand on my arm. Tony, who had driven up with me instead of seeing his horses work.

'Come on,' he said. 'Let's get out of here.'

I nodded and went down with him in the lift, out into the hall, and towards the front door. Outside there we could see a bunch of newspaper reporters waylaying Cranfield with their notebooks at the ready, and I stopped dead at the sight.

'Let's wait till they've gone,' I said.

'They won't go. Not before they've chewed you up too.'

We waited, hesitating, and a voice called behind me, 'Hughes.'

I didn't turn round. I felt I owed no one the slightest politeness. The footsteps came up behind me and he finally came to a halt in front.

Lord Ferth. Looking tired.

'Hughes. Tell me. Why in God's name did you do it?'

I looked at him stonily.

'I didn't.'

He shook his head. 'All the evidence . . .'

'You tell me,' I said, rudely, 'why decent men like Stewards so easily believe a lot of lies.'

I turned away from him, too. Twitched my head at Tony and made for the front door. To hell with the Press. To hell with the Stewards and Mr Kessel. And to hell with everything to do with racing. The upsurge

55

She looked at me suspiciously, but decided not to pursue it. 'My coat is in your bedroom.'

'I'll fetch it for you.'

'Thank you.'

I walked across the sitting-room and into the bedroom. Her coat was lying on my bed in a heap. Black and white fur, in stripes going round. I picked it up and turned, and found she had followed me.

'Thank you so much.' She presented her back to me and put her arms in the coat-putting-on position. On went the coat. She swivelled slowly, buttoning up the front with shiny black saucers. 'This flat really is fantastic. Who is your decorator?'

'Chap called Kelly Hughes.'

She raised her eyebrows. 'I know the professional touch when I see it.'

'Thank you.'

She raised the chin. 'Oh well, if you won't say . . .'

'I would say. I did say. I did the flat myself. I've been whitewashing pigsties since I was six.'

She wasn't quite sure whether to be amused or offended, and evaded it by changing the subject.

'That picture . . . that's your wife, isn't it?'

I nodded.

'I remember her,' she said. 'She was always so sweet to me. She seemed to know what I was feeling. I was really awfully sorry when she was killed.'

I looked at her in surprise. The people Rosalind had

of fury took me out of the building and fifty yards along the pavement in Portman Square and only evaporated into grinding misery when we had climbed into the taxi Tony whistled for.

Tony thumped up the stairs to the darkened flat. I heard him calling.

'Are you there, Kelly?'

I unrolled myself from the bed, stood up, stretched, went out into the sitting-room and switched on the lights. He was standing in the far doorway, blinking, his hands full of tray.

'Poppy insisted,' he explained.

He put the tray down on the table and lifted off the covering cloth. She'd sent hot chicken pie, a tomato, and about half a pound of Brie.

'She says you haven't eaten for two days.'

'I suppose not.'

'Get on with it, then.' He made an instinctive line for the whisky bottle and poured generously into two tumblers.

'And here. For once, drink this.'

I took the glass and a mouthful and felt the fire trickle down inside my chest. The first taste was always the best. Tony tossed his off and ordered himself a refill.

I ate the pie, the tomato, and the cheese. Hunger, I

hadn't consciously felt rolled contentedly over and slept.

'Can you stay a bit?' I asked.

'Natch.'

'I'd like to tell you about the Enquiry.'

'Shoot,' he said with satisfaction. 'I've been waiting.'

I told him all that had happened, almost word for word. Every detail had been cut razor sharp into my memory in the way that only happens in disasters.

Tony's astonishment was plain. 'You were framed!'

'That's right.'

'But surely no one can get away with that?'

'Someone seems to be doing all right.'

'But was there *nothing* you could say to prove . . .'

'I couldn't think of anything yesterday, which is all that matters. It's always easy to think of all the smart clever things one *could* have said, afterwards, when it's too late.'

'What would you have said, then?'

'I suppose for a start I should have asked who had given that so-called enquiry agent instructions to search my flat. Acting on instructions, he said. Well, *whose* instructions? I didn't think of asking, yesterday. Now I can see that it could be the whole answer.'

'You assumed the Stewards had instructed him?'

'I suppose so. I didn't really think. Most of the time I was so shattered that I couldn't think clearly at all.'

'Maybe it *was* the Stewards.'

57

'Well, no. I suppose it's barely possible they might
have sent an investigator, though when you look at it
in cold blood it wouldn't really seem likely, but it's a
tear drop to the Atlantic that they wouldn't have supplied him with five hundred quid and a forged note and
told him to photograph them somewhere distinctive in
my flat. But that's what he did. Who instructed him?'

'Even if you'd asked, he wouldn't have said.'

'I guess not. But at least it might have made the
Stewards think a bit too.'

Tony shook his head. 'He would still have said he
found the money behind Rosalind's picture. His word
against yours. Nothing different.'

He looked gloomily into his glass. I looked gloomily
into mine.

'That bloody little Charlie West,' I said. 'Someone
got at him, too.'

'I presume you didn't in fact say "Brakes on,
chaps"?'

'I did say it, you see. Not in the Lemonfizz, of course,
but a couple of weeks before, in that frightful novice
'chase at Oxford, the day they abandoned the last two
races because it was snowing. I was hitting every fence
on that deadly bad jumper that old Almond hadn't
bothered to school properly, and half the other runners
were just as green, and a whole bunch of us had got
left about twenty lengths behind the four who were
any use, and sleet was falling, and I didn't relish ending

up with a broken bone at nought degrees centigrade, so as we were handily out of sight of the stands at that point I shouted, "OK. Brakes on, chaps," and a whole lot of us eased up thankfully and finished the race a good deal slower than we could have done. It didn't affect the result, of course. But there you are. I did say it. What's more, Charlie West heard me. He just shifted it from one race to another.'

'The bastard.'

'I agree.'

'Maybe no one got at him. Maybe he just thought he'd get a few more rides if you were out of the way.'

I considered it and shook my head. 'I wouldn't have thought he was *that* much of a bastard.'

'You never know.' Tony finished his drink and absent-mindedly replaced it. 'What about the bookmaker?'

'Newtonnards? I don't know. Same thing, I suppose. Someone has it in for Cranfield too. Both of us, it was. The Stewards couldn't possibly have warned off one of us without the other. We were knitted together so neatly.'

'It makes me livid,' Tony said violently. 'It's wicked.'

I nodded. 'There was something else, too, about that Enquiry. Some undercurrent, running strong. At least, it was strong at the beginning. Something between Lord Gowery and Lord Ferth. And then Andy Tring, he was sitting there looking like a wilted lettuce.' I shook my head in puzzlement. 'It was like a couple of heavy animals lurking in the undergrowth, shaping up to fight each other. You couldn't see them, but there was a sort of quiver in the air. At least, that's how it seemed at one point...'

'Stewards are men,' Tony said with bubble-bursting matter-of-factness. 'Show me any organization which doesn't have some sort of power struggle going on under its gentlemanly surface. All you caught was a whiff of the old brimstone. State of nature. Nothing to do with whether you and Cranfield were guilty or not.'

He half convinced me. He polished off the rest of the whisky and told me not to forget to get some more.

Money. That was another thing. As from yesterday I had no income. The welfare state didn't pay unemployment benefits to the self-employed, as all jockeys remembered every snow-bound winter.

'I'm going to find out,' I said abruptly.

'Find out what?'

'Who framed us.'

'Up the Marines,' Tony said unsteadily. 'Over the top, boys. Up and at 'em.' He picked up the empty bottle and looked at it regretfully. 'Time for bed, I guess. If you need any help with the campaign, count on my Welsh blood to the last clot.'

He made an unswerving line to the door, turned, and gave me a grimace of friendship worth having.

'Don't fall down the stairs,' I said.

PART TWO

MARCH

CHAPTER FOUR

Roberta Cranfield looked magnificent in my sitting-room. I came back from buying whisky in the village and found her gracefully draped all over my restored Chippendale. The green velvet supported a lot of leg and a deep purple size-ten wool dress, and her thick long hair the colour of dead beech leaves clashed dramatically with the curtains. Under the hair she had white skin, incredible eyebrows, amber eyes, photogenic cheekbones and a petulant mouth.

She was nineteen, and I didn't like her.

'Good morning,' I said.

'Your door was open.'

'It's a habit I'll have to break.'

I peeled the tissue wrapping off the bottle and put it with the two chunky glasses on the small silver tray I had once won in a race sponsored by some sweet manufacturers. Troy weight, twenty-four ounces: but ruined by the inscription, K. HUGHES, WINNING JOCKEY, STARCHOCS SILVER STEEPLECHASE. Starchocs indeed. And

I never ate chocolates. Couldn't afford to, from the weight point of view.

She flapped her hand from a relaxed wrist, indicating the room.

'This is all pretty lush.'

I wondered what she had come for. I said, 'Would you like some coffee?'

'Coffee and cannabis.'

'You'll have to go somewhere else.'

'You're very prickly.'

'As a cactus,' I agreed.

She gave me a half-minute unblinking stare with her liquid eyes. Then she said, 'I only said cannabis to jolt you.'

'I'm not jolted.'

'No. I can see that. Waste of effort.'

'Coffee, then?'

'Yes.'

I went into the kitchen and fixed up the percolator. The kitchen was white and brown and copper and yellow. The colours pleased me. Colours gave me the sort of mental food I imagined others got from music. I disliked too much music, loathed the type of stuff you couldn't escape in restaurants and airliners, didn't own a record-player, and much preferred silence.

She followed me in from the sitting-room and looked around her with mild surprise.

'Do all jockeys live like this?'

'Naturally.'

'I don't believe it.'

She peered into the pine-fronted cupboard I'd taken the coffee from.

'Do you cook for yourself?'

'Mostly.'

'*Recherché* things like *shashlik*?' An undercurrent of mockery.

'Steaks.'

I poured the bubbling coffee into two mugs and offered her cream and sugar. She took the cream, generously, but not the sugar, and perched on a yellow-topped stool. Her copper hair fitted the kitchen, too.

'You seem to be taking it all right,' she said.

'What?'

'Being warned off.'

I didn't answer.

'A cactus,' she said, 'isn't in the same class.'

She drank the coffee slowly, in separate mouthfuls, watching me thoughtfully over the mug's rim. I watched her back. Nearly my height, utterly self-possessed, as cool as the stratosphere. I had seen her grow from a demanding child into a selfish fourteen-year-old, and from there into a difficult-to-please debutante and from there to a glossy imitation model girl heavily tinged with boredom. Over the eight years I had ridden for her father we had met briefly and spoken seldom, usually in parade rings and outside the weighing-room, and on the occasions when she did speak to me she seemed to be aiming just over the top of my head.

'You're making it difficult,' she said.

'For you to say why you came?'

She nodded. 'I thought I knew you. Now it seems I don't.'

'What did you expect?'

'Well . . . Father said you came from a farm cottage with pigs running in and out of the door.'

'Father exaggerates.'

She lifted her chin to ward off the familiarity, a gesture I'd seen a hundred times in her and her brothers. A gesture copied from her parents.

'Hens,' I said, 'not pigs.'

She gave me an up-stage stare. I smiled at her faintly and refused to be reduced to the ranks. I watched the wheels tick over while she worked out how to approach a cactus, and gradually the chin came down.

'Actual hens?'

Not bad at all. I could feel my own smile grow genuine.

'Now and then.'

'You don't look like . . . I mean . . .'

'I know exactly what you mean,' I agreed. 'And it's high time you got rid of those chains.'

'Chains? What are you talking about?'

'The fetters in your mind. The iron bars in your soul.'

'My mind is all right.'

'You must be joking. It's chock-a-block with ideas half a century out of date.'

'I didn't come here to . . .' she began explosively, and then stopped.

'You didn't come here to be insulted,' I said ironically.

'Well, as you put it in that well-worn hackneyed phrase, no, I didn't. But I wasn't going to say that.'

'What did you come for?'

She hesitated. 'I wanted you to help me.'

'To do what?'

'To . . . to *cope* with Father.'

I was surprised, first that Father needed coping with, and second that she needed help to do it.

'What sort of help?'

'He's . . . he's so *shattered*.' Unexpectedly there were tears standing in her eyes. They embarrassed and angered her, and she blinked furiously so that I shouldn't see. I admired the tears but not her reason for trying to hide them.

'Here are you,' she said in a rush, 'walking about as cool as you please and buying whisky and making coffee as if no screaming avalanche had poured out on you and smothered your life and made every thought an absolute bloody hell, and maybe you don't understand how anyone in that state needs help, and come to that I don't understand why *you* don't need help, but anyway, Father *does*.'

'Not from me,' I said mildly. 'He doesn't think enough of me to give it any value.'

She opened her mouth angrily and shut it again and took two deep controlling breaths. 'And it looks as though he's right.'

'Ouch,' I said ruefully. 'What sort of help, then?'

'I want you to come and talk to him.'

My talking to Cranfield seemed likely to be as therapeutic as applying itching powder to a baby. However, she hadn't left me much room for kidding myself that fruitlessness was a good reason for not trying.

'When?'

'Now . . . Unless you have anything else to do.'

'No,' I said carefully. 'I haven't.'

She made a face and an odd little gesture with her hands. 'Will you come now, then . . . please?'

She herself seemed surprised about the real supplication in that 'please'. I imagined that she had come expecting to instruct, not to ask.

'All right.'

'Great.' She was suddenly very cool, very employer's daughter again. She put her coffee mug on the draining board and started towards the door. 'You had better follow me, in your car. It's no good me taking you, you'll need your own car to come back in.'

'That is so,' I agreed.

been sweetest to had invariably been unhappy. She had had a knack of sensing it, and of giving succour without being asked. I would not have thought of Roberta Cranfield as being unhappy, though I supposed from twelve to fifteen, when she had known Rosalind, she could have had her troubles.

'She wasn't bad, as wives go,' I said flippantly, and Miss Cranfield disapproved of that, too.

We left the flat and this time I locked the door, though such horses as I'd had had already bolted. Roberta had parked her Sunbeam Alpine behind the stables and across the doors of the garage where I kept my Lotus. She backed and turned her car with aggressive poise, and I left a leisurely interval before I followed her through the gates, to avoid a competition all the eighteen miles to her home.

Cranfield lived in an early Victorian house in a hamlet four miles out of Lambourn. A country gentleman's residence, estate agents would have called it: built before the Industrial Revolution had invaded Berkshire and equally impervious to the social revolution a hundred years later. Elegant, charming, timeless, it was a house I liked very much. Pity about the occupants.

I drove up the back drive as usual and parked alongside the stable yard. A horsebox was standing there with its ramp down, and one of the lads was leading a

horse into it. Archie, the head lad, who had been helping, came across as soon as I climbed out of the car.

'This is a God-awful bloody business,' he said. 'It's
wicked, that's what it is. Downright bloody wicked.'

'The horses are going?'

'Some owners have sent boxes already. All of them
will be gone by the day after tomorrow.' His weather-
beaten face was a mixture of fury, frustration, and
anxiety. 'All the lads have got the sack. Even me. And
the missus and I have just taken a mortgage on one
of the new houses up the road. Chalet bungalow, just
what she'd always set her heart on. Worked for years,
she has, saving for it. Now she won't stop crying. We
moved in only a month ago, see? How do you think
we're going to keep up the payments? Took every
pound we had, what with the deposit and the solicitors,
and curtains and all. Nice little place, too, she's got it
looking real nice. And it isn't as if the Guvnor really
fiddled the blasted race. That Cherry Pie, anyone could
see with half an eye he was going to be good some day.
I mean, if the Guvnor had done it, like, somehow all
this wouldn't be so bad. I mean, if he deserved it, well
serve him right, and I'd try and get a bit of compensation from him because we're going to have a right
job selling the house again. I'll tell you, because there's
still two of them empty, they weren't so easy to sell in
the first place, being so far out of Lambourn . . . I'll tell
you straight, I wish to God we'd never moved out of

71

the Guvnor's cottage, dark and damp though it may be ... George,' he suddenly shouted at a lad swearing and tugging at a reluctant animal, 'don't take it out on the horse, it isn't *his* fault ...' He bustled across the yard and took the horse himself, immediately quietening it and leading it without trouble into the horsebox.

He was an excellent head lad, better than most, and a lot of Cranfield's success was his doing. If he sold his house and got settled in another job, Cranfield wouldn't get him back. The training licence might not be lost for ever, but the stable's main prop would be.

I watched another lad lead a horse round to the waiting box. He too looked worried. His wife, I knew, was on the point of producing their first child.

Some of the lads wouldn't care, of course. There were plenty of jobs going in racing stables, and one lot of digs was much the same as another. But they too would not come back. Nor would most of the horses, nor many of the owners. The stable wasn't being suspended for a few months. It was being smashed.

Sick and seething with other people's fury as well as my own, I walked down the short stretch of drive to the house. Roberta's Alpine was parked outside the front door and she was standing beside it looking cross.

'So there you are. I thought you'd ratted.'

'I parked down by the yard.'

'I can't bear to go down there. Nor can Father. In

fact, he won't move out of his dressing-room. You'll have to come upstairs to see him.'

She led the way through the front door and across thirty square yards of Persian rug. When we had reached the foot of the stairs the door of the library was flung open and Mrs Cranfield came through it. Mrs Cranfield always flung doors open, rather as if she suspected something reprehensible was going on behind them and she was intent on catching the sinners in the act. She was a plain woman who wore no make-up and dressed in droopy woollies. To me she had never talked about anything except horses, and I didn't know whether she could. Her father was an Irish baron, which may have accounted for the marriage.

'My father-in-law, Lord Coolihan . . .' Cranfield was wont to say: and he was wont to say it far too often. I wondered whether, after Gowery, he was the tiniest bit discontented with the aristocracy.

'Ah, there you are, Hughes,' Mrs Cranfield said. 'Roberta told me she was going to fetch you. Though what good you can do I cannot understand. After all, it was you who got us into the mess.'

'I what?'

'If you'd ridden a better race on Squelch, none of this would have happened.'

I bit back six answers and said nothing. If you were hurt enough you lashed out at the nearest object. Mrs Cranfield continued to lash.

'Dexter was thoroughly shocked to hear that you had been in the habit of deliberately losing races.'

'So was I,' I said dryly.

Roberta moved impatiently. 'Mother, do stop it. Come along, Hughes. This way.'

I didn't move. She went up three steps, paused, and looked back. 'Come on, what are you waiting for?'

I shrugged. Whatever I was waiting for, I wouldn't get it in that house. I followed her up the stairs, along a wide passage, and into her father's dressing-room.

There was too much heavy mahogany furniture of a later period than the house, a faded plum-coloured carpet, faded plum plush curtains, and a bed with an Indian cover.

On one side of the bed sat Dexter Cranfield, his back bent into a bow and his shoulders hunched round his ears. His hands rolled loosely on his knees, fingers curling, and he was staring immovably at the floor.

'He sits like that for hours,' Roberta said on a breath beside me. And, looking at him, I understood why she had needed help.

'Father,' she said, going over and touching his shoulder. 'Kelly Hughes is here.'

Cranfield said, 'Tell him to go and shoot himself.'

She saw the twitch in my face, and from her expression thought that I minded, that I believed Cranfield too thought me the cause of all his troubles. On the whole I decided not to crystallize her fears by saying I thought Cranfield had said shoot because shoot was in his mind.

'Hop it,' I said, and jerked my head towards the door.

The chin went up like a reflex. Then she looked at the husk of her father, and back to me, whom she'd been to some trouble to bring, and most of the starch dissolved.

'All right. I'll be down in the library. Don't go without . . . telling me.'

I shook my head, and she went collectedly out of the room, shutting the door behind her.

I walked to the window and looked at the view. Small fields trickling down into the valley. Trees all bent one way by the wind off the Downs. A row of pylons, a cluster of council-house roofs. Not a horse in sight. The dressing-room was on the opposite side of the house to the stables.

'Have you a gun?' I asked.

No answer from the bed. I went over and sat down beside him. 'Where is it?'

His eyes slid a fraction in my direction and then back. He had been looking past me. I got up and went to the table beside his bed, but there was nothing lethal on it, and nothing in the drawer.

I found it behind the high mahogany bedhead. A finely wrought Purdey more suitable for pheasants. Both barrels were loaded. I unloaded them.

'Very messy,' I remarked. 'Very inconsiderate. And anyway, you didn't mean to do it.'

I wasn't at all sure about that, but there was no harm in trying to convince him.

'What are you doing here?' he said indifferently.

'Telling you to snap out of it. There's work to be done.'

'Don't speak to me like that.'

'How, then?'

His head came up a little, just like Roberta's. If I made him angry, he'd be halfway back to his normal self. And I could go home.

'It's useless sitting up here sulking. It won't achieve anything at all.'

'*Sulking?*' He was annoyed, but not enough.

'Someone took our toys away. Very unfair. But nothing to be gained by grizzling in corners.'

'*Toys* . . . You're talking nonsense.'

'Toys, licences, what's the difference. The things we prized most. Someone's snatched them away. Tricked us out of them. And nobody except us can get them back. Nobody else will bother.'

'We can apply,' he said without conviction.

'Oh, we can apply. In six months' time, I suppose. But there's no guarantee we'd get them. The only sensible thing to do is to start fighting back right now and find out who fixed us. Who, and why. And after that I'll wring his bloody neck.'

He was still staring at the floor, still hunched. He couldn't even look me in the face yet, let alone the world. If he hadn't been such a climbing snob, I thought uncharitably, his present troubles wouldn't have produced such a complete cave-in. He was on the verge of literally not being able to bear the public disgrace of being warned off.

Well, I wasn't so sure I much cared for it myself. It was all very well knowing that one was not guilty, and even having one's closest friends believe it, but one could hardly walk around everywhere wearing a notice proclaiming 'I am innocent. I never done it. It were all a stinking frame-up.'

'It's not so bad for you,' he said.

'That's perfectly true.' I paused. 'I came in through the yard.'

He made a low sound of protest.

'Archie seems to be seeing to everything himself. And he's worried about his house.'

Cranfield made a waving movement of his hand as much as to ask how did I think he could be bothered with Archie's problems on top of his own.

'It wouldn't hurt you to pay Archie's mortgage for a bit.'

'*What?*' That finally reached him. His head came up at least six inches.

'It's only a few pounds a week. Peanuts to you. Life

77

or death to him. And if you lose him you'll never get so many winners again.'

'You ... you ...' He spluttered. But he still didn't look up.

'A trainer is as good as his lads.'

'That's stupid.'

'You've got good lads just now. You've chucked out the duds, the rough and lazy ones. It takes time to weed out and build up a good team, but you can't get a high ratio of winners without one. You might get your licence back but you won't get these lads back and it'll take years for the stable to recover. If it ever does. And I hear you have already given them all the sack.'

'What else was there to do?'

'You could try keeping them on for a month.'

His head came up a little more. 'You haven't the slightest idea what that would cost me. The wages come to more than four hundred pounds a week.'

'There must still be quite a lot to come in in training fees. Owners seldom pay in advance. You won't have to dig very deep into your own pocket. Not for a month, anyway, and it might not take as long as that.'

'What might not?'

'Getting our licences back.'

'Don't be so bloody ridiculous.'

'I mean it. What is it worth to you? Four weeks' wages for your lads? Would you pay that much if there was a chance you'd be back in racing in a month? The owners would send their horses back, if it was as quick as that. Particularly if you tell them you confidently expect to be back in business almost immediately.'

'They wouldn't believe it.'

'They'd be uncertain. That should be enough.'

'There isn't a chance of getting back.'

'Oh yes there damn well is,' I said forcefully. 'But only if you're willing to take it. Tell the lads you're keeping them on for a bit. Especially Archie. Go down to the yard and tell them now.'

'*Now*.'

'Of course,' I said impatiently. 'Probably half of them have already read the Situations Vacant columns and written to other trainers.'

'There isn't any point.' He seemed sunk in fresh gloom. 'It's all hopeless. And it couldn't have happened, it simply could *not* have happened at a worse time. Edwin Byler was going to send me his horses. It was all fixed up. Now of course he's telephoned to say it's all off, his horses are staying where they are, at Jack Roxford's.'

To train Edwin Byler's horses was to be presented with a pot of gold. He was a North country businessman who had made a million or two out of mail order, and had used a little of it to fulfil a long held ambition to own the best string of steeplechasers in Britain. Four of his present horses had in turn cost more than anyone had paid before. When he wanted, he bid. He only wanted the best, and he had bought enough of them to put him for the two previous seasons at the top of the Winning Owners' list. To have been going to train Edwin Byler's horses, and now not to be going to, was a refined cruelty to pile on top of everything else.

To have been going to *ride* Edwin Byler's horses . . . as I would no doubt have done . . . that too was a thrust where it hurt.

'There's all the more point, then,' I said. 'What more do you want in the way of incentive? You're throwing away without a struggle not only what you've got but what you might have . . . Why in the Hell don't you get off your bed and behave like a gentleman and show some spirit?'

'Hughes!' He was outraged. But he still sat. He still wouldn't look at me.

I paused, considering him. Then, slowly, I said, 'All right, then. I'll tell you why you won't. You won't because . . . to some degree . . . you are in fact guilty. You made sure Squelch wouldn't win. And you backed Cherry Pie.'

That got him. Not just his head up, but up, trembling, on to his feet.

CHAPTER FIVE

'How dare you?'

'Frankly, just now I'd dare practically anything.'

'You said we were framed.'

'So we were.'

Some of his alarm subsided. I stoked it up again.

'You handed us away on a plate.'

He swallowed, his eyes flicking from side to side, looking everywhere except at me.

'I don't know what you mean.'

'Don't be so weak,' I said impatiently. 'I rode Squelch, remember? Was he his usual self? He was not.'

'If you're suggesting,' he began explosively, 'that I doped . . .'

'Oh, of course not. Anyway, they tested him, didn't they? Negative result. Naturally. No trainer needs to dope a horse he doesn't want to win. It's like swatting a fly with a bull-dozer. There are much more subtle methods. Undetectable. Even innocent. Maybe you

81

should be kinder to yourself and admit that you quite innocently stopped Squelch. Maybe you even did it subconsciously, wanting Cherry Pie to win.'

'Bull,' he said.

'The mind plays tricks,' I said. 'People often believe they are doing something for one good reason, while they are subconsciously doing it for another.'

'Twaddle.'

'The trouble comes sometimes when the real reason rears its ugly head and slaps you in the kisser.'

'Shut up.' His teeth and jaw were clenched tight.

I drew a deep breath. I'd been guessing, partly. And I'd guessed right.

I said, 'You gave Squelch too much work too soon before the race. He lost the Lemonfizz on the gallops at home.'

He looked at me at last. His eyes were dark, as if the pupils had expanded to take up all the iris. There was a desperate sort of hopelessness in his expression.

'It wouldn't have been so bad,' I said, 'if you had admitted it to yourself. Because then you would never have risked not engaging a lawyer to defend us.'

'I didn't mean to over-train Squelch,' he said wretchedly. 'I didn't realize it until afterwards. I did back him, just as I said at the Enquiry.'

I nodded. 'I imagined you must have done. But you backed Cherry Pie as well.'

He explained quite simply, without any of his usual

'Well, who was the middle-aged man who put the bets on for you?'

'Just a friend. There's no need to involve him. I want to keep him out of it.'

'Could Newtonnards have seen you talking to him by the parade ring before the first race?'

'Yes,' he said with depression. 'I did talk to him. I gave him the money to bet with.'

And he still hadn't seen any danger signals. Had taken Monty Midgley's assurance at its face value. Hadn't revealed the danger to me. I could have throttled him.

'What did you do with the winnings?'

'They're in the safe downstairs.'

'And you haven't been able to admit to anyone that you've got them.'

'No.'

I thought back. 'You lied about it at the Enquiry.'

'What else was there to do?'

By then, what indeed. Telling the truth hadn't done much for me.

'Let's see, then.' I moved over to the window again, sorting things out. 'Cherry Pie won on his merits. You backed him because he looked like coming into form rather suddenly. Squelch had had four hard races in two months, and a possibly over-zealous training gallop. These are the straight facts.'

'Yes . . . I suppose so.'

'No trainer should lose his licence because he didn't tell the world he might just possibly have a flier. I never see why the people who put in all the work shouldn't have the first dip into the well.'

Owners, too, were entitled. Cherry Pie's owner, however, had died three weeks before the Lemonfizz, and Cherry Pie had run for the executors. Someone was going to have a fine time deciding his precise value at the moment of his owner's death.

'It means, anyway, that you do have a fighting fund,' I pointed out.

'There's no point in fighting.'

'You,' I said exasperatedly, 'are so soft that you'd make a marshmallow look like granite.'

His mouth slowly opened. Before that morning I had never given him anything but politeness. He was looking at me as if he'd really noticed me, and it occurred to me that if we did indeed get our licences back he would remember that I'd seen him in pieces, and maybe find me uncomfortable to have around. He paid me a retainer, but only on an annual contract. Easy enough to chuck me out, and retain someone else. Expediently, and not too pleased with myself for it, I took the worst crags out of my tone.

'I presume,' I said, 'that you do want your licence back?'

'There isn't a chance.'

85

'If you'll keep the lads for a month, I'll get it back for you.'

Defeatism still showed in every sagging muscle, and he didn't answer.

I shrugged. 'Well, I'm going to try. And if I give you your licence back on a plate it will be just too bad if Archie and the lads have gone.' I walked towards the door and put my hand on the knob. 'I'll let you know how I get on.'

Twisted the knob. Opened the door.

'Wait,' he said.

I turned round. A vestige of starch had returned, mostly in the shape of the reappearance of the mean lines round his mouth. Not so good.

'I don't believe you can do it. But as you're so cocksure, I'll make a bargain with you. I'll pay the lads for two weeks. If you want me to keep them on for another two weeks after that, you can pay them yourself.'

Charming. He'd made two thousand pounds out of Cherry Pie and had over-trained Squelch and was the direct cause of my being warned off. I stamped on a violent inner tremble of anger and gave him a cold answer.

'Very well. I agree to that. But you must make a bargain with me too. A bargain that you'll keep your mouth tight shut about your guilt feelings. I don't want to be sabotaged by you hairshirting it all over the place

86

and confessing your theoretical sins at awkward moments.'

'I am unlikely to do that,' he said stiffly.

I wasn't so sure. 'I want your word on it,' I said.

He drew himself up, offended. It at least had the effect of straightening his backbone.

'You have it.'

'Fine.' I held the door open for him. 'Let's go down to the yard, then.'

He still hesitated, but finally made up his mind to it, and went before me through the door and down the stairs.

Roberta and her mother were standing in the hall, looking as if they were waiting for news at a pithead after a disaster. They watched the reappearance of the head of the family with a mixture of relief and apprehension, and Mrs Cranfield said tentatively, 'Dexter? . . .'

He answered irritably, as if he saw no cause for anxiety in his having shut himself away with a shotgun for thirty-six hours, 'We're going down to the yard.'

'Great,' said Roberta practically smothering any tendency to emotion from her mother, 'I'll come too.'

Archie hurried to meet us and launched into a detailed account of which horses had gone and which were about to go next. Cranfield hardly listened and certainly didn't take it in. He waited for a gap in the flow, and when he'd waited long enough, impatiently interrupted.

'Yes, yes, Archie, I'm sure you have everything in hand. That is not what I've come down for, however. I want you to tell the lads at once that their notice to leave is withdrawn for one month.'

Archie looked at me, not entirely understanding.

'The sack,' I said, 'is postponed. Pending attempts to get wrongs righted.'

'Mine too?'

'Absolutely,' I agreed. 'Especially, in fact.'

'Hughes thinks there is a chance we can prove ourselves innocent and recover our licences,' Cranfield said formally, his own disbelief showing like two heads. 'In order to help me keep the stable together while he makes enquiries, Hughes has agreed to contribute one half towards your wages for one month.' I looked at him sharply. That was not at all what I had agreed. He showed no sign of acknowledging his reinterpretation (to put it charitably) of the offer I had accepted, and went authoritatively on. 'Therefore, as your present week's notice still has five days to run, none of you will be required to leave here for five weeks. In fact,' he added grudgingly, 'I would be obliged if you would all stay.'

Archie said to me, 'You really mean it?' and I watched the hope suddenly spring up in his face and thought that maybe it wasn't only my own chance of a future that was worth eight hundred quid.

'That's right,' I agreed. 'As long as you don't all spend the month busily fixing up to go somewhere else at the end of it.'

'What do you take us for?' Archie protested.

'Cynics,' I said, and Archie actually laughed.

I left Cranfield and Archie talking together with most of the desperation evaporating from both of them, and walked away to my aerodynamic burnt-orange car. I didn't hear Roberta following me until she spoke in my ear as I opened the door.

'Can you really do it?' she said.

'Do what?'

'Get your licences back.'

'It's going to cost me too much not to. So I guess I'll have to or . . .'

'Or what?'

I smiled. 'Or die in the attempt.'

It took me an hour to cross into Gloucestershire and almost half as long to sort out the geography of the village of Downfield, which mostly seemed to consist of cul-de-sacs.

The cottage I eventually found after six misdirections from local inhabitants was old but not beautiful, well painted but in dreary colours, and a good deal more trustworthy than its owner.

When Mrs Charlie West saw who it was, she tried to shut the front door in my face. I put out a hand that was used to dealing with strong horses and pulled her by the wrist, so that if she slammed the door she would be squashing her own arm.

She screeched loudly. An inner door at the back of the hall opened all of six inches, and Charlie's round face appeared through the crack. A distinct lack of confidence was discernible in that area.

'He's hurting me,' Mrs West shouted.

'I want to talk to you,' I said to Charlie over her shoulder.

Charlie West was less than willing. Abandoning his teenage wife, long straight hair, Dusty Springfield eyelashes, beige lipstick and all, he retreated a pace and quite firmly shut his door. Mrs West put up a loud and energetic defence to my attempt to establish further contact with Master Charlie, and I went through the hall fending off her toes and fists.

Charlie had wedged a chair under the door handle.

I shouted through the wood. 'Much as you deserve it, I haven't come here to beat you up. Come out and talk.'

No response of any sort. I rattled the door. Repeated my request. No results. With Mrs West still stabbing around like an agitated hornet I went out of the front door and round the outside to try to talk to him through the window. The window was open, and the sitting-room inside was empty.

I turned round in time to see Charlie's distant back-view disappearing across a field and into the next parish. Mrs West saw him too, and gave a nasty smile.

'So there,' she said triumphantly.

'Yes,' I said. 'I'm sure you must be very proud of him.'

The smile wobbled. I walked back down their garden path, climbed into the car, and drove away.

Round one slightly farcically to the opposition.

Two miles away from the village I stopped the car in a farm gateway and thought it over. Charlie West had been a great deal more scared of me than I would have supposed, even allowing for the fact that I was a couple of sizes bigger and a fair amount stronger. Maybe Charlie was as much afraid of my fury as of my fists. He almost seemed to have been expecting that I would attempt some sort of retaliation, and certainly after what he had done, he had a right to. All the same, he still represented my quickest and easiest route to who, if not to why.

After a while I started up again and drove on into the nearest town. Remembered I hadn't eaten all day, put away some rather good cold beef at three-thirty in a home-made café geared more to cake and scones, dozed in the car, waited until dark, and finally drove back again to Charlie's village.

There were lights on in several rooms of his cottage. The Wests were at home. I turned the car and re-tracked about a hundred yards, stopping half on and half off a grassy verge. Climbed out. Stood up.

Plan of attack: vague. I had had some idea of ringing the front-door bell, disappearing and waiting for either Charlie or his dolly wife to take one incautious step outside to investigate. Instead, unexpected allies materialized in the shape of one small boy and one large dog.

The boy had a torch, and was talking to his dog, who paused to dirty up the roadside five yards ahead.

'What the hell d'you think you were at, you bloody great nit, scoffing our Mum's stewing steak? Gor blimey mate, don't you ever learn nothing? Tomorrow's dinner gone down your useless big gullet and our Dad will give us both a belting this time I shouldn't wonder, not just you, you senseless rotten idiot. Time you knew the bloody difference between me Mum's stewing steak and dog meat, it is straight, though come to think of it there isn't all that difference, 'specially as maybe your eyes don't look at things the same. Do they? I damn well wish you could talk, mate.'

I clicked shut the door of the car and startled him,

and he swung round with the torch searching wildly. The beam caught me and steadied on my face.

The boy said, 'You come near me and I'll set my dog on you.' The dog, however, was still squatting and showed no enthusiasm.

'I'll stay right here, then,' I said amicably, leaning back against the car. 'I only want to know who lives in that cottage over there, where the lights are.'

'How do I know? We only come to live here the day before yesterday.'

'Great . . . I mean, that must be great for you, moving.'

'Yeah. Sure. You stay there, then. I'm going now.' He beckoned to the dog. The dog was still busy.

'How would it be if you could offer your Mum the price of the stewing steak? Maybe she wouldn't tell your Dad, then, and neither you nor the dog would get a belting.'

'Our Mum says we mustn't talk to strange men.'

'Hmm. Well, never mind then. Off you go.'

'I'll go when I'm ready,' he said belligerently. A natural born rebel. About nine years old, I guessed.

'What would I have to do for it?' he said, after a pause.

'Nothing much. Just ring the front-door bell of that cottage and tell whoever answers that you can't stop your dog eating the crocuses they've got growing all along the front there. Then when they come out to see, just nip off home as fast as your dog can stagger.'

It appealed to him. 'Steak probably cost a good bit,' he said.

'Probably.' I dug into my pocket and came up with a small fistful of pennies and silver. 'This should leave a bit over.'

'He doesn't really have to eat the crocuses, does he?'

'No.'

'OK, then.' Once his mind was made up he was jaunty and efficient. He shovelled my small change into his pocket, marched up to Charlie's front door, and told Mrs West, who cautiously answered it, that she was losing her crocuses. She scolded him all the way down the path, and while she was bending down to search for the damage, my accomplice quietly vanished. Before Mrs West exactly realized she had been misled I had stepped briskly through her front door and shut her out of her own house.

When I opened the sitting-room door Charlie said, without lifting his eyes from a racing paper, 'It wasn't him again, then.'

'Yes,' I said, 'it was.'

Charlie's immature face crumpled into a revolting state of fear and Mrs West leaned on the door bell. I shut the sitting-room door behind me to cut out some of the din.

'What are you so afraid of?' I said loudly.

'Well . . . you . . .'

'And so you damn well ought to be,' I agreed. I took a step towards him and he shrank back into his armchair. He was brave enough on a horse, which made this abject cringing all the more unexpected, and all the more unpleasant. I took another step. He fought his way into the upholstery.

Mrs West gave the door bell a rest.

'Why did you do it?' I said.

He shook his head dumbly, and pulled his feet up on to the chair seat in the classic womb position. Wishful regression to the first and only place where the world couldn't reach him.

'Charlie, I came here for some answers, and you're going to give them to me.'

Mrs West's furious face appeared at the window and she started rapping hard enough to break the glass. With one eye on her husband to prevent him making another bolt for it, I stepped over and undid the latch.

'Get out of here,' she shouted. 'Go on, get out.'

'You get in. Through here, I'm not opening the door.'

'I'll fetch the police.'

'Do what you like. I only want to talk to your worm of a husband. Get in or stay out, but shut up.'

She did anything but. Once she was in the room it took another twenty minutes of fruitless slanging before I could ask Charlie a single question without her loud voice obliterating any chance of an answer.

Charlie himself tired of it first and told her to stop, but at least her belligerence had given him a breathing space. He put his feet down on the floor again and said it was no use asking those questions, he didn't know the answers.

'You must do. Unless you told those lies about me out of sheer personal spite.'

'No.'

'Then why?'

'I'm not telling you.'

'Then I'll tell you something, you little louse. I'm going to find out who put you up to it. I'm going to stir everything up until I find out, and then I'm going to raise such a stink about being framed that sulphur will smell like sweet peas by comparison, and you, Master Charlie West, *you* will find yourself without a licence, not me, and even if you get it back you'll never live down the contempt everyone will feel for you.'

'Don't you talk to my Charlie like that!'

'Your Charlie is a vicious little liar who would sell you too for fifty pounds.'

'It wasn't fifty,' she snapped triumphantly. 'It was five hundred.'

Charlie yelled at her and I came as near to hitting him as the distance between my clenched teeth. Five hundred pounds. He'd lied my licence away for a handout that would have insulted a tout.

'That does it,' I said. 'And now you tell me who paid you.'

The girl wife started to look as frightened as Charlie, and it didn't occur to me then that my anger had flooded through that little room like a tidal wave.

Charlie stuttered, 'I d . . . d . . . don't know.'

I took a pace towards him and he scrambled out of his chair and took refuge behind it.

'K . . . k . . . keep away from me. I don't know. I don't know.'

'That isn't good enough.'

'He really doesn't know,' the girl wailed. 'He really doesn't.'

'He does,' I repeated furiously.

The girl began to cry. Charlie seemed to be on the verge of copying her.

'I never saw . . . never saw the bloke. He telephoned.'

'And how did he pay you?'

'In two . . . in two packages. In one-pound notes. A hundred of them came the day before the Enquiry, and I was to get . . .' His voice trailed away.

'You were to get the other four hundred if I was warned off?'

He nodded, a fractional jerk. His head was tucked into his shoulders, as if to avoid a blow.

'And have you?'

'What?'

'Have you had it yet? The other four hundred?'

97

His eyes widened, and he spoke in jerks. 'No . . . but . . . of course . . . it . . . will . . . come.'

'Of course it won't,' I said brutally. 'You stupid treacherous little ninny.' My voice sounded thick, and each word came out separately and loaded with fury.

Both of the Wests were trembling, and the girl's eye make-up was beginning to run down her cheeks.

'What did he sound like, this man on the telephone?'

'Just . . . just a man,' Charlie said.

'And did it occur to you to ask *why* he wanted me warned off?'

'I said . . . you hadn't done anything to harm me . . . and he said . . . you never know . . . supposing one day he does . . .'

Charlie shrank still farther under my astounded glare.

'Anyway . . . five hundred quid . . . I don't earn as much as you, you know.' For the first time there was a tinge of spite in his voice, and I knew that in truth jealousy had been a factor, that he hadn't in fact done it entirely for the money. He'd got his kicks, too.

'You're only twenty,' I said. 'What exactly do you expect?'

But Charlie expected everything, always, to be run entirely for the best interests of Charlie West.

I said, 'And you'll be wise to spend that money carefully, because, believe me, it's going to be the most expensive hundred quid you've ever earned.'

'Kelly...' He was halfway to entreaty. Jealous, greedy, dishonest, and afraid. I felt not the remotest flicker of compassion for him, only a widening anger that the motives behind his lies were so small.

'And when you lose your licence for this, and I'll see that you do, you'll have plenty of time to understand that it *serves you right.*'

The raw revenge in my voice made a desert of their little home. They both stood there dumbly with wide miserable eyes, too broken up to raise another word. The girl's beige mouth hung slackly open, mascara half-way to her chin, long hair straggling in wisps across her face and round her shoulders. She looked sixteen. A child. So did Charlie. The worst vandals are always childish.

I turned away from them and walked out of their cottage, and my anger changed into immense depression on the drive home.

CHAPTER SIX

At two o'clock in the morning the rage I'd unleashed on the Wests looked worse and worse.

To start with, it had achieved nothing helpful. I'd known before I went there that Charlie must have had a reason for lying about me at the Enquiry. I now knew the reason to be five hundred pounds. Marvellous. A useless scrap of information out of a blizzard of emotion.

Lash out when you're hurt . . . I'd done that, all right. Poured out on them the roaring bitterness I'd smothered under a civilized front ever since Monday.

Nor had I given Charlie any reason to do me any good in future. Very much the reverse. He wasn't going to be contrite and eager to make amends. When he'd recovered himself he'd be sullen and vindictive.

I'd been taught the pattern over and over. Country A plays an isolated shabby trick. Country B is outraged and exacts revenge. Country A is forced to express apologies and meekly back down, but thoroughly resents it. Country A now holds a permanent grudge, and harms Country B whenever possible. One of the classic variations in the history of politics and aggression. Also applicable to individuals.

To have known about the pitfalls and jumped in regardless was a mite galling. It just showed how easily good sense lost out to anger. It also showed me that I wasn't going to get results that way. A crash course in detection would have been handy. Failing that, I'd have to start taking stock of things coolly, instead of charging straight off again towards the easiest looking target, and making another mess of it.

Cool stock-taking...

Charlie West hadn't wanted to see me because he had a guilty conscience. It followed that everyone else who had a guilty conscience wouldn't want to see me. Even if they didn't actually spring off across the fields, they would all do their best to avoid my reaching them. I was going to have to become adept – and fast – at entering their lives when their backs were turned.

If Charlie West didn't know who had paid him, and I believed that he didn't, it followed that perhaps no one else who had lied knew who had persuaded them to. Perhaps it had all been done on the telephone. Long-distance leverage. Impersonal and undiscoverable.

Perhaps I had set myself an impossible task and I

101

should give up the whole idea and emigrate to Australia.

Except that they had racing in Australia, and I wouldn't be able to go. The banishment covered the world. Warned off. Warned off.

Oh God.

All right, so maybe I did let the self-pity catch up with me for a while. But I was privately alone in my bed in the dark, and I'd jeered myself out of it by morning.

Looking about as ragged as I felt, I got up at six and pointed the Lotus's smooth nose towards London, NW7, Mill Hill.

Since I could see no one at the races I had to catch them at home, and in the case of George Newtonnards, bookmaker, home proved to be a sprawling pink-washed ranch-type bungalow in a prosperous suburban road. At eight-thirty a.m. I hoped to find him at breakfast, but in fact he was opening his garage door when I arrived. I parked squarely across the entrance to his drive, which was hardly likely to make me popular, and he came striding down towards me to tell me to move.

I climbed out of the car. When he saw who it was, he stopped dead. I walked up the drive to meet him, shivering a little in the raw east wind and regretting I wasn't snug inside a fur-collared jacket like his.

'What are you doing here?' he said sharply.

'I would be very grateful if you would just tell me one or two things . . .'

'I haven't time.' He was easy, self-assured, dealing with a small-sized nuisance. 'And nothing I can say will help you. Move your car, please.'

'Certainly . . . Could you tell me how it was that you came to be asked to give evidence against Mr Cranfield?'

'How it was? . . .' He looked slightly surprised. 'I received an official letter, requiring me to attend.'

'Well, why? I mean, how did the Stewards know about Mr Cranfield's bet on Cherry Pie? Did you write and tell them?'

He gave me a cool stare. 'I hear,' he said, 'that you are maintaining you were framed.'

'News travels.'

A faint smile. 'News always travels – towards me. An accurate information service is the basis of good bookmaking.'

'How did the Stewards know about Mr Cranfield's bet?'

'Mm. Well, yes, that I don't know.'

'Who, besides you, knew that you believed that Cranfield had backed Cherry Pie?'

'He did back him.'

'Well, who besides you knew that he had?'

'I haven't time for this.'

'I'll be happy to move my car... in a minute or two.'

His annoyed glare gradually softened round the edges into a half-amused acceptance. A very smooth civilized man, George Newtonnards.

'Very well. I told a few of the lads... other book-makers, that is. I was angry about it, see? Letting myself be taken to the cleaners like that. Me, at my age, I should know better. So maybe one of them passed on the word to the Stewards, knowing the Enquiry was coming up. But no, I didn't do it myself.'

'Could you guess which one might have done? I mean, do you know of anyone who has a grudge against Cranfield?'

'Can't think of one.' He shrugged. 'No more than against any other trainer who tries it on.'

'Tries it on?' I echoed, surprised. 'But he doesn't.'

'Oh yeah?'

'I ride them,' I protested. 'I should know.'

'Yes,' he said sarcastically. 'You should. Don't come the naïve bit with me, chum. Your friend Chris Smith, him with the cracked skull, he's a proper artist at strangulation, wouldn't you say? Same as you are. A fine pair, the two of you.'

'You believe I pulled Squelch, then?'

'Stands to reason.'

'All the same, I didn't.'

'Tell it to the Marines.' A thought struck him. 'I

don't know any bookmakers who have a grudge against Cranfield, but I sure know one who has a grudge against *you*. A whopping great life-sized grudge. One time, he was almost coming after you with a chopper. You got in his way proper, mate, you did indeed.'

'How? And who?'

'You and Chris Smith, you were riding two for Cranfield . . . about six months ago. It was . . . right at the beginning of the season anyway . . . in a novice 'chase at Fontwell. Remember? There was a big holiday crowd in from the South Coast because it was a bit chilly that day for lying on the beach . . . anyway, there was a big crowd all primed with holiday money . . . and there were you and Chris Smith on these two horses, and the public fancying both of them, and Pelican Jobberson asked you which was off, and you said you hadn't an earthly on yours, so he rakes in the cash on you and doesn't bother to balance his book, and then you go and ride a hell of a finish and win by a neck, when you could have lost instead without the slightest trouble. Pelican went spare and swore he'd be even with you when he got the chance.'

'I believed what I told him,' I said. 'It was that horse's first attempt over fences. No one could have predicted he'd have been good enough to win.'

'Then why did you?'

'The owner wanted to, if possible.'

'Did he bet on it?'

'The owner? No. It was a woman. She never bets much. She just likes to see her horses win.'

'Pelican swore you'd backed it yourself, and put him off so that you could get a better price.'

'You bookmakers are too suspicious for your own good.'

'Hard experience proves us right.'

'Well, he's wrong this time,' I insisted. 'This bird friend of yours. If he asked me ... and I don't remember him asking ... then I told him the truth. And anyway, any bookmaker who asks jockeys questions like that is asking for trouble. Jockeys are the worst tipsters in the world.'

'Some aren't,' he said flatly. 'Some are good at it.'

I skipped that. 'Is he still angry after all these months? And if so, would he be angry enough not just to tell the Stewards that Cranfield backed Cherry Pie, but to bribe other people to invent lies about us?'

His eyes narrowed while he thought about it. He pursed his mouth, undecided. 'You'd better ask him yourself.'

'Thanks.' Hardly an easy question.

'Move your car now?' he suggested.

'Yes.' I walked two steps towards it, then stopped and turned back. 'Mr Newtonnards, if you see the man who put the money on for Mr Cranfield, will you find out who he is ... and let me know?'

'Why don't you ask Cranfield?'

'He said he didn't want to involve him.'

'But you do?'

'I suppose I'm grasping at anything,' I said. 'But yes, I think I do.'

'Why don't you just quieten down and take it?' he said reasonably. 'All this thrashing about . . . you got copped. So, you got copped. Fair enough. Sit it out, then. You'll get your licence back, eventually.'

'Thank you for your advice,' I said politely, and went and moved my car out of his gateway.

It was Thursday. I should have been going to Warwick to ride in four races. Instead, I drove aimlessly back round the North Circular Road wondering whether or not to pay a call on David Oakley, enquiry agent and imaginative photographer. If Charlie West didn't know who had framed me, it seemed possible that Oakley might be the only one who did. But even if he did, he was highly unlikely to tell me. There seemed no point in confronting him, and yet nothing could be gained if I made no attempt.

In the end I stopped at a telephone box and found his number via enquiries.

A girl answered. 'Mr Oakley isn't in yet.'

'Can I make an appointment?'

She asked me what about.

'A divorce.'

She said Mr Oakley could see me at 11.30, and asked me my name.

'Charles Crisp.'

'Very well, Mr Crisp. Mr Oakley will be expecting you.'

I doubted it. On the other hand, he, like Charlie West, might in general be expecting some form of protest.

From the North Circular Road I drove ninety miles up the M1 motorway to Birmingham and found Oakley's office above a bicycle and radio shop half a mile from the town centre.

His street door, shabby black, bore a neat small nameplate stating, simply, 'Oakley'. There were two keyholes, Yale and Chubb, and a discreetly situated peephole. I tried the handle of this apparent fortress, and the door opened easily under my touch. Inside, there was a narrow passage with pale blue walls leading to an uncarpeted staircase stretching upwards.

I walked up, my feet sounding loud on the boards. At the top there was a small landing with another shabby black door, again similarly fortified. On this door, another neat notice said, 'Please ring'. There was a bell push: I gave it three seconds' work.

The door was opened by a tall strong-looking girl dressed in a dark coloured leather trouser-suit. Under the jacket she wore a black sweater, and under the trouser legs, black leather boots. Black eyes returned

my scrutiny, black hair held back by a tortoiseshell
band fell straight to her shoulders before curving
inwards. She seemed at first sight to be about twenty-
four, but there were already wrinkle lines round her
eyes, and the deadness in their expression indicated too
much familiarity with dirty washing.

'I have an appointment,' I said. 'Crisp.'

'Come in.' She opened the door wider and left it for
me to close.

I followed her into the room, a small square office
furnished with a desk, typewriter, telephone, and four
tall filing cabinets. On the far side of the room there
was another door. Not black; modern flat hardboard,
painted grey. More keyholes. I eyed them thoughtfully.

The girl opened the door, said through it, 'It's Mr
Crisp,' and stood back for me to pass her.

'Thank you,' I said. Took three steps forwards, and
shut myself in with David Oakley.

His office was not a great deal larger than the ante-
room, and no thrift had been spared with the furniture.
There was dim brown linoleum, a bentwood coat stand,
a small cheap armchair facing a grey metal desk, and
over the grimy window, in place of curtains, a tough-
looking fixed frame covered with chicken wire. Outside
the window there were the heavy bars and supports of
a fire escape. The Birmingham sun, doing its best
against odds, struggled through and fell in wrinkled
honeycomb shadows on the surface of an ancient safe.

In the wall on my right, another door, firmly closed. With yet more keyholes.

Behind the desk in a swivel chair sat the proprietor of all this glory, the totally unmemorable Mr Oakley. Youngish. Slender. Mouse-coloured hair. And this time, sunglasses.

'Sit down, Mr Crisp,' he said. Accentless voice, entirely emotionless, as before. 'Divorce, I believe? Give me the details of your requirements, and we can arrive at a fee.' He looked at his watch. 'I can give you just ten minutes, I'm afraid. Shall we get on?'

He hadn't recognized me. I thought I might as well take advantage of it.

'I understand you would be prepared to fake some evidence for me ... photographs?'

He began to nod, and then grew exceptionally still. The unrevealing dark glasses were motionless. The pale straight mouth didn't twitch. The hand lying on the desk remained loose and relaxed.

Finally he said, without any change of inflection, 'Get out.'

'How much do you charge for faking evidence?'

'Get out.'

I smiled. 'I'd like to know how much I was worth.'

'Dust,' he said. His foot moved under the desk.

'I'll pay you in gold dust, if you'll tell me who gave you the job.'

He considered it. Then he said, 'No.'

The door to the outer office opened quietly behind me.

Oakley said calmly, 'This is not a Mr Crisp, Didi. This is a Mr Kelly Hughes. Mr Hughes will be leaving.'

'Mr Hughes is not ready,' I said.

'I think Mr Hughes will find he is,' she said.

I looked at her over my shoulder. She was carrying a large black-looking pistol with a very large black-looking silencer. The whole works were pointing steadily my way.

'How dramatic,' I said. 'Can you readily dispose of bodies in the centre of Birmingham?'

'Yes,' Oakley said.

'For a fee, of course, usually,' Didi added.

I struggled not to believe them, and lost. All the same . . .

'Should you decide after all to sell the information I need, you know where to find me.' I relaxed against the back of the chair.

'I may have a liking for gold dust,' he said calmly. 'But I am not a fool.'

'Opinions differ,' I remarked lightly.

There was no reaction. 'It is not in my interest that you should prove you were . . . shall we say . . . set up.'

'I understand that. Eventually, however, you will wish that you hadn't helped to do it.'

He said smoothly. 'A number of other people have

said much the same, though few, I must confess, as quietly as you.'

It occurred to me suddenly that he must be quite used to the sort of enraged onslaught I'd thrown at the Wests, and that perhaps that was why his office . . . Didi caught my wandering glance and cynically nodded.

'That's right. Too many people tried to smash the place up. So we keep the damage to a minimum.'

'How wise.'

'I'm afraid I really do have another appointment now,' Oakley said. 'So if you'll excuse me? . . .'

I stood up. There was nothing to stay for.

'It surprises me,' I remarked, 'that you're not in jail.'

'I am clever,' he said matter-of-factly. 'My clients are satisfied, and people like you, . . . impotent.'

'Someone will kill you, one day.'

'Will you?'

I shook my head. 'Not worth it.'

'Exactly,' he said calmly. 'The jobs I accept are never what the victims would actually kill me for. I really am not a fool.'

'No,' I said.

I walked across to the door and Didi made room for me to pass. She put the pistol down on her desk in the outer office and switched off a red bulb which glowed brightly in a small switchboard.

'Emergency signal?' I enquired. 'Under his desk.'

'You could say so.'

'Is that gun loaded?'

Her eyebrows rose. 'Naturally.'

'I see.' I opened the outer door. She walked over to close it behind me as I went towards the stairs.

'Nice to have met you, Mr Hughes,' she said unemotionally. 'Don't come back.'

I walked along to my car in some depression. From none of the three damaging witnesses at the Enquiry had I got any change at all, and what David Oakley had said about me being impotent looked all too true.

There seemed to be no way of proving that he had simply brought with him the money he had photographed in my flat. No one at Corrie had seen him come or go: Tony had asked all the lads, and none of them had seen him. And Oakley would have found it easy enough to be unobserved. He had only had to arrive early, while everyone was out riding on the Downs at morning exercise. From seven-thirty to eight-thirty the stable yard would be deserted. Letting himself in through my unlocked door, setting up his props, loosing off a flash or two, and quietly retreating ... The whole process would have taken him no more than ten minutes.

It was possible he had kept a record of his shady transactions. Possible, not probable. He might need to keep some hold over his clients, to prevent their later

113

denouncing him in fits of resurgent civil conscience. If he did keep such records, it might account for the multiplicity of locks. Or maybe the locks were simply to discourage people from breaking in to search for records, as they were certainly discouraging me.

Would Oakley, I wondered, have done what Charlie West had done, and produced his lying testimony for a voice on the telephone? On the whole, I decided not. Oakley had brains where Charlie had vanity, and Oakley would not involve himself without his clients up tight too. Oakley had to know who had done the engineering.

But stealing that information . . . or beating it out of him . . . or tricking him into giving it . . . as well as buying it from him . . . every course looked as hopeless as the next. I could only ride horses. I couldn't pick locks, fights, or pockets. Certainly not Oakley's.

Oakley and Didi. They were old at the game. They'd invented the rules. Oakley and Didi were senior league.

How did anyone get in touch with Oakley, if they needed his brand of service?

He could scarcely advertise.

Someone had to know about him.

I thought it over for a while, sitting in my car in the car park wondering what to do next. There was only one person I knew who could put his finger on the pulse of Birmingham if he wanted to, and the likelihood was that in my present circumstances he wouldn't want to.

However . . .

I started the car, threaded a way through the one-way streets, and found a slot in the crowded park behind the Great Stag Hotel. Inside, the ritual of Business Lunch was warming up, the atmosphere thickening nicely with the smell of alcohol, the resonance of fruity voices, the haze of cigars. The Great Stag Hotel attracted almost exclusively a certain grade of wary, prosperous, level-headed businessmen needing a soft background for hard options, and it attracted them because the landlord, Teddy Dewar, was that sort of man himself.

I found him in the bar, talking to two others almost indistinguishable from him in their dark grey suits, white shirts, neat maroon ties, seventeen-inch necks, and thirty-eight-inch waists.

A faint glaze came over his professionally noncommittal expression when he caught sight of me over their shoulders. A warned-off jockey didn't rate too high with him. Lowered the tone of the place, no doubt.

I edged through to the bar on one side of him and ordered whisky.

'I'd be grateful for a word with you,' I said.

He turned his head a fraction in my direction, and

without looking at me directly answered. 'Very well. In a few minutes.'

No warmth in the words. No ducking of the unwelcome situation, either. He went on talking to the two men about the dicky state of oil shares, and eventually smoothly disengaged himself and turned to me.

'Well, Kelly . . .' His eyes were cool and distant, waiting to see what I wanted before showing any real feeling.

'Will you lunch with me?' I made it casual.

His surprise was controlled. 'I thought . . .'

'I may be banned,' I said, 'but I still eat.'

He studied my face. 'You mind.'

'What do you expect . . .? I'm sorry it shows.'

He said neutrally, 'There's a muscle in your jaw . . . Very well: if you don't mind going in straightaway.'

We sat against the wall at an inconspicuous table and chose beef cut from a roast on a trolley. While he ate his eyes checked the running of the dining-room, missing nothing. I waited until he was satisfied that all was well and then came briefly to the point.

'Do you know anything about a man called David Oakley? He's an enquiry agent. Operates from an office about half a mile from here.'

'David Oakley? I can't say I've ever heard of him.'

'He manufactured some evidence which swung things against me at the Stewards' Enquiry on Monday.'

'Manufactured?' There was delicate doubt in his voice.

'Oh yes,' I sighed. 'I suppose it sounds corny, but I really was not guilty as charged. But someone made sure it looked like it.' I told him about the photograph of money in my bedroom.

'And you never had this money?'

'I did not. And the note supposed to be from Cranfield was a forgery. But how could we prove it?'

He thought it over.

'You can't.'

'Exactly,' I agreed.

'This David Oakley who took the photograph ... I suppose you got no joy from him.'

'No joy is right.'

'I don't understand precisely why you've come to me.' He finished his beef and laid his knife and fork tidily together. Waiters appeared like genii to clear the table and bring coffee. He waited still noncommittally while I paid the bill.

'I expect it is too much to ask,' I said finally. 'After all, I've only stayed here three or four times, I have no claim on you personally for friendship or help ... and yet, there's no one else I know who could even begin to do what you could ... if you will.'

'What?' he said succinctly.

'I want to know how people are steered towards David Oakley, if they want some evidence faked. He

117

as good as told me he is quite accustomed to do it. Well . . . how does he get his clients? Who recommends him? I thought that among all the people you know, you might think of someone who could perhaps pretend he wanted a job done . . . or pretend he had a friend who wanted a job done . . . and throw out feelers, and see if anyone finally recommended Oakley. And if so, who.'

He considered it. 'Because if you found one contact you might work back from there to another . . . and eventually perhaps to a name which meant something to you? . . .'

'I suppose it sounds feeble,' I said resignedly.

'It's a very outside chance,' he agreed. There was a long pause. Then he added, 'All the same, I do know of someone who might agree to try.' He smiled briefly, for the first time.

'That's . . .' I swallowed. 'That's marvellous.'

'Can't promise results.'

CHAPTER SEVEN

Tony came clomping up my stairs on Friday morning after first exercise and poured half an inch of Scotch into the coffee I gave him. He drank the scalding mixture and shuddered as the liquor bit.

'God,' he said. 'It's cold on the Downs.'

'Rather you than me,' I said.

'Liar,' he said amicably. 'It must feel odd to you, not riding.'

'Yes.'

He sprawled in the green armchair. 'Poppy's got the morning ickies again. I'll be glad when this lousy pregnancy is over. She's been ill half the time.'

'Poor Poppy.'

'Yeah . . . Anyway, what it means is that we ain't going to that dance tonight. She says she can't face it.'

'Dance? . . .'

'The Jockey's Fund dance. You know. You've got the tickets on your mantel over there.'

119

'Oh ... yes. I'd forgotten about it. We were going together.'

'That's right. But now, as I was saying, you'll have to go without us.'

'I'm not going at all.'

'I thought you might not.' He sighed and drank deeply. 'Where did you get to yesterday?'

'I called on people who didn't want to see me.'

'Any results?'

'Not many.' I told him briefly about Newtonnards and David Oakley, and about the hour I'd spent with Andrew Tring.

It was because the road home from Birmingham led near his village that I'd thought of Andrew Tring, and my first instinct anyway was to shy away from even the thought of him. Certainly visiting one of the Stewards who had helped to warn him off was not regulation behaviour for a disbarred jockey. If I hadn't been fairly strongly annoyed with him I would have driven straight on.

He was disgusted with me for calling. He opened the door of his prosperous sprawling old manor house himself and had no chance of saying he was out.

'Kelly! What are you doing here?'

'Asking you for some explanation.'

'I've nothing to say to you.'

'You have indeed.'

He frowned. Natural good manners were only just

preventing him from retreating and shutting the door in my face. 'Come in then. Just for a few minutes.'

'Thank you,' I said without irony, and followed him into a nearby small room lined with books and containing a vast desk, three deep armchairs and a colour television set.

'Now,' he said, shutting the door and not offering the armchairs, 'why have you come?'

He was four years older than me, and about the same size. Still as trim as when he rode races, still outwardly the same man. Only the casual, long-established changing-room friendliness seemed to have withered somewhere along the upward path from amateurship to Authority.

'Andy,' I said, 'do you really and honestly believe that Squelch race was rigged?'

'You were warned off,' he said coldly.

'That's far from being the same thing as guilty.'

'I don't agree.'

'Then you're stupid,' I said bluntly. 'As well as scared out of your tiny wits.'

'That's enough, Kelly. I don't have to listen to this.' He opened the door again and waited for me to leave. I didn't. Short of throwing me out bodily he was going to have to put up with me a little longer. He gave me a furious stare and shut the door again.

I said more reasonably, 'I'm sorry. Really, I'm sorry. It's just that you rode against me for at least five years... I'd have thought you wouldn't so easily believe I'd deliberately lose a race. I've never yet lost a race I could win.'

He was silent. He knew that I didn't throw races. Anyone who rode regularly knew who would and who wouldn't, and in spite of what Charlie West had said at the Enquiry, I was not an artist at stopping one because I hadn't given it the practice.

'There was that money,' he said at last. He sounded disillusioned and discouraged.

'I never had it. Oakley took it with him into my flat and photographed it there. All that so-called evidence, the whole bloody Enquiry in fact, was as genuine as a lead sixpence.'

He gave me a long doubtful look. Then he said, 'There's nothing I can do about it.'

'What are you afraid of?'

'Stop saying I'm afraid,' he said irritably. 'I'm not afraid. I just can't do anything about it, even if what you say is true.'

'It is true ... and maybe you don't think you are afraid, but that's definitely the impression you give. Or maybe ... are you simply overawed? The new boy among the old powerful prefects. Is that it? Afraid of putting a foot wrong with them?'

'Kelly!' he protested; but it was the protest of a touched nerve.

I said unkindly, 'You're a gutless disappointment,'

and took a step towards his door. He didn't move to open it for me. Instead he put up a hand to stop me, looking as angry as he had every right to.

'That's not fair. Just because I can't help you . . .'

'You could have done. At the Enquiry.'

'You don't understand.'

'I do indeed. You found it easier to believe me guilty than to tell Gowery you had any doubts.'

'It wasn't as easy as you think.'

'Thanks,' I said ironically.

'I don't mean . . .' He shook his head impatiently. 'I mean, it wasn't all as simple as you make out. When Gowery asked me to sit with him at the Enquiry I believed it was only going to be a formality, that both you and Cranfield had run the Lemonfizz genuinely and were surprised yourselves by the result. Colonel Midgley told me it was ridiculous having to hold the Enquiry at all, really. I never expected to be caught up in having to warn you off.'

'Did you say,' I said, 'that Lord Gowery asked you to sit with him?'

'Of course. That's the normal procedure. The Stewards sitting at an Enquiry aren't picked out of a hat . . .'

'There isn't any sort of rota?'

'No. The Disciplinary Steward asks two colleagues to officiate with him . . . and that's what put me on the spot, if you must know, because I didn't want to say no to Lord Gowery . . .' He stopped.

'Go on,' I urged without heat. 'Why not?'

'Well because . . .' He hesitated, then said slowly, 'I suppose in a way I owe it to you . . . I'm sorry Kelly, desperately sorry, I do know you don't usually rig races . . . I'm in an odd position with Gowery and it's vitally important I keep in with him.'

I stifled my indignation. Andrew Tring's eyes were looking inward and from his expression he didn't very much like what he could see.

'He owns the freehold of the land just north of Manchester where our main pottery is.' Andrew Tring's family fortunes were based not on fine porcelain but on smashable teacups for institutions. His products were dropped by washers-up in schools and hospitals from Waterloo to Hong Kong, and the pieces in the world's dustbins were his perennial licence to print money.

He said, 'There's been some redevelopment round there and that land is suddenly worth about a quarter of a million. And our lease runs out in three years . . . We have been negotiating a new one, but the old one was for ninety-nine years and no one is keen to renew for that long . . . The ground rent is in any case going to be raised considerably, but if Gowery changes his mind and wants to sell that land for development, there's nothing we can do about it. We only own the buildings . . . We'd lose the entire factory if he didn't renew the lease . . . And we can only make cups and saucers so cheaply because our overheads are small . . .

If we have to build or rent a new factory our prices will be less competitive and our world trade figures will slump. Gowery himself has the final say as to whether our lease will be renewed or not, and on what terms . . . so you see, Kelly, it's not that I'm afraid of him . . . there's so much more at stake . . . and he's always a man to hold it against you if you argue with him.'

He stopped and looked at me gloomily. I looked gloomily back. The facts of life stared us stonily in the face.

'So that's that,' I agreed. 'You are quite right. You can't help me. You couldn't, right from the start. I'm glad you explained . . .' I smiled at him twistedly, facing another dead end, the last of a profitless day.

'I'm sorry, Kelly . . .'

'Sure,' I said.

Tony finished his fortified breakfast and said, 'So there wasn't anything sinister in Andy Tring's lily-livered bit on Monday.'

'It depends what you call sinister. But no, I suppose not.'

'What's left, then?'

'Damn all,' I said in depression.

'You can't give up,' he protested.

'Oh no. But I've learned one thing in learning nothing, and that is that I'm getting nowhere because

I'm me. First thing Monday morning I'm going to hire me my own David Oakley.'

'Attaboy,' he said. He stood up. 'Time for second lot, I hear.' Down in the yard the lads were bringing out the horses, their hooves scrunching hollowly on the packed gravel.

'How are they doing?' I asked.

'Oh . . . so so. I sure hate having to put up other jocks. Given me a bellyful of the whole game, this business has.'

When he'd gone down to ride I cleaned up my already clean flat and made some more coffee. The day stretched emptily ahead. So did the next day and the one after that, and every day for an indefinite age.

Ten minutes of this prospect was enough. I searched around and found another straw to cling to: telephoned to a man I knew slightly at the BBC. A cool secretary said he was out, and to try again at eleven.

I tried again at eleven. Still out. I tried at twelve. He was in then, but sounded as if he wished he weren't.

'Not Kelly Hughes, the . . .' His voice trailed off while he failed to find a tactful way of putting it.

'That's right.'

'Well . . . er . . . I don't think . . .'

'I don't want anything much,' I assured him resignedly. 'I just want to know the name of the outfit who make the films of races. The camera patrol people.'

'Oh.' He sounded relieved. 'That's the Racecourse

Technical Services. Run by the Levy Board. They've a virtual monopoly, though there's one other small firm operating sometimes under licence. Then there are the television companies, of course. Did you want any particular race? Oh ... the Lemonfizz Crystal Cup, I suppose.'

'No,' I said. 'The meeting at Reading two weeks earlier.'

'Reading ... Reading ... Let's see, then. Which lot would that be?' He hummed a few out-of-tune bars while he thought it over. 'I should think ... yes, definitely the small firm, the Cannot Lie people. Cannot Lie, Ltd. Offices at Woking, Surrey. Do you want their number?'

'Yes, please.'

He read it to me.

'Thank you very much,' I said.

'Any time ... er ... well ... I mean ...'

'I know what you mean,' I agreed. 'But thanks anyway.'

I put down the receiver with a grimace. It was still no fun being everyone's idea of a villain.

The BBC man's reaction made me decide that the telephone might get me nil results from the Cannot Lie brigade. Maybe they couldn't lie, but they would certainly evade. And anyway, I had the whole day to waste.

The Cannot Lie office was a rung or two up the

127

luxury ladder from David Oakley's, which wasn't saying a great deal. A large rather bare room on the second floor of an Edwardian house in a side street. A rickety lift large enough for one slim man or two starving children. A well-worn desk with a well-worn blonde painting her toenails on top of it.

'Yes?' she said, when I walked in.

She had lilac panties on, with lace. She made no move to prevent me seeing a lot of them.

'No one in?' I asked.

'Only us chickens,' she agreed. She had a South London accent and the smart back-chatting intelligence that often goes with it. 'Which do you want, the old man or our Alfie?'

'You'll do nicely,' I said.

'Ta.' She took it as her due, with a practised come-on-so-far-but-no-further smile. One foot was finished. She stretched out her leg and wiggled it up and down to help with the drying.

'Going to a dance tonight,' she explained. 'In me peep-toes.'

I didn't think anyone would concentrate on the toes. Apart from the legs she had a sharp pointed little bosom under a white cotton sweater and a bright pink patent leather belt clasping a bikini-sized waist. Her body looked about twenty years old. Her face looked as if she'd spent the last six of them hopping.

'Paint the other one,' I suggested.

'You're not in a hurrry?'

'I'm enjoying the scenery.'

She gave a knowing giggle and started on the other foot. The view was even more hair-raising than before. She watched me watching, and enjoyed it.

'What's your name?' I asked.

'Carol. What's yours?'

'Kelly.'

'From the Isle of Man?'

'No. The land of our fathers.'

She gave me a bright glance. 'You catch on quick, don't you?'

I wished I did. I said regretfully, 'How long do you keep ordinary routine race films?'

'Huh? For ever, I suppose.' She changed mental gear effortlessly, carrying straight on with her uninhibited painting. 'We haven't destroyed any so far, that's to say. Course, we've only been in the racing business eighteen months. No telling what they'll do when the big storeroom's full. We're up to the eyebrows in all the others with films of motor races, golf matches, three-day events, any old things like that.'

'Where's the big storeroom?'

'Through there.' She waved the small pink enamelling brush in the general direction of a scratched once-cream door. 'Want to see?'

'If you don't mind.'

'Go right ahead.'

She had finished the second foot. The show was over. With a sigh I removed my gaze and walked over to the door in question. There was only a round hole where most doors have a handle. I pushed against the wood and the door swung inwards into another large high room, furnished this time with rows of free standing bookshelves, like a public library. The shelves, however, were of bare functional wood, and there was no covering on the planked floor.

Well over half the shelves were empty. On the others were rows of short wide box files, their backs labelled with neat typed strips explaining what was to be found within. Each box proved to contain all the films from one day's racing, and they were all efficiently arranged in chronological order. I pulled out the box for the day I rode Squelch and Wanderlust at Reading, and looked inside. There were six round cans of sixteen-millimetre film, numbered one to six, and space enough for another one, number seven.

I took the box out to Carol. She was still sitting on top of the desk, dangling the drying toes and reading through a woman's magazine.

'What have you found then?'

'Do you lend these films to anyone who wants them?'

'Hire, not lend. Sure.'

'Who to?'

'Anyone who asks. Usually it's the owners of the

horses. Often they want prints made to keep, so we make them.'

'Do the Stewards often want them?'

'Stewards? Well, see, if there's any doubt about a race the Stewards see the film on the racecourse. That van the old man and our Alfie's got develops it on the spot as soon as it's collected from the cameras.'

'But sometimes they send for them afterwards?'

'Sometimes, yeah. When they want to compare the running of some horse or other.' Her legs suddenly stopped swinging. She put down the magazine and gave me a straight stare.

'Kelly . . . Kelly Hughes?'

I didn't answer.

'Hey, you're not a bit like I thought.' She put her blonde head on one side, assessing me. 'None of those sports writers ever said anything about you being smashing looking and dead sexy.'

I laughed. I had a crooked nose and a scar down one cheek from where a horse's hoof had cut my face open, and among jockeys I was an also-ran as a bird-attracter.

'It's your eyes,' she said. 'Dark and sort of smiley and sad and a bit withdrawn. Give me the happy shivers, your eyes do.'

'You read all that in a magazine,' I said.

'I never!' but she laughed.

'Who asked for the film that's missing from the box?' I said. 'And what exactly did they ask for?'

She sighed exaggeratedly and edged herself off the desk into a pair of bright pink sandals.

'Which film is that?' She looked at the box and its reference number, and did a Marilyn Monroe sway over to a filing cabinet against the wall. 'Here we are. One official letter from the Stewards' secretary saying please send film of last race at Reading...'

I took the letter from her and read it myself. The words were quite clear: 'the last race at Reading'. Not the sixth race. The last race. And there had been seven races. It hadn't been Carol or the Cannot Lie Co who had made the mistake.

'So you sent it?'

'Of course. Off to the authorities, as per instructions.' She put the letter back in the files. 'Did you in, did it?'

'Not that film, no.'

'Alfie and the old man say you must have made a packet out of the Lemonfizz, to lose your licence over it.'

'Do you think so too?'

'Stands to reason. Everyone thinks so.'

'Man in the street?'

'Him too.'

'Not a cent.'

'You're a nit, then,' she said frankly. 'Whatever did you do it for?'

'I didn't.'

'Oh yeah?' She gave me a knowing wink. 'I suppose you have to say that, don't you?'

'Well,' I said, handing her the Reading box to put back in the storeroom. 'Thanks anyway.' I gave her half a smile and went away across the expanse of mottled linoleum to the door out.

I drove home slowly, trying to think. Not a very profitable exercise. Brains seemed to have deteriorated into a mushy blankness.

There were several letters for me in the mailbox on my front door, including one from my parents. I unfolded it walking up the stairs, feeling as usual a million miles away from them on every level.

My mother had written the first half in her round regular handwriting on one side of a large piece of lined paper. As usual there wasn't a full stop to be seen. She punctuated entirely with commas.

Dear Kelly,

Thanks for your note, we got it yesterday, we don't like reading about you in the papers, I know you said you hadn't done it, son, but no smoke without fire is what Mrs Jones the post office says, and it is not nice for us what people are saying about you round here, all the airs and graces they say you are and pride goes before a fall and all that, well the pullets have started laying at last, we are painting your old room for Auntie Myfanwy who is coming to live here her arthritis is too bad for those stairs she has, well Kelly, I wish I could say we want you to come home but your Da is that angry and now Auntie Myfanwy needs the room anyway, well son, we never wanted you to go for a jockey, there was that nice job at the Townhall in Tenby you could have had, I don't like to say it but you have disgraced us, son, there's horrid it is going into the village now, everyone whispering, your loving Mother.

I took a deep breath and turned the page over to receive the blast from my father. His writing was much like my mother's as they had learned from the same teacher, but he had pressed so hard with his ballpoint that he had almost dug through the paper.

Kelly,

You're a damned disgrace boy. It's soft saying you didn't do it. They wouldn't of warned you off if you didn't do it. Not lords and such. They know what's right. You're lucky you're not here I would give you a proper belting. After all that scrimping your Ma did to let you go off to the University. And people said you would get too ladidah to speak to us, they were right. Still, this is worse, being a cheat. Don't you come back here, your Ma's that upset, what with that cat Mrs Jones saying things. It would

be best to say don't send us any more money into
the bank. I asked the manager but he said only you
can cancel a banker's order so you'd better do it.
Your Ma says it's as bad as you being in prison, the
disgrace and all.

He hadn't signed it. He wouldn't know how to, we had
so little affection for each other. He had despised me
from childhood for my liking school, and had mocked
me unmercifully all the way to college. He showed his
jolly side only to my two older brothers, who had had
what he considered a healthy contempt for education:
one of them had gone into the Merchant Navy and the
other lived next door and worked alongside my father
for the farmer who owned the cottages.

When in the end I had turned my back on all the
years of learning and taken to racing my family had
again all disapproved of me, though I guessed they
would have been pleased enough if I'd chosen it all
along. I'd wasted the country's money, my father said;
I wouldn't have been given all those grants if they'd
known that as soon as I was out I'd go racing. That
was probably true. It was also true that since I'd been
racing I'd paid enough in taxes to send several other
farm boys through college on grants.

I put my parents' letter under Rosalind's photograph. Even she had been unable to reach their
approval, because they thought I should have married

a nice girl from my own sort of background, not the student daughter of a colonel.

They had rigid minds. It was doubtful now if they would ever be pleased with me, whatever I did. And if I got my licence back, as like as not they would think I had somehow cheated again.

You couldn't take aspirins for that sort of pain. It stayed there, sticking in knives. Trying to escape it I went into the kitchen, to see if there was anything to eat. A tin of sardines, one egg, the dried-up remains of some Port Salut.

Wrinkling my nose at that lot I transferred to the sitting-room and looked at the television programmes.

Nothing I wanted to see.

I slouched in the green velvet armchair and watched the evening slowly fade the colours into subtle greys. A certain amount of peace edged its way past the dragging gloom of the last four days. I wondered almost academically whether I would get my licence back before or after I stopped wincing at the way people looked at me, or spoke to me, or wrote about me. Probably the easiest course would be to stay out of sight, hiding myself away.

Like I was hiding away at that minute, by not going to the Jockeys' Fund dance.

The tickets were on the mantel. Tickets for Tony and Poppy, and for me and the partner I hadn't got around to inviting. Tickets which were not going to be used, which I had paid twelve fund-raising guineas for.

I sat in the dark for half an hour thinking about the people who would be at the Jockeys' Fund dance.

Then I put on my black tie and went to it.

CHAPTER EIGHT

I went prepared to be stared at.

I was stared at.

Also pointed out and commented on. Discreetly, however, for the most part. And only two people decisively turned their backs.

The Jockeys' Fund dance glittered as usual with titles, diamonds, champagne, and talent. Later it might curl round the edges into spilled drinks, glassy eyes, raddled make-up, and slurring voices, but the gloss wouldn't entirely disappear. It never did. The Jockeys' Fund dance was one of the great social events of the steeplechasing year.

I handed over my ticket and walked along the wide passage to where the lights were low, the music hot, and the air thick with smoke and scent. The opulent ballroom of the Royal Country Hotel, along the road from Ascot racecourse.

Around the dancing area there were numbers of large circular tables with chairs for ten or twelve round each, most of them occupied already. According to the chart in the hall, at table number thirty-two I would find the places reserved for Tony and me, if in fact they were still reserved. I gave up looking for table thirty-two less than halfway down the room because whenever I moved a new battery of curious eyes swivelled my way. A lot of people raised a hello but none of them could hide their slightly shocked surprise. It was every bit as bad as I'd feared.

A voice behind me said incredulously, 'Hughes!'

I knew the voice. I turned round with an equal sense of the unexpected. Roberta Cranfield. Wearing a honey-coloured silk dress with the top smothered in pearls and gold thread and her copper hair drawn high with a trickle of ringlets down the back of her neck.

'You look beautiful,' I said.

Her mouth opened. 'Hughes!'

'Is your father here?'

'No,' she said disgustedly. 'He wouldn't face it. Nor would Mother. I came with a party of neighbours but I can't say I was enjoying it much until you turned up.'

'Why not?'

'You must be joking. Just look around. At a rough guess fifty people are rubber-necking at you. Doesn't it make you cringe inside? Anyway, I've had quite enough of it myself this evening, and I didn't even *see* the damned race, let alone get myself warned off.' She stopped. 'Come and dance with me. If we're hoisting the flag we may as well do it thoroughly.'

'On one condition,' I said.

'What's that?'

'You stop calling me Hughes.'

'What?'

'Cranfield, I'm tired of being called Hughes.'

'Oh!' It had obviously never occurred to her. 'Then . . . Kelly . . . how about dancing?'

'Enchanted, Roberta.'

She gave me an uncertain look. 'I still feel I don't know you.'

'You never bothered.'

'Nor have you.'

That jolted me. It was true. I'd disliked the idea of her. And I didn't really know her at all.

'How do you do?' I said politely. 'Come and dance.'

We shuffled around in one of those affairs which look like formalized jungle rituals, swaying in rhythm but never touching. Her face was quite calm, remotely smiling. From her composure one would have guessed her to be entirely at ease, not the target of turned heads, assessing glances, half-hidden whispers.

'I don't know how you do it,' she said.

'Do what?'

'Look so . . . so matter of fact.'

'I was thinking exactly the same about you.'

She smiled, eyes crinkling and teeth gleaming, and incredibly in the circumstances she looked happy.

We stuck it for a good ten minutes. Then she said we would go back to her table, and made straight off to it without waiting for me to agree. I didn't think her party would be pleased to have me join them, and half of them weren't.

'Sit down and have a drink, my dear fellow,' drawled her host, reaching for a champagne bottle with a languid hand. 'And tell me all about the bring-back-Cranfield campaign. Roberta tells me you are working on a spot of reinstatement.'

'I haven't managed it yet,' I said deprecatingly.

'My dear chap . . .' He gave me an inspecting stare down his nose. He'd been in the Guards, I thought. So many ex-Guards' officers looked at the world down the sides of their noses: it came of wearing those blinding hats. He was blond, in his forties, not unfriendly. Roberta called him Bobbie.

The woman the other side of him leaned over and drooped a heavy pink satin bosom perilously near her brimming glass.

'Do tell me,' she said, giving me a thorough gaze from heavily made-up eyes, 'what made you come?'

'Natural cussedness,' I said pleasantly.

'Oh.' She looked taken aback. 'How extraordinary.'

'Joined to the fact that there was no reason why I shouldn't.'

141

'And are you enjoying it?' Bobbie said. 'I mean to say, my dear chap, you are somewhat in the position of a rather messily struck-off doctor turning up four days later at the British Medical Association's grandest function.'

I smiled. 'Quite a parallel.'

'Don't needle him Bobbie,' Roberta protested.

Bobbie removed his stare from me and gave it to her instead. 'My dear Roberta, this cookie needs no little girls rushing to his defence. He's as tough as old oak.'

A disapproving elderly man on the far side of the pink bosom said under his breath. 'Thick skinned, you mean.'

Bobbie heard, and shook his head. 'Vertebral,' he said. 'Different altogether.' He stood up. 'Roberta, my dear girl, would you care to dance?'

I stood up with him.

'No need to go, my dear chap. Stay. Finish your drink.'

'You are most kind,' I said truthfully. 'But I really came tonight to have a word with one or two people . . . If you'll excuse me, I'll try to find them.'

He gave me an odd formal little inclination of the head, halfway to a bow. 'Come back later, if you'd care to.'

'Thank you,' I said. 'Very much.'

He took Roberta away to dance and I went up the

stairs to the balcony which encircled the room. There were tables all round up there too, but in places one could get a good clear view of most people below. I spent some length of time identifying them from the tops of their heads.

There must have been about six hundred there, of whom I knew personally about a quarter. Owners, trainers, jockeys, Stewards, pressmen, two or three of the bigger bookmakers, starters, judges, Clerks of Courses, and all the others, all with their wives and friends and chattering guests.

Kessel was there, hosting a party of twelve almost exactly beneath where I stood. I wondered if his anger had cooled since Monday, and decided if possible not to put it to the test. He had reputedly sent Squelch off to Pat Nikita, a trainer who was a bitter rival of Cranfield's, which had been rubbing it in a bit. The report looked likely to be true, as Pat Nikita was among the party below me.

Cranfield and Nikita regularly claimed each other's horses in selling races and were apt to bid each other up spitefully at auctions. It was a public joke. So in choosing Nikita as his trainer, Kessel was unmistakably announcing worldwide that he believed Cranfield and I had stopped his horse. Hardly likely to help convince that we hadn't.

At one of the most prominent tables, near the dancing space, sat Lord Ferth, talking earnestly to a large lady in pale blue ostrich feathers. All the other chairs round the table were askew and unoccupied, but while I watched the music changed to a Latin rhythm, and most of the party drifted back. I knew one or two of them slightly, but not well. The man I was chiefly looking for was not among them.

Two tables away from Lord Ferth sat Edwin Byler, gravely beckoning to the waiter to fill his guests' glasses, too proud of his home-made wealth to lift the bottle himself. His cuddly little wife on the far side of the table was loaded with half the stock of Hatton Garden and was rather touchingly revelling in it.

Not to be going to ride Edwin Byler's string of super horses . . . The wry thrust of regret went deeper than I liked.

There was a rustle behind me and the smell of Roberta's fresh flower scent. I turned towards her.

'Kelly? . . .'

She really looked extraordinarily beautiful.

'Kelly . . . Bobbie suggested that you should take me in to supper.'

'That's generous of him.'

'He seems to approve of you. He said . . .' She stopped abruptly. 'Well, never mind what he said.'

We went down the stairs and through an archway to the supper room. The light there was of a heartier wattage. It didn't do any damage to Roberta.

Along one wall stretched a buffet table laden with

144

aspic-shining cold meats and oozing cream gateaux. Roberta said she had dined at Bobbie's before coming on to the dance and wasn't hungry, but we both collected some salmon and sat down at one of the twenty or so small tables clustered into half of the room.

Six feet away sat three fellow jockeys resting their elbows among a debris of empty plates and coffee cups.

'Kelly!' One of them exclaimed in a broad northern voice. 'My God. Kelly. Come over here, you old so and so. Bring the talent with you.'

The talent's chin began its familiar upward tilt.

'Concentrate on the character, not the accent,' I said.

She gave me a raw look of surprise, but when I stood up and picked up her plate, she came with me. They made room for us, admired Roberta's appearance, and didn't refer to anyone being warned off. Their girls, they explained, were powdering their noses, and when the noses reappeared, immaculate, they all smiled goodbye and went back to the ballroom.

'They were kind.' She sounded surprised.

'They would be.'

She fiddled with her fork, not looking at me. 'You said the other day that my mind was in chains. Was that what you meant ... that I'm inclined to judge people by their voices ... and that it's wrong?'

'Eton's bred its rogues,' I said. 'Yes.'

'Cactus. You're all prickles.'

'Original sin exists.' I said mildly. 'So does original

145

virtue. They both crop up regardless. No respecters of birth.'

'Where did you go to school?'

'In Wales.'

'You haven't a Welsh accent. You haven't any accent at all. And that's odd really, considering you are only . . .' Her voice trailed away and she looked aghast at her self-betrayal. 'Oh dear . . . I'm sorry.'

'It's not surprising,' I pointed out. 'Considering your father. And anyway, in my own way I'm just as bad. I smothered my Welsh accent quite deliberately. I used to practise in secret, while I was still at school, copying the BBC news announcers. I wanted to be a Civil Servant, and I was ambitious, and I knew I wouldn't get far if I sounded like the son of a Welsh farm labourer. So in time this became my natural way of talking. And my parents despise me for it.'

'Parents!' she said despairingly. 'Why can we never escape them? Whatever we are, it is because of *them*. I want to be *me*.' She looked astonished at herself. 'I've never felt like this before. I don't understand . . .'

'Well I do.' I said, smiling. 'Only it happens to most people around fifteen or sixteen. Rebellion, it's called.'

'You're mocking me.' But the chin stayed down.

'No.'

We finished the salmon and drank coffee. A large loudly chattering party collected food from the buffet and pushed the two tables next to us together so that

146

they could all sit at one. They were well away on a tide of alcohol and bonhomie, loosened and expansive. I watched them idly. I knew four of them, two trainers, one wife, one owner.

One of the trainers caught sight of me and literally dropped his knife.

'That's Kelly Hughes,' he said disbelievingly. The whole party turned round and stared. Roberta drew a breath in distress. I sat without moving.

'What are you doing here?'

'Drinking coffee,' I said politely.

His eyes narrowed. Trevor Norse was not amused. I sighed inwardly. It was never good to antagonize trainers, it simply meant one less possible source of income: but I'd ridden for Trevor Norse several times already, and knew that it was practically impossible to please him anyway.

A heavy man, six feet plus, labouring under the misapprehension that size could substitute for ability. He was much better with owners than with horses, tireless at cultivating the one and lazy with the other.

His brainless wife said brightly, 'I hear you're paying Dexter's lads' wages, because you're sure you'll get your licence back in a day or two.'

'What's all that?' Norse said sharply. 'Where did you hear all that nonsense?'

'Everyone's talking about it, darling,' she said protestingly.

'Who's everyone?'

She giggled weakly. 'I heard it in the ladies, if you must know. But it's quite true, I'm sure it is. Dexter's lads told Daphne's lads in the local pub, and Daphne told Miriam, and Miriam was telling us in the ladies . . .'

'Is it true?' Norse demanded.

'Well, more or less,' I agreed.

'Good Lord.'

'Miriam said Kelly Hughes says he and Dexter were framed, and that he's finding out who did it.' Mrs Norse giggled at me. 'My *dear*, isn't it all such fun.'

'Great,' I said dryly. I stood up, and Roberta also.

'Do you know Roberta Cranfield?' I said formally, and they all exclaimed over her, and she scattered on them a bright artificial smile, and we went back and tried another dance.

It wasn't altogether a great idea because we were stopped halfway round by Daddy Leeman of the *Daily Witness* who raked me over with avid eyes and yelled above the music was it true I was claiming I'd been framed. He had a piercing voice. All the nearby couples turned and stared. Some of them raised sceptical eyebrows at each other.

'I really can't stand a great deal more of this,' Roberta said in my ear. 'How can you? Why don't you go home now?'

'I'm sorry,' I said contritely. 'You've been splendid. I'll take you back to Bobbie.'

'But you? . . .'

'I haven't done what I came for. I'll stay a bit longer.'

She compressed her mouth and started to dance again. 'All right. So will I.'

We danced without smiling.

'Do you want a tombola ticket?' I asked.

'No.' She was astonished.

'You might as well. I want to go down that end of the room.'

'Whatever for?'

'Looking for someone. Haven't been down that end at all.'

'Oh. All right, then.'

She stepped off the polished wood on to the thick dark carpet, and threaded her way to the clear aisle which led down to the gaily decorated tombola stall at the far end of the ballroom.

I looked for the man I wanted, but I didn't see him. I met too many other eyes, most of which hastily looked away.

'I hate them,' Roberta said fiercely. 'I hate people.'

I bought her four tickets. Three of them were blanks. The fourth had a number which fitted a bottle of vodka.

'I don't like it much,' she said, holding it dubiously.

'Nor do I.'

'I'll give it to the first person who's nice to you.'

'You might have to drink it yourself.'

We went slowly back down the aisle, not talking.

A thin woman sprang up from her chair as we approached her table and in spite of the embarrassed holding-back clutches of her party managed to force her way out into our path. We couldn't pass her without pushing. We stopped.

'You're Roberta Cranfield, aren't you?' she said. She had a strong-boned face, no lipstick, angry eyes, and stiffly regimented greying hair. She looked as if she'd had far too much to drink.

'Excuse us,' I said gently, trying to go past.

'Oh no you don't,' she said. 'Not until I've had my say.'

'Grace!' wailed a man across the table. I looked at him more closely. Edwin Byler's trainer, Jack Roxford. 'Grace dear, leave it. Sit down, dear,' he said.

Grace dear had no such intentions. Grace dear's feelings were far too strong.

'Your father's got exactly what he deserves, my lass, and I can tell you I'm glad about it. Glad.' She thrust her face towards Roberta's, glaring like a mad woman. Roberta looked down her nose at her, which I would have found as infuriating as Grace did.

'I'd dance on his grave,' she said furiously. 'That I would.'

'Why?' I said flatly.

She didn't look at me. She said to Roberta, 'He's a bloody snob, your father. A bloody snob. And he's got what he deserved. So there. You tell him that.'

'Excuse me,' Roberta said coldly, and tried to go forwards.

'Oh no you don't.' Grace clutched at her arm. Roberta shook her hand off angrily. 'Your bloody snob of a father was trying to get Edwin Byler's horses away from us. Did you know that? Did you know that? All those grand ways of his. Thought Edwin would do better in a bigger stable, did he? Oh, I heard what he said. Trying to persuade Edwin he needed a grand top-drawer trainer now, not poor little folk like us, who've won just rows of races for him. Well, I could have laughed my head off when I heard he'd been had up. I'll tell you. Serves him right, I said. What a laugh.'

'Grace,' said Jack Roxford despairingly. 'I'm sorry, Miss Cranfield. She isn't really like this.'

He looked acutely embarrassed. I thought that probably Grace Roxford was all too often like this. He had the haunted expression of the for-ever apologizing husband.

'Cheer up then, Mrs Roxford,' I said loudly. 'You've got what you want. You're laughing. So why the fury?'

'Eh?' She twisted her head round at me, staggering a fraction. 'As for you, Kelly Hughes, you just asked for what you got, and don't give me any of that crap we've been hearing this evening that you were framed, because you know bloody well you weren't. People like you and Cranfield, you think you can get away with murder, people like you. But there's justice somewhere

151

in this world sometimes and you won't forget that in a hurry, will you now, Mr Clever Dick.'

One of the women of the party stood up and tried to persuade her to quieten down, as every ear for six tables around was stretched in her direction. She was oblivious to them. I wasn't.

Roberta said under her breath,'Oh God.'

'So you go home and tell your bloody snob of a father,' Grace said to her, 'that it's a great big laugh him being found out. That's what it is, a great big laugh.'

The acutely embarrassed woman friend pulled her arm, and Grace swung angrily round from us to her. We took the brief opportunity and edged away round her back, and as we retreated we could hear her shouting after us, her words indistinct above the music except for 'laugh' and 'bloody snob'.

'She's *awful*,' Roberta said.

'Not much help to poor old Jack,' I agreed.

'I do hate scenes. They're so messy.'

'Do you think all strong emotions are messy?'

'That's not the same thing,' she said. 'You can have strong emotions without making scenes. Scenes are disgusting.'

I sighed. 'That one was.'

'Yes.'

She was walking, I noticed, with her neck stretched very tall, the classic signal to anyone watching that she was not responsible or bowed down or amused at being involved in noise and nastiness. Rosalind, I reflected nostalgically, would probably have sympathetically agreed with dear disturbed Grace, led her off to some quiet mollifying corner, and reappeared with her eating out of her hand. Rosalind had been tempestuous herself and understood uncontrollable feelings.

Unfortunately at the end of the aisle we almost literally bumped into Kessel, who came in for the murderous glance from Roberta which had been earned by dear Grace. Kessel naturally misinterpreted her expression and spat first.

'You can tell your father that I had been thinking for some time of sending my horses to Pat Nikita, and that this business has made me regret that I didn't do it a long time ago. Pat has always wanted to train for me. I stayed with your father out of a mistaken sense of loyalty, and just look how he repaid me.'

'Father has won a great many races for you,' Roberta said coldly. 'And if Squelch had been good enough to win the Lemonfizz Cup, he would have done.'

Kessel's mouth sneered. It didn't suit him.

'As for you, Hughes, it's a disgrace you being here tonight and I cannot think why you were allowed in. And don't think you can fool me by spreading rumours that you are innocent and on the point of proving it. That's all piffle, and you know it, and if you have any ideas you can reinstate yourself with me that way, you are very much mistaken.'

He turned his back on us and bristled off, pausing triumphantly to pat Nikita on the shoulder, and looking back to make sure we had noticed. Very small of him.

'There goes Squelch,' I said resignedly.

'He'll soon be apologizing and sending him back,' she said, with certainty.

'Not a hope. Kessel's not the humble-pie kind. And Pat Nikita will never let go of that horse. Not to see him go back to your father. He'd break him down first.'

'Why are people so jealous of each other!' she exclaimed.

'Born in them,' I said. 'And almost universal.'

'You have a very poor opinion of human nature.' She disapproved.

'An objective opinion. There's as much good as bad.'

'You can't be objective about being warned off,' she protested.

'Er . . . no,' I conceded. 'How about a drink?'

She looked instinctively towards Bobbie's table, and I shook my head. 'In the bar.'

'Oh . . . still looking for someone?'

'That's right. We haven't tried the bar yet.'

'Is there going to be another scene?'

'I shouldn't think so.'

'All right, then.'

We made our way slowly through the crowd. By

then the fact that we were there must have been known to almost everyone in the place. Certainly the heads no longer turned in open surprise, but the eyes did, sliding into corners, giving us a surreptitious once-over, probing and hurtful. Roberta held herself almost defiantly straight.

The bar was heavily populated, with cigar smoke lying in a haze over the well-groomed heads and the noise level doing justice to a discotheque. Almost at once through a narrow gap in the cluster I saw him standing against the far wall, talking vehemently. He turned his head suddenly and looked straight at me, meeting my eyes briefly before the groups between us shifted and closed the line of sight. In those two seconds, however, I had seen his mouth tighten and his whole face compress into annoyance; and he had known I was at the dance, because there was no surprise.

'You've seen him,' Roberta said.

'Yes.'

'Well . . . who is it?'

'Lord Gowery.'

She gasped. 'Oh no, Kelly.'

'I want to talk to him.'

'It can't do any good.'

'You never know.'

'Annoying Lord Gowery is the last, positively the

last way of getting your licence back. Surely you can see that?'

'Yes . . . he's not going to be kind, I don't think. So would you mind very much if I took you back to Bobbie first?'

She looked troubled. 'You won't say anything silly? It's Father's licence as well, remember.'

'I'll bear it in mind,' I said flippantly. She gave me a sharp suspicious glance, but turned easily enough to go back to Bobbie.

Almost immediately outside the bar we were stopped by Jack Roxford, who was hurrying towards us through the throng.

'Kelly,' he said, half panting with the exertion. 'I just wanted to catch you . . . to say how sorry I am that Grace went off the deep end like that. She's not herself, poor girl . . . Miss Cranfield, I do apologize.'

Roberta unbent a little. 'That's all right, Mr Roxford.'

'I wouldn't like you to believe that what Grace said . . . all those things about your father . . . is what I think too.' He looked from her to me, and back again, the hesitant worry furrowing his forehead. A slight, unaggressive man of about forty-five; bald crown, nervous eyes, permanently worried expression. He was a reasonably good trainer but not enough of a man of the world to have achieved much personal stature. To me, though I had never ridden for him, he had always been friendly, but his restless anxiety-state made him tiring to be with.

'Kelly,' he said, 'if it's really true that you were both framed, I do sincerely hope that you get your licences back. I mean, I know there's a risk that Edwin will take his horses to your father, Miss Cranfield, but he did tell me this evening that he won't do so now, even if he could ... But please believe me, I hold no dreadful grudge against either of you, like poor Grace ... I do hope you'll forgive her.'

'Of course, Mr Roxford,' said Roberta, entirely placated. 'Please don't give it another thought. And oh!' she added impulsively, 'I think you've earned this!' and into his astonished hands she thrust the bottle of vodka.

CHAPTER NINE

When I went back towards the bar I found Lord Gowery had come out of it. He was standing shoulder to shoulder with Lord Ferth, both of them watching me walk towards them with faces like thunder.

I stopped four feet away, and waited.

'Hughes,' said Lord Gowery for openers, 'you shouldn't be here.'

'My lord,' I said politely. 'This isn't Newmarket Heath.'

It went down badly. They were both affronted. They closed their ranks.

'Insolence will get you nowhere,' Lord Ferth said, and Lord Gowery added, 'You'll never get your licence back, if you behave like this.'

I said without heat, 'Does justice depend on good manners?'

They looked as if they couldn't believe their ears. From their point of view I was cutting my own throat, though I had always myself doubted that excessive meekness got licences restored any quicker than they would have been without it. Meekness in the accused brought out leniency in some judges, but severity in others. To achieve a minimum sentence, the guilty should always bone up on the character of their judge, a sound maxim which I hadn't had the sense to see applied even more to the innocent.

'I would have thought some sense of shame would have kept you away,' Lord Ferth said.

'It took a bit of an effort to come,' I agreed.

His eyes narrowed and opened again quickly.

Gowery said, 'As to spreading these rumours . . . I say categorically that you are not only not on the point of being given your licence back, but that your suspension will be all the longer in consequence of your present behaviour.'

I gave him a level stare and Lord Ferth opened his mouth and shut it again.

'It is no rumour that Mr Cranfield and I are not guilty,' I said at length. 'It is no rumour that two at least of the witnesses were lying. These are facts.'

'Nonsense,' Gowery said vehemently.

'What you believe, sir,' I said, 'doesn't alter the truth.'

'You are doing yourself no good, Hughes.' Under his heavy authoritative exterior he was exceedingly angry. All I needed was a bore hole and I'd get a gusher.

I said, 'Would you be good enough to tell me who suggested to you or the other Stewards that you should seek out and question Mr Newtonnards?'

There was the tiniest shift in his eyes. Enough for me to be certain.

'Certainly not.'

'Then will you tell me upon whose instructions the enquiry agent David Oakley visited my flat?'

'I will not.' His voice was loud, and for the first time, alarmed.

Ferth looked in growing doubt from one of us to the other.

'What is all this about?' he said.

'Mr Cranfield and I were indeed wrongly warned off,' I said. 'Someone sent David Oakley to my flat to fake that photograph. And I believe Lord Gowery knows who it was.'

'I most certainly do not,' he said furiously. 'Do you want to be sued for slander?'

'I have not slandered you, sir.'

'You said . . .'

'I said you knew who sent David Oakley. I did not say that you knew the photograph was a fake.'

'And it wasn't,' he insisted fiercely.

'Well,' I said. 'It was.'

There was a loaded, glaring silence. Then Lord Gowery said heavily, 'I'm not going to listen to this,' and turned on his heel and dived back into the bar.

Lord Ferth, looking troubled, took a step after him.

I said, 'My lord, may I talk to you?' And he stopped and turned back to me and said, 'Yes, I think you'd better.'

He gestured towards the supper room next door and we went through the archway into the brighter light. Nearly everyone had eaten and gone. The buffet table bore shambled remains and all but two of the small tables were unoccupied. He sat down at one of these and pointed to the chair opposite. I took it, facing him.

'Now,' he said. 'Explain.'

I spoke in a flat calm voice, because emotion was going to repel him where reason might get through. 'My lord, if you could look at the Enquiry from my point of view for a minute, it is quite simple. I know that I never had any five hundred pounds or any note from Mr Cranfield, therefore I am obviously aware that David Oakley was lying. It's unbelievable that the Stewards should have sent him, since the evidence he produced was faked. So someone else did. I thought Lord Gowery might know who. So I asked him.'

'He said he didn't know.'

'I don't altogether believe him.'

'Hughes, that's preposterous.'

'Are you intending to say, sir, that men in power positions are infallibly truthful?'

He looked at me without expression in a lengthening

silence. Finally he said, as Roberta had done, 'Where did you go to school?'

In the usual course of things I kept dead quiet about the type of education I'd had because it was not likely to endear me to either owners or trainers. Still, there was a time for everything, so I told him.

'Coedlant Primary, Tenby Grammar, and LSE.'

'LSE ... you don't mean ... the London School of Economics?' He looked astonished.

'Yes.'

'My God ...'

I watched while he thought it over. 'What did you read there?'

'Politics, philosophy, and economics.'

'Then what on earth made you become a jockey?'

'It was almost an accident,' I said. 'I didn't plan it. When I'd finished my final exams I was mentally tired, so I thought I'd take a sort of paid holiday working on the land ... I knew how to do that, my father's a farmhand. I worked at harvesting for a farmer in Devon and every morning I used to ride his 'chasers out at exercise, because I'd ridden most of my life, you see. He had a permit, and he was dead keen. And then his brother, who raced them for him, broke his shoulder at one of the early Devon meetings, and he put me up instead, and almost at once I started winning ... and then it took hold of me ... so I didn't get around to being a Civil Servant, as I'd always vaguely intended, and ... well ... I've never regretted it.'

'Not even now?' he said with irony.

I shook my head. 'Not even now.'

'Hughes ...' His face crinkled dubiously. 'I don't know what to think. At first I was sure you were not the type to have stopped Squelch deliberately ... and then there was all that damning evidence. Charlie West saying you had definitely pulled back ...'

I looked down at the table. I didn't after all want an eye for an eye, when it came to the point.

'Charlie was mistaken,' I said. 'He got two races muddled up. I did pull back in another race at about that time ... riding a novice 'chaser with no chance, well back in the field. I wanted to give it a good schooling race. That was what Charlie remembered.'

He said doubtfully, 'It didn't sound like it.'

'No,' I agreed. 'I've had it out with Charlie since. He might be prepared to admit now that he was talking about the wrong race. If you will ask the Oxford Stewards, you'll find that Charlie said nothing to them directly after the Lemonfizz, when they made their first enquiries, about me not trying. He only said it later, at the Enquiry in Portman Square.' Because in between some beguiling seducer had offered him five hundred pounds for the service.

'I see.' He frowned. 'And what was it that you asked Lord Gowery about Newtonnards?'

'Newtonnards didn't volunteer the information to the Stewards about Mr Cranfield backing Cherry Pie, but he did tell several bookmaker colleagues. Someone told the Stewards. I wanted to know who.'

'Are you suggesting that it was the same person who sent Oakley to your flat?'

'It might be. But not necessarily.' I hesitated, looking at him doubtfully.

'What is it?' he said.

'Sir, I don't want to offend you, but would you mind telling me why you sat in at the Enquiry? Why there were four of you instead of three, when Lord Gowery, if you'll forgive me saying so, was obviously not too pleased at the arrangement.'

His lips tightened. 'You're being uncommonly tactful all of a sudden.'

'Yes, sir.'

He looked at me steadily. A tall thin man with high cheekbones, strong black hair, hot fiery eyes. A man whose force of character reached out and hit you, so that you'd never forget meeting him. The best ally in the whole 'chasing set up, if I could only reach him.

'I cannot give you my reasons for attending,' he said with some reproof.

'Then you had some . . . reservations . . . about how the Enquiry would be conducted?'

'I didn't say that,' he protested. But he had meant it.

'Lord Gowery chose Andrew Tring to sit with him

164

at the hearing, and Andrew Tring wants a very big concession from him just now. And he chose Lord Plimborne as the third Steward, and Lord Plimborne continually fell asleep.'

'Do you realize what you're saying?' He was truly shocked.

'I want to know how Lord Gowery acquired all that evidence against us. I want to know why the Stewards' Secretaries sent for the wrong film. I want to know why Lord Gowery was so biased, so deaf to our denials, so determined to warn us off.'

'That's slanderous . . .'

'I want you to ask him,' I finished flatly.

He simply stared.

I said, 'He might tell you. He might just possibly tell you. But he'd never in a million years tell *me*.'

'Hughes . . . You surely don't expect . . .'

'That wasn't a straight trial, and he knows it. I'm just asking you to tackle him with it, to see if he will explain.'

'You are talking about a much respected man,' he said coldly.

'Yes, sir. He's a baron, a rich man, a Steward of long standing. I know all that.'

'And you *still* maintain? . . .'

'Yes.'

His hot eyes brooded. 'He'll have you in court for this.'

'Only if I'm wrong.'

'I can't possibly do it,' he said, with decision.

'And please, if you have one, use a tape-recorder.'

'I told you . . .'

'Yes, sir, I know you did.'

He got up from the table, paused as if about to say something, changed his mind, and as I stood up also, turned abruptly and walked sharply away. When he had gone I found that my hands were trembling, and I followed him slowly out of the supper room feeling a battered wreck.

I had either resurrected our licences or driven the nails into them, and only time would tell which.

Bobbie said, 'Have a drink, my dear fellow. You look as though you've been clobbered by a steamroller.'

I took a mouthful of champagne and thanked him, and watched Roberta swing her body to a compelling rhythm with someone else. The ringlets bounced against her neck. I wondered without disparagement how long it had taken her to pin them on.

'Not the best of evenings for you, old pal,' Bobbie observed.

'You never know.'

He raised his eyebrows, drawling down his nose, 'Mission accomplished?'

'A fuse lit, rather.'

He lifted his glass. 'To a successful detonation.'

'You are most kind,' I said formally.

The music changed gear and Roberta's partner brought her back to the table.

I stood up. 'I came to say goodbye,' I said. 'I'll be going now.'

'Oh not yet,' she exclaimed. 'The worst is over. No one's staring any more. Have some fun.'

'Dance with the dear girl,' Bobbie said, and Roberta put out a long arm and pulled mine, and so I went and danced with her.

'Lord Gowery didn't eat you then?'

'He's scrunching the bones at this minute.'

'Kelly! If you've done any damage . . .'

'No omelettes without smashing eggs, love.'

The chin went up. I grinned. She brought it down again. Getting quite human, Miss Cranfield.

After a while the hot rhythm changed to a slow smooch, and couples around us went into clinches. Bodies to bodies, heads to heads, eyes shut, swaying in the dimming light. Roberta eyed them coolly and prickled when I put my arms up to gather her in. She danced very straight, with four inches of air between us. Not human enough.

We ambled around in that frigid fashion through three separate wodges of glutinous music. She didn't come any closer, and I did nothing to persuade her, but equally she seemed to be in no hurry to break it up. Composed, cool, off-puttingly gracious, she looked as flawless in the small hours as she had when I'd arrived.

'I'm glad you were here,' I said.

She moved her head in surprise. 'It hasn't been exactly the best Jockeys' Fund dance of my life . . . but I'm glad I came.'

'Next year this will be all over, and everyone will have forgotten.'

'I'll dance with you again next year,' she said.

'It's a pact.'

She smiled, and just for a second a stray beam of light shimmered on some expression in her eyes which I didn't understand.

She was aware of it. She turned her head away, and then detached herself altogether, and gestured that she wanted to go back to the table. I delivered her to Bobbie, and she sat down immediately and began powdering a non-shiny nose.

'Goodnight,' I said to Bobbie. 'And thank you.'

'My dear fellow. Any time.'

'Goodnight, Roberta.'

She looked up. Nothing in the eyes. Her voice was collected. 'Goodnight, Kelly.'

I lowered myself into the low-slung burnt-orange car in the park and drove away thinking about her. Roberta

Cranfield. Not my idea of a cuddly bed mate. Too cold, too controlled, too proud. And it didn't go with that copper hair, all that rigidity. Or maybe she was only rigid to me because I was a farm labourer's son. Only that, and only a jockey . . . and her father had taught her that jockeys were the lower classes dear and don't get your fingers dirty . . .

Kelly, I said to myself, you've a fair-sized chip on your shoulder, old son. Maybe she does think like that, but why should it bother you? And even if she does, she spent most of the evening with you . . . although she was really quite careful not to touch you too much. Well . . . maybe that was because so many people were watching . . . and maybe it was simply that she didn't like the thought of it.

I was on the short cut home that led round the south of Reading, streaking down deserted back roads, going fast for no reason except that speed had become a habit. This car was easily the best I'd ever had, the only one I had felt proud of. Mechanically a masterpiece and with looks to match. Even thirty thousand miles in the past year hadn't dulled the pleasure I got from driving it. Its only fault was that like so many other sports cars it had a totally inefficient heater, which in spite of coaxing and overhauls stubbornly refused to do more than demist the windscreen and raise my toes one degree above frostbite. If kicked, it retaliated with a smell of exhaust.

I had gone to the dance without a coat, and the night was frosty. I shivered and switched on the heater to maximum. As usual, damn all.

There was a radio in the car, which I seldom listened to, and a spare crash helmet, and my five-pound racing saddle which I'd been going to take to Wetherby races.

Depression flooded back. Fierce though the evening had been, in many ways I had forgotten for a while the dreariness of being banned. It could be a long slog now, after what I had said to the Lords Gowery and Ferth. A very long slog indeed. Cranfield wouldn't like the gamble. I wasn't too sure that I could face telling him, if it didn't come off.

Lord Ferth . . . would he or wouldn't he? He'd be torn between loyalty to an equal and a concept of justice. I didn't know him well enough to be sure which would win. And maybe anyway he would shut everything I'd said clean out of his mind, as too far-fetched and preposterous to bother about.

Bobbie had been great, I thought. I wondered who he was. Maybe one day I'd ask Roberta.

Mrs Roxford . . . poor dear Grace. What a life Jack must lead . . . Hope he liked vodka . . .

I took an unexpectedly sharp bend far too fast. The wheels screeched when I wrenched the nose round and the car went weaving and skidding for a hundred yards before I had it in control again. I put my foot gingerly back on the accelerator and still had in my mind's eye the solid trunks of the row of trees I had just missed by centimetres.

God, I thought, how could I be so careless. It rocked me. I was a careful driver, even if fast, and I'd never had an accident. I could feel myself sweating. It was something to sweat about.

How stupid I was, thinking about the dance, not concentrating on driving, and going too fast for these small roads. I rubbed my forehead, which felt tense and tight, and kept my speed down to forty.

Roberta had looked beautiful . . . keep your mind on the road, Kelly, for God's sake . . . Usually I drove semi-automatically without having to concentrate every yard of the way. I found myself going slower still, because both my reactions and my thoughts were growing sluggish. I'd drunk a total of about half a glass of champagne all evening, so it couldn't be that.

I was simply going to sleep.

I stopped the car, got out, and stamped about to wake myself up. People who went to sleep at the wheels of sports cars on the way home from dances were not a good risk.

Too many sleepless nights, grinding over my sorry state. Insulting the lions seemed to have released the worst of that. I felt I could now fall unconscious for a month.

I considered sleeping there and then, in the car. But the car was cold and couldn't be heated. I would drive on, I decided, and stop for good if I felt really dozy again. The fresh air had done the trick; I was wide awake and irritated with myself.

The beam of my headlights on the cats' eyes down the empty road was soon hypnotic. I switched on the radio to see if that would hold my attention, but it was all soft and sweet late-night music. Lullaby. I switched it off.

Pity I didn't smoke. That would have helped.

It was a star-clear night with a bright full moon. Ice crystals sparkled like diamond dust on the grass verges, now that I'd left the wooded part behind. Beautiful but unwelcome, because a hard frost would mean no racing tomorrow at Sandown ... With a jerk I realized that that didn't matter to me any more.

I glanced at the speedometer. Forty. It seemed very fast. I slowed down still further to thirty-five, and nodded owlishly to myself. Anyone would be safe at thirty-five.

The tightness across my forehead slowly developed into a headache. Never mind, only an hour to home, then sleep ... sleep ... sleep ...

It's no good, I thought fuzzily. I'll have to stop and black out for a bit, even if I do wake up freezing, or I'll black out without stopping first, and that will be that.

The next layby, or something like tha ...

I began looking, forgot what I was looking for, took

my foot still farther off the accelerator and reckoned that thirty miles an hour was quite safe. Maybe twenty five . . . would be better.

A little farther on there were some sudden bumps in the road surface and my foot slipped off the accelerator altogether. The engine stalled. Car stopped.

Oh well, I thought. That settles it. Ought to move over to the side though. Couldn't see the side. Very odd.

The headache was pressing on my temples, and now that the engine had stopped I could hear a faint ringing in my ears.

Never mind. Never mind. Best to go to sleep. Leave the lights on . . . no one came along that road much . . . not at two in the morning . . . but have to leave the lights on just in case.

Ought to pull in to the side.

Ought to . . .

Too much trouble. Couldn't move my arms properly, anyway, so couldn't possibly do it.

Deep, deep in my head a tiny instinct switched itself to emergency.

Something was wrong. Something was indistinctly but appallingly wrong.

Sleep. Must sleep.

Get out, the flickering instinct said. Get out of the car.

Ridiculous.

Get out of the car.

Unwillingly, because it was such an effort, I struggled weakly with the handle. The door swung open. I put one leg out and tried to pull myself up, and was swept by a wave of dizziness. My head was throbbing. This wasn't . . . it couldn't be . . . just ordinary sleep.

Get out of the car . . .

My arms and legs belonged to someone else. They had me on my feet . . . I was standing up . . . didn't remember how I got there. But I was out.

Out.

Now what?

I took three tottering steps towards the back of the car and leant against the rear wing. Funny, I thought, the moonlight wasn't so bright any more.

The earth was trembling.

Stupid. Quite stupid. The earth didn't tremble.

Trembling. And the air was wailing. And the moon was falling on me. Come down from the sky and rushing towards me . . .

Not the moon. A great roaring wailing monster with a blinding moon eye. A monster making the earth tremble. A monster racing to gobble me up, huge and dark and faster than the wind and unimaginably terrifying . . .

I didn't move. Couldn't.

The one-thirty mail express from Paddington to Plymouth ploughed into my sturdy little car and carried its crumpled remains half a mile down the track.

CHAPTER TEN

I didn't know what had happened. Didn't understand. There was a tremendous noise of tearing metal and a hundred-mile-an-hour whirl of ninety-ton diesel engine one inch away from me, and a thudding catapulting scrunch which lifted me up like a rag doll and toppled me somersaulting through the air in a kaleidoscopic black arc.

My head crashed against a concrete post. The rest of my body felt mangled beyond repair. There were rainbows in my brain, blue, purple, flaming pink, with diamond-bright pin stars. Interesting while it lasted. Didn't last very long. Dissolved into an embracing inferno in which colours got lost in pain.

Up the line the train had screeched to a stop. Lights and voices were coming back that way.

The earth was cold, hard, and damp. A warm stream ran down my face. I knew it was blood. Didn't care much. Couldn't think properly, either. And didn't really want to.

More lights. Lots of lights. Lots of people. Voices. A voice I knew.

'Roberta, my dear girl, don't look.'

'It's Kelly!' she said. Shock. Wicked, unforgettable shock. 'It's Kelly.' The second time, despair.

'Come away, my dear girl.'

She didn't go. She was kneeling beside me. I could smell her scent, and feel her hand on my hair. I was lying on my side, face down. After a while I could see a segment of honey silk dress. There was blood on it.

I said, 'You're ruining . . . your dress.'

'It doesn't matter.'

It helped somehow to have her there. I was grateful that she had stayed. I wanted to tell her that. I tried . . . and meant . . . to say 'Roberta'. What in fact I said was . . . 'Rosalind'.

'Oh Kelly . . .' Her voice held a mixture of pity and distress.

I thought groggily that she would go away, now that I'd made such a silly mistake, but she stayed, saying small things like, 'You'll be all right soon,' and sometimes not talking at all, but just being there. I didn't know why I wanted her to stay. I remembered that I didn't even like the girl.

All the people who arrive after accidents duly arrived. Police with blue flashing lights. Ambulance waking the neighbourhood with its siren. Bobbie took Roberta away, telling her there was no more she could

177

do. The ambulance men scooped me unceremoniously on to a stretcher and if I thought them rough it was only because every movement brought a scream up as far as my teeth and heaven knows whether any of them got any farther.

By the time I reached the hospital the mists had cleared. I knew what had happened to my car. I knew that I wasn't dying. I knew that Bobbie and Roberta had taken the backroads detour like I had, and had reached the level crossing not long after me.

What I didn't understand was how I had come to stop on the railway. That crossing had drop-down-fringe gates, and they hadn't been shut.

A young dark-haired doctor with tired dark-ringed eyes came to look at me, talking to the ambulance men.

'He'd just come from a dance,' they said. 'The police want a blood test.'

'Drunk?' said the doctor.

The ambulance men shrugged. They thought it possible.

'No,' I said. 'It wasn't drink. At least . . .'

They didn't pay much attention. The young doctor stooped over my lower half, feeling the damage with slender gentle fingers. 'That hurts? Yes.' He parted my hair, looking at my head. 'Nothing much up there. More blood than damage.' He stood back. 'We'll get your pelvis X-rayed. And that leg. Can't tell what's what until after that.'

A nurse tried to take my shoes off. I said very loudly, 'Don't.'

She jumped. The doctor signed to her to stop. 'We'll do it under an anaesthetic. Just leave him for now.'

She came instead and wiped my forehead.

'Sorry,' she said.

The doctor took my pulse. 'Why ever did you stop on a level crossing?' he said conversationally. 'Silly thing to do.'

'I felt . . . sleepy. Had a headache.' It didn't sound very sensible.

'Had a bit to drink?'

'Almost nothing.'

'At a dance?' He sounded sceptical.

'Really,' I said weakly. 'I didn't.'

He put my hand down. I was still wearing my dinner jacket, though someone had taken off my tie. There were bright scarlet blotches down my white shirt and an unmendable tear down the right side of my black trousers.

I shut my eyes. Didn't do much good. The screaming pain showed no signs of giving up. It had localized into my right side from armpit to toes, with repercussions up and down my spine. I'd broken a good many bones racing, but this was much worse. Much. It was impossible.

'It won't be long now,' the doctor said comfortingly. 'We'll have you under.'

'The train didn't hit me,' I said. 'I got out of the car . . . I was leaning against the back of it . . . the train hit the car . . . not me.'

I felt sick. How long? . . .

'If it had hit you, you wouldn't be here.'

'I suppose not . . . I had this thumping headache . . . needed air . . .' Why couldn't I pass out, I thought. People always passed out, when it became unbearable. Or so I'd always believed.

'Have you still got the headache?' he asked clinically.

'It's gone off a bit. Just sore now.' My mouth was dry. Always like that, after injuries. The least of my troubles.

Two porters came to wheel me away, and I protested more than was stoical about the jolts. I felt grey. Looked at my hands. They were quite surprisingly red.

X-ray department. Very smooth, very quick. Didn't try to move me except for cutting the zip out of my trousers. Quite enough.

'Sorry,' they said.

'Do you work all night?' I asked.

They smiled. On duty, if called.

'Thanks,' I said.

Another journey. People in green overalls and white masks, making soothing remarks. Could I face taking my coat off? No? Never mind then. Needle into vein in back of hand. Marvellous. Oblivion rolled through

180

me in grey and black and I greeted it with a sob of welcome.

The world shuffled back in the usual way, bit by uncomfortable bit, with a middle-aged nurse patting my hand and telling me to wake up dear, it was all over.

I had to admit that my wildest fears were not realized. I still had two legs. One I could move. The other had plaster on. Inside the plaster it gently ached. The scream had died to a whisper. I sighed with relief.

What was the time? Five o'clock, dear.

Where was I? In the recovery ward, dear. Now go to sleep again and when you wake up you'll be feeling much better, you'll see.

I did as she said, and she was quite right.

Mid-morning, a doctor came. Not the same one as the night before. Older, heavier, but just as tired looking.

'You had a lucky escape,' he said.

'Yes, I did.'

'Luckier than you imagine. We took a blood test. Actually we took two blood tests. The first one alcohol. With practically negative results. Now this interested us, because who except a drunk would stop a car on a level crossing and get out and lean against it? The casualty doctor told us you swore you hadn't been drinking and that anyway you seemed sober enough to him . . . but that you'd had a bad headache which was now better . . . We gave you a bit of thought, and we looked at those very bright scarlet stains on your shirt . . . and tested your blood again . . . and there it was!' He paused triumphantly.

'What?'

'Carboxyhaemoglobin.'

'*What*?'

'Carbon monoxide, my dear chap. Carbon-monoxide poisoning. Explains everything, don't you see?'

'Oh . . . but I thought . . . with carbon monoxide . . . one simply blacked out.'

'It depends. If you got a large dose all at once that would happen, like it does to people who get stuck in snow drifts and leave their engines running. But a trickle, that would affect you more slowly. But it would all be the same in the end, of course. The haemoglobin in the red corpuscles has a greater affinity for carbon monoxide than for oxygen, so it mops up any carbon monoxide you breathe in, and oxygen is disregarded. If the level of carbon monoxide in your blood builds up gradually . . . you get gradual symptoms. Very insidious they are too. The trouble is that it seems that when people feel sleepy they light a cigarette to keep themselves awake, and tobacco smoke itself introduces significant quantities of carbon monoxide into the body, so the cigarette may be the final knock out. Er ... do you smoke?'

'No.' And to think I'd regretted it.

'Just as well. You obviously had quite a dangerous concentration of CO in any case.'

'I must have been driving for half an hour ... maybe forty minutes. I don't really know.'

'It's a wonder you stopped safely at all. Much more likely to have crashed into something.'

'I nearly did ... on a corner.'

He nodded. 'Didn't you smell exhaust fumes?'

'I didn't notice. I had too much on my mind. And the heater burps out exhaust smells sometimes. So I wouldn't take much heed, if it wasn't strong.' I looked down at myself under the sheets. 'What's the damage?'

'Not much now,' he said cheerfully. 'You were lucky there too. You had multiple dislocations ... hip, knee, and ankle. Never seen all three before. Very interesting. We reduced them all successfully. No crushing or fractures, no severed tendons. We don't even think there will be a recurring tendency to dislocate. One or two frayed ligaments round your knee, that's all.'

'It's a miracle.'

'Interesting case, yes. Unique sort of accident, of course. No direct force involved. We think it might have been air impact ... that it sort of blew or stretched you apart. Like being on the rack, eh?' He chuckled. 'We put plaster on your knee and ankle, to give them a chance to settle, but it can come off in three or four weeks. We don't want you to put weight on your hip yet, either. You can have some physiotherapy. But take it easy for a while when you leave here. There was a lot of spasm in the muscles, and all your ligaments and so on were badly stretched. Give everything time to subside properly before you run a mile.' He smiled, which turned halfway through into a yawn. He smothered it apologetically. 'It's been a long night . . .'

'Yes,' I said.

I went home on Tuesday afternoon in an ambulance with a pair of crutches and instructions to spend most of my time horizontal.

Poppy was still sick. Tony followed my slow progress up the stairs apologizing that she couldn't manage to have me stay, the kids were exhausting her to distraction.

'I'm fine on my own.'

He saw me into the bedroom, where I lay down in my clothes on top of the bedspread, as per instructions. Then he made for the whisky and refreshed himself after my labours.

'Do you want anything? I'll fetch you some food, later.'

'Thanks,' I said. 'Could you bring the telephone in here?'

He brought it in and plugged the lead into the socket beside my bed.

'OK?'

'Fine,' I said.

'That's it, then.' He tossed off his drink quickly and made for the door, showing far more haste than usual and edging away from me as though embarrassed.

'Is anything wrong?' I said.

He jumped. 'No. Absolutely nothing. Got to get the kids their tea before evening stables. See you later, pal. With the odd crust.' He smiled sketchily and disappeared.

I shrugged. Whatever it was that was wrong, he would tell me in time, if he wanted to.

I picked up the telephone and dialled the number of the local garage. Its best mechanic answered.

'Mr Hughes . . . I heard . . . Your beautiful car.' He commiserated genuinely for half a minute.

'Yes,' I said. 'Look, Derek, is there any way that exhaust gas could get into the car through the heater?'

He was affronted. 'Not the way I looked after it. Certainly not.'

'I apparently breathed in great dollops of carbon monoxide,' I said.

'Not through the heater . . . I can't understand it.' He paused, thinking. 'They take special care not to let that happen, see? At the design stage. You could only get exhaust gas through the heater if there was a loose or worn gasket on the exhaust manifold *and* a crack or break in the heater tubing *and* a tube connecting the two together, and you can take it from me, Mr Hughes, there was nothing at all like that on your car. Maintained perfect, it is.'

'The heater does sometimes smell of exhaust. If you remember, I did mention it, some time ago.'

'I give the whole system a thorough check then, too. There wasn't a thing wrong. Only thing I could think of was the exhaust might have eddied forwards from the back of the car when you slowed down, sort of, and got whirled in through the fresh-air intake, the one down beside the heater.'

'Could you possibly go and look at my car? At what's left of it? . . .'

'There's a good bit to do here,' he said dubiously.

'The police have given me the name of the garage where it is now. Apparently all the bits have to stay there until the insurance people have seen them. But you know the car . . . it would be easier for you to spot anything different with it from when you last serviced it. Could you go?'

'D'you mean,' he paused. 'You don't mean . . . there might be something . . . well . . . *wrong* with it?'

'I don't know,' I said. 'But I'd like to find out.'

'It would cost you,' he said warningly. 'It would be working hours.'

'Never mind. If you can go, it will be worth it.'

'Hang on, then.' He departed to consult. Came back. 'Yes, all right. The Guvnor says I can go first thing in the morning.'

'That's great,' I said. 'Call me when you get back.'

'It couldn't have been a gasket,' he said suddenly.

'Why not?'

'You'd have heard it. Very noisy. Unless you had the radio on?'

'No.'

'You'd have heard a blown gasket,' he said positively. 'But there again, if the exhaust was being somehow fed straight into the heater . . . perhaps not. The heater would damp the noise, same as a silencer . . . but I don't see how it could have happened. Well . . . all I can do is take a look.'

I would have liked to have gone with him. I put down the receiver and looked gloomily at my right leg. The neat plaster casing stretched from well up my thigh down to the base of my toes, which were currently invisible inside a white hospital theatre sock. A pair of Tony's slacks, though too long by six inches, had slid up easily enough over the plaster, decently hiding it, and as far as looks went, things were passable.

I sighed. The plaster was a bore. They'd designed it somehow so that I found sitting in a chair uncomfortable. Standing and lying down were both better. It wasn't going to stay on a minute longer than I could help, either. The muscles inside it were doing themselves no good in immobility. They would be getting flabby, unfit, wasting away. It would be just too ironic if I got my licence back and was too feeble to ride.

Tony came back at eight with half a chicken. He didn't want to stay, not even for a drink.

'Can you manage?' he said.

'Sure. No trouble.'

'Your leg doesn't hurt, does it?'

'Not a flicker,' I said. 'Can't feel a thing.'

'That's all right then.' He was relieved: wouldn't look at me squarely: went away.

Next morning, Roberta Cranfield came.

'Kelly?' she called. 'Are you in?'

'In the bedroom.'

She walked across the sitting-room and stopped in the doorway. Wearing the black-and-white striped fur coat, hanging open. Underneath it, black pants and a stagnant-pond-coloured sweater.

'Hullo,' she said. 'I've brought you some food. Shall I put it in the kitchen?'

'That's pretty good of you.'

She looked me over. I was lying, dressed, on top of the bedspread, reading the morning paper. 'You look comfortable enough.'

'I am. Just bored. Er ... not now you've come, of course.'

'Of course,' she agreed. 'Shall I make some coffee?'

'Yes, do.'

She brought it back in mugs, shed her fur, and sat loose limbed in my bedroom armchair.

'You look a bit better today,' she observed.

'Can you get that blood off your dress?'

She shrugged. 'I chucked it at the cleaners. They're trying.'

'I'm sorry about that . . .'

'Think nothing of it.' She sipped her coffee. 'I rang the hospital on Saturday. They said you were OK.'

'Thanks.'

'Why on earth did you stop on the railway?'

'I didn't know it was the railway, until too late.'

'But how did you get there, anyway, with the gates down?'

'The gates weren't down.'

'They were when we came along,' she said. 'There were all those lights and people shouting and screaming and we got out of the car to see what it was all about, and someone said the train had hit a car . . . and then I saw you, lying spark out with your face all covered in blood, about ten feet up the line. Nasty. Very nasty. It was, really.'

'I'm sorry . . . I'd had a couple of lungfuls of carbon monoxide. What you might call diminished responsibility.'

She grinned. 'You're some moron.'

The gates must have shut after I'd stopped on the line. I hadn't heard them or seen them. I must, I supposed, have been more affected by the gas than I remembered.

'I called you Rosalind,' I said apologetically.

'I know.' She made a face. 'Did you think I was her?'

'No . . . It just came out. I meant to say Roberta.'

She unrolled herself from the chair, took a few steps, and stood looking at Rosalind's picture. 'She'd have been glad . . . knowing she still came first with you after all this time.'

The telephone rang sharply beside me and interrupted my surprise. I picked up the receiver.

'Is that Kelly Hughes?' The voice was cultivated, authoritative, loaded indefinably with power. 'This is Wykeham Ferth speaking. I read about your accident in the papers . . . a report this morning says you are now home. I hope . . . you are well?'

'Yes, thank you, my lord.'

It was ridiculous, the way my heart had bumped. Sweating palms, too.

'Are you in any shape to come to London?'

'I'm . . . I've got plaster on my leg . . . I can't sit in a car very easily, I'm afraid.'

'Hm.' A pause. 'Very well. I will drive down to Corrie instead. It's Harringay's old place, isn't it?'

'That's right. I live in a flat over the yard. If you walk into the yard from the drive, you'll see a green door with a brass letter box in the far corner. It won't be locked. There are some stairs inside. I live up there.'

'Right,' he said briskly. 'This afternoon? Good. Expect me at . . . er . . . four o'clock. Right?'

'Sir . . .' I began.

'Not now, Hughes. This afternoon.'

I put the receiver down slowly. Six hours' suspense. Damn him.

'What an absolutely heartless letter,' Roberta exclaimed.

I looked at her. She was holding the letter from my parents, which had been under Rosalind's photograph.

'I dare say I shouldn't have been so nosey as to read it,' she said unrepentantly.

'I dare say not.'

'How *can* they be so beastly?'

'They're not really.'

'This sort of thing always happens when you get one bright son in a family of twits,' she said disgustedly.

'Not always. Some bright sons handle things better than others.'

'Stop clobbering yourself.'

'Yes, ma'am.'

'Are you going to stop sending them money?'

'No. All they can do about that is not spend it . . . or give it to the local cats' and dogs' home.'

'At least they had the decency to see they couldn't take your money *and* call you names.'

'Rigidly moral man, my father,' I said. 'Honest to

191

the last farthing. Honest for its own sake. He taught me a lot that I'm grateful for.'

'And that's why this business hurts him so much?'

'Yes.'

'I've never ... Well. I know you'll despise me for saying it ... but I've never thought about people like your father before as ... well ... *people.*'

'If you're not careful,' I said, 'those chains will drop right off.'

She turned away and put the letter back under Rosalind's picture.

'Which university did you go to?'

'London. Starved in a garret on a grant. Great stuff.'

'I wish ... how odd ... I wish I'd trained for something. Learned a job.'

'It's hardly too late,' I said, smiling.

'I'm nearly twenty. I didn't bother much at school with exams ... no one made us. Then I went to Switzerland for a year, to a finishing school ... and since then I've just lived at home ... What a waste!'

'The daughters of the rich are always at a disadvantage,' I said solemnly.

'Sarcastic beast.'

She sat down again in the armchair and told me that her father really seemed to have snapped out of it at last, and had finally accepted a dinner invitation the night before. All the lads had stayed on. They spent most of their time playing cards and football, as the only horses left in the yard were four half-broken two-year-olds and three old 'chasers recovering from injuries. Most of the owners had promised to bring their horses back at once, if Cranfield had his licence restored in the next few weeks.

'What's really upsetting Father now is hope. With the big Cheltenham meeting only a fortnight away, he's biting his nails about whether he'll get Breadwinner back in time for him to run in his name in the Gold Cup.'

'Pity Breadwinner isn't entered in the Grand National. That would give us a bit more leeway.'

'Would your leg be right in time for the Gold Cup?'

'If I had my licence, I'd saw the plaster off myself.'

'Are you any nearer . . . with the licences?'

'Don't know.'

She sighed. 'It was a great dream while it lasted. And you won't be able to do much about it now.'

She stood up and came over and picked up the crutches which were lying beside the bed. They were black tubular metal with elbow supports and hand grips.

'These are much better than those old fashioned under-the-shoulder affairs,' she said. She fitted the crutches round her arms and swung around the room a bit with one foot off the floor. 'Pretty hard on your hands, though.'

She looked unselfconscious and intent. I watched

193

her. I remembered the revelation it had been in my childhood when I first wondered what it was like to be someone else.

Into this calm sea Tony appeared with a wretched face and a folded paper in his hand.

'Hi,' he said, seeing Roberta. A very gloomy greeting.

He sat down in the armchair and looked at Roberta standing balanced on the crutches with one knee bent. His thoughts were not where his eyes were.

'What is it, then?' I said. 'Out with it.'

'This letter . . . came yesterday,' he said heavily.

'It was obvious last night that something was the matter.'

'I couldn't show it to you then, not straight out of hospital. And I don't know what to do, Kelly pal, sure enough I don't.'

'Let's see, then.'

He handed me the paper worriedly. I opened it up. A brief letter from the racing authorities. Bang bang, both barrels.

Dear Sir,

It has been brought to our attention that a person warned off Newmarket Heath is living as a tenant in your stable yard. This is contrary to the regulations, and you should remedy the situation as soon as possible. It is perhaps not necessary to warn you that your own training licence might have to be reviewed if you should fail to take the steps suggested.

'Sods,' Tony said forcefully. 'Bloody sods.'

CHAPTER ELEVEN

Derek from the garage came while Roberta was clearing away the lunch she had stayed to cook. When he rang the door bell she went downstairs to let him in.

He walked hesitatingly across the sitting-room looking behind him to see if his shoes were leaving dirty marks and out of habit wiped his hands down his trousers before taking the one I held out to him.

'Sit down,' I suggested. He looked doubtfully at the khaki velvet armchair, but in the end lowered himself gingerly into it. He looked perfectly clean. No grease, no filthy overalls, just ordinary slacks and sports jacket. He wasn't used to it.

'You all right?' he said.

'Absolutely.'

'If you'd been in that car . . .' He looked sick at what he was thinking, and his vivid imagination was one of the things which made him a reliable mechanic. He didn't want death on his conscience. Young, fair haired, diffident, he kept most of his brains in his fingertips and outside of cars used the upstairs lot sparingly.

'You've never seen nothing like it,' he said. 'You wouldn't know it was a car, you wouldn't straight. It's all in little bits . . . I mean, like, bits of metal that don't look as if they were ever part of anything. Honestly. It's like twisted shreds of stuff.' He swallowed. 'They've got it collected up in tin baths.'

'The engine too?'

'Yeah. Smashed into fragments. Still, I had a look. Took me a long time, though, because everything is all jumbled up, and honest you can't tell what anything used to be. I mean, I didn't think it was a bit of exhaust manifold that I'd picked up, not at first, because it wasn't any shape that you'd think of.'

'You found something?'

'Here.' He fished in his trouser pocket. 'This is what it was all like. This is a bit of the exhaust manifold. Cast iron, that is, you see, so of course it was brittle, sort of, and it had shattered into bits. I mean, it wasn't sort of crumpled up like all the aluminium and so on. It wasn't bent, see, it was just in bits.'

'Yes, I do see,' I said. The anxious lines on his forehead dissolved when he saw that he had managed to tell me what he meant. He came over and put the small black jagged-edged lump into my hands. Heavy for its size. About three inches long. Asymmetrically curved. Part of the side wall of a huge tube.

'As far as I can make out, see,' Derek said, pointing, 'it came from about where the manifold narrows down to the exhaust pipe, but really it might be anywhere. There were quite a few bits of manifold, when I looked, but I couldn't see the bit that fits into this, and I dare say it's still rusting away somewhere along the railway line. Anyway, see this bit here . . .' He pointed a stubby finger at a round dent in part of one edge. 'That's one side of a hole that was bored in the manifold wall. Now don't get me wrong, there's quite a few holes might have been drilled through the wall. I mean, some people have exhaust-gas temperature gauges stuck into the manifold . . . and other gauges too. Things like that. Only, see, there weren't no gauges in your manifold, now, were there?'

'You tell me,' I said.

'There weren't, then. Now you couldn't really say what the hole was for, not for certain you couldn't. But as far as I know, there weren't any holes in your manifold last time I did the service.'

I fingered the little semi-circular dent. No more than a quarter of an inch across.

'However did you spot something so small?' I asked.

'Dunno, really. Mind you, I was there a good couple of hours, picking through those tubs. Did it methodical, like. Since you were paying for it and all.'

'Is it a big job . . . drilling a hole this size through an exhaust manifold? Would it take long?'

'Half a minute, I should think.'

'With an electric drill?' I asked.

'Oh yeah, sure. If you did it with a hand drill, then it would take five minutes. Say nearer eight or ten, to be on the safe side.'

'How many people carry drills around in their tool kits?'

'That, see, it depends on the chap. Now some of them carry all sorts of stuff in their cars. Proper work benches, some of them. And then others, the tool kit stays strapped up fresh from the factory until the car's dropping to bits.'

'People do carry drills, then?'

'Oh yeah, sure. Quite a lot do. Hand drills, of course. You wouldn't have much call for an electric drill, not in a tool kit, not unless you did a lot of repairs, like, say on racing cars.'

He went and sat down again. Carefully, as before.

'If someone drilled a hole this size through the manifold, what would happen?'

'Well, honestly, nothing much. You'd get exhaust gas out through the engine, and you'd hear a good lot of noise, and you might smell it in the car, but it would sort of blow away, see, it wouldn't come in through the heater. To do that, like I said before, you'd have to put some tubing into the hole there and then stick the other end of the tubing into the heater. Mind you that would be pretty easy, you wouldn't need a drill. Some heater tubes are really only cardboard.'

'Rubber tubing from one end to the other?' I suggested.

He shook his head. 'No. Have to be metal. Exhaust gas, that's very hot. It'd melt anything but metal.'

'Do you think anyone could do all that on the spur of the moment?'

He put his head on one side, considering. 'Oh sure, yeah. If he'd got a drill. Like, say the first other thing he needs is some tubing. Well, he's only got to look around for that. Lots lying about, if you look. The other day, I used a bit of a kiddy's old cycle frame, just the job it was. Right, you get the tube ready first and then you fit a drill nearest the right size, to match. And Bob's your uncle.'

'How long, from start to finish?'

'Fixing the manifold to the heater? Say, from scratch, including maybe having to cast around for a bit of tube, well, at the outside half an hour. A quarter, if you had something all ready handy. Only the drilling would take any time, see? The rest would be like stealing candy from a baby.'

Roberta appeared in the doorway shrugging herself into the stripy coat. Derek stood up awkwardly and didn't know where to put his hands. She smiled at him sweetly and unseeingly and said to me, 'Is there anything else you want, Kelly?'

'No. Thank you very much.'

'Think nothing of it. I'll see . . . I might come over again tomorrow.'

'Fine,' I said.

'Right.'

She nodded, smiled temperately, and made her usual poised exit. Derek's comment approached, 'Cor.'

'I suppose you didn't see any likely pieces of tube in the wreckage?' I asked.

'Huh?' He tore his eyes away with an effort from the direction Roberta had gone. 'No, like it was real bad. Lots of bits, you couldn't have told what they were. I never seen anything like it. Sure, I seen crashes, stands to reason. Different, this was.' He shivered.

'Did you have any difficulty with being allowed to search?'

'No, none. They didn't seem all that interested in what I did. Just said to help myself.' Course, I told them it was my car, like. I mean, that I looked after it. Mind you, they were right casual about it, anyway, because when I came away they were letting this other chap have a good look too.'

'Which other chap?'

'Some fellow. Said he was an insurance man, but he didn't have a notebook.'

I felt like saying Huh? too. I said, 'Notebook?'

'Yeah, sure, insurance men, they're always crawling

round our place looking at wrecks and never one without a notebook. Write down every blessed detail, they do. But this other chap, looking at your car, he didn't have any notebook.'

'What did he look like?'

He thought.

'That's difficult, see. He didn't look like anything, really. Medium, sort of. Not young and not old really either. A nobody sort of person, really.'

'Did he wear sunglasses?'

'No. He had a hat on, but I don't know if he had ordinary glasses. I can't actually remember. I didn't notice that much.'

'Was he looking through the wreckage as if he knew what he wanted?'

'Uh . . . don't know, really. Strikes me he was a bit flummoxed, like, finding it was all in such small bits.'

'He didn't have a girl with him?'

'Nope.' He brightened. 'He came in a Volkswagen, an oldish grey one.'

'Thousands of those about,' I said.

'Oh yeah, sure. Er . . . was this chap important?'

'Only if he was looking for what you found.'

He worked it out.

'Cripes,' he said.

*

Lord Ferth arrived twenty minutes after he'd said, which meant that I'd been hopping round the flat on my crutches for half an hour, unable to keep still.

He stood in the doorway into the sitting-room holding a briefcase and bowler hat in one hand and unbuttoning his short fawn overcoat with the other.

'Well, Hughes,' he said. 'Good afternoon.'

'Good afternoon, my lord.'

He came right in, shut the door behind him, and put his hat and case on the oak chest beside him.

'How's the leg?'

'Stagnating,' I said. 'Can I get you some tea . . . coffee . . . or a drink?'

'Nothing just now . . .' He laid his coat on the chest and picked up the briefcase again, looking round him with the air of surprise I was used to in visitors. I offered him the green armchair with a small table beside it. He asked where I was going to sit.

'I'll stand,' I said. 'Sitting's difficult.'

'But you don't stand all day!'

'No. Lie on my bed, mostly.'

'Then we'll talk in your bedroom.'

We went through the door at the end of the sitting-room and this time he murmured aloud.

'Whose flat is this?' he asked.

'Mine.'

He glanced at my face, hearing the dryness in my voice. 'You resent surprise?'

203

'It amuses me.'

'Hughes ... it's a pity you didn't join the Civil Service. You'd have gone all the way.'

I laughed. 'There's still time ... Do they take in warned-off jockeys at the Administrative Grade?'

'So you can joke about it?'

'It's taken nine days. But yes, just about.'

He gave me a long straight assessing look, and there was a subtle shift somewhere in both his manner to me and in his basic approach, and when I shortly understood what it was I was shaken, because he was taking me on level terms, level in power and understanding and experience: and I wasn't level.

Few men in his position would have thought that this course was viable, let alone chosen it. I understood the compliment. He saw, too, that I did, and I knew later that had there not been this fundamental change of ground, this cancellation of the Steward-jockey relationship, he would not have said to me all that he did. It wouldn't have happened if he hadn't been in my flat.

He sat down in the khaki velvet armchair, putting the briefcase carefully on the floor beside him. I took the weight off my crutches and let the bed springs have a go.

'I went to see Lord Gowery,' he said neutrally. 'And I can see no reason not to tell you straight away that you and Dexter Cranfield will have your warning off rescinded within the next few days.'

'Do you mean it?' I exclaimed. I tried to sit up. The plaster intervened.

Lord Ferth smiled. 'As I see it, there is no alternative. There will be a quiet notice to that effect in next week's Calendar.'

'That is, of course,' I said, 'all you need to tell me.'

He looked at me levelly. 'True. But not all you want to know.'

'No.'

'No one has a better right . . . and yet you will have to use your discretion about whether you tell Dexter Cranfield.'

'All right.'

He sighed, reached down to open the briefcase, and pulled out a neat little tape-recorder.

'I did try to ignore your suggestion. Succeeded, too, for a while. However . . .' He paused, his fingers hovering over the controls. 'This conversation took place late on Monday afternoon, in the sitting-room of Lord Gowery's flat near Sloane Square. We were alone . . . you will see that we were alone. He knew, though, that I was making a recording.' He still hesitated. 'Compassion. That's what you need. I believe you have it.'

'Don't con me,' I said.

He grimaced. 'Very well.'

The recording began with the self-conscious platitudes customary in front of microphones, especially when no one wants to take the first dive into the deep end. Lord Ferth had leapt, eventually.

'Norman, I explained why we must take a good look at this Enquiry.'

'Hughes is being ridiculous. Not only ridiculous, but downright slanderous. I don't understand why you should take him seriously.' Gowery sounded impatient.

'We have to, even if only to shut him up.' Lord Ferth looked across the room, his hot eyes gleaming ironically. The recording ploughed on, his voice like honey. 'You know perfectly well, Norman, that it will be better all round if we can show there is nothing whatever in these allegations he is spreading around. Then we can emphatically confirm the suspension and squash all the rumours.'

Subtle stuff. Lord Gowery's voice grew easier, assured now that Ferth was still an ally. As perhaps he was. 'I do assure you, Wykeham, that if I had not sincerely believed that Hughes and Dexter Cranfield were guilty, I would not have warned them off.'

There was something odd about that. Both Ferth and Gowery had thought so too, as there were several seconds of silence on the tape.

'But you do still believe it?' Ferth said eventually.

'Of course.' He was emphatic. 'Of course I do.' Much too emphatic.

'Then ... er ... taking one of Hughes' questions

first ... How did it come about that Newtonnards was called to the Enquiry?'

'I was informed that Cranfield had backed Cherry Pie with him.'

'Yes ... but who informed you?'

Gowery didn't reply.

Ferth's voice came next, with absolutely no pressure in it.

'Um ... Have you any idea how we managed to show the wrong film of Hughes racing at Reading?'

Gowery was on much surer ground. 'My fault, I'm afraid. I asked the Secretaries to write off for the film of the last race. Didn't realize there were seven races. Careless of me, I'll admit. But of course, as it was the wrong film, it was irrelevant to the case.'

'Er ...' said Lord Ferth. But he hadn't yet been ready to argue. He cleared his throat and said, 'I suppose you thought it would be relevant to see how Hughes had ridden Squelch last time out.'

After another long pause Gowery said, 'Yes.'

'But in the event we didn't show it.'

'No.'

'Would we have shown it if, after having sent for it, we found that the Reading race bore out entirely Hughes' assertion that he rode Squelch in the Lemonfizz in exactly the same way as he always did?'

More silence. Then he said quietly, 'Yes,' and he sounded very troubled.

'Hughes asked at the Enquiry that we should show the right film,' Ferth said.

'I'm sure he didn't.'

'I've been reading the transcript. Norman, I've been reading and re-reading that transcript all weekend and frankly, that is why I'm here. Hughes did in fact suggest that we should show the right film, presumably because he knew it would support his case . . .'

'Hughes was guilty!' Gowery broke in vehemently. 'Hughes was guilty. I had no option but to warn him off.'

Lord Ferth pressed the stop button on the tape-recorder.

'Tell me,' he said, 'what you think of that last statement?'

'I think,' I said slowly, 'that he did believe it. Both from that statement and from what I remember of the Enquiry. His certainty that day shook me. He believed me guilty so strongly that he was stone deaf to anything which looked even remotely likely to assault his opinion.'

'That was your impression?'

'Overpowering,' I said.

Lord Ferth took his lower lip between his teeth and shook his head, but I gathered it was at the general situation, not at me. He pressed the start button again. His voice came through, precise, carefully without emotion, gentle as vaseline.

'Norman, about the composition of the Enquiry . . . the members of the Disciplinary Committee who sat with you . . . What guided you to choose Andrew Tring and old Plimborne?'

'What guided me?' He sounded astonished at the question. 'I haven't any idea.'

'I wish you'd cast back.'

'I can't see that it has any relevance . . . but let's see . . . I suppose I had Tring in my mind anyway, as I'm in the middle of some business negotiations with him. And Plimborne . . . well, I just saw him snoozing away in the Club. I was talking to him later in the lobby, and I asked him just on the spur of the moment to sit with me. I don't see the point of your asking.'

'Never mind. It doesn't matter. Now . . . about Charlie West. I can see that of course you would call the rider of the third horse to give evidence. And it is clear from the transcript that you knew what the evidence would be. However, at the preliminary enquiry at Oxford West said nothing at all about Hughes having pulled his horse back. I've consulted all three of the Oxford Stewards this morning. They confirm that West did not suggest it at the time. He asserted it, however, at the Enquiry, and you knew what he was going to say, so . . . er . . . how did you know?'

More silence.

Ferth's voice went on a shade anxiously. 'Norman, if you instructed a Stipendiary Steward to interview

209

West privately and question him further, for heaven's sake say so. These jockeys stick together. It is perfectly reasonable to believe that West wouldn't speak up against Hughes to begin with, but might do so if pressed with questions. Did you send a Stipendiary?'

Gowery said faintly, 'No.'

'Then how did you know what West was going to say?'

Gowery didn't answer. He said instead, 'I did instruct a Stipendiary to look up all the races in which Cranfield had run two horses and compile me a list of all the occasions when the lesser-backed had won. And as you know, it is the accepted practice to bring up everything in a jockey's past history at an Enquiry. It was a perfectly normal procedure.'

'I'm not saying it wasn't,' Ferth's voice said, puzzled.

Ferth stopped the recorder and raised his eyebrows at me.

'What d'you make of *that*?'

'He's grabbing for a rock in a quicksand.'

He sighed, pressed the starter again and Gowery's voice came back.

'It was all there in black and white . . . It was quite true . . . they'd been doing it again and again.'

'What do you mean, it was quite true? Did someone *tell* you they'd been doing it again and again?'

More silence. Gowery's rock was crumbling.

Again Ferth didn't press him. Instead he said in the same unaccusing way, 'How about David Oakley?'

'Who?'

'David Oakley. The enquiry agent who photographed the money in Hughes' flat. Who suggested that he should go there?'

No answer.

Ferth said with the first faint note of insistence, 'Norman, you really must give some explanation. Can't you see that all this silence just won't do? We *have* to have some answers if we are going to squash Hughes' rumours.'

Gowery reacted with defence in his voice. 'The evidence against Cranfield and Hughes was collected. What does it matter who collected it?'

'It matters because Hughes asserts that much of it was false.'

'No,' he said fiercely. 'It was not false.'

'Norman,' Ferth said, 'is that what you believe . . . or what you *want* to believe?'

'Oh . . .' Gowery's exclamation was more of anguish than surprise. I looked sharply across at Ferth. His dark eyes were steady on my face. His voice went on, softer again. Persuasive.

'Norman, was there any reason why you *wanted* Cranfield and Hughes warned off?'

'No.' Half a shout. Definitely a lie.

'Any reason why you should go so far as to manufacture evidence against them, if none existed?'

'Wykeham!' He was outraged. 'How can you say that! You are suggesting ... You are suggesting ... something so dishonourable ...'

Ferth pressed the stop button. 'Well?' he said challengingly.

'That was genuine,' I said. 'He didn't manufacture it himself. But then I never thought he did. I just wanted to know where he got it from.'

Ferth nodded. Pressed the start again.

His voice. 'My dear Norman, you lay yourself open to such suggestions if you will not say how you came by all the evidence. Do you not see? If you will not explain how you came by it, you cannot be too surprised if you are thought to have procured it yourself.'

'The evidence was genuine!' he asserted. A rearguard action.

'You are still trying to convince yourself that it was.'

'No! It was.'

'Then where did it come from?'

Gowery's back was against the wall. I could see from the remembered emotion twisting Ferth's face that this had been a saddening and perhaps embarrassing moment.

'I was sent,' said Gowery with difficulty, 'a package. It contained ... various statements ... and six copies of the photograph taken in Hughes' flat.'

'Who sent it to you?'

Gowery's voice was very low. 'I don't know.'

'You don't know?' Ferth was incredulous. 'You warned two men off on the strength of it, and you don't know where it came from?'

A miserable assenting silence.

'You just accepted all that so-called evidence on its face value?'

'It was all true.' He clung to it.

'Have you still got that package?'

'Yes.'

'I'd like to see it.' A touch of iron in Ferth's voice.

Gowery hadn't argued. There were sounds of moving about, a drawer opening and closing, a rustling of papers.

'I see,' Ferth said slowly. 'These papers do, in fact, look very convincing.'

'Then you see why I acted on them,' Gowery said eagerly, with a little too much relief.

'I can see why you should consider doing so . . . after making a careful check.'

'I did check.'

'To what extent?'

'Well . . . the package only came four days before the Enquiry. On the Thursday before. I had the Secretaries send out the summonses to Newtonnards, Oakley, and West immediately. They were asked to confirm by telegram that they would be attending, and

213

they all did so. Newtonnards was asked to bring his records for the Lemonfizz Cup. And then of course I asked a Stipendiary to ask the Totalizator people if anyone had backed Cherry Pie substantially, and he collected those affidavits . . . the ones we produced at the Enquiry. There was absolutely no doubt whatsoever that Cranfield had backed Cherry Pie. He lied about it at the Enquiry. That made it quite conclusive. He was entirely guilty, and there was no reason why I should not warn him off.'

Ferth stopped the recorder. 'What do you say to that?' he asked.

I shrugged. 'Cranfield did back Cherry Pie. He was stupid to deny it, but admitting it was, as he saw it, cutting his own throat. He told me that he backed him – through this unidentified friend – with Newtonnards and on the Tote, and not with his normal bookmaker, because he didn't want Kessel to know, as Kessel and the bookmaker are tattleswapping buddies. He in fact put a hundred pounds on Cherry Pie because he thought the horse might be warming up to give everyone a surprise. He also put two hundred and fifty pounds on Squelch, because reason suggested that *he* would win. And where is the villainy in that?'

Ferth looked at me levelly. 'You didn't know he had backed Cherry Pie, not at the Enquiry.'

'I tackled him with it afterwards. It had struck me by then that that had to be true, however hard he had denied it. Newtonnards might have lied or altered his books, but no one can argue against Tote tickets.'

'That was one of the things which convinced me too,' he admitted.

He started the recorder. He himself was speaking and now there was a distinct flavour in his voice of cross examination. The whole interview moved suddenly into the shape of an Enquiry of its own. 'This photograph . . . didn't it seem at all odd to you?'

'Why should it?' Gowery said sharply.

'Didn't you ask yourself how it came to be taken?'

'No.'

'Hughes says Oakley took the money and the note with him and simply photographed them in his flat.'

'No.'

'How can you be sure?' Ferth pounced on him.

'No!' Gowery said again. There was a rising note in his voice, the sound of pressure approaching blow-up.

'Who sent Oakley to Hughes' flat?'

'I've told you, I don't know.'

'But you're sure that is a genuine photograph?'

'Yes. Yes it is.'

'You are sure beyond doubt?' Ferth insisted.

'Yes!' The voice was high, the anxiety plain, the panic growing. Into this screwed up moment Ferth dropped one intense word, like a bomb.

'*Why?*'

CHAPTER TWELVE

The tape ran on for nearly a minute. When Gowery finally answered his voice was quite different. Low, broken up, distressed to the soul.

'It had ... to be true. I said at first ... I couldn't warn them off if they weren't guilty ... and then the package came ... and it was such a relief ... they really were guilty ... I could warn them off ... and everything would be all right.'

My mouth opened. Ferth watched me steadily, his eyes narrowed with the pity of it.

Gowery went on compulsively. Once started, he needed to confess.

'If I tell you ... from the beginning ... perhaps you will understand. It began the day after I was appointed to substitute for the Disciplinary Steward at the Cranfield-Hughes Enquiry. It's ironic to think of it now, but I was quite pleased to be going to do it ... and then ... and then ...' He paused and took an effortful control of his voice. 'Then, I had a telephone call.' Another pause. 'This man said . . . said . . . I must warn Cranfield off.' He cleared his throat. 'I told him I would do no such thing, unless Cranfield was guilty. Then he said . . . then he said . . . that he knew things about me . . . and he would tell everyone . . . if I didn't warn Cranfield off. I told him I couldn't warn him off if he wasn't guilty . . . and you see I didn't think he *was* guilty. I mean, racehorses are so unpredictable, and I saw the Lemonfizz myself and although after that crowd demonstration it was obvious the Stewards would have Cranfield and Hughes in, I was surprised when they referred it to the Disciplinary Committee . . . I thought that there must have been circumstances that I didn't know of . . . and then I was asked to take the Enquiry . . . and I had an open mind . . . I told the man on the telephone that no threats could move me from giving Cranfield a fair judgement.'

Less jelly in his voice while he remembered that first strength. It didn't last.

'He said . . . in that case . . . I could expect . . . after the Enquiry . . . if Cranfield got off . . . that my life wouldn't be worth living . . . I would have to resign from the Jockey Club . . . and everyone would know . . . And I said again that I would not warn Cranfield off unless I was convinced of his guilt, and that I would not be blackmailed, and I put down the receiver and cut him off.'

'And then,' Ferth suggested, 'you began to worry?'

'Yes.' Little more than a whisper.

'What exactly did he threaten to publish?'

'I can't ... can't tell you. Not criminal ... not a matter for the police ... but ...'

'But enough to ruin you socially?'

'Yes ... I'm afraid so ... yes, completely.'

'But you stuck to your guns?'

'I was desperately worried ... I couldn't ... how could I? ... take away Cranfield's livelihood just to save myself ... It would have been dishonourable ... and I couldn't see myself living with it ... and in any case I couldn't just warn him off, just like that, if there was no proof he was guilty ... So I did worry ... couldn't sleep ... or eat ...'

'Why didn't you ask to be relieved of the Enquiry?'

'Because he told me ... if I backed out ... it would count the same with him as letting Cranfield off ... so I had to go on, just in case some proof turned up.'

'Which it did,' Ferth said drily. 'Conveniently.'

'Oh ...' Again the anguish. 'I didn't realize ... I didn't indeed ... that it might have been the black-mailer who had sent the package. I didn't wonder very much who had sent it. It was release ... that's all I could see ... it was a heaven-sent release from the most unbearable ... I didn't question ... I just believed it ... believed it absolutely ... and I was so grateful ... so grateful ...'

Four days before the Enquiry, that package had

come. He must have been sweating for a whole week, taking a long bleak look at the wilderness. Send a St Bernard to a dying mountaineer and he's unlikely to ask for the dog licence.

'When did you begin to doubt?' Ferth said calmly.

'Not until afterwards. Not for days. It was Hughes . . . at the dance. You told me he was insisting he'd been framed and was going to find out who . . . and then he asked me directly who had sent Oakley to his flat . . . and it . . . Wykeham, it was *terrible*. I realized . . . what I'd done. Inside, I did know . . . but I couldn't admit it to myself . . . I shut it away . . . they *had* to be guilty . . .'

There was another long silence. Then Gowery said, 'You'll see to it . . . that they get their licences back?'

'Yes,' Ferth said.

'I'll resign . . .' He sounded desolate.

'From the Disciplinary Committee, I agree,' Ferth said reasonably. 'As to the rest . . . we will see.'

'Do you think the . . . the blackmailer . . . will tell . . . everyone . . . anyway, when Cranfield has his licence back?'

'He would have nothing to gain.'

'No, but . . .'

'There are laws to protect you.'

'They couldn't.'

'What does he in fact have over you?'

'I . . . I . . . oh, God.' The tape stopped abruptly, cutting off words that were disintegrating into gulps.

Ferth said, 'I switched it off. He was breaking down. One couldn't record that.'

'No.'

'He told me what it was he was being blackmailed about. I think I am prepared to tell you also, although he would hate it if he knew. But you only.'

'Only,' I said. 'I won't repeat it.'

'He told me . . .' His nose wrinkled in distaste. 'He told me that he has . . . he suffers from . . . unacceptable sexual appetites. Not homosexual. Perhaps that would have been better . . . simpler . . . he wouldn't now-adays have been much reviled for that. No. He says he belongs to a sort of club where people like him can gratify themselves fairly harmlessly, as they are all there because they enjoy . . . in varying forms . . . the same thing.' He stopped. He was embarrassed.

'Which is what?' I said matter-of-factly.

He said, as if putting a good yard of clean air between himself and the world, 'Flagellation.'

'That old thing!' I said.

'What?'

'The English disease. Shades of Fanny Hill. Sex tang-led up with self-inflicted pain, like nuns with their little disciplines and sober citizens paying a pound a lash to be whipped.'

'Kelly!'

'You must have read their coy little advertisements? "Correction given". That's what it's all about. More

widespread than most people imagine. Starts with hus-
bands spanking their wives regularly before they bed
them, and carries right on up to the parties where they
all dress up in leather and have a right old orgy. I don't
actually understand why anyone should get fixated on
leather or rubber or hair, or on those instead of anything else. Why not coal, for instance . . . or silk? But
they do, apparently.'

'In this case . . . leather.'

'Boots and whips and naked bosoms?'

Ferth shook his head in disbelief. 'You take it so
coolly.'

'Live and let live,' I said. 'If that's what they feel
compelled to do . . . why stop them? As he said, they're
not harming anyone, if they're in a club where everyone
else is the same.'

'But for a Steward,' he protested. 'A member of the
Disciplinary Committee!'

'Gives you pause,' I agreed.

He looked horrified. 'But there would be nothing
sexual in his judgement on racing matters.'

'Of course not. Nothing on earth as unsexual as
racing.'

'But one can see . . . he would be finished in the
racing world, if this got out. Even I . . . I cannot think
of him now without this . . . this perversion . . . coming
into my mind. It would be the same with everyone.
One can't respect him any more. One can't like him.'

'Difficult,' I agreed.

'It's ... horrible.' In his voice, all the revulsion of the normal for the deviation. Most racing men were normal. The deviation would be cast out. Ferth felt it. Gowery knew it. And so did someone else ...

'Don't they wear masks, at this club?' I asked.

Ferth looked surprised. 'Why, yes, they do. I asked him who could know about him ... in order to blackmail him ... and he said he didn't know, they all wore masks. Hoods, actually, was the word he used. Hoods ... and aprons ...' He was revolted.

'All leather?'

He nodded. 'How can they?'

'They do less harm than the ones who go out and rape small children.'

'I'm glad I ... ' he said passionately.

'Me too,' I said. 'But it's just luck.' Gowery had been unlucky, in more ways than one. 'Someone may have seen him going in, or leaving afterwards.'

'That's what he thinks. But he says he doesn't know the real names of any of his fellow members. They all call each other by fanciful made-up names, apparently.'

'There must be a secretary ... with a list of members?'

Ferth shook his head. 'I asked him that. He said he'd never given his own name to anyone there. It wasn't expected. There's no annual subscription, just ten pounds in cash every time he attends. He says he goes about once a month, on average.'

'How many other members are there?'

'He didn't know the total number. He says there are never fewer than ten, and sometimes thirty or thirty-five. More men than women, usually. The club isn't open every day; only Mondays and Thursdays.'

'Where is it?'

'In London. He wouldn't tell me exactly where.'

'He wants . . . needs . . . to keep on going,' I said.

'You don't think he will!'

'After a while. Yes.'

'Oh no . . .'

'Who introduced him to the club, do you know?'

'He said it couldn't be the person who introduced him to the club. She was a prostitute . . . he'd never told her his real name.'

'But she understood his needs.'

He sighed. 'It would seem so.'

'Some of those girls make more money out of whipping men than sleeping with them.'

'How on earth do you know?'

'I had digs once in the next room to one. She told me.'

'Good Lord.' He looked as if he'd turned over a stone and found creepy-crawlies underneath. He had plainly no inkling of what it was like to *be* a creepy-crawly. His loss.

'Anyway,' he said slowly, 'you will understand why he accepted that package at its face value.'

'And why he chose Lord Plimborne and Andy Tring.'

Lord Ferth nodded. 'At the end, when he'd recovered a little, he understood that he'd chosen them for the reasons you said, but he believed at the time that they were impulsive choices. And he is now, as you would expect, a very worried and troubled man.'

'Was he,' I asked, 'responsible for this?'

I held out to him the letter Tony had received from the Stewards' Secretaries. He stood up, came to take it, and read its brief contents with exasperation.

'I don't know,' he said explosively. 'I really don't know. When did this arrive?'

'Tuesday. Postmarked noon on Monday.'

'Before I saw him . . . He didn't mention it.'

'Could you find out if it was his doing?'

'Do you mean . . . it will be all the more impossible to forgive him?'

'No. Nothing like that. I was just wondering if it was our little framer-blackmailer at work again. See those words "It has been brought to our attention"? . . . What I'd like to know is who brought it.'

'I'll find out,' he agreed positively. 'That shouldn't be difficult. And of course, disregard the letter. There won't be any question now of your having to move.'

'How are you going to work it? Giving our licences back. How are you going to explain it?'

He raised his eyebrows. 'We never have to give reasons for our decisions.'

I smothered a laugh. The system had its uses.

Lord Ferth sat down in the chair again and put the letter in his briefcase. Then he packed up the tape-recorder and tucked that away too. Then with an air of delicately choosing his words he said, 'A scandal of this sort would do racing a great deal of harm.'

'So you want me to take my licence back and shut up?'

'Er . . . yes.'

'And not chase after the blackmailer, in case he blows the gaffe?'

'Exactly.' He was relieved that I understood.

'No.' I said.

'Why not?' Persuasion in his voice.

'Because he tried to kill me.'

'*What?*'

I showed him the chunk of exhaust manifold, and explained. 'Someone at the dance,' I said. 'That means that our blackmailer is one of about six hundred people, and from there it shouldn't be too hard. You can more or less rule out the women, because few of them would drill through cast iron wearing an evening dress. Much too conspicuous, if anyone saw them. That leaves three hundred men.'

'Someone who knew your car,' he said. 'Surely that would narrow it down considerably?'

'It might not. Anyone could have seen me getting out of it at the races. It was a noticeable car, I'm afraid. But I arrived late at the dance. The car was parked right at the back.'

'Have you . . .' he cleared his throat. 'Are the police involved in this?'

'If you mean are they at present investigating an attempted murder, then no, they are not. If you mean, am I going to ask them to investigate, et cetera, then I haven't decided.'

'Once you start the police on something, you can't stop them.'

'On the other hand if I don't start them the black-mailer might have another go at me, with just a fraction of an inch more success. Which would be quite enough.'

'Um.' He thought it over. 'But if you made it clear to everyone now that you are not any longer trying to find out who framed you . . . he might not try again.'

I said curiously, 'Do you really think it would be best for racing if we just leave this blackmailing murderer romping around free?'

'Better than a full-blown scandal.'

The voice of Establishment diplomacy.

'And if he doesn't follow your line of reasoning . . . and he does kill me . . . how would that do for a scandal?'

He didn't answer. Just looked at me levelly with the hot eyes.

'All right, then,' I said. 'No police.'

'Thank you.'

'Us, though. We'll have to do it ourselves. Find him and deal with him.'

'How do you mean?'

'I'll find him. You deal with him.'

'To your satisfaction, I suppose,' he said ironically.

'Absolutely.'

'And Lord Gowery?'

'He's yours entirely. I shan't tell Dexter Cranfield anything at all.'

'Very well.' He stood up, and I struggled off the bed on to the crutches.

'Just one thing,' I said. 'Could you arrange to have that package of Lord Gowery's sent to me here?'

'I have it with me.' Without hesitation he took a large manila envelope out of the briefcase and put it on the bed. 'You'll understand how he fell on it with relief.'

'Things being as they were,' I agreed. He walked across the sitting-room to the way out, stopping by the chest to put on his coat.

'Can Cranfield tell his owners to shovel their horses back?' I said. 'The sooner the better, you see, if they're to come back in time for Cheltenham.'

'Give me until tomorrow morning. There are several other people who must know first.'

'All right.'

He held out his hand. I transferred the right crutch to the left, and shook it.

He said, 'Perhaps one day soon... when this is over ... you will dine with me?'

'I'd like to,' I said.

'Good.' He picked up his bowler and his briefcase, swept a last considering glance round my flat, nodded to me as if finalizing a decision, and quietly went away.

I telephoned to the orthopod who regularly patched me up after falls.

'I want this plaster off.'

He went into a long spiel of which the gist was two or three more weeks.

'Monday,' I said.

'I'll give you up.'

'Tuesday I start getting it off with a chisel.'

I always slept in shirt-and-shorts pyjamas, which had come in very handy in the present circs. Bedtime that day I struggled into a lime-green and white checked lot I had bought in an off moment at Liverpool the year before with my mind more on the imminent Grand National than on what they would do to my yellow complexion at six on a winter's morning.

Tony had gloomily brought me some casseroled beef and had stayed to celebrate when I told him I wouldn't have to leave. I was out of whisky again in consequence.

When he'd gone I went to bed and read the pages which had sent me to limbo. And they were, indeed, convincing. Neatly typed, well set out, written in authoritative language. Not at first, second, or even third sight the product of malevolence. Emotionless. Cool. Damaging.

'Charles Richard West is prepared to testify that during the course of the race, and in particular at a spot six furlongs from the winning post on the second circuit, he heard Hughes say that he (Hughes) was about to ease his horse so that it should be in no subsequent position to win. Hughes' precise words were, "OK. Brakes on chaps".'

The four other sheets were equally brief, equally to the point. One said that through an intermediary Dexter Cranfield had backed Cherry Pie with Newtonnards. The second pointed out that an investigation of the past form would show that on several other occasions Cranfield's second string had beaten his favourite. The third suggested watching the discrepancies in Hughes' riding in the Lemonfizz and in the last race at Reading ... and there it was in black and white, 'the last race at Reading.' Gowery hadn't questioned it or checked; had simply sent for the last race at Reading. If he had shown it privately to Plimborne and Tring only, and not to me as well, no one might ever have realized it was the wrong race. This deliberate piece of misleading had in fact gone astray, but only just. And the rest hadn't. Page four stated categorically that Cranfield had bribed Hughes not to win, and photographic evidence to prove it was hereby attached.

There was also a short covering note of explanation.

'These few facts have come to my notice. They should clearly be laid before the appropriate authorities, and I am therefore sending them to you, sir, as Steward in command of the forthcoming Enquiry.'

The typewriting itself was unremarkable, the paper medium-quality quarto. The paper clip holding the sheets together was sold by the hundred million, and the buff envelope in which they'd been sent cost a penny or two in any stationer's in the country.

There were two copies only of the photograph. On the back, no identifications.

I slid them all back into the envelope, and put it in the drawer of the table beside my bed. Switched out the light. Lay thinking of riding races again with a swelling feeling of relief and excitement. Wondered how poor old Gowery was making out, going fifteen rounds with his conscience. Thought of Archie and his mortgage ... Kessel having to admit he'd been wrong ... Roberta stepping off her dignity ... the blackmailer biting his nails in apprehension ... sweet dreams every one ... slid into the first easy sleep since the Enquiry.

*

I woke with a jolt, knowing I'd heard a sound which had no business to be there.

A pen-sized flashlight was flickering round the inside of one of the top drawers of the dressing chest. A dark shape blocked off half of its beam as an arm went into the drawer to feel around. Cautious. Very quiet, now.

I lay watching through slit-shut eyes, wondering how close I was this time to the pearly gates. Inconveniently my pulse started bashing against my eardrums as fear stirred up the adrenals, and inside the plaster all the hairs on my leg fought to stand on end.

Trying to keep my breathing even and make no rustle with the sheets I very cautiously slid one arm over the side of the bed and reached down to the floor for a crutch. Any weapon handy was better than none.

No crutches.

I felt around, knowing exactly where I'd laid them beside me, feeling nothing but carpet under my fingers.

The flashlight moved out of the drawer and swung in a small arc while the second top drawer was opened, making the same tiny crack as it loosened which had woken me with the other. The scrap of light shone fractionally on my two crutches propped up against the wall by the door.

I drew the arm very slowly back into bed and lay still. If he'd meant just to kill me, he would have done it by now: and whatever he intended I had little chance of avoiding. The plaster felt like a ton, chaining me immobile.

A clammy crawling feeling all over my skin. Jaw tight, clenched with tension. Dryness in the mouth. Head feeling as if it were swelling. I lay and tried to beat the physical sensations, tried to will them away.

No noticeable success.

He finished with the drawers. The flashlight swung over the khaki chair and steadied on the polished oak chest behind it, against the wall. He moved over there soundlessly and lifted the lid. I almost cried out to him not to, it would wake me. The lid always creaked loudly. I really didn't want him to wake me, it was much too dangerous.

The lid creaked sharply. He stopped dead with it six inches up. Lowered it back into place. It creaked even louder.

He stood there, considering. Then there were quick soft steps on the carpet, a hand fastening in my hair and yanking my head back, and the flashlight beam full in my eyes.

'Right, mate. You're awake. So you'll answer some questions.'

I knew the voice. I shut my eyes against the light and spoke in as bored a drawl as I could manage.

'Mr Oakley, I presume?'

'Clever Mr Hughes.'

He let go of my hair and stripped the bedclothes off

with one flick. The flashlight swung away and fell on top of them. I felt his grip on my neck and the front of my shirt as he wrenched me off the bed and on to the floor. I fell with a crash

'That's for starters,' he said.

CHAPTER THIRTEEN

He was fast, to give him his due. Also strong and ruthless and used to this sort of thing.

'Where is it?' he said.

'What?'

'A chunk of metal with a hole in it.'

'I don't know what you're talking about.'

He swung his arm and hit me with something hard and knobbly. When it followed through to the tiny light I could see what it was. One of my own crutches. Delightful.

I tried to disentangle my legs and roll over and stand up. He shone the light on me to watch. When I was half up he knocked me down again.

'Where is it?'

'I told you . . .'

'We both know, chum, that you have this chunk of metal. I want it. I have a customer for it. And you're going to hand it over like a good little warned-off crook.'

'Go scratch yourself.'

I rolled fast and almost missed the next swipe. It landed on the plaster. Some flakes came off. Less work for Tuesday.

'You haven't a hope,' he said. 'Face facts.'

The facts were that if I yelled for help only the horses would hear.

Pity.

I considered giving him the chunk of metal with the hole in it. Correction, half a hole. He didn't know it was only half a hole. I wondered whether I should tell him. Perhaps he'd be only half as savage.

'Who wants it?' I said.

'Be your age.' He swung the crutch.

Contact.

I cursed.

'Save yourself, chum. Don't be stupid.'

'What is this chunk of metal?'

'Just hand it over.'

'I don't know what you're looking for.'

'Chunk of metal with a hole in it.'

'What chunk of metal?'

'Look, chum, what does it matter what chunk of metal? The one you've got.'

'I haven't.'

'Stop playing games.' He swung the crutch. I grunted. 'Hand it over.'

'I haven't . . . got . . . any chunk of metal.'

'Look chum, my instructions are as clear as glass. You've got some lump of metal and I've come to fetch it. Understand? Simple. So save yourself, you stupid crumb.'

'What is he paying for it?'

'You still offering more?'

'Worth a try.'

'So you said before. But nothing doing.'

'Pity.'

'Where's the chunk? . . .'

I didn't answer, heard the crutch coming, rolled at the right instant, and heard it thud on the carpet, roughly where my nose had been.

The little flashlight sought me out. He didn't miss the second time, but it was only my arm, not my face.

'Didn't you ask what it was?' I said.

'None of your bloody business. You just tell me' . . . bash . . . 'where' . . . bash . . . 'it is.'

I'd had about enough. Too much, in fact. And I'd found out all I was likely to, except how far he was prepared to go, which was information I could do without.

I'd been trying to roll towards the door. Finally made it near enough. Stretched backwards over my head and felt my fingers curl round the bottom of the other crutch still propped against the wall.

The rubber knob came into my hand, and with one

scything movement I swept the business end round viciously at knee level.

It caught him square and unexpected on the back of the legs just as he himself was in mid swing, and he overbalanced and crashed down half on top of me. I reached out and caught something, part of his coat, and gripped and pulled, and tried to swing my plaster leg over his body to hold him down.

He wasn't having any. We scrambled around on the floor, him trying to get up and me trying to stop him, both of us scratching and punching and gouging in a thoroughly unsportsmanlike manner. The flashlight had fallen away across the far side of the room and shone only on the wall. Not enough light to be much good. Too much for total evasion of his efficient fists.

The bedside table fell over with a crash and the lamp smashed. Oakley somehow reached into the ruins and picked up a piece of glass, and I just saw the light shimmer on it as he slashed it towards my eyes. I dodged it by a millimetre in the last half-second.

'You bugger,' I said bitterly.

We were both gasping for breath. I loosed the grip I had on his coat in order to have both hands free to deal with the glass, and as soon as he felt me leave go he was heaving himself back on to his feet.

'Now,' he said, panting heavily, 'where bloody is it?'

I didn't answer. He'd got hold of a crutch again. Back to square one. On the thigh, that time.

I was lying on the other crutch. The elbow supports were digging into my back. I twisted my arm underneath me and pulled out the crutch, hand-swung it at him just as he was having a second go. The crutches met and crashed together in the air. I held on to mine for dear life and rolled towards the bed.

'Give . . . up . . .' he said.

'Get . . . stuffed.'

I made it to the bed and lay in the angle between it and the floor. He couldn't get a good swing at me there. I turned the crutch round, and held it by the elbow and hand grips with both of my own. To hit me where I was lying he had to come nearer.

He came. His dark shadow was above me, exaggerated by the dim torchlight. He leant over, swinging. I shoved the stick end of the crutch hard upwards. It went into him solidly and he screeched sharply. The crutch he had been swinging dropped harmlessly on top of me as he reeled away, clutching at his groin.

'I'll . . . kill you . . . for that . . .' His voice was high with pain. He groaned, hugging himself.

'Serves . . . you . . . right,' I said breathlessly.

I pulled myself across the floor, dragging the plaster, aiming for the telephone which had crashed on to the floor with the little table. Found the receiver. Pulled the cord. The telephone bumped over the carpet into my hand.

Put my finger on the button. Small ting. Dialling tone. Found the numbers. Three . . . nine . . . one . . .

'Yeah?' Tony's voice, thick with sleep.

Dead careless, I was. Didn't hear a thing. The crutch swung wickedly down on the back of my head and I fell over the telephone and never told him to gallop to the rescue.

I woke where Oakley had left me, still lying on the floor over the telephone, the receiver half in and half out of my hand.

It was daylight, just. Grey and raw and raining. I was stiff. Cold. Had a headache.

Remembered bit by bit what had happened. Set about scraping myself off the carpet.

First stop, back on to the bed, accompanied by bedclothes. Lay there feeling terrible and looking at the mess he had made of my room.

After he'd knocked me out, he had nothing to be quiet about. Everything had been pulled out of the closet and drawers and flung on the floor. Everything smashable was smashed. The sleeves of some of my suits were ripped and lying in tatters. Rosalind's picture had been torn into four pieces and the silver frame twisted and snapped. It had been revenge more than a search. A bad loser, David Oakley.

What I could see of the sitting-room through the

open door seemed to have received the same treatment.

I lay and ached in most places you could think of.

Didn't look to see if Oakley had found the piece of manifold because I knew he wouldn't have. Thought about him coming, and about what he'd said.

Thought about Cranfield.

Thought about Gowery.

Once I got the plaster off and could move about again, it shouldn't take me too long now to dig out the enemy. A bit of leg work. Needed two legs.

Oakley would shortly be reporting no success from the night's work. I wondered if he would be sent to try again. Didn't like that idea particularly.

I shifted on the bed, trying to get comfortable. I'd been concussed twice in five days once before, and got over it. I'd been kicked along the ground by a large field of hurdlers, which had been a lot worse than the crutches. I'd broken enough bones to stock a cemetery and this time they were all whole. But all the same I felt sicker than after racing falls, and in the end realized my unease was revulsion against being hurt by another man. Horses, hard ground, even express trains, were impersonal. Oakley had been a different type of invasion. The amount you were mentally affected by a pain always depended on how you got it.

I felt terrible. Had no energy at all to get up and tidy the mess.

Shut my eyes to blot it out. Blotted myself out, too. Went to sleep.

A voice said above my head, 'Won't you ever learn to keep your door shut?'

I smiled feebly. 'Not if you're coming through it.'

'Finding you flat out is becoming a habit.'

'Try to break it.'

I opened my eyes. Broad daylight. Still raining.

Roberta was standing a foot from the bed wearing a blinding yellow raincoat covered in trickling drops. The copper hair was tied up in a pony tail and she was looking around her with disgust.

'Do you realize it's half past ten?' she said.

'No.'

'Do you always drop your clothes all over the place when you go to bed?'

'Only on Wednesdays.'

'Coffee?' she said abruptly, looking down at me.

'Yes, please.'

She picked her way through the mess to the door, and then across the sitting-room until she was out of sight. I rubbed my hand over my chin. Bristly. And there was a tender lump on the back of my skull and a sore patch all down one side of my jaw, where I hadn't dodged fast enough. Bruises in other places set up a morning chorus. I didn't listen.

She came back minus the raincoat and carrying two steaming mugs which she put carefully on the floor.

241

Then she picked up the bedside table and transferred the mugs to its top.

The drawer had fallen out of the table, and the envelope had fallen out of the drawer. But Oakley hadn't apparently looked into it: hadn't known it was there to find.

Roberta picked up the scattered crutches and brought them over to the bed.

'Thanks,' I said.

'You take it very calmly.'

'I've seen it before,' I pointed out.

'And you just went to sleep?'

'Opted out,' I agreed.

She looked more closely at my face and rolled my head over on the pillow. I winced. She took her hand away.

'Did you get the same treatment as the flat?'

'More or less.'

'What for?'

'For being stubborn.'

'Do you mean,' she said incredulously, 'that you could have avoided all this ... and didn't?'

'If there's a good reason for backing down, you back down. If there isn't, you don't.'

'And all this ... isn't a good enough reason?'

'No.'

'You're crazy,' she said.

'You're so right,' I sighed, pushed myself up a bit, and reached for the coffee.

'Have you called the police?' she asked.

I shook my head. 'Not their quarrel.'

'Who did it, then?'

I smiled at her. 'Your father and I have got our licences back.'

'*What?*'

'It'll be official some time today.'

'Does Father know? How did it happen? Did you do it?'

'No, he doesn't know yet. Ring him up. Tell him to get on to all the owners. It'll be confirmed in the papers soon, either today's evening editions, or tomorrow's dailies.'

She picked the telephone off the floor and sat on the edge of my bed, and telephoned to her father with real joy and sparkling eyes. He wouldn't believe it at first.

'Kelly says it's true,' she said.

He argued again, and she handed the telephone to me.

'You tell him.'

Cranfield said, 'Who told you?'

'Lord Ferth.'

'Did he say why?'

'No,' I lied. 'Just that the sentences had been

reviewed . . . and reversed. We're back, as from today. The official notice will be in next week's Calendar.'

'No explanation at all?' he insisted.

'They don't have to give one,' I pointed out.

'All the same . . .'

'Who cares why?' I said. 'The fact that we're back . . . that's all that matters.'

'Did you find out who framed us?'

'No.'

'Will you go on trying?'

'I might do,' I said. 'We'll see.'

He had lost interest in that. He bounded into a stream of plans for the horses, once they were back. 'And it will give me great pleasure to tell Henry Kessel . . .'

'I'd like to see his face,' I agreed. But Pat Nikita would never part with Squelch, nor with Kessel, now. If Cranfield thought Kessel would come crawling apologetically back, he didn't know his man. 'Concentrate on getting Breadwinner back,' I suggested. 'I'll be fit to ride in the Gold Cup.'

'Old Strepson promised Breadwinner would come back at once . . . and Pound Postage of his . . . that's entered in the National, don't forget.'

'I haven't,' I assured him, 'forgotten.'

He ran down eventually and disconnected, and I could imagine him sitting at the other end still wondering whether to trust me.

Roberta stood up with a spring, as if the news had filled her with energy.

'Shall I tidy up for you?'

'I'd love some help.'

She bent down and picked up Rosalind's torn picture.

'They didn't have to do that,' she said in disgust.

'I'll get the bits stuck together and re-photographed.'

'You'd hate to lose her . . .'

I didn't answer at once. She looked at me curiously, her eyes dark with some unreadable expression.

'I lost her,' I said slowly. 'Rosalind . . . Roberta . . . you are so unalike.'

She turned away abruptly and put the pieces on the chest of drawers where they had always stood.

'Who wants to be a carbon copy?' she said, and her voice was high and cracking. 'Get dressed . . . while I start on the sitting-room.' She disappeared fast and shut the door behind her.

I lay there looking at it.

Roberta Cranfield. I'd never liked her.

Roberta Cranfield. I couldn't bear it . . . I was beginning to love her.

She stayed most of the day, helping me clear up the mess.

Oakley had left little to chance: the bathroom and

kitchen both looked as if they'd been gutted by a whirl-wind. He'd searched everywhere a good enquiry agent could think of, including in the lavatory cistern and the refrigerator; and everywhere he'd searched he'd left his trail of damage.

After midday, which was punctuated by some scram-bled eggs, the telephone started ringing. Was it true, asked the *Daily Witness* in the shape of Daddy Leeman, that Cranfield and I? . . . 'Check with the Jockey Club,' I said.

The other papers had checked first. 'May we have your comments?' they asked.

'Thrilled to bits,' I said gravely. 'You can quote me.'

A lot of real chums rang to congratulate, and a lot of pseudo chums rang to say they'd never believed me guilty anyway.

For most of the afternoon I lay flat on the sitting-room floor with my head on a cushion talking down the telephone while Roberta stepped around and over me nonchalantly, putting everything back into place.

Finally she dusted her hands off on the seat of her black pants, and said she thought that that would do. The flat looked almost as good as ever. I agreed grate-fully that it would do very well.

'Would you consider coming down to my level?' I asked.

She said calmly, 'Are you speaking literally, meta-phorically, intellectually, financially, or socially?'

'I was suggesting you might sit on the floor.'

'In that case,' she said collectedly, 'yes.' And she sank gracefully into a cross-legged sprawl.

I couldn't help grinning. She grinned companionably back.

'I was scared stiff of you when I came here last week,' she said.

'You were *what*?'

'You always seemed so aloof. Unapproachable.'

'Are we talking about me . . . or you?'

'You, of course,' she said in surprise. 'You always made me nervous. I always get sort of . . . strung up . . . when I'm nervous. Put on a bit of an act, to hide it, I suppose.'

'I see,' I said slowly.

'You're still a pretty good cactus, if you want to know . . . but . . . well, you see people differently when they've been bleeding all over your best dress and looking pretty vulnerable . . .'

I began to say that in that case I would be prepared to bleed on her any time she liked, but the telephone interrupted me at halfway. And it was old Strepson, settling down for a long cosy chat about Breadwinner and Pound Postage.

Roberta wrinkled her nose and got to her feet.

'Don't go,' I said, with my hand over the mouthpiece.

'Must. I'm late already.'

'Wait.' I said. But she shook her head, fetched the

247

yellow raincoat from the bath, where she'd put it, and edged herself into it.

''Bye,' she said.

'Wait . . .'

She waved briefly and let herself out of the door. I struggled up on to my feet, and said, 'Sir . . . could you hold on a minute . . .' into the telephone, and hopped without the crutches over to the window. She looked up when I opened it. She was standing in the yard, tying on a headscarf. The rain had eased to drizzle.

'Will you come tomorrow?' I shouted down.

'Can't tomorrow. Got to go to London.'

'Saturday?'

'Do you want me to?'

'Yes.'

'I'll try, then.'

'Please come.'

'Oh . . .' She suddenly smiled in a way I'd never seen before. 'All right.'

Careless I might be about locking my front door, but in truth I left little about worth stealing. Five hundred pounds would never have been lying around on my chest of drawers for enquiry agents to photograph.

When I'd converted the flat from an old hay loft I'd built in more than mod cons. Behind the cabinet in the kitchen which housed things like fly killer and soap powder, and tucked into a crafty piece of brickwork, lay a maximum security safe. It was operated not by keys or combinations, but by electronics. The manufacturers had handed over the safe itself and also the tiny ultrasonic transmitter which sent out the special series of radio waves which alone would release the lock mechanism, and I'd installed them myself: the safe in the wall and the transmitter in a false bottom to the cabinet. Even if anyone found the transmitter, they had still to find the safe and to know the sequence of frequencies which unlocked it.

A right touch of the Open Sesame. I'd always liked gadgets.

Inside the safe there were, besides money and some racing trophies, several pieces of antique silver, three paintings by Houthuesen, two Chelsea figures, a Meissen cup and saucer, a Louis XIV snuff box, and four uncut diamonds totalling twenty-eight carats. My retirement pension, all wrapped in green baize and appreciating nicely. Retirement for a steeplechase jockey could lurk in the very next fall: and the ripe age of forty, if one lasted that long, was about the limit.

There was also a valueless lump of cast iron, with a semi-circular dent in it. To these various treasures I added the envelope which Ferth had given me, because it wouldn't help if I lost that either.

Bolting my front door meant a hazardous trip down the stairs, and another in the morning to open it. I decided it could stay unlocked as usual. Wedged a chair under the door into my sitting-room instead.

During the evening I telephoned to Newtonnards in his pink washed house in Mill Hill.

'Hallo,' he said. 'You've got your licence back then. Talk of the meeting it was at Wincanton today, soon as the Press Association chaps heard about it.'

'Yes, it's great news.'

'What made their lordships change their minds?'

'I've no idea ... Look, I wondered if you'd seen that man again yet, the one who backed Cherry Pie with you.'

'Funny thing,' he said, 'but I saw him today. Just after I'd heard you were back in favour, though, so I didn't think you'd be interested any more.'

'Did you by any chance find out who he is?'

'I did, as a matter of fact. More to satisfy my own curiosity, really. He's the Honourable Peter Foxcroft. Mean anything to you?'

'He's a brother of Lord Middleburg.'

'Yeah. So I'm told.'

I laughed inwardly. Nothing sinister about Cranfield refusing to name his mysterious pal. Just another bit of ladder climbing. He might be one rung up being in a position to use the Hon. P. Foxcroft as a runner: but he would certainly be five rungs down involving him in a messy Enquiry.

'There's one other thing...' I hesitated. 'Would you ... could you ... do me a considerable favour?'

'Depends what it is.' He sounded cautious but not truculent. A smooth, experienced character.

'I can't offer much in return.'

He chuckled. 'Warning me not to expect tip offs when you're on a hot number?'

'Something like that,' I admitted.

'OK then. You want something for strictly nothing. Just as well to know where we are. So shoot.'

'Can you remember who you told about Cranfield backing Cherry Pie?'

'Before the Enquiry, you mean?'

'Yes. Those bookmaker colleagues you mentioned.'

'Well...' he sounded doubtful.

'If you can,' I said, 'could you ask *them* who *they* told?'

'Phew.' He half breathed, half whistled down the receiver. 'That's some favour.'

'I'm sorry. Just forget it.'

'Hang on, hang on. I didn't say I wouldn't do it. It's a bit of a tall order, though, expecting them to remember.'

'I know. Very long shot. But I still want to know who told the Stewards about the bet with you.'

'You've got your licence back. Why don't you let it rest?'

'Would you?'

251

He sighed. 'I don't know. All right then, I'll see what I can do. No promises, mind. Oh, and by the way, it can be just as useful to know when one of your mounts is *not* fit or likely to win. If you take my meaning.'

'I take it,' I said smiling. 'It's a deal.'

I put down the receiver reflecting that only a minority of bookmakers were villains, and that most of them were more generous than they got credit for. The whole tribe were reviled for the image of the few. Like students.

CHAPTER FOURTEEN

Oakley didn't come. No one came. I took the chair from under the door knob to let the world in with the morning. Not much of the world accepted the invitation.

Made some coffee. Tony came while I was standing in the kitchen drinking it and put whisky into a mug of it for himself by way of breakfast. He'd been out with one lot of horses at exercise and was waiting to go out with the other, and spent the interval discussing their prospects as if nothing had ever happened. For him the warning off was past history, forgotten. His creed was that of newspapers; today is important, tomorrow more so, but yesterday is nothing.

He finished the coffee and left, clapping me cheerfully on the shoulder and setting up a protest from an Oakley bruise. I spent most of the rest of the day lying flat on my bed, answering the telephone, staring at the ceiling, letting Nature get on with repairing a few ravages, and thinking.

Another quiet night. I had two names in my mind, juggling them. Two to work on. Better than three hundred. But both could be wrong.

Saturday morning the postman brought the letters right upstairs, as he'd been doing since the era of plaster. I thanked him, sorted through them, dropped a crutch, and had the usual awkward fumble picking it up. When I opened one of the letters I dropped both the crutches again in surprise.

Left the crutches on the floor. Leant against the wall and read.

Dear Kelly Hughes,

I have seen in the papers that you have had your licence restored, so perhaps this information will be too late to be of any use to you. I am sending it anyway because the friend who collected it is considerably out of pocket over it, and would be glad if you could reimburse him. I append also his list of expenses.

As you will see he went to a good deal of trouble over this, though to be fair he also told me that he had enjoyed doing it. I hope it is what you wanted.

Sincerely,
Teddy Dewar.
Great Stag Hotel, Birmingham.

Clipped behind the letter were several other sheets of varying sizes. The top one was a schematic presentation of names which looked at first glance like an inverted family tree. There were clumps of three or four names inside two-inch circles. The circles led via arrows to other circles below and sometimes beside them, but the eye was led downwards continually until all the arrows had converged to three circles, and then to two, and finally to one. And the single name in the bottom circle was David Oakley.

Behind the page was an explanatory note.

I knew one contact, the J.L. Jones underlined in the third row of circles. From him I worked in all directions, checking people who knew of David Oakley. Each clump of people heard about him from one of the people in the next clump. Everyone on the page, I guarantee, has heard either directly or indirectly that Oakley is the man to go to if one is in trouble. I posed as a man in trouble, as you suggested, and nearly all that I talked to either mentioned him of their own accord, or agreed when I brought him up as a possibility.

I only hope that one at least of these names has some significance for you, as I'm afraid the expenses were rather high. Most of the investigation was conducted in pubs or hotels, and it was sometimes necessary to get the contact tight before he would divulge.

Faithfully,

B.R.S. Timieson.

The expense list was high enough to make me whistle. I turned back to the circled names, and read them carefully through.

Looking for one of two.

One was there.

Perhaps I should have rejoiced. Perhaps I should have been angry. Instead, I felt sad.

I doubled the expenses and wrote out a cheque with an accompanying note:

'This is really magnificent. Cannot thank you enough. One of the names has great significance, well worth all your perseverance. My eternal thanks.'

I wrote also a grateful letter to Teddy Dewar saying the information couldn't have been better timed, and enclosing the envelope for his friend Timieson.

As I was sticking on the stamp the telephone rang. I hopped over to it and lifted the receiver.

George Newtonnards.

'Spent all last evening on the blower. Astronomical phone bill, I'm going to have.'

'Send me the account,' I said resignedly.

'Better wait to see if I've got results,' he suggested. 'Got a pencil handy?'

'Just a sec.' I fetched a writing pad and ballpoint. 'OK. Go ahead.'

'Right then. First, here are the chaps I told.' He dictated five names. 'The last one, Pelican Jobberson, is the one who holds a fierce grudge against you for that bum steer you gave him, but as it happens he didn't tell the Stewards or anyone else because he went off to Casablanca the next day for a holiday. Well . . . here are the people Harry Ingram told . . .' He read out three names. 'And these are the people Herbie Subbing told . . .' Four names. 'These are the people Dimmie Ovens told . . .' Five names. 'And Clobber Mackintosh, he really spread it around . . .' Eight names. 'That's all they can remember. They wouldn't swear there was no one else. And of course, all those people they've mentioned could have passed the info on to someone else . . . I mean, things like this spread out in ripples.'

'Thanks anyway,' I said sincerely. 'Thank you very much indeed for taking so much trouble.'

'Has it been any help?'

'Oh yes, I think so. I'll let you know, some time.'

'And don't forget. The obvious non-winner . . . give me the wink.'

'I'll do that,' I promised. 'If you'll risk it, after Pelican Jobberson's experience.'

'He's got no sense,' he said. 'But I have.'

257

He rang off, and I studied his list of names. Several were familiar and belonged to well-known racing people: the bookmakers' clients, I supposed. None of the names were the same as those on Timieson's list of Oakley contacts, but there was something...

For ten minutes I stood looking at the paper wondering what was hovering around the edge of consciousness, and finally, with a thud, the association clicked.

One of the men Herbie Subbing had told was the brother-in-law of the person I had found among the Oakley contacts.

I thought for a while, and then opened the newspaper and studied the programme for the day's racing, which was at Reading. Then I telephoned to Lord Ferth at his London house, and reached him via a plummy-voiced manservant.

'Well, Kelly?...' There was something left of Wednesday's relationship. Not all, but something.

'Sir,' I said, 'are you going to Reading races?'

'Yes, I am.'

'I haven't yet had any official notice of my licence being restored... Will it be all right for me to turn up there? I would particularly like to talk to you.'

'I'll make sure you have no difficulty, if it's important.' There was a faint question in his tone, which I answered.

'I know,' I said, 'who engineered things.'

'Ah... Yes. Then come. Unless the journey would

be too uncomfortable for you? I could, you know, come on to Corrie after the races. I have no engagements tonight.'

'You're very thoughtful. But I think our engineer will be at the races too . . . or at least there's a very good chance of it.'

'As you like,' he agreed. 'I'll look out for you.'

Tony had two runners at the meeting and I could ask him to take me. But there was also Roberta . . . she was coming over, probably, and she too might take me. I smiled wryly to myself. She might take me anywhere. Roberta Cranfield. Of all people.

As if by telepathy the telephone rang, and it was Roberta herself on the other end. She sounded breathless and worried.

'Kelly! I can't come just yet. In fact . . .' The words came in a rush. 'Can you come over here?'

'What's the matter?'

'Well . . . I don't really know if *anything's* the matter . . . seriously, that is. But Grace Roxford has turned up here.'

'Dear Grace?'

'Yes . . . look, Kelly, she's just sitting in her car outside the house sort of glaring at it. Honestly, she looks a bit mad. We don't know quite what to do. Mother wants to call the police, but, I mean, one *can't* . . .

Supposing the poor woman has come to apologize or something, and is just screwing herself up?'

'She's still sitting in the car?'

'Yes. I can see her from here. Can you come? I mean ... Mother's useless and you know how dear Grace feels about *me* ... She looks pretty odd, Kelly.' Definite alarm in her voice.

'Where's your father?'

'Out on the gallops with Breadwinner. He won't be back for about an hour.'

'All right then. I'll get Tony or someone to drive me over. As soon as I can.'

'That's great,' she said with relief. 'I'll try and stall her till you come.'

It would take half an hour to get there. More, probably. By then dear Grace might not still be sitting in her car ...

I dialled three nine one.

'Tony,' I said urgently. 'Can you drop everything instantly and drive me to Cranfield's? Grace Roxford has turned up there and I don't like the sound of it.'

'I've got to go to Reading,' he protested.

'You can go on from Cranfield's when we've sorted Grace out ... and anyway, I want to go to Reading too, to talk to Lord Ferth. So be a pal, Tony. Please.'

'Oh all right. If you want it that much. Give me five minutes.'

He took ten. I spent some of them telephoning to

Jack Roxford. He was surprised I should be calling him.

'Look, Jack,' I said, 'I'm sorry to be upsetting you like this, but have you any idea where your wife has gone?'

'Grace?' More surprise, but also anxiety. 'Down to the village, she said.'

The village in question was roughly forty miles from Cranfield's house.

'She must have gone some time ago,' I said.

'I suppose so . . . what's all this about?' The worry was sharp in his voice.

'Roberta Cranfield has just telephoned to say that your wife is outside their house, just sitting in her car.'

'Oh God,' he said. 'She can't be.'

'I'm afraid she is.'

'Oh *no* . . .' he wailed. 'She seemed better this morning . . . quite her old self . . . it seemed safe to let her go and do the shopping . . . she's been so upset, you see . . . and then you and Dexter got your licences back . . . it's affected her . . . it's all been so awful for her.'

'I'm just going over there to see if I can help,' I said.

'But . . . can you come down and collect her?'

'Oh *yes*,' he said. 'I'll start at once. Oh poor dear Grace . . . Take care of her, till I come.'

'Yes,' I said reassuringly, and disconnected.

I made it without mishap down the stairs and found

DICK FRANCIS

Tony had commandeered Poppy's estate car for the journey. The back seat lay flat so that I could lie instead of sit, and there were even cushions for my shoulders and head.

'Poppy's idea,' Tony said briefly, helping me climb in through the rear door. 'Great girl.'

'She sure is,' I said gratefully, hauling in the crutches behind me. 'Lose no time, now, friend.'

'You sound worried.' He shut the doors, switched on and drove away with minimum waste of time.

'I am, rather. Grace Roxford is unbalanced.'

'But surely not dangerous?'

'I hope not.'

I must have sounded doubtful because Tony's foot went heavily down on the accelerator. 'Hold on to something,' he said. We rocked round corners. I couldn't find any good anchorage: had to wedge my useful foot against the rear door and push myself off the swaying walls with my hands.

'OK?' he shouted.

'Uh . . . yes,' I said breathlessly.

'Good bit of road just coming up.' We left all the other traffic at a standstill. 'Tell me if you see any cops.'

We saw no cops. Tony covered the eighteen miles through Berkshire in twenty-three minutes. We jerked to a stop outside Cranfield's house, and the first thing I saw was that there was no one in the small grey Volkswagen standing near the front door.

Tony opened the back of the car with a crash and unceremoniously tugged me out.

'She's probably sitting down cosily having a quiet cup of tea,' he said.

She wasn't.

Tony rang the front-door bell and after a lengthy interval Mrs Cranfield herself opened it.

Not her usual swift wide-opening fling. She looked at us through a nervous six inches.

'Hughes. What are you doing here? Go away.'

'Roberta asked me to come. To see Grace Roxford.'

'Mrs Roxford is no longer here.' Mrs Cranfield's voice was as strung up as her behaviour.

'Isn't that her car?' I pointed to the Volkswagen.

'No,' she said sharply.

'Whose is it, then?'

'The gardener's. Now Hughes, go away at once. Go away.'

'Very well,' I said, shrugging. And she instantly shut the door.

'Help me back into the car,' I said to Tony.

'Surely you're not just *going*?'

'Don't argue,' I said. 'Get me into the car, drive away out through the gates, then go round and come back in through the stable entrance.'

'That's better.' He shuffled me in, threw in the crutches, slammed the door and hustled round to the driving seat.

'Don't rush so,' I said. 'Scratch your head a bit. Look disgusted.'

'You think she's watching?' He didn't start the car: looked at me over his shoulder.

'I think Mrs Cranfield would never this side of doomsday allow her gardener to park outside her front door. Mrs Cranfield was doing her best to ask for help.'

'Which means,' he added slowly, 'that Grace Roxford is very dangerous indeed.'

I nodded with a dry mouth. 'Drive away, now.'

He went slowly. Rolled round into the back drive, accelerated along that, and stopped with a jerk beside the stables. Yet again he helped me out.

'There's a telephone in the small office in the yard,' I said. 'Next to the tackroom. Look up in the classified directory and find a local doctor. Tell him to come smartish. Then wait here until Dexter Cranfield comes back with the horses, and stop him going into the house.'

'Kelly, couldn't you be exaggerating? . . .

I'll never be able to stop Cranfield.'

'Tell him no one ever believes anything tragic will happen until it has.'

He looked at me for two seconds, then wheeled away into the yard.

I peg-legged up the back drive and tried the back door. Open. It would be. For Cranfield to walk easily through it. And to what?

I went silently along into the main hall, and listened. There was no sound in the house.

Tried the library first, juggling the crutches to get a good grip on the door handle, sweating lest I should drop one with a crash. Turned the handle, pressed the door quietly inwards.

The library was uninhabited. A large clock on the mantel ticked loudly. Out of time with my heart.

I left the door open. Went slowly, silently towards the small sitting-room beside the front door. Again the meticulously careful drill with the handle. If they'd seen me come, they would most probably be in this room.

The door swung inwards. Well oiled. No creaks. I saw the worn chintz covers on the armchairs, the elderly rugs, the debris of living, scattered newspapers, a pair of spectacles on some letters, a headscarf and a flower basket. No people.

On the other side of the hall there were the double doors into the large formal drawing-room, and at the back, beyond the staircase, the doors to the dining-room and to Dexter Cranfield's own study, where he kept his racing books and did all his paper work.

I swung across to the study, and opened the door. It was quiet in there. Dust slowly gravitated. Nothing else moved.

That left only the two large rooms downstairs, and the whole of upstairs. I looked at the long broad flight uneasily. Wished it were an escalator.

The dining-room was empty. I shifted back through the hall to the double doors of the drawing-room. Went through the crutch routine with more difficulty, because if I were going in there I would need both doors open, and to open both doors took both hands. I managed it in the end by hooking both crutches over my left arm like walking sticks, and standing on one leg.

The doors parted and I pushed them wide. The quarter-acre of drawing-room contained chairs of gold brocade upholstery, a pale cream Chinese carpet and long soft blue curtains. A delicate, elegant, class-conscious room designed for Cranfield's glossiest aspirations.

Everything in there was motionless. A tableau.

I hitched the crutches into place, and walked forwards. Stopped after a very few paces. Stopped because I had to.

Mrs Cranfield was there. And Roberta. And Grace Roxford. Mrs Cranfield was standing by the fireplace, hanging on to the shoulder-high mantel as if needing support. Roberta sat upright in an armless wooden chair set out of its usual place in a large clear area of carpet. Behind her and slightly to one side, and with one hand firmly grasping Roberta's shoulder, stood Grace Roxford.

Grace Roxford held the sort of knife used by fishmongers. Nearly a foot long, razor sharp, with a point like a needle. She was resting the lethal end of it against Roberta's neck.

'Kelly!' Roberta said. Her voice was high and a trifle wavery, but the relief in it was overwhelming. I feared it might be misplaced.

Grace Roxford had a bright colour over her taut cheekbones and a piercing glitter in her eyes. Her body was rigid with tension. The hand holding the knife trembled in uneven spasms. She was as unstable as wet gelignite; but she still knew what she was doing.

'You went away, Kelly Hughes,' she said. 'You went away.'

'Yes, Grace,' I agreed. 'But I came back to talk to Roberta.'

'You come another step,' she said, 'and I'll cut her throat.'

Mrs Cranfield drew a breath like a sob, but Roberta's expression didn't change. Grace had made that threat already. Several times, probably. Especially when Tony and I had arrived at the front door.

She was desperately determined. Neither I nor the Cranfields had room to doubt that she wouldn't do as she said. And I was twenty feet away from her and a cripple besides.

'What do you want, Grace?' I said, as calmly as possible.

'Want? Want?' Her eyes flickered. She seemed to be trying to remember what she wanted. Then her rage sharpened on me like twin darts, and her purpose came flooding back.

'Dexter Cranfield ... bloody snob ... I'll see he doesn't get those horses ... I'm going to kill him, see, kill him ... then he can't get them, can he? No ... he can't.'

Again there was no surprise either in Roberta or her mother. Grace had told them already what she'd come for.

'Grace, killing Mr Cranfield won't help your husband.'

'Yes. Yes. Yes. Yes.' She nodded sharply between each yes, and the knife jumped against Roberta's neck. Roberta shut her eyes for a while and swayed on the chair.

I said, 'How do you hope to kill him, Grace?'

She laughed. It got out of control at halfway and ended in a maniacal high-pitched giggle. 'He'll come here, won't he? He'll come here and stand beside me, because he'll do just what I say, won't he? Won't he?'

I looked at the steel blade beside Roberta's pearly skin and knew that he would indeed do as she said. As I would.

'And then, see,' she said, 'I'll just stick the knife into *him*, not into her. See? See?'

'I see,' I said.

She nodded extravagantly and her hand shook.

'And then what?' I asked.

'Then what?' She looked puzzled. She hadn't got any further than killing Cranfield. Beyond that lay only darkness and confusion. Her vision didn't extend to consequences.

'Edwin Byler could send his horses away to someone else,' I said.

'No. No. Only Dexter Cranfield. Only him. Telling him he ought to have a more snobbish trainer. Taking him away from us. I'm going to kill him. Then he can't have those horses.' The words tumbled out in a vehement monotone, all the more frightening for being clearly automatic. These were thoughts she'd had in her head for a very long time.

'It would have been all right, of course,' I said slowly. 'If Mr Cranfield hadn't got his licence back.'

'Yes!' It was a bitterly angry shriek.

'I got it back for him,' I said.

'They just gave it back. They just gave it back. They shouldn't have done that. They shouldn't.'

'They didn't just give it back,' I said. 'They gave it back because I made them.'

'You couldn't . . .'

'I told everyone I was going to. And I did.'

'No. No. No.'

'Yes,' I said flatly.

Her expression slowly changed, and highly frightening it was too. I waited while it sank into her disorganized brain that if Byler sent his horses to Cranfield after all it was me alone she had to thank for it. I watched the intention to kill widen to embrace me too.

The semi-cautious restraint in her manner towards me was transforming itself into a vicious glare of hate.

I swallowed. I said again, 'If I hadn't made the Stewards give Mr Cranfield's licence back, he would still be warned off.'

Roberta said in horror, 'No, Kelly. Don't. Don't do it.'

'Shut up,' I said. 'Me or your father ... which has more chance? And run, when you can.'

Grace wasn't listening. Grace was grasping the essentials and deciding on a course of action.

There was a lot of white showing round her eyes.

'I'll kill you,' she said. 'I'll kill you.'

I stood still. I waited. The seconds stretched like centuries.

'Come here,' she said. 'Come here, or I'll cut her throat.'

CHAPTER FIFTEEN

I took myself crutch by crutch towards her. When I was halfway there Mrs Cranfield gave a moaning sigh and fainted, falling awkwardly on the rug and scattering the brass fire irons with a nerve-shattering crash.

Grace jumped. The knife snicked into Roberta's skin and she cried out. I stood half unbalanced, freezing into immobility, trying to will Grace not to disintegrate into panic, not to go over the edge, not to lose the last tiny grip she had on her reason. She wasn't far off stabbing everything in sight.

'Sit still,' I said to Roberta with dreadful urgency and she gave me a terrified look and did her best not to move. She was trembling violently. I had never thought I could pray. I prayed.

Grace was moving her head in sharp birdlike jerks. The knife was still against Roberta's neck. Grace's other hand still grasped Roberta's shoulder. A thread of blood trickled down Roberta's skin and was blotted up in a scarlet patch by her white jersey.

No one went to help Roberta's mother. I didn't even dare to look at her, because it meant turning my eyes away from Grace.

'Come here,' Grace said. 'Come here.'

Her voice was husky, little more than a loud whisper. And although she was watching me come with unswerving murder in her eyes, I was inexpressibly thankful that she could still speak at all, still think, still hold a purpose.

During the last few steps I wondered how I was going to dodge, since I couldn't jump, couldn't bend my knees, and hadn't even my hands free. A bit late to start worrying. I took the last step short so that she would have to move to reach me and at the same time eased my elbow out of the right-hand crutch.

She was almost too fast. She struck at me instantly, in a flashing thrust directed at my throat, and although I managed to twist the two inches needed to avoid it, the hissing knife came close enough, through the collar of my coat. I brought my right arm up and across, crashing crutch against her as she prepared to try again.

Out of the corner of my eye I saw Roberta wrench herself out of Grace's clutching grasp, and half stumble, half fall as she got away from the chair.

'Kill you,' Grace said. The words were distorted. The meaning clear. She had no thought of self-defence. No thought at all, as far as I could see. Just one single burning obsessive intention.

I brought up the left-hand crutch like a pole to push her away. She dived round it and tried to plunge her knife through my ribs, and in throwing myself away from that I over-balanced and half fell down, and she was standing over me with her arm raised like a priest at a human sacrifice.

I dropped one crutch altogether. Useless warding off a knife with a bare hand. I tried to shove the other crutch round into her face, but got it tangled up against an armchair.

Grace brought her arm down. I fell right to the floor as soon as I saw her move and the knife followed me harmlessly, all the impetus gone by the time it reached me. Another tear in my coat.

She came down on her knees beside me, her arm going up again.

From nowhere my lost crutch whistled through the air and smashed into the hand which held the knife. Grace hissed like a snake and dropped it, and it fell point down into my plaster. She twisted round to see who had hit her and spread out her hands towards the crutch that Roberta was aiming at her again.

She caught hold of it and tugged. I wriggled round on the floor, stretched until I had my fingers round the handle of the knife, and threw it as hard as I could towards the open door into the hall.

Grace was too much for Roberta. Too much for me. She was appallingly, insanely, strong. I heaved myself up on to my left knee and clasped my arms tight round her chest from behind, trying to pin her arms down to her sides. She shook me around like a sack of feathers, struggling to get to her feet.

She managed it, lifting me with her, plaster and all. She knew where I'd thrown the knife. She started to go that way, dragging me with her still fastened to her back like a leech.

'Get that knife and run to the stables,' I gasped to Roberta. A girl in a million. She simply ran and picked up the knife and went on running, out into the hall and out of the house.

Grace started yelling unintelligibly and began trying to unclamp the fingers I had laced together over her thin breastbone. I hung on for everyone's dear life, and when she couldn't dislodge them she began pinching wherever she could reach with fierce hurting spite.

The hair which she usually wore screwed into a fold up the back of her neck had come undone and was falling into my face. I could see less and less of what was going on. I knew only that she was still headed towards the doorway, still unimaginably violent, and mumbling now in a continuous flow of senseless words interspersed with sudden shrieks.

She reached the doorway and started trying to get free of me by crashing me against the jamb. She had a hard job of it, but she managed it in the end, and when she felt my weight fall off her she turned in a flash, sticking out her hands with rigid fingers towards my neck.

Her face was a dark congested crimson. Her eyes were stretched wide in a stark screaming stare. Her lips were drawn back in a tight line from her teeth.

I had never in all my life seen anything so terrifying. Hadn't imagined a human could look like that, had never visualized homicidal madness.

She would certainly have killed me if it hadn't been for Tony, because her strength made a joke of mine. He came tearing into the hall from the kitchen and brought her down with a rugger tackle about the knees, and I fell too, on top of her, because she was trying to tear my throat out in handfuls, and she didn't leave go.

It took all Tony could do, all Archie could do, all three other lads could do to unlatch her from me and hold her down on the floor. They sat on her arms and legs and chest and head, and she threshed about convulsively underneath them.

Roberta had tears streaming down her face and I hadn't any breath left to tell her to cheer up, there was no more danger, no more . . . no more . . . I leant weakly against the wall and thought it would be too damned silly to pass out now. Took three deep breaths instead. Everything steadied again, reluctantly.

Tony said, 'There's a doctor on his way. Don't think he's expecting this, though.'

'He'll know what to do.'

'Mother!' exclaimed Roberta suddenly. 'I'd forgotten about her.' She hurried past me into the drawing-room and I heard her mother's voice rising in a disturbed, disorientated question.

Grace was crying out, but her voice sounded like seagulls and nothing she said made sense. One of the lads said sympathetically. 'Poor thing, oughtn't we to let her get up?' and Tony answered fiercely, 'Only under a tiger net.'

'She doesn't know what's happening,' I said wearily. 'She can't control what she does. So don't for God's sake let go of her.'

Except for Tony's resolute six foot they all sat on her gingerly and twice she nearly had them off. Finally and at long last the front door bell rang, and I hopped across the hall to answer it.

It was the local doctor, looking tentative, wondering no doubt if it were a hoax. But he took one look at Grace and was opening his case while he came across the hall. Into her arm he pushed a hypodermic needle and soon the convulsive threshing slackened, and the high-pitched crying dulled to murmurs and in the end to silence.

The five men slowly stood up and stepped away from her, and she lay there looking shrunk and crumpled, her greying hair falling in streaks away from her flaccidly relaxing face. It seemed incredible that such thin limbs, such a meagre body, could have put out such strength.

We all stood looking down at her with more awe than pity, watching while the last twitches shook her and she sank into unconscious peace.

Half an hour later Grace still lay on the floor in the hall, but with a pillow under her head and a rug keeping her warm.

Dexter Cranfield had come back from watching the horses work and walked unprepared into the aftermath of drama. His wife's semi-hysterical explanations hadn't helped him much.

Roberta told him that Grace had come to kill him because he had his licence back and that she was the cause of his losing it in the first place, and he stamped around in a fury which I gathered was mostly because the source of our troubles was a woman. He basically didn't like women. She should have been locked up years ago, he said. Spiteful, petty minded, scheming, interfering . . . just like a woman, he said. I listened to him gravely and concluded he had suffered from a bossy nanny.

The doctor had done some intensive telephoning, and presently an ambulance arrived with two compassionate-looking men and a good deal of special equipment. The front door stood wide open and the prospect of Grace's imminent departure was a relief to everyone.

Into this active bustling scene drove Jack Roxford.

He scrambled out of his car, took a horrified look at the ambulance, and ploughed in through the front door. When he saw Grace lying there with the ambulance men preparing to lift her on to a stretcher, he went down on his knees beside her.

'Grace dear . . .' He looked at her more closely. She was still unconscious, very pale now, looking wizened and sixty. 'Grace dear!' There was anguish in his voice. 'What's the matter with her?'

The doctor started to break it to him. Cranfield interrupted the gentle words and said brutally. 'She's raving mad. She came here trying to kill me and she could have killed my wife and daughter. It's absolutely disgraceful that she should have been running around free in that state. I'm going to see my solicitors about it.'

Jack Roxford only heard the first part. His eyes went to the cut on Roberta's neck and the blood-stain on her jersey, and he put his hand over his mouth and looked sick.

'Grace,' he said. 'Oh, Grace . . .'

There was no doubt he loved her. He leant over her, stroking the hair away from her forehead, murmuring to her, and when he finally looked up there were tears in his eyes and on his cheeks.

'She'll be all right, won't she?'

The doctor shifted uncomfortably and said one

would have to see, only time would tell, there were marvellous treatments nowadays . . .

The ambulance men loaded her gently on to the stretcher and picked it up.

'Let me go with her,' Jack Roxford said. 'Where are you taking her? Let me go with her.'

One of the ambulance men told him the name of the hospital and advised him not to come.

'Better try this evening, sir. No use you waiting all day, now, is it?' And the doctor added that Grace would be unconscious for some time yet and under heavy sedation after that, and it was true, it would be better if Roxford didn't go with her.

The uniformed men carried Grace out into the sunshine and loaded her into the ambulance, and we all followed them out into the drive. Jack Roxford stood there looking utterly forlorn as they shut the doors, consulted finally with the doctor, and with the minimum of fuss, drove away.

Roberta touched his arm. 'Can't I get you a drink, Mr Roxford?'

He looked at her vaguely, and then his whole face crumpled and he couldn't speak.

'Don't, Mr Roxford,' Roberta said with pity. 'She isn't in any pain, or anything.'

He shook his head. Roberta put her arm across his shoulders and steered him back into the house.

'Now what?' Tony said. 'I've really got to get to

Reading, pal. Those runners of mine have to be declared for the second race.'

I looked at my watch. 'You could spare another quarter of an hour. I think we should take Jack Roxford with us. He's got a runner too, incidentally, though I imagine he doesn't much care about that ... Except that it's one of Edwin Byler's. But he's not fit to drive anywhere himself, and the races would help to keep him from brooding too much about Grace.'

'Yeah. A possible idea,' Tony grinned.

'Go into the house and see if you can persuade him to let you take him.'

'OK.' He went off amiably, and I passed the time swinging around the drive on my crutches and peering into the cars parked there. I'd be needing a new one ... probably choose the same again, though.

I leant against Tony's car and thought about Grace. She'd left on me a fair legacy of bruises from her pinches to add to the crop grown by Oakley. Also my coat would cost a fortune at the invisible menders, and my throat felt like a well-developed case of septic tonsils. I looked gloomily down at my plastered leg. The dangers of detection seemed to be twice as high as steeplechasing. With luck, I thought with a sigh, I could now go back to the usual but less frequent form of battery.

Tony came out of the house with Roberta and Jack Roxford. Jack looked dazed, and let Tony help him into the front of the estate car as if his thoughts were miles away. As indeed they probably were.

I scrunched across the gravel towards Roberta.

'Is your neck all right?' I asked.

'Is yours?'

I investigated her cut more closely. It wasn't deep. Little more than an inch long.

'There won't be much of a scar,' I said.

'No,' she agreed.

Her face was close to mine. Her eyes were amber with dark flecks.

'Stay here,' she said abruptly. 'You don't have to go to the races.'

'I've an appointment with Lord Ferth . . . Best to get this business thoroughly wrapped up.'

'I suppose so.' She looked suddenly very tired. She'd had a wearing Saturday morning.

'If you've nothing better to do,' I suggested, 'would you come over tomorrow . . . and cook me some lunch?'

A small smile tugged at her mouth and wrinkled her eyes.

'I fell hopelessly in love with you,' she said, 'when I was twelve.'

'And then it wore off?'

'Yes.'

'Pity,' I said.

Her smile broadened.

'Who is Bobbie?' I asked.

'Bobbie? Oh . . . he's Lord Iceland's son.'

'He would be.'

She laughed. 'Father wants me to marry him.'

'That figures.'

'But Father is going to be disappointed.'

'Good,' I said.

'Kelly,' yelled Tony. 'Come on, for Hell's sakes, or I'll be late.'

'Goodbye,' she said calmly. 'See you tomorrow.'

Tony drove to Reading races with due care and attention and Jack Roxford sat sunk in gloomy silence from start to finish. When we stopped in the car park he stepped out of the car and walked dazedly away towards the entrance without a word of thanks or explanation.

Tony watched him go and clicked his tongue. 'That woman isn't worth it.'

'She is, to him,' I said.

Tony hurried off to declare his horses, and I went more slowly through the gate looking out for Lord Ferth.

It felt extraordinary being back on a racecourse. Like being let out of prison. The same people who had looked sideways at me at the Jockey's Fund dance now slapped me familiarly on the back and said they were delighted to see me. Oh yeah, I thought ungratefully. Never kick a man once he's up.

Lord Ferth was standing outside the weighing-room in a knot of people from which he detached himself when he saw me coming.

'Come along to the Steward's dining-room,' he said. 'We can find a quiet corner there.'

'Can we postpone it until after the third race?' I asked. 'I want my cousin Tony to be there as well, and he has some runners . . .'

'Of course,' he agreed. 'Later would be best for me too, as it happens. After the third, then.'

I watched the first three races with the hunger of an exile returned. Tony's horse, my sometime mount, finished a fast fourth, which augured well for next time out, and Byler's horse won the third. As I hurried round to see how Jack Roxford would make out in the winner's enclosure I almost crashed into Kessel. He looked me over, took in the plaster and crutches, and said nothing at all. I watched his cold expressionless face with one to match. After ramming home the point that he had no intention of apologizing he turned brusquely on his heel and walked away.

'Get that,' Tony said in my ear. 'You could sue him for defamation.'

'He's not worth the effort.'

From Charlie West, too, I'd had much the same reaction. Defiance, slightly sullen variety. I shrugged resignedly. That was my own fault, and only time would tell.

Tony walked with me to the winner's enclosure. Byler was there, beaming. Jack Roxford still looked lost. We watched Byler suggest a celebration drink, and Jack shake his head vaguely as if he hadn't understood.

'Go and fish Jack out,' I said to Tony. 'Tell him you're still looking after him.'

'If you say so, pal.' He obligingly edged through the crowd, took Jack by the elbow, said a few explanatory words to Byler, and steered Jack out.

I joined them and said neutrally, 'This way,' and led them along towards the Stewards' dining-room. They both went through the door, taking off their hats and hanging them on the pegs inside.

The long tables in the Stewards' dining-room had been cleared from lunch and laid for tea, but there was no one in there except Lord Ferth. He shook hands with Tony and Jack and invited them to sit down around one end of a table.

'Kelly? . . .' he suggested.

'I'll stand,' I said. 'Easier.'

'Well now,' Ferth said, glancing curiously at Tony and Jack, 'you told me, Kelly, that you knew who had framed you and Dexter Cranfield.'

I nodded.

Tony said regretfully, 'Grace Roxford. Jack's wife.'

Jack looked vaguely down at the tablecloth and said nothing at all.

Tony explained to Lord Ferth just what had happened at Cranfield's and he looked more and more upset.

'My dear Roxford,' he said uncomfortably, 'I'm so sorry. So very sorry.' He looked up at me. 'One could never have imagined that she ... that Grace Roxford of all people ... could have framed you.'

'That's right,' I said mildly. 'She didn't.'

CHAPTER SIXTEEN

Both Tony and Jack sat up as if electrified.

Lord Ferth said, 'But you said...' And Tony answered, 'I thought there was no doubt... She tried to kill Kelly... she was going to kill Cranfield too.'

'She tried to kill me this time,' I agreed. 'But not the time before. It wasn't she who fiddled with my car.'

'Then *who*?' Lord Ferth demanded.

'Her husband.'

Jack stood up. He looked a lot less lost.

I poked Tony on the shoulder with my crutch, and he took the hint and stood up too. He was sitting between Jack and the door.

'Sit down, Mr Roxford,' Ferth said authoritatively, and after a pause, slowly, he obeyed.

'That's nonsense,' he said protestingly. 'I didn't touch Kelly's car. No one could have arranged that accident.'

'You couldn't have imagined I would be hit by a train,' I agreed. 'But some sort of smash, yes, definitely.'

'But Grace...' began Tony, still bewildered.

'Grace,' I said prosaically, 'has in most respects displayed exactly opposite qualities to the person who engineered Cranfield's and my suspension. Grace has been wild, accusing, uncontrolled, and emotional. The planning which went into getting us warned off was cool, careful, efficient, and brutal.'

'Mad people are very cunning,' Tony said doubtfully.

'It wasn't Grace,' I said positively. 'It was Jack.'

There was a pause. Then Jack said in a rising wail, 'Why ever did she have to go to Cranfield's this morning? Why ever couldn't she leave things alone?'

'It wouldn't have done any good,' I said, 'I already knew it was you.'

'That's impossible.'

Ferth cleared his throat. 'I think ... er ... you'd better tell us, Kelly, what your grounds are for making this very serious accusation.'

'It began,' I said, 'when Dexter Cranfield persuaded Edwin Byler to take his horses away from Roxford and send them to him. Cranfield did no doubt persuade Byler, as Grace maintained, that he was a more highly regarded trainer socially than Roxford. Social standing means a great deal to Mr Cranfield, and he is apt to expect that it does to everyone else. And in Edwin Byler's case, he was very likely right. But Jack had trained Byler's horses from the day he bought his first, and as Byler's fortune and string grew, so did Jack's prosperity and prestige. To lose Byler was to him a total disaster. A return to obscurity. The end of every-thing. Jack isn't a bad trainer, but he hasn't the person-ality to make the top ranks. Not without an accident . . . a gift from Heaven . . . like Byler. And you don't find two Bylers in your yard in one lifetime. So almost from the start I wondered about Jack; from as soon as Cranfield told me, two days after the Enquiry, that Byler had been going to transfer his horses. Because I felt such a wrench of regret, you see, that I was not going to ride them . . . and I realized that that was nothing compared to what Jack would have felt if he'd lost them.'

'I didn't feel so bad as that,' said Jack dully.

'I had an open mind,' I said, 'because Pat Nikita had much the same motive, only the other way round. He and Cranfield detest each other. He had been trying to coax Kessel away from Cranfield for years, and getting Cranfield warned off was one way of clinching things. Then there were various people with smaller motives, like Charlie West, who might have hoped to ride Squelch for Nikita if I were out of the way. And there was a big possibility that it was someone else altogether, someone I hadn't come across, whose motive I couldn't even suspect.'

'So why must it be Mr Roxford?' Ferth said.

I took the paper Teddy Dewar had sent me out of my pocket and handed it to him, explaining what it meant.

'That shows a direct link between Oakley and the people in the circles. One of those people is Jack Roxford. He did, you see, know of Oakley's existence. He knew Oakley would agree to provide faked evidence.'

'But . . .' Lord Ferth began.

'Yes, I know,' I said. 'Circumstantial. Then there's this list of people from George Newtonnards.' I gave him the list, and pointed. 'These are the people who definitely knew that Cranfield had backed Cherry Pie with Newtonnards. Again this is not conclusive, because other people might have known, who are not on this list. But that man,' I pointed to the name in Herbie Subbings' list of contacts, 'that man is Grace Roxford's brother. Jack's brother-in-law.'

Ferth looked at me levelly. 'You've taken a lot of trouble.'

'It was taken for me,' I said, 'by Teddy Dewar and his friend, and by George Newtonnards.'

'They acted on your suggestions, though.'

'Yes.'

'Anything else?'

'Well.' I said. 'There are those neatly typed sheets of accusations which were sent to Lord Gowery. So untypical, by the way, of Grace. We could compare the typewriter with Jack's . . . Typewriters are about as distinctive as finger prints. I haven't had an opportunity to do that yet.'

289

Jack looked up wildly. The typewriter made sense to him. He hadn't followed the significance of the lists.

Ferth said slowly, 'I obtained from the Stewards' Secretaries the letter which pointed out to them that a disqualified person was living in a racing stable. As far as I remember, the typing is the same as in the original accusations.'

'Very catty, that,' I said. 'More like Grace. Revengeful, and without much point.'

'I never wrote to the Stewards' Secretaries,' Jack said.

'Did Grace?'

He shook his head. I thought perhaps he didn't know. It didn't seem to be of any great importance. I said instead: 'I looked inside the boot of Jack's car this morning, while he was in Mr Cranfield's house. He carries a great big tool kit, including a hand drill.'

'No,' Jack said.

'Yes, indeed. Also you have an old grey Volkswagen, the one Grace drove today. That car was seen by the mechanic from my garage when you went to pick over the remains of my car. I imagine you were hoping to remove any tell-tale drill holes which might have led the insurance company to suspect attempted murder, but Derek was there before you. And you either followed him or asked the garage whether he'd taken anything from the wreckage, because you sent David Oakley to my flat to get it back. Oakley didn't know the significance of what he was looking for. A chunk of metal with a hole in it. That was all he knew. He was there to earn a fee.'

'Did he find it?' Ferth asked.

'No. I still have it. Can one prove that a certain drill made a certain hole?'

Ferth didn't know. Jack didn't speak.

'When you heard, at the dance,' I said, 'that I was trying to find out who had framed Cranfield and me, you thought you would get rid of me, in case I managed it. Because if I managed it, you'd lose far more than Byler's horses ... so while I was talking to Lord Ferth and dancing with Roberta, you were out at the back of the car park rigging up your booby trap. Which,' I added calmly, remembering the blazing hell of the dislocations, 'I find hard to forgive.'

'I'll strangle him,' Tony said forcefully.

'What happens to him,' I shook my head, 'depends on Lord Ferth.'

Ferth regarded me squarely. 'You find him. I deal with him.'

'That was the agreement.'

'To your satisfaction.'

'Yes.'

'And what *is* your satisfaction?'

I didn't know.

Tony moved restlessly, looking at his watch. 'Lord

Ferth, Kelly, look, I'm sorry, but I've got a horse to
saddle for the last race . . . I'll have to go now.'

'Yes, of course,' said Lord Ferth. 'But we'd all be
obliged if you wouldn't talk about what you've learned
in here.'

Tony looked startled. 'Sure. If you say so. Not a
word.' He stood up and went over to the door. 'See
you after,' he said to me. 'You secretive so-and-so.'

As he went out a bunch of Stewards and their wives
came in chattering for their tea. Lord Ferth went over
to them and exerted the flashing eyes, and they all went
into reverse. A waiter who had materialized behind
them was stationed outside the door with instructions
to send all customers along to the members' tea room.

While this was going on Jack looked steadfastly
down at the tablecloth and said not a word. I didn't
feel like chatting to him idly either. He'd cost me too
much.

Lord Ferth came briskly back and sat down.

'Now then, Roxford,' he said in his most businesslike
way, 'we've heard Kelly's accusations. It's your turn
now to speak up in your defence.'

Jack slowly lifted his head. The deep habitual lines
of worry were running with sweat.

'It was someone else.' His voice was dead.

'It certainly wasn't Grace,' I said, 'because Lord
Gowery was quite clear that the person who tried to
blackmail him on the telephone was a man.' So was

the person who had got at Charlie West a man, or so he'd said.

Jack Roxford jerked.

'Yes, Roxford, we know about Lord Gowery,' Ferth said.

'You *can't* . . .'

'You belong to the same club,' I said assertively, as if I knew.

For Jack Roxford, too, the thought of that club was the lever which opened the floodgates. Like Gowery before him he broke into wretched pieces.

'You don't understand . . .'

'Tell us then,' Ferth said. 'And we'll try.'

'Grace . . . we . . . I . . . Grace didn't like . . .' He petered out.

I gave him a shove. 'Grace liked her sex natural and wouldn't stand for what you wanted.'

He gulped. 'Soon after we were married we were having rows all the time, and I hated that. I loved her, really I did. I've always loved her. And I felt . . . all tangled up . . . she didn't understand that when I beat her it was because of love . . . she said she'd leave me and divorce me for cruelty . . . so I asked a girl I'd known . . . a street girl, who didn't mind . . . I mean . . . she let you, if you paid well enough . . . if I could go on seeing her . . . but she said she'd given that up now . . . but there was a club in London . . . and I went there . . . and it was a terrific relief . . . and then I was

293

all right with Grace . . . but of course we didn't . . . well, hardly ever . . . but somehow . . . we could go on being married.'

Lord Ferth looked revolted.

'I couldn't believe it at first,' Jack said more coherently, 'when I saw Lord Gowery there. I saw him in the street, just outside. I thought it was just a coincidence. But then, one night, inside the club, I was sure it was him, and I saw him again in the street another time . . . but I didn't say anything. I mean, how could I? And anyway, I knew how he felt . . . you don't go there unless you must . . . and you can't keep away.'

'How long have you known that Lord Gowery went to the same club?' I asked.

'Oh . . . two or three years. A long time. I don't know exactly.'

'Did he know you were a member?'

'No. He hadn't a clue. I spoke to him once or twice on the racecourse about official things . . . He didn't have any idea.'

'And then,' Ferth said thoughtfully, 'you read that he had been appointed in Colonel Midgley's place to officiate at the Cranfield-Hughes Enquiry, and you saw what you thought was a good chance of getting Cranfield out of racing, and keeping Byler's horses yourself.'

Jack sat huddled in his chair, not denying it.

'And when Lord Gowery declined to be blackmailed,

you couldn't bear to give up the idea, and you set about faking evidence that would achieve your ends.'

A long silence. Then Jack said in a thick disjointed voice. 'Grace minded so much . . . about Cranfield taking our horses. She went on and on about it . . . morning, noon, and night. Couldn't stop. Talk, talk, talk. All the time. Saying she'd like to kill Cranfield . . . and things like that. I mean . . . she's always been a bit nervy . . . a bit strung up . . . but Cranfield was upsetting her . . . I got a bit frightened for her sometimes, she was that violent about him . . . Well, it was really because of that that I tried to get Cranfield warned off . . . I mean, he was better warned off than Grace trying to kill him.'

'Did you truly believe she would?' I asked.

'She was ranting about it all the time . . . I didn't know if she really would . . . but I was so afraid . . . I didn't want her to get into trouble . . . dear dear Grace . . . I wanted to help her . . . and make things right again . . . so I set about it . . . and it wasn't too difficult really, not once I'd set my mind to it.'

Ferth gave me a twisted smile. I gave him a similar one back and reflected that marriage could be a deadly institution. Grace's strung-up state would have been aggravated by the strain of living with a sexually odd man, and Jack would have felt guilty about it and wanted to make it up to her. Neither of them had been rationally inclined, and the whole situation had boiled up claustrophobically inside their agonized private world. Having dear Grace harping on endlessly would have driven many a stronger man to explosive action: but Jack couldn't desert her, because he had to stay with his horses, and he couldn't drive her away because he loved her. The only way he'd seen of silencing his wife had been to ruin Cranfield.

'Why me?' I said, trying to keep out the bitterness. 'Why me too?'

'Eh?' He squinted at me, half focussing. 'You ... well ... I haven't anything against you personally ... But I thought it was the only way to make it a certainty ... Cranfield couldn't have swindled that race without Squelch's jockey being in the know.'

'That race was no swindle,' I said.

'Oh ... I know that. Those stupid Oxford Stewards ... still, they gave me such an opportunity ... when I heard about Lord Gowery being in charge. And then, when I'd fixed up with Charlie West and Oakley ... Grace's brother told me, just told me casually, mind you, that his bookmaker had told him that Cranfield had backed Cherry Pie, and do you know what, I couldn't stop laughing. Just like Grace, I felt ... dead funny, it was, that he really had backed Cherry Pie ...'

'What was that about Charlie West?' Ferth said sharply.

'I paid him ... to say Kelly pulled Squelch back. I

telephoned and asked him . . . if Kelly ever did anything like that . . . and he said once, in a novice 'chase, Kelly had said, "OK. Brakes on, chaps," and I told him to say Kelly had said that in the Lemonfizz Cup because it sounded so convincing, didn't it, saying something Kelly really had said . . .'

Ferth looked at me accusingly. 'You shielded West.'

I shrugged ruefully. Jack paid no attention: didn't hear.

He went on miserably: 'Grace was all right before the dance. She was wonderfully calm again, after Cranfield was warned off. And then Edwin Byler said that we would be keeping his horses for always . . . and we were happy . . . in our way . . . and then we heard . . . that Kelly was at the dance . . . saying he'd been framed . . . and was just on the point of finding out who . . . and Grace saw Cranfield's daughter and just boiled over all over again, nearly as bad as before . . . and I thought . . . if Kelly was dead . . . it would be all right again . . .'

Ferth slowly shook his head. The reasoning which had led Jack Roxford step by step from misfortune to crime defeated him.

'I thought he wouldn't feel anything,' Jack said. 'I thought that you just blacked out suddenly from carbon monoxide. I thought it would be like going to sleep . . . he wouldn't know about it. Just wouldn't wake up.'

'You didn't drill a big enough hole,' I said without

irony. 'Not enough gas came through at once to knock me out.'

'I couldn't find a large enough tube,' he said with macabre sense. 'Had to use a piece I had. It was a bit narrow. That was why.'

'I see,' I said gravely. So close. Not a few inches from the express train. One eighth of an inch extra in the tube's diameter would have done it.

'And you went to look for the pieces of manifold, afterwards?'

'Yes . . . but you know about that. I was furious with Oakley for not finding it . . . he said he tried to make you tell, but you wouldn't . . . and I said it didn't surprise me . . .'

'Why didn't you ask *him* to kill me?' I said matter-of-factly.

'Oh, I did. He said he didn't kill. He said he would dispose of the body if I did it, but he never did the job himself. Not worth it, he said.'

That sounded like the authentic Oakley. Straight from the agent's mouth.

'But you couldn't risk it?' I suggested.

'I didn't have any chance. I mean . . . I didn't like to leave Grace alone much . . . she was so upset . . . and then, you were in hospital . . . and then you went back to your flat . . . and I did try to shift you out into the open somewhere . . .'

'You did write to the Stewards' Secretaries,' Ferth exclaimed. 'After all.'

'Yes . . . but it was too late . . . wasn't it . . . She really meant it . . . poor Grace, poor Grace . . . why did I let her go out . . . But she seemed so much better this morning . . . and now . . . and now . . .' His face screwed up and turned red as he tried not to cry. The thought of Grace as he'd last seen her was too much for him. The tears rolled. He sniffed into a handkerchief.

I wondered how he would have felt if he'd seen Grace as I'd seen her. But probably the uncritical love he had would have survived even that.

'Just sit here quietly a moment, Roxford,' Lord Ferth directed, and he himself stood up and signed for me to walk with him over to the door.

'So what do we do with him?' he said.

'It's gone too far now,' I said reluctantly, 'to be entirely hushed up. And he's if anything more danger-ous than Grace . . . She will live, and he will very likely see everything for ever in terms of her happiness. Anyone who treats her badly in any way could end up as a victim of his scheming. End up ruined . . . or dead. People like nurses . . . or relations . . . or even people like me, who did her no harm at all. Anybody . . .'

Ferth said, 'You seem to understand his mind. I must say that I don't. But what you say makes sense. We cannot just take away his licence and leave it at that . . . It isn't a racing matter any more. But Lord Gowery . . .'

'Lord Gowery will have to take his chance,' I said without satisfaction. 'Very likely you can avoid busting open his reputation ... but it's much more important to stop Jack Roxford doing the same sort of thing again.'

'Yes,' he said. 'It is.' He spread out his hands sideways in a pushing gesture as if wanting to step away from the decision. 'All this is so *distressing.*'

I looked down the room at Jack, a huddled defeated figure with nervous eyes and an anxious forehead. He was picking at the tablecloth with his fingers, folding it into senseless little pleats. He didn't look like a villain. No hardened criminal. Just a tenacious little man with a fixed idea, to make up to dear Grace for being what he was.

Nothing was more useless than sending him to prison, and nothing could do him more harm: yet that, I imagined, was where he would go. Putting his body in a little cage wouldn't straighten the kinks in his mind. The system, for men like him, was screwy.

He stood up slowly and walked unsteadily towards us.

'I suppose,' he said without much emotion, 'that you are going to get the police. I was wondering ... please ... don't tell them about the club ... I won't say Lord Gowery goes there ... I won't tell anybody ever ... I never really wanted to ... it wouldn't have done any good, would it? I mean, it wouldn't have kept those horses in my yard . . . wouldn't have made a scrap of difference . . . So do you think anyone need know about . . . the club?'

'No,' said Ferth with well-disguised relief. 'They need not.'

A faint smile set up a rival set of creases to the lines of anxiety. 'Thank you.' The smile faded away. The lost look deepened. 'How long . . . do you think I'll get?'

Ferth moved uncomfortably. 'No point in worrying about that until you have to.'

'You could probably halve it,' I said.

'How?' He was pathetically hopeful. I flung him the rope.

'By giving evidence at another trial I have in mind, and taking David Oakley down with you.'

PART THREE

MARCH

EPILOGUE

Yesterday I rode Breadwinner in the Cheltenham Gold Cup.

A horse of raw talent with more future than past. A shambling washy chestnut carrying his head low. No one's idea of equine beauty.

Old Strepson watched him slop around the parade ring and said with a sigh, 'He looks half asleep.'

'Hughes will wake him up,' Cranfield said condescendingly.

Cranfield stood in the chill March sunshine making his usual good stab at arrogance. The mean calculating lines round his mouth seemed to have deepened during the past month, and his manner to me was if anything more distant, more master-servant, than ever before. Roberta said she had told him that I had in some way managed to get our licences back, but he saw no reason to believe her and preferred the thought of divine intervention.

Old Strepson said conversationally, 'Kelly says

Breadwinner was a late foal and a late developer, and won't reach his true strength until about this time next year.'

Cranfield gave me a mouth-tightening mind-your-own-business glare, and didn't seem to realize that I'd given him an alibi if the horse didn't win and built him up into one heck of a good trainer if it did. Whatever low opinion Cranfield held of me, I reciprocated it in full.

Farther along the parade ring stood a silent little group of Kessel, Pat Nikita, and their stable jockey, Al Roach. They were engaged in running poor old Squelch, and their interest lay not so fiercely in winning as in finishing at all costs in front of Breadwinner. Kessel himself radiated so much hatred that I thought it was probably giving him a headache. Hating did that. The day I found it out, I gave up hating.

Grace's hatred-headache must have been unbearable . . .

Grace's recovery was still uncertain. Ferth had somehow wangled the best available psychiatrist on to her case, and had also arranged for him to see Jack. Outside the weighing-room when I had arrived, he had jerked his head for me to join him, and told me what the psychiatrist had reported.

'He says Jack is sane according to legal standards, and will have to stand trial. He wouldn't commit himself about Grace's chances. He did say, though, that from all points of view their enforced separation was a godsend. He said he thought their only chance of leading fairly normal lives in the future was to make the separation total and permanent. He said a return to the same circumstances could mean a repeat of the whole cycle.'

I looked at Ferth gloomily. 'What a cold, sad, depressing solution.'

'You never know,' he said optimistically, 'once they get over it, they might both feel ... well ... released.'

I smiled at him. He said abruptly, 'Your outlook is catching, dammit ... How about that dinner?'

'Any time,' I said.

'Tomorrow, then? Eight o'clock. The Caprice, round the corner from the Ritz ... The food's better there than at my club.'

'Fine,' I said.

'And you can tell me how the police are getting on with David Oakley ...'

I'd had the Birmingham police on my telephone and doorstep for much of the past week. They had almost fallen on my neck and sobbed when I first went to them with enough to make an accusation stick, and had later promised to deliver to me, framed, one of the first fruits of their search warrant: a note from Cranfield to Jack Roxford dated two years earlier, thanking him for not bidding him up at an auction after a selling race and enclosing a cheque for fifty pounds. Across the bottom of the page Cranfield had written:

As agreed. Thanks. D.C.

It was the note Oakley had photographed in my flat. Supplied by Roxford, who had suggested the photograph.

Kept by Oakley, as a hold over Roxford.

The police also told me that Jack Roxford had drawn six hundred pounds in new notes out of his bank during the two weeks before the Enquiry, and David Oakley had paid three hundred of the same notes into his own account five days later.

Clever, slippery Mr Oakley had been heard to remark that he regretted not having slaughtered Kelly Hughes.

The bell rang for the jockeys to mount, and Cranfield and old Strepson and I walked over to where Breadwinner waited.

The one jockey missing from the day's proceedings was Charlie West, whose licence had been suspended for the rest of the season. And it was only thanks to Hughes' intervention, Ferth had told him forcefully, that he hadn't got his deserts and been warned off for life. Whether Charlie West would feel an atom of gratitude was another matter.

I swung up easily on to Breadwinner and fitted my right foot carefully into the stirrup. A compromise between me and the orthopod had seen the plaster off seven days previously, but the great surgeon's kind parting words had been, 'You haven't given that leg enough time and if it dislocates again it's your own bloody fault.'

I had told him that I couldn't afford to have Cranfield engage another jockey for Breadwinner with all the horse's future races at stake. Old Strepson was the grateful type who didn't dislodge a jockey who had won for him, and if some other jockey won the Gold Cup on Breadwinner I would lose the mount for life: and it was only this argument which had grudgingly brought out the saw.

I gathered up the reins and walked the horse quietly round the ring while everyone sorted themselves out into the right order for the parade down the course. Apart from the Grand National, the Cheltenham Gold Cup was the biggest steeplechase of the year. In prestige, probably the greatest of all. All the stars turned out for it, meeting each other in level terms. Bad horses hadn't a hope.

There were nine runners. Breadwinner was the youngest, Squelch the most experienced, and a bad-tempered grey called Ironclad, the favourite.

DICK FRANCIS

Al Roach, uninfected by Kessel, lined up beside me at the start and gave me his usual wide friendly Irish grin. 'Now Kelly my bhoy,' he said, 'tell me how you ride this little fellow, now.'

'You want to be warned off?' I said.

He chuckled. 'What's the owner got against you, Kelly me bhoy?'

'I was right and he was wrong, and he can't forgive that.'

'Peculiar fellow, he is, that Kessel . . .'

The tapes went up and we were away. Three and a quarter miles, twenty-one jumps, two whole circuits of the course.

Nothing much happened on the first circuit. No horses fell and no jockeys got excited, and going past the stands and outward bound for the second time a fair-sized sheet would have covered the lot. The next mile sorted the men from the boys, and the bunch flattened out into a relentless, thundering, muscle-straining procession in which hope and sweat and tactics merged into a rushing private world of conflict. Speed . . . jumping at near-disaster rate . . . gambling on the horse's coordination . . . stretching your own . . . a race like the Gold Cup showed you what you were made of . . .

Coming to the second last fence, Ironclad was leading Squelch by three lengths which could have been ten, and he set himself right with all the time in the world. Squelch followed him over, and four lengths behind Breadwinner strained forwards to be third.

Between the last two fences the status quo was unchanged, Breadwinner making no impression on Squelch, nor Squelch on Ironclad. Oh well, I thought resignedly. Third. That wasn't really too bad for such a young horse. One couldn't have everything. And there was always Pound Postage in the Grand National, two weeks on Saturday . . .

Ironclad set himself right for the last fence, launched himself muscularly into the air, crossed the birch with a good foot of air beneath him . . . and pitched forwards on to his nose on landing.

I couldn't believe it. Shook up Breadwinner with a bang of renewed hope and drove him into the last fence for the jump of his young life.

Squelch was over it first, of course. Squelch the sure-footed trained-to-the-minute familiar old rascal . . . Irony of ironies, to be beaten to the Gold Cup by Squelch.

Breadwinner did the best he could to catch him, and I saw that as in the Lemonfizz, Squelch was dying from tiredness. Length by length my gangling chestnut pegged back the gap, straining, stretching, quivering to get past . . . but the winning post was too near . . . it was no good . . . there wasn't time . . .

Al Roach looked round to see who was pressing him. Saw me. Knew that Breadwinner was of all others the one he had to beat. Was seized with panic. If he had sat still, he would have won by two lengths. Instead, he picked up his whip and hit Squelch twice down the flank.

You stupid ass, I thought breathlessly. He hates that. He'll stop. He always stops if you hit him ...

Squelch's tail swished in fury. His rhythmic stride broke up into bumps. He shook his head violently from side to side.

I saw Al's desperate face as Breadwinner caught him ... and the winning post was there and gone in a flash ... and neither of us knew even then which had won.

The photograph gave it to Breadwinner by a nostril. And if I got booed by the crowd after the Lemonfizz they made up for it after the Gold Cup.

Kessel, predictably, was purple with fury, and he seemed on the brink of explosion when someone remarked loudly that Squelch would have won if Hughes had been riding him. I laughed. Kessel looked almost as murderous as Grace.

Old Strepson was pale with emotion but even the Gold Cup did not raise much observable joy in Cranfield; and I found out later that Edwin Byler had just told him he wouldn't be sending him his horses after all. Grace's psychiatrist had written to say that Grace's ultimate sanity might depend on Cranfield not having the horses, and Byler said he felt he owed the Roxfords something ... sorry and all that, but there it was.

Roberta with her mother had been there patting Breadwinner in the winner's enclosure, and when I came out of the weighing-room twenty minutes later after changing into street clothes, she was leaning against the rails there, waiting.

'You're limping,' she said calmly.

'Unfit, that's all.'

'Coffee?' she suggested.

'Yes,' I said.

She walked sedately ahead of me into the coffee room. Her copper hair still shone after she'd stepped out of the sunshine, and I liked the simple string-coloured coat which went underneath it.

I bought her some coffee and sat at a little plastic-topped table and looked at the litter left by the last occupants; empty coffee cups, plates with crumbs, cigarette butts, and a froth-lined beer glass. Roberta packed them coolly to one side and ignored them.

'Winning and losing,' she said. 'That's what it's all about.'

'Racing?'

'Life.'

I looked at her.

She said, 'Today is marvellous, and being warned off was terrible. I suppose everything goes on like that ... up and down ... always.'

'I suppose so,' I agreed.

'I've learned a lot, since the Enquiry.'

'So have I ... about you.'

'Father says I must remember your background ...'

'That's true,' I said. 'You must.'

'Father's mind has chains on. Iron bars in his soul. His head's chock-a-block with ideas half a century out of date.' She mimicked my own words with pompous mischief.

I laughed. 'Roberta ...'

'Please tell me ...'

She hesitated. '... At the level crossing ... when you called me Rosalind ... was it her you wanted?'

'No,' I said slowly, 'it was you ... In her place.'

She sighed contentedly.

'That's all right, then,' she said. 'Isn't it?'

RAT RACE

INTRODUCTION

I learned to fly in the Royal Air Force during the Second World War, and in the course of the 1940s flew Spitfire fighters and later Wellington and Lancaster bombers, amassing hundreds of hours in the air. On the thrifty novelist's premiss of not wasting any of life's experiences I decided to base one of my stories on flying (but not in wartime), the result being a book called *Flying Finish*.

My wife, Mary, helping me with earlier research for that book, undertook to go up for three flights in a light aircraft to find out about up-to-date civilian air regulations, which of course hadn't been in existence during the War. To our mutual surprise, Mary at once developed an enormous enthusiasm and aptitude at the controls, and in time became a qualified pilot herself.

From this almost accidental beginning she went on to take an Instrument Rating – approximately a master's degree in flying – and was commissioned to write a flying teaching book for absolute beginners which became recommended reading in British Airways pilot training schools.

We bought three light aircraft, two of them to lease to a flying training school and one, a fast little sports-car equivalent, for Mary to fly personally. People like jockeys, trainers and owners began asking her to fly them to the races, and eventually as a result we set up a small professional air-taxi and charter operation, employing six experienced British Airways pilots in their spare time – not Mary herself – to fly our paying passengers round the British Isles and Europe. Mary arranged the flights, smoothed their way and ran the records and business side.

Rat Race is about taxi flying. (Never waste experiences!) While I wrote the book, our own taxi business filled our days so that I was constantly surrounded by the raw materials of the story. Aircraft became the book's central characters, air procedures its structural bones. One might even say that page by page and hour by hour I lived and breathed the same basic concerns as my chief character, pilot Matt Shore.

As *Rat Race* is fiction, Matt Shore's more dangerous problems did *not* arise, I'm glad to say, in the seven years of our own air-taxi firm's life. We sold the successful little business finally to one of our chief customers and it is operating still, though changed and expanded, concentrating more on Euro-businessmen as passengers and less on the racing scene.

CHAPTER ONE

I picked four of them up at White Waltham in the new
Cherokee Six 300 that never got a chance to grow old.
The pale-blue upholstery still had a new leather smell
and there wasn't a scratch on the glossy white fuselage.
A nice little aeroplane, while it lasted.

They had ordered me for noon but they were already
in the bar when I landed at eleven-forty. Three double
whiskies and a lemonade.

Identification was easy: several chairs round a small
table were draped with four lightweight raincoats, three
binocular cases, two copies of the *Sporting Life* and
one very small racing saddle. The four passengers were
standing nearby in the sort of spread-about group
indicative of people thrown together by business rather
than natural friendship. They were not talking to each
other, though it looked as though they had been. One, a
large man, had a face full of anger. The smallest, evidently a jockey, was flushed and rigid. The two others, an
elderly man and a middle-aged woman, were steadfastly

319

staring at nothing in particular in the way that meant a lot of furious activity was going on inside their heads.

I walked towards the four of them across the large lounge reception room and spoke to an indeterminate spot in mid-air.

'Major Tyderman?'

The elderly man, who said 'Yes?', had been made a major a good long time ago. Nearer seventy than sixty; but still with a tough little body, wiry little moustache, sharp little eyes. He had thin salt-and-pepper hair brushed sideways across a balding crown and he carried his head stiffly, with his chin tucked back into his neck. Tense: very tense. And wary, looking at the world with suspicion.

He wore a lightweight speckled fawn suit vaguely reminiscent in cut of his military origins, and unlike the others had not parked his binoculars but wore them with the strap diagonally across his chest and the case facing forwards on his stomach, like a sporran. Club badges of metal and coloured cardboard hung in thick clusters at each side.

'Your aeroplane is here, Major,' I said. 'I'm Matt Shore . . . I'm flying you.'

He glanced over my shoulder, looking for someone else.

'Where's Larry?' he asked abruptly.

'He left,' I said. 'He got a job in Turkey.'

The Major's gaze came back from the search with a click. 'You're new,' he said accusingly.

'Yes,' I agreed.

'I hope you know the way.'

He meant it seriously. I said politely, 'I'll do my best.'

The second of the passengers, the woman on the Major's left, said flatly, 'The last time I flew to the races, the pilot got lost.'

I looked at her, giving her my best approximation to a confidence-boosting smile. 'The weather's good enough today not to have any fear of it.'

It wasn't true. There were cu-nims forecast for the June afternoon. And anyone can get lost any time if enough goes wrong. The woman gave me a disillusioned stare and I stopped wasting my confidence builder. She didn't need it. She had all the confidence in the world. She was fifty and fragile looking, with greying hair cut in a straight-across fringe and a jaw-length bob. There were two mild brown eyes under heavy dark eyebrows and a mouth that looked gentle; yet she held herself and behaved with the easy authority of a much higher command than the Major's. She was the only one of the group not outwardly ruffled.

The Major had been looking at his watch. 'You're early,' he said. 'We've got time for the other half.' He turned to the barman and ordered refills, and as an afterthought said to me, 'Something for you?'

I shook my head. 'No, thank you.'

The woman said indifferently, 'No alcohol for eight hours before a flight. Isn't that the rule?'

'More or less,' I agreed.

321

The third passenger, the large angry looking man, morosely watched the barman push the measure up twice on the Johnnie Walker. 'Eight hours. Good God,' he said. He looked as if eight hours seldom passed for him without topping up. The bulbous nose, the purple thread veins on his cheeks, the swelling paunch, they had all cost a lot in Excise duty.

The atmosphere I had walked into slowly subsided. The jockey sipped his low calorie lemonade, and the bright pink flush faded from his cheek bones and came out in fainter mottles on his neck. He seemed about twenty-one or two, reddish haired, with a naturally small frame and a moist looking skin. Few weight problems, I thought. No dehydration. Fortunate for him.

The Major and his large friend drank rapidly, muttered unintelligibly, and removed themselves to the Gents. The woman eyed the jockey and said in a voice which sounded more friendly than her comment, 'Are you out of your mind, Kenny Bayst? If you go on antagonizing Major Tyderman you'll be looking for another job.'

Kenny Bayst flicked his eyes to me and away again, compressing his rosebud mouth. He put the half-finished lemonade on the table and picked up one of the raincoats and the racing saddle.

'Which plane?' he said to me. 'I'll stow my gear.'

He had a strong Australian accent with a resentful bite to it. The woman watched him with what would have passed for a smile but for the frost in her eyes.

'The baggage door is locked,' I said. 'I'll come over with you.' To the woman I said, 'Can I carry your coat?'

'Thank you.' She indicated the coat which was obviously hers, a shiny rust-coloured affair with copper buttons. I picked it up, and also the businesslike binoculars lying on top, and followed Kenny Bayst out of the door.

After ten fuming paces he said explosively, 'It's too damn easy to blame the man on top.'

'They always blame the pilot,' I said mildly. 'Fact of life.'

'Huh?' he said. 'Oh yeah. Too right. They do.'

We reached the end of the path and started across the grass. He was still oozing grudge. I wasn't much interested.

'For the record,' I said, 'What are the names of my other passengers? Besides the Major, that is.'

He turned his head in surprise. 'Don't you know her? Our Annie Villars? Looks like someone's cosy old granny and has a tongue that would flay a kangaroo. Everyone knows our little Annie.' His tone was sour and disillusioned.

'I don't know much about racing,' I said.

'Oh? Well, she's a trainer, then. A damned good trainer, I'll say that for her, I wouldn't stay with her else. Not with that tongue of hers. I'll tell you, sport, she can roust her stable lads out of the gallops in words a sergeant-major never thought of. But sweet as milk with the owners. Has them eating out of her little hand.'

'The horses, too?'

'Uh? Oh, yeah. The horses love her. She can ride like a jock, too, when she's a mind to. Not that she does it much now. She must be getting on a bit. Still, she knows what she's at, true enough. She knows what a horse can do and what it can't, and that's most of the battle in this game.'

His voice held resentment and admiration in roughly equal amounts.

I said, 'What is the name of the other man? The big one.'

This time it was pure resentment: no admiration. He spat the name out syllable by deliberate syllable, curling his lips away from his teeth.

'Mister Eric Goldenberg.'

Having got rid of the name he shut his mouth tight and was clearly taking his employer's remarks to heart. We reached the aircraft and stowed the coats and his saddle in the baggage space behind the rear seats.

'We're going to Newbury first, aren't we?' he asked. 'To pick up Colin Ross?'

'Yes.'

He gave me a sardonic look. 'Well, you *must* have heard of Colin Ross.'

'I guess,' I agreed, 'that I have.'

It would have been difficult not to, since the champion jockey was twice as popular as the Prime Minister and earned six times as much. His face appeared on half the billboards in Britain encouraging the populace to drink more milk and there was even a picture strip about him in a children's comic. Everyone, but everyone, had heard of Colin Ross.

Kenny Bayst climbed in through the rear end door and sat in one of the two rear seats. I took a quick look round the outside of the aircraft, even though I'd done a thorough preflight check on it not an hour ago, before I left base. It was my first week, my fourth day, my third flight for Derrydown Sky Taxis, and after the way Fate had clobbered me in the past, I was taking no chances.

There were no nuts loose, no rivets missing on the sharp-nosed little six-seater. There were eight quarts of oil where there should have been eight quarts of oil, there were no dead birds clogging up the air intakes to the engine, there were no punctures in the tyres, no cracks in the green or red glass over the navigation lights, no chips in the propeller blades, no loose radio aerials. The pale-blue cowling over the engine was securely clipped down, and the matching pale-blue cowlings over the struts and wheels of the fixed undercarriage were as solid as rocks.

By the time I'd finished the other three passengers were coming across the grass. Goldenberg was doing the talking with steam still coming out of his ears, while the Major nodded agreement in unhappy little jerks and Annie Villars looked as if she wasn't listening. When they arrived within earshot Goldenberg was saying '. . . can't lay the horse unless we're sure he'll pull it . . .' But he stopped with a snap when the Major gestured sharply in my direction. He need hardly have bothered. I had no curiosity about their affairs.

On the principle that in a light aircraft it is better to have the centre of gravity as far forward as possible, I asked Goldenberg to sit in front in the right-hand seat beside me, and put the Major and Annie Villars in the centre two seats, and left Kenny in the last two, with the empty one ready for Colin Ross. The four rear seats were reached by the port side door, but Goldenberg had to climb in by stepping up on the low wing on the starboard side and lowering into his seat through the forward door. He waited while I got in before him and moved over to my side, then squeezed his bulk in through the door and settled heavily into his seat.

They were all old hands at air taxis: they had their safety belts fastened before I did mine, and when I looked round to check that they were ready to go, the Major was already deep in the *Sporting Life*. Kenny Bayst was cleaning his nails with fierce little jabs, relieving his frustration by hurting himself.

I got clearance from the tower and lifted the little aeroplane away for the twenty-mile hop across Berkshire. Taxi flying was a lot different from the airlines, and finding racecourses looked more difficult to me than being radar vectored into Heathrow. I'd never before flown a racecourse trip, and I'd asked my predecessor Larry about it that morning when he'd come into the office to collect his cards.

'Newbury's a cinch,' he said offhandedly. 'Just point

its nose at that vast runway the Yanks built at Green-
ham Common. You can practically see it from Scotland.
The racecourse is just north of it, and the landing strip is
parallel with the white rails of the finishing straight.
You can't miss it. Good long strip. No problems. As for
Haydock, it's just where the M6 motorway crosses the
East Lancs road. Piece of cake.'

He took himself off to Turkey, stopping on one foot
at the doorway for some parting advice. 'You'll have to
practise short landings before you go to Bath; and avoid
Yarmouth in a heatwave. It's all yours now, mate, and
the best of British luck.'

It was true that you could see Greenham Common
from a long way off, but on a fine day it would anyway
have been difficult to lose the way from White Waltham
to Newbury; the main railway line to Exeter ran more
or less straight from one to the other. My passengers
had flown into Newbury before, and the Major helpfully
told me to look out for the electric cables strung across
the approach. We landed respectably on the newly
mown grass and taxied along the strip towards the
grandstand end, braking to a stop just before the boundary fence.

Colin Ross wasn't there.

I shut down the engine, and in the sudden silence
Annie Villars remarked, 'He's bound to be late. He said
he was riding work for Bob Smith, and Bob's never on
time getting his horses out.'

The other three nodded vaguely but they were still

not on ordinarily chatty terms with each other, and after about five minutes of heavy silence I asked Goldenberg to let me out to stretch my legs. He grunted and mumbled at having to climb out on to the wing to let me past him and I gathered I was breaking Derrydown's number one rule: never annoy the customers, you're going to need them again.

Once I was out of their company, however, they did start talking. I walked round to the front of the aircraft and leant against the leading edge of the wing; and looked up at the scattered clouds in the blue-grey sky and thought unprofitably about this and that. Behind me their voices rose acrimoniously, and when they opened the door wide to get some air, scraps of what they were saying floated across.

'. . . simply asking for a dope test.' Annie Villars.

'. . . if you can't ride a losing race better than last time . . . find someone else.' Goldenberg.

'. . . very difficult position . . .' Major Tyderman.

A short sharp snap from Kenny, and Annie Villars' exasperated exclamation. 'Bayst!'

'. . . not paying you more than last time.' The Major, very emphatically.

Indistinct protest from Kenny, and a violently clear reaction from Goldenberg: 'Bugger your licence.'

Kenny my lad, I thought remotely, if you don't watch out you'll end up like me, still with a licence but with not much else.

A Ford-of-all-work rolled down the road past the

grandstands, came through the gate in the boundary fence, and bounced over the turf towards the aircraft. It stopped about twenty feet away, and two men climbed out. The larger, who had been driving, went round to the back and pulled out a brown canvas and leather overnight grip. The smaller one walked on over the grass. I took my weight off the wing and stood up. He stopped a few paces away, waiting for the larger man to catch up. He was dressed in faded blue jeans and a whitish cotton sweater with navy-blue edgings. Black canvas shoes on his narrow feet. He had nondescript brownish hair over an exceptionally broad forehead, a short straight nose, and a delicate feminine looking chin. All his bones were fine and his waist and hips would have been the despair of Victorian maidens. Yet there was something unmistakably masculine about him: and more than that, he was mature. He looked at me with the small still smile behind the eyes which is the hallmark of those who know what life is really about. His soul was old. He was twenty-six.

'Good morning,' I said.

He held out his hand, and I shook it. His clasp was cool, firm, and brief.

'No Larry?' he inquired.

'He's left. I'm Matt Shore.'

'Fine,' he said noncommittally. He didn't introduce himself. He knew there was no need. I wondered what it was like to be in that position. It hadn't affected Colin Ross. He had none of the 'I am' aura which often clings around the notably successful, and from the extreme understatement of his clothes I gathered that he avoided it consciously.

'We're late, I'm afraid,' he said. 'Have to bend the throttle.'

'Do my best . . .'

The larger man arrived with the grip, and I stowed it in the forward luggage locker between the engine wall and the forward bulkhead of the cabin. By the time the baggage door was securely fastened Colin Ross had found his empty seat and strapped himself into it. Goldenberg with heavy grunts moved out again so that I could get back to my left-hand place. The larger man, who was apparently the dilatory trainer Bob Smith, said his hellos and goodbyes to the passengers, and stood watching afterwards while I started the engine and taxied back to the other end of the strip to turn into wind for take-off.

The flight north was uneventful: I went up the easy way under the Amber One airway, navigating on the radio beacons at Daventry, Lichfield and Oldham. Manchester control routed us right round the north of their zone so that I had to drop down southwards towards Haydock racecourse, and there it was, just as Larry had said, near the interchange of the two giant roads. We touched down on the grass strip indicated in the centre of the course, and I taxied on and parked where the Major told me to, near the rails of the track itself, a mere hundred yards from the grandstand.

The passengers disembarked themselves and their belongings and Colin Ross looked at his watch. A faint smile hovered and was gone. He made no comment. He said merely, 'Are you coming in to the races?'

I shook my head. 'Think I'll stay over here.'

'I'll arrange with the man on the gate to let you into the paddock, if you change your mind.'

'Thanks,' I said in surprise. 'Thanks very much.'

He nodded briefly and set off without waiting for the others, ducking under the white-painted rails and trudging across the track.

'Pilots' perks,' Kenny said, taking his raincoat from my hand and putting his arm forward for the saddle. 'You want to take advantage.'

'Maybe I will,' I said, but I didn't mean to. Horse racing began and ended with the Derby as far as I was concerned, and also I was a non-gambler by nature.

Annie Villars said in her deceptively gentle voice, 'You do understand that we're all going on to Newmarket after the races, and not back to Newbury?'

'Yes,' I assured her. 'That's what I was told.'

'Good.'

'If we don't go to jail,' Kenny said under his breath. Goldenberg looked at me sharply to see if I'd heard that, and I gave no sign of it. Whatever they were about, it was as little my concern as who killed Cock Robin.

Major Tyderman pushed at his moustache with a hand rigid with nervous energy and said, 'Last race at four-thirty. Need a drink after that. Ready to start back at, say, five-fifteen. That all right with you?'

'Perfectly, Major,' I nodded.

'Right,' he said. 'Good.' His gaze was flicking from one to another of his travelling companions, assessing and suspicious. His eyes narrowed fiercely at Kenny Bayst, opened and narrowed again rapidly on Goldenberg, relaxed on Annie Villars and went cold on the vanishing back of Colin Ross. The thoughts behind the outward physical reactions were unguessable, and when he finally looked back at me he didn't really see me, he was busy with the activity inside his head.

'Five-fifteen,' he repeated vaguely. 'Good.'

Kenny said to me, 'Don't waste your money in the three-thirty, sport'; and Goldenberg raised his fist with a face going purple with anger and nearly hit him.

Annie Villars' voice rapped into him, the steel sticking through the cream with a vengeance, the top-brass quality transcendent and withering.

'Control your temper, you stupid man.'

Goldenberg's mouth literally dropped open, to reveal a bottom row of unappetising brown stained teeth. His raised fist lowered slowly, and he looked altogether foolish.

'As for you,' she said to Kenny, 'I told you to keep your tongue still, and that was your last chance.'

'Are you sacking me?' he asked.

'I'll decide that at the end of the afternoon.'

Kenny showed no anxiety about keeping his job, and

I realized that in fact what he had been doing was trying to provoke them into getting rid of him. He'd got himself into nutcrackers and while they squeezed he couldn't get out.

I became mildly curious to see what would happen in the three-thirty. It would help to pass the afternoon.

They straggled off towards the stands, Kenny in front, the Major and Goldenberg together, with Annie Villars several paces behind. The Major kept stopping and looking back and waiting for her, but every time just as she reached him he turned and went off again in front, so that as a piece of courtesy, the whole thing was wasted. He reminded me vividly of an aunt who had taken me for childhood walks in just that way. I remembered quite clearly that it had been infuriating.

I sighed, shut the baggage doors and tidied up the aeroplane. Annie Villars had been smoking thin brown cigars. Goldenberg had been eating indigestion tablets, each from a square wrapper. The Major had left his *Sporting Life* in a tumbled heap on the floor.

While I was fiddling around with the debris, two more aeroplanes flew in, a four-seat high-winged Cessna and a six-seat twin-engined Aztec.

I watched their touchdowns with an uncritical eye, though I wouldn't have given the Aztec pilot a gold medal for his double bounce. Several small men disgorged themselves and made a dart like a flock of starlings across the track towards the paddock. They were followed by three or four larger and slower-moving people slung around with binoculars and what I later learned to be bags for carrying sets of racing colours. Finally out of each aircraft popped the most leisurely of all the inmates, a man dressed very much as I was, in dark trousers, white shirt, neat dark tie.

They strolled towards each other and lit cigarettes. After a while, not wanting to seem unsociable, I wandered across to join them. They turned and watched me come, but with no welcome in unsmiling faces.

'Hello,' I said moderately. 'Nice day.'

'Perhaps,' said one.

'You think so?' said the other.

They offered me fish-eyed stares but no cigarette. I had grown hardened to that sort of thing. I turned half away from them and read the names of the firms they flew for, which were painted on the tails of their aircraft. It was the same name on both. Polyplane Services.

How dreary of them, I thought, to be so antagonistic. I gave them the benefit of a very small doubt and made one more approach.

'Have you come far?'

They didn't answer. Just gave me the stares, like two cod.

I laughed at them as if I thought their behaviour pathetic, which in fact I did, and turned on my heel to go back to my own territory. When I'd gone ten steps one of them called after me, 'Where's Larry Gedge?' He didn't sound as if he liked Larry any better than me.

I decided not to hear: if they really wanted to know,

they could come and ask nicely. It was their turn to cross the grass.

They didn't bother. I wasn't particularly sorry. I had long ago learned that pilots were not all one great happy brotherhood. Pilots could be as bloodyminded to each other as any group on earth.

I climbed back into my seat in the Cherokee and sorted out my maps and flight plans for the return journey. I had four hours to do it in and it took me ten minutes. After that I debated whether to go over to the stands and find some lunch, and decided I wasn't hungry. After that I yawned. It was a habit.

I had been depressed for so long that it had become a permanent state of mind. Expectations might lift the edge of the cloud every time one took a new job, but life never turned out to be as good as the hopes. This was my sixth job since I'd gone to learn flying with stars in my eyes, my fourth since the stars had faded for good. I had thought that taxi flying might be interesting, and after crop spraying, which I'd been doing last, anything would be; and perhaps it would indeed be interesting, but if I'd thought it might be free of gripe and bad temper I'd been kidding myself. For here it all was, as usual. Squabbling passengers and belligerent competitors and no discernible joy anywhere.

There was a small buffet on the side of the fuselage and the jar and sound of someone stepping up on to the wing. The slightly open door was pushed wide with a crash, and into its space appeared a girl, bending at the waist and knees and neck so that she could look inside and across at me.

She was slim and dark haired and she was wearing large square sunglasses. Also she had a blue linen dress and long white boots. She looked great. The afternoon instantly improved.

'You lousy bloody skunk,' she said.

It really was one of those days.

CHAPTER TWO

'Wow,' she said. 'Wrong man.' She took off the sun-glasses and folded them away in the white handbag which hung from her shoulder by a thick red, white and blue cord.

'Think nothing of it.'

'Where's Larry?'

'Gone to Turkey.'

'Gone?' she said blankly. 'Do you mean literally gone already, or planning to go, or what?'

I looked at my watch. 'Took off from Heathrow twenty minutes ago, I believe.'

'Damn,' she said forcibly. 'Bloody damn.'

She straightened up so that all I could see of her was from the waist down. A pleasant enough view for any poor aviator. The legs looked about twenty-three years old and there was nothing wrong with them.

She bent down again. Nothing wrong with the rest of her, either.

'When will he be back?'

'He had a three-year contract.'

'Oh, *hell*.' She stared at me in dismay for a few seconds, then said, 'Can I come in there and talk to you for a minute?'

'Sure,' I agreed, and moved my maps and stuff off Goldenberg's seat. She stepped down into the cockpit and slid expertly into place. By no means her first entrance into a light aircraft. I wondered about Larry. Lucky Larry.

'I suppose he didn't give you . . . a parcel . . . or anything . . . to give me, did he?' she said gloomily.

'Nothing, I'm afraid.'

'He's an absolute beast then . . . er, is he a friend of yours?'

'I've met him twice, that's all.'

'He's pinched my hundred quid,' she said bitterly.

'He pinched? . . .'

'He bloody has. Not to mention my handbag and keys and everything.' She stopped and compressed her mouth in anger. Then she added, 'I left my handbag in this aeroplane three weeks ago, when we flew to Doncaster. And Larry has been saying ever since that he'll bring it on the next trip to the races and give it to Colin to give to me, and for three solid weeks he's kept on forgetting it. I suppose he knew he was going to Turkey and he thought if he could put it off long enough he would never have to give my bag back.'

'Colin . . . Colin Ross?' I asked. She nodded abstractedly.

'Is he your husband?'

She looked startled, then laughed. 'Good Lord, no. He's my brother. I saw him just now in the paddock and I said, "Has he brought my handbag?" and he shook his head and started to say something, but I belted off over here in a fury without stopping to listen, and I suppose he was going to tell me it wasn't Larry who had come in the plane . . . Oh damn it, I *hate* being robbed. Colin would have lent him a hundred quid if he was that desperate. He didn't have to pinch it.'

'It was a lot of money to have in a handbag,' I suggested.

'Colin had just given it to me, you see. In the plane. Some owner had handed him a terrific present in readies, and he gave me a hundred of it to pay a bill with, which was really sweet of him, and I can hardly expect him to give me another hundred just because I was silly enough to leave the first one lying about . . .' Her voice tailed off in depression.

'The bill,' she added wryly, 'is for flying lessons.'

I looked at her with interest. 'How far have you got?'

'Oh, I've got my licence,' she said. 'These were instrument flying lessons. And radio navigation, and all that jazz. I've done about ninety-five hours, altogether. Spread over about four years, though, sad to say.'

That put her in the experienced-beginner class and the dangerous time bracket. After eighty hours flying, pilots are inclined to think they know enough. After a hundred hours, they are sure they don't. Between the two, the accident rate is at its peak.

DICK FRANCIS

She asked me several questions about the aeroplane, and I answered them. Then she said, 'Well, there's no point in sitting here all afternoon,' and began to lever herself out on to the wing. 'Aren't you coming over to the races?'

'No,' I shook my head.

'Oh come on,' she said. 'Do.'

The sun was shining and she was very pretty. I smiled and said 'OK,' and followed her out on to the grass. It is profitless now to speculate on the different course things would have taken if I'd stayed where I was.

I collected my jacket from the rear baggage compartment and locked all the doors and set off with her across the track. The man on the gate duly let me into the paddock and Colin Ross' sister showed no sign of abandoning me once we were inside. Instead she diagnosed my almost total ignorance and seemed pleased to be able to start dispelling it.

'You see that brown horse over there,' she said, steering me towards the parade ring rails, 'That one walking round the far end, number sixteen, that's Colin's mount in this race. It's come out a bit light but it looks well in its coat.'

'It does?'

She looked at me in amusement. 'Definitely.'

'Shall I back it, then?'

'It's all a joke to you.'

'No,' I protested.

'Oh yes indeed,' she nodded. 'You're looking at this

race meeting in the way I'd look at a lot of spiritualists. Disbelieving and a bit superior.'

'Ouch.'

'But what you're actually seeing is a large export industry in the process of marketing its wares.'

'I'll remember that.'

'And if the industry takes place out of doors on a nice fine sunny day with everyone enjoying themselves, well, so much the better.'

'Put that way,' I agreed, 'it's a lot more jolly than a car factory.'

'You will get involved,' she said with certainty.

'No.' I was equally definite.

She shook her head. 'You will, you know, if you do much racecourse taxi work. It'll bust through that cool shell of yours and make you feel something, for a change.'

I blinked. 'Do you always talk like that to total strangers?'

'No,' she said slowly. 'I don't.'

The bright little jockeys flooded into the parade ring and scattered to small earnest owner-trainer groups where there were a lot of serious conversations and much nodding of heads. On the instructions of Colin Ross' sister I tried moderately hard to take it all seriously. Not with much success.

Colin Ross' sister . . .

'Do you have a name?' I asked.

'Often.'

'Thanks.'

She laughed. 'It's Nancy. What's yours?'

'Matt Shore.'

'Hm. A flat matt name. Very suitable.'

The jockeys were thrown up like confetti and landed in their saddles, and their spindly shining long-legged transportation skittered its way out on to the track. Two-year-olds, Nancy said.

She walked me back towards the stands and proposed to smuggle me into the 'Owners and Trainers'. The large official at the bottom of the flight of steps beamed at her until his eyes disappeared and he failed to inspect me for the right bit of cardboard.

It seemed that nearly everyone on the small rooftop stand knew Nancy, and obvious that they agreed with the beaming official's assessment. She introduced me to several people whose interest collapsed like a soufflé in a draught when they found I didn't understand their opening bids.

'He's a pilot,' Nancy explained apologetically. 'He flew Colin here today.'

'Ah,' they said. 'Ah.'

Two of my other passengers were there. Annie Villars was watching the horses canter past with an intent eye and a pursed mouth: the field-marshal element was showing strongly, the feminine camouflage in abeyance. Major Tyderman, planted firmly with his legs apart and his chin tucked well back into his neck, was scribbling notes into his racecard. When he looked up he saw us, and made his way purposefully across.

'I say,' he said to me, having forgotten my name. 'Did I leave my *Sporting Life* over in the plane, do you know?'

'Yes, you did, Major.'

'Blast,' he said. 'I made some notes on it . . . Must get it you know. Have to go across after this race.'

'Would you like me to fetch it?' I asked.

'Well, that's very good of you, my dear chap. But . . . no . . . couldn't ask it. Walk will do me good.'

'The aircraft's locked, Major,' I said. 'You'll need the keys.' I took them out of my pocket and gave them to him.

'Right.' He nodded stiffly. 'Good.'

The race started away off down the track and was all over long before I sorted out the colours of Colin Ross. In the event, it wasn't difficult. He had won.

'How's Midge?' Annie Villars said to Nancy, restoring her giant raceglasses to their case.

'Oh, much better, thank you. Getting on splendidly.'

'I'm so glad. She's had a bad time, poor girl.'

Nancy nodded and smiled, and everyone trooped down the stairs to the ground.

'Well now,' Nancy said. 'How about some coffee? And something to munch, perhaps?'

'You must have others you'd prefer to be with . . . I won't get into trouble, you know, on my own.'

Her lips twitched. 'Today I need a bodyguard. I

elected you for the job. Desert me if you like, but if you want to please, stick.'

'Not difficult,' I said.

'Great. Coffee, then.'

It was iced coffee, rather good. Halfway through the turkey sandwiches the reason why Nancy wanted me with her drifted up to the small table where we sat and slobbered all over her. She fended off what looked to me like a random assembly of long hair, beard, beads, fringes and a garment like a tablecloth with a hole in it, and yelled to me through the undergrowth, 'Buddy, your job starts right now.'

I stood up, reached out two hands, caught hold of an assortment of wool and hair, and pulled firmly back-wards. The result resolved itself into a youngish man sitting down with surprise much more suddenly than he'd intended.

'Nancy,' he said in an aggrieved voice.

'This is Chanter,' she said to me. 'He's never grown out of the hippie thing, as you can see.'

'I'm an artist,' he said. He had an embroidered band across his forehead and round his head: like the horses' bridles, I thought fleetingly. All the hair was clean and there were shaven parts on his jaw just to prove that it wasn't from pure laziness that he let everything grow. On closer inspection I was sure that it was indeed a dark-green chenille tablecloth, with a central hole for his head. Underneath that he wore low-slung buckskin trousers fringed from hip to ankle, and a creepy crêpy dim mauve shirt curved to fit his concave stomach. Various necklaces and pendants on silver chains hung round his neck. Under all the splendour he had dirty bare feet.

'I went to art school with him,' Nancy said resignedly. 'That was in London. Now he's at Liverpool, just down the road. Any time I come racing up here, he turns up too.'

'Uh,' Chanter said profoundly.

'Do you get grants for ever?' I asked: not sneeringly; I simply wanted to know.

He was not offended. 'Look, man, like, up here I'm the fuzz.'

I nearly laughed. Nancy said, 'You know what he means, then?'

'He teaches,' I said.

'Yeah, man, that's what I said.' He took one of the turkey sandwiches. His fingers were greenish with black streaks. Paint.

'You keep your impure thoughts off this little bird,' he said to me, spitting out bits of bread. 'She's strictly my territory. But strictly, man.'

'Zat so?'

'Zat definitely, but definitely . . . is . . . so, man.'

'How come?'

He gave me a look which was as off beat as his appearance.

'I've still got the salt to put on this little bird's tail,' he said. 'Shan't be satisfied till it's there . . .'

Nancy was looking at him with an expression which

345

meant that she didn't know whether to laugh at him or be afraid of him. She couldn't decide whether he was Chanter the amorous buffoon or Chanter the frustrated sex maniac. Nor could I. I understood her needing help when he was around.

'He only wants me because I won't,' she said.

'The challenge bit,' I nodded. 'Affront to male pride, and all that.'

'Practically every other girl has,' she said.

'That makes it worse.'

Chanter looked at me broodingly. 'You're a drag, man. I mean, cubic.'

'To each his scene,' I said ironically.

He took the last of the sandwiches, turned his back studiously towards me and said to Nancy, 'Let's you and me lose this dross, huh?'

'Let's you and me do nothing of the sort, Chanter. If you want to tag along, Matt comes in the deal.'

He scowled at the floor and then suddenly stood up so that all the fringes and beads danced and jingled.

'Come on, then. Let's get a look at the horses. Life's a-wasting.'

'He really can draw,' Nancy said as we followed the tablecloth out into the sunshine.

'I wouldn't doubt it. I'll bet half of what he does is caricature, though, with a strong element of cruelty.'

'How d'you know?' she said, startled.

'He just seems like that.'

He padded along beside us in his bare feet and was a

sufficiently unusual sight on a racecourse to attract a barrage of stares ranging from amusement to apoplexy. He didn't seem to notice. Nancy looked as if she were long used to it.

We came to a halt against the parade ring rails where Chanter rested his elbows and exercised his voice.

'Horses,' he said. 'I'm not for the Stubbs and Munnings thing. When I see a racehorse I see a machine, and that's what I paint, a horse-shaped machine with pistons thumping away and muscle fibres like connecting rods and a crack in the crank case with the oil dripping away drop by drop into the body cavity . . .' He broke off abruptly but with the same breath finished. 'How's your sister?'

'She's much better,' Nancy said, not seeming to see any great change of subject. 'She's really quite well now.'

'Good,' he said, and went straight on with his lecture. 'And then I draw some distant bulging stands with hats flying off and everyone cheering and all the time the machine is bursting its gut . . . I see components, I see what's happening to the bits . . . the stresses . . . I see colours in components too . . . nothing on earth is a whole . . . nothing is ever what it seems . . . everything is components.' He stopped abruptly, thinking about what he'd said.

After a suitably appreciative pause, I asked, 'Do you ever sell your paintings?'

'Sell them?' He gave me a scornful, superior stare. 'No, I don't. Money is disgusting.'

'It's more disgusting when you haven't got it,' Nancy said.

'You're a renegade, girl,' he said fiercely.

'Love on a crust,' she said, 'is fine when you're twenty, but pretty squalid when you're sixty.'

'I don't intend to be sixty. Sixty is strictly for grandfathers. Not my scene at all.'

We turned away from the rails and came face to face with Major Tyderman, who was carrying his *Sporting Life* and holding out the aircraft's keys. His gaze swept over Chanter and he controlled himself admirably. Not a twitch.

'I locked up again,' he said, handing me the bunch.

'Thanks, Major.'

He nodded, glanced once more at Chanter, and retreated in good order.

Even for Nancy's sake the official wouldn't let Chanter up the steps to the Owners and Trainers. We watched at grass level with Chanter muttering 'stinking bourgeois' at regular intervals.

Colin Ross finished second. The crowd booed and tore up a lot of tickets. Nancy looked as though she were long used to that, too.

Between the next two races we sat on the grass while Chanter gave us the uninterrupted benefit of his views on the evils of money, racialism, war, religion and marriage. It was regulation stuff, nothing new. I didn't say I

348

thought so. During the discourse he twice without warning stretched over and put his hand on Nancy's breast. Each time without surprise she picked it off again by the wrist and threw it back at him. Neither of them seemed to think it needed comment.

After the next race (Colin was third) Chanter remarked that his throat was dry, and Nancy and I obediently followed him off to the Tattersalls bar for lubrication. Coca-Colas for three, splashed out of the bottles by an overworked barmaid. Chanter busily juggled the three glasses so that it was I who paid, which figured.

The bar was only half full but a great deal of space and attention was being taken up by one man, a large tough-looking individual with a penetrating Australian accent. He had an obviously new white plaster cast on his leg and a pair of crutches which he hadn't mastered. His loud laugh rose above the general buzz as he constantly apologised for knocking into people.

'Haven't got the hang of these props yet . . .'

Chanter regarded him, as he did most things, with some disfavour.

The large Australian went on explaining his state to two receptive acquaintances.

'Mind you, can't say I'm sorry I broke my ankle. Best investment I ever made.' The laugh rang out infectiously and most people in the bar began to grin. Not Chanter, of course.

'See, I only paid my premium the week before, and

then I fell down these steps and I got a thousand quid for it. Now that ain't whistling, that ain't, eh? A thousand bleeding quid for falling down a flight of steps.' He laughed again hugely, enjoying the joke. 'Come on mates,' he said, 'Drink up, and let's go and invest some of this manna from Heaven on my good friend Kenny Bayst.'

I jumped a fraction and looked at my watch. Coming up to three-thirty. Kenny Bayst clearly hadn't told his good friend not to speculate. Absolutely none of my business. Telling him myself would be the worst favour I could do for Kenny Bayst.

The large Australian swung himself out of the bar, followed by the two mates. Chanter's curiosity overcame his disinclination to show himself at a loss.

'Who,' he said crossly, 'is going to give that schmo a thousand quid for breaking his ankle?'

Nancy smiled. 'It's a new insurance fund, specially for people who go racing. Accident insurance. I don't really know. I've heard one or two people mention it lately.'

'Insurance is immoral,' Chanter said dogmatically, sliding round behind her and laying his hand flat on her stomach. Nancy picked it off and stepped away. As a bodyguard, I didn't seem to be doing much good.

Nancy said she particularly wanted to see this race properly, and left Chanter looking moody at the bottom of the staircase. Without asking her I followed her up the steps: a period alone with Chanter held no attractions.

Kenny Bayst, according to my slantways look at Nancy's racecard, was riding a horse called Rudiments: number seven, owned by the Duke of Wessex, trained by Miss Villars, carrying olive green with silver crossbelts and cap. I watched the horse canter down pa t the stands on the olive-green grass and reflected that the Duke of Wessex had chosen colours which were as easy to distinguish as coal on a black night.

I said to Nancy, 'What did Rudiments do in his last race?'

'Hm?' she said absentmindedly, all her attention on the rose-pink and white shape of her brother. 'Did you say Rudiments?'

'That's right. I brought Kenny Bayst and Annie Villars here, as well.'

'Oh. I see.' She looked down at her racecard. 'Last time out . . . it won. Time before that, it won. Time before that, it came fourth.'

'It's good, then?'

'Fairly, I suppose.' She wrinkled her nose at me. 'I told you you'd get involved.'

I shook my head. 'Just curious.'

'Same thing.'

'Is it favourite?'

'No, Colin is. But . . . you can see over there, on that big board . . . see? . . . Rudiments is second favourite on the Tote at about three to one.'

351

'Well . . .' I said. 'What does it mean, to lay a horse?'

'It means to stand a bet. It's what bookmakers do. What the Tote does, really, come to that.'

'Can people do it who aren't bookmakers?'

'Oh sure. They do. Say the bookmakers are offering three to one, and you yourself don't think the horse will win, you could say to your friends, I'll lay you four to one; so they'd bet with you because you were offering more. Also, no betting tax. Private wager, you see.'

'And if the horse wins, you pay out?'

'You sure do.'

'I see,' I said. And I did. Eric Goldenberg had laid Rudiments the last time it had run because Kenny Bayst had agreed to lose, and then he'd gone and won. Their tempers were still on the dicky side as a result: and they had been arguing today about whether or not to try again.

'Colin thinks he'll win this,' Nancy said. 'I do hope so.'

Bonanza for Bayst, I thought.

It was a seven furlong race, it seemed. The horses accelerated from standing to 30 mph in times which would have left a Porsche gasping. When they swung away round the far bend Rudiments was as far as I was concerned invisible, and until the last hundred yards I didn't see him once. Then all of a sudden there he was, boxed in in a bunch on the rails and unable to get past Colin Ross directly in front.

Kenny didn't find his opening. He finished the race in

third place, still pinned in by Colin in front and a dappled grey alongside. I couldn't begin to tell whether or not he had done it on purpose.

'Wasn't that *great*?' Nancy exclaimed to the world in general, and a woman on the far side of her agreed that it was, and asked after the health of her sister Midge.

'Oh, she's fine, thanks,' Nancy said. She turned to me and there was less joy in her eyes than in her voice. 'Come over here,' she said. 'You can see them unsaddling the winner.'

The Owners and Trainers turned out to be on the roof of the weighing room. We leaned over the rails at the front and watched Colin and Kenny unbuckle the saddle girths, loop the saddles over their arms, pat their steaming horses, and disappear into the weighing room. The group in the winner's enclosure were busy slapping backs and unburdening to the Press. The group in the third enclosure wore small tight smiles and faraway eyes. I still couldn't tell if they were ecstatic and hiding it, or livid and ditto.

The horses were led away and the groups dispersed. In their place appeared Chanter, staring up and waving his arm.

'Come on down,' he shouted.

'No inhibitions, that's his trouble,' Nancy said. 'If we don't go down, he'll just go on shouting.'

He did. An official strode up manfully to ask him to belt up and buzz off, but it was like ripples trying to push over Bass Rock.

'Come on down, Nancy.' Fortissimo.

She pushed herself away from the rails and took enough steps to be out of his sight.

'Stay with me,' she said. It was more than half a question.

'If you want it.'

'You've seen what he's like. And he's been mild, today. Mild. Thanks to you.'

'I've done absolutely nothing.'

'You're here.'

'Why do you come to Haydock, if he always bothers you too much?'

'Because I'm bloody well not letting him frighten me away.'

'He loves you,' I said.

'No. Can't you tell the difference, for God's sake?'

'Yes,' I said.

She looked startled, then shook her head. 'He loves Chanter, full stop.'

She took three more steps towards the stairs, then stopped again.

'Why is it that I talk to you as if I'd known you for years?'

To a certain extent I knew, but I smiled and shook my head. No one cares to say straight out that it's because one is as negative as wallpaper.

Chanter's plaintive voice floated up the steps. 'Nancy, come on down . . .'

She took another step, and then stopped again. 'Will

354

you do me another favour? I'm staying up here a few more days with an aunt, but I bought a present for Midge this morning and I've given it to Colin to take home. But he's got a memory like a string vest for everything except horses, so would you check with him that he hasn't left it in the changing room, before you take off?'

'Sure,' I said. 'Your sister . . . I gather she's been ill.'

She looked away up at the sun-filled sky and down again and straight at me, and in a shattering moment of awareness I saw the pain and the cracks behind the bright public façade.

'Has been. Will be,' she said. 'She's got leukaemia.'

After a pause she swallowed and added the unbearable bit.

'She's my identical twin.'

CHAPTER THREE

After the fifth race Chanter gloomily announced that about fifty plastic students were waiting for him to pat their egos and that although he despised the system he was likely to find eating a problem if he actually got the sack. His farewell to Nancy consisted in wiping his hands all over her, front and back, and giving her an open-mouthed kiss which owing to her split-second evasive action landed on her ear.

He glared at me as if it were my fault. Nancy not relenting, he scowled at her and muttered something about salt, and then twirled around on his bare heel so that the tablecloth and all the hair and fringes and beads swung out with centrifugal force, and strode away at high speed towards the exit.

'The soles of his feet are like leather,' she said. 'Disgusting.' But from the hint of indulgence in her face I gathered that Chanter's cause wasn't entirely lost.

She said she was thirsty again and could do with a Coke, and since she seemed to want me still to tag along, I tagged. This time, without Chanter, we went to the members' bar in the Club enclosure, the small downstairs one that was open to the main entrance hall.

The man in the plaster cast was there again. Different audience. Same story. His big cheerful booming voice filled the little bar and echoed round the whole hall outside.

'You can't hear yourself think,' Nancy said.

In a huddle in a far corner were Major Tyderman and Eric Goldenberg, sitting at a small table with what looked like treble whiskies in front of them. Their heads were bent towards each other, close, almost touching, so that they could each hear what the other was saying amid the din, yet not be overheard. Relations between them didn't seem to be at their most cordial. There was a great deal of rigidity in their down-bent faces, and no friendliness in the small flicking glances they occasionally gave each other.

'The *Sporting Life* man,' Nancy said, following my gaze.

'Yes. The big one is a passenger too.'

'They don't look madly happy.'

'They weren't madly happy coming up here, either.'

'Owners of chronic losers?'

'No – well, I don't think so. They came up because of that horse Rudiments which Kenny Bayst rode for Annie Villars, but they aren't down in the racecard as its owners.'

She flicked back through her card. 'Rudiments. Duke

of Wessex. Well, neither of those two is him, poor old booby.'

'Who, the Duke?'

'Yes,' she said, 'Actually I suppose he isn't all that old, but he's dreadfully dim. Big important looking man with a big important looking rank, and as sweet as they come, really, but there's nothing but cotton wool upstairs.'

'You know him well?'

'I've met him often.'

'Subtle difference.'

'Yes.'

The two men scraped back their chairs and began to make their way out of the bar. The man in the plaster cast caught sight of them and his big smile grew even bigger.

'Say, if it isn't Eric Goldenberg, of all people. Come over here, me old sport, come and have a drink.'

Goldenberg looked less than enthusiastic at the invitation and the Major sidled away quickly to avoid being included, giving the Australian a glance full of the dislike of the military for the flamboyant.

The man in the cast put one arm clumsily round Goldenberg's shoulder, the crutch swinging out widely and knocking against Nancy.

'Say,' he said. 'Sorry, lady. I haven't got the hang of these things yet.'

'That's all right,' she said, and Goldenberg said something to him that I couldn't hear, and before we knew where we were we had been encompassed into the Australian's circle and he was busy ordering drinks all round.

Close to, he was a strange-looking man because his face and hair were almost colourless. The skin was whitish, the scalp, half bald, was fringed by silky hair that had been fair and was turning white, the eyelashes and eyebrows made no contrast, and the lips of the smiling mouth were creamy pale. He looked like a man made up to take the part of a large cheerful ghost. His name, it appeared, was Acey Jones.

'Aw, come on,' he said to me in disgust. 'Coke is for milksops, not men.' Even his eyes were pale: a light indeterminate bluey grey.

'Just lay off him, Ace,' Goldenberg said. 'He's flying me home. A drunken pilot I can do without.'

'A pilot, eh?' The big voice broadcast the information to about fifty people who weren't in the least interested. 'One of the fly boys? Most pilots I know are a bunch of proper tearaways. Live hard, love hard, drink hard. Real characters, those guys.' He said it with an expansive smile which hid the implied slight. 'C'mon now, sport, live dangerously. Don't disillusion all these people.'

'Beer, then, please,' I said.

Nancy was equally scornful, but for opposite reasons. 'Why did you climb down?'

'Antagonizing people when you don't have to is like

casting your garbage on the waters. One day it may come floating back, smelling worse.'

She laughed. 'Chanter would say that was immoral. Stands must be made on principles.'

'I won't drink more than half of the beer. Will that do?'

'You're impossible.'

Acey Jones handed me the glass and watched me take a mouthful and went on a bit about hell-raising and beating up the skies and generally living the life of a high-powered gypsy. He made it sound very attractive and his audience smiled and nodded their heads and none of them seemed to know that the picture was fifty years out of date, and that the best thing a pilot can be is careful: sober, meticulous, receptive, and careful. There are old pilots and foolish pilots, but no old foolish pilots. Me, I was old, young, wise, foolish, thirty-four. Also depressed, divorced and broke.

After aviation, Acey Jones switched back to insurance and told Goldenberg and Nancy and me and the fifty other people about getting a thousand pounds for breaking his ankle, and we had to listen to it all again, reacting with the best we could do in surprised appreciation.

'No, look, no kidding, sport,' he said to Goldenberg with his first sign of seriousness. 'You want to get yourself signed up with this outfit. Best fiver I've ever spent . . .'

Several of the fifty onlookers edged nearer to listen,

and Nancy and I filtered towards the outside of the group. I put down the tasted beer on an inconspicuous table out in the hall while Nancy dispatched the bottom half of her Coke, and from there we drifted out into the air.

The sun was still shining, but the small round white clouds were expanding into bigger round clouds with dark-grey centres. I looked at my watch. Four-twenty. Still nearly an hour until the time the Major wanted to leave. The longer we stayed the bumpier the ride was likely to be, because the afternoon forecast for scattered thunderstorms looked accurate.

'Cu-nims forming,' Nancy said, watching them. 'Nasty.'

We went and watched her brother get up on his mount for the last race and then we went up on the Owners and Trainers and watched him win it, and that was about that. She said goodbye to me near the bottom of the steps, outside the weighing room.

'Thanks for the escort duty . . .'

'Enjoyed it . . .'

She had smooth gilded skin and greyish-brown eyes. Straight dark eyebrows. Not much lipstick. No scent. Very much the opposite of my blonde, painted, and departed wife.

'I expect,' she said, 'that we'll meet again, because I sometimes fly with Colin, if there's a spare seat.'

'Do you ever take him yourself?'

'Good Lord no.' She laughed. 'He wouldn't trust me

to get him there on time. And anyway, there are too many days when the weather is beyond what I can do. Maybe one day, though . . .'

She held out her hand and I shook it. A grip very like her brother's, and just as brief.

'See you, then,' she said.

'I hope so.'

She nodded with a faint smile and went away. I watched her neat blue and white back view and stifled a sudden unexpected inclination to run after her and give her a Chanter type farewell.

When I walked across the track towards the aeroplane I met Kenny Bayst coming back from it with his raincoat over his arm. His skin was blotched pink again with fury, clashing with his carroty hair.

'I'm not coming back with you,' he said tightly. 'You tell Miss Annie effing Villars that I'm not coming back with you. There's no bloody pleasing her. Last time I nearly got the push for winning and this time I nearly got the push for not winning. You'd think that both times I'd had the slightest choice in the matter. I'll tell you straight, sport, I'm not coming back in your bloody little aeroplane having them gripe gripe gripe at me all the way back.'

'All right,' I said. I didn't blame him.

'I've just been over to fetch my raincoat. I'll go home by train . . . or get a lift.'

'Raincoat . . . but the aircraft is locked.'

'No it isn't. I just got my raincoat out of the back. Now you tell them I've had enough, right?' I nodded, and while he hurried off I walked on towards the aeroplane puzzled and a bit annoyed. Major Tyderman had said he had locked up again after he had fetched his *Sporting Life*, but apparently he hadn't.

He hadn't. Both the doors on the port side were unlocked, the passenger door and the baggage locker. I wasn't too pleased because Derrydowns had told me explicitly never to leave the aircraft open as they'd had damage done by small boys on several occasions: but all looked well and there were no signs of sticky fingers.

I did all the external checks again and glanced over the flight plan for the return. If we had to avoid too many thunderclouds it might take a little longer to reach Newmarket, but unless there was one settled and active over the landing field there should be no problem.

The passengers of the two Polyplane aircraft assembled by ones and twos, shovelled themselves inside, shut the doors, and were trundled down to the far end of the course. One after the other the two aeroplanes raced back over the grass and lifted away, wheeling like black darts against the blue, grey and white patchwork of the sky.

Annie Villars came first of my lot. Alone, composed, polite; giving nothing away. She handed me her coat and binoculars and I stored them for her. She thanked

363

me. The deceptive mild brown eyes held a certain blankness and every few seconds a spasmodic tightening belied the gentle set of her mouth. A formidable lady, I thought. What was more, she herself knew it. She was so conscious of the strength and range of her power that she deliberately manufactured the disarming exterior in order not exactly to hide it, but to make it palatable. Made a nice change, I thought ironically, from all those who put up a big tough front to disguise their inner lack.

'Kenny Bayst asked me to tell you that he has got a lift home to Newmarket and won't be coming back by air,' I said.

A tiny flash of fire in the brown eyes. The gentle voice, completely controlled, said 'I'm not surprised.' She climbed into the aeroplane and strapped herself into her seat and sat there in silence, looking out over the emptying racecourse with eyes that weren't concentrating on the grass and the trees.

Tyderman and Goldenberg returned together, still deep in discussion. The Major's side mostly consisted of decisive nods, but it was pouring out of Goldenberg. Also he was past worrying about what I overheard.

'I would be surprised if the little shit hasn't been double crossing us all the time and collecting from some bookmaker or other even more than he got from us. Making fools of us, that's what he's been doing. I'll murder the little sod. I told him so, too.'

'What did he say?' the Major asked.

'Said I wouldn't get the chance. Cocky little bastard.'

They thrust their gear angrily into the baggage compartment and stood talking by the rear door in voices rumbling like the distant thunder.

Colin Ross came last, slight and inconspicuous, still wearing the faded jeans and the now crumpled sweat shirt.

I went a few steps to meet him. 'Your sister Nancy asked me to check with you whether you had remembered to bring the present for Midge.'

'Oh damn . . .' More than irritation in his voice there was weariness. He had ridden six hard races, won three of them. He looked as if a toddler could knock him down.

'I'll get it for you, if you like.'

'Would you?' He hesitated, then with a tired flap of his wrist said, 'Well, I'd be grateful. Go into the weighing room and ask for my valet, Ginger Mundy. The parcel's on the shelf over my peg. He'll get it for you.'

I nodded and went back across the track. The parcel, easily found, proved to be a little smaller than a shoe box and was wrapped in pink and gold paper with a pink bow. I took it over to the aeroplane and Colin put it on Kenny Bayst's empty seat.

The Major had already strapped himself in and was drumming with his fingers on his binocular case, which was as usual slung around him. His body was still stiff with tension. I wondered if he ever relaxed.

Goldenberg waited without a smile while I clam-

bered across into my seat, and followed me in and clipped shut the door in gloomy silence. I sighed, started
the engine, and taxied down to the far end of the course.
Ready for take-off I turned round to my passengers and
tried a bright smile.

'All set?'

I got three grudging nods for my pains. Colin Ross
was asleep. I took the hilarious party off the ground
without enthusiasm, skirted the Manchester zone, and
pointed the nose in the general direction of Newmarket.
Once up in the sky it was all too clear that the air had
become highly unstable. At lower levels, rising pockets
of heat from the built-up areas bumped the aeroplane
about like a puppet, and to enormous heights great
heaps of cumulo-nimbus cloud were boiling up all
round the horizon.

Airsick-making weather. I looked round to see if
an issue of waterproof bags was going to be required.
Needn't have bothered. Colin was still asleep and the
other three had too much on their minds to worry about
a few lurches. I told Annie Villars where the bags were
to be found if wanted, and she seemed to think I had
insulted her.

Although by four thousand feet the worst of the
bumps were below us, the flight was a bit like a bending
race as I tracked left and right to avoid the dark tower-
ing cloud masses. Mostly we stayed in the sunshine:
occasionally raced through the small veiling clouds
which were dotted among the big ones. I wanted to

avoid even the medium-sized harmless ones, as these sometimes hid a dangerous whopper just behind, and at a hundred and fifty miles an hour there was little chance to dodge. Inside every well grown cumulo-nimbus there were vertical rushing air currents which could lift and drop even an airliner like a yoyo. Also one could meet hailstones and freezing rain. Nobody's idea of a jolly playground. So it was a good idea to avoid the black churning brutes, but it was a rougher ride than one should aim for with passengers.

Everyone knows the horrible skin-prickling heart-thudding feeling when the normal suddenly goes wrong. Fear, it's called. The best place to feel it is not with a jerk at four thousand feet in a battlefield of cu-nims.

I was used to far worse weather; to bad, beastly, even lethal weather. It wasn't the state of the sky which distracted me, which set the fierce little adrenalin-packed alarm bell ringing like crazy.

There was something wrong with the aeroplane.

Nothing much. I couldn't even tell what it was. But something. Something . . .

My instinct for safety was highly developed. Over-developed, many had said, when it had got me into trouble. Bloody coward, was how they'd put it.

You couldn't ignore it, though. When the instinct switched to danger you couldn't risk ignoring it, not with passengers on board. What you could do when you were alone was a different matter, but civil commercial pilots seldom got a chance to fly alone.

Nothing wrong with the instruments. Nothing wrong with the engine.

Something wrong with the flying controls.

When I swerved gently to avoid yet another lurking cu-nim the nose of the aircraft dropped and I had a shade of difficulty pulling it up again. Once level nothing seemed wrong. All the gauges seemed right. Only the instinct remained. Instinct and the memory of a slightly sluggish response.

The next time I made a turn, the same thing happened. The nose wanted to drop, and it needed more pressure than it should have done to hold it level. At the third turn, it was worse.

I looked down at the map on my knees. We were twenty minutes out of Haydock ... south of Matlock ... approaching Nottingham. Another eighty nautical miles to Newmarket.

It was the hinged part of the tailplane which raised or lowered the aircraft's nose. The elevators, they were called. They were linked by wires to the control column in such a way that when you pushed the control column forward the tail went up and tipped the nose down. And vice versa.

The wires ran through rings and over pulleys, between the cabin floor and the outer skin of the fuselage. There wasn't supposed to be any friction.

Friction was what I could feel.

I thought perhaps one of the wires had somehow come off one of the pulleys during the bumpy ride. I'd never heard of it happening before, but that didn't mean it couldn't. Or perhaps a whole pulley had come adrift, or had broken in half . . . If something was rolling around loose it could affect the controls fairly seriously.

I turned to the cheerful company.

'I'm very sorry, but there will be a short delay on the journey. We're going to land for a while at the East Midlands Airport, near Nottingham, while I get a quick precautionary check done to the aircraft.'

I met opposition.

Goldenberg said belligerently, 'I can't see anything wrong.' His eyes swept over the gauges, noticing all the needles pointing to the green safety segments on all the engine instruments. 'It all looks the same as it always does.'

'Are you sure it's necessary?' Annie Villars said. 'I particularly want to get back to see my horses at evening stables.'

The Major said 'Damn it all!' fiercely and frowned heavily and looked more tense than ever.

They woke up Colin Ross.

'The pilot wants to land here and make what he calls a precautionary check. We want to go straight on. We don't want to waste time. There isn't anything wrong with the plane, as far as we can see . . .'

Colin Ross' voice came across, clear and decisive. 'If he says we're going down, we're going down. He's the boss.'

I looked round at them. Except for Colin they were

all more moody and gloomy than ever. Colin unexpectedly gave me a flicker of a wink. I grinned as much to myself as to him, called up East Midlands on the radio, announced our intention to land, and asked them to arrange for a mechanic to be available for a check.

On the way down I regretted it. The friction seemed no worse: if anything it was better. Even in the turbulent air near the ground I had no great trouble in moving the elevators. I'd made a fool of myself and the passengers would be furious and Derrydowns would be scathing about the unnecessary expense, and at any time at all I would be looking for my seventh job.

It was a normal landing. I parked where directed on the apron and suggested everyone got out and went into the airport for a drink, as the check would take half an hour, and maybe more.

They were by then increasingly annoyed. Up in the air they must have had a lingering doubt that I was right about landing. Safe on the ground, they were becoming sure it was unnecessary.

I walked some of the way across the tarmac with them towards the airport passengers' doors, then peeled off to go to the control office for the routine report after landing, and to ask for the mechanic to come for a look-see as soon as possible. I would fetch them from the bar, I said, once the check was done.

'Hurry it up,' Goldenberg said rudely.

'Most annoying. Most annoying indeed.' The Major.

'I was away last night . . . particularly wanted to get

back this evening. Might as well go by road, no point in paying for speed if you don't get it . . .' Annie Villars' irritation overcoming the velvet glove.

Colin Ross said, 'If your horse coughs, don't race it.'

The others looked at him sharply. I said, 'Thanks' gratefully, and bore off at a tangent to the left. I saw them out of the side of my vision, looking briefly back towards the aircraft and then walking unenthusiastically towards the big glass doors.

There was a crack behind me like a snapping branch, and a monstrous boom, and a roaring gust of air.

I'd heard that sequence before. I spun round, appalled.

Where there had stood a smart little blue and white Cherokee there was an exploding ball of fire.

CHAPTER FOUR

The bomb had taken a fraction of a second to detonate. The public impact lasted three days. The investigations dragged on for weeks.

Predictably, the dailies went to town on 'Colin Ross Escapes Death by One Minute' and 'Champion Jockey wins Race against Time'. Annie Villars, looking particularly sweet and frail, said in a television news interview that we had all been fantastically lucky. Major Tyderman was quoted as saying, 'Fortunately there was something wrong with the plane, and we landed for a check. Otherwise . . .' And Colin Ross had apparently finished his sentence for him; 'Otherwise we would all have been raining down on Nottingham in little bits.'

That was after they had recovered, of course. When I reached them at a run near the airport doors their eyes were stretched wide and their faces were stiff with shock. Annie Villars' mouth had dropped open and she was shaking from head to foot. I put my hand on her arm. She looked at me blankly and then made a small mewing sound and crumpled against me in a thoroughly un-

Napoleonic faint. I caught her on the way down and lifted her up in my arms to save her falling on the shower-soaked tarmac. She weighed even less than she looked.

'God,' said Goldenberg automatically. 'God.' His mind and tongue seemed to be stuck on the single word.

The Major's mouth was trembling and he was losing the battle to keep it still with his teeth. Sweat stood out in fine drops on his forehead and he was breathing in short shocked gasps.

Holding Annie Villars I stood beside them and watched the death throes of the aeroplane. The first explosion had blown it apart and almost immediately the fuel tanks had ignited and finished the job. The wreckage lay strewn in burning twisted pieces over a radius of wet tarmac, the parts looking too small ever to have formed the whole. Rivers of burning petrol ran among them, and great curling orange and yellow flames roared round the largest piece, which looked like the front part of the cabin.

My seat. My hot, hot seat.

Trouble followed me around like the rats of Hamelin.

Colin Ross looked as shocked as the others but his nerves were of sterner stuff. 'Was that . . . a bomb?'

'Nothing but,' I said flippantly.

He looked at me sharply. 'It's not funny.'

'It's not tragic, either,' I said. 'We're still here.'

A lot of the stiffness left his face and body. The beginnings of a smile appeared. 'So we are,' he said.

Someone in the control tower had pressed the panic

button. Fire engines screamed up and foam poured out
of the giant hoses on to the pathetic scraps. The equipment was designed to deal with jumbos. It took about
ten seconds to reduce the Cherokee sized flames to
black memories.

Three or four airport cars buzzed around like gnats and
one filled with agitated officials dashed in our direction.

'Are you the people who came in that aircraft?'

The first of the questions. By no means the last. I
knew what I was in for. I had been taken apart before.

'Which is the pilot? Will you come with us, then, and
your passengers can go to the manager's office . . . Is the
lady injured?'

'Fainted,' I said.

'Oh . . .' he hesitated. 'Can someone else take her?'
He looked at the others. Goldenberg, large and flabby;
the Major, elderly; Colin, frail. His eyes passed over
Colin and then went back, widening, the incredulity
fighting against recognition.

'Excuse me . . . are you? . . .'

'Ross,' said Colin flatly. 'Yes.'

They rolled out the red carpet, after that. They produced smelling salts and a ground hostess for Annie
Villars, stiff brandies for the Major and Goldenberg,
autograph books for Colin Ross. The manager himself
took charge of them. And someone excitedly rang up
the national press.

*

The Board of Trade investigators were friendly and polite. As usual. And persistent, scrupulous, and ruthless. As usual.

'Why did you land at East Midlands?'

Friction.

'Had you any idea there was a bomb on board?'

No.

'Had you made a thorough pre-flight investigation?'

Yes.

'And no bomb?'

No.

Did I know that I was nevertheless responsible for the safety of the aircraft and could technically be held responsible for having initiated a flight with a bomb on board?

Yes.

We looked at each other. It was an odd rule. Very few people who took off with a bomb on board lived to be held responsible. The Board of Trade smiled, to show they knew it was silly to think anyone would take off with a bomb, knowing it was there.

'Did you lock the aircraft whenever you left it?'

I did.

'And did it remain locked?'

The knife was in. I told them about the Major. They already knew.

'He says he is sure that he relocked the doors,' they said. 'But even so wasn't it your responsibility to look after the safety of the aircraft, not his?'

Quite so.

'Wouldn't it have been prudent of you to accompany him to fetch the paper?'

No comment.

'The safety of the aircraft is the responsibility of the captain.'

Whichever way you turned, it came back to that.

This was my second interview with the Board of Trade. The first, the day after the explosion, had been friendly and sympathetic, a fact-finding mission during which the word responsibility had not cropped up once. It had hovered delicately in the wings. Inevitably it would be brought on later and pinned to someone's chest.

'During the past three days we have interviewed all your passengers, and none of them has any idea who would have wanted to kill them, or why. We now feel we must go more carefully into the matter of opportunity, so we do hope you don't mind answering what may be a lot of questions. Then we can piece together a statement for you, and we would be glad if you would sign it . . .'

'Do all I can,' I said. Dig my own grave. Again.

'They all agreed that the bomb must have been in the gift wrapped parcel which you yourself carried on board.'

Nice.

'And that the intended victim was Colin Ross.'

I sucked my teeth.

'You don't think so?'

'I honestly have no idea who it was intended for,' I said. 'But I don't think the bomb was in the parcel.'

'Why not?'

'His sister bought it, that morning.'

'We know.' He was a tall man, with inward looking eyes as if they were consulting a computer in his head, feeding in every answer he was given and waiting for the circuits to click out a conclusion. There was no aggression anywhere in his manner, no vengeance in his motivation. A fact-finder, a cause-seeker: like a truffle hound. He knew the scent of truth. Nothing would entice him away.

'And it sat on a shelf in the changing room all afternoon,' I said. 'And no one is allowed into the changing room except jockeys and valets.'

'We understand that that is so,' He smiled. 'Could the parcel have been the bomb? Weightwise?'

'I suppose so.'

'Miss Nancy Ross says it contained a large fancy bottle of bath oil.'

'No pieces in the wreckage?' I asked.

'Not a thing.' The tall man's nose wrinkled. 'I've seldom seen a more thorough disintegration.'

We were sitting in what was called the crew room in the Derrydowns office on the old RAF airfield near Buckingham. Such money as Derrydowns spent on appearances began in the manager's office and ended in the passengers' waiting lounge across the hall. The crew room looked as if the paint and the walls were coming up to their silver wedding. The linoleum had long passed the age of consent. Three of the four cheap armchairs looked as if they had still to reach puberty but the springs in the fourth were so badly broken that it was more comfortable to sit on the floor.

Much of the wall space was taken up by maps and weather charts and various Notices to Airmen, several of them out of date. There was a duty roster upon which my name appeared with the utmost regularity and a notice typed in red capitals to the effect that anyone who failed to take the aircraft's documents with him on a charter flight would get the sack. I had duly taken all the Cherokee's records and maintenance certificates with me, as the Air Navigation Order insisted. Now they were burned to a crisp. I hoped someone somewhere saw some sense in it.

The tall man looked carefully round the dingy room. The other, shorter, broader, silent, sat with his green bitten HB poised over his spiral bound notebook.

'Mr Shore, I understand you hold an Airline Transport Pilot's Licence. And a Flight Navigator's certificate.'

He had been looking me up. I knew he would have.

I said flatly, 'Yes.'

'This taxi work is hardly ... well ... what you were intended for.'

I shrugged.

'The highest possible qualifications ...' He shook his head. 'You were trained by BOAC and flew for them for nine years. First Officer. In line for Captain. And then you left.'

'Yes.' And they never took you back. Policy decision. Never.

He delicately consulted his notes. 'And then you flew as Captain for a private British airline until it went into liquidation? And after that for a South American airline, who, I believe, dismissed you. And then all last year a spot of gun running, and this spring some crop spraying. And now this.'

They never let go. I wondered who had compiled the list.

'It wasn't guns. Food and medical supplies in, refugees and wounded out.'

He smiled faintly. 'To some remote African airstrip on dark nights? Being shot at?'

I looked at him.

He spread out his hands, 'Yes, I know. All legal and respectable, and not our business, of course.' He cleared his throat . . . 'Weren't you the . . . er . . . the subject . . . of an investigation about four years ago? While you were flying for British Interport?'

I took in a slow breath. 'Yes.'

'Mm.' He looked up, down, and sideways. 'I've read an outline of that case. They didn't suspend your licence.'

'No.'

'Though on the face of it one might have expected them to.'

I didn't answer.

'Did Interport pay the fine for you?'

'No.'

'But they kept you on as Captain. You were convicted of gross negligence, but they kept you on.' It was halfway between a statement and a question.

'That's right,' I said.

If he wanted all the details, he could read the full report. He knew it and I knew it. He wasn't going to get me to tell him.

He said, 'Yes ... well. Who put this bomb in the Cherokee? When and how?'

'I wish I knew.'

His manner hadn't changed. His voice was still friendly. We both ignored his tentative shot at piling on the pressure.

'You stopped at White Waltham and Newbury ...'

'I didn't lock up at White Waltham. I parked on the grass outside the reception lounge. I could see the aeroplane most of the time, and it was only on the ground for half an hour. I got there early ... I can't see that anyone had a chance, or could rely on having a chance, to put a bomb on board at White Waltham.'

'Newbury?'

'They all stayed in their seats except me. Colin Ross came ... We put his overnight bag in the front baggage locker ...'

The tall man shook his head. 'The explosion was further back. Behind the captain's seat, at the very least.

The blast evidence makes it certain. Some of the metal parts of the captain's seat were embedded in the instrument panel.'

'One minute,' I said reflectively. 'Very nasty.'

'Yes . . . Who had an opportunity at Haydock?'

I sighed inwardly. 'I suppose anyone, from the time I gave the keys to Major Tyderman until I went back to the aircraft.'

'How long was that?'

I'd worked it out. 'Getting on for three hours. But . . .'

'But what?'

'No one could have counted on the aircraft being left unlocked.'

'Trying to wriggle out?'

'Do you think so?'

He dodged an answer: said: 'I'll give it to you that no one could have known whether it would be locked or unlocked. You just made it easy.'

'All right,' I said. 'If you'll also bear in mind that pickers and stealers unlock cars every day of the week, and that aircraft keys are the same type. Anyone who could manufacture and plant a bomb could open a little old lock.'

'Possibly,' he said, and repeated, 'But you made it easy.'

Damn Major Tyderman, I thought bleakly. Stupid, careless old fool. I stifled the thought that I probably would have gone across with him, or insisted on fetching his newspaper for him, if I hadn't been unwilling to walk away and leave Nancy.

'Who could have had access . . . leaving the matter of locks?'

I shrugged one shoulder. 'All the world. They had only to walk across the track.'

'The aircraft was parked opposite the stands, I believe, in full view of the crowds.'

'Yes. About a hundred yards, in fact, from the stands. Not close enough for anyone to see exactly what some-one was doing, if he seemed to be walking round peering in through the windows. People do that, you know, pretty often.'

'You didn't notice anyone, yourself?'

I shook my head. 'I looked across several times during the afternoon. Just a casual glance, though. I wasn't thinking about trouble.'

'Hm.' He reflected for a few seconds. Then he said, 'Two of the Polyplanes were there as well, I believe.'

'Yes.'

'I think I'd better talk to the pilots, to see if they noticed anything.'

I didn't comment. His eyes suddenly focused on mine, sharp and black.

'Were they friendly?'

'The pilots? Not particularly.'

'How's the feud?'

'What feud?'

He stared at me assessingly. 'You're not that dumb.

No one could work for Derrydown and not know that they and Polyplanes are permanently engaged in scratching each others' eyes out.'

I sighed. 'I don't give a damn.'

'You will, when they start reporting you.'

'Reporting me? For what? What do you mean?'

He smiled thinly. 'If you infringe the rules by as much as one foot, Polyplanes will be on to us before your wheels have stopped rolling. They're doing their best to put Derrydowns out of business. Most of it we shrug off as simply spite. But if they catch you breaking the regulations, and can produce witnesses, we'd have to take action.'

'Charming.'

He nodded. 'Aviation will never need a special police force to detect crime. Everyone is so busy informing on everyone else. Makes us laugh, sometimes.'

'Or cry,' I said.

'That too.' He nodded wryly. 'There are no permanent friendships in aviation. The people you think are your friends are the first to deny they associate with you at the faintest hint of trouble. The cock crows until it's hoarse, in aviation.' The bitterness in his voice was unmistakable. But impersonal, also.

'You don't approve.'

'No. It makes our job easier, of course. But I like less and less the sight of people scrambling to save themselves at any cost to others. It diminishes them. They are small.'

'You can't always blame them for not always wanting to be involved. Aviation law cases are so fierce, so unforgiving . . .'

'Did your friends at Interport rally round and cheer you up?'

I thought back to those weeks of loneliness. 'They waited to see.'

He nodded. 'Didn't want to be contaminated.'

'It's a long time ago,' I said.

'You never forget rejection,' he said. 'It's a trauma.'

'Interport didn't reject me. They kept me on for another year, until they went bust. And,' I added, 'I didn't have anything to do with *that*.'

He gently laughed. 'Oh I know. My masters in that Government put on one of its great big squeezes and by one means or another forced them out of business.'

I didn't pursue it. The history of aviation was littered with the bodies of murdered air firms. Insolvency sat like a vulture in every boardroom in the industry and constantly pecked away at the bodies before they were dead. British Eagle, Handley Page, Beagle, the list of corpses was endless. Interport had been one of the largest, and Derrydowns, still struggling, one of the smallest, but their problems were identical. Huge inexorable costs. Fickle variable income. Write the sum in red.

I said, 'There is one other place, of course, where the bomb could have been put on board.' I stopped.

'Spell it out, then.'

'Here.'

The tall investigator and his silent friend with the pencil went down to the hangar to interview old Joe.

Harley called me into his office.

'Have they finished?'

'They've gone to ask Joe if he put the bomb in the Cherokee.'

Harley was irritated, which was with him a common state of mind. 'Ridiculous.'

'Or if Larry did.'

'*Larry . . .* '

'He left for Turkey that afternoon,' I pointed out. 'Would he have planted a legacy?'

'No.' Short, snappy and vehement.

'Why did he leave?'

'He wanted to.' He gave me a sharp glance bordering on dislike. 'You sound like the Board of Trade.'

'Sorry,' I said in conciliation. 'Must be catching.'

Harley's office dated back to a more prosperous past. There was a carpet of sorts on the floor and the walls had been painted within living memory, and his good-quality desk had mellowed instead of chipping. Limp blue curtains framed the big window looking out over the airfield and several good photographs of aeroplanes had been framed and hung. Customers, when they visited him, were allowed the nearly new lightweight armchair. Crew sat on the wooden upright.

Harley himself was proprietor, manager, chief flying instructor, booking clerk and window cleaner. His staff consisted of one qualified mechanic past retiring age, one part-time boy helper, one full-time taxi pilot (me) and one part-time pilot who switched from taxiing to teaching, whichever was required, and on alternate days taught in a flying club twenty miles to the north.

Derrydown's other assets had been, before the Cherokee blew up, three useful aircraft and one bright girl.

The remaining two aircraft were a small single engined trainer, and a twin-engined eight-year-old Aztec equipped with every possible flying aid, for which Harley was paying through the nose on a five year lease.

The girl, Honey, his brother's daughter, worked for love and peanuts and was the keystone which held up the arch. I knew her voice better than her face, as she sat up in the control tower all day directing such air traffic as came along. Between times she typed all the letters, kept the records, did the accounts, answered the telephone if her uncle didn't and collected landing fees from visiting pilots. She was reputed to be suffering from a broken heart about Larry and consequently came down from her crow's nest as seldom as possible.

'She's made puff balls out of her eyes, crying for that louse,' was how my part-time colleague put it. 'But you

wait just a week or two. She'll lie down for you instead. Never refused a good pilot yet, our Honey hasn't.'

'How about you?' I asked, amused.

'Me? She'd squeezed me like a lemon long before that goddamned Larry ever turned up.'

Harley said crossly, 'We've lost two charters since the bomb. They say the Aztec's too expensive, they would rather go by road.' He ran his hand over his head. 'There's another Cherokee Six up at Liverpool that's available to lease. I've just been talking to them on the phone. It sounds all right. They're bringing it across here tomorrow afternoon, so you can take it up when you get back from Newmarket and see what you think.'

'How about the insurance on the old one?' I asked idly. 'It would be cheaper in the long run to buy rather than lease.'

'It was on hire purchase,' he said gloomily. 'We'll be lucky if we get a penny. And it's not really your business.'

Harley was slightly plump and slightly bald and just not quite forceful enough to lift Derrydowns up by its bootstraps. His manner to me was more bossy than friendly, a reaction I understood well enough.

'The last person on earth to put a bomb on any aircraft would be Joe,' he said explosively. 'He looks after them like a mother. He *polishes* them.'

It was true. The Derrydowns aircraft sparkled outside and were shampooed inside. The engines ran like silk. The general, slightly misleading, air of prosperity which clung around the public face of the firm was mostly Joe's work.

The Board of Trade came back from the hangar looking vaguely sheepish. The rough side of Joe's tongue, I guessed. At sixty-nine and with savings in the bank, he was apt to lay down his own laws. He had taken exception to my theory that a pulley on the elevator wires had come adrift. No such thing was possible in one of his aircraft, he had told me stiffly, and I could take my four gold rings away and I knew what I could do with them. As I hadn't worn my captain's jacket for nearly two years I told him the moths had beaten me to it, and although it was a feeble joke he gave me a less sour look and told me that it couldn't have been a broken pulley, he was sure it couldn't, and if it was, it was the manufacturer's fault, not his.

'It saved Colin Ross' life,' I pointed out. 'You should claim a medal for it.' Which opened his mouth and shut him up.

The Board of Trade trooped into Harley's office. The tall man sat in the armchair and Green Pencil on the hard one. Harley behind his desk. I leant against the wall, on my feet.

'Well now,' said the tall man. 'It seems as if everyone on this airfield had a chance to tamper with the Cherokee. Everyone in the company, and any customers who happened to be here that morning, and any member of the public wandering around for a look-see. We've assumed the bomb was aimed at Colin Ross, but we don't really know that. If it was, someone had a pretty accurate idea of when he would be in the aircraft.'

'Last race four-thirty. He was riding in it,' Harley said. 'Doesn't take too much figuring to assume that at five-forty he'd be in the air.'

'Five forty-seven,' said the tall man. 'Actually.'

'Any time about then,' said Harley irritably.

'I wonder what the bomb was in,' said the tall man reflectively. 'Did you look inside the first-aid tin?'

'No,' I said, startled. 'I just checked that it was there. I've never looked inside it. Or inside the fire extinguishers, or under the seats or inside the life jacket covers . . .'

The tall man nodded. 'It could have been in any of those places. Or it could after all have been in that fancy parcel.'

'Ticking away,' said Harley.

I peeled myself slowly off the wall. 'Suppose,' I said hesitantly, 'suppose it wasn't in any of those places. Suppose it was deeper, out of sight. Somewhere between the cabin wall and the outer skin . . . like a limpet mine, for instance. Suppose that that bumpy ride . . . and all those turns I did to avoid the cu-nims . . . dislodged it, so that it was getting jammed in the elevator wires . . . Suppose that was what I could feel . . . and why I decided to land . . . and that what saved us . . . was the bomb itself.'

CHAPTER FIVE

The next day I took five jockeys and trainers from New-market to Newcastle races and back in the Aztec and listened to them grousing over the extra expense, and in the evening I tried out the replacement Cherokee, which flew permanently left wing down on the auto pilot, had an unserviceable fuel flow meter, and an over-load somewhere on the electrical circuit.

'It isn't very good,' I told Harley. 'It's old and noisy and it probably drinks fuel and I shouldn't think the battery's charging properly.'

He interrupted me. 'It flies. And it's cheap. And Joe will fix it. I'm taking it.'

'Also it's orange and white, just like the Polyplanes.'

He gave me an irritable glare. 'I'm not blind. I know it is. And it's not surprising, considering it used to belong to them.'

He waited for me to protest so that he could slap me down, so I didn't. I shrugged instead. If he wanted to admit to his bitterest rivals that his standards were down to one of their third hand clapped out old buggies, that was his business.

He signed the lease on the spot and gave it to the pilot who had brought the aeroplane to take back with him on the train, and the pilot smiled a pitying smile and went off shaking his head.

The orange and white Cherokee went down to the hangar for Joe to wave his wand over, and I walked round the perimeter track to home sweet home.

One caravan, pilots' for the use of. Larry had lived in it before me, and others before him: Harley's taxi pilots stayed, on average, eight months, and most of them settled for the caravan because it was easiest. It stood on a dusty square of concrete which had once been the floor of a RAF hut, and it was connected to the mains electricity, water and drainage which had served the long departed airmen.

As caravans go it must once have held up its head, but generations of beer drinking bachelors had left tiny teeth marks of bottle-caps along the edges of all the fitments, and circular greasy head marks on the wall above every seat. Airport dirt had clogged the brown haircord into a greyish cake, relieved here and there by darker irregular stains. Shabby pin-ups of superhuman mammalian development were stuck to the walls with Sellotape, and a scatter of torn-off patches of paint showed where dozens of others had been stuck before. Tired green curtains had opened and shut on a thousand hangovers. The fly-blown mirror had stared back at a lot of disillusion, and the bed springs sagged from the weight of a bored succession of pilots with nothing to do except Honey.

I had forgotten to get anything to eat. There was half a packet of cornflakes in the kitchen and a jar of instant coffee. Neither was much use, as yesterday's half pint of milk had gone sour in the heat. I damned it all and slouched on the two seat approximation to a sofa, and resignedly dragged out of my pocket the two letters which had lain unopened there since this morning.

One was from a television rental firm who said they confirmed that they were transferring the rental from Larry's name to mine, as requested, and could I now be so good as to pay immediately the six weeks for which he was in arrears. The other, from Susan, said briefly that I was late with the alimony yet again.

I put down both the letters and stared unseeingly through the opposite window towards the darkening summer sky. All the empty airfield stretched away into the dusk, calm, quiet, undemanding and shadowy, everything I needed for a few repairs to the spirit. The only trouble was, the process was taking longer than I'd expected. I wondered sometimes whether I'd ever get back to where I'd once been. Maybe if you'd hashed up your life as thoroughly as I had, there was never any going back. Maybe one day soon I'd stop wanting to. Maybe one day I would accept the unsatisfactory present not as a healing period but as all there ever was going to be. That would be a pity, I thought. A pity to let the void take over for always.

I had three pounds in my pocket and sixteen in the bank, but I had finally paid all my debts. The crippling fine, the divorce, and the mountainous bills Susan had run up everywhere in a cold orgy of hatred towards me in the last weeks we were together: everything had been settled. The house had always been in her name because of the nature of my job, and she had clung on to that like a leech. She was still living in it, triumphant, collecting a quarter of everything I earned and writing sharp little letters if I didn't pay on the nail.

I didn't understand how love could curdle so abysmally: looking back, I still couldn't understand. We had screamed at each other: hit each other, intending to hurt. Yet when we married at nineteen we'd been entwined in tenderness, inseparable and sunny. When it started to go wrong she said it was because I was away so much, long ten-day tours to the West Indies all the time, and all she had was her job as a doctor's secretary and the dull endless housework. In an uprush of affection and concern for her I resigned from BOAC and joined Interport instead, where I flew short-haul trips, and spent most of my nights at home. The pay was a shade less good, the prospects a lot less good, but for three months we were happier. After that there was a long period in which we both tried to make the best of it, and a last six months in which we had torn each other's nerves and emotions to shreds.

393

Since then I had tried more or less deliberately not to feel anything for anybody. Not to get involved. To be private, and apart, and cold. An ice-pack after the tempest.

I hadn't done anything to improve the caravan, to stamp anything of myself upon it. I didn't suppose I would, because I didn't feel the need. I didn't want to get involved, not even with a caravan.

And certainly not with Tyderman, Goldenberg, Annie Villars and Colin Ross.

All of them except Goldenberg were on my next racing trip.

I had spent two more days in the Aztec, chauffeuring some business executives on their regular monthly visit to subsidiary factories in Germany and Luxembourg, but by Saturday Joe had tarted up the replacement Cherokee so I set off in that. The fuel meter still resolutely pointed to nought, which was slightly optimistic, but the electrical fault had been cured: no overload now on the generator. And if it still flew one wing low, at least the wing in question sparkled with a new shine. The cabin smelt of soap and air freshener, and all the ash trays were empty.

The passengers were to be collected that day at Cambridge, and although I flew into the aerodrome half an hour early, the Major was already there, waiting on a seat in a corner of the entrance hall.

I saw him before he saw me, and as I walked towards him he took the binoculars out of their case and put them on the low table beside him. The binoculars were smaller than the case suggested. In went his hand again and out came a silver and pigskin flask. The Major took a six-second swig and with a visible sigh screwed the cap back into place.

I slowed down and let him get the binoculars back on top of his courage before I came to a halt beside him and said good morning.

'Oh . . . Good morning,' he said stiffly. He stood up, fastening the buckle of the case and giving it a pat as it swung into its usual facing forwards position on his stomach. 'All set?'

'The others are not here yet. It's still early.'

'Ah. No. Of course.' He wiped his moustache care-fully with his hand and tucked his chin back into his neck. 'No bombs today, I hope?'

He wasn't altogether meaning to joke.

'No bombs,' I assured him.

He nodded, not meeting my eyes. 'Very upsetting, last Friday. Very upsetting, you know.' He paused. 'Nearly didn't come, today, when I heard that Colin . . . er . . .' He stopped.

'I'll stay in the aeroplane all afternoon,' I promised him.

The Major nodded again, sharply. 'Had a Board of Trade fellow come to see me. Did you know that?'

'They told me so.'

'Been to see you too, I suppose.'

'Yes.'

'They get about a bit.'

'They're very thorough. They'll go a hundred miles to get a single answer to a simple question.'

He looked at me sharply. 'Speaking from bitter experience?'

I hadn't known there was any feeling in my voice. I said, 'I've been told they do.'

He grunted. 'Can't think why they don't leave it to the police.'

No such luck, I thought. There was no police force in the world as tenacious as the British Board of Trade.

Annie Villars and Colin Ross arrived together, deep in a persuasive argument that was getting nowhere.

'Just say you'll ride my horses whenever you can.'

'. . . too many commitments.'

'I'm not asking a great deal.'

'There are reasons, Annie. Sorry, but no.' He said it with an air of finality, and she looked startled and upset.

'Good morning,' she said to me abstractedly. 'Morning, Rupert.'

'Morning, Annie,' said the Major.

Colin Ross had achieved narrow pale-grey trousers and a blue open-necked shirt.

'Morning, Matt,' he said.

The Major took a step forward, bristling like a terrier. 'Did I hear you turning down Annie's proposition?'

'Yes, Major.'

'Why?' he asked in an aggrieved tone. 'Our money is as good as anyone else's, and her horses are always fit.'

'I'm sorry, Major, but no. Just let's leave it at that.'

The Major looked affronted and took Annie Villars off to see if the bar was open. Colin sighed and sprawled in a wooden armchair.

'God save me,' he said, 'from crooks.'

I sat down too. 'She doesn't seem crooked to me.'

'Who, Annie? She isn't really. Just not one hundred per cent permanently scrupulous. No, it's that crummy slob Goldenberg that I don't like. She does what he says, a lot too much. I'm not taking indirect riding orders from him.'

'Like Kenny Bayst?' I suggested.

He looked at me sideways. 'The word gets around, I see. Kenny reckons he's well out of it. Well I'm not stepping in.' He paused reflectively. 'The Board of Trade investigator who came to see me asked if I thought there was any significance in Bayst having cried off the return trip the other day.'

'What did you say?'

'I said I didn't. Did you?'

'I confess I wondered, because he did go across to the aeroplane after the races, and he certainly felt murderous, but . . .'

'But,' he agreed, 'would Kenny Bayst be cold blooded enough to kill you and me as well?' He shook his head. 'Not Kenny, I wouldn't have thought.'

'And besides that,' I nodded, 'he only came to the steaming boil after he lost the three-thirty, and just how would he rustle up a bomb at Haydock in a little over one hour?'

'He would have to have arranged it in advance.'

'That would mean that he knew he would lose the race . . .'

'It's been done,' said Colin dryly.

There was a pause. Then I said, 'Anyway, I think we had it with us all the time. Right from before I left base.'

He swivelled his head and considered it. 'In that case . . . Larry?'

'Would he?'

'God knows. Sneaky fellow. Pinched Nancy's hundred quid. But a bomb . . . and what was the point?'

I shook my head.

Colin said, 'Bombs are usually either political or someone's next of kin wanting to collect the insurance.'

'Fanatics or family . . .' I stifled the beginnings of a yawn.

'You don't really care, do you?' he said.

'Not that much.'

'It doesn't disturb you enough to wonder whether the bomb merchant will try again?'

'About as much as it's disturbing you.'

He grinned. 'Yes . . . well. It would be handy to know for sure whose name was on that one. One would look so damn silly taking fiddly precautions if it was the Major who finally got clobbered. Or you.'

'Me?' I said in astonishment.

'Why not?'

I shook my head. 'I don't stand in anyone's way to anything.'

'Someone may think you do.'

'Then they're nuts.'

'It takes a nut . . . a regular psycho . . . to put a bomb in an aeroplane . . .'

Tyderman and Annie Villars came back from the direction of the bar with two more people, a man and a woman.

'Oh Christ,' Colin said under his breath. 'Here comes my own personal Chanter.' He looked at me accusingly. 'You didn't tell me who the other passengers were.'

'I don't know them. Who are they? I don't do the bookings.'

We stood up. The woman, who was in her thirties but dressed like a teenager, made a straight line for Colin and kissed him exuberantly on the cheek.

'Colin, darling, there was a spare seat and Annie said I could come. Wasn't that absolutely super of her?'

Colin glared at Annie who pretended not to notice.

The girl-woman had a strong upper-class accent, white knee socks, a camel-coloured high-waisted dress, several jingling gold bracelets, streaky fair brown long hair, a knock-you-down exotic scent and an air of expecting everyone to curl up and die for her.

She latched her arm through Colin's so that he couldn't disentangle without giving offence, and said

with a somehow unattractive gaiety, 'Come along everyone, let's take the plunge. Isn't it all just too unnerving,
flying around with Colin these days.'

'You don't actually have to come,' Colin said without
quite disguising his wishes.

She seemed oblivious. 'Darling,' she said. 'Too rivet-
ing. Nothing would stop me.'

She moved off towards the door, followed by the
Major and Annie and the new man together, and finally
by me. The new man was large and had the same air as
the woman of expecting people to jump to it and
smooth his path. The Major and Annie Villars were
busy smoothing it, their ears bent deferentially to catch
any falling crumbs of wisdom, their heads nodding in
agreement over every opinion.

The two just-teenage girls I had stationed beside the
locked aircraft were still on duty, retained more by
the promise of Colin's autograph than by my money.
They got both, and were delighted. No one, they anxiously insisted, had even come close enough to ask what
they were doing. No one could possibly have put a piece
of chewing gum on to the aeroplane, let alone a bomb.

Colin, signing away, gave me a sidelong look of
amusement and appreciation and said safety came
cheap at the price. He was less amused to find that the
affectionate lady had stationed herself in one of the rear
seats and was beckoning him to come and sit beside her.

'Who is she?' I asked.

'Fenella Payne-Percival. Fenella pain in the neck.'

I laughed. 'And the man?'

'Duke of Wessex. Annie's got a horse running for him today.'

'Not Rudiments again?'

He looked up in surprise from the second autograph book.

'Yes. That's right. Bit soon, I would have thought.' He finished the book and gave it back. 'Kenny Bayst isn't riding it.' His voice was dry.

'You don't say.'

The passengers had sorted themselves out so that Annie and the Duke sat in the centre seats, with the Major waiting for me to get in before him into the first two. He nodded his stiff little nod as I stepped up on to the wing, and pushed at his moustache. Less tense, slightly less rigid, than last time. The owner was along instead of Goldenberg and Kenny wasn't there to stir things up. No coup today, I thought. No coup to go wrong.

The flight up was easy and uneventful, homing to the radio beacon on the coast at Ottringham and tracking away from it on a radial to Redcar. We landed without fuss on the racecourse and the passengers yawned and unbuckled themselves.

'I wish every racecourse had a landing strip,' Colin sighed. 'It makes the whole day so much easier. I hate all those dashes from airport to course by taxi.'

The racecourses which catered for aeroplanes were in a minority, which seemed a shame considering there was room enough on most, if anyone cared enough. Harley constantly raved in frustration at having to land ten or fifteen miles away and fix up transportation for the passengers. All the conveniently placed RAF air-fields with superb runways who either refused to let private aircraft land at all, or shut their doors firmly at 5 pm weekdays and all day on Saturdays had him on the verge of tears. As also did all the airfields whose owners said they wouldn't take the responsibility of having an aircraft land there or take off if they didn't have a fire engine standing by, even though Harley's own insurance didn't require it.

'The English are as air-minded as earth worms,' Harley said.

On the other hand Honey had tacked a list to the office wall which started in big red letters 'God Bless...' and continued with all the friendly and accommodating places like Kempton Park, which let you land up the five furlong straight (except during five furlong races) and RAF stations like Wroughton and Leeming and Old Sarum, who really tried for you, and the airfields who could let you land when they were officially shut, and all the privately owned strips whose owners generously agreed to you using them any time you liked.

Harley's view of Heaven was an open public landing field outside every town and a windsock and a flat four furlongs on every racecourse. It wasn't much to ask, he said plaintively. Not in view of the dozens of enormous airfields which had been built during World War Two and were now disused and wasted.

He could dream, I thought. There was never any money for such schemes, except in wars.

The passengers stretched themselves on to the grass. Fenella Payne-Percival made little up and down jumps of excitement like a small girl, the Major patted his binocular case reassuringly, Annie Villars efficiently picked up her own belongings and directed a look of melting feminine helplessness towards the Duke, Colin looked at his watch and smiled, and the Duke himself glanced interestedly around and said, 'Nice day, what?'

A big man, he had a fine looking head with thick greying hair, eyebrows beginning to sprout, and a strong square jaw, but there wasn't enough living stamped on his face for a man in his fifties, and I remembered what Nancy had said of him: sweet as they come, but nothing but cottonwool upstairs.

Colin said to me, 'Are you coming into the paddock?'

I shook my head. 'Better stay with the aeroplane, this time.'

The Duke said, 'Won't you need some lunch, my dear chap?'

'It's kind of you, sir, but I often don't have any.'

'Really?' He smiled. 'Must have my lunch.'

Annie Villars said, 'We'll leave soon after the last. About a quarter to five.'

'Right,' I agreed.

'Doesn't give us time for a drink, Annie,' complained the Duke.

She swallowed her irritation. 'Any time after that, then.'

'I'll be here,' I said.

'Oh do come on,' said Fenella impatiently. 'The pilot can look after himself, can't he? Let's get going, do. Come on, Colin darling.' She twined her arm in his again and he all but squirmed. They moved away towards the paddock obediently, with only Colin looking back. I laughed at the desperation on his face and he stuck out his tongue.

There were three other aircraft parked in a row. One private, one from a Scottish taxi firm, and one Polyplane. All the pilots seemed to have gone in to the races, but when I climbed out half way through the afternoon to stretch my legs, I found the Polyplane pilot standing ten yards away, staring at the Cherokee with narrowed eyes and smoking a cigarette.

He was one of the two who had been at Haydock. He seemed surprised that I was there.

'Hello,' I said equably. Always a sucker.

He gave me the old hard stare. 'Taking no chances today, I see.'

I ignored the sneer in his voice. 'That's right.'

'We got rid of that aircraft,' he said sarcastically nodding towards it, 'because we'd flown the guts out of it. It's only suitable now for minor operators like you.'

'It shows signs of the way you flew it,' I agreed

politely: and that deadly insult did nothing towards cooling the feud.

He compressed his lips and flicked the end of his cigarette away into the grass. A thin trickle of blue smoke arose from among the tangled green blades. I watched it without comment. He knew as well as I did that smoking near parked aircraft was incredibly foolish, and on all airfields, forbidden.

He said, 'I'm surprised you take the risk of flying Colin Ross. If your firm are proved to be responsible for his death you'll be out of business.'

'He's not dead yet.'

'If I were him I wouldn't risk flying any more with Derrydowns.'

'Did he, by any chance,' I asked, 'once fly with Poly-planes? Is all this sourness due to his having transferred to Derrydowns instead?'

He gave me a bitter stare. 'No,' he said.

I didn't believe him. He saw that I didn't. He turned on his heel and walked away.

Rudiments won the big race. The dim green colours streaked up the centre of the track at the last possible moment and pushed Colin on the favourite into second place. I could hear the boos all the way from the stands.

An hour until the end of racing. I yawned, leaned back in my seat, and went to sleep.

A young voice saying 'Excuse me,' several times,

woke me up. I opened my eyes. He was about ten, slightly shy, ultra well bred. Squatting down on the wing, he spoke through the open door.

'I say, I'm sorry to wake you, but my uncle wanted me to come over and fetch you. He said you hadn't had anything to eat all day. He thinks you ought to. And besides, he's had a winner and he wants you to drink his health.'

'Your uncle is remarkably kind,' I said, 'but I can't leave the aeroplane.'

'Well, actually, he thought of that. I've brought my father's chauffeur over with me, and he is going to sit here for you until you come back.' He smiled with genuine satisfaction at these arrangements.

I looked past him out of the door, and there, sure enough, was the chauffeur, all togged up in dark green with a shining peak to his cap.

'OK,' I said. 'I'll get my jacket.'

He walked with me along the paddock, through the gate, and across to the members' bar.

'Awfully nice chap, my uncle,' he said.

'Unusually thoughtful,' I agreed.

'Soft, my mother says,' he said dispassionately. 'He's her brother. They don't get along very well.'

'What a pity.'

'Oh, I don't know. If they were frightfully chummy she would always be wanting to come with me when I go to stay with him. As it is, I go on my own, and we have some fantastic times, him and me. That's how I know how super he is.' He paused. 'Lots of people think he's terribly thick, I don't know why.' There was a shade of anxiety in his young voice. 'He's really awfully kind.'

I reassured him. 'I only met him this morning, but I think he's very nice.'

His brow cleared. 'You do? Oh, good.'

The Duke was knee deep in cronies all armed with glasses of champagne. His nephew disappeared from my side, dived through the throng, and reappeared tugging at his uncle's arm.

'What?' The kind brown eyes looked round; saw me. 'Oh yes.' He bent down to talk, and presently the boy came back.

'Champagne or coffee?'

'Coffee, please.'

'I'll get it for you.'

'I'll get it,' I suggested.

'No. Let me. Do let me. Uncle gave me the money.' He marched off to the far end of the counter and ordered a cup of coffee and two rounds of smoked salmon sandwiches, and paid for them with a well crushed pound note.

'There,' he said triumphantly. 'How's that?'

'Fine,' I said. 'Terrific. Have a sandwich.'

'All right.'

We munched companionably.

'I say,' he said, 'look at that man over there, he looks like a ghost.'

I turned my head. Big blond man with very pale skin. Pair of clumsy crutches. Large plaster cast. Acey Jones.

Not so noisy today. Drinking beer very quietly in a far corner with a nondescript friend.

'He fell down some steps and broke his ankle and collected a thousand pounds from an insurance policy,' I said.

'Golly,' said the boy. 'Almost worth it.'

'He thinks so, too.'

'Uncle has something to do with insurance. Don't know what, though.'

'An underwriter?' I suggested.

'What's that?'

'Someone who invests money in insurance companies, in a special sort of way.'

'He talks about Lloyd's, sometimes. Is it something to do with Lloyd's?'

'That's right.'

He nodded and looked wistfully at the sandwiches.

'Have another,' I suggested.

'They're yours, really.'

'Go on. I'd like you to.'

He gave me a quick bright glance and bit into number two.

'My name's Matthew,' he said.

I laughed. 'So is mine.'

'Is it really? Do you really mean it?'

'Yes.'

'Wow.'

There was a step behind me and the deep Eton-sounding voice said, 'Is Matthew looking after you all right?'

'Great sir, thank you,' I said.

'His name is Matthew too,' said the boy.

The Duke looked from one of us to the other. 'A couple of Matts, eh? Don't let too many people wipe their feet on you.'

Matthew thought it a great joke but the touch of sadness in the voice was revealing. He was dimly aware that despite his ancestry and position, one or two sharper minds had wiped their feet on *him*.

I began to like the Duke.

'Well done with Rudiments, sir,' I said.

His face lit up. 'Splendid, wasn't it? Absolutely splendid. Nothing on earth gives me more pleasure than seeing my horses win.'

I went back to the Cherokee just before the last race and found the chauffeur safe and sound and reading *Doctor Zhivago*. He stretched, reported nothing doing, and ambled off.

All the same I checked the aircraft inch by inch inside and even unscrewed the panel to the aft baggage compartment so that I could see into the rear part of the fuselage, right back to the tail. Nothing there that shouldn't be. I screwed the panel on again.

Outside the aircraft, I started in the same way.

Started only: because when I was examining every
hinge in the tail plane I heard a shout from the next
aircraft.

I looked round curiously but without much haste.

Against that side of the Polyplane which faced away
from the stands, two large men were laying into Kenny
Bayst.

CHAPTER SIX

The pilot of the Polyplane was standing aside and watching. I reached him in six strides.

'For God's sake,' I said. 'Come and help him.'

He gave me a cold stolid stare. 'I've got my medical tomorrow. Do it yourself.'

In three more steps I caught one of the men by the fist as he lifted it high to smash into the crumpling Kenny, bent his arm savagely backwards and kicked him hard in the left hamstring. He fell over on his back with a shout of mixed anger, surprise, and pain, closely echoed in both emotion and volume by his colleague, who received the toe of my shoe very solidly at the base of his spine.

Bashing people was their sort of business, not mine, and Kenny hadn't enough strength left to stand up, let alone fight back, so that I got knocked about a bit here and there. But I imagined that they hadn't expected any serious opposition, and it must have been clear to them from the beginning that I didn't play their rules.

They had big fists all threateningly bunched and the

hard round sort of toecaps which cowards hide behind. I kicked their knees with vigour, stuck my fingers out straight and hard towards their eyes, and chopped the sides of my palms at their throats.

I'd had enough of it before they had. Still, I outlasted them for determination, because I really did not want to fall down and have their boots bust my kidneys. They got tired in the end and limped away quite suddenly, as if called off by a whistle. They took with them some damaged knee cartilage, aching larynxes, and one badly scratched eye; and they left behind a ringing head and a set of sore ribs.

I leaned against the aeroplane getting my breath back and looking down at Kenny where he sat on the grass. There was a good deal of blood on his face. His nose was bleeding, and he had tried to wipe it with the back of his hand.

I bent down presently and helped him up. He came to his feet without any of the terrible slowness of the severely injured and there was nothing wrong with his voice.

'Thanks, sport.' He squinted at me. 'Those sods said they were going to fix me so my riding days were over ... God ... I feel crook ... here, have you got any whisky ... aah ... Jesus ...' He bent double and vomited rakingly on to the turf.

Straightening up afterwards he dragged a large handkerchief out of his pocket and wiped his mouth, looking in dismay at the resulting red stains.

'I'm bleeding . . .'

'It's your nose, that's all.'

'Oh . . .' He coughed weakly. 'Look, sport, thanks. I guess thanks isn't enough . . .' His gaze sharpened on the Polyplane pilot still standing aloof a little way off. 'That bastard didn't lift a finger . . . they'd have crippled me and he wouldn't come . . . I shouted.'

'He's got his medical tomorrow,' I said.

'Sod his bloody medical . . .'

'If you don't pass your medical every six months, you get grounded. If you get grounded for long in the taxi business you lose either your whole job or at least half your income . . .'

'Yeah,' he said. 'And your own medical, when does that come up?'

'Not for two months.'

He laughed a hollow, sick sounding laugh. Swallowed. Swayed. Looked suddenly very small and vulnerable.

'You'd better go over and see the doctor,' I suggested.

'Maybe . . . but I've got the ride on Volume Ten on Monday . . . big race . . . opportunity if I do well of a better job than I've had with Annie Villars . . . don't want to miss it . . .' He smiled twistedly. 'Doesn't do jockeys any good to be grounded either, sport.'

'You're not in very good shape.'

'I'll be all right. Nothing broken . . . except maybe my nose. That won't matter; done it before.' He coughed again. 'Hot bath. Spell in the sauna. Good as new by Monday. Thanks to you.'

'How about telling the police?'

'Yeah. Great idea.' He was sarcastic. 'Just imagine their sort of questions. "Why was anyone trying to cripple you, Mr Bayst?" "Well, officer, I'd promised to fiddle their races see, and this sod Goldenberg, I beg his pardon, gentlemen, Mr Eric Goldenberg, sticks these two heavies on to me to get his own back for all the lolly he had to cough up when I won ..." "And why did you promise to fiddle the race, Mr Bayst?" "Well, officer, I done it before you see and made a handy bit on the side ..." ' He gave me a flickering glance and decided he'd said enough. 'Guess I'll see how it looks tomorrow. If I'm in shape to ride Monday I'll just forget it happened.'

'Suppose they try again?'

'No.' He shook his head a fraction. 'They don't do it twice.'

He picked himself off the side of the fuselage and looked at his reflection in the Polyplane's window, licked his handkerchief and wiped most of the blood off his face.

The nose had stopped bleeding. He felt it gingerly between thumb and forefinger.

'It isn't moving. Can't feel it grate. It did, when I broke it.'

Without the blood he looked pale under the red hair

but not leaden. 'Guess I'll be all right. Think I'll get into the plane and sit down, though . . . Came in it, see . . .'

I helped him in. He sagged down weakly in his seat and didn't look like someone who would be fit to ride a racehorse in forty-six hours.

'Hey,' he said, 'I never asked you . . . are you OK yourself?'

'Yes . . . Look, I'll get your pilot to fetch you some whisky.'

His reaction showed how unsettled he still felt. 'That would be . . . fair dinkum. He won't go though.'

'He will,' I said.

He did. British aviation was a small world. Everyone knew someone who knew someone else. News of certain sorts travelled slowly but surely outwards and tended to follow one around. He got the message. He also agreed to buy the whisky himself.

By the time he came back, bearing a full quarter bottle and a scowl, the last race was over and the passengers for all the aeroplanes were turning up in little groups. Kenny began to look less shaky, and when two other jockeys arrived with exclamations and consolations, I went back to the Cherokee.

Annie Villars was waiting, not noticeably elated by her win with Rudiments.

'I thought you said you were going to stay with the plane,' she said. Ice cracked in her voice.

'Didn't take my eyes off it.'

She snorted. I did a quick double check inside, just to

415

be sure, but no one had stored anything aboard since my last search. The external check I did more slowly and more thoroughly. Still nothing.

The thumping I'd collected started to catch up. The ringing noise in my head was settling into a heavy ache. Various soggy areas on my upper arms were beginning to stiffen. My solar plexus and adjacent areas felt like Henry Cooper's opponents on the morning after.

'Did you know,' I said to Annie Villars conversationally, 'that two men just had a go at beating up Kenny Bayst?'

If she felt any compassion she controlled it admirably. 'Is he badly hurt?'

'An uncomfortable night should see him through.'

'Well then . . . I dare say he deserved it.'

'What for?'

She gave me a direct stare. 'You aren't deaf.'

I shrugged: 'Kenny thinks Mr Goldenberg arranged it.'

She hadn't known it was going to happen. Didn't know whether Goldenberg was responsible or not. I saw her hesitating, summing the information up.

In the end she said vaguely, 'Kenny never could keep his tongue still,' and a minute later, under her breath, 'Stupid thing to do. Stupid man.'

Major Tyderman, the Duke of Wessex and Fenella Payne-in-the-neck arrived together, the Duke still talking happily about his winner.

'Where's Colin?' asked Fenella. 'Isn't he here after

416

all? What a frantic nuisance. I asked for him at the weighing room and that man, who did he say he was? His valet, oh yes, of course . . . his valet, said that he had already gone to the plane.' She pouted, thrusting out her lower lip. There was champagne in her eyes and petulance in her voice. The gold bracelets jingled. The heavy scent didn't seem to have abated during the afternoon. I thought Colin had dodged very neatly. The Major also had been included in the celebrations. He looked slightly fuzzy round the eyes and a lot less rigid everywhere else. The hand that pushed at the wiry moustache looked almost gentle. The chin was still tucked well back into the neck, but there was nothing aggressive any more: it seemed suddenly only the mannerism of one who used suspiciousness instead of understanding to give himself a reputation for shrewdness.

The Duke asked the Major if he minded changing places on the way home so that he, the Duke, could sit in front. 'I like to see the dials go round,' he explained.

The Major, full of ducal champagne, gracefully agreed. He and Fenella climbed aboard and I waited outside with the Duke.

'Is there anything the matter, my dear chap?' he said.

'No, sir.'

He studied me slowly. 'There is, you know.'

I put my fingers on my forehead and felt the sweat. 'It's a hot day,' I said.

Colin came eventually. He too was sweating: his now

crumpled open shirt had great dark patches under the arms. He had ridden five races. He looked thin and exhausted.

'Are you all right?' he said abruptly.

'I *knew*,' said the Duke.

'Yes, thank you.'

Colin looked back to where the Polyplane still waited on the ground.

'Is Kenny bad?'

'A bit sore. He didn't want anyone to know.'

'One of the jockeys with him on the trip came back over and told us. Kenny said you saved him from a fate worse than death, or words to that effect.'

'What?' said the Duke.

Colin explained. They looked at me suspiciously.

'I'm fit to fly, if that's what's worrying you.'

Colin made a face. 'Yeah, boy, it sure is.' He grinned, took a deep breath, and dived into the back with the tentacly Fenella. The Duke folded himself after me into the front seats and we set off.

There was thick cloud over the Humber at Ottringham and all the way south to Cambridge. As he could see just about as far forward as the propeller, the Duke asked me what guarantee there was that we wouldn't collide with another aircraft.

There wasn't any guarantee. Just probability.

'The sky is huge,' I said. 'And there are strict rules for flying in clouds. Collisions practically never happen.'

His hands visibly relaxed. He shifted into a more

comfortable position. 'How do you know where we are?' he asked.

'Radio,' I said. 'Radio beams from transmitters on the ground. As long as that needle on the dial points centrally downwards, we are going straight to Ottringham, where the signal is coming from.'

'Fascinating,' he said.

The replacement Cherokee had none of the sophistication of the one which had been blown up. That had had an instrument which locked the steering on to the radio beam and took the aircraft automatically to the transmitter. After the attentions of Kenny Bayst's assailants I regretted not having it around.

'How will we know when we get to Cambridge?' asked the Duke.

'The needle on that other dial down there will swing from pointing straight up and point straight down. That will mean we have passed over the top of the transmitter at Cambridge.'

'Wonderful what they think of,' said the Duke.

The needles came up trumps. We let down through the cloud over Cambridge into an overcast, angry looking afternoon and landed on the shower soaked tarmac. I taxied them over close to the buildings, shut down the engine, and took off my head set, which felt a ton heavier than usual.

'Wouldn't have missed it,' said the Duke. 'Always motored everywhere before, you know.' He unfastened his safety belt. 'Annie persuaded me to try flying. Just once, she said. But I'll be coming with you again, my dear chap.'

'That's great, sir.'

He looked at me closely, kindly. 'You want to go straight to bed when you get home, Matthew. Get your wife to tuck you up nice and warm, eh?'

'Yes,' I said.

'Good, good.' He nodded his fine head and began to heave himself cumbersomely out of the door and on to the wing. 'You made a great hit with my nephew, my dear chap. And I respect Matt's opinion. He can spot good 'uns and bad 'uns a mile off.'

'He's a nice boy,' I said.

The Duke smiled happily. 'He's my heir.'

He stepped down from the wing and went round to help Annie Villars put on her coat. No doubt I should have been doing it. I sat with my belt still fastened, feeling too rough to be bothered to move. I didn't relish the thought of the final hop back to Buckingham, up into the clouds again and with no easy well-placed transmitter to help me down at the other end. I'd have to go round the Luton complex . . . could probably get a steer home from there, from the twenty-four hour radar . . .

I ached. I thought of the caravan. Cold little harbour.

The passengers collected their gear, shut the rear door, waved, and walked off towards the buildings. I looked at the map, picked out a heading, planned the return journey in terms of time and the cross references

I'd need to tell me when I'd got to Buckingham, if the radar should be out of service. After that I sat and stared at the flight plan and told myself to get on with it. After that I rested my head on my hand and shut my eyes.

Ridiculous wasting time, I thought. Cambridge airport charged extra for every minute they stayed open after six o'clock, and the passengers were already committed to paying for more than an hour. Every moment I lingered cost them more still.

There was a tap on the window beside me. I raised my head more quickly than proved wise. Colin Ross was standing there, watching me with a gleam of humour. I twisted the catch and opened the window flap on its hinge.

'Fit to fly, didn't you say?' he said.

'That was two hours ago.'

'Ah yes. Makes a difference.' He smiled faintly. 'I just wondered, if you don't feel like going on, whether you'd care to let me take you home for the night? Then, you can finish the trip tomorrow. It might be a fine day, tomorrow.'

He had flown a great deal and understood the difficulties. All the same, I was surprised he had troubled to come back.

'It might,' I agreed. 'But I could stay in Cambridge . . .'

'Get out of there and fix the hangarage,' he said calmly.

'I'll have to check with Derrydowns . . .'

'Check, then.'

I climbed too slowly out of the aeroplane and struggled into my jacket. We walked together across into the building.

'Call your wife, too,' he said.

'Haven't got one.'

'Oh.' He looked at me with speculative curiosity.

'No,' I said. 'Not that. Married twelve years, divorced three.'

Humour crinkled the skin round his eyes. 'Better than me,' he said. 'Married two years, divorced four.'

Harley answered at the first ring.

'Where are you? Cambridge? ... No, come back now, if you stay at Cambridge we'll have to pay the hangarage.' I hadn't told him about the fight, about the way I felt.

'I'll pay it,' I said. 'You can deduct it from my salary. Colin Ross has asked me to stay with him.' That would clinch it. Harley saw the importance of pleasing, and Colin Ross was his best customer.

'Oh ... that's different. All right then. Come back in the morning.'

I went into the Control office and arranged for the aircraft to be stowed under cover for the night, one last overtime job for the staff before they all went home. After that I sank into the Ross Aston Martin and let the world take care of itself.

*

He lived in an ordinary looking brick built bungalow on the outskirts of Newmarket. Inside, it was colourful and warm, with a large sitting-room stocked with deep luxurious velvet upholstered armchairs.

'Sit down,' he said.

I did. Put my head back. Shut my eyes.

'Whisky or brandy?' he asked.

'Whichever you like.'

I heard him pouring. It sounded like a tumblerful.

'Here,' he said.

I opened my eyes and gratefully took the glass. It was brandy and water. It did a grand job.

There were sounds of pans from the kitchen and a warm smell of roasting chicken. Colin's nose twitched.

'Dinner will be ready soon . . . I'll go and tell the cooks there will be one extra.'

He went out of the room and came back almost immediately with his two cooks.

I stood up slowly. I hadn't given it a thought; was quite unprepared.

They looked at first sight like two halves of one whole. Nancy and Midge. Same dark hair, tied high on the crown with black velvet bows. Same dark eyes, straight eyebrows, spontaneous smiles.

'The bird man himself,' Nancy said. 'Colin, how did you snare him?'

'Potted a sitting duck . . .'

'This is Midge,' she said. 'Midge . . . Matt.'

'Hi,' she said. 'The bomb man, aren't you?'

When you looked closer, you could see. She was thinner than Nancy, and much paler, and she seemed fragile where Nancy was strong: but without the mirror comparison with her sister there was no impression of her being ill.

'First and last bomb, I hope,' I said.

She shivered. 'A lot too ruddy close.'

Colin poured each of them a Dubonnet and took whisky for himself. 'Bombs, battles . . . some introduction you've had to racing.'

'An eventful change from crop spraying,' I agreed.

'Is that a dull job?' Midge asked, surprised.

'Dull and dangerous. You get bored to death trudging up and down some vast field for six hours a day . . . It's all low flying, you see, so you have to be wide awake, and after a while you start yawning. One day maybe you get careless and touch the ground with your wing in a turn, and you write off an expensive machine, which is apt to be unpopular with the boss.'

Nancy laughed. 'Is that what you did?'

'No . . . I went to sleep for a second in the air one day and woke up twenty feet from a pylon. Missed it by millimetres. So I quit while everything was still in one piece.'

'Never mind,' Midge said. 'The next plane you touched disintegrated beautifully.'

They laughed together, a united family, close.

Colin told them about Kenny Bayst's fracas and they exclaimed sympathetically, which made me feel a humbug: Colin habitually drove himself to exhaustion and Midge was irretrievably afflicted, and all I had were a few minor bruises.

Dinner consisted simply of the hot roast chicken and a tossed green salad, with thick wedges of cheese afterwards. We ate in the kitchen with our elbows on the scarlet table, and chewed the bones. I hadn't passed a more basically satisfying evening for many a long weary year.

'What are you thinking?' Nancy demanded. 'At this moment?'

'Making a note to fall frequently sick at Cambridge.'

'Well,' said Midge. 'Don't bother. Just come any time.' She looked inquiringly at her sister and brother and they nodded. 'Just come,' she repeated. 'Whenever it's handy.'

The old inner warning raised its urgent head: don't get involved, don't feel anything, don't risk it.

Don't get involved.

I said, 'Nothing I'd like better,' and didn't know whether I meant it or not.

The two girls stacked the plates in a dishwasher and made coffee. Nancy poured cream carefully across the top of her cup.

'Do you think that bomb was really intended for Colin?' she asked suddenly.

I shrugged. 'I don't know. It could just as well have been intended for Major Tyderman or Annie Villars or Goldenberg, or even Kenny Bayst, really, because it must have been on board before he decided not to come. Or it might have been intended for putting the firm out of action ... for Derrydowns, itself, if you see what I mean, because if Colin had been killed, Derrydowns would probably have gone bust.'

'I can't see why anyone would want to kill Colin,' Midge said. 'Sure, people are jealous of him, but jealousy is one thing and killing five people is another ...'

'Everyone seems to be taking it so calmly,' Nancy suddenly exploded. 'Here is this bloody bomb merchant running around loose with no one knowing just what he'll do next, and no one seems to be trying to find him and lock him up.'

'I don't see how they can find him,' Colin said. 'And anyway, I don't suppose he will risk trying it again.'

'Oh you ... you ... *ostrich*,' she said bitterly. 'Doesn't it occur to you that you don't just lightly put a bomb in an aeroplane? Whoever did it must have had an overwhelming reason, however mad it was, and since the whole thing went wrong they still have the same motive rotting away inside them, and what do you think Midge and I will do if next time you get blown to bits?'

I saw Midge looking at her with compassion and understood the extent of Nancy's fear. One day she was certainly going to lose her sister. She couldn't face losing her brother as well.

'It won't happen,' he said calmly.

They looked at him, and at me. There was a long, long pause. Then Midge picked up the wishbone of the chicken and held it out for me to pull. It snapped with the biggest side in her fist.

'I wish,' she said seriously, 'that Colin would stop cutting his toenails in the bath.'

CHAPTER SEVEN

I slept on a divan bed in Colin's study, a small room crammed with racing trophies, filing cabinets and form books. Every wall was lined by rows of framed photographs of horses passing winning posts and owners proudly leading them in. Their hooves thudded through my head most of the night, but all was peace by morning.

Colin brought me a cup of tea, yawning in his dark woolly bathrobe. He put the cup down on the small table beside the divan and pulled back the curtains.

'It's drizzling cats and dogs,' he announced. 'There's no chance of you flying this morning so you may as well relax and go back to sleep.'

I looked out at the misty rain. Didn't mind a bit.

'It's my day off,' I said.

'Couldn't be better.'

He perched his bottom on the edge of the desk.

'Are you OK this morning?'

'Fine,' I said. 'That hot bath loosened things a lot.'

'Every time you moved yesterday evening you could see it hurt.'

I made a face. 'Sorry.'

'Don't be. In this house you say ouch.'

'So I've noticed,' I said dryly.

He grinned. 'Everyone lives on a precipice. All the time. And Midge keeps telling me and Nancy that if we're not careful she'll outlive us both.'

'She's marvellous.'

'Yes, she is.' He looked out of the window. 'It was a terrible shock at first. Terrible. But now . . . I don't know . . . we seem to have accepted it. All of us. Even her.'

I said hesitantly, 'How long? . . .'

'How long will she live? No one knows. It varies so much, apparently. She's had it, they think, for about three years now. It seems a lot of people have it for about a year before it becomes noticeable enough to be diagnosed, so no one knows when it started with Midge. Some people die within days of getting it. Some have lived for twenty years. Nowadays, with all the modern treatments, they say the average after diagnosis is from two to six years, but it will possibly be ten. We've had two . . . We just believe it will be ten . . . and that makes it much easier . . .'

'She doesn't look especially ill.'

'Not at the moment. She had pneumonia a short while ago and the odd thing about that is that it reverses leukaemia for a while. Any fever does it, apparently. Actually makes her better. So do doses of radiation on her arms and legs, and other bones and organs. She's had several relapses and several good long spells of being well. It just goes on like that . . . but her blood is different, and her bones are changing inside all the time . . . I've seen pictures of what is happening . . . and one day . . . well, one day she'll have a sort of extreme relapse, and she won't recover.'

'Poor Midge . . .'

'Poor all of us.'

'What about . . . Nancy? Being her twin . . .'

'Do identical bodies get identical blood diseases, do you mean?' He looked at me across the room, his eyes in shadow. 'There's that too. They say the chances are infinitesimal. They say there are only eighteen known cases of leukaemia occurring twice in the same family unit. You can't catch it, and you can't inherit it. A girl with leukaemia can have a baby, and the baby won't have leukaemia. You can transfuse blood from someone with leukaemia into someone without it, and he won't catch it. They say there's no reason why Nancy should develop it any more than me or you or the postman. But they don't *know*. The books don't record any cases of an identical twin having it, or what became of the other one.' He paused. Swallowed, 'I think we are all more afraid of Nancy getting it too than of anything on earth.'

I stayed until the sky cleared up at five o'clock. Colin spent most of the day working out which races he wanted to ride in during the coming week and answering telephone calls from owners and trainers anxious to engage him. Principally he rode for a stable half a mile down the road, he said, but the terms of his retainer there gave him a good deal of choice.

He worked at a large chart with seven columns, one for each day of the week. Under each day he listed the various meetings, and under each meeting he listed the names, prizes and distances of the races. Towards the end of the afternoon there was a horse's name against a fair proportion of races, especially, I noticed, those with the highest rewards.

He grinned at my interest. 'A business is a business,' he said.

'So I see. A study in time and motion.'

On three of the days he proposed to ride at two meetings.

'Can you get me from Brighton to Windsor fast enough for two races an hour and a half apart? Three o'clock race at Brighton. Four-thirty, Windsor. And on Saturday, three o'clock race at Bath, four-thirty at Brighton?'

'With fast cars both ends, don't see why not.'

'Good.' He crossed out a couple of question marks and wrote ticks instead. 'And next Sunday, can you take me to France?'

'If Harley says so.'

'Harley will say so,' he said with certainty.

'Don't you ever take a day off?'

He raised his eyebrows in surprise. 'Today,' he said, 'is off. Hadn't you noticed?'

'Er . . . yes.'

'The horse I was going over to ride today went lame on Thursday. Otherwise I was going to Paris. BEA, though, for once.'

Nancy said with mock resignation, 'The dynamo whirs non-stop from March to November in England and Europe and then goes whizzing off to Japan and so on, and around about February there might be a day or two when we can all flop back in armchairs and put our feet up.'

Midge said, 'We put them up in the Bahamas last time. It was gorgeous. All that hot sun . . .'

The others laughed. 'It rained the whole of the first week.'

The girls cooked steaks for lunch. 'In your honour,' Midge said to me. 'You're too thin.'

I was fatter than any of them; which wasn't saying much.

Midge cleared the things away afterwards and Nancy covered the kitchen table with maps and charts.

'I really am flying Colin to the races one day soon, and I wondered if you'd help . . .'

'Of course.'

She bent over the table, the long dark hair swinging down over her neck. Don't get involved, I said to myself. Just don't.

'Next week, to Haydock. If the weather's good enough.'

'She's doing you out of a job,' Midge observed, wiping glasses.

'Wait till it thunders.'

'Beast,' Nancy said.

She had drawn a line on the map. She wanted me to tell her how to proceed in the Manchester control zone, and what to do if they gave her instructions she didn't understand.

'Ask them to repeat them. If you still don't understand, ask them to clarify.'

'They'll think I'm stupid,' she protested.

'Better that than barging on regardless and crashing into an airliner.'

'OK,' she sighed. 'Point taken.'

'Colin deserves a medal,' Midge said.

'Just shut up,' Nancy said. 'You're all bloody rude.'

When the drizzle stopped they all three took me back to Cambridge, squashing into the Aston Martin. Midge drove, obviously enjoying it. Nancy sat half on Colin and half on me, and I sat half on the door handle.

They stood in a row, and waved when I took off. I rolled the wings in salute and set course for Buckingham, and tried to ignore the regret I felt to be leaving.

Honey was up in the control tower at Derrydowns, Sunday or no Sunday, and Harley was aloft in the trainer giving someone a lesson. When he heard me on the radio he said snappily 'And about time too,' and I remembered the dimensions of my bank balance and didn't snap back. Chanter, I thought wryly, would have plain despised me.

I left the Cherokee Six in the hangar and walked round to the caravan. It seemed emptier, more sordid, more dilapidated than before. The windows all needed cleaning. The bed wasn't made. Yesterday's milk had gone sour again, and there was still no food.

I sat for a while watching the evening sun struggle through the breaking clouds, watching Harley's pupil stagger through some ropy landings, wondering how long it would be before Derrydowns went broke, and wondering if I could save enough before that happened to buy a car. Harley was paying me forty-five pounds a week, which was more than he could afford and less than I was worth. Of that, Susan, taxes and insurance would be taking exactly half, and with Harley deducting four more for my rent it wasn't going to be easy.

Impatiently I got up and cleaned all the windows, which improved my view of the airfield but not of the future.

When the light began to fade I had a visitor. A ripe shapely girl in the minimum of green cotton dress. Long fair hair. Long legs. Large mouth. Slightly protruding teeth. She walked with a man-eating sway and spoke with the faintest of lisps.

Honey Harley, come down from her tower.

She knocked on her way in. All the same if I'd been naked. As it was, I had my shirt off from the window cleaning and for Honey, it seemed, that was invitation enough. She came over holding out a paper in one hand and putting the other lightly on my shoulder. She let it slide down against my skin to halfway down my back and then brought it up again to the top.

'Uncle and I were making out the list for the next week. We wondered if you fixed anything up with Colin Ross.'

I moved gently away, picked up a nylon sweater, and put it on.

'Yes ... he wants us Tuesday, Friday, Saturday and Sunday.'

'Great.'

She followed me across the small space. One step farther backwards and I'd be in my bedroom. Internally I tried to stifle a laugh. I stepped casually round her, back towards the door. Her face showed nothing but businesslike calm.

'Look,' she said, 'Monday, that's tomorrow, then, you collect a businessman at Coventry, take him to Rotterdam, wait for him, and bring him back. That's in the Aztec. Tuesday, Colin Ross. Wednesday, nothing yet. Thursday, probably a trainer in Lambourn wanting to

DICK FRANCIS

look at a horse for sale in Yorkshire, he'll let us know, and then Colin Ross again all the end of the week.'

'OK.'

'And the Board of Trade want to come out and see you again. I told them early Tuesday or Wednesday.'

'All right.' As usual, the automatic sinking of the heart even at the words Board of Trade: though this time, surely, surely, my responsibility was a technicality. This time, surely, I couldn't get ground to bits.

Honey sat down on the two-seat sofa and crossed her legs. She smiled.

'We haven't seen much of each other yet, have we?'

'No,' I said.

'Can I have a cigarette?'

'I'm sorry . . . I don't smoke . . . I haven't any.'

'Oh. Well, give me a drink, then.'

'Look, I really am sorry . . . all I can offer you is black coffee . . . or water.'

'Surely you've got some beer?'

'Afraid not.'

She stared at me. Then she stood up, went into the tiny kitchen, and opened all the cupboards. I thought it was because she thought I was lying, but I'd done her an injustice. Sex minded she might be, but no fool.

'You've no car, have you? And the shops and the pub are nearly two miles away.' She came back frowning, and sat down again. 'Why didn't you ask someone to give you a lift?'

'Didn't want to be a bother.'

436

She considered it. 'You've been here three weeks and you don't get paid until the end of the month. So ... have you any money?'

'Enough not to starve,' I said. 'But thanks all the same.'

I'd sent ten pounds to Susan and told her she'd have to wait for the rest until I got my pay cheque. She'd written back short and to the point. Two months, by then, don't forget. As if I could. I had under four pounds left in the world and too much pride.

'Uncle would give you an advance.'

'I wouldn't like to ask him.'

A small smile lifted the corners of her mouth. 'No, I can see that, as he's so intent on slapping you down.'

'Is he?'

'Don't pretend to be surprised. You know he is. You give him a frightful inferiority complex and he's getting back at you for it.'

'It's silly.'

'Oh sure. But you are the two things he longs to be and isn't, a top class pilot and an attractive man. He needs you badly for the business, but he doesn't have to like it. And don't tell me you didn't know all that, because it's been obvious all along that you understand, otherwise you would have lost your temper with him every day at the treatment he's been handing out.'

'You see a lot from your tower,' I said smiling.

'Sure. And I'm very fond of my uncle. And I love this little business, and I'd do anything to keep us afloat.'

437

She said it with intense feeling. I wondered whether 'anything' meant sleeping with the pilots, or whether that came under the heading of pleasure, not profit. I didn't intend to find out. Not getting involved included Honey, in the biggest possible way.

I said, 'It must have been a blow to the business, losing that new Cherokee.'

She pursed her mouth and put her head on one side. 'Not altogether. In fact, absolutely the reverse. We had too much capital tied up in it. We had to put down a lump sum to start with, and the HP instalments were pretty steep ... I should think when everything's settled, and we get the insurance, we will have about five thousand pounds back, and with that much to shore us up we can keep going until times get better.'

'If the aircraft hadn't blown up, would you have been able to keep up with the HP?'

She stood up abruptly, seeming to think that she had already said too much. 'Let's just leave it that things are all right as they are.'

The daylight was fading fast. She came and stood close beside me, not quite touching.

'You don't smoke, you don't eat, you don't drink,' she said softly. 'What else don't you do?'

'That too.'

'Not ever?'

'Not now. Not here.'

'I'd give you a good time.'

'Honey ... I just ... don't want to.'

438

She wasn't angry. Not even hurt. 'You're cold,' she said judiciously. 'An iceberg.'

'Perhaps.'

'You'll thaw,' she said. 'One of these days.'

The Board of Trade had sent the same two men, the tall one and the silent one, complete with notebook and bitten green pencil. As before, I sat with them in the crew room and offered them coffee from the slot machine in the passengers' lounge. They accepted, and I went and fetched three plastic cupfuls. The staff as well as the customers had to buy their coffee or whatever from the machine. Honey kept it well stocked. It made a profit.

Outside on the airfield my part-time colleague, Ron, was showing a new pupil how to do the external checks. They crept round the trainer inch by inch. Ron talked briskly. The pupil, a middle-aged man, nodded as if he understood.

The tall man was saying in effect that they had got nowhere with the bomb.

'The police have been happy to leave the investigations with us, but frankly in these cases it is almost impossible to find the identity of the perpetrator. Of course if someone on board is a major political figure, or a controversial agitator . . . Or if there is a great sum of personal insurance involved . . . But in this case there is nothing like that.'

439

'Isn't Colin Ross insured?' I asked.

'Yes, but he has no new policy, or anything exceptional. And the beneficiaries are his twin sisters. I cannot believe . . .'

'Impossible,' I said with conviction.

'Quite so.'

'How about the others?'

He shook his head. 'They all said, in fact, that they ought to be better insured than they were.' He coughed discreetly. 'There is, of course, the matter of yourself.'

'What do you mean?'

His sharp eyes stared at me unblinkingly.

'Several years ago you took out a policy for the absolute benefit of your wife. Although she is now your ex-wife, she would still be the beneficiary. You can't change that sort of policy.'

'Who told you all this?'

'She did,' he said. 'We went to see her in the course of our inquiries.' He paused. 'She didn't speak kindly of you.'

I compressed my mouth. 'No. I can imagine. Still, I'm worth more to her alive than dead. She'll want me to live as long as possible.'

'And if she wanted to get married again? Your alimony payments would stop then, and a lump sum from insurance might be welcome.'

I shook my head. 'She might have killed me in a fury three years ago, but not now, cold bloodedly, with other people involved. It isn't in her nature. And besides, she doesn't know anything about bombs and she had no opportunity . . . You'll have to cross out that theory too.'

'She has been going out occasionally with an executive from a firm specializing in demolitions.'

He kept his voice dead even, but he had clearly expected more reaction than he got. I wasn't horrified or even much taken aback.

'She wouldn't do it. Or put anyone else up to doing it. Ordinarily, she was too . . . too kind hearted. Too sensible, anyway. She used to be so angry whenever innocent passengers were blown up . . . she would never do it herself. Never.'

He watched me for a while in the special Board of Trade brand of unnerving silence. I didn't see what I could add. Didn't know what he was after.

Outside on the airfield the trainer started up and taxied away. The engine noise faded. It was very quiet. I sat. I waited.

Finally he stirred. 'All in all, for all our trouble, we have come up with only one probability. And even that gets us no nearer knowing who the bomb was intended for, or who put it on board.'

He put his hand in his inner pocket and brought out a stiff brown envelope. Out of that he shook on to the crew room table a twisted piece of metal. I picked it up and looked at it. Beyond the impression that it had once been round and flat, like a button, it meant nothing.

'What is it?'

'The remains,' he said, 'of an amplifier.'

441

I looked up, puzzled. 'Out of the radio?'

'We don't think so.' He chewed his lip. 'We think it was in the bomb. We found it embedded in what had been the tail plane.'

'Do you mean . . . it wasn't a time bomb after all?'

'Well . . . probably not. It looks as if it was exploded by a radio transmission. Which puts, do you see, a different slant on things.'

'What difference? I don't know much about bombs. How does a radio bomb differ from a time bomb?'

'They can differ a lot, though in many the actual explosive is the same. In those cases it's just the trigger mechanism that's different.' He paused. 'Well, say you have a quantity of plastic explosive. Unfortunately that's all too easy to get hold of, nowadays. In fact, if you happen to be in Greece, you can go into any hardware shop and buy it over the counter. On its own, it won't explode. It needs a detonator. Gunpowder, old-fashioned gunpowder, is the best. You also need something to ignite the gunpowder before it will detonate the plastic. Are you with me?'

'Faint but pursuing,' I said.

'Right. The easiest way to ignite gunpowder, from a distance, that is, is to pack it round a thin filament of fuse wire. Then you pass an electric current through the filament. It becomes red hot, ignites the gunpowder . . .'

'And boom, you have no Cherokee Six.'

'Er, yes. Now, in this type of bomb you have a battery, a high voltage battery about the size of a sixpence, to provide the electric current. The filament will heat up if you bend it round and fasten one end to one terminal of the battery, and the other to the other.'

'Clear,' I said. 'And the bomb goes off immediately.'

He raised his eyes to Heaven. 'Why did I ever start this? Yes, it would go off immediately. So it is necessary to have a mechanism that will complete the circuit after the manufacturer is safely out of the way.'

'By a spring?' I suggested.

'Yes. You hold the circuit open by a hair spring on a catch. When the catch is removed, the spring snaps the circuit shut, and that's that. Right? Now, the catch can be released by a time mechanism like an ordinary alarm clock. Or it can be released by a radio signal from a distance, via a receiver, an amplifier and a solenoid, like mechanisms in a space craft.'

'What is a solenoid, exactly?'

'A sort of electric magnet, a coil with a rod in the centre. The rod moves up and down inside the coil, when a pulse is passed through the coil. Say the top of the rod is sticking up out of the coil to form the catch on the spring, when the rod moves down into the coil the spring is released.'

I considered it. 'What is there to stop someone detonating the bomb by accident, by unknowingly transmitting on the right frequency? The air is packed with radio waves . . . surely radio bombs are impossibly risky?'

He cleared his throat. 'It is possible to make a

combination type release mechanism. One could make a bomb in which, say, three radio signals had to be received in the correct order before the circuit could be completed. For such a release mechanism, you would need three separate sets of receivers, amplifiers and solenoids to complete the circuit . . . We were exceptionally fortunate to find this amplifier. We doubt if it was the only one . . .'

'It sounds much more complicated than the alarm clock.'

'Oh yes, it is. But also more flexible. You are not committed to a time in advance to set it off.'

'So no one had to know what time we would be leaving Haydock. They would just have to see us go.'

'Yes . . . Or be told you had gone.'

I thought a bit. 'It does put a different slant, doesn't it?'

'I'd appreciate your thinking.'

'You must be thinking the same,' I protested. 'If the bomb could be set off at any hour, any day, any week even, it could have been put in the aircraft at any time after the last maintenance check.'

He smiled thinly. 'And that would let you halfway off the hook?'

'Half way,' I agreed.

'But only half.'

'Yes.'

He sighed. 'I've sprung this on you. I'd like you to think it over, from every angle. Seriously. Then tell me if anything occurs to you. If you care at all to find out what happened, that is, and maybe prevent it happening again.'

'You think I don't care?'

'I got the impression.'

'I would care now,' I said slowly, 'if Colin Ross were blown up.'

He smiled. 'You are less on your guard, today.'

'You aren't sniping at me from behind the bushes.'

'No . . .' He was surprised. 'You're very observant, aren't you?'

'More a matter of atmosphere.'

He hesitated. 'I have now read the whole of the transcript of your trial.'

'Oh.' I could feel my face go bleak. He watched me.

'Did you know,' he said, 'that someone has added to the bottom of it in pencil a highly libellous statement?'

'No,' I said. Waited for it.

'It says that the Chairman of Interport is of the undoubtedly correct opinion that the First Officer lied on oath throughout, and that it was because of the First Officer's own gross negligence, not that of Captain Shore, that the airliner strayed so dangerously off course.'

Surprised, shaken, I looked away from him, out of the window, feeling absurdly vindicated and released. If that postscript was there for anyone who read the transcript to see, then maybe my name hadn't quite so much mud on it as I'd thought. Not where it mattered anyway.

I said without heat, 'The Captain is always responsible. Whoever does what.'

'Yes.'

A silence lengthened. I brought my thoughts back from four years ago and my gaze from the empty airfield.

'Thank you,' I said.

He smiled very slightly. 'I wondered why you hadn't lost your licence . . . or your job. It didn't make sense to me that you hadn't. That's why I read the transcript, to see if there was any reason.'

'You're very thorough.'

'I like to be.'

'Interport knew one of us was lying : . . we both said the other had put the ship in danger . . . but I was the Captain. It inevitably came back to me. It was, in fact, my fault.'

'He wilfully disobeyed your instructions . . .'

'And I didn't find out until it was nearly too late.'

'Quite . . . but he need not have lied about it.'

'He was frightened,' I sighed. 'Of what would happen to his career.'

He let half a minute slip by without comment. Then he cleared his throat and said, 'I suppose you wouldn't like to tell me why you left the South American people?'

I admired his delicate approach. 'Gap in the dossier?' I suggested.

His mouth twitched. 'Well, yes.' A pause. 'You are of course not obliged . . .'

'No,' I said. 'Still . . .' Something for something. 'I refused to take off one day because I didn't think it was safe. They got another pilot who said it was. So he took off, and nothing happened. And they sacked me. That's all.'

'But,' he said blankly, 'it's a Captain's absolute right not to take off if he thinks it's unsafe.'

'There's no BALPA to uphold your rights there, you know. They said they couldn't afford to lose custom to other airlines because their Captains were cowards. Or words to that effect.'

'Good gracious.'

I smiled. 'Probably the Interport business accounted for my refusal to take risks.'

'But then you went to Africa and took them,' he protested.

'Well . . . I needed money badly, and the pay was fantastic. And you don't have the same moral obligation to food and medical supplies as to airline passengers.'

'But the refugees and wounded, coming out?'

'Always easier flying out than in. No difficulties finding the home base, not like groping for some jungle clearing on a black night.'

He shook his head wonderingly, giving me up as a bad job.

'What brought you back here to something as dull as crop spraying?'

I laughed. Never thought I could laugh in front of the Board of Trade. 'The particular war I was flying in ended. I was offered another one a bit further south, but I suppose I'd had enough of it. Also I was nearly solvent again. So I came back here, and crop spraying was the first thing handy.'

'What you might call a chequered career,' he commented.

'Mild compared with some.'

'Ah yes. That's true.' He stood up and threw his empty coffee beaker into the biscuit tin which served as a waste paper basket. 'Right then . . . You'll give a bit of thought to this bomb business?'

'Yes.'

'We'll be in touch with you again.' He fished in an inner pocket and produced a card. 'If you should want me, though, you can find me at this number.'

'OK.'

He made a wry face. 'I know how you must feel about us.'

'Never mind,' I said. 'Never mind.'

CHAPTER EIGHT

For most of that week I flew where I was told to, and thought about radio bombs, and sat on my own in the caravan in the evenings.

Honey didn't come back, but on the day after her visit I had returned from Rotterdam to find a large bag of groceries on the table: eggs, butter, bread, tomatoes, sugar, cheese, powdered milk, tins of soup. Also a pack of six half pints of beer. Also a note from Honey: 'Pay me next week.'

Not a bad guy, Honey Harley. I took up eating again. Old habits die hard.

Tuesday I took Colin and four assorted others to Wolverhampton races, Wednesday, after the Board of Trade departed, I took a politician to Cardiff to a Union strike meeting, and Thursday I took the racehorse trainer to various places in Yorkshire and Northumberland to look at some horses to see if he wanted to buy any.

Thursday evening I made myself a cheese and tomato sandwich and a cup of coffee, and ate them looking at the pin-ups, which were curling a bit round the edges. After I'd finished the sandwich I unstuck the Sellotape and took all the bosomy ladies down. The thrusting pairs of heavily ringed nipples regarded me sorrowfully, like spaniels' eyes. Smiling, I folded them decently over and dropped them in the rubbish bin. The caravan looked just as dingy, however, without them.

Friday morning, when I was in Harley's office filing flight records, Colin rang Harley and said he wanted me to stay overnight at Cambridge, ready again for Saturday.

Harley agreed. 'I'll charge Matt's hotel bill to your account.'

Colin said, 'Fine. But he can stay with me again if he likes.'

Harley relayed the message. Did I like? I liked.

Harley put down the receiver. 'Trying to save money,' he said disparagingly, 'having you to stay.' He brightened: 'I'll charge him the hangarage, though.'

I took the Cherokee over to Cambridge and fixed for them to give it shelter that night. When Colin came he was with four other jockeys: three I didn't know, and Kenny Bayst. Kenny said how was I. I was fine, how was he? Good as new, been riding since Newbury, he said.

Between them they had worked out the day's shuttle. All to Brighton, Colin to White Waltham for Windsor, aeroplane to return to Brighton, pick up the others, return to White Waltham, return to Cambridge.

'Is that all right?' Colin asked.

'Sure. Anything you say.'

He laughed. 'The fusses we used to have when we used to ask this sort of thing . . .'

'Don't see why,' I said.

'Larry was a lazy sod . . .'

They loaded themselves on board and we tracked down east of the London control zone and over the top of Gatwick to Shoreham airport for Brighton. When we landed Colin looked at his watch and Kenny nodded and said, 'Yeah, he's always faster than Larry. I've noticed it too.'

'Harley will give him the sack,' Colin said dryly, unfastening his seatbelt.

'He won't, will he?' Kenny sounded faintly anxious. Quicker journeys meant smaller bills.

'It depends on how many customers he pinches from Polyplanes through being fast.' Colin grinned at me. 'Am I right?'

'You could be,' I agreed.

They went off laughing about it to the waiting taxi. A couple of hours later Colin came back at a run in his breeches and colours and I whisked him over to White Waltham. He had won, it appeared, at Brighton. A close finish. He was still short of breath. A fast car drove right up to the aircraft as soon as I stopped and had him off down the road to Windsor in a cloud of dust. I went more leisurely back to Shoreham and collected the others at the end of their programme. It was a hot sunny day, blue and hazy. They came back sweating.

Kenny had ridden a winner and had brought me a

bottle of whisky as a present. I said he didn't need to give me a present.

'Look, sport, if it weren't for you, I wouldn't be riding any more bleeding winners. So take it.'

'All right,' I said. 'Thanks.'

'Thanks yourself.'

They were tired and expansive. I landed at White Waltham before Colin arrived back from Windsor, and the other four yawned and gossiped, opening all the doors and fanning themselves.

'. . . gave him a breather coming up the hill.'

'That was no breather. That was the soft bugger dropping his bit. Had to give him a sharp reminder to get him going again.'

'Can't stand that fellow Fossel . . .'

'Why do you ride for him then?'

'Got no choice, have I? Small matter of a retainer . . .'

'. . . What chance you got on Candlestick?'

'Wouldn't finish in the first three if it started now . . .'

'Hey,' said Kenny Bayst, leaning forward and tapping me on the shoulder. 'Got something that might interest you, sport.' He pulled a sheet of paper out of his trouser pocket. 'How about this, then?'

I took the paper and looked at it. It was a leaflet, high quality printing on good glossy paper. An invitation to all racegoers to join the Racegoers' Accident Fund.

'I'm not a racegoer,' I said.

'No, read it. Go on,' he urged. 'It came in the post this morning. I thought you'd be interested, so I brought it.'

I read down the page. 'Up to one thousand pounds for serious personal injury, five thousand pounds for accidental death. Premium five pounds. Double the premium double the insurance. The insurance everyone can afford. Stable lads, buy security for your missus. Jockeys: out of work but in the money. Race crowds, protect yourself against road accidents on the way home. Trainers who fly to meetings, protect yourself against bombs!'

'Damn it,' I said.

Kenny laughed. 'I thought you'd like it.'

I handed the leaflet back, smiling. 'Yeah. The so-and-sos.'

'Might not be a bad idea, at that.'

Colin's hired car drove up and decanted the usual spent force. He climbed wearily into his seat, clipped shut his belt, and said, 'Wake me at Cambridge.'

'How did it go?' Kenny asked.

'Got that sod Export home by a whisker ... But as for Uptight,' he yawned, 'They might as well send him to the knackers. Got the slows right and proper, that one has.'

We woke him at Cambridge. It was a case of waking most of them, in point of fact. They stretched their way on to the tarmac, shirt necks open, ties hanging loose, jackets on their arms. Colin had no jacket, no tie: for him, the customary jeans, the rumpled sweat shirt, the air of being nobody, of being one in a crowd, instead of a crowd in one.

Nancy and Midge had come in the Aston Martin to pick us up.

'We brought a picnic,' Nancy said, 'as it's such a super evening. We're going to that place by the river.'

They had also brought swimming trunks for Colin and a pair of his for me. Nancy swam with us, but Midge said it was too cold. She sat on the bank wearing four watches on her left arm and stretching her long bare legs in the sun.

It was cool and quiet and peaceful in the river after the hot sticky day. The noise inside my head of engine throb calmed to silence. I watched a moorhen gliding along by the reeds, twisting her neck cautiously to fasten me with a shiny eye, peering suspiciously at Colin and Nancy floating away ahead. I pushed a ripple towards her with my arm. She rode on it like a cork. Simple being a moorhen, I thought. But it wasn't really. All of nature had its pecking order. Everywhere, someone was the pecked.

Nancy and Colin swam back. Friendly eyes, smiling faces. Don't get involved, I thought. Not with anyone. Not yet.

The girls had brought cold chicken and long crisp cos lettuce leaves with a tangy sauce to dip them in. We ate while the sun went down, and drank a cold bottle of Chablis, sitting on a large blue rug and throwing the chewed bones into the river for the fishes to nibble.

When she had finished Midge lay back on the rug and shielded her eyes from the last slanting rays.

'I wish this could go on for ever,' she said casually. 'The summer, I mean. Warm evenings. We get so few of them.'

'We could go and live in the south of France, if you like,' Nancy said.

'Don't be silly . . . Who would look after Colin?'

They smiled, all three of them. The unspoken things were all there. Tragic. Unimportant.

The slow dusk drained all colours into shades of grey. We lazed there, relaxing, chewing stalks of grass, watching the insects flick over the surface of the water, talking a little in soft summer evening murmuring voices.

'We both lost a stone in Japan, that year we went with Colin . . .'

'That was the food more than the heat.'

'I never did get to like the food . . .'

'Have you ever been to Japan, Matt?'

'Used to fly there for BOAC.'

'BOAC?' Colin was surprised. 'Why ever did you leave?'

'Left to please my wife. Long time ago, now, though.'

'Explains how you fly.'

'Oh sure . . .'

'I like America better,' Midge said. 'Do you remember Mr Kroop in Laurel, where you got those riding boots made in a day?'

'Mm . . .'

'And we kept driving round that shopping centre there and getting lost in the one way streets . . .'

'Super that week was . . .'

'Wish we could go again . . .'

There was a long regretful silence. Nancy sat up with a jerk and slapped her leg.

'Bloody mosquitoes.'

Colin scratched lazily and nodded. 'Time to go home.'

We wedged back into the Aston Martin. Colin drove. The twins sat on my legs, leaned on my chest and twined their arms behind my neck for balance. Not bad, not bad at all. They laughed at my expression.

'Too much of a good thing,' Nancy said.

When we went to bed they both kissed me good-night, with identical soft lips, on the cheek.

Breakfast was brisk, businesslike, and accompanied throughout by telephone calls. Annie Villars rang to ask if there was still a spare seat on the Cherokee.

'Who for?' Colin asked cautiously. He made a face at us. 'Bloody Fenella,' he whispered over the mouthpiece. 'No, Annie, I'm terribly sorry, I've promised Nancy . . .'

'You have?' Nancy said. 'First I've heard of it.'

He put the receiver down. 'I rescue you from Chanter, now it's your turn.'

'Rescue my foot. You're in and out of the weighing room all day. Fat lot of good that is.'

'Do you want to come?'

'Take Midge,' she said. 'It's her turn.'

'No, you go,' Midge said. 'Honestly, I find it tiring. Especially as it's one of those rush from course to course days. I'll go along to the meeting here next week. That will do me fine.'

'Will you be all right?'

'Naturally I will. I'll lie in the sun in the garden and think of you all exhausting yourselves racing round in circles.'

When it turned out that there were two other empty seats as well, in spite of Nancy being there, Annie Villars gave Colin a reproachful look of carefully repressed annoyance and said it would have been useful to have had along Fenella to share the cost. Why else did Colin think she had suggested it?

'I must have miscounted,' said Colin happily. 'Too late to get her now.'

We flew to Bath without incident, Nancy sitting in the right-hand seat beside me and acting as co-pilot. It was clear that she intensely enjoyed it, and there was no pain in it for me either. I could see what Larry had meant about practising short landings, as the Bath runways were incredibly short, but we got down in fair order and parked alongside the opposition's Cessna.

Colin said, 'Lock the aeroplane and come into the races. You can't for ever stand on guard.'

The Polyplane pilot was nowhere to be seen. I hoped for the best, locked up, and walked with the others into the racecourse next door.

The first person we saw was Acey Jones, balancing on

his crutches with the sun making his pale head look fairer than ever.

'Oh yes. Colin,' Nancy said. 'Do you want me to send a fiver to the Accident Insurance people? You remember, the leaflet which came yesterday? That man reminded me . . . he got a thousand pounds from the fund for cracking his ankle. I heard him say so, at Haydock.'

'If you like,' he agreed. 'A fiver won't break the bank. May as well.'

'Bobbie Wessex is sponsoring it,' Annie commented.

'Yes,' Nancy added. 'It was on the leaflet.'

'Did you see the bit about the bombs?' I asked.

Annie and Nancy both laughed. 'Someone in insurance has got a sense of humour, after all.'

Annie hustled off to the weighing room to see her runner in the first race, and Colin followed her, to change.

'Lemonade?' I suggested to Nancy.

'Pints of it. Whew, it's hot.'

We drank it in a patch of shade, out on the grass. Ten yards away, loud and clear, Eric Goldenberg was conducting a row with Kenny Bayst.

'. . . And don't you think, sport, that you can set your guerrillas on me and expect me to do you favours afterwards, because if you think that you've got another think coming.'

'What guerrillas?' Goldenberg demanded, not very convincingly.

'Oh come off it. Set them to cripple me. At Redcar.'

'Must have been those bookmakers you swindled while you were busy double crossing us.'

'I never double crossed you.'

'Don't give me that crap,' Goldenberg said heavily. 'You know bloody well you did. You twisty little bastard.'

'If you think that, why the frigging hell are you asking me to set up another touch for you now?'

'Bygones are bygones.'

'Bygones bloody aren't.' Kenny spat on the ground at Goldenberg's feet and removed himself to the weighing room. Goldenberg watched him go with narrowed eyes and a venomous twist to his mouth. The next time I saw him he was holding a well-filled glass and adding substantially to his paunch, while muttering belligerently to a pasty slob who housed all his brains in his biceps. The slob wasn't one of the two who had lammed into Kenny at Redcar. I wondered if Goldenberg intended mustering reinforcements.

'What do you think of Kenny Bayst?' I asked Nancy.

'The big little Mister I-Am from Down Under,' she said. 'He's better than he used to be, though. He came over here thinking everyone owed him a living, as he'd had a great big successful apprenticeship back home.'

'Would he lose to order?'

'I expect so.'

'Would he agree to lose to order, take the money, back himself, and try to win?'

She grinned. 'You're learning fast.'

We watched Colin win the first race. Annie Villars' horse finished third from last. She stood glumly looking at its heaving sides while Kenny's successor made the best of explaining away his own poor showing.

'Annie should have kept Kenny Bayst,' Nancy said.

'He wanted out.'

'Like Colin doesn't want in,' she nodded. 'Annie's being a bit of a fool this season.'

Before the third race we went back to the aeroplane. The Polyplane pilot was standing beside it, peering in through the windows. He was not the stand off merchant from Redcar, but his colleague from Haydock.

'Good afternoon,' Nancy said.

'Good afternoon, Miss Ross.' He was polite in the way that is more insolent than rudeness. Not the best method, I would have thought, of seducing Colin's custom back from Derrydowns. He walked away, back to his Cessna, and I went over the Cherokee inch by inch looking for anything wrong. As far as I could see, there was nothing. Nancy and I climbed aboard and I started the engine to warm it up ready to take off.

Colin and Annie arrived in a hurry and loaded themselves in, and we whisked off across southern England to Shoreham. Colin and Annie again jumped into a waiting taxi and vanished. Nancy stayed with me and the Cherokee, and we sat on the warm grass and watched little aeroplanes landing and taking off, and talked now and then without pressure about flying, racing, life in general.

Towards the end of the afternoon she asked, 'Will you go on being a taxi pilot all your life?'

'I don't know. I don't look far ahead any more.'

'Nor do I,' she said.

'No.'

'We've been happy, these last few weeks, with Midge being so much better. I wish it would last.'

'You'll remember it.'

'That's not the same.'

'It's only special because of what's coming,' I said.

There was a long pause while she thought about it. At length she asked, disbelievingly, 'Do you mean that it is because Midge is dying that we are so happy now?'

'Something like that.'

She turned her head; considered me. 'Tell me something else. I need something else.'

'Comfort?'

'If you like.'

I said, 'You've all three been through the classic progression, these last two years. All together, not just Midge herself. Shock, disbelief, anger and in the end acceptance . . .' I paused. 'You've come through the dark tunnel. You're out in the sun the other end. You've done most of your grieving already. You are a most extraordinarily strong family. You'll remember this summer because it will be something worth remembering.'

'Matt . . .'

There were tears in her eyes. I watched the bright little dragonfly aeroplanes dart and go. They could heal me, the Ross family, I thought. Their strength could heal me. If it would take nothing away from them. If I could be sure.

'What was Colin's wife like?' I asked, after a while.

'Oh . . .' She gave a laugh which was half a sniff. 'A bit too much like Fenella. He was younger then. He didn't know how to duck. She was thirty-three and bossy and rich, and he was twenty and madly impressed by her. To be honest, Midge and I thought she was fabulous too. We were seventeen and still wet behind the ears. She thought it would be marvellous being married to a genius, all accolades and champagne and glamour. She didn't like it when it turned out to be mostly hard work and starvation and exhaustion . . . so she left him for a young actor who'd just had rave notices for his first film, and it took Colin months to get back to being himself from the wreck she'd made of him.'

'Poor Colin.' Or lucky Colin. Strong Colin. Months . . . it was taking me years.

'Yeah . . .' She grinned. 'He got over it. He's got some bird now in London. He slides down to see her every so often when he thinks Midge and I aren't noticing.'

'I must get me a bird,' I said idly. 'One of these days.'

'You haven't got one?'

I shook my head. I looked at her. Straight eyebrows,

straight eyes, sensible mouth. She looked back. I wanted to kiss her. I didn't think she would be angry.

'No,' I said absentmindedly. 'No bird.'

Take nothing away from them. Nothing from Midge.

'I'll wait a while longer,' I said.

Several days, several flights later I telephoned the Board of Trade. Diffidently. Sneering at myself for trying to do their job for them, for thinking I might have thought of something they hadn't worked out for themselves. But then, I'd been on the flight with the bomb, and they hadn't. I'd seen things, heard things, felt things that they hadn't.

Partly for my own sake, but mainly because of what Nancy had said about the bomb merchant still running around loose with his motives still rotting away inside him, I had finally found myself discarding the thought that it was none of my business, that someone else could sort it all out, and coming round to the view that if I could in fact come up with anything it might be a profitable idea.

To which end I wasted a lot of brain time chasing down labyrinths of speculation, and fetched up against a series of reasons why not.

There was Larry, for instance. Well, what about Larry? Larry had had every chance to put the bomb on board, right up to two hours before I set off to collect the passengers from White Waltham. But however strong a motive he had to kill Colin or ruin Derrydowns, and none had so far appeared bar a few trivial frauds, if it was true it was a radio and not a time bomb he couldn't have set it off because when it exploded he was in Turkey. If it had been Larry, a time bomb would have been the only simple and practical way.

Then Susan . . . Ridiculous as I thought it, I went over again what the Board of Trade man had said: she was going out occasionally with a demolitions expert. Well, good luck to her. The sooner she got married again the better off I'd be. Only trouble was, the aversion therapy of that last destructive six months seemed to have been just as successful with her as it had been with me.

I couldn't believe that any executive type in his right mind would bump off his occasional girlfriend's ex-husband for the sake of about six thousand pounds of insurance, especially as the longer I lived, the greater would be the sum she eventually collected. I had three years ago stopped paying any more premiums, but the value of the pay-off automatically went on increasing.

Apart from knowing her incapable of the cold-blooded murder of innocent people, I respected her mercenary instincts. The longer I lived the better off she would be on all counts. It was as simple as that.

Honey Harley . . . had said she would do 'anything' to keep Derrydowns in business, and the blowing up of the Cherokee had eased the financial situation. One couldn't sell things which were being bought on the hire purchase, and if one couldn't keep up the instalments the aircraft technically belonged to the HP company, who might sell it at a figure which did little more than cover themselves, leaving a molehill for Derrydowns to salvage. Insurance, on the other hand, had done them proud: paid off the HP and left them with capital in hand.

Yet killing Colin Ross would have ruined Derrydowns completely. Honey Harley would never have killed any of the customers, let alone Colin Ross. And the same applied to Harley himself, all along the line.

The Polyplane people, then? Always around, always belligerent, trying their damnedest to put Derrydowns out of business and win back Colin Ross. Well . . . the bomb would have achieved the first object but have put the absolute dampers on the second. I couldn't see even the craziest Polyplane pilot killing the golden goose.

Kenny Bayst . . . livid with Eric Goldenberg, Major Tyderman and Annie Villars. But as I'd said to Colin, where would he have got a bomb from in the time, and would he have killed Colin and me too? It didn't seem possible, any of it. No to Kenny Bayst.

Who, then?

Who?

Since I couldn't come up with anyone else, I went back over the possibilities all over again. Larry, Susan, the Harleys, Polyplanes, Kenny Bayst . . . Looked at them up, down, and sideways. Got nowhere. Made some coffee, went to bed, went to sleep.

Woke up at four in the morning with the moon

shining on my face. And one fact hitting me with a bang. Up, down and sideways. Look at things laterally. Start from the bottom.

I started from the bottom. When I did that, the answer rose up and stared me in the face. I couldn't believe it. It was too darned simple.

In the morning I made a lengthy telephone call to a long lost cousin, and two hours later got one back. And it was then, expecting a flat rebuff, that I rang up the Board of Trade.

The tall polite man wasn't in. He would, they said, call back later.

When he did, Harley was airborne with a pupil and Honey answered in the tower. She buzzed through to the crew room, where I was writing up records.

'The Board of Trade want you. What have you been up to?'

'It's only that old bomb,' I said soothingly.

'Huh.'

When the tall man came on the line, she was still listening on the tower extension.

'Honey,' I said. 'Quit.'

'I beg your pardon,' said the Board of Trade.

Honey giggled, but she put her receiver down. I heard the click.

'Captain Shore?' the voice said reprovingly.

'Er, yes.'

'You wanted me?'

'You said . . . if I thought of any angle on the bomb.'

'Indeed yes.' A shade of warmth.

'I've been thinking,' I said, 'about the transmitter which was needed to set it off.'

'Yes?'

'How big would the bomb have been?' I asked. 'All that plastic explosive and gunpowder and wires and solenoids?'

'I should think quite small . . . you would probably pack a bomb like that into a flat tin about seven inches by four by two inches deep. Possibly even smaller. The tighter they are packed the more fiercely they explode.'

'And how big would the transmitter have to be to send perhaps three different signals?'

'Nowadays, not very big. If size were important . . . a pack of cards, perhaps. But in this case I would have thought . . . larger. The transmissions must have had to carry a fairly long way . . . and to double the range of a signal you have to quadruple the power of the transmitter, as no doubt you know.'

'Yes . . . I apologize for going through all this the long way, but I wanted to be sure. Because although I don't know *why*, I've a good idea of *when* and *who*.'

'What did you say?' His voice sounded strangled.

'I said . . .'

'Yes, yes,' he interrupted. 'I heard. When . . . when, then?'

'It was put on board at White Waltham. Taken off again at Haydock. And put back on again at Haydock.'

'What do you mean?'

'It came with one of the passengers.'

'Which one?'

'By the way,' I said. 'How much would such a bomb cost?'

'Oh . . . about eighty pounds or so,' he said impatiently. 'Who? . . .'

'And would it take a considerable expert to make one?'

'Someone used to handling explosives and with a working knowledge of radio.'

'I thought so.'

'Look,' he said, 'look, will you please stop playing cat and mouse. I dare say it amuses you to tease the Board of Trade . . . I don't say I absolutely blame you, but will you please tell me which of the passengers had a bomb with him?'

'Major Tyderman,' I said.

'Major . . .' He took an audible breath. 'Are you meaning to say now that it wasn't the bomb rolling around on the elevator wires which caused the friction which persuaded you to land? . . . That Major Tyderman was carrying it around unknown to himself all the afternoon? Or what?'

'No,' I said, 'And no.'

'For God's sake . . .' He was exasperated. 'I suppose you couldn't simplify the whole thing by telling me exactly who planted the bomb on Major Tyderman? Who intended to blow him up?'

'If you like.'

He took a shaking grip. I smiled at the crew room wall.

'Well, who?'

'Major Tyderman,' I said. 'Himself.'

Silence. Then a protest.

'Do you mean suicide? It can't have been. The bomb went off when the aeroplane was on the ground . . .'

'Precisely,' I said.

'What?'

'If a bomb goes off in an aeroplane, everyone automatically thinks it was intended to blow up in the air and kill all the people on board.'

'Yes, of course.'

'Suppose the real intended victim was the aeroplane itself, not the people?'

'But why?'

'I told you, I don't know why.'

'All right,' he said. 'All right.' He took a deep breath. 'Let's start from the beginning. You are saying that Major Tyderman, intending to blow up the aeroplane for reasons unknown, took a bomb with him to the races.'

'Yes.'

'What makes you think so?'

'Looking back . . . He was rigidly tense all day, and he wouldn't be parted from his binocular case, which was large enough to contain a bomb of the size you described.'

'That's absurdly circumstantial,' he protested.

'Sure,' I agreed. 'Then it was the Major who borrowed the keys from me, to go over to the aircraft to fetch the *Sporting Life* which he had left there. He wouldn't let me go, though I offered. He came back saying he had locked up again, and gave me back the keys. Of course he hadn't locked up. He wanted to create a little confusion. While he was over there he unscrewed the back panel of the luggage bay and put the bomb behind it, against the fuselage. Limpet gadget, I expect, like I said before, which came unstuck on the bumpy flight.'

'He couldn't have foreseen you'd land at East Midlands . . .'

'It didn't matter where we landed. As soon as everyone was clear of the aircraft, he was ready to blow it up.'

'That's sheer guess work.'

'He did it in front of my eyes, at East Midlands. I saw him look round, to check there was no one near it. Then he was fiddling with his binocular case . . . sending the signals. They could have been either very low or super-high frequencies. They didn't have very far to go. But more important, the transmitter would have been very low powered . . . and very small.'

'But . . . by all accounts . . . and yours too . . . he was severely shocked after the explosion.'

'Shocked by the sight of the disintegration he had been sitting on all day. And acting a bit, too.'

He thought it over at length. Then he said, 'Wouldn't someone have noticed that the Major wasn't using binoculars although he was carrying the case?'

'He could say he'd just dropped them and they were broken ... and anyway, he carries a flask in that case normally as well as the race glasses ... lots of people must have seen him taking a swig, as I have ... they wouldn't think it odd ... they might think he'd brought the flask but forgotten the glasses.'

I could imagine him shaking his head. 'It's a fantastic theory altogether. And not a shred of evidence. Just a guess.' He paused. 'I'm sorry, Mr Shore, I'm certain you've done your best, but ...'

I noticed he'd demoted me from Captain. I smiled thinly.

'There's one other tiny thing,' I said gently.

'Yes?' He was slightly, very slightly apprehensive, as if expecting yet more fantasy.

'I got in touch with a cousin in the army, and he looked up some old records for me. In World War Two Major Tyderman was in the Royal Engineers, in charge of a unit which spent nearly all of its time in England.'

'I don't see ...'

'They were dealing,' I said, 'with unexploded bombs.'

CHAPTER NINE

It was the next day that Nancy flew Colin to Haydock. They went in the four-seater 140 horse power small version Cherokee which she normally hired from her flying club for lessons and practice, and they set off from Cambridge shortly before I left there myself with a full load in the replacement Six. I had been through her flight plan with her and helped her all I could with the many technicalities and regulations she would meet in the complex Manchester control zone. The weather forecast was for clear skies until evening, there would be radar to help her if she got lost, and I would be listening to her nearly all the time on the radio as I followed her up.

Colin grinned at me. 'Harley would be horrified at the care you're taking to look after her. "Let them frighten themselves silly," he'd say, "then he'll fly with us all the time, with none of this do-it-yourself nonsense".'

'Yeah,' I agreed. 'And Harley wants you safe, too, don't forget.'

'Did he tell you to help us?'

'Not actually, no.'

'Thought not.'

Harley had said crossly, 'I don't want them making a habit of it. Persuade Colin Ross she isn't experienced enough.'

Colin didn't need persuading: he knew. He also wanted to please Nancy. She set off with shining eyes, like a child being given a treat.

The Derrydowns Six had been hired by an un-clued-up trainer who had separately agreed to share the trip with both Annie Villars and Kenny Bayst. Even diluted by the hiring trainer, the large loud-voiced owner of the horse he was running, and the jockey who was to ride it, the atmosphere at loading time was poisonous.

Jarvis Kitch, the hiring trainer, who could have helped, retreated into a huff.

'How was I to know,' he complained to me in aggrieved anger, 'that they loathe each other's guts?'

'You couldn't,' I said soothingly.

'They just rang up and asked if there was a spare seat. Annie yesterday, Bayst the day before. I said there was. How was I to know? . . .'

'You couldn't.'

The loud-voiced owner, who was evidently footing the bill, asked testily what the hell it mattered, they would be contributing their share of the cost. He had a north country accent and a bullying manner, and he was the sort of man who considered that when he bought a

473

man's services he bought his soul. Kitch subsided hastily: the small attendant jockey remained cowed and silent throughout. The owner, whose name I later discovered from the racecard was Ambrose, then told me to get a move on as he hadn't hired me to stand around all day on the ground at Cambridge.

Annie Villars suggested in embarrassment that the captain of an aircraft was like the captain of a ship.

'Nonsense,' he said, 'In a two bit little outfit like this he's only a chauffeur. Taking me from place to place isn't he? For hire?' He nodded. 'Chauffeur.' His voice left no one in any doubt about his opinion on the proper place of chauffeurs.

I sighed, climbed aboard, strapped myself in. Easy to ignore him, as it was far from the first time in my life I'd met that attitude. All the same, hardly one of the jolliest of trips.

The Cherokee Six cruised at fifty miles an hour faster than the One Forty, so that I passed Nancy somewhere on the way up. I could hear her calling the various flight information regions on the radio, as she could hear me. It was companionable, in an odd sort of way. And she was doing all right.

I landed at Haydock a few minutes before her, and unloaded the passengers in time to watch her come in. She put on a show to impress the audience, touching down like a feather on the grass. I grinned to myself. Not bad for a ninety-hour amateur. It hadn't been the easiest of trips either. There would be no holding her, after this.

She rolled to a stop a little way along the rails from me and I finished locking the Six and walked over to tell her she would smash the undercarriage next time she thumped an aeroplane down like that.

She made a face at me, excited and pleased. 'It was super. Great. The Liverpool radar people were awfully kind. They told me exactly which headings to fly round the control zone and then told me they would put me smack overhead the racecourse, and they did.'

Colin was proud of her and teased her affectionately. 'Sure, we've got here, but we've got to go home yet.'

'Going home's always easier,' she said confidently. 'And there are none of those difficult control zone rules round Cambridge.'

We walked together across the track to the paddock, ducking under the rails. Nancy talked the whole way, as high as if she'd taken benzedrine. Colin grinned at me. I grinned back. Nothing as intoxicating as a considerable achievement.

We left him at the weighing room and went off to have some coffee.

'Do you know it's only four weeks since we were at Haydock before?' she said. 'Since the bomb. Only four weeks. I seem to have known you half my life.'

'I hope you'll know me for the other half,' I said.

'What did you say?'

'Nothing . . . Turkey sandwiches all right?'

'Mm, lovely.' She looked at me, unsure. 'What did you mean?'

'Just one of those pointless things people say.'

'Oh.'

She bit into the soft thick sandwich. She had good straight teeth. I was being a fool, I thought. A fool to get involved, a fool to grow fond of her. I had nothing but a lot of ruins to offer anyone, and she had the whole world to choose from, the sister of Colin Ross. If I was an iceberg, as Honey said, I'd better stay an iceberg. When ice melted, it made a mess.

'You've clammed up,' she said, observing me.

'I haven't.'

'Oh yes, you have. You do, sometimes. You look relaxed and peaceful, and then something inside goes snap shut and you retreat out into the stratosphere. Somewhere very cold.' She shivered. 'Freezing.'

I drank my coffee and let the stratosphere do its stuff. The melting edges safely refroze.

'Will Chanter be here today?' I asked.

'God knows.' She shrugged. 'Do you want him to be?'

'No.' It sounded more vehement than I meant.

'That's something, anyhow,' she said under her breath.

I let it go. She couldn't mean what it sounded like. We finished the sandwiches and went out to watch Colin ride, and after that while we were leaning against the parade ring rails Chanter appeared out of nowhere and smothered Nancy in hair and fringes and swirling fabric, as closely as if he were putting out a fire with a carpet.

She pushed him away. 'For God's sake . . .'

He was unabashed. 'Aw Nancy. C'mon now. You and me, we'd have everything going for us if you'd just loosen up.'

'You're a bad trip, Chanter, as far as I'm concerned.'

'You've never been on any real trip, chick, that's your problem.'

'And I'm not going,' she said firmly.

'A little acid lets you into the guts of things.'

'Components,' I agreed. 'Like you said before. You see things in fragments.'

'Huh?' Chanter focussed on me. 'Nancy, you still got this creep in tow? You must be joking.'

'He sees things whole,' she said. 'No props needed.'

'Acid isn't a prop, it's a doorway,' he declaimed.

'Shut the door,' she said. 'I'm not going through.'

Chanter scowled at me. The green chenille tablecloth had been exchanged for a weird shapeless tunic made of irregular shaped pieces of fabrics, fur, leather and metal all stapled together instead of sewn.

'This is your doing, man, you're bad news.'

'It's not his doing,' Nancy said. 'The drug scene is a drag. It always was. Maybe at art school I thought getting woozy on pot was a gas, but not any more. I've grown up, Chanter. I've told you before, I've grown up.'

'He's brainwashed you.'

She shook her head. I knew she was thinking of

Midge. Face something big enough, and you always grow up.

'Don't you have any classes today?' she asked.

He scowled more fiercely. 'The sods are out on strike.'

She laughed. 'Do you mean the students?'

'Yeah. Demanding the sack for the deputy Head for keeping a record of what demos they go to.'

I asked ironically, 'Which side are you on?'

He peered at me. 'You bug me, man, you do really.'

For all that, he stayed with us all afternoon, muttering, scowling, plonking his hands on Nancy whenever he got the chance. Nancy bore his company as if she didn't altogether dislike it. As for me, I could have done without it. Easily.

Colin won two races, including the day's biggest. Annie Villars' horse came second, Kenny Bayst won a race on an objection. The loud voiced Ambrose's horse finished fourth, which didn't bode well for sweetness and light on the way home.

The way home was beginning to give me faint twinges of speculation. The weak warm front which had been forecast for late evening looked as if it were arriving well before schedule. From the south-west the upper winds were drawing a strip of cloud over the sky like a sheet over a bed.

Nancy looked up when the sun went in.

'Golly, where did all that cloud come from?'

'It's the warm front.'

'Damn . . . do you think it will have got to Cambridge?'

'I'll find out for you, if you like.'

I telephoned to Cambridge and asked them for their actual and forecast weather. Nancy stood beside me inside the telephone box and Chanter fumed suspiciously outside. I had to ask Cambridge to repeat what they'd said. Nancy smelled faintly of a fresh flowering scent. 'Did you say two thousand feet?' Yes, said Cambridge with exaggerated patience, we've told you twice already.

I put down the receiver. 'The front isn't expected there for three or four hours, and the forecast cloud base even then is as high as two thousand feet, so you should be all right.'

'Anyway,' she said, 'I've done dozens of practice letdowns at Cambridge. Even if it should be cloudy by the time we get back, I'm sure I could do it in earnest.'

'Have you ever done it without an instructor?'

She nodded. 'Several times. On fine days, of course.'

I pondered. 'You aren't legally qualified yet to carry passengers in clouds.'

'Don't look so fraught. I won't have to. They said it was clear there now, didn't they? And if the base is two thousand feet when I get there, I can keep below that easily.'

'Yes, I suppose you can.'

'And I've got to get back, haven't I?' she said reasonably.

'Mm . . .'

Chanter pulled open the telephone box door. 'You taking a lease on that space, man?' he inquired. He put his arm forward over Nancy's chest a millimetre south of her breasts and scooped her out. She half disappeared into the enveloping fuzz and re-emerged blushing.

'Chanter, for God's sake, we're at the races!'

'Transfer to my pad, then.'

'No, thank you.'

'Women,' he said in disgust. 'Goddamn women. Don't know what's good for them.'

'How's that for a right-wing reactionary statement?' I inquired of the air in general.

'You cool it, man. Just cool it.'

Nancy smoothed herself down and said, 'Both of you cool it. I'm going back to the aeroplane now to get set for going home, and you're not coming with me, Chanter. I can't concentrate with you crawling all over me.'

He stayed behind with a bad grace, complaining bitterly when she took me with her.

'He's impossible,' she said as we walked across the track. But she was smiling.

Spreading the map out on the wing I went through the flight plan with her, step by step, as that was what she wanted. She was going back as we'd come, via the radio beacon at Lichfield: not a straight line but the easiest way to navigate. As she had said, it was a simpler business going home. I worked out the times between points for her and filled them in on her planning sheet.

'You are five times as quick at it as I am,' she sighed.

'I've had a spot more practice.'

I folded the map and clipped the completed plan on to it. 'See you at Cambridge,' I said. 'With a bit of luck.'

'Meany.'

'Nancy . . .'

'Yes?'

I didn't exactly know what I wanted to say. She waited.

After a while I said earnestly, 'Take care.'

She half smiled. 'I will, you know.'

Colin came across the track dragging his feet. 'God, I'm tired,' he said. 'How's my pilot?'

'Ready, willing, and if it's your lucky day, able.'

I did the external checks for her while they climbed aboard. No bombs to be seen. Didn't expect any. She started the engine after I'd given her the all clear, and they both waved as she taxied off. She turned into the wind at the far end of the field, accelerated quickly, and lifted off into the pale-grey sky. The clouds were a shade lower than they had been. Nothing to worry about. Not if it was clear at Cambridge. I strolled across to the Derrydowns Six. Annie Villars and Kenny Bayst were both there already, studiously looking in opposite directions. I unlocked the doors, and Annie embarked without a word. Kenny gave her a sour look and stayed outside on the ground. I congratulated him on his winner. It all helped, he said.

Ambrose's trainer and jockey trickled back looking pensive, and finally Ambrose came himself, reddish in the face and breathing out beer fumes in a sickly cloud. As soon as he reached the aircraft he leaned towards me and gave me the full benefit.

'I've left me hat in the cloakroom,' he said. 'Hop over and fetch it for me.'

Kenny and the other two were all of a sudden very busy piling themselves aboard and pretending they hadn't heard. Short of saying 'Fetch it yourself' and losing Harley a customer, I was stuck with it. I trudged back across the track, through the paddock, into the members' gents, and collected the hat off the peg it was hanging on. Its band was so greasy that I wondered how Ambrose had the nerve to let anyone see it.

Turned, made for the door. Felt my arm clutched in a fiercely urgent grip.

I swung round. The hands holding on to my arm like steel grabs belonged to Major Tyderman.

'Major,' I exclaimed in surprise. I hadn't seen him there all through the afternoon.

'Shore!' He was far more surprised to see me. And more than surprised. Horrified. The colour was draining out of his face while I watched.

'Shore . . . What are you doing here? Did you come back?'

Puzzled, I said, 'I came over for Mr Ambrose's hat.'

'But . . . you flew . . . you took off with Colin and Nancy Ross.'

I shook my head. 'No, I didn't. Nancy was flying.'

'But . . . you came with them.' He sounded agonized.

'I didn't. I flew the Six here with five passengers.' The extreme state of his shock got through to me like a tidal wave. He was clinging on to my arm now more for support than to attract my attention.

'Major,' I said, the terrible, terrifying suspicion shaking in my voice, 'you haven't put another bomb on that aircraft? Not . . . oh God . . . another bomb?'

'I . . . I . . .' His voice strangled in his throat.

'Major.' I disengaged my arm and seized both of his. Ambrose's hat fell and rolled unnoticed on the dirty floor. 'Major.' I squeezed him viciously. '*Not another bomb?*'

'No . . . but . . .'

'But *what*?'

'I thought . . . you were flying them . . . I thought you were with them . . . you would be able to cope . . .'

'Major.' I shook him, gripping as if I'd pull his arms in two. 'What have you done to that aeroplane?'

'I saw you . . . come with them, when they came. And go back . . . and look at the map . . . and do the checks . . . I was sure . . . it was you that was flying . . . and you . . . you . . . could deal with . . . but Nancy Ross . . . Oh my God . . .'

I let go one of his arms and slapped him hard in the face.

'*What have you done to that aeroplane?*'

'You can't . . . do anything . . .'

'I'll get her back. Get her down on the ground at once.'

He shook his head. 'You won't . . . be able to . . . She'll have no radio . . . I put . .' He swallowed and put his hand to his face where I'd hit him. 'I put . . . a plaster . . . nitric acid . . . on the lead . . . to the master switch . . .'

I let go of his other arm and simply looked at him, feeling the coldness sink in. Then I blindly picked up Ambrose's hat and ran out of the door. Ran. Ran across the paddock, across the track, down to the aircraft. I didn't stop to slap it out of the Major what he'd done it for. Didn't think of it. Thought only of Nancy with her limited experience having to deal with a total electrical failure.

She could do it, of course. The engine wouldn't stop. Several of the instruments would go on working. The altimeter, the air-speed indicator, the compass, none of those essentials would be affected. They worked on magnetism, air pressure and engine driven gyroscopes, not electricity.

All the engine instruments would read zero, and the fuel gauge would register empty. She wouldn't know how much fuel she had left. But she did know, I thought, that she had enough for at least two hours' flying.

The worst thing was the radio. She would have no communication with the ground, nor could she receive any signals from the navigation beacons. Well . . . dozens of people flew without radio, without even having it installed at all. If she was worried about getting lost, she could land at the first suitable airfield.

It might not have happened yet, I thought. Her radio might still be working. The nitric acid might not yet have eaten through the main electrical cable.

While I was on the ground I was too low down for them to hear me, but if I got up in the air fast enough I could tell the Manchester control people the situation, get them to relay the facts to her, tell her to land at an airfield as soon as she could . . . A fairly simple matter to repair the cable, once she was safe on the ground.

I gave Ambrose his hat. He was still outside on the grass, waiting for me to climb through to the left hand seat. I shifted myself across on to it with no seconds wasted and he hauled himself up after me. By the time he'd strapped himself in I had the engine running, my head-set in place, and the radios warming up.

'What's the rush?' Ambrose inquired, as we taxied at just under take-off speed down to the far end.

'Have to send a radio message to Colin Ross, who's in the air ahead of us.'

'Oh . . .' He nodded heavily. He knew the Rosses had come up when we had, knew that Nancy was flying. 'All right then.'

I thought fleetingly that if he thought I couldn't even hurry without getting his permission first he was in for a moderate shock. I wasn't taking him back to Cambridge until I was certain Nancy and Colin were safe.

As there was only one head-set on board Ambrose couldn't hear any incoming transmissions, and with the microphone close against my lips I doubted if he could hear over the engine noise anything I sent outwards. I thought I would delay as long as possible inviting his objections.

Two hundred feet off the ground I raised the Air Traffic Controller at Liverpool. Explained that Nancy's radio might be faulty; asked if he had heard her.

Yes, he had. He'd given her radar clearance out of the control zone, and handed her on to Preston Information. Since I had to stay on his frequency until I was out of the zone myself, I asked him to find out from Preston if they still had contact with her.

'Stand by,' he said.

After a long two minutes he came back. 'They did have,' he said briefly. 'They lost her in the middle of one of her transmissions. They can't raise her now.'

Sod the Major, I thought violently. Stupid, dangerous little man.

I kept my voice casual. 'Did they have her position?'

'Stand by.' A pause. He came back. 'She was on track to Lichfield, ETA Lichfield five three, flying visual on top at flight level four five.'

'On top?' I repeated with apprehension.

'Affirmative.'

We had been climbing steadily ourselves. We went

into thin cloud at two thousand feet and came through it into the sunshine at four thousand. Everywhere below us in all directions spread the cottonwool blanket, hiding the earth beneath. She would have to climb to that height as well, because the Pennines to the east of Manchester rose to nearly three thousand feet and the high ridges would have been sticking up into the clouds. With no room for her between the clouds and the hills she would have had either to go back, or go up. She wouldn't see any harm in going up. With radio navigation and a good forecast for Cambridge it was merely the sensible thing to do.

'Her destination is Cambridge,' I said. 'Can you check the weather there?'

'Stand by.' A much longer pause. Then his voice, dead level, spelling it out. 'Cambridge actual weather, cloud has spread in fast from the south-west, now eight eighths cover, base twelve hundred feet, tops three thousand five hundred.'

I didn't acknowledge him at once: was digesting the appalling implications.

'Confirm weather copied,' he said baldly.

'Weather copied.'

'Latest meteorological reports indicate total cloud cover over the entire area south of the Tees.' He knew exactly what he was saying. The laconic non-panic voice was deliberately unexcited. Nancy was flying above the cloud layer with no means of telling where she was. She couldn't see the ground and couldn't ask anyone for directions. Eventually she would have to come down, because she would run out of fuel. With the gauge out of action, she couldn't tell exactly how long she could stay airborne, and it was essential for her to go down through the clouds while the engine was still running, so that she could find somewhere to land once she was underneath. But if she went down too soon, or in the wrong place, she could all too easily fly into a cloud-covered hill. Even for a highly experienced pilot it was a sticky situation.

I said, with the same studied artificial calm, 'Can the RAF radar stations find her and trace her where she goes? I know her flight plan ... I made it out for her. She is likely to stick to it, as she thinks it is still clear at Cambridge. I could follow ... and find her.'

'Stand by.' Again the pause for consultations. 'Change frequency to Birmingham radar on one one eight zero five.'

'Roger,' I said. 'And thanks very much.'

'Good luck,' he said. 'You'll need it.'

CHAPTER TEN

He had explained the situation to Birmingham. I gave the radar controller Nancy's planned track and air speed and estimated time for Lichfield, and after a few moments he came back and said there were at least ten aircraft on his screen which were possibles, but he had no way of telling who they were. 'I'll consult with the RAF Wymeswold . . . they may not be as busy as we are . . . they can concentrate on it more.'

'Tell them that at about five three she will change her heading to one two five.'

'Roger,' he said. 'Stand by.'

He came back. 'RAF Wymeswold say they will watch for her.'

'Great,' I said.

After a few moments he said in an incredulous voice, 'We have a report that Colin Ross is aboard the non-radio aircraft. Can you confirm?'

'Affirmative,' I said. 'The pilot is his sister.'

'Good God,' he said. 'Then we'd better find her.'

I had got them to route me straight through the

control zone instead of round it, and was making for Northwich, and then the Lichfield beacon. We had taken off, I calculated, a good thirty minutes behind her, and in spite of the short cut and the Six's superior speed it would be barely possible to overtake her before Cambridge. I looked at my watch for about the twentieth time. Five-fifty. At five fifty-three she would be turning over Lichfield . . . except that she wouldn't know she was at Lichfield. If she turned as scheduled, it would be on her part simply blind faith.

Birmingham radar called me up. 'Cambridge report a steady deterioration in the weather. The cloud base is now eight hundred feet.'

'Roger,' I said flatly.

After another five minutes, during which five fifty-three came and went in silence, he said, 'Wymeswold report that an aircraft on their screen has turned from one six zero on to one two five, but it is five miles north-east of Lichfield. The aircraft is unidentified. They will maintain surveillance.'

'Roger,' I said.

She could be drifting north-east, I thought, because the wind from the south-west was stronger than it had been on the northward journey, and I hadn't made enough allowance for it on the flight plan. I pressed the transmit button and informed the radar man.

'I'll tell them,' he said.

We flew on. I looked round at the passengers. They looked variously bored, thoughtful and tired. Probably none of them would notice when we left our direct course to go and look for Nancy: but they'd certainly notice if or when we found her.

'Wymeswold report the aircraft they were watching has turned north on to zero one zero.'

'Oh no,' I said.

'Stand by . . .'

Too easy, I thought despairingly. It had been too easy. The aircraft which had turned on to the right heading at the right time at roughly the right place hadn't been the right aircraft after all. I took three deep deliberate breaths. Concentrated on the fact that wherever she was she was in no immediate danger. She could stay up for more than another hour and a half.

I had over an hour in which to find her. In roughly three thousand square miles of sky as featureless as the desert. Piece of cake.

'Wymeswold report that the first aircraft has apparently landed at East Midlands, but that they have another possibility ten miles east of Lichfield, present heading one two zero. They have no height information.'

'Roger,' I said again. No height information meant that the blip on their screen could be flying at anything up to thirty thousand feet or more, not four thousand five hundred.

'Stand by.'

I stood by. Metaphorically bit my nails. Slid a sidelong glance at Ambrose and went unhurriedly about checking our own height, speed, direction. Lichfield dead ahead, eleven minutes away. Forty minutes to Cambridge. Too long. Have to go faster. Pushed the throttle open another notch and came up against the stops. Full power. Nothing more to be done.

'Possible aircraft now tracking steady one zero five. Present track if maintained will take it thirty miles north of Cambridge at estimated time two zero.'

'Roger.' I looked at my watch. Did a brief sum. Pressed the transmit button. 'That's the wrong aircraft. It's travelling too fast. At ninety knots she couldn't reach the Cambridge area before three five or four zero.'

'Understood.' A short silence. 'Retune now to RAF Cottesmore, Northern Radar, one two two decimal one. I'm handing you on to them.'

I thanked him. Retuned. Cottesmore said they were in the picture, and looking. They had seven unidentified aircraft travelling from west to east to the south of them, all at heights unknown.

Seven. She could be any one of them. She could have gone completely haywire and turned round and headed back to Manchester. I felt my skin prickle. Surely she would have enough sense not to fly straight into a control zone without radio. And anyway, she still believed it was clear at Cambridge . . .

I reached the Lichfield beacon. Turned on to course for Cambridge. Informed Cottesmore radar that I had

492

done so. They didn't have me on their screen yet, they said: I was still too far away.

I tracked doggedly on towards Cambridge over the cottonwool wastes. The sun shone hotly into the cabin, and all the passengers except Ambrose went to sleep.

'One unidentified aircraft has landed at Leicester,' Cottesmore radar said. 'Another appears to be heading directly for Peterborough.'

'That leaves five?' I asked.

'Six . . . there's another now farther to the west.'

'It may be me.'

'Turn left thirty degrees for identification.'

I turned, flew on the new heading.

'Identified,' he said. 'Return to former heading.'

I turned back on track, stifling the raw anxiety which mounted with every minute. They must find her, I thought. They *must*.

Cottesmore said, 'One aircraft which passed close to the south of us five minutes ago has now turned north.'

Not her.

'The same aircraft has now flown in a complete circle and resumed a track of one one zero.'

It might be her. If she had spotted a thin patch. Had gone to see if she could see the ground and get down safely to below the cloud. Had found she couldn't: had gone on again in what she thought was the direction of Cambridge.

'That might be her,' I said. Or someone else in the

same difficulties. Or someone simply practising turns. Or anything.

'That particular aircraft has now turned due south . . . slightly west . . . now round again to south-east . . . back to one one zero.'

'Could be looking for thin patches in the cloud,' I said.

'Could be. Stand by.' A pause. Then his voice, remote and careful. 'Cloud base in this area is down to six hundred feet. Eight eighths cover. No clear patches.'

Oh Nancy . . .

'I'm going to look for that one,' I said. 'Can you give me a steer to close on its present track?'

'Will do,' he said. 'Turn left on to zero nine five. You are thirty miles to the west. I estimate your ground speed at one fifty knots. The aircraft in question is travelling at about ninety-five knots.'

In the twelve minutes it would take me to reach the other aircraft's present position, it would have shifted twenty miles farther on. Catching up would take twenty-five to thirty minutes.

'The aircraft in question is circling again . . . now tracking one one zero . . .'

The more it circled, the sooner I'd catch it. But if it wasn't Nancy at all . . . I thrust the thought violently out of my mind. If it wasn't we might never find her.

Ambrose touched my arm, and I had been concentrating so hard that I jumped.

'We're off course,' he said dogmatically. He tapped

the compass. 'We're going due east. We'd better not be lost.'

'We're under radar control,' I said matter-of-factly.

'Oh . . .' He was uncertain. 'I see.'

I would have to tell him, I thought. Couldn't put it off any longer. I explained the situation as briefly as I could, leaving out Major Tyderman's part in it and shouting to make myself heard over the noise of the engine.

He was incredulous. 'Do you mean we're chasing all over the sky looking for Colin Ross?'

'Directed by radar,' I said briefly.

'And who,' he asked belligerently, 'is going to pay for this? I am certainly not. In fact you have been totally irresponsible in changing course without asking my permission first.'

Cottesmore reported, 'The aircraft is now overhead Stamford, and circling again.'

'Roger,' I said. And for God's sake, Nancy, I thought, don't try going down through the cloud just there. There were some hills round about and a radio mast five hundred feet high.

'Steer one zero zero to close.'

'One zero zero.'

'Aircraft has resumed its former heading.'

I took a considerable breath of relief.

'Did you hear what I said?' Ambrose demanded angrily.

'We have a duty to go to the help of an aircraft in trouble,' I said.

'Not at my expense, we don't.'

'You will be charged,' I said patiently, 'only the normal amount for the trip.'

'That's not the point. You should have asked my permission. I am seriously displeased. I will complain to Harley. We should not have left our course. Someone else should have gone to help Colin Ross. Why should we be inconvenienced?'

'I am sure he will be pleased to hear your views,' I said politely. 'And no doubt he will pay any expenses incurred in his rescue.'

He glared at me speechlessly, swept by fury.

Annie Villars leaned forward and tapped me on the shoulder.

'Did I hear you say that Colin Ross is lost? Up here, do you mean? On top of the clouds?'

I glanced round. They were all awake, all looking concerned.

'Yes,' I said briefly. 'With no radio. The radar people think they may have found him. We're going over to see . . . and to help.'

'Anything we can do . . .' Annie said. 'Of course, call on us.'

I smiled at her over my shoulder. Ambrose turned round to her and started to complain. She shut him up smartly. 'Do you seriously propose we make no attempt to help? You must be out of your mind. It is our clear and absolute duty to do whatever we can. And a captain doesn't have to consult his passengers before he goes to help another ship in distress.'

He said something about expense. Annie said crisply, 'If you are too mean to pay a few extra pounds as your share of perhaps saving the life of Colin Ross, I shall be pleased to contribute the whole amount myself.'

'Atta girl,' Kenny Bayst said loudly. Annie Villars looked startled, but not displeased. Ambrose swivelled to face forwards. He had turned a dark purplish red. I hoped it was shame and embarrassment, not an incipient thrombosis.

'The aircraft is circling again,' Cottesmore reported. 'Its position now is just south of Peterborough... Remain on your present heading... I am handing you on now to Wytton... no need for you to explain to them... they know the situation.'

'Thank you very much,' I said.

'Good luck...'

Wytton, the next in the chain, the RAF master station north-east of Cambridge, was crisp, cool, efficient.

'Cloud base at Cambridge six hundred feet, no further deterioration in past half-hour. Visibility three kilometres in light rain. Surface wind two four zero, ten knots.'

'Weather copied,' I said automatically. I was looking at the map. Another radio mast, this one seven hundred feet high, south of Peterborough. Go on, Nancy, I thought, go on, further east. Don't try there. Not there . . .

Wytton said, 'Aircraft now back on one one zero.'

I rubbed a hand round the back of my neck. I could feel the sweat.

'Steer zero nine five. You are now ten miles west of the aircraft.'

'I'm climbing to flight level eight zero. To see better.'

'Cleared to eight zero.'

The altimeter hands crept round to eight thousand feet. The blanket of white fleece spread out unbroken in all directions to the horizon, soft and pretty in the sun. The passengers murmured, perhaps realizing for the first time the extent of Nancy's predicament. Mile after mile after mile of emptiness, and absolutely no way of telling where she was.

'Aircraft's circling again . . . Maintain zero nine five. You are now seven miles to the west.'

I said over my shoulder to Annie Villars, 'We'll see them soon . . . Would you take this notebook . . .' I handed her the spiral bound reporters' notebook I used for jotting during flight, 'and make some letters out of the pages? As big as you can. We will need, you see, to hold them up in the window, so that Nancy and Colin can read what we want them to do.'

And let it be them, I thought coldly. Just let it be them, and not some other poor lost souls. Because we'd have to stay to help. We couldn't leave them to struggle and look somewhere else for the ones we wanted . . .

Annie Villars fumbled in her handbag and produced a small pair of scissors.

'Which letters?' she said economically. 'You say, and I'll write them down, and then make them.'

'Right . . . FOLWBASE. That will do to start with.'

I twisted my head and saw her start snipping. She was making them full page size and as bold as possible. Satisfied, I looked forward again, scanning the sunny waste, searching for a small black cigarette shape moving ahead.

'Turn on to one zero five,' Wytton said. 'The aircraft is now in your one o'clock position five miles ahead.'

I looked down over to the right of the aircraft's nose. Ambrose reluctantly looked out of the window in sulky silence.

'*There*,' Kenny Bayst said. 'Over there, down there.' I looked where he was pointing . . . and there it was, slightly more over to our right, beginning another circling sweep over a darker patch of cloud which might have been a hole, but wasn't.

'Contact,' I said to Wytton. 'Closing in now.'

'Your intentions?' he asked unemotionally.

'Lead them up to the Wash, descend over the sea, follow the river and railway from King's Lynn to Cambridge.'

'Roger. We'll advise Marham. They'll give you radar coverage over the sea.'

I put the nose down, built up the speed, and overhauled the other aircraft like an E-type catching a bicycle. The nearer we got the more I hoped . . . it was a low-winged aeroplane . . . a Cherokee . . . white with red markings . . . and finally the registration number . . . and someone frantically waving a map at us from the window.

The relief was overpowering.

'It's them,' Annie said, and I could only nod and swallow.

I throttled back and slowed the Six until it was down to Nancy's cruising speed, then circled until I came up on her left side, and about fifty yards away. She had never done any formation flying. Fifty yards was the closest it was safe to go to her and even fifty yards was risking it a bit. I kept my hand on the throttle, my eyes on her, and an extra pair of eyes I didn't know I had, fixed on the heading.

To Annie Villars I said, 'Hold up the letters for "follow". Slowly. One by one.'

'Right.' She held them flat against the window beside her. We could see Colin's head leaning back behind Nancy's. When Annie finished the word we saw him wave his hand, and after that Nancy waved her map against her window, which showed up better.

'Wytton,' I reported. 'Is it the right aircraft. They are following us to the Wash. Can you give me a steer to King's Lynn?'

'Delighted,' he said. 'Steer zero four zero, and call Marham on frequency one one nine zero.'

'Thanks a lot,' I said with feeling.

500

'You're very welcome.'

Good guys, I thought. Very good guys, sitting in their darkened rooms wearing headsets and staring at their little dark circular screens, watching the multitude of yellow dots which were aircraft swimming slowly across like tadpoles. They'd done a terrific job, finding the Rosses. Terrific.

'Can you make a figure four?' I asked Annie Villars.

'Certainly.' The scissors began to snip.

'When you have, would you hold up the O, then the four, then the O again?'

'With pleasure.'

She held up the figures. Nancy waved the map. We set off north-eastwards to the sea, Nancy staying behind us to the right, with me flying looking over my shoulder to keep a steady distance between us. I judged it would take thirteen minutes at her speed to reach the sea, five to ten to let down, and twenty or so more to return underneath the cloud base to Cambridge. Her fuel by the time she got there would be low, but there was less risk of her running dry than of hitting a hill or trees or a building by going down over the land. Letting down over the sea was in these circumstances the best procedure whenever possible.

'We're going to need some more letters,' I told Annie.

'Which?'

'Um . . . R, I, V, and N, D, C, and a T, and a nine.'

'Right.'

Out of the corner of my eye I could see Annie Villars snipping and Kenny Bayst, sitting behind her, sorting out the letters she had already made so that she could easily pick them out when they were needed. There was, I thought to myself, with a small internal smile, a truce in operation in that area.

Marham radar reported, 'You have four miles to run to the coast.'

'Hope the tide's in,' I said facetiously.

'Affirmative,' he said with deadpan humour. 'High water eighteen forty hours BST.'

'And . . . er . . . the cloud base?'

'Stand by.' Down in his dark room he couldn't see the sky. He had to ask the tower dwellers above.

'Cloud base between six and seven hundred feet above sea level over the entire area from the Wash to Cambridge. Visibility two kilometres in drizzle.'

'Nice,' I said with irony.

'Very.'

'Could I have the regional pressure setting?'

'Nine nine eight millibars.'

'Nine nine eight,' I repeated, and took my hand off the throttle enough to set that figure on the altimeter subscale. To Annie Villars I said, 'Can you make an eight, as well?'

'I expect so.'

'Crossing the coast,' Marham said.

'Right . . . Miss Villars, will you hold up SEA?'

She nodded and did so. Nancy waved the map.

'Now hold up SET, then nine nine eight, then MBS.'

'S . . . E . . . T,' she repeated, holding them against the window. 'Nine, nine, eight.' She paused. 'There's no M cut out.'

'W upside down,' Kenny Bayst said, and gave it to her.

'Oh yes. M . . . B . . . S. What does MBS mean?'

'Millibars,' I said.

Nancy waved the map, but I said to Annie, 'Hold up the nine nine eight again, it's very important.'

She held them up. We could see Nancy's head nodding as she waved back vigorously.

'Why is it so important?' Annie said.

'Unless you set the altimeter to the right pressure on the subscale, it doesn't tell you how high you are above the sea.'

'Oh.'

'Now would you hold up BASE, then six zero zero, then FT.'

'Right . . . Base . . . six hundred . . . feet.'

There was a distinct pause before Nancy waved, and then it was a small, half-hearted one. She must have been horrified to find that the clouds were so low: she must have been thanking her stars that she hadn't tried to go down through them. Highly frightening piece of information, that six hundred feet.

'Now,' I said to Annie, 'hold up FOLLOW RIVER AND RAIL ONE NINE ZERO TO CAMBRIDGE.'

'Follow . . . river . . . and . . . rail . . . one . . . nine . . .

zero . . . to . . . Cambridge . . . no G . . . never mind, C will do, then E.' She spelt it out slowly. Nancy waved.

'And just one more . . . four zero, then N, then M.'

'Forty nautical miles,' she said triumphantly. She held them up and Nancy waved.

'Now hold up FOLLOW again.'

'Right.'

I consulted Marham, took Nancy out to sea a little further, and led her round in a circle until we were both heading just west of south on one nine zero, and in a straight line to the railway and river from King's Lynn to Cambridge.

'Hold up DOWN,' I said.

She did it without speaking. Nancy gave a little wave. I put the nose of the Six down towards the clouds and accelerated to a hundred and forty knots so that there would be no possibility of her crashing into the back of us. The white fleecy layer came up to meet us, embraced us in sunlit feathery wisps, closed lightly around us, became denser, darker, an anthracite fog pressing on the windows. The altimeter unwound, the clock needles going backwards through 3,000 feet, 2,000 feet, 1,000 feet, still no break at 800 feet, 700 . . . and there, there at last the mist receded a little and became drizzly haze, and underneath us, pretty close underneath, were the restless rainswept dark greeny grey waves.

The passengers were all silent. I glanced round at them. They were all looking down at the sea in varying states of awe. I wondered if any of them knew I had just broken two laws and would undoubtedly be prosecuted again by the Board of Trade. I wondered if I would ever, ever, learn to keep myself out of trouble.

We crossed the coast over King's Lynn and flew down the river to Ely and Cambridge, just brushing through the misty cloud base at seven hundred feet. The forward visibility was bad, and I judged it silly to go back and wait for Nancy, because we might collide before we saw each other. I completed the journey as briefly as possible and we landed on the wet tarmac and taxied round towards the airport buildings. When I stopped the engine, everyone as if moved by one mind climbed out and looked upwards; even Ambrose.

The drizzle was light now, like fine mist. We stood quietly in it, getting damp, listening for the sound of an engine, watching for the shadow against the sky. Minutes ticked past. Annie Villars looked at me anxiously. I shook my head, not knowing exactly what I meant.

She couldn't have gone down too far . . . hit the sea . . . got disorientated in the cloud . . . lost when she came out of it . . . still in danger.

The drizzle fell. My heart also.

But she hadn't made any mistakes.

The engine noise crept in as a hum, then a buzz, then a definite rhythm. The little red and white aeroplane appeared suddenly against the right-hand sky, and she was circling safely round the outskirts of the field and coming sedately down to land.

'Oh . . .' Annie Villars said, and wiped two surprising tears of relief out of her eyes.

Ambrose said sulkily, 'That's all right then. Now I hope we can get off home,' and stomped heavily away towards the buildings.

Nancy taxied round and stopped her Cherokee a short distance away. Colin climbed out on the wing, grinned hugely in our direction, and waved.

'He's got no bloody nerves,' Kenny said. 'Not a bleeding nerve in his whole body.'

Nancy came out after him, jumping down on to the tarmac and staggering a bit as she landed on wobbly knees. I began to walk towards them. She started slowly to meet me, and then faster, and then ran, with her hair swinging out and her arms stretched wide. I held her round the waist and swung her up and round in the air and when I put her down she wrapped her arms behind my neck and kissed me.

'Matt . . .' She was half laughing, half crying, her eyes shining, her cheeks a burning red, the sudden release of tension making her tremble down to her fingertips.

Colin reached us and gave me a buffet on the shoulder.

'Thanks, chum.'

'Thank the RAF. They found you on their radar.'

'But how did you know? . . .'

'Long story,' I said. Nancy was still holding on to me as if she would fall down if she let go. I made the most of it by kissing her again, on my own account.

She laughed shakily and untwined her arms. 'When you came . . . I can't tell you . . . it was such a relief . . .'

Annie Villars came up and touched her arm and she turned to her with the same hectic overexcitement.

'Oh . . . *Annie.*'

'Yes, dear,' she said calmly. 'What you need now is a strong brandy.'

'I ought to see to . . .' she looked vaguely in my direction, and back to the Cherokee.

'Colin and Matt will see to everything.'

'All right, then . . .' She let herself be taken off by Annie Villars, who had recovered her poise and assumed total command as a good general should. Kenny and the other jockey and trainer meekly followed.

'Now,' said Colin. 'How on earth did you know we needed you?'

'I'll show you,' I said abruptly. 'Come and look.' I walked him back to the little Cherokee, climbed up on to the wing and lay down on my back across the two front seats, looking up under the control panel.

'What on earth . . .?'

The device was there. I showed it to him. Very neat, very small. A little polythene-wrapped packet swinging free on a rubber band which was itself attached to the cable leading to the master switch. Nearer the switch one wire of the two wire cable had been bared: the two severed ends of copper showed redly against the black plastic casing.

507

I left everything where it was and eased myself out on to the wing.

'What is it? What does it mean?'

'Your electric system was sabotaged.'

'For God's sake . . . why?'

'I don't know,' I sighed. 'I only know who did it. The same person who planted the bomb a month ago. Major Rupert Tyderman.'

He stared at me blankly. 'It doesn't make sense.'

'Not much. No.'

I told him how the Major had set off the bomb while we were safely on the ground, and that today he had thought I was flying Nancy's Cherokee and could get myself out of trouble.

'But that's . . . that means . . .'

'Yes,' I said.

'He's trying to make it look as though someone's trying to kill me.'

I nodded. 'While making damn sure you survive.'

CHAPTER ELEVEN

The Board of Trade came down like the hounds of Hell and it wasn't the tall reasonable man I faced this time in the crew room but a short hard-packed individual with an obstinate jaw and unhumorous eyes. He refused to sit down: preferred to stand. He had brought no silent note-taker along. He was strictly a one man band. And hot on percussion.

'I must bring to your attention the Air Navigation Order Nineteen sixty-six.' His voice was staccato and uncompromising, the traditional politeness of his department reduced to the thinnest of veneers.

I indicated that I was reasonably familiar with the order in question. As it ruled every cranny of a professional pilot's life, this was hardly surprising.

'We have been informed that on Friday last you contravened Article 25, paragraph 4, subsection a, and Regulation 8, paragraph 2.'

I waited for him to finish. Then I said, 'Who informed you?'

He looked at me sharply. 'That is beside the point.'

'Could it have been Polyplanes?'

His eyelids flickered in spite of himself. 'If we receive a complaint which can be substantiated we are bound to investigate.'

The complaint could be substantiated, all right. Saturday's newspapers were still strewn around the crew room this Monday morning, all full of the latest attempt on Colin Ross' life. Front page stuff. Also minute details from all my passengers about how we had led him out to sea and brought him home under the 700 foot cloud base.

Only trouble was, it was illegal in a single-engine aeroplane like the Six to take paying customers out over the sea as low as I had, and to land them at an airport where the cloud base was lower than one thousand feet.

'You admit that you contravened Section . . .'

I interrupted him. 'Yes.'

He opened his mouth and shut it again. 'Er, I see.' He cleared his throat. 'You will receive a summons in due course.'

'Yes,' I said again.

'Not your first, I believe.' An observation, not a sneer.

'No,' I said unemotionally.

A short silence. Then I said, 'How did that gadget work? The nitric acid package on the rubber band.'

'That is not your concern.'

I shrugged. 'I can ask any schoolboy who does chemistry.'

He hesitated. He was not of the stuff to give anything

away. He would never, as the tall man had, say or imply that there could be any fault in his Government or the Board. But having searched his conscience and no doubt his standing orders, he felt able after all to come across.

'The package contained fluffy fibreglass soaked in a weak solution of nitric acid. A section of wire in the cable to the master switch had been bared, and the fibreglass wrapped around it. The nitric acid slowly dissolved the copper wire, taking, at that concentration, probably about an hour and a half to complete the process.' He stopped, considering.

'And the rubber band?' I prompted.

'Yes ... well, nitric acid, like water, conducts electricity, so that while the fibreglass was still in position the electrical circuit would be maintained, even though the wire itself had been completely dissolved. To break the circuit the fibreglass package had to be removed. This was done by fastening it under tension via the rubber band to a point further up the cable. When the nitric acid dissolved right through the wire and the two ends parted, there was nothing to stop the rubber band contracting and pulling the fibreglass package away. Er ... do I make myself clear?'

'Indeed,' I agreed, 'you do.'

He seemed to give himself a little mental and physical shake, and turned with sudden energy towards the door.

'Right,' he said briskly. 'Then I need a word with Mr Harley.'

'Did you get a word with Major Tyderman?' I asked.

After the merest hiatus he said again, 'That is not your concern.'

'Perhaps you have seen him already?'

Silence.

'Perhaps, though, he is away from home?'

More silence. Then he turned to me in stiff exasperation. 'It is not your business to question me like this. I cannot answer you any more. It is I who am here to inquire into you, not the other way round.' He shut his mouth with a snap and gave me a hard stare. 'And they even warned me,' he muttered.

'I hope you find the Major,' I said politely, 'before he plants any more little devices in inconvenient places.'

He snorted and strode before me out of the crew room and along to Harley's office. Harley knew what he was there for and had been predictably furious with me ever since Friday.

'Mr Shore admits the contraventions,' the Board of Trade said.

'He'd be hard pushed not to,' Harley said angrily, 'considering every RAF base across the country told him about the low cloud base at Cambridge.'

'In point of fact,' agreed the Board of Trade, 'he should then have returned immediately to Manchester which was then still within the legal limit, and waited there until conditions improved, instead of flying all the way to East Anglia and leaving himself with too small a fuel margin to go to any cloud-free airport. The proper course was certainly to turn back right at the beginning.'

'And to hell with Colin Ross,' I said conversationally.

Their mouths tightened in chorus. There was nothing more to be said. If you jumped red traffic lights and broke the speed limit rushing someone to hospital to save his life, you would still be prosecuted for the offences. Same thing exactly. Same impasse. Humanity versus law, an age-old quandary. Make your choice and lie on it.

'I'm not accepting any responsibility for what you did,' Harley said heavily. 'I will state categorically, and in court if I have to, that you were acting in direct opposition to Derrydowns' instructions, and that Derrydowns disassociates itself entirely from your actions.'

I thought of asking him if he'd like a basin for the ritual washing of hands. I also thought that on the whole I'd better not.

He went on, 'And of course if there is any fine involved you will pay it yourself.'

Always my bad luck, I reflected, to cop it when the firm was too nearly bankrupt to be generous. I said merely, 'Is that all, then? We have a charter, if you remember . . .'

They waved me away in disgust and I collected my gear and flew off in the Aztec to take a clutch of businessmen from Elstree to The Hague.

*

By the time, the previous Friday, that Colin and I had locked Nancy's Cherokee and ensured that no one would touch it, the first cohorts of the local press had come galloping up with ash on their shirt fronts, and the Board of Trade, who neither slumbered nor slept, were breathing heavily down the STD.

Aircraft radios are about as private as Times Square: it appeared that dozens of ground-based but air-minded Midlands enthusiasts had been listening in to my conversation with Birmingham radar and had jammed the switchboard at Cambridge ringing up to find out if Colin Ross was safe. Undaunted, they had conveyed to Fleet Street the possibility of his loss. His arrival in one piece was announced on a television news broadcast forty minutes after we landed. The great British media had pulled out every finger they possessed. Nancy and Annie Villars had answered questions until their throats were sore and had finally taken refuge in the Ladies Cloaks. Colin was used to dealing with the press, but by the time he extricated himself from their ever increasing news-hungry numbers he too was pale blue from tiredness.

'Come on,' he said to me. 'Let's get Nancy out and go home.'

'I'll have to ring Harley . . .'

Harley already knew and was exploding like a fire-cracker. Someone from Polyplanes, it appeared, had telephoned at once to inform him with acid sweetness that his so highly qualified chief pilot had broken every law in sight and put Derrydowns thoroughly in the cart. The fact that his best customer was still alive to pay another day didn't seem to have got through to Harley at all. Polyplanes had made him smart, and it was all my fault.

I stayed in Cambridge by promising to foot the bill for hangarage again, and went home with Nancy and Colin.

Home.

A dangerous, evocative word. And the trouble was, it *felt* like home. Only the third time I'd been there, and it was already familiar, cosy, undemanding, easy . . . It was no good feeling I belonged there, because I didn't.

Saturday morning I spent talking to the police face to face in Cambridge and the Board of Trade in London on the telephone. Both forces cautiously murmured that they might perhaps ask Major Rupert Tyderman to help them with their inquiries. Saturday afternoon I flew Colin back to Haydock without incident, Saturday night I again stayed contentedly at Newmarket, Sunday I took him to Buckingham, changed over to the Aztec, and flew him to Ostend. Managed to avoid Harley altogether until I got back Sunday evening, when he lay in wait for me as I taxied down to the hangar and bitched on for over half an hour about sticking to the letter of the law. The gist of his argument was that left to herself Nancy would have come down safely somewhere over the flat land of East Anglia. Bound to have done. She wouldn't have hit any of the radio masts or power station chimneys which scattered the area and which had stuck up into the clouds like needles. They were all marked there, disturbing her, on the map. She had known that if she had to go down at random she had an average chance of hitting one. The television mast at Mendlesham stretched upwards for more than a thousand feet . . . But, said Harley, she would have missed the lot. Certain to have done.

'What would you have felt like, in her position?' I asked.

He didn't answer. He knew well enough. As pilot, as businessman, he was a bloody fool.

On Tuesday morning he told me that Colin had telephoned to cancel his trip to Folkestone that day, but that I would still be going in the Six, taking an owner and his friends there from Nottingham.

I imagined that Colin had changed his intention to ride at Folkestone and gone to Pontefract instead, but it wasn't so. He had, I found, flown to Folkestone. And he had gone in a Polyplane.

I didn't know he was there until after the races when he came back to the airport in a taxi. He climbed out of it in his usual wilted state, surveyed the row of parked aircraft, and walked straight past me towards the Polyplane.

'Colin,' I said.

He stopped, turned his head, gave me a straight stare. Nothing friendly in it, nothing at all.

'What's the matter?' I said puzzled. 'What's happened?'

He looked away from me, along to the Polyplane. I followed his glance. The pilot was standing there smirking. He was the one who had refused to help Kenny Bayst, and he had been smirking vigorously all afternoon.

'Did you come with him?' I asked.

'Yes, I did.' His voice was cold. His eyes also.

I said in surprise, 'I don't get it . . .'

Colin's face turned from cold to scorching. 'You . . . you . . . I don't think I can bear to talk to you.'

A feeling of unreality clogged my tongue. I simply looked at him in bewilderment.

'You've properly bust us up . . . Oh, I dare say you didn't mean to . . . but Nancy has lit off out of the house and I left Midge at home crying . . .'

I was appalled. 'But why? On Sunday morning when we left, everything was fine . . .'

'Yesterday,' he said flatly. 'Nancy found out yesterday, when she went to the airfield for a practice session. It absolutely overthrew her. She came home in a dreadful mood and raged round the house practically throwing things and this morning she packed a suitcase and walked out . . . neither Midge nor I could stop her and Midge is frantically distressed . . .' He stopped, clenched his jaw, and said with shut teeth, 'Why the hell didn't you have the guts to tell her yourself?'

'Tell her what?'

'*What?*' He thrust his hand into the pocket of his faded jeans and brought out a folded wad of newspaper. 'This.'

I took it from him. Unfolded it. Felt the woodenness take over in my face; knew that it showed.

He had handed me the most biting, the most damaging, of the tabloid accounts of my trial and conviction for negligently putting the lives of eighty seven people in jeopardy. A one-day wonder to the general public; long forgotten. But always lying there in the files, if anyone wanted to dig it up.

'That wasn't all,' Colin said. 'He told her also that you'd been sacked from another airline for cowardice.'

'Who told her?' I said dully. I held out the cutting. He took it back.

'Does it matter?'

'Yes, it does.'

'He had no axe to grind. That's what convinced her.'

'No axe . . . did he say that?'

'I believe so. What does it matter?'

'Was it a Polyplane pilot who told her? The one, for instance, who is flying you today?' Getting his own back, I thought, for the way I'd threatened him at Redcar.

Colin's mouth opened.

'No axe to grind,' I said bitterly. 'That's a laugh.

They've been trying to prise you loose from Derry-downs all summer and now it looks as if they've done it.'

I turned away from him, my throat physically closing. I didn't think I could speak. I expected him to walk on, to walk away, to take himself to Polyplanes and my future to the trash can.

Instead of that he followed me and touched my arm. 'Matt . . .'

I shook him off. 'You tell your precious sister,' I said thickly, 'that because of the rules I broke leading her back to Cambridge last Friday I am going to find myself in court again, and convicted and fined and in debt again . . . and this time I did it with my eyes open . . . not like that . . .' I pointed to the newspaper clipping with a hand that trembled visibly, 'when I had to take the rap for something that was mostly not my fault.'

'Matt!' He was himself appalled.

'And as for the cowardice bit, she's got her facts wrong . . . Oh, I've no doubt it sounded convincing and dreadful . . . Polyplanes had a lot to gain by upsetting her to the utmost . . . but I don't see . . . I don't see why she was more upset than just to persuade you not to fly with me . . .'

'Why didn't you tell her yourself?'

I shook my head. 'I probably might have done, one day. I didn't think it was important.'

'Not important!' He was fierce with irritation. 'She seems to have been building up some sort of hero image of you, and then she discovered you had clay feet in all

519

directions . . . Of course you should have told her, as you were going to marry her. That was obviously what upset her most . . .'

I was speechless. My jaw literally dropped. Finally I said foolishly, 'Did you say *marry* . . . ?'

'Well, yes, of course,' he said impatiently, and then seemed struck by my state of shock. 'You were going to marry her, weren't you?'

'We've never . . . even talked about it.'

'But you must have,' he insisted. 'I overheard her and Midge discussing it on Sunday evening, after I got back from Ostend. "When you are married to Matt," Midge said. I heard her distinctly. They were in the kitchen, washing up. They were deciding you would come and live with us in the bungalow . . . They were sharing out the bedrooms . . .' His voice tailed off weakly. 'It isn't . . . it isn't true?'

I silently shook my head.

He looked at me in bewilderment. 'Girls,' he said. 'Girls.'

'I can't marry her,' I said numbly. 'I've hardly enough for a licence . . .'

'That doesn't matter.'

'It does to me.'

'It wouldn't to Nancy,' he said. He did a sort of double take. 'Do you mean . . . she wasn't so far out . . . after all?'

'I suppose . . . not so far.'

He looked down at the cutting in his hand, and suddenly screwed it up. 'It looked so bad,' he said with a tinge of apology.

'It was bad,' I said.

He looked at my face. 'Yes. I see it was . . .'

A taxi drew up with a jerk and out piled my passengers, all gay and flushed with a winner and carrying a bottle of champagne.

'I'll explain to her,' Colin said. 'I'll get her back . . .' His expression was suddenly horrified. Shattered.

'Where has she gone?' I asked.

He screwed up his eyes as if in pain.

'She said . . .' He swallowed. 'She went . . . to Chanter.'

I sat all evening in the caravan wanting to smash something. Smash the galley. Smash the windows. Smash the walls.

Might have felt better if I had.

Chanter . . .

Couldn't eat, couldn't think, couldn't sleep.

Never had listened to my own advice: don't get involved. Should have stuck to it, stayed frozen. Icy. Safe.

Tried to get back to the Arctic and not feel anything, but it was too late. Feeling had come back with a vengeance and of an intensity I could have done without. I hadn't known I loved her. Knew I liked her, felt easy with her, wanted to be with her often and for a long

521

time to come. I'd thought I could stop at friendship, and didn't realize how far, how deep I had already gone.

Oh Nancy . . .

I went to sleep in the end by drinking half of the bottle of whisky Kenny Bayst had given me, but it didn't do much good. I woke up at six in the morning to the same dreary torment and with a headache on top.

There were no flights that day to take my mind off it.

Nancy and Chanter . . .

At some point in the morning I telephoned from the coinbox in the customers' lounges to the art school in Liverpool, to ask for Chanter's home address. A crisp secretarial female voice answered: very sorry, absolutely not their policy to divulge the private addresses of their staff. If I could write, they would forward the letter.

'Could I speak to him, then, do you think?' I asked: though what good that would do, Heaven alone knew.

'I'm afraid not, because he isn't here. The school is temporarily closed, and we are not sure when it will reopen.'

'The students,' I remembered, 'are on strike?'

'That . . . er . . . is so,' she agreed.

'Can't you possibly tell me how I could get in touch with Chanter?'

'Oh dear . . . You are the second person pressing me to help . . . but honestly, to tell you the truth we don't know where he lives... he moves frequently and seldom bothers to keep us up to date.' Secretarial disapproval and despair in the tidy voice. 'As I told Mr Ross, with all the best will in the world, I simply have no idea where you could find him.'

I sat in the crew room while the afternoon dragged by. Finished writing up all records by two-thirty, read through some newly arrived information circulars, calculated I had only three weeks and four days to run before my next medical, worked out that if I bought four cups of coffee every day from Honey's machine, I was drinking away one fifteenth of my total week's spending money, decided to make it water more often, looked up when Harley came stalking in, received a lecture on loyalty (mine to him), heard that I was on the next day to take a Wiltshire trainer to Newmarket races, and that if I gave Polyplanes any more grounds for reporting me or the firm to the Board of Trade, I could collect my cards.

'Do my best not to,' I murmured. Didn't please him.

Looked at the door swinging shut behind his back.

Looked at the clock. Three twenty-two.

Chanter and Nancy.

Back in the caravan, the same as the evening before. Tried turning on the television. Some comedy about

American suburban life punctuated by canned laughter. Stood five minutes of it, and found the silence afterwards almost as bad.

Walked halfway round the airfield, cut down to the village, drank half a pint in the pub, walked back. Total, four miles. When I stepped into the caravan it was still only nine o'clock.

Honey Harley was waiting for me, draped over the sofa with maximum exposure of leg. Pink checked cotton sun-dress, very low cut.

'Hi,' she said with self possession. 'Where've you been?'

'For a walk.'

She looked at me quizzically. 'Got the Board of Trade on your mind?'

I nodded. That, and other things.

'I shouldn't worry too much. Whatever the law says or does, you couldn't have just left the Rosses to flounder.'

'Your uncle doesn't agree.'

'Uncle,' she said dispassionately, 'is a nit. And anyway, play your cards right, and even if you do get a fine, Colin Ross will pay it. All you'd have to do would be to ask.'

I shook my head.

'You're daft,' she said. 'Plain daft.'

'You may be right.'

She sighed, stirred, stood up. The curvy body rippled in all the right places. I thought of Nancy: much flatter, much thinner, less obviously sexed and infinitely more desirable. I turned abruptly away from Honey. Like hitting a raw nerve, the thought of Chanter, with his hair and his fringes . . . and his hands.

'OK, iceberg,' she said, mistakenly, 'relax. Your virtue is quite safe. I only came down, to start with, to tell you there was a phone call for you, and would you please ring back.'

'Who? . . .' I tried hard to keep it casual.

'Colin Ross,' Honey said matter-of-factly. 'He wants you to call some time this evening, if you can. I said if it was about a flight I could deal with it, but apparently it's something personal.' She finished the sentence halfway between an accusation and a question and left me ample time to explain.

I didn't. I said, 'I'll go up now, then, and use the telephone in the lounge.'

She shrugged. 'All right.'

She walked up with me, but didn't quite have the nerve to hover close enough to listen. I shut the lounge door in front of her resigned and humorously rueful face.

Got the number.

'Colin? Matt.'

'Oh good,' he said. 'Look. Nancy rang up today while Midge and I were at the races . . . I took Midge along on the Heath because she was so miserable at home, and now of course she's even more miserable that she missed Nancy . . . anyway, our cleaning woman answered the telephone, and Nancy left a message.'

'Is she . . . I mean, is she all right?'

'Do you mean, is she with Chanter?' His voice was strained. 'She told our cleaner she had met an old art school friend in Liverpool and was spending a few days camping with her near Warwick.'

'*Her?*' I exclaimed.

'Well, I don't know. I asked our Mrs Williams, and she then said she *thought* Nancy said "her", but of course she would think that, wouldn't she?'

'I'm afraid she would.'

'But anyway, Nancy had been much more insistent that Mrs Williams tell me something else . . . it seems she has seen Major Tyderman.'

'She didn't!'

'Yeah . . . She said she saw Major Tyderman in the passenger seat of a car on the Stratford road out of Warwick. Apparently there were some roadworks, and the car stopped for a moment just near her.'

'He could have been going anywhere . . . from anywhere . . .'

'Yes,' he agreed in depression. 'I rang the police in Cambridge to tell them, but Nancy had already been through to them, when she called home. All she could remember about the driver was that he wore glasses. She thought he might have had dark hair and perhaps a moustache. She only glanced at him for a second because she was concentrating on Tyderman. Also she hadn't taken the number, and she's hopeless on the make of cars, so altogether it wasn't a great deal of help.'

'No . . .'

'Anyway, she told Mrs Williams she would be coming home on Saturday. She said if I would drive to Warwick races instead of flying, she would come home with me in the car.'

'Well . . . thank God for that.'

'If for nothing else,' he said aridly.

527

CHAPTER TWELVE

I flew the customers from Wiltshire to Newmarket and parked the Six as far as possible from the Polyplane. When the passengers had departed standwards, I got out of the fuggy cabin and into the free air, lay propped on one elbow on the grass, loosened my tie, opened the neck of my shirt. Scorching hot day, a sigh of wind over the Heath, a couple of small cumulus clouds defying evaporation, blue sky over the blue planet.

A suitable day for camping.

Wrenched my thoughts away from the profitless grind: Nancy despised me, despised herself, had chosen Chanter as a refuge, as a steadfast known quantity, had run away from the near-stranger who had not seemed what he seemed, and gone to where she knew she was wanted. Blind, instinctive, impulsive flight. Reckless, understandable, forgivable flight . . .

I could take Chanter, I thought mordantly. I could probably take the thought and memory of Chanter, if only she would settle for me in the end.

It was odd that you had to lose something you didn't

even know you had, before you began to want it more than anything on earth.

Down at the other end of the row of aircraft the Polyplane pilot was strolling about, smoking again. One of these fine days he would blow himself up. There was no smile in place that afternoon: even from a hundred yards one could detect the gloom in the heavy frowns he occasionally got rid of in my direction.

Colin had booked with Harley for the week ahead. Polyplanes must have been wondering what else they would have to do to get him back.

They played rough, no doubt of that. Informing on Derrydowns to the Board of Trade, discrediting their pilot, spreading smears that they weren't safe. But would they blow up a Derrydowns aircraft? Would they go as far as that?

They would surely have had to be certain they would gain from it, before they risked it. But in fact they hadn't gained. No one had demonstrably been frightened away from using Derrydowns, particularly not Colin Ross. If the bomb had been meant to look like an attack on Colin's life, why should Colin think he would be any safer in a Polyplane?

If they had blown up the aircraft with passengers aboard, that would have ruined Derrydowns. But even if they had been prepared to go that far, they wouldn't have chosen a flight with Colin Ross on it.

And why Major Tyderman, when their own pilots could get near the Derrydowns aircraft without much comment? That was easier ... they needed a bomb expert. Someone completely unsuspectable. Someone even their pilots didn't know. Because if the boss of Polyplanes had taken the dark step into crime, he wouldn't want chatty employees like pilots spilling it into every aviation bar from Prestwick to Lydd.

The second aeroplane, though, that Tyderman had sabotaged, hadn't been one of the Derrydowns at all. On the other hand, he had thought it was. I stood up, stretched, watched the straining horses scud through the first race, saw in the distance a girl with dark hair and a blue dress and thought for one surging moment it was Nancy. It wasn't Nancy. It wasn't even Midge. Nancy was in Warwickshire, living in a tent.

I thrust my balled fists into my pockets. Not the slightest use thinking about it. Concentrate on something else. Start from the bottom again, as before. Look at everything the wrong way up.

No easy revelation this time. Just the merest flicker of speculation.

Harley? ...

He had recovered ill-invested capital on the first occasion. He had known Colin would not rely often on his sister's skill after the second. But would Harley go so far? ... And Harley had known I wasn't flying Colin, though Tyderman had thought I was.

Rats on treadwheels, I thought, go round and round in small circles and get nowhere, just like me.

I sighed. It wasn't much use trying to work it all

out when I obviously lacked about fifty pieces of vital information. Decision: did I or did I not start actively looking for some of the pieces? If I didn't, a successor to Major Tyderman might soon be around playing another lot of chemical tricks on aeroplanes, and if I did, I could well be heading myself for yet more trouble.

I tossed a mental coin. Heads you do, tails you don't. In mid-toss I thought of Nancy. All roads led back to Nancy. If I just let everything slide and lay both physically and metaphorically on my back on the grass in the sun, I'd have nothing to think about except what I hated to think about. Very poor prospect. Almost anything else was better.

Took the plunge, and made a start with Annie Villars. She was standing in the paddock in a sleeveless dark-red dress, her greying short hair curling neatly under a black straw hat chosen more for generalship than femininity. From ten paces the authority was clearly uppermost: from three, one could hear the incongruously gentle voice, see the non-aggression in the consciously curved lips, realize that the velvet glove was being given a quilted lining.

She was talking to the Duke of Wessex. She was saying, 'Then if you agree, Bobbie, we'll ask Kenny Bayst to ride it. This new boy has no judgement of pace, and for all his faults, Kenny does know how to time a race.'

The Duke nodded his distinguished head and smiled at her benevolently. They caught sight of me hovering near them and both turned towards me with friendly expressions, one deceptively, and one authentically vacant.

'Matt,' smiled the Duke. 'My dear chap. Isn't it a splendid day?'

'Beautiful, sir,' I agreed. As long as one could obliterate Warwickshire.

'My nephew Matthew,' he said. 'Do you remember him?'

'Of course I do, sir.'

'Well . . . it's his birthday soon, and he wants . . . he was wondering if for a birthday present I would give him a flight in an aeroplane. With you, he said. Especially with you.'

I smiled. 'I'd like to do that very much.'

'Good, good. Then . . . er . . . how do you suggest we fix it?'

'I'll arrange it with Mr Harley.'

'Yes. Good. Soon then. He's coming down to stay with me tomorrow as it's the end of term and his mother is off somewhere in Greece. So next week, perhaps?'

'I'm sure that will be all right.'

He beamed happily. 'Perhaps I'll come along too.'

Annie Villars said patiently, 'Bobbie, we ought to go and see about saddling your horse.'

He looked at his watch. 'By jove, yes. Amazing where the afternoon goes to. Come along, then.' He gave me another large smile, transferred it intact to Annie, and obediently moved off after her as she started purposefully towards the saddling boxes.

I bought a racecard. The Duke's horse was a two-year-old maiden called Thundersticks. I watched the Duke and Annie watch Thundersticks walk round the parade ring, one with innocent beaming pride, the other with judicious non-commitment. The pace-lacking boy rode a bad race, even to my unpractised eye: too far out in front over the first furlong, too far out the back over the last. Just as well the Duke's colours were inconspicuous, I thought. He took his disappointment with charming grace, reassuring Annie that the colt would do better next time. Sure to. Early days yet. She smiled at him in soft agreement and bestowed on the jockey a look which would have bored a hole through steel plating.

After they had discussed the sweating colt's performance yard by yard, and patted him and packed him off with his lad towards the stables, the Duke took Annie away to the bar for a drink. After that she had another loser for another owner and another thoughtful detour for refreshment, so that I didn't manage to catch her on her own until between the last two races.

She listened without comment to me explaining that I thought it might be possible to do something positive about solving the Great Bomb Mystery, if she would help.

'I thought it was solved already.'

'Not really. No one knows why.'

'No. Well, I don't see how I can help.'

'Would you mind telling me how well Major

Tyderman and Mr Goldenberg know each other, and how they come to have any say in how Rudiments should run in its various races?'

She said mildly, 'It's none of your business.'

I knew what the mildness concealed. 'I know that.'

'And you are impertinent.'

'Yes.'

She regarded me straightly, and the softness gradually faded out of her features to leave taut skin over the cheekbones and a stern set to the mouth.

'I am fond of Midge and Nancy Ross,' she said. 'I don't see how anything I can tell you will help, but I certainly want no harm to come to those two girls. That last escapade was just a shade too dangerous, wasn't it? And if Rupert Tyderman could do that...' She paused, thinking deeply. 'I will be obliged if you will keep anything I may tell you to yourself.'

'I will.'

'Very well... I've known Rupert for a very long time. More or less from my childhood. He is about fifteen years older... When I was a young girl I thought he was a splendid person, and I didn't understand why people hesitated when they talked about him.' She sighed. 'I found out, of course, when I was older. He had been wild, as a youth. A vandal when vandalism wasn't as common as it is now. When he was in his twenties he borrowed money from all his relations and friends for various grand schemes, and never paid them back. His family bought him out of one mess where he had sold a picture entrusted to him for safe keeping and spent the proceeds . . . Oh, lots of things like that. Then the war came and he volunteered immediately, and I believe all during the war he did very well. He was in the Royal Engineers, I think . . . but afterwards, after the war ended, he was quietly allowed to resign his commission for cashing dud cheques with his fellow officers.'

She shook her head impatiently. 'He has always been a fool to himself . . . Since the war he has lived on some money his grandfather left in trust, and on what he could cadge from any friends he had left.'

'You included?' I suggested.

She nodded. 'Oh yes. He's always very persuasive. It's always for something extremely plausible, but all the deals fall through . . .' She looked away across the Heath, considering. 'And then this year, back in February or March, I think, he turned up one day and said he wouldn't need to borrow any more from me, he'd got a good thing going which would make him rich.'

'What was it?'

'He wouldn't say. Just told me not to worry, it was all legal. He had gone into partnership with someone with a cast iron idea for making a fortune. Well, I'd heard that sort of thing from him so often before. The only difference was that this time he didn't want money . . .'

'He wanted something else?'

'Yes.' She frowned. 'He wanted me to introduce him to Bobbie Wessex. He said . . . just casually . . . how much he'd like to meet him, and I suppose I was so relieved not to find him cadging five hundred or so that I instantly agreed. It was very silly of me, but it didn't seem important . . .'

'What happened then?'

She shrugged. 'They were both at the Doncaster meeting at the opening of the flat season, so I introduced them. Nothing to it. Just a casual racecourse introduction. And then,' she looked annoyed, 'the next time Rupert turned up with that man Goldenberg, saying Bobbie Wessex had given him permission to decide how Rudiments should be run in all his races. I said he certainly wasn't going to do that, and telephoned to Bobbie. But,' she sighed, 'Rupert had indeed talked him into giving him carte blanche with Rudiments. Rupert is an expert persuader, and Bobbie, well, poor Bobbie is easily open to suggestion. Anyone with half an eye could see that Goldenberg was as straight as a corkscrew but Rupert said he was essential as someone had got to put the bets on, and he, Rupert, couldn't, as no bookmaker would accept his credit and you had to have hard cash for the Tote.'

'And then the scheme went wrong,' I said.

'The first time Rudiments won, they'd both collected a lot of money. I had told them the horse would win. Must win. It started at a hundred to six, first time out, and they were both as high as kites afterwards.'

'And next time Kenny Bayst won again when he wasn't supposed to, when they had laid it?'

She looked startled. 'So you did understand what they were saying.'

'Eventually.'

'Just like Rupert to let it out. No sense of discretion.'

I sighed. 'Well, thank you very much for being so frank. Even if I still can't see what connection Rudiments has with Major Tyderman blowing up one aircraft and crippling another.'

She twisted her mouth. 'I told you,' she said, 'right at the beginning, that nothing I said would be of any help.'

Colin stopped beside me in pink and green silks on his way from the weighing room to the parade ring for the last race. He gave me a concentrated inquiring look which softened into something like compassion.

'The waiting's doing you no good,' he said.

'Has she telephoned again?'

He shook his head. 'Midge won't leave the house, in case she does.'

'I'll be at Warwick races on Saturday . . . flying some people up from Kent . . . Will you ask her . . . just to talk to me?'

'I'll wring her stupid little neck,' he said.

I flew the customers back to Wiltshire and the Six back to Buckingham. Harley, waiting around with bitter eyes, told me the Board of Trade had let him know they were definitely proceeding against me.

'I expected they would.'

'But that's not what I wanted to speak to you about. Come into the office.' He was unfriendly, as usual. Snappy. He picked up a sheet of paper from his desk and waved it at me.

'Look at these times. I've been going through the bills Honey has sent out since you've been here. All the times are shorter. We've had to charge less . . . we're not making enough profit. It's got to stop. D'you understand? Got to stop.'

'Very well.'

He looked nonplussed: hadn't expected such an easy victory.

'And I'm taking on another pilot.'

'Am I out, then?' I found I scarcely cared.

He was surprised. 'No. Of course not. We simply seem to be getting too much taxi work just lately for you to handle on your own, even with Don's help.'

'Maybe we're getting more work because we're doing the jobs faster and charging less,' I suggested.

He was affronted. 'Don't be ridiculous.'

Another long evening in the caravan, aching and empty.

Nowhere to go, no way of going, and nothing to spend when I got there. That didn't matter, because wherever I went, whatever I spent, the inescapable thoughts lay in wait. Might as well suffer them alone and cheaply as anywhere else.

For something to do, I cleaned the caravan from end to end. When it was finished, it looked better, but I, on the whole, felt worse. Scrambled myself two eggs, ate them unenthusiastically on toast. Drank a dingy cup of dried coffee, dried milk.

Switched on the television. Old movie, circa 1950, pirates, cutlasses, heaving bosoms. Switched off.

Sat and watched night arrive on the airfield. Tried to concentrate on what Annie Villars had told me, so as not to think of night arriving over the fields and tents of Warwickshire. For a long time, had no success at all.

Look at everything upside down. Take absolutely nothing for granted.

The middle of the night produced out of a shallow restless sleep a singularly wild idea. Most sleep-spawned revelations from the subconscious wither and die of ridicule in the dawn, but this time it was different. At five, six, seven o'clock, it still looked possible. I traipsed in my mind through everything I had seen and heard since the day of the bomb, and added a satisfactory answer to why to the answer to who.

That Friday I had to set off early in the Aztec to Germany with some television cameramen from Denham,

wait while they took their shots, and bring them home
again. In spite of breaking Harley's ruling about speed
into pin-sized fragments it was seven-thirty before I
climbed stiffly out of the cockpit and helped Joe push
the sturdy twin into the hangar.

'Need it for Sunday, don't you?' he asked.

'That's right. Colin Ross to France.' I stretched and
yawned, and picked up my heavy flight bag with all its
charts and documents.

'We're working you hard.'

'What I'm here for.'

He put his hands in his overall pockets. 'You're light
on those aeroplanes, I'll give you that. Larry, now, Larry
was heavy-handed. Always needing things repaired, we
were, before you came.'

I gave him a sketch of an appreciative smile and
walked up to fill in the records in the office. Harley
and Don were both still flying, Harley giving a lesson,
and Don a sight-seeing trip in the Six, and Honey was
still traffic-copping up in the tower. I climbed up there
to see her and ask her a considerable favour.

'Borrow my Mini?' she repeated in surprise. 'Do you
mean now, this minute?'

I nodded. 'For the evening.'

'I suppose I could get Uncle to take me home,' she
reflected. 'If you'll fetch me in the morning?'

'Certainly.'

'Well . . . all right. I don't really need it this evening.
Just fill it up with petrol before you hand it back.'

'OK. And thanks a lot.'

She gave me a frankly vulgar grin. 'Minis are too small for what you want.'

I managed to grin back. 'Yeah . . .'

Given the wheels, make the appointment. A pleasant male voice answered the telephone, polite and quiet.

'The Duke of Wessex? Yes, this is his house. Who is speaking please?'

'Matthew Shore.'

'One moment, sir.'

The one moment stretched to four minutes, and I fed a week's beer money into the greedy box. At last the receiver at the other end was picked up and with slightly heavy breathing the Duke's unmistakable voice said, 'Matt? My dear chap, what can I do for you?'

'If you are not busy this evening, sir, could I call in to see you for a few minutes?'

'This evening? Busy? Hm . . . Is it about young Matthew's flight?'

'No, sir, something different. I won't take up much of your time.'

'Come by all means, my dear chap, if you want to. After dinner, perhaps? Nine o'clock, say?'

'Nine o'clock,' I confirmed. 'I'll be there.'

The Duke lived near Royston, west of Cambridge. Honey's Mini ate up the miles like Billy Bunter so that it was nine o'clock exactly when I stopped at a local garage to ask for directions to the Duke's house. On Honey's radio, someone was reading the news. I listened idly at first while the attendant finished filling up the car in front, and then with sharp and sickened attention. 'Racehorse trainer Jarvis Kitch and owner Dobson Ambrose, whose filly Scotchbright won the Oaks last month, were killed today in a multiple traffic accident just outside Newmarket. The Australian jockey Kenny Bayst, who was in the car with them, was taken to hospital with multiple injuries. His condition tonight is said to be fair. Three stable lads, trapped when a lorry crushed their car, also died in the crash.'

Mechanically I asked for, got, and followed, the directions to the Duke's house. I was thinking about poor large aggressive Ambrose and his cowed trainer Kitch, hoping that Kenny wasn't too badly hurt to race again, and trying to foresee the ramifications.

There was nothing else on the news except the weather forecast: heatwave indefinitely continuing.

No mention of Rupert Tyderman. But Tyderman, that day, had been seen by the police.

CHAPTER THIRTEEN

The Duke's manservant was as pleasant as his voice: a short, assured, slightly pop-eyed man in his later forties with a good deal of the Duke's natural benevolence in his manner. The house he presided over opened to the public, a notice read, every day between March 1st and November 30th. The Duke, I discovered, lived privately in the upper third of the south-west wing.

'The Duke is expecting you, sir. Will you come this way?'

I followed. The distance I followed accounted for the length of time I had waited for the Duke to come to the telephone and also his breathlessness when he got there. We went up three floors, along a two-furlong straight, and up again, to the attics. The attics in eighteenth-century stately homes were a long way from the front hall.

The manservant opened a white-painted door and gravely showed me in.

'Mr Shore, your Grace.'

'Come in, come in, my dear chap,' said the Duke.

I went in, and smiled with instant, spontaneous delight. The square low-ceilinged room contained a vast toy electric train set laid out on an irregular ring of wide green-covered trestle tables. A terminus, sidings, two small towns, a branch line, tunnels, gradients, viaducts, the Duke had the lot. In the centre of the ring, he and his nephew Matthew stood behind a large control table pressing the switches which sent about six different trains clanking on different courses round the complex.

The Duke nudged his nephew. 'There you are, what did we say? He likes it.'

Young Matthew gave me a fleeting glance and went back to some complicated point changing. 'He was bound to. He's got the right sort of face.'

The Duke said, 'You can crawl in here best under that table with the signal box and level crossing.' He pointed, so I went down on hands and knees and made the indicated journey. Stood up in the centre. Looked around at the rows of lines and remembered the hopeless passion I'd felt in toy shops as a child: my father had been an underpaid schoolmaster who had spent his money on books.

The two enthusiasts showed me where the lines crossed and how the trains could be switched without crashing. Their voices were filled with contentment, their eyes shining, their faces intent.

'Built this lot up gradually, of course,' the Duke said. 'Started when I was a boy. Then for years I never came up here. Not until young Matthew got old enough. Now, as I expect you can see, we have great times.'

'We're thinking of running a branch line right through that wall over there into the next attic,' Matthew said. 'There isn't much room in here.'

The Duke nodded. 'Next week, perhaps. For your birthday.'

Young Matthew gave him a huge grin and deftly let a pullman cross three seconds in front of a chugging goods. 'It's getting dark,' he observed. 'Lighting up time.'

'So it is,' agreed the Duke.

Matthew with a flourish pressed a switch, and they both watched my face. All round the track, and on all the stations and signal boxes and in the signals themselves, tiny electric lights suddenly shone out. The effect, to my eyes, was enchanting.

'There you are,' said the Duke. 'He likes it.'

'Bound to,' young Matthew said.

They played with the trains for another whole hour, because they had worked out a timetable and they wanted to see if they could keep to it before they pinned it up on the notice board in the terminal. The Duke apologized, not very apologetically, for keeping me waiting, but it was, he explained, Matthew's first evening out of school, and they had been waiting all through the term for this occasion.

At twenty to eleven the last shuttle service stopped at the buffers in the terminal and Matthew yawned.

With the satisfaction of a job well done the two railway-men unfolded several large dustsheets and laid them carefully over the silent tracks, and then we all three crawled back under the table which held the level crossing.

The Duke led the way down the first flight and along the two furlongs, and we were then, it appeared, in his living quarters.

'You'd better cut along to bed, now, Matthew,' he said to his nephew. 'See you in the morning. Eight o'clock sharp, out in the stables.'

'Sure thing,' Matthew said. 'And after that, the races.' He sighed with utter content. 'Better than school,' he said.

The Duke showed me into a smallish white-painted sitting-room furnished with Persian rugs, leather arm-chairs, and endless sporting prints.

'A drink?' he suggested, indicating a tray.

I looked at the bottles. 'Whisky, please.'

He nodded, poured two, added water, gave me the glass and waved me to an armchair.

'Now, my dear chap? . . .'

It suddenly seemed difficult, what I had come to ask him, and what to explain. He was so transparently honest, so incapable of double dealing: I wondered if he could comprehend villainy at all.

'I was talking to Annie Villars about your horse Rudiments,' I said.

A slight frown lowered his eyebrows. 'She was

annoyed with me for letting her friend Rupert Tyderman advise me . . . I do so dislike upsetting Annie, but
I'd promised . . . Anyway, she has sorted it all out splendidly, I believe, and now that her friend has turned out
to be so extraordinary, with that bomb, I mean, I don't
expect he will want to advise me about Rudiments any
more.'

'Did he, sir, introduce to you any friend of his?'

'Do you mean Eric Goldenberg? Yes, he did. Can't
say I really liked the fellow, though. Didn't trust him,
you know. Young Matthew didn't like him, either.'

'Did Goldenberg ever talk to you about insurance?'

'Insurance?' he repeated. 'No, I can't remember
especially that he did.'

I frowned. It had to be insurance.

It had to be.

'It was his other friend,' said the Duke, 'who
arranged the insurance.'

I stared at him. 'Which other friend?'

'Charles Carthy-Todd.'

I blinked. 'Who?'

'Charles Carthy-Todd,' he repeated patiently. 'He
was an acquaintance of Rupert Tyderman. Tyderman
introduced us one day. At Newmarket races, I think it
was. Anyway, it was Charles who suggested the
insurance. Very good scheme, I thought it was. Sound.
Very much needed. An absolute boon to a great many
people.'

'The Racegoers' Accident Fund,' I said. 'Of which you are Patron.'

'That's right.' He smiled contentedly. 'So many people have complimented me on giving it my name. A splendid undertaking altogether.'

'Could you tell me a little more about how it was set up?'

'Are you interested in insurance, my dear chap? I could get you an introduction at Lloyd's . . . but . . .'

I smiled. To become an underwriter at Lloyd's one had to think of a stake of a hundred thousand pounds as loose change. The Duke, in his quiet good natured way, was a very rich man indeed.

'No sir. It's just the Accident Fund I'm interested in. How it was set up, and how it is run.'

'Charles sees to it all, my dear chap. I can't seem to get the hang of these things at all, you know. Technicalities, and all that. Much prefer horses, don't you see?'

'Yes, sir, I do see. Could you perhaps, then, tell me about Mr Carthy-Todd? What he's like, and so on.'

'He's about your height but much heavier and he has dark hair and wears spectacles. I think he has a moustache . . . yes, that's right, a moustache.'

I was jolted. The Duke's description of Charles Carthy-Todd fitted almost exactly the impression Nancy had had of Tyderman's companion. Dozens of men around, though, with dark hair, moustache, glasses . . .

'I really meant, sir, his . . . er . . . character.'

'My dear chap. Sound. Very sound. A thoroughly

good fellow. An expert in insurance, spent years with a big firm in the city.'

'And . . . his background?' I suggested.

'Went to Rugby. Then straight into an office. Good family, of course.'

'You've met them?'

He looked surprised at the question. 'Not actually, no. Business connection, that's what I have with Charles. His family came from Herefordshire, I think. There are photographs in our office . . . land, horses, dogs, wife and children, that sort of thing. Why do you ask?'

I hesitated. 'Did he come to you with the Accident Scheme complete?'

He shook his fine head. 'No, no, my dear chap. It arose out of conversation. We were saying how sad it was for the family of that small steeplechase trainer who was drowned on holiday and what a pity it was that there wasn't some scheme which covered everyone engaged in racing, not just the jockeys. Then of course when we really went into it we broadened it to include the racing public as well. Charles explained that the more premiums we collected the more we could pay out in compensation.'

'I see.'

'We have done a great deal of good already.' He smiled happily. 'Charles was telling me the other day that we have settled three claims for injuries so far, and that those clients are so pleased that they are telling everyone else to join in.'

I nodded. 'I've met one of them. He'd broken his ankle and received a thousand pounds.'

He beamed. 'There you are, then.'

'When did the scheme actually start?'

'Let me see. In May, I should think. Towards the end of May. About two months ago. It took a little while to organize, of course, after we'd decided to go ahead.'

'Charles did the organizing?'

'My dear chap, of course.'

'Did you take advice from any of your friends at Lloyd's?'

'No need, you know. Charles is an expert himself. He drew up all the papers. I just signed them.'

'But you read them first?'

'Oh yes,' he said reassuringly, then smiled like a child. 'Didn't understand them much, of course.'

'And you yourself guaranteed the money?' Since the collapse of cut-price car insurance firms, I'd read somewhere, privately run insurance schemes had to show a minimum backing of fifty thousand pounds before the Board of Trade would give them permission to exist.

'That's right.'

'Fifty thousand pounds?'

'We thought a hundred thousand might be better. Gives the scheme better standing, more weight, don't you see?'

'Charles said so?'

'He knows about such things.'

'Yes.'

'But of course I'll never have to find that money. It's only a guarantee of good faith, and to comply with the law. The premiums will cover the compensation and Charles' salary and all the costs. Charles worked it all out. And I told him right at the beginning that I didn't want any profit out of it, just for lending it my name. I really don't need any profit. I told him just to add my share into the paying out fund, and he thought that was a most sensible suggestion. Our whole purpose, you see, is to do good.'

'You're a singularly kind, thoughtful and generous man,' I said.

It made him uncomfortable. 'My dear chap . . .'

'And after tonight's news, I think several widows in Newmarket will bless you.'

'What news?'

I told him about the accident in which Kitch and Ambrose and the three stable lads had died. He was horrified.

'Oh, the poor fellows. The poor fellows. One can only hope that you are right, and that they had joined our scheme.'

'Will the premiums you have already collected be enough to cover many large claims all at once?'

He wasn't troubled. 'I expect so. Charles will have seen to all that. But even if they don't, I will make up the difference. No one will suffer. That's what guaranteeing means, do you see?'

'Yes, sir.'

'Kitch and Ambrose,' he said. 'The poor fellows.'

'And Kenny Bayst is in hospital, badly hurt.'

'Oh dear.' His distress was genuine. He really cared.

'I know that Kenny Bayst was insured with you. At least, he told me he was going to be. And after this I should think you would be flooded with more applications.'

'I expect you're right. You seem to understand things, just like Charles does.'

'Did Charles have any plans for giving the scheme a quick boost to begin with?'

'I don't follow you, my dear chap.'

'What happened to the Accident Fund,' I asked casually, 'after that bomb exploded in the aeroplane which had been carrying Colin Ross?'

He looked enthusiastic. 'Do you know, a lot of people told me they would join. It made them think, they said. I asked Charles if they had really done anything about it, and he said yes, quite a few inquiries had come in. I said that as no one had been hurt, the bomb seemed to have done the Fund a lot of good, and Charles was surprised and said so it had.'

Charles had met the Duke through Rupert Tyderman. Rupert Tyderman had set off the bomb. If ever there was a stone cold certainty, it was that Charles Carthy-Todd was the least surprised on earth that cash had followed combustion. He had reckoned it would. He had reckoned right.

'Charles sent out a pamphlet urging everyone to insure against bombs on the way home,' I said.

The Duke smiled. 'Yes, that's right. I believe it was very effective. We thought, do you see, that as no one had been hurt, there would be no harm in it.'

'And as it was Colin Ross who was on board, the bomb incident was extensively covered on television and in the newspapers . . . and had a greater impact on your Fund than had it been anyone else.'

The Duke's forehead wrinkled. 'I'm not sure I understand.'

'Never mind, sir. I was just thinking aloud.'

'Very easy habit to fall into. Do it myself, you know, all the time.'

Carthy-Todd and Tyderman's second sabotage, I thought to myself, hadn't been as good. Certainly by attacking Colin they'd achieved the same impact and national coverage, but I would have thought it was too obviously slanted at one person to have had much universal effect. Could be wrong, though . . .

'This has been the most interesting chat,' said the Duke. 'But my dear fellow, the evening is passing. What was it that you wanted to see me about?'

'Er . . .' I cleared my throat. 'Do you know, sir, I'd very much like to meet Mr Carthy-Todd. He sounds a most go-ahead, enterprising man.'

The Duke nodded warmly.

'Do you know where I could find him?'

'Tonight, do you mean?' He was puzzled.

'No, sir. Tomorrow will do.'

'I suppose you might find him at our office. He's sure to be there, because he knows I will be calling in myself. Warwick races, do you see?'

'The Accident Fund office . . . is in Warwick?'

'Of course.'

'Silly of me,' I said. 'I didn't know.'

The Duke twinkled at me. 'I see you haven't joined the Fund.'

'I'll join tomorrow. I'll go to the office. I'll be at Warwick too, for the races.'

'Great,' he said. 'Great. The office is only a few hundred yards from the racecourse.' He put two fingers into an inside pocket and brought out a visiting card. 'There you are, my dear chap. The address. And if you're there about an hour before the first race, I'll be there too, and you can meet Charles. You'll like him, I'm sure of that.'

'I'll look forward to it,' I said. I finished my whisky and stood up. 'It was kind of you to let me come . . . and I think your trains are absolutely splendid . . .'

His face brightened. He escorted me all the way down to the front door, talking about young Matthew and the plans they had for the holidays. Would I fix Matthew's flight for Thursday, he asked. Thursday was Matthew's birthday. He would be eleven.

'Thursday it is,' I agreed. 'I'll do it in the evening, if there's a charter fixed for that day.'

'Most good of you, my dear chap.'

I looked at the kind, distinguished, uncomprehending face. I knew that if his partner Charles Carthy-Todd skipped with the accumulated premiums before paying out the Newmarket widows, as I was privately certain he would, the honourable Duke of Wessex would meet every penny out of his own coffers. In all probability he could afford it, but that wasn't the point. He would be hurt and bewildered and impossibly distressed at having been tangled up in a fraud, and it seemed to me especially vicious that anyone should take advantage of his vulnerable simplicity and goodness.

Charles Carthy-Todd was engaged in taking candy from a mentally retarded child and then making it look as though the child had stolen it in the first place. One couldn't help but feel protective. One couldn't help but want to stop it.

I said impulsively, 'Take care of yourself, sir.'

'My dear chap . . . I will.'

I walked down the steps from his front door towards Honey's Mini waiting in the drive, and looked back to where he stood in the yellow oblong of light. He waved a hand gently and slowly closed the door, and I saw from his benign slightly puzzled expression that he was still not quite sure why I had come.

*

It was after one o'clock when I got back to the caravan. Tired, hungry, miserable about Nancy, I still couldn't stay asleep. Three o'clock, I was awake again, tangling the sheets as if in fever. I got up and splashed my itching eyes with cold water: lay down, got up, went for a walk across the airfield. The cool starry night came through my shirt and quietened my skin but didn't do much for the hopeless ache between my ears.

At eight in the morning I went to fetch Honey, filling her tank with the promised petrol at the nearest garage. She had made a gallon or two on the deal, I calculated. Fair enough.

What was not fair enough, however, was the news with which she greeted me.

'Colin Ross wants you to ring him up. He rang yesterday evening about half an hour after you'd buzzed off.'

'Did he say . . . what about?'

'He did ask me to write you a message, but honestly, I forgot. I was up in the tower until nine, and then Uncle was impatient to get home, and I just went off with him and forgot all about coming down here with the message . . . and anyway, what difference would a few hours make?'

'What was the message?'

'He said to tell you his sister didn't meet anyone called Chanter at Liverpool. Something about a strike, and this Chanter not being there. I don't know . . . there were two aircraft in the circuit and I wasn't paying all that much attention. Come to think of it, he did seem pretty anxious I should give you the message last night, but like I said, I forgot. Sorry, and all that. Was it important?'

I took a deep breath. Thinking about the past night, I could cheerfully have strangled her. 'Thanks for telling me.'

She gave me a sharp glance. 'You looked bushed. Have you been making love all night? You don't look fit to fly.'

'Seldom felt better,' I said with truth. 'And no, I haven't.'

'Save yourself for me.'

'Don't bank on it.'

'Louse.'

When I rang Colin's number from the telephone in the lounge it was Midge who answered. The relief in her voice was as overwhelming as my own.

'Matt! . . .' I could hear her gulp, and knew she was fighting against tears. 'Oh, Matt . . . I'm so glad you've rung. She didn't go after Chanter. She didn't. It's all right. Oh dear . . . just a minute . . .' She sniffed and paused, and when she spoke again she had her voice under control. 'She rang yesterday evening and we talked to her for a long time. She said she was sorry if she had upset us, she had really left because she was so angry with herself, so humiliated at having made up such silly dreams about you . . . she said it was all her own fault, that you hadn't deceived her in any way, she had deceived herself . . . she wanted to tell us that it wasn't because she was angry with you that she ran out, but because she felt she had made such a fool of herself . . . Anyway, she said she had cooled off a good deal by the time her train got to Liverpool and she was simply miserable by then, and then when she found Chanter had gone away because of the strike she said she was relieved, really. Chanter's landlady told Nancy where he had gone . . . somewhere in Manchester, to do a painting of industrial chimneys, she thought . . . but Nancy decided it wasn't Chanter she wanted . . . and she didn't know what to do, she still felt muddled . . . and then outside the art school she met a girl who had been a student with us in London. She was setting off for a camping holiday near Stratford and . . . well . . . Nancy decided to go with her. She said a few days' peace and some landscape painting would put her right . . . so she rang up here and it was our cleaning woman who answered . . . Nancy swears she told her it was Jill she was with, and not Chanter, but of course we never got that part of the message . . .' She stopped, and when I didn't answer immediately she said anxiously, 'Matt, are you still there?'

'Yes.'

'You were so quiet.'

'I was thinking about the last four days.'

Four wretched, dragging days. Four endless grinding nights. All unnecessary. She hadn't been with Chanter at all. If she'd suffered about what she'd imagined about me, so had I from what I'd imagined about her. Which made us, I guessed, about quits.

'Colin told her she should have asked you about that court case instead of jumping to conclusions,' Midge said.

'She didn't jump, she was pushed.'

'Yes. She knows that now. She's pretty upset. She doesn't really want to face you at Warwick ... after making such a mess of things ...'

'I shan't actually slaughter her.'

She half laughed. 'I'll defend her. I'm driving over with Colin. I'll see you there too.'

'That's marvellous.'

'Colin's out on the gallops just now. We're setting off after he's come in and had something to eat.'

'Tell him to drive carefully. Tell him to think of Ambrose.'

'Yes ... Isn't it awful about that crash?'

'Have you heard what happened, exactly?'

'Apparently Ambrose tried to pass a slow lorry on a bend and there was another one coming the other way ... he ran into it head on and one of the lorries overturned and crushed another car with three stable lads in it. There's quite a lot about it in today's *Sporting Life*.'

'I expect I'll see it. And Midge ... thank Colin for his message last night.'

'I will. He said he didn't want you to worry any longer. He seemed to think you were almost as worried about her as we were.'

'Almost,' I agreed wryly. 'See you at Warwick.'

CHAPTER FOURTEEN

Honey had arranged for me to fly a Mr and Mrs White-knight and their two young daughters down to Lydd, where the daughters were to meet friends and leave on the car air ferry to Le Touquet for a holiday in France. After waving the daughters off, the Whiteknights wanted to belt back to see their horse run in the first race at Warwick, which meant, since there was no race-course strip, landing at Coventry and hailing a cab.

Accordingly I loaded them up at Buckingham and pointed the nose of the Six towards Kent. The two daughters, about fourteen and sixteen, were world-weary and disagreeable, looking down their noses at everything with ingrained hostility. Their mother behaved to me with the cool graciousness of condescension, and autocratically bossed the family. Mr White-knight, gruff, unconsulted, a downtrodden universal provider, out of habit brought up the rear.

At Lydd, after carrying the daughters' suitcases unthanked into the terminal, I went back to the Six to wait through the farewells. Mr Whiteknight had obligingly left his *Sporting Life* on his seat. I picked it up and read it. There was a photograph of the Ambrose crash. The usual mangled metal, pushed to the side of the road, pathetic result of impatience.

I turned to the middle page, to see how many races Colin was riding at Warwick. He was down for five, and in most of them was favourite.

Alongside the Warwick programme, there was an advertisement in bold black letters.

'Colin Ross has insured with us. Why don't you?' Underneath in smaller type it went on, '*You* may not be lucky enough to survive two narrow escapes. Don't chance it. Cut out the proposal form printed below and send it with five pounds to the Racegoers' Accident Fund, Avon Street, Warwick. Your insurance cover starts from the moment your letter is in the post.'

I put the paper down on my knee, looked into space, and sucked my teeth.

Major Tyderman had told Annie Villars that he and a partner of his had something going for them that would make them rich. She had thought he meant control of Rudiments, but of course it hadn't been that. The manoeuvring with Rudiments had come about simply because Tyderman couldn't resist a small swindle on the side, even when he was engaged in a bigger one.

Tyderman had got Annie to introduce him to the Duke so that he in his turn could produce Carthy-Todd. Goldenberg was incidental, needed only for placing bets. Carthy-Todd was central, the moving mind, the instigator. Everyone else, Tyderman, the Duke, Colin, Annie, myself, all of us were pieces on his chess-board, to be shoved around until the game was won.

Clean up and clear out, that was how he must have decided to play. He hadn't waited for the Fund to grow slowly and naturally, he'd blown up an aeroplane and used Colin Ross for publicity. He would only have stayed anyway until the claims began mounting, and if the crash victims at Newmarket were in fact insured he would be off within the week. He would stay just long enough to collect the crash-inspired rush of new premiums, and that would be that. A quick transfer to a Swiss bank. A one-way ticket to the next happy hunting ground.

I didn't know how to stop him. There would be no proof that he meant to defraud until after he'd done it. I could produce nothing to back up my belief. No one was going to lurch into drastic action on what was little more than a guess. I could perhaps telephone to the Board of Trade . . . but the Board of Trade and I were hardly on speaking terms. The tall man might listen. He had, after all, once asked for my thoughts. Maybe the aircraft section had a hotline to the insurance section. And maybe not.

With a sigh I folded up Mr Whiteknight's newspaper and glanced again at the crash on the front page. Down in one corner in the left-hand column, beside the account of the accident, a paragraph heading caught my eye.

Tyderman, it said. I read the dry meagre lines underneath with a vague and then mounting feeling of alarm.

'A man believed to be Major Rupert Tyderman was found dead early yesterday beside the main London to South Wales railway line, between Swindon and Bristol. His death, at first attributed to a fall from a train, was later established as having been the result of a stab wound. The police, who had wanted to interview Major Tyderman, are making inquiries.'

The Whiteknight parents were walking back across the apron by the time I'd decided what to do. They were displeased when I met them and said I was going to make a telephone call. There wasn't time, they said.

'Check on the weather,' I lied. They looked up at the hazy heatwave sky and gave me deservedly bitter looks. All the same, I went on my way.

The Duke's polite manservant answered.

'No, Mr Shore, I'm very sorry, His Grace left for Warwick half an hour ago.'

'Was young Matthew with him?'

'Yes, sir.'

'Do you know if he was planning to go to the Accident Fund office before he went to the racecourse?'

'I believe so, sir. Yes.'

I put the receiver down, feeling increasingly fearful. Rupert Tyderman's death put the game into a different league. Lives had been at risk before, in the aeroplanes; the basic callousness was there; but on those occasions the intention had been expressly not to kill. But now, if

Carthy-Todd had decided to clear up behind him . . .
if Tyderman's blunder with Nancy's aeroplane, which
had led to his uncovering, had also led directly to his
death . . . if Carthy-Todd had stopped Tyderman giving
evidence against him . . . then would he, could he possibly, also kill the simple, honest, truth-spilling
Duke . . .?

He wouldn't, I thought coldly. He couldn't.

I didn't convince myself one little bit.

The Whiteknights had no cause for complaint about the
speed at which I took them to Coventry, though they
consented only with bad grace when I asked to share
their taxi to the races. I parted from them at the main
gate and walked back towards the town centre, looking
for the office of the Accident Fund. As the Duke had
said, it wasn't far: less than a quarter of a mile.

It was located on the first floor of a small moderately
well kept town house which fronted straight on to the
pavement. The ground floor seemed to be uninhabited,
but the main door stood open and a placard on the
wall just inside announced 'Racegoers' Accident Fund.
Please walk up.'

I walked up. On the first landing there was a wash
room, a secretary's office, and, at the front of the house,
a door with a Yale lock and a knocker in the shape of a
horse's head. I flipped the knocker a couple of times
and the door came abruptly open.

'Hello,' said young Matthew, swinging it wide. 'Uncle was just saying you would miss us. We're just going along to the races.'

'Come along in, my dear chap,' said the Duke's voice from inside the room.

I stepped into the office. At first sight a plushy one: wall to wall plum coloured carpet, but of penny-pinching quality, two fat looking easy chairs with cheap foam seats, a pair of shoulder high metal filing cabinets and a modern afrormosia desk. The atmosphere of a solid, sober, long established business came exclusively from the good proportions of the bay windowed room, the mouldings round the nineteenth-century ceiling, the carved wood and marble slab of the handsome fireplace, and some dark old gilt framed oils on the walls. The office had been chosen with genius to convince, to reassure, to charm. And as clients of insurance companies seldom if ever visited its office, this one must have been designed to convince, to reassure, to charm only the Duke himself.

The Duke introduced me to the man who had been sitting and who now stood behind the desk.

'Charles Carthy-Todd . . . Matthew Shore.'

I shook his hand. He'd seen me before, as I'd seen him. Neither of us gave the slightest sign of it. I hoped he had not distinguished in me the minute subsidence of tension which I saw in him. The tension I felt hadn't subsided in the slightest.

He was all the Duke had said: a man with good

presence, good voice, a thorough-going public school gent. He would have had to have been, to net the Duke; and there were all those silver framed photographs, which the Duke had mentioned, standing around to prove it.

He had dark hair with the merest sprinkling of grey, a compact little moustache, pinkish tan, slightly oily-looking skin, and heavy black-framed glasses assisting his greyish-blue eyes.

The Duke was sitting comfortably in an armchair in the bay window, his splendid head haloed by the shining day behind. His knees were crossed, his hands relaxed, and he was smoking a cigar. From his general air of pleased well-being, it was easy to see the pride he held in his beautiful benevolent fund. I wished sincerely for his sake that he wasn't going to have to wake up.

Charles Carthy-Todd sat down and continued with what he had been going to do when I arrived, offering young Matthew a piece of chocolate-covered orange peel from a half-empty round red and gold tin. Matthew took it, thanked him, ate it, and watched him with anxious reserve. Like the Duke, I trusted young Matthew's instinct. All too clearly, it had switched to amber, if not to red. I hoped for all our sakes that he would have the good manners to keep quiet.

'Give Matthew a proposal form, Charles,' the Duke said contentedly. 'That's what he's come for, you know, to join the Fund.'

Carthy-Todd obediently rose, crossed to the filing

cabinet, pulled open the top drawer, and lifted out two separate sheets of paper. One, it appeared, was the proposal form: the other, a lavishly curlicued certificate of insurance. I filled in the spaces on the ultra-simple proposal while Carthy-Todd inscribed my name and number on the certificate; then I handed over a fiver, which left me with enough to live on cornflakes until pay day, and the transaction was complete.

'Take care of yourself now, Matt,' joked the Duke, and I smiled and said I would.

The Duke looked at his watch. 'Good gracious!' He stood up. 'Come along now, everybody. Time we went along to the racecourse. And no more excuses, Charles, I insist on you lunching with me.' To me he explained, 'Charles very rarely goes to the races. He doesn't much care for it, do you see? But as the course is so very close . . .'

Carthy-Todd's aversion to race meetings was to my mind completely understandable. He wished to remain unseen, anonymous, unrecognizable, just as he'd been all along. Charles would choose which meetings he went to very carefully indeed. He would never, I imagined, turn up without checking with the Duke whether he was going to be there too.

We walked back to the racecourse, the Duke and Carthy-Todd in front, young Matthew and me behind. Young Matthew slowed down a little and said to me in a quiet voice, 'I say, Matt, have you noticed something strange about Mr Carthy-Todd?'

I glanced at his face. He was half anxious, half puzzled, wanting reassurance.

'What do you think is strange?'

'I've never seen anyone before with eyes like that.'

Children were incredibly observant. Matthew had
seen naturally what I had known to look for.

'I shouldn't mention it to him. He might not care
for it.'

'I suppose not.' He paused. 'I don't frightfully like
him.'

'I can see that.'

'Do you?'

'No,' I said.

He nodded in satisfaction. 'I didn't think you would.
I don't know why Uncle's so keen on him. Uncle,' he
added dispassionately, 'doesn't understand about
people. He thinks everyone is as nice as he is. Which
they're not.'

'How soon can you become his business manager?'

He laughed. 'I know all about trustees. I've got them.
Can't have this and can't do that, that's all they ever say,
Mother says.'

'Does your Uncle have trustees?'

'No, he hasn't. Mother's always beefing on about
Uncle not being fit to control all that lucre and one day
he'll invest the lot in a South Sea Bubble. I asked Uncle
about it and he just laughed. He told me he has a stockbroker who sees to everything and Uncle just goes on
getting richer and when he wants some money for

something he just tells the stockbroker and he sells some shares and sends it along. Simple. Mother fusses over nothing. Uncle won't get into much trouble about money because he knows that he doesn't know about it, if you see what I mean?'

'I wouldn't like him to give too much to Mr Carthy-Todd,' I said.

He gave me a flashing look of understanding. 'So that's what I felt . . . Do you think it would do any good if I sort of tried to put Uncle off him a bit?'

'Couldn't do much harm.'

'I'll have a go,' he said. 'But he's fantastically keen on him.' He thought deeply and came up with a grin. 'I must say,' he said, 'that he has awfully good chocolate orange peel.'

Annie Villars was upset about Kenny Bayst. 'I went to see him for a few moments this morning. He's broken both legs and his face was cut by flying glass. He won't be riding again before next season, he says. Luckily he's insured with the Racegoers' Fund. Sent them a tenner, he told me, so he's hoping to collect two thousand pounds at least. Marvellous thing, that Fund.'

'Did you join?'

'I certainly did. After that bomb. Didn't know it was Rupert, then, of course. Still, better to do things at once rather than put them off, don't you agree?'

'Were Kitch and the stable lads insured too, do you know?'

She nodded. 'They were all Kitch's own lads. He'd advised them all to join. Even offered to deduct the premium from their wages bit by bit. Everyone in New-market is talking about it, saying how lucky it was. All the stable lads in the town who hadn't already joined are sending their fivers along in the next few days.'

I hesitated. 'Did you read about Rupert Tyderman in the *Sporting Life*?'

A twinge of regret twisted her face: her mouth for the first time since I had known her took on a soft curve that was not consciously constructed.

'Poor Rupert . . . What an end, to be murdered.'

'There isn't any doubt, then?'

She shook her head. 'When I saw the report, I rang the local newspaper down at Kemble . . . that's where they found him. He was lying, they said, at the bottom of an embankment near a road bridge over the railway. The local theory is that he could have been brought there by car during the night, and not fallen from a train at all . . .' She shook her head in bewilderment. 'He had one stab wound below his left shoulder-blade, and he had been dead for hours when he was found.'

It took a good deal of lying-in-wait to catch the Duke without Carthy-Todd at his elbow, but I got him in the end.

'I've left my wallet in the Accident Fund office,' I said. 'Must have left it on the desk when I paid my premium . . . Do you think, sir, that you could let me have a key, if you have one, so that I can slip along and fetch it?'

'My dear chap, of course.' He produced a small bunch from his pocket and sorted out a bright new yale. 'Here you are. That's the one.'

'Very kind, sir. I won't be long.' I took a step away and then turned back, grinning, making a joke.

'What happens, sir, if it's you who gets killed in a car crash? What happens to the Fund then?'

He smiled back reassuringly in a patting-on-the-shoulder avuncular manner. 'All taken care of, my dear chap. Some of the papers I signed, they dealt with it. The Fund money would be guaranteed from a special arrangement with my estate.'

'Did Charles see to it?'

'Naturally. Of course. He understands these things, you know.'

Between the Duke and the main gate a voice behind me crisply shouted.

'Matt.'

I stopped and turned. It was Colin, hurrying towards me, carrying the saddle from the loser he'd partnered in the first race.

'Can't stop more than a second,' he said. 'Got to

change for the next. You weren't leaving, were you? Have you seen Nancy?'

'No. I've been looking. I thought . . . perhaps . . .'

He shook his head. 'She's here. Up there, on the balcony, with Midge.'

I followed where he was looking, and there they were, distant, high up, talking with their heads together, two halves of one whole.

'Do you know which is Nancy?' Colin asked.

I said without hesitation, 'The one on the left.'

'Most people can't tell.'

He looked at my expression and said with exasperation, 'If you feel like that about her, why the bloody hell don't you let her know? She thinks she made it all up . . . she's trying to hide it but she's pretty unhappy.'

'She'd have to live on peanuts.'

'For crying out loud, what does that matter? You can move in with us. We all want you. Midge wants you . . . and now, not some distant time when you think you can afford it. Time for us is now, this summer. There may not be much after this.' He hitched the saddle up on his arm and looked back towards the weighing room. 'I'll have to go. We'll have to talk later. I came after you now, though, because you looked as though you were leaving.'

'I'm coming back soon.' I turned and walked along with him towards the weighing room. 'Colin . . . I ought to tell someone . . . you never know . . .' He gave me a puzzled glance and in three brief sentences I told him

573

why the Accident Fund was a fraud, how he and the bomb had been used to drum up business, and in what way Carthy-Todd was a fake.

He stopped dead in his tracks. 'Good God,' he said. 'The Fund was such a great idea. What a bloody shame.'

Saturday afternoon. The Board of Trade had gone home to its lawn mowing and the wife and kids. I put down the telephone and considered the police.

The police were there, on the racecourse, all ready and able. But willing? Hardly. They were there to direct the traffic; a crime not yet committed would not shift them an inch.

Both lots, if they believed me, might eventually arrive on Carthy-Todd's doorstep. By appointment, probably; especially the Board of Trade.

There would be no Carthy-Todd to welcome them in. No records. No Fund. Possibly no Duke . . .

I always told myself to stay out of trouble.

Never listened.

No clocks ticked in Carthy-Todd's office. The silence was absolute. But it was only in my mind that it was ominous and oppressive. Carthy-Todd was safe at the races and I should have a clear hour at least: or so my brain told me. My nerves had other ideas.

I found myself tiptoeing across to the desk.

Ridiculous. I half laughed at myself and put my feet down flat on the soundless carpet.

Nothing on the desk top except a blotter without blots, a tray of pens and pencils, a green telephone, a photograph of a woman, three children and a dog in a silver frame, a desk diary, closed, and the red and gold tin of chocolate orange peel.

The drawers contained stationery, paper clips, stamps, and a small pile of the 'insure against bombs on the way home' brochures. Two of the four drawers were completely empty.

Two filing cabinets. One unlocked. One locked. The top of the three drawers of the unlocked cabinet contained the packets of proposal forms and insurance certificates, and a third packet containing claim forms; in the second, the completed and returned forms of those insured, filed in a rank of folders from A–Z; and the third, almost empty, contained three folders only, one marked 'Claims settled', one 'Claims pending', and the other 'Receipts'.

'Claims settled' embraced the records of two separate outgoing payments of one thousand pounds, one to Acey Jones and one to a trainer in Kent who had been kicked in the face at evening stables. Three hundred pounds had been paid to a stable girl in Newmarket in respect of fracturing her wrist in a fall from a two-year-old at morning exercise. The claim forms, duly filled in, and with doctor's certificates attached, were stamped 'paid' with a date.

'Claims pending' was fatter. There were five letters of application for claim forms, annotated 'forms sent', and two forms completed and returned, claiming variously for a finger bitten off by a hungry hurdler and a foot carelessly left in the path of a plough. From the dates, the claimants had only been waiting a month for their money, and few insurance companies paid out quicker than that.

The thin file 'Receipts' was in many ways the most interesting. The record took the form of a diary, with the number of new insurers entered against the day they paid their premiums. From sporadic twos and threes during the first week of operation the numbers had grown like a mushroom.

The first great spurt was labelled in the margin in small tidy handwriting 'A. C. Jones, etc.' The second, an astronomical burst, was noted 'Bomb!' The third, a lesser spurt, 'Pamphlet'. The fourth, a noticeable upthrust, 'Electric failure'. After that, the daily average had gone on climbing steadily. The word, by then, had reached pretty well every ear.

The running total in two months had reached five thousand, four hundred and seventy-two. The receipts, since some insurers had paid double premiums for double benefits, stood at £28,040.

With the next inrush of premiums after the Kitch-Ambrose accident (which Carthy-Todd certainly had not engineered, as only non-claiming accidents were any good to him) there would almost have been enough in the kitty to settle all the claims. I sighed, frowning. It was, as Colin had said, a bloody shame. The Duke's view of the Fund was perfectly valid. Run by an honest man, and with its ratio of premiums to pay-off slightly adjusted, it could have done good all round.

I slammed the bottom drawer shut with irritation and felt the adrenalin race through my veins as the noise reverberated round the empty room.

No one came. My nerves stopped registering tremble; went back to itch.

The locked second cabinet was proof only against casual eyes. I tipped it against the wall and felt underneath, and sure enough it was the type worked on one connecting rod up the back: pushed the rod up from the bottom and all the drawers became unlocked.

I looked through all of them quickly, the noise I had made seeming to act as an accelerator. Even if I had all the time in the world, I wanted to be out of there, to be gone.

The top drawer contained more folders of papers. The middle drawer contained a large grey metal box. The bottom drawer contained two cardboard boxes and two small square tins.

Taking a deep breath I started at the top. The folders contained the setting-up documents of the Fund and the papers which the Duke had so trustingly signed. The legal language made perfect camouflage for what Carthy-Todd had done. I had to read them twice, to take a strong grip and force myself to concentrate, before I understood the two covenants the Duke had given him.

The first, as the Duke had said, transferred one hundred thousand pounds from his estate into a guarantee trust for the Fund, in the event of his death. The second one at first sight looked identical, but it certainly wasn't. It said in essence that if the Duke died within the first year of the Fund, a further one hundred thousand pounds from his estate was to be paid into it.

In both cases, Carthy-Todd was to be sole Trustee.

In both cases, he was given absolute discretion to invest or use the money in any way he thought best.

Two hundred thousand pounds . . . I stared into space. Two hundred thousand pounds if the Duke died. A motive to make tongue-silencing look frivolous.

The twenty-eight thousand of the Fund money was only the beginning. The bait. The jackpot lay in the dead Duke.

His heirs would have to pay. Young Matthew, to be precise. The papers looked thoroughly legal, with signatures witnessed and stamped, and in fact it seemed one hundred per cent certain that Carthy-Todd wouldn't have bothered with them at all if they were not foolproof.

He wouldn't waste much more time, I thought. Not with the claims for the Ambrose accident coming in. With the Duke dead, the two hundred thousand would have to be paid almost at once, because the covenants would be a first charge on his estate, like debts. There

578

would be no having to wait around for probate. If Carthy-Todd could stave off the claims for a while, he could skip with both the Duke's money and the whole Fund.

I put the papers back in their folder, back in the drawer. Closed it. Gently. My heart thumped.

Second drawer. Large metal box. One could open it without removing it from the cabinet. I opened it. Lots of space, but few contents. Some cottonwool, cold cream, glue, and a half used stick of greasepaint. I shut the lid, shut the drawer. Only to be expected.

Bottom drawer. Knelt on the floor. Two small square tins, one empty, one full and heavy and fastened all round with adhesive tape. Looked inside the two cardboard boxes first and felt the breath go out of my body as if I'd been kicked.

The cardboard boxes contained the makings of a radio bomb. Solenoids, transmitters, fuse wire, a battery and a small container of gunpowder in the first box. Plastic explosive wrapped in tin foil in the other.

I sat on my heels looking at the small square heavy tin. Heard in my mind the tall man from the Board of Trade: the tighter you pack a bomb the more fiercely it explodes.

Decided not to open the small square tin. Felt the sweat stand out in cold drops on my forehead.

I shut the bottom drawer with a caution which seemed silly when I remembered the casual way I'd tilted the whole cabinet over to open it. But then the bomb wouldn't get the signal where it was, not with those precious documents in the cabinet just above.

I wiped my hand over my face. Stood up. Swallowed.

I'd found everything I came to find, and more. All except for one thing. I glanced round the office, looking for somewhere else. Somewhere to hide something big . . .

There was a door in the corner behind Carthy-Todd's desk which I assumed connected with the secretary's office next door. I went over to it. Tried the handle. It was locked.

I let myself out of Carthy-Todd's office and went into the secretary's room, whose door was shut but had no keyhole. Stared, in there, at an L-shaped blank wall. No connecting door to Carthy-Todd. It was a cupboard, with the door on his side.

I went back to Carthy-Todd's office and stood contemplating the door. If I broke it open, he would know. If I didn't, I could only guess at what was inside. Evidence of a fraud committed, that would spur the Board of Trade to action. Evidence that would make the Duke rescind his covenants, or at least re-write them so that they were no longer death warrants . . .

Carthy-Todd hadn't been expecting trouble. He had left the key to the cupboard on his desk in the tray of pens and pencils. I picked up the single key which lay there, and it fitted.

Opened the cupboard door. It squeaked on its hinges, but I was too engrossed to notice.

There he was. Mr Acey Jones. The crutches, leaning against the wall. The white plaster cast lying on the floor.

I picked up the cast and looked at it. It had been slit neatly down the inside leg from the top to the ankle. One could put one's foot into it like a boot, with the bare toes sticking out of the end and the metal walking support under the arch. There were small grip-clips like those used on bandages sticking into the plaster all down the opening. Put your foot into the cast, fasten the clips, and bingo, you had a broken ankle.

Acey Jones, loudly drumming up business for the Fund.

Acey Jones, Carthy-Todd. Confidence tricksters were the best actors in the world.

I didn't hear him come.

I put the cast back on the floor just where it had been, and straightened up and started to shut the cupboard door, and saw him moving out of the corner of my eye as he came into the room. I hadn't shut the office door behind me, when I'd gone back. I hadn't given myself any time at all.

His face went rigid with fury when he saw what I'd seen.

'Meddling pilot,' he said. 'When the Duke told me he'd given you the key . . .' He stopped, unable to speak for rage. His voice was different, neither the Eton of

Carthy-Todd, nor the Australian of Acey Jones. Just ordinary uninflected English. I wondered fleetingly where he came from, who he really was . . . a thousand different people, one for every crime.

Unblinking behind the black-framed glasses the pale blue-grey eyes all but sizzled. The incongruous white eyelashes, which Matthew had noticed, gave him now a fierce fanatical ruthlessness. The decision he was coming to wasn't going to be for my good.

He put his hand into his trouser pocket and briefly pulled it out again. There was a sharp click. I found myself staring at the knife which had snapped out, and thought with a horrific shiver of Rupert Tyderman tumbling down dead beside the railway line . . .

He took a step sideways and kicked shut the office door. I twisted round towards the mantelshelf to pick up whatever I could find there . . . a photograph, a cigarette box . . . anything I could use as a weapon or a shield.

I didn't even get as far as taking anything into my hand, because he didn't try to stab me with the knife.

He threw it.

CHAPTER FIFTEEN

It hit me below the left shoulder and the jolt threw me forward on my twisting legs so that I hit my forehead solidly on the edge of the marble slab mantelshelf. Blacking out, falling, I put out a hand to stop myself, but there was nothing there, only the empty black hollow of the fireplace, and I went on, right down, smashing and crashing amongst the brass fire irons . . . but I heard them only dimly . . . and then not at all.

I woke up slowly, stiffly, painfully, after less than a quarter of an hour. Everything was silent. No sound. No people. Nothing.

I couldn't remember where I was or what had happened. Not until I tried to get up. Then the tearing soreness behind my shoulder stung me straight back into awareness.

Had a knife sticking in my back.

Lying face down among the fire irons I felt gingerly round with my right hand. My fingers brushed like feathers against the hilt. I cried out at my own touch. It was frightful.

Stupid the things you think of in moments of disaster. I thought: damn it, only three weeks and one day to my medical. I'll never pass it . . .

Never pull knives out of wounds, they say. It makes the bleeding worse. You can die from pulling knives out of wounds. Well . . . I forgot all that. I could see only that Acey-Carthy-Todd had left me for dead and if he found me alive when he came back he would almost certainly finish the job. Therefore I had to get out of his office before he came back. And it seemed incongruous, really, to walk round Warwick with a knife in one's back. So I pulled it out.

I pulled it out in two stages and more or less fainted after each. Kidded myself it was concussion from the mantelshelf, but I was crying as well. No stoic, Matt Shore.

When it was out I lay where I was for a while, looking at it, snivelling weakly and feeling the sticky warmth slowly spread, but being basically reassured because I was pretty sure by then that the knife had not gone through into my lung. It must have been deflected by hitting my shoulder blade: it had been embedded to three or four inches, but slanting, not straight in deep. I wasn't going to die. Or not yet.

After a while I got up on to my knees. I didn't have all the time in the world. I put my right hand on Carthy-Todd's desk: pulled myself to my feet.

Swayed. Thought it would be much much worse if I

fell down again. Leant my hip against the desk and looked vaguely round the office.

The bottom drawer of the second filing cabinet was open.

Shouldn't be. I'd shut it.

Open.

I shifted myself off the desk and tried a few steps. Tottered. Made it. Leant gingerly against the wall. Looked down into the drawer.

The cardboard boxes were still there. The empty tin was still there. The small heavy tin wasn't.

Realized coldly that the future no longer meant simply getting myself to safety out of that office, but getting to the Duke before the bomb did.

It was only four hundred yards . . . Only . . .

I'd have to do it, I thought, because if I hadn't searched the office Carthy-Todd wouldn't now be in a tearing hurry. When I didn't turn up to ferry home the Whiteknights, or turn up anywhere again for that matter, except with a stab wound in a ditch, the Duke would say where I had been last . . . and Carthy-Todd would want to avoid a police investigation like a slug shrinking away from salt. He wouldn't wait for that. He would obliterate my tracks.

There was something else missing from the office. I didn't know what it was, just knew it was something. It niggled for a moment, but was gone. Didn't think it could be important . . .

Walked with deliberation to the door. Opened it,

went outside. Stopped dead at the top of the stairs, feeling dizzy and weak.

Well. Had to get down them somehow. Had to.

The handrail was on the left-hand side. I couldn't bear to lift my left arm. Turned round, hung on tightly, and went down backwards.

'There you are,' I said aloud. 'You bloody can.' Didn't convince myself. It took Carthy-Todd to convince.

I laughed weakly. I was a fully paid up insurer with the Fund. Like to see Carthy-Todd pay my claim . . . a thousand smackers for a knife in the back. Lovely.

Rolled out into the hot sunlit street as light headed as a blond.

Blond Acey Jones . . .

Acey Jones was being pushed. Hurried. Knowing I'd found him out but still believing he could retrieve the situation. Still make his two hundred thousand. If he kept his nerve. If he killed the Duke immediately, this afternoon, and somehow made it look like an accident. If he dumped me somewhere later, as he had the Major . . .

He would think he could still do it. He didn't know I'd told Colin, didn't know that Colin knew he was Carthy-Todd . . .

The empty street had got much longer during the afternoon. Also it wouldn't stay absolutely still. It shimmered. It undulated. The pavement was uneven. Every time I put my foot down the paving stones reached up and stabbed me in the back.

I passed only an elderly woman on the way. She was muttering to herself. I realized that I was, too.

Half-way. I squinted along at the gate of the car park. Had to make it. Had to. And that wasn't all. Had to find someone to go and fetch the Duke, so that I could explain . . . explain . . .

Felt myself falling and put a hand out towards the wall. Mustn't shut my eyes . . . I'd be done for . . . spun heavily against the bricks and shuddered at the result. Rested my head against the wall, trying not to weep. Couldn't spare the time. Had to get on.

I pushed myself back into a moderately upright walking position. My feet couldn't tell properly how far it was down to the pavement: half the time I was climbing imaginary steps.

Weird.

Something warm on my left hand. I looked down. My head swam. Blood was running down my fingers, dripping on to the pavement. Looked up again, along to the course. Head swam again. Didn't know if it was concussion or heat or loss of blood. Only knew it reduced the time factor. Had to get there. Quickly.

One foot in front of the other, I told myself . . . just go on doing that: one foot in front of the other. And you'll get there.

Concentrate.

I got there. Gate to the car park. And no official guarding it. At that time in the afternoon, they'd given up expecting further customers.

587

I said 'Ohh . . .' in weak frustration. Have to go still further. Have to find someone . . . I turned in to the car park. Through the car park there was a gate into the paddock. Lots of people there. Lots . . .

I went between the cars, staggering, holding on to them, feeling my knees bending, knowing the dizzy weakness was winning and caring less and less about the jagged pain of every step. Had to find someone. Had to.

Someone suddenly called to me from quite close.

'Matt!'

I stopped. Looked slowly round. Midge was climbing out of Colin's parked Aston Martin down the row and running to catch me up.

'Matt,' she said, 'We've been looking for you. I came back to the car because I was tired. Where have you been?'

She put her hand with friendship on my left arm.

I said thickly, 'Don't . . . touch me.'

She took her hand away with a jerk. 'Matt!'

She looked at me more closely, at first in puzzlement and then in anxiety. Then she looked at her fingers, and where she'd grasped my coat there were bright red smears.

'It's blood,' she said blankly.

I nodded a fraction. My mouth was dry. I was getting very tired.

'Listen . . . Do you know the Duke of Wessex?'

'Yes. But . . .' she protested.

'Midge,' I interrupted. 'Go and find him. Bring him

588

here . . . I know it sounds stupid . . . but someone is trying to kill him . . . with a bomb.'

'Like Colin? But that wasn't . . .'

'Fetch him, Midge,' I said. 'Please.'

'I can't leave you. Not like this.'

'You must.'

She looked at me doubtfully.

'Hurry.'

'I'll get you some help, too,' she said. She turned lightly on her heel and half walked, half ran towards the paddock. I leant the bottom of my spine against a shiny grey Jaguar and wondered how difficult it would be to prevent Carthy-Todd from planting his bomb. That tin . . . it was small enough to fit into a binocular case . . . probably identical with the one which had destroyed the Cherokee. I would have sweated at the thought of so much confined explosive power if I hadn't been sweating clammily already.

Why didn't they come? My mouth was drier . . . The day was airless . . . I moved restlessly against the car. After I'd told the Duke, he'd have to go off somewhere and stay safely out of sight until the Board of Trade had dealt with Carthy-Todd . . .

I dispassionately watched the blood drip from my fingers on to the grass. I could feel that all the back of my coat was soaked. Couldn't afford a new one, either. Have to get it cleaned, and have the slit invisibly mended. Get myself mended, too, as best I could. Harley wouldn't keep the job for me. He'd have to get someone else in my place. The Board of Trade doctors wouldn't let me fly again for weeks and weeks. If you gave a pint of blood as a donor, they grounded you for over a month . . . I'd lost more than a pint involuntarily, by the looks of things . . . though a pint would make a pretty good mess, if you spilled it.

I lifted my lolling head up with a jerk. Got to stay awake until they came. Got to explain to the Duke . . .

Things were beginning to fuzz round the edges. I licked my dry lips. Didn't do much good. Didn't have any moisture in my tongue either.

I finally saw them, and it seemed a long way off, coming through the gate from the paddock. Not just Midge and the Duke, but two others as well. Young Matthew, jigging along in front.

And Nancy.

Chanter had receded into the unimportant past. I didn't give him a thought. Everything was as it had been before, the day she flew to Haydock. Familiar, friendly, trusting. The girl I hadn't wanted to get involved with, who had melted a load of ice like an acetylene torch.

Across the sea of cars Midge pointed in my direction and they began to come towards me, crossing through the rows. When they were only twenty or so yards away, on the far side of the row in front of me, they unaccountably stopped.

Come on, I thought. For God's sake come on.

They didn't move.

With an effort I pushed myself upright from the

Jaguar and took the few steps past its bonnet, going towards them. On my left, six cars along, was parked what was evidently the Duke's Rolls. On the bonnet stood a bright red and gold tin. Matthew was pointing, wanting to cross over and fetch it, and Midge was saying urgently, 'No, come on, Matt said to come quickly, and he's bleeding . . .'

Matthew gave her a concerned look and then nodded, but at the last second temptation was too much and he ran over and picked up the tin and started back to join them.

Bright red and gold tin. Containing sticks of orange peel dipped in chocolate. It had been on the desk. And afterwards . . . not on the desk. Something missing. Red and gold tin.

Missing from Carthy-Todd's desk.

My heart bumped. I shouted, and my voice came out hopelessly weak.

'Matthew, throw it to me.'

He looked up doubtfully. The others began to walk through the rows of cars towards him. They would reach him before I could. They would be standing all together, Nancy and Midge and the Duke and young Matthew, who knew too that I'd been in Carthy-Todd's office that day.

I scanned the car park desperately, but he was there. He'd put the tin on the car and simply waited for them to come out of the races. The last race was about to start . . . the horses had gone down to the post and at that moment the loudspeakers were announcing 'They're under starter's orders' . . . He knew it wouldn't be long before they came . . . He was standing over nearer the rails of the course with his black head showing and the sun glinting on his glasses. He had meant just to kill young Matthew and the Duke, but now there were Nancy and Midge as well . . . and he didn't know he couldn't get away with it . . . didn't know Colin knew . . . and he was too far away for me to tell him . . . I couldn't shout . . . could barely talk.

'Matthew, throw me the tin.' It was a whisper, nothing more.

I began to walk towards him, holding out my right arm. Stumbled. Swayed. Frightened him.

The others were closing on him.

No more time. I took a breath. Straightened up.

'Matthew,' I said loudly. 'To save your life, throw me that tin. Throw it now. At once.'

He was upset, uncertain, worried.

He threw the tin.

It was taking Carthy-Todd several seconds to press the transmission buttons. He wasn't as adept at it as Rupert Tyderman. He wouldn't be able to see that he had missed his opportunity with the Duke, and that now there was only me. But whatever he did, he'd lost the game.

The red-gold tin floated towards me like a blazing sun and seemed to take an eternity crossing the fifteen feet from Matthew. I stretched my right arm forward to meet it and when it landed on my hand I flung it with a bowling action high into the air behind where I was standing, back as far as I could over the parked rows, because behind them, at the rear, there was empty space.

The bomb went off in the air. Three seconds out of my hand, six seconds out of Matthew's. Six seconds. As long a time as I had ever lived.

The red and gold tin disintegrated into a cracking fireball like the sun, and the blast of it knocked both young Matthew and me with a screeching jolt flat to the ground. The windows in most of the cars in the car park crashed into splinters, and the two Fords just below the explosion were thrown about like toys. Nancy and Midge and the Duke, still sheltered between two cars, rocked on their feet and clung to each other for support.

Along in the stands, we heard later, no one took much notice. The race had started and the commentator's voice was booming out, filling everyone's ears with the news that Colin Ross was lying handy and going nicely on the favourite half a mile from home.

Young Matthew picked himself smartly up and said in amazement, 'What was that?'

Midge completed the four bare steps to his side and held his hand.

'It was a bomb,' she said in awe. 'Like Matt said, it was a bomb.'

I was trying to get myself up off the grass. Even though the Duke was for the present safe, the Fund money was not. Might as well try for set and match . . .

On my knees, I said to Matthew, 'Can you see Carthy-Todd anywhere? It was his tin . . . his bomb . . .'

'Carthy-Todd?' repeated the Duke vaguely. 'It can't be. Impossible. He wouldn't do a thing like that.'

'He just did,' I said. I was having no success in getting up any further. Had nothing much left. A strong arm slid under my right armpit, helping me. A soft calm voice said in my ear, 'You look as if you'd be better staying down.'

'Nancy . . .'

'How did you get into this state?'

'Carthy-Todd . . . had a knife . . .'

'There he is!' Matthew suddenly shouted. 'Over there.'

I wobbled to my feet. Looked where Matthew was pointing. Carthy-Todd, running between the rows. Nancy looked too.

'But that's,' she said incredulously, 'that's the man I saw in the car with Major Tyderman. I'd swear to it.'

'You may have to,' I said.

'He's running to get out,' Matthew shouted. 'Let's head him off.'

It was almost a game to him, but his enthusiasm infected several other racegoers who had come early out of the races and found their windows in splinters.

'Head him off,' I heard a man shout, and another, 'There, over there. Head him off.'

I leaned in hopeless weakness against a car, and

dimly watched. Carthy-Todd caught sight of the growing number converging on him. Hesitated. Changed course. Doubled back on his tracks. Made for the only free and open space he could see. The green grass behind him. The racecourse itself.

'Don't . . .' I said. It came out a whisper, and even if I'd had a microphone he wouldn't have heard.

'Oh God,' Nancy said beside me. 'Oh no.'

Carthy-Todd didn't see his danger until it was too late. He ran blindly out across the course looking over his shoulder at the bunch of men who had suddenly, aghast, stopped chasing him.

He ran straight in front of the thundering field of three-year-olds sweeping round the last bend to their final flying effort up the straight.

Close bunched, they had no chance of avoiding him. He went down under the pounding hooves like a rag into a threshing machine, and a second later the flowing line of horses broke up into tumbling chaos . . . crashing at thirty miles an hour . . . legs whirling . . . jockeys thudding to the ground like bright blobs of paint . . . a groaning shambles on the bright green turf . . . and side-stepping, swaying, looking over their shoulders, the rear ones in the field swerved past and went on to a finish that no one watched.

Nancy said in anguish, 'Colin!' and ran towards the rails. The pink and white silks lay still, a crumpled bundle curled in a protective ball. I followed her, plod by plod, feeling that I couldn't go any further, I simply couldn't. One car short of the rails, I stopped. I clung on to it, sagging. The tide was going out.

The pink and white ball stirred, unrolled itself, stood up. Relief made me even weaker. Crowds of people had appeared on the course, running, helping, gawping . . . closing in like a screen round the strewn bodies . . . I waited for what seemed an age, and then Colin and Nancy reappeared through a thronging wall of people and came back towards the car park.

'Only stunned for a second,' I heard him say to a passing inquirer. 'I shouldn't go over there . . .' But the inquirer went on, looking avid.

Nancy saw me and waved briefly, and ducked under the rails with Colin.

'He's dead,' she said abruptly. She looked sick. 'That man . . . he . . . he was Acey Jones . . . Colin said you knew . . . his hair was lying on the grass . . . but it was a wig . . . and there was this bald white head and that pale hair . . . and you could see the line of grease paint . . . and the black moustache . . .' Her eyes were wide. Full of horror.

'Don't think about it,' Colin said. He looked at me. 'She shouldn't have come over . . .'

'I had to . . . you were lying there,' she protested. He went on looking at me. His expression changed. He said, 'Nancy said you were hurt. She didn't say . . . how badly.' He turned abruptly to Nancy and said, 'Fetch the doctor.'

'I tried to before,' she said. 'But he said he was on

duty and couldn't see to Matt before the race in case he was needed . . .' She tailed off and looked over at the crowd on the course. 'He'll be over there . . . seeing to those two jockeys . . .' She looked back at Colin with sudden fright. 'Midge said Matt had cut his arm . . . Is it worse? . . .'

'I'll fetch him,' Colin said grimly, and ran back to the battlefield. Nancy looked at me with such flooding anxiety that I grinned.

'Not as bad as all that,' I said.

'But you were walking . . . you threw that bomb with such force . . . I didn't realize . . . You do look ill . . .'

The Duke and young Matthew and Midge reappeared from somewhere. I hadn't seen them come. Things were getting hazier.

The Duke was upset. 'My dear chap,' he said over and over again. 'My dear chap . . .'

'How did you know it was a bomb?' Matthew asked.

'Just knew.'

'That was a pretty good throw.'

'Saved our lives,' said the Duke. 'My dear chap . . .'

Colin was back.

'He's coming,' he said. 'Immediately.'

'Saved our lives . . .' said the Duke again. 'How can we repay . . .'

Colin looked at him straightly. 'I'll tell you how, sir. Set him up in business . . . or take over Derrydowns . . . give him an air taxi business, based near Newmarket. He'll make you a profit. He'll have me for a customer, and Annie, and Kenny . . . and in fact the whole town, because the Fund can go on now, can't it?' He looked at me inquiringly, and I fractionally nodded. 'It may cost a bit to put right,' Colin said, 'but your Fund can go on, sir, and do all the good it was meant to . . .'

'An air taxi business. Take over Derrydowns,' the Duke repeated. 'My dear Colin, what a splendid idea. Of course. Of course.'

I tried to say something . . . anything . . . to begin to thank him for so casually thrusting the world into my fingers . . . but I couldn't say anything . . . couldn't speak. I could feel my legs collapsing. Could do nothing any more to stop them. Found myself kneeling on the grass, keeping myself from falling entirely by hanging on to a door handle of the car. Didn't want to fall. Hurt too much.

'Matt!' Nancy said. She was down on her knees beside me. Midge too. And Colin.

'Don't bloody die,' Nancy said.

I grinned at her. Felt light-headed. Grinned at Colin. Grinned at Midge.

'Want a lodger?' I asked.

'Soon as you like,' Colin said.

'Nancy,' I said. 'Will you . . . will you . . .'

'You nit,' she said. 'You great nit.'

My hand slipped out of the door handle. Colin caught me as I fell. Everything drifted quietly away, and by the time I reached the ground I couldn't feel anything at all.

SMOKESCREEN

With thanks to Jane and Christopher Coldrey

INTRODUCTION

In 1971 I was asked to go to South Africa to take part in the Johannesburg International Horse Show, a two-week-long entertainment similar to the Olympia and Wembley indoor horse shows in London and Canada's Royal Winter Fair in Toronto. The invited party of about twenty international horse people included Olympic show-jumpers Piero d'Inzeo and Anneli Drummond Hay, who jumped local borrowed horses to dazzling effect. I went in the capacity of judge of varying classes of riding horses, a task which meant setting the horses in order according to their looks, and then riding them to see if they moved with presence, appointing winners overall.

My wife Mary and I stayed with the Show Director Christopher Coldrey on his farm out in the country, and in between performances he introduced us to South African private life. We spent a free weekend of three scorching days in the Kruger Park Game Reserve, eyeball to eyeball with lion, elephant, impala and giraffe, and were shown the back roads and hidden places by one of the senior game wardens. Naturally (for me) we went also to race meetings, and there met a man who invited us down his gold mine, offering a private conducted tour and invaluable knowledge.

Smokescreen, written after our return to England, unsurprisingly unfolds against a background of South African racing, a gold mine and blazing heat in the Kruger Park Game Reserve; and to this day, if I glance into the book, the beauty and the powerful sweet scent of the South African countryside fill my memory.

Edward Lincoln, the chief character, is an English film star, and for the authentic background of his job my wife and I went to the British film studios at Pinewood, where we were comprehensively shown how movies are made. We already counted many actors among our friends, as Mary had earlier worked behind the scenes in the theatre, so usefully I knew how good actors behave and think.

As a mix of all these experiences, together with humour and, of course, make believe, *Smokescreen* evolved.

This is not a political book, just a matter of fun and suspense.

CHAPTER ONE

Sweating, thirsty, hot, uncomfortable, and tired to the point of explosion.

Cynically, I counted my woes.

Considerable, they were. Considerable, one way and another.

I sat in the driving seat of a custom-built aerodynamic sports car, the cast-off toy of an oil sheik's son. I had been sitting there for the best part of three days. Ahead, the sun-dried plain spread gently away at some distant brown and purple hills, and hour by hour their hunched shapes remained exactly where they were on the horizon, because the 150 mph Special was not moving.

Nor was I. I looked morosely at the solid untarnishable handcuffs locked round my wrists. One of my arms led through the steering wheel, and the other was outside it, so that in total effect I was locked on to the wheel, and in consequence firmly attached to the car.

There was also the small matter of seat belts. The Special would not start until the safety harness was fastened. Despite the fact that the key was missing from the ignition, the harness was securely fastened: one strap over my stomach, one diagonally across my chest.

I could not bring my legs up from their stretched-forward sports car position in order to break the steering wheel with my feet. I had tried it. I was too tall, and couldn't bend my knees far enough. And apart from that, the steering wheel was not of possibly breakable plastic. People who built spectacularly expensive cars like the Special didn't mess around with plastic wheels. This was one of the small-diameter leather-covered metal type, as durable as the Mont Blanc.

I was thoroughly fed up with sitting in the car. Every muscle in my legs, up my spine and down my arms protested energetically against the constraint. A hard band of heaviness behind my eyes was tightening into a perceptible ache.

It was time to make another determined effort to get free, though I knew from countless similar attempts that it couldn't be done.

I tugged, strained, used all my strength against the straps and the handcuffs: struggled until fresh sweat rolled down my face; and couldn't, as before, progress even a millimetre towards freedom.

I put my head back against the padded headrest, and rolled my face around towards the open window beside me, on my right.

I shut my eyes. I could feel the slash of sunlight cut across my cheek and neck and shoulder with all the vigour of 15.00 hours in July at 37° North. I could feel the heat on my left eyelid. I let lines of frustration and pain develop across my forehead, put a certain grimness into my mouth, twitched a muscle along my jaw, and swallowed with an abandonment of hope.

After that I sat still, and waited.

The desert plain was very quiet.

I waited.

Then Evan Pentelow shouted 'Cut' with detectable reluctance, and the cameramen removed their eyes from the view-finders. No whisper of wind fluttered the large bright-coloured umbrellas which shielded them and their apparatus. Evan fanned himself vigorously with his shooting schedule, creating the breeze that nature had neglected, and others in the small group in the shade of portable green polystyrene sun-shelters came languidly to life, the relentless heat having hours ago drained their energy. The sound mixer took off his ear-phones, hung them over the back of his chair, and fiddled slowly with the knobs on his Nagra recorder, and the electricians kindly switched off the clutch of minibrute lamps which had been ruthlessly reinforcing the sun.

I looked into the lens of the Arriflex which had been recording every sweating pore at a distance of six feet from my right shoulder. Terry, behind his camera, mopped his neck with a dusty handkerchief, and Simon added to his Picture Negative Report for the processing laboratory.

Further back, from a different angle, the Mitchell, with its thousand-feet magazine, had shot the same scene. Lucky, who operated it, was busily not meeting my eye, as he had been since breakfast. He believed I was angry with him, because, although he swore it was not his fault, the last lot of film he had shot the day before had turned out to be fogged. I had asked him quite mildly in the circumstances just to be sure that today there should be no more mishaps, as I reckoned I couldn't stand many more retakes of Scene 623.

Since then, we had retaken it six times. With, I grant you, a short break for lunch.

Evan Pentelow had apologized to everyone, loudly and often, that we would just have to go on and on shooting the scene until I got it right. He changed his mind about how it should go after every second take, and although I followed a good many of his minutely detailed directions, he had not yet once pronounced himself satisfied.

Every single member of the team who had come to southern Spain to complete the location shots was aware of the animosity behind the tight-reined politeness with which he spoke to me, and behind that with which I answered him. The unit, I had heard, had opened a book on how long I would hang on to my temper.

The girl who carried the precious key to the handcuffs walked slowly over from the furthest green shelter, where the continuity, make-up, and wardrobe girls sat exhaustedly on spread-out towels. Tendrils of damp hair clung to the girl's neck as she opened the door of the car and fitted the key into the hole. They were regulation

British police handcuffs, fastening with a stiffish screw instead of a ratchet, and she always had some difficulty in pushing the key round its last few all-important turns.

She looked at me apprehensively, knowing that I couldn't be far from erupting. I achieved at least the muscle movements of a smile, and relief at not being bawled at gave her impetus to finish taking off the hand-cuffs smoothly and quickly.

I unfastened the seat harness and stood up stiffly outside in the sun. It was a good ten degrees cooler than inside the Special.

'Get back in,' Evan said. 'We'll have to take it again.'

I inhaled a lungful straight from the Sahara, and counted five in my mind. Then I said, 'I'm going over to the caravan for a beer and a pee, and we'll shoot it again when I come back.'

They wouldn't pay out the pool on that, I thought in amusement. That might be a crack in the volcano, but it wasn't Krakatoa. I wondered if they would let me take a bet on the flashpoint myself.

No one had bothered to put the canvas over the Mini-moke, to shield it from the sun. I climbed into the little buggy where it was parked behind the largest shelter, and swore as the seat leather scorched through my thin cotton trousers. The steering wheel was hot enough to fry eggs.

The legs of my trousers were rolled up to the knee, and on my feet were flip-flops. They contrasted oddly with the formal white shirt and dark tie which I wore above, but then the Arriflex angle cut me off at the knee, and the Mitchell higher still, above the waist.

I drove the Moke without haste to where the semi-circle of caravans was parked, two hundred yards away in a hollow. An apology for a tree cast a patch of thinnish shade that was better than nothing for the Moke, so I stopped it there and walked over to the caravan assigned to me as a dressing-room.

The air-conditioning inside hit like a cold shower, and felt marvellous. I loosened my tie, undid the top button of my shirt, fetched a can of beer from the refrigerator, and sat down wearily on the divan to drink it.

Evan Pentelow was busy paying off an old resentment, and unfortunately there was no way I could stop him. I had worked with him only once before, on his first major film and my seventh, and by the end of it we had detested each other. Nothing had improved by my subsequently refusing to sign for films if he were to direct, a circumstance which had cut him off from at least two smash hits he might otherwise have collared.

Evan was the darling of those critics who believed that actors couldn't act unless the director told them inch by inch what to do. Evan never gave directions by halves: he liked to see his films called 'Evan Pentelow's latest', and he achieved that by making the gullible believe that step by tiny step the whole thing stemmed from his talent, and his alone. Never mind how old a hand an actor was, Evan remorselessly taught him his business. Evan never *discussed* how a scene should be played, how a word should be inflected. He dictated.

He had cut some great names down to size, down to notices like 'Pentelow has drawn a sympatic performance from Miss Five-Star Blank . . .' He resented everyone, like me, who wouldn't give him the chance.

There was no doubt that he was an outstanding director in that he had a visual imagination of a very high quality. Most actors positively liked to work with him, as their salaries were generous and his films never went unsung. Only uncompromising bloody asses like myself believed that at least nine-tenths of a performance should be the actor's own work.

I sighed, finished the beer, visited the loo, and went out to the Moke. Apollo still raged away in the brazen sky, as one might say if one had a taste for that sort of thing.

The original director of the glossy action thriller on which we were engaged had been a quiet-spoken sophisticate who usually lifted the first elbow before breakfast and had died on his feet at 10 AM, from a surfeit of Scotch. It happened during a free weekend which I had spent alone in Yorkshire walking on the hills, and I had returned to the set on Tuesday to find Evan already ensconced and making his stranglehold felt.

There was about an eighth of the film still to do. The sly smile that he had put on when he saw me arrive had been pure clotted malice.

Protestations to the management had brought soothing noises but no joy.

'No one else of that calibre was free . . . can't take risks with the backers' money, can we, not as things are these days . . . got to look at it realistically . . . Sure, Link, I know you won't work with him ordinarily, but this is a *crisis*, dammit . . . it isn't actually in your contract in black and white this time, you know, because I checked . . . well, actually, we were relying on your good nature, I suppose . . .'

I interrupted dryly, 'And on the fact that I'll be collecting four per cent of the gross?'

The management cleared its throat. 'Er, we wouldn't ourselves have made the mistake of reminding you . . . but since you mention it . . . yes.'

Amused, I had finally given in, but with foreboding, as the location scenes of the car all lay ahead. I had known Evan would be difficult: hadn't reckoned, though, that he would be the next best thing to sadistic.

I stopped the Moke with a jerk behind the shelter and pulled the canvas cover over it to stop it sizzling. I had been away exactly twelve minutes, but when I walked round into the shelter Evan was apologizing to the camera crews for my keeping them hanging around in this heat. Terry made a disclaiming gesture, as I could see perfectly well that he had barely finished loading the Arriflex with a fresh magazine out of the ice box. No one bothered to argue. At a hundred degrees in the shade, no one but Evan had any energy.

'Right,' he said briskly. 'Get into the car, Link. Scene 623, Take 10. And let's for hell's sake get this one right.'

I said nothing. Of the nine previous takes, three had been fogged: that left today's six; and I knew, as everyone else knew, that Evan could have used any one of them.

I got into the car. We retook the scene twice more.

Evan managed to shake his head dubiously even after that, but the head cameraman told him the light was getting too yellow, and even if they took any more it would be no good, as they wouldn't be able to match it to the scene which went before. Evan gave in only because he could come up with no possible reason for going on, for which Apollo had my thanks.

The unit packed up. The girl came limply across and undid the handcuffs. Two general duty men began to wrap up the Special in dust-sheets and pegged-down tarpaulins, and Terry and Lucky began to dismantle their cameras and pack them in cases, to take them away for the night.

In twos and threes everyone straggled across to the caravans, with me driving Evan in the Moke and saying not a word to him on the way. The coach had arrived from the small nearby town of Madroledo, bringing the two night-watchmen. Coach was a flattering word for it: an old airport runabout bus with a lot of room for equipment and minimum comfort for passengers. The company said they had stipulated a luxury touring coach with air-conditioning, but the bone-shaker was what had actually turned up.

The hotel in Madroledo where the whole unit was staying was in much the same category. The small inland town, far from the tourist beat, offered amenities that package holiday operators would have blanched at; but the management had had to install us there, they said, because the best hotels on the coast at Almeria were booked solid by hundreds of Americans engaged on making an epic western in the next bit of desert to ours.

In fact I much preferred even the rough bits of this film to the last little caper I had been engaged on, a misty rock-climbing affair in which I had spent days and days clinging to the ledges while the effects men showered buckets of artificial rainstorm over my head. It was never much good my complaining about the occasional wringers I got put through: I'd started out as a sort of stunt man, they said, so what was a little cold, a little heat? Get out there on the ledges, they said. Get out there in the car. And just concentrate on how much lolly you're stacking away to comfort you later through arthritis. Never fear, they said, we won't let you come to any real harm, not so long as the insurance premiums are so high, and not so long as almost every film you make covers its production costs in the first month of showing. Such charming people, those managements, with dollar signs for eyes, cash registers for hearts.

Cooler and cleaner, the entire unit met for before-dinner drinks in Madroledo's idea of an American Bar.

Away out on the plain in the warm night the Special sat under its guarding floodlights, a shrouded hump, done with the day. By tomorrow night, I thought, or at least the day after, we would have completed all the scenes which needed me stuck in the driving seat. Provided Evan could think of no reason for reshooting Scene 623 yet again, we only had 624 and 625 to do, the cavalry-to-the-rescue bits. We had done Scenes 622 and 621, which showed the man waking from a drugged sleep and assessing his predicament, and the helicopter shots were also in the can; the wide-circling and then narrowing aerial views which established the Special in its bare lonely terrain, and gave glimpses of the man slumped inside. Those were to be the opening shots of the film and the background to the credits, the bulk to the story being told afterwards in one long flashback to explain why the car and the man were where they were.

In the bar Terry and the Director of Photography were holding a desultory discussion about focal lengths, punctuating every wise thought with draughts of sangria. The Director, otherwise known professionally as the lighting cameraman, and personally as Conrad, patted me gently on the shoulder and pressed an almost cold glass into my hand. We had all grown to like this indigenous thirst quencher, a rough red local wine diluted by ice and a touch of the fruit salads.

'There you are, dear boy, it does wonders for the dehydration,' he said, and then in the same breath finished his broken-off sentence to Terry. 'So he used an eighteen-millimetre wide-angle and of course every scrap of tension evaporated from the scene.'

Conrad spoke from the strength of an Oscar on the sideboard, and called everyone 'dear boy', from chairmen downwards. Aided by a naturally resonant bass voice and a droopy cultivated moustache, he had achieved the notable status of 'a character' in a business which specialized in them, but behind the flamboyance there was a sharp technician's mind which saw life analytically at twenty-four frames per second and thought in Eastman-colour.

Terry said, 'Beale Films won't use him now because of the time he shot two thousand feet one day at Ascot without an 85 filter, and there wasn't another race meeting due there until a month after they ran into compensation time . . .'

Terry was fat, bald, forty, and had given up earlier aspirations to climb to Director of Photography with his name writ large in credits. He had settled instead for being a steady, reliable, experienced, and continually in-work craftsman, and Conrad always liked to have him on his team.

Simon joined us and Conrad gave him, too, a glass of sangria. Simon, the clapper/loader of Terry's crew, had less assurance than he ought to have had at twenty-three, and was sometimes naïve to the point where one speculated about arrested development. His job entailed operating the clapper board before every shot, keeping careful records of the type and footage of film used, and loading the raw film into the magazines which were used in the cameras.

Terry himself had taught him how to load the magazines, a job which meant winding unexposed film on to reels, in total darkness and by feel only. Everyone, to begin with, learned how to do it with unwanted exposed film in a well-lit room, and practised it over and over until they could do it with their eyes shut. When Simon could do this faultlessly, Terry sent him to load some magazines in earnest, and it was not until after a long day's shooting that the laboratory discovered all the film to be completely black.

Simon, it appeared, had done exactly what he had been taught: gone into the loading room and threaded the film on to the magazine with his eyes shut. And left the electric light on while he did it.

He took a sip of his pink restorer, looked at the others in bewilderment, and said, 'Evan told me to write "print" against every one of those shots we took today.' He searched their faces for astonishment and found none. 'But, I say,' he protested, 'if all the first takes were good enough to print, why on earth did he go on doing so many?'

No one answered except Conrad, who looked at him with pity and said, 'Work it out, dear boy. Work it out.' But Simon hadn't the equipment.

The bar room was large and cool, with thick white-painted walls and a brown tiled floor: pleasant in the daytime, when we were seldom there, but too stark at night because of the glaring striplighting some insensitive soul had installed on the ceiling. The four girls, sitting languidly round a table with half-empty glasses of lime juice and Bacardi and soda, took on a greenish tinge as the sunlight faded outside, and aged ten years. The pouches beneath Conrad's eyes developed shadows, and Simon's chin receded too far for flattery.

Another long evening stretched ahead, exactly like the nine that had gone before: several hours of shop and gossip punctuated by occasional brandies, cigars and a Spanish-type dinner. I hadn't even any lines to learn for the next day, as my entire vocal contribution to Scenes 624 and 625 was to be a variety of grunts and mumbles. I would be glad, I thought, by God I would be glad, to get back home.

We went in to eat in a private dining-room as uninviting as the bar. I found myself between Simon and the handcuffs girl, two-thirds of the way along one side of the long table at which we all sat together haphazardly. About twenty-five of us, there were: all technicians of some sort except me and the actor due to amble to the rescue as a Mexican peasant. The group had been cut to a minimum, and our stay scheduled for as short a time as possible: the management had wanted even the desert scenes shot at Pinewood like the rest of the film, or at least on some dried-up bit of England, but the original director had stuck out for the authentic shimmer of real heat, damn and bless his departed spirit.

There was an empty space around the far side of the table.

No Evan.

'He's telephoning,' the handcuffs girl said. 'I think he's been telephoning ever since we came back.'

I nodded. Evan telephoned the management most evenings, though not normally at great length. He was probably having difficulty getting through.

'I'll be glad to go home,' the girl said, sighing. Her first location job, which she had looked forward to, was proving disappointing; boring, too hot and no fun. Jill – her real name was Jill, though Evan had started calling her Handcuffs, and most of the unit had copied him – slid a speculative look sideways at my face, and added, 'Won't you?'

'Yes,' I said neutrally.

Conrad, sitting opposite, snorted loudly. 'Handcuffs, dear girl, that's cheating. Anyone who prods him has her bet cancelled.'

'It wasn't a prod,' she said defensively.

'Next best thing.'

'Just how many of you are in this pool?' I asked sarcastically.

'Everyone except Evan,' Conrad admitted cheerfully. 'Quite a healthy little jackpot it is.'

'And has anyone lost their money yet?'

Conrad chuckled. 'Most of them, dear boy. This afternoon.'

'And you,' I said, 'have you?'

He narrowed his eyes at me and put his head on one side. 'You've a temper that blows the roof off, but usually on behalf of someone else.'

'He can't answer your question, you see,' Jill explained to me. 'That's against the rules too.'

But I had worked with Conrad on three previous films, and he had indeed told me where he had placed his bet.

Evan came back from telephoning, walked purposefully to his empty chair, and splashed busily into his turtle soup. Intent, concentrated, he stared at the table and either didn't hear, or didn't wish to hear, Terry's tentative generalities.

I looked at Evan thoughtfully. At forty he was wiry, of medium height and packed with aggressive energy. He had undisciplined black curling hair, a face in which even the bones looked determined, and fierce hot brown eyes. That evening the eyes were looking inwards, seeing visions in his head; and the tumultuous activity going on in there showed unmistakably in the tension in his muscles. His spoon was held in rigid fingers, and his neck and back were as stiff as stakes.

I didn't like his intensity, not at any time or in any circumstances. It always set up in me the unreasonable reaction of wanting to avoid doing what he was pressing for, even when his ideas made good sense. That evening he was building up a good head of steam, and my own antipathy rose to match.

He shovelled his way briskly through the anglicized

paella which followed, and pushed his empty plate away decisively.

'Now . . .' he said: and everybody listened. His voice sounded loud and high, strung up with his inner urgency. It would have been impossible to sit in that room and ignore him.

'As you know, this film we are making is called *Man in a Car.*'

We knew.

'And as you know, the car has figured in at least half the scenes that have been shot.'

We knew that too, better than he did, as we had been with it all through.

'Well . . .' he paused, looking round the table, collecting eyes. 'I have been talking to the producer, and he agrees . . . I want to change the emphasis . . . change the whole shape of the film. There are going to be a number of flashbacks now, and not just one. The story will jump back every time from the desert scene and each desert shot will give an impression of the days passing, and show the man growing weaker. There is to be no rescue, as such. This means, I'm afraid, Stephen . . .' He looked directly at the other actor, '. . . that your part is out entirely, but you will of course be paid what was agreed.' He turned back to the unit in general. 'We are going to scrap those cool witty scenes of reunion with the girl that you did at Pinewood. Instead, we will end the film with the reverse of the opening. That is to say, a helicopter shot that starts with the car in close-up and gradually recedes from it until it is merely a dot on the plain. The view will widen just at the end to indicate a peasant walking along a ridge of hill, leading a donkey, and everyone who sees the film can decide for himself whether the peasant rescues the man, or passes by without seeing him.'

He cleared his throat into a wholly attentive silence. 'This of course means that we shall have to do much more work here on location. I estimate that we will be here for at least another two weeks, as there will have to be many more scenes of Link in the car.'

Someone groaned. Evan looked fiercely in the direction of the protest, and silenced it effectively. Only Conrad made any actual comment.

'I'm glad I'm behind the camera, and not in front of it,' he said slowly. 'Link's showing wear and tear already.'

I pushed the last two bits of chicken around with my fork, not really seeing my plate. Conrad was staring across at me: I could feel his eyes. And all the others', too. It was the actor in me, I knew, which kept them waiting while I ate a mouthful, drank some wine, and finally looked up again at Evan.

'All right,' I said.

A sort of quiver ran through the unit, and I realized they had all been holding their breath for the explosion of the century. But setting my own feelings aside, I had to admit that what Evan had suggested made excellent film sense, and I trusted to that instinct, if not to his humanity. There was a lot I would do, to make a good film.

He was surprised at my unconditional agreement, but also excited by it. Visions poured out of him, faster than his tongue.

'There will be tears . . . and skin cracks, and sun blisters . . . and terrible thirst . . . and muscles and tendons quivering with strain like violin strings, and hands curled with cramp . . . and agony and frightful despair . . . and the scorching, inexorable, thunderous silence . . . and towards the end, the gradual disintegration of a human soul . . . so that even if he is rescued he will be different . . . and there won't be a single person who sees the film who doesn't leave exhausted and wrung out and filled with pictures he'll never forget.'

The camera crews listened with an air of we've-seen-all-this-before and the make-up girl began looking particularly thoughtful. It was only I who seemed to see it from the inside looking out, and I felt a shudder go through my gut as if it had been a real dying I was to do, and not pretence. It was foolish. I shook myself; shook off the illusion of personal involvement. To be any good, acting had to be deliberate, not emotional.

He paused in his harangue, waiting with fixed gaze for me to answer him, and I reckoned that if I were not to let him stampede all over me it was time to contribute something myself.

'Noise,' I said calmly.

'What . . .?'

'Noise,' I repeated. 'He would make a noise, too, at first. Shouting for help. Shouting from fury, and hunger, and terror. Shouting his bloody head off.'

Evan's eyes widened and embraced the truth of it.

'Yes,' he said. He took a deep ecstatic breath at the thought of his idea taking actual shape. '. . . Yes.'

Some of the inner furnace died down to a saner, more calculating heat.

'Will you do it?' he said.

I knew he meant not Would I just get through the scenes somehow, but Would I put into them the best I could. And he might well ask, after his behaviour to me that day. I would, I thought; I would make it bloody marvellous; but I answered him flippantly.

'There won't be a dry eye in the house.'

He looked irritated and disappointed, which would do no harm. The others relaxed and began talking, but some undercurrent of excitement had awoken, and it was the best evening we had had since we arrived.

So we went back to the desert plain for another two weeks, and it was lousy, but the glossy little adventure turned into an eventual box-office blockbuster which even the critics seemed to like.

I got through the whole fortnight with my temper intact; and in consequence Conrad, who had guessed right, won his bet and scooped the pool.

CHAPTER TWO

England in August seemed green and cool in comparison when I got back. At Heathrow I collected my car, a production line BMW, darkish blue, ordinarily jumbled registration number, nothing Special about it, and drove westwards into Berkshire with a feeling of ease.

Four o'clock in the afternoon.

Going home.

I found myself grinning at nothing in particular. Like a kid out of school, I thought. Going home to a summer evening.

The house was middle-sized, part old, part new, built on a gentle slope outside a village far up the Thames. There was a view down over the river, and lots of evening sun, and an unsignposted lane to approach by, that most people missed.

There was a boy's bicycle lying half on the grass, half on the drive, and some gardening tools near a half-weeded flowerbed. I stopped the car outside the garage, looked at the shut front door, and walked round the house to the back.

I saw all four of them before they saw me; like looking in through a window. Two small boys splashing in the pool with a black and white beach ball. A slightly faded sun umbrella nearby, with a little girl lying on an air bed in its shade. A young woman with short chestnut hair, sitting on a rug in the sun, hugging her knees.

One of the boys looked up and saw me standing watching them from across the lawn.

'Hey,' he shouted. 'Dad's home,' and ducked his brother.

I walked towards them, smiling. Charlie unstuck herself from the rug and came unhurriedly to meet me.

'Hi,' she said. 'I'm covered in oil.' She put her mouth forward for a kiss and held my face between the insides of her wrists.

'What on earth have you been doing with yourself?' she asked. 'You look terribly thin.'

'It was hot in Spain,' I said. I walked back to the pool beside her, stripping off my loosened tie, and then my shirt.

'You didn't get very sunburned.'

'No . . . Sat in the car most of the time . . .'

'Did it go all right?'

I made a face. 'Time will tell . . . How are the kids?'

'Fine.'

I had been away a month. It might have been a day. Any father coming home to his family after a day's work.

Peter levered himself out of the pool via his stomach and splashed across the grass.

'What did you bring us?' he demanded.

'Pete, I've *told* you . . .' Charlie said, exasperated. 'If you ask, you won't *get*.'

'You won't get much this time anyway,' I told him. 'We were miles from any decent shops. And go and pick your bike up off the drive.'

'Oh, honestly,' he said. 'The minute you're home, we've done something wrong.' He retreated round the house, his backview stiff with protest.

Charlie laughed. 'I'm glad you're back . . .'

'Me too.'

'Dad, look at me. Look at me do this, Dad.'

I obediently watched while Chris turned some complicated sort of somersault over the beach ball and came up with a triumphant smile, shaking water out of his eyes and waiting for praise.

'Jolly good,' I said.

'Watch me again, Dad . . .'

'In a minute.'

Charlie and I walked over to the umbrella, and looked down at our daughter. She was five years old, brown-haired, and pretty. I sat down beside the air bed and tickled her tummy. She chuckled, and smiled at me deliciously.

'How's she been?'

'Same as usual.'

'Shall I take her in the pool?'

'She came in with me this morning . . . but she loves it. It wouldn't do her any harm to go again.'

Charlie squatted down beside her. 'Daddy's home, little one,' she said. But to Libby, our little one, the words themselves meant almost nothing. Her mental development had slowed to a snail's pace after the age of ten months, when her skull had been fractured. Peter, who had been five then, had lifted her out of her pram, wanting to be helpful and bring her indoors for lunch. But Charlie, going out to fetch her, had seen him trip and fall and it had been Libby's head which struck the stone step on the terrace of the flat we then occupied in London. The baby had been stunned, but after an hour or two the doctors could find nothing wrong with her.

It was only two or three weeks later that she felt sick, and later still, when she was surviving a desperate illness, that the hospital doctors told us she had had a hair-line fracture at the base of the brain, which had become infected and given her meningitis. We were so relieved that she was alive that we scarcely took notice of the cautiously phrased warnings . . . 'We must not be surprised if she were a little late in developing . . .' Of course she would be a little late after being so ill. But she would soon catch up, wouldn't she? And we dismissed the dubious expression, and that unfamiliar word 'retarded'.

During the next year we learned what it meant, and in facing such a mammoth disaster had also discovered much about ourselves. Before the accident, our marriage had been shaking towards disintegration under the onslaughts of prosperity and success: after it, we had gradually cemented ourselves together again, with a much clearer view of what was really important, and what was not.

We had left the bright lights, the adulation, and the whoopee, and gone to live in the country, where anyway both of us had our original roots. Better for the kids, we said; and knew it was better for us, too.

Libby's state no longer caused us any acute grief. It was just part of life, accepted and accustomed. She was treated with good humour by the boys, with love by Charlie, and with gentleness by me; and as she was seldom ill and seemed to be happy enough, it could have been a lot worse.

It had proved harder in the end to grow skins against the reactions of strangers, but after all these years neither Charlie nor I gave a damn what anyone said. So maybe Libby couldn't talk yet, couldn't walk steadily, fed herself messily, and was not reliably continent: but she was our daughter, and that was that.

I went into the house, changed into swimming trunks, and took her with me into the pool. She was slowly learning to swim, and had no fear of the water. She splashed around happily in my grasp, patted my face with wet palms and called me 'Dada', and wound her arms around my neck and clung to me like a little limpet.

After a bit I handed her over to Charlie to dry, and played water polo (of sorts) with Peter and Chris, and after twenty minutes of that decided that even Evan Pentelow was a lesser task master.

'More, Dad,' they said, and 'I *say*, Dad, you aren't getting out already, are you?'

'Yes,' I said firmly, and dried myself sitting beside Charlie on the rug.

She put the kids to bed while I unpacked, and I read them stories while she cooked, and we spent the evening by ourselves, eating chicken and watching an old movie (from before my days) on television. After that we stacked the dishes in the washer and went to bed.

We had no one else living in the house with us. On four mornings a week a woman walked up from the village to help with the chores, and there was also a retired nurse there who would always come to look after Libby and the boys if we wanted to go out. These arrangements were Charlie's own choice: I had married a quiet, intelligent girl who had grown into a practical, down-to-earth, and, to her own surprise, domesticated woman. Since we had left London she had developed an added strength which one could only call serenity, and although she could on occasion lose her temper as furiously as I could, her foundations were now built on rock.

A lot of people in the film world, I knew, thought my wife unexciting and my home life a drag, and expected me to break out in blondes and red-heads, like a rash. But I had very little in common with the sort of larger-than-life action man I played in film after film. They were my work, and I worked hard at them, but I didn't take them home.

Charlie snuggled beside me under the duvet and put

her head on my chest. I smoothed my hands over her bare skin, feeling the ripple deep in her abdomen and the faint tremble in her legs.

'OK?' I asked, kissing her hair.

'Very . . .'

We made love in the simple, ordinary way, as we always did; but because I had been away a month it was one of the best times, one of the breathtaking, fundamental, indescribable times which became a base to live from. Certainty begins here, I thought. With this, what else did one need?

'Fantastic,' Charlie sighed. 'That was *fantastic.*'

'Remind us to do it less often.'

She laughed. 'It does improve with keeping . . .'

'Mm.' I yawned.

'I say,' she said, 'I was reading a magazine in the dentist's waiting-room this morning while Chris was having his teeth done, and there was a letter in it on the sob-stuff page, from a woman who had a bald fat middle-aged husband she didn't fancy, and she was asking for advice on her sex life. And do you know what advice they gave her?' There was a smile in her voice. 'It was, "Imagine you are sleeping with Edward Lincoln".'

'That's silly.' I yawned again.

'Yeah . . . Actually, I thought of writing in and asking what advice they would give *me.*'

'Probably tell you to imagine you're sleeping with some fat bald middle-aged man you don't fancy.'

She chuckled. 'Maybe I will be, in twenty years' time.'

631

'You are so kind.'

'Think nothing of it.'

We drifted contentedly to sleep.

I had a racehorse, a steeplechaser, in training with a thriving stable about five miles away, and I used to go over when I was not working and ride out with the string at morning exercise. Bill Tracker, the energetic trainer, did not in general like to have owners who wanted to ride their horses, but he put up with my intermittent presence on the same two counts as his stable lads did, namely that my father had once been a head lad along in Lambourn, and that I had also at one time earned my living by riding, even if not in races.

There wasn't much doing in August, but I went over, a couple of days after my return, and rode out on the Downs. The new jumping season had barely begun, and most of the horses, including my own, were still plodding round the roads to strengthen their legs. Bill generously let me take out one of the more forward hurdlers which was due to have its first run in two weeks or so, and as usual I much appreciated the chance he gave me to ride to some useful purpose, and to shake the dust off the one skill I had been born with.

I had learned to ride before I could walk, and had grown up intending to be a jockey. But the fates weren't kind: I was six feet tall when I was seventeen, and whatever special something it took to be a racer, I hadn't got.

The realization had been painful. The switch to jigging along in films, a wretched second best.

Ironic, to remember that.

The Downs were wide and windy and covered in breathable air: nice and primaeval still, except for the power station on the horizon and the distant slash of the motorway. We walked and trotted up to the gallops, cantered, galloped where and when bidden, and walked down again, cooling the horses off; and it was absolutely great.

I stayed to breakfast with the Trackers and rode my own horse afterwards with the second lot round the roads, cursing like the rest of the lads at the cars which didn't slow down to pass. I relaxed easily in the saddle and smiled as I remembered how my father had yelled himself hoarse at me – 'Sit *up*, you bloody boy. And keep your elbows *in*.'

Evan Pentelow and Madroledo were in another world.

When I got back the boys were squabbling noisily over whose turn it was with the unbroken roller skates, and Charlie was making a cake.

'Hi,' she said. 'Did you have a good ride?'

'Great.'

'Fine . . . Well there weren't any calls, except Nerissa rang . . . Will you two be *quiet*, we can't hear ourselves think . . .'

'It's *my* turn,' Peter yelled.

'If you two don't both shut up I'll twist your ears,' I said.

They shut up. I'd never carried out the often repeated threat, but they didn't like the idea of it. Chris immediately pinched the disputed skates and disappeared out of the kitchen, and Peter gave chase with muted yells.

'Kids!' Charlie said disgustedly.

I scooped out a fingerful of raw cake mixture and got my wrist slapped.

'What did Nerissa want?'

'She wants us to go to lunch.' Charlie paused, with the wooden spoon dropping gouts of chocolate goo into the bowl. 'She was a bit . . . well . . . odd, in a way. Not her usual brisk self. Anyway, she wanted us to go today . . .'

'Today!' I said, looking at the clock.

'Oh, I told her we couldn't, that you wouldn't be back until twelve. So she asked if we could make it tomorrow.'

'Why the rush?'

'Well, I don't know, darling. She just said, could we come as soon as poss. Before you got tied up in another film, she said.'

'I don't start the next one until November.'

'Yes, I told her that. Still, she was pretty insistent. So I said we'd love to go tomorrow unless you couldn't, in which case I'd ring back this lunch time.'

'I wonder what she wants,' I said. 'We haven't seen her for ages. We'd better go, don't you think?'

'Oh yes, of course.'

So we went.

It is just as well one can never foresee the future.

Nerissa was a sort of cross between an aunt, a god-mother, and a guardian, none of which I had ever actually had. I had had a stepmother who loved her two precious children exclusively, and a busy father nagged by her to distraction. Nerissa, who had owned three horses in the yard where my father reigned, had given me first sweets, then pound notes, then encouragement, and then, as the years passed, friendship. It had never been a close relationship, but always a warmth in the background.

She was waiting for us, primed with crystal glasses and a decanter of dry sherry on a silver tray, in the summer sitting-room of her Cotswold house, and she rose to meet us when she heard her manservant bringing us through the hall.

'Come on, my dears, come in,' she said. 'How lovely to see you. Charlotte, I love you in yellow . . . and Edward, how very thin you are . . .'

She had her back to the sunlight which poured in through the window framing the best view in Gloucestershire, and it was only when we each in turn kissed her offered cheek that we could see the pitiful change in her.

The last time I had seen her she had been an attract-ive woman of fifty plus, with young blue eyes and an apparently indestructible vitality. Her walk seemed to be on the edge of dancing, and her voice held a wise sense of humour. She came from the blue-blooded end of the Stud Book and had what my father had succinctly described as 'class'.

But now, within three months, her strength had vanished and her eyes were dull. The gloss on her hair, the spring in her step, the laugh in her voice: all were gone. She looked nearer seventy than fifty, and her hands trembled.

'Nerissa,' Charlie exclaimed in a sort of anguish, for she, like me, held her in much more than affection.

'Yes, dear. Yes,' Nerissa said comfortingly. 'Now sit down, dear, and Edward shall pour you some sherry.'

I poured all three of us some of the fine pale liquid, but Nerissa hardly sipped hers at all. She sat in a gold brocade chair in a long-sleeved blue linen dress, with her back to the sun and her face in shadow.

'How are those two little monkeys?' she asked. 'And how is dear little Libby? And Edward, my dear, being so thin doesn't suit you . . .' She talked on, making practised conversation and looking interested in our answers, and gave us no opening to ask what was the matter with her.

When she went into the dining-room it was with the help of a walking stick and my arm, and the feather-light lunch which had been geared to her needs did nothing to restore my lost pounds. Afterwards, we went slowly back to the summer-room for coffee.

'Do smoke, Edward dear . . . There are some cigars in

the cupboard. You know how I love the smell . . . and so few people smoke here, nowadays.'

I imagined they didn't because of her condition, but if she wanted it, I would, even though I rarely did, and only in the evening. They were Coronas, but a little dry from old age. I lit one, and she inhaled the smoke deeply, and smiled with real pleasure.

'That's so good,' she said.

Charlie poured the coffee but again Nerissa hardly drank. She settled back gently into the same chair as before, and crossed her elegant ankles.

'Now, my dears,' she said calmly, 'I shall be dead by Christmas.'

We didn't even make any contradictory noises. It was all too easy to believe.

She smiled at us. 'So sensible, you two are. No silly swooning, or making a fuss.' She paused. 'It appears I have some stupid ailment, and they tell me there isn't much to be done. As a matter of fact, it's what they *do* do which is making me feel so ill. Before, it wasn't so bad . . . but I have had to have X-rays so often . . . and now all these horrid cytotoxic drugs, and really, they make me most unwell.' She managed another smile. 'I've asked them to stop, but you know what it's like . . . if they can, they say they must. Quite an unreasonable view to take, don't you think? Anyway, my dears, that need not trouble you . . .'

'But you would like us to do something for you?' Charlie suggested.

Nerissa looked surprised. 'How did you know I had anything like that in mind?'

'Oh . . . Because you wanted us in a hurry . . . and you must have known for weeks how ill you were.'

'Edward, how clever your Charlotte is,' she said. 'Yes, I do want something . . . want Edward to do something for me, if he will.'

'Of course,' I said.

A dry amusement crept back into her voice. 'Wait until you hear what it is, before you promise so glibly.'

'OK.'

'It is to do with my horses.' She paused to consider, her head inclined to one side. 'They are running so badly.'

'But,' I said, in bewilderment, 'they haven't been out yet, this season.'

She still had two steeplechasers trained in the yard where I had grown up, and although since my father's death I had no direct contact with them, I knew they had won a couple of races each the season before.

She shook her head. 'Not the jumpers, Edward. My other horses. Five colts and six fillies, running on the flat.'

'On the flat? I'm sorry . . . I didn't realize you had any.'

'In South Africa.'

'Oh.' I looked at her a bit blankly. 'I don't know anything about South African racing. I'm awfully sorry. I'd love to be of use to you . . . but I don't know enough to begin to suggest why your horses there are running badly.'

'It's nice of you, Edward dear, to look disappointed. But you really can help me, you know. If you will.'

'Just tell him how,' Charlie said, 'and he'll do it. He'll do anything for you, Nerissa.'

At that time, and in those circumstances, she was right. The finality of Nerissa's condition made me sharply aware of how much I had always owed her: not in concrete terms as much as in the feeling that she was *there*, interested and caring about what I did. In my motherless teens, that had meant a lot.

She sighed. 'I've been writing to my trainer out there about it, and he seems very puzzled. He doesn't know why my horses are running badly, because all the others he trains are doing all right. But it takes so long for letters to pass . . . the postal services at both ends seem to be so erratic these days. And I wondered, Edward, my dear, if you could possibly . . . I mean, I know it's a good deal to ask . . . but could you possibly give me a week of your time, and go out there and find out what's happening?'

There was a small silence. Even Charlie did not rush to say that of course I would go, although it was clear already that it would have to be a matter of how, not of whether.

Nerissa went on persuasively, 'You see, Edward, you do know about racing. You know what goes on in a stable, and things like that. You could see, couldn't you, if there is something wrong with their training? And then of course you are so good at investigating things . . .'

'I'm what?' I asked. 'I've never investigated anything in my life.'

She fluttered a hand. 'You know how to find things out, and nothing ever deflects you.'

'Nerissa,' I said suspiciously, 'you've been seeing my films.'

'Well, of course. I've seen nearly all of them.'

'Yes, but that's not me. Those investigating supermen, they're just acting.'

'Don't be silly, Edward dear. You couldn't do all the things you do in films without being brave and determined and very clever at finding things out.'

I looked at her in a mixture of affection and exasperation. So many people mistook the image for the man, but that she should . . .

'You've known me since I was eight,' I protested. 'You know I'm not brave or particularly determined. I'm ordinary. I'm me. I'm the boy you gave sweets to, when I was crying because I'd fallen off a pony, and said "never mind" to, when I didn't have the nerve to be a jockey.'

She smiled indulgently. 'But since then you've learned to fight. And look at that last picture, when you were clinging to a ledge by one hand with a thousand foot drop just below you . . .'

'Nerissa, dear Nerissa,' I interrupted her. 'I'll go to South Africa for you. I really will. But those fights in films . . . most of the time that isn't me, it's someone my

size and shape who really does know judo. I don't. I can't
fight at all. It's just my face in close-ups. And those
ledges I was clinging to . . . certainly they were on a real
rock face, but I was in no danger. I wouldn't have fallen
a thousand feet, but only about ten, into one of those
nets they use under trapeze acts in circuses. I did fall,
two or three times. And there wasn't really a thousand
feet below me; not sheer anyway. We filmed it in the
Valley of Rocks in North Devon, where there are a lot
of little plateaux among the rock faces, to stand the
cameras on.'

She listened with an air of being completely unconvinced. I reckoned it was useless to go on: to tell her that
I was not a crack shot, couldn't fly an aeroplane or
beat Olympic skiers downhill, couldn't speak Russian or
build a radio transmitter or dismantle bombs, and would
tell all at the first threat of torture. She knew different,
she'd seen it with her own eyes. Her expression told
me so.

'Well, all right,' I said, capitulating. 'I do know what
should and should not go on in a racing stable. In
England, anyway.'

'And,' she said complacently, 'you can't say it wasn't
you who did all that trick riding when you first went into
films.'

I couldn't. It was. But it had been nothing unique.

'I'll go and look at your horses, and see what your
trainer says,' I said; and thought that if had no reasons to
offer, I would be most unlikely to find any.

'Dear Edward, so kind . . .' She seemed suddenly weaker, as if the effort of persuading me had been too much. But when she saw the alarm on Charlie's face, and on mine, she raised a reassuring smile.

'Not yet, my dears. Another two months, perhaps . . . Two months at least, I think.'

Charlie shook her head in protest, but Nerissa patted her hand. 'It's all right, my dear. I've come to terms with it. But I want to arrange things . . . which is why I want Edward to see about the horses, and I really ought to explain . . .'

'Don't tire yourself,' I said.

'I'm not . . . tired,' she said, obviously untruthfully. 'And I want to tell you. The horses used to belong to my sister, Portia, who married and went to live in South Africa thirty years ago. After she was widowed she stayed there because all her friends were there, and I've been out to visit her several times over the years. I know I've told you about her.'

We nodded.

'She died last winter,' I said.

'Yes . . . a great sorrow.' Nerissa looked a good deal more upset about her sister's death than about her own. 'She had no close relatives except me, and she left me nearly everything she had inherited from her husband. And all her horses, too.' She paused, as much to gather her forces as her thoughts. 'They were yearlings. Expensive ones. And her trainer wrote to me to ask if I wanted to sell them, as of course owing to the African horsesickness quarantine laws we cannot bring South African horses to England. But I thought it might be fun . . . interesting . . . to run them in South Africa, and then sell them for stud. But now . . . well, now I won't be here when they are old enough for stud, and meanwhile their value has dropped disastrously.'

'Dearest Nerissa,' Charlie said. 'Does it matter?'

'Oh yes. Yes, my dear, it does,' she said positively. 'Because I'm leaving them to my nephew, Danilo, and I don't like the idea of leaving him something worthless.'

She looked from one of us to the other. 'I can't remember – have you ever met Danilo?'

Charlie said, 'No,' and I said, 'Once or twice, when he was a small boy. You used to bring him to the stables.'

'That's right, so I did. And then of course my brother-in-law divorced that frightful woman, Danilo's mother, and took him to live in California with him. Well . . . Danilo has been back in England recently, and he has grown into such a nice young man. And isn't that lucky, my dears? Because, you see, I have so few relatives. In fact, really, Danilo is the only one, and even he is not a blood relative, his father being dear John's youngest brother, do you see?'

We saw. John Cavesey, dead sixteen years or more, had been a country gent with four hunters and a sense of humour. He had also had Nerissa, no children, one brother, one nephew, and five square miles of Merrie England.

After a pause Nerissa said, 'I'll cable to Mr Arknold

... that's my trainer ... to tell him you're coming to look into things, and to book some rooms for you.'

'No, don't do that. He might resent your sending anyone, and I'd get no cooperation from him at all. I'll fix the rooms, and so on. And if you cable him, just say I might be calling in, out of interest, while I'm in South Africa on a short visit.'

She smiled slowly and sweetly, and said, 'You see, my dear, you do know how to investigate, after all.'

CHAPTER THREE

I flew to Johannesburg five days later, equipped with a lot of facts and no faith in my ability to disentangle them.

Charlie and I had driven home from Nerissa's in a double state of depression. Poor Nerissa, we said. And poor us, losing her.

'And you've only just come home,' Charlie added.

'Yes,' I sighed. 'Still . . . I couldn't have said no.'

'No.'

'Not that it'll do much good.'

'You never know, you might spot something.'

'Very doubtful.'

'But,' she said with a touch of anxiety, 'you will do your best?'

'Of course, love.'

She shook her head. 'You're cleverer than you think.'

'Yeah,' I said. 'Sure.'

She made a face, and we went some way in silence. Then she said, 'When you went out to look at those two young chasers in her paddock, Nerissa told me what is the matter with her.'

'Did she?'

Charlie nodded. 'Some ghastly thing called Hodgkin's disease, which makes her glands swell, or something, and turn cellular, whatever that really means. She didn't know very clearly herself, I don't think. Except that it is absolutely fatal.'

Poor Nerissa.

'She also told me,' Charlie went on, 'that she has left us a keepsake each in her will.'

'Has she really?' I turned my head to look at Charlie. 'How kind of her. Did she say what?'

'Keep your eyes on the road, for heaven's sake. No, she didn't say what. Just something to remember her by. She said she had quite enjoyed herself, drawing up her new will and giving people presents in it. Isn't she amazing?'

'She is.'

'She really meant it. And she is so pleased that her nephew has turned out well. I've never seen anyone like that before . . . dying, and quite calm about it . . . and even enjoying things, like making a will . . . and knowing . . . knowing . . .'

I glanced at her sideways. Tears on Charlie's cheeks. She seldom cried, and didn't like to be watched.

I kept my eyes on the road.

I telephoned my agent and stunned him.

'But,' he stuttered, 'you never go anywhere, you

always refuse . . . you thumped my table and shouted about it . . .'

'Quite,' I agreed. 'But now I want a good reason for going to South Africa, so are any of my films due to open there soon, or are they not?'

'Well . . .' he sounded thoroughly disorganized. 'Well, I'll have to look it up. And are you sure,' he added in disbelief, 'that if one of them is due to open, you really and truly want me to tell them you'll turn up in person?'

'That's what I said.'

'Yes. I just don't believe it.'

He rang back an hour later.

'There are two coming up. They are showing *One Way to Moscow* in Cape Town, starting Monday week. That's the first in a series of six revivals, so although *Moscow* itself is pretty old, you could turn up to give the whole lot a boost. Or there's the opening of *Rocks* in Johannesburg. But that's not until September 14th. Three weeks off. Is that soon enough?'

'Not really.' I pondered. 'It will have to be the Johannesburg one, though.'

'All right. I'll fix it. And . . . er . . . does the sudden change of heart extend to chat shows and newspaper interviews?'

'No, it does not.'

'I was afraid of that.'

*

I had taken home from Nerissa's house all her trainer's letters, all the South African Racing Calendars, news-paper cuttings and magazines she had been sent, and all the details of breeding and racing form of her eleven non-winning youngsters. A formidable bulk of paper, it had proved; and not miraculously easy to understand.

The picture which emerged, though, was enough to make anyone think, let alone the owner of the horses in question. Nine of the eleven had run nicely when they began their racing careers, and between December and May had clocked up a joint total of fourteen wins. Since the middle of May, none of them had finished nearer than fourth.

As far as I could judge from a limited squint at the leading-sires tables and the breeding notes section of the South African *Horse and Hound*, all of them were of impeccable pedigree, and certainly, from the amounts she had laid out, Nerissa's sister Portia had bought no bargains. None of them had so far won enough prize money to cover their purchase price, and with every resounding defeat their future stud value, too, slid a notch towards zero.

As a bequest, the South African horses were a lump of lead.

Charlie came with me to Heathrow to see me off, as I had been home only nine days, which hadn't been long enough for either of us. While we were waiting at the check-in counter half a dozen ladies asked for my auto-graph for their daughters – nephews – grandchildren –

and a few eyes swivelled our way; and presently a dark-uniformed airline official appeared at our side and offered a small private room for waiting in. They were pretty good about that sort of thing, as I came through the airport fairly often, and we accepted gratefully.

'It's like being married to two people,' Charlie sighed, sitting down. 'The public you, and the private you. Quite separate. Do you know, if I see one of the films, or even a clip of one on the box, I look at the pictures of you, and I think, I slept with that man last night. And it seems extraordinary, because that public you doesn't really belong to me at all, but to all the people who pay to see you. And then you come home again, and you're just you, my familiar husband, and the public you is some other fellow . . .'

I looked at her affectionately. 'The private me has forgotten to pay the telephone bill.'

'Well, damn it, I reminded you sixteen times . . .'

'Will you pay it, then?'

'Well, I suppose so. But the telephone bill is one of your jobs. Checking all those cables, and those phone calls to America – I don't know what they should be. We're probably being overcharged, if you don't check it.'

'Have to risk it.'

'Honestly!'

'It will be set off against tax, anyway.'

'I suppose so.'

I sat down beside her. The unpaid telephone bill was as good as anything else to talk about: we no longer needed to say aloud what we were saying to each other underneath. In all our life together we had taken good-byes casually, and hellos, too. A lot of people mistook it for not caring. It was perhaps too much the opposite. We needed each other like bees and honey.

When I landed at Jan Smuts International Airport six-teen hours later, I was met by a nervous man with damp palms who introduced himself as the South African Dis-tribution Manager for Worldic Cinemas.

'Wenkins,' he said. 'Clifford Wenkins. So nice to see you.'

He had restless eyes and a clipped South African accent. About forty. Never going to be successful. Talk-ing a little too loudly, a little too familiarly, with the sort of uneasy bonhomie I found hardest to take.

As politely as possible I removed my sleeve from his grasp.

'Nice of you to come,' I said; and wished he hadn't.

'Couldn't let Edward Lincoln arrive without a recep-tion, you know.' He laughed loudly, out of nerves. I wondered idly why he should be so painfully self-conscious: as Distribution Manager he surely met film actors before breakfast every month of the year.

'Car over here.' He walked crabwise in front of me with his arms extended fore and aft, as if to push a path for me with the one and usher me along it with the other. There were not enough people around for it to be remotely necessary.

I followed him, carrying my suitcase and making an effort to suffer his attentions gladly.

'Not far,' he said anxiously, looking up placatingly at my face.

'Fine,' I said.

There was a group of about ten people just inside the main doors. I looked at them in disillusion: their clothes and the way they stood had 'media' stamped all over them, and it was without surprise that I saw the tape-recorders and cameras sprout all over as soon as we drew near.

'Mr Lincoln, what do you think of South Africa?'

'Hey, Link, how about a big smile . . .?'

'Is there any truth in the rumour . . .?'

'Our readers would like your views on . . .'

'Give us a smile . . .'

I tried not to stop walking, but they slowed us down to a crawl. I smiled at them collectively and said soothing things like 'I'm glad to be here. This is my first visit. I am looking forward to it very much,' and eventually we persevered into the open air.

Clifford Wenkins's dampness extended to his brow, though the sunshine at 6,000 feet above sea level was decidedly chilly.

'Sorry,' he said, 'but they would come.'

'Marvellous how they knew the right day and the

right time, when my flight was only booked yesterday morning.'

'Er . . . yes,' he agreed weakly.

'I expect they are often willing to arrange publicity for people, when you want them to.'

'Oh yes, indeed,' he agreed warmly.

I smiled at him. One could hardly blame him for using me as payment for past and future services, and I knew it was widely considered irrational that I preferred to avoid interviews. In many countries the media gave you a rough passage if you wouldn't let them milk you for copy, and the South Africans had been more civil than most.

Wenkins rubbed his beaded forehead with one of the damp palms, and said, 'Let me take your suitcase.'

I shook my head. 'It isn't heavy,' I said, and besides, I was a good deal bigger than he was.

We walked across the car park to his car, and I experienced for the first time the extraordinary smell of Africa. A blend of hot sweet odours with a kink of mustiness; a strong disturbing smell which stayed in my nostrils for three or four days, until my scenting nerves got used to it and disregarded it. But my first overriding impression of South Africa was the way it smelt.

Smiling too much, sweating too much, talking too much, Clifford Wenkins drove me down the road to Johannesburg. The airport lay east of the city, out on the bare expanses of the Transvaal, and we were a good half-hour reaching our destination.

'I hope everything will be all right for you,' Wenkins said. 'We don't often get . . . I mean, well . . .' He laughed jerkily. 'Your agent was telling me on the telephone not to arrange any receptions or parties or radio shows or anything . . . I mean, we usually put on that sort of show for visiting stars . . . that is, er, of course, if Worldic are handling their films . . . but, er, we haven't done anything like that for you, and it seems all wrong to me . . . but then, your agent insisted . . . and then, your room . . . not in the city, he said. Not in the city itself, and not in a private house, he said, so I hope you will like . . . I mean, we were shattered . . . er, that is, honoured . . . to hear you were coming . . .'

Mr Wenkins, I thought, you would get a lot further on in life if you didn't chatter so much. And aloud I said, 'I'm sure everything will be fine.'

'Yes, well . . . Er, if you don't want the usual round of things, though, what am I to arrange for you? I mean, there is a fortnight before the premiere of *Rocks*, don't you see? So what . . .?'

I didn't answer that one straight away. Instead I said, 'This premiere . . . How much of a thing are you making of it?'

'Oh.' He laughed again at nothing funny. 'Er, well, big, of course. Invitations. Tickets in aid of charity. All the glitter, old boy . . . er, I mean . . . sorry . . . er, well. Worldic said to push the boat right out, you see, once they'd got over the shock, that is.'

'I do see.' I sighed slightly. I had chosen to do the

damn thing, I thought. So I ought, in all fairness, to give them value for their trouble.

'Look,' I said, 'if you want to, and if you think anyone would want to come, go ahead and arrange some sort of drinks and canapés affair either before or after the showing of the film, and I'll go to that. And one morning soon, if you'd like to, you could ask all those good friends of yours at the airport, and any others in their trade that you want to include, to meet us somewhere for coffee or a drink or something. How would that do?'

For once he was dumb. I looked across at him. His mouth was opening and shutting like a fish.

I laughed in my throat. Nerissa had a lot to answer for.

'The rest of the time, don't worry about me. I'll amuse myself all right. For one thing, I'll go to the races.'

'Oh,' He finally overcame the jaw problem and got the two halves into proper working order. 'Er . . . I could get someone to take you there, if you like.'

'We'll see,' I said noncommittally.

The journey ended at the Iguana Rock, a very pleasant country hotel on the northern edge of the city. The management gave me a civil greeting and a luxurious room and indicated that a clap of the hands would bring anything from iced water to dancing girls, as required.

'I would like to hire a car,' I said, and Wenkins gushed forth to say it was all arranged, he had arranged it, a chauffeur-driven pumpkin would be constantly on call, courtesy of Worldic.

I shook my head. 'Courtesy of me,' I said. 'Didn't my agent tell you that I intended to pay all the expenses of my trip myself?'

'Well, he did, yes, but . . . Worldic say they'd like to pick up the tab . . .'

'No,' I said.

He laughed nervously. 'No . . . well, I see, er, I mean . . . yes.' He spluttered to a stop. The eyes darted around restlessly, the hands gestured vaguely, the meaningless smile twitched his mouth convulsively, and he couldn't stand still on his two feet. I didn't usually throw people into such a tizzy, and I wondered what on earth my agent could have said to him, to bring him to such a state.

He managed eventually to get himself out of the Iguana Rock and back to his car, and his departure was a great relief. Within an hour, however, he was on the telephone.

'Would tomorrow, er, morning . . . suit you for, er, I mean, the Press?'

'Yes,' I said.

'Then, er, would you ask your driver to take you to, er, Randfontein House, er . . . the Dettrick Room . . . that's a reception room, you see, which we hire for this, well, sort of thing.'

'What time?'

'Oh ... say eleven thirty. Could you ... er ... get there at about eleven thirty?'

'Yes,' I said briefly again, and after a few further squirms he said he would look forward ... er ... to seeing me then.

I put the receiver down, finished unpacking, drank some coffee, summoned up the pumpkin, and went briskly off to the races.

CHAPTER FOUR

Flat racing in South Africa took place on Wednesdays and Saturdays throughout the year, but only occasionally on other days. Accordingly, it had seemed good sense to arrive in Johannesburg on Wednesday morning and go to the only race-meeting in South Africa that day, at Newmarket.

I paid to go in and bought a race-card. One of Nerissa's constant failures, I saw, was due to have another go later in the afternoon.

Newmarket was Newmarket the world over. Stands, cards, horses, bookmakers; atmosphere of bustle and purpose; air of tradition and order. All were much the same. I wandered across to the parade ring, where the runners for the first race were already walking round. Same little clumps of owners and trainers standing in hopeful conversations in the middle. Same earnest race-goers leaning on the rails and studying the wares.

Differences were small. The horses, to English eyes, looked slightly smaller-framed and had very upright fetlocks, and they were led round, not by white stable lads in their own darkish clothes, but by black stable-boys in long white coats.

On the principle of only backing horses I knew something about, I kept my hands in my pockets. The jockeys in their bright silks came out and mounted, the runners went away down the track and scurried back, hooves rattling on the bone-dry ground, and I strolled down from the stands to search for and identify Nerissa's trainer, Greville Arknold. He had a runner in the following race, and somewhere he would be found, saddling it up.

In the event, I hardly had to look. On my way to the saddling boxes, a young man touched me on the arm.

'I say,' he said, 'Aren't you Edward Lincoln?'

I nodded and half smiled, and kept on walking.

'Guess I'd better introduce myself. Danilo Cavesey. I believe you know my aunt.'

That stopped me, all right. I put out my hand, and he shook it warmly.

'I heard you were coming, of course. Aunt Nerissa cabled Greville you were on your way out here for some film premiere, and would he look out for you at the races. So I was kind of expecting you, you see.'

His accent was a slow Californian drawl full of lazy warmth. It was instantly clear why Nerissa had liked him: his sun-tanned, good-looking face, his open, pleasant expression, his clean, casual, blond-brown hair, all were in the best tradition of American youth.

'She didn't say you were in South Africa,' I commented, surprised.

'Well, no.' He wrinkled his nose disarmingly. 'I don't believe she knows. I only flew out here a few days ago, on a vacation. Say, how is the old girl? She wasn't all that sprightly when I last visited with her.'

He was smiling happily. He didn't know.

I said, 'She's pretty ill, I'm afraid.'

'Is that so? I'm sure sorry to hear that. I must write her, tell her I'm out here, tell her I'm taking a look-see into the state of the horses.'

'The state of the horses?' I echoed.

'Oh sure. Aunt Nerissa's horses out here are not running good. Stinking bad, to be accurate.' He grinned cheerfully. 'I shouldn't bet on number eight in the fourth race, if you want to die rich.'

'Thanks,' I said. 'She did mention to me that they were not doing so well just now.'

'I'll bet she did. They wouldn't win if you gave them ten minutes start and nobbled the others.'

'Is there any reason for it, do you know?'

'Search me,' he shrugged. 'Greville's real chewed up about it. Says he hasn't had anything like this happen before.'

'Not a virus?' I suggested.

'Can't be. Otherwise all the others would get it too, not just Aunt Nerissa's. We've been talking it over, you see. Greville just hasn't an idea.'

'I'd like to meet him,' I said casually.

'Oh sure. Yes, indeed. But say, why don't we get out of this wind and have ourselves a beer or something?

Greville has this starter now, but he'll be happy to see us later on.'

'All right,' I agreed, and we went and had ourselves the beer. Danilo was right: the south wind was cold and spring was still a hint and a memory.

Danilo, I judged, was about twenty years old. He had bright blue eyes and blond-brown eyelashes, and his teeth were California-straight. He had the untouched air of one to whom the rigours of life had not yet happened; a boy not necessarily spoilt, but to whom much had been given.

He was at Berkeley University studying Political Science, he said, with one more year to do. 'This time next summer I'll be all through with college . . .'

'What do you plan to do after that?' I asked, making conversation.

There was a flash of amusement in the blue eyes. 'Oh, I guess I'll have to think of something, but I've nothing lined up right now.'

The future could take care of itself, I thought, and reflected that for golden boys like Danilo it usually did.

We watched the next race together. Greville's starter finished third, close up.

'Too bad,' Danilo sighed. 'I just had it on the nose, not across the boards.'

'Did you lose much?' I asked sympathetically.

'I guess not. Just a few rand.'

Rands came just under two to the pound sterling, or

a little over one to the dollar. He couldn't have done himself much harm.

We walked down from the stands and over towards the unsaddling enclosures. 'Do you know something?' he said. 'You're not a bit what I expected.'

'In what way?' I asked, smiling.

'Oh, I guess . . . For a big movie star, I expected some sort of, well, *presence*. You know?'

'Off the screen, movie actors are as dim as anyone else.'

He glanced at me suspiciously, but I wasn't laughing at him. I meant it. He had a much more naturally luminous personality than I had. I might have been an inch or two taller, an inch or two broader across the shoulders, but the plus factor had nothing to do with size.

The man stalking round the horse which had finished third, peering judiciously at its legs and running a probing hand along its loins, was a burly thickset man with an air of dissatisfaction.

'That's Greville,' Danilo nodded, following my gaze.

The trainer spoke briefly to a woman Danilo identified to me as the horse's owner. His manner, from twenty feet away, looked brusque and far from conciliatory. I knew trainers had to grow hard skins if they were to stay sane: one could not for ever be apologizing to owners if their horses got beaten, one had to make them realize that regardless of the oats and exercise crammed into them, maybe other people's horses could actually run

661

faster: but Greville Arknold appeared plainly disagreeable.

After a while the horses were led away and the crowd
thinned out. Arknold listened, with a pinched mouth
and a stubborn backward tilt of the head, to what looked
almost like apologies from the woman owner. She came
to a stop, got no melting response from him, shrugged,
turned slowly, and walked away.

Arknold's gaze rose from down his nose and fastened
on Danilo. He stared for a moment, then raised his
eyebrows questioningly. Danilo very slightly jerked
his head in my direction, and Arknold transferred his
attention to me.

Again the slow appraisal. Then he came across.

Danilo introduced us with an air of what fun it was
for us to know each other. A mutual privilege.

Great.

I didn't take to Greville Arknold, neither then nor
ever after. Yet he was pleasant enough to me: smiled,
shook hands, said he was glad to meet me, said that Mrs
Cavesey had cabled to say I might be coming to the
races, and to look after me if I did.

He had a flat-sounding Afrikaaner accent, and like
many South Africans he was, I discovered later, trilin-
gual in English, Afrikaans and Zulu. He had a face
formed of thick slabs of flesh, lips so thin that they hardly
existed, the scars of old acne over his chin and down his
neck, and a bristly ginger moustache one inch by two

below his nose. And for all the smiling and the welcoming chat, he had cold eyes.

'Your horse ran well just then,' I suggested conversationally.

The recent anger reappeared at once in his manner. 'That stupid woman insisted that her horse ran today when I wanted to run it Saturday instead. He had a hard race at Turffontein last Saturday. He needed another three days' rest.'

'She looked as if she were apologizing,' I said.

'*Ja*. She was. Too late, of course. She should have had more sense. Decent colt, that. Would have won on Saturday. No sense. Owners always ought to do what a trainer says. They pay for expert knowledge, don't they? So they always ought to do what the experts say.'

I smiled vaguely, noncommittally. As an owner myself, even of only one moderate steeplechasing gelding, I disagreed with him about always. Sometimes, even usually, yes. But always, no. I knew of at least one Grand National winner which would never have gone to the start if the owner had paid attention to the trainer's advice.

'I see Mrs Cavesey has a runner in the fourth,' I said.

The dogmatic look faded to be replaced by a slight frown.

'*Ja*,' Arnold said. 'I expect she may have mentioned to you that her horses are not doing well.'

'She told me you had no idea why,' I nodded.

He shook his head. 'I cannot understand it. They get

the same treatment as all the others. Same food, same exercise, everything. They are not ill. I have had a veterinarian examine them, several times. It is worrying. Very.'

'It must be,' I agreed sympathetically.

'And dope tests!' he said. 'We must have had a hundred dope tests. All negative, the whole lot.'

'Do they look fit?' I asked. 'I mean, would you expect them to do better, from the way they look?'

'See for yourself.' He shrugged. 'That is . . . I don't know how much of a judge of a horse you are . . .'

'Bound to be a pretty good one, I'd say,' said Danilo positively. 'After all, it's no secret his old man was a stable hand.'

'Is that so?' he said. 'Then perhaps you would like to see round the stables? Maybe you could even come up with some suggestion about Mrs Cavesey's string, you never know.'

The irony in his voice made it clear that he thought that impossible. Which meant that either he really did not know what was the matter with the horses, or he did know, but was absolutely certain that I would not find out.

'I'd like to see the stables very much,' I said.

'Good. Then you shall. How about tomorrow evening? Walk round with me, at evening stables. Four-thirty?'

I nodded.

'That's fixed then. And you, Danilo. Do you want to come as well?'

'That would be just fine, Greville. I sure would like that.'

So it was settled; and Danilo said he would come and pick me up at the Iguana Rock himself.

Chink, Nerissa's runner in the fourth race, looked good enough in the parade ring, with a healthy bloom on his coat and muscles looking strong and free and loose. There wasn't a great deal of substance about him, but he had an intelligent head and strong, well-placed shoulders. Nerissa's sister Portia had given twenty-five thousand rand for him as a yearling on the strength of his breeding, and he had won only one race, his first, way back in April.

'What do you think of him, Link?' Danilo asked, leaning his hip against the parade ring rail.

'He looks fit enough,' I said.

'Yeah. They all do, Greville says.'

Chink was being led around by two stable lads, one each side. Nothing wrong with Arknold's security arrangements.

Because of the upright fetlocks I found it hard to judge the degree of spring in Chink's stride. All the horses looked to me as if they were standing on their toes, a condition I imagined was caused by living from birth on hard dry ground. Certainly he went down to the post moving no more scratchily than the others, and he lined up in the stalls and bounded out of them with no trouble. I watched every step of his journey through my Zeiss eight by fifties.

He took the first half mile without apparent effort, lying about sixth, nice and handy, just behind the leading bunch. When they turned into the straight for home, the leaders quickened, but Chink didn't. I saw the head of the jockey bob and the rest of his body become energetically busy trying to keep the horse going: but when a jockey has to work like that on a horse a long way out, he might as well not bother. Chink had run out of steam, and the best rider in the world could have done nothing about that.

I put down my race glasses. The winner fought a ding-dong, the crowd roared, and Chink returned unsung, unbacked, unwatched, and a good thirty lengths later.

With Danilo I went down to where he was being unsaddled, and joined Greville Arknold in his aura of perplexed gloom.

'There you are,' he said. 'You saw for yourself.'

'I did,' I agreed.

Chink was sweating and looked tired. He stood still, with drooping head, as if he felt the disgrace.

'What do you think?' Arknold asked.

I silently shook my head. He had in fact looked plainly like a slow horse, yet on his breeding, and the fast time of the race he had won, he should not be.

He and the other ten could not all have bad hearts, or bad teeth, or blood disorders, all undetected. Not after those thorough veterinary investigations. And not *all* of them. It was impossible.

They had not all been ridden every time by the same jockey. There were, I had discovered from Nerissa's racing papers, very few jockeys in South Africa compared with England: only thirteen jockeys and twenty-two apprentices riding on the Natal tracks near Durban, the supposed centre of the sport.

There were four main racing areas: the Johannesburg tracks in the Transvaal, the Pietermaritzburg-Durban tracks in Natal, the Port Elizabeth tracks in the Eastern Cape, and the Cape Town tracks in Cape Province. Various ones of Nerissa's horses had been to all four areas, had been ridden by the local bunch of jockeys, and had turned in the same results.

Fast until May, dead slow from June onwards.

The fact that they moved around meant that it probably could not be attributed to something in their base quarters.

No illness. No dope. No fixed address. No common jockey.

All of which pointed to one solution. One source of disaster.

The trainer himself.

It was easy enough for a trainer to make sure a horse of his didn't win, if he had a mind to. He merely had to give it too severe an exercise gallop too soon before a race. Enough races had in sober fact been lost that way by accident for it to be impossible to prove that anyone had done it on purpose.

Trainers seldom nobbled their own horses because they had demonstrably more to gain if they won. But it looked to me as if it had to be Arknold who was responsible, even if the method he was using turned out to be the simplest in the world.

I thought the solution to Nerissa's problem lay in transferring her string to a different trainer.

I thought I might just as well go straight home and tell her so.

Two nasty snags.

I was committed to a premiere two weeks off.

And I might guess who and how, about the horses.

But I had no idea *why*.

CHAPTER FIVE

The ladies and gentlemen of the Press (or in the other words a partially shaven, polo-neck-sweatered, elaborately casual and uniformed mob) yawned to their feet when I reached the Dettrick Room in Randfontein House within ticking distance of half past eleven.

Clifford Wenkins had met me in the hall, twittering as before, and with wetter than ever palms. We rode up in the lift together, with him explaining to me exactly whom he had asked, and who had come. Interviewers from two radio programmes. He hoped I wouldn't mind? They would be happy just to tape my answers to their questions. Just into a microphone. If I didn't mind? And then there were the dailies, the weeklies, the ladies' magazines, and one or two people who had flown up especially from Cape Town and Durban.

I wished I hadn't suggested it. Too late to run away.

The only thing to do, I thought, as the lift hissed to a halt and the doors slid open, was to put on a sort of performance. To act.

'Wait a minute,' I said to Wenkins.

He stopped with me outside the lift as the doors shut again behind us.

'What is it?' he asked anxiously.

'Nothing. I just need a few seconds, before we go in.'

He didn't understand, though what I was doing was not a process by any means confined to professional actors. Girding up the loins, the Bible called it. Getting the adrenalin on the move. Making the heart beat faster. Shifting the mental gears into top. Politicians could do it in three seconds flat.

'OK,' I said.

He sighed with relief, walked across the hallway, and opened a heavy polished door opposite.

We went in.

They unfolded themselves from sofas and carpet, pushed themselves tiredly off the walls, stubbed out one or two cigarettes and went on puffing at others.

'Hi,' said one of the men: and the others, like a sort of jungle pack, watched and waited. He was one of those who had been at the airport. He had no reason, as none of them had, to believe I would now be any different.

'Hullo,' I said.

Well, I could always do it, if I really wanted to. Almost every well-trained actor can.

I watched them loosen, saw the tiredness go out of their manner and the smile creep into their eyes. They wouldn't now chew me to bits in their columns, even if they still came across with those carefully sharpened questions they all had ready in their notebooks.

670

The man who had said hi, their apparently natural leader, put out his hand to be shaken, and said, 'I'm Roderick Hodge of the *Rand Daily Star*. Features Editor.'

Late thirties, but trying to ignore the passage of time: young hair-cut, young clothes, young affectation of speech. A certain *panache* about him, but also some of the ruthless cynicism of experienced journalists.

I shook his hand and smiled at him as a friend. I needed him to be one.

'Look,' I said. 'Unless you are all in a hurry, why don't we sit down again, and then you can all ask whatever you like, perhaps in groups, maybe I can move around a bit, and then everyone might have more time for things than if I just sort of stand here in front of you.'

They thought that was all right. No one was in much of a hurry, they said. Roderick said dryly that no one would go before the booze started flowing, and the atmosphere started mellowing nicely into an all-pals-together trade meeting.

They mostly asked the personal questions first.

According to their calculations, I was thirty-three. Was that right?

It was.

And married? Yes. Happily? Yes. My first or second marriage? First. And her first? Yes.

They wanted to know how many children I had, with their names and ages. They asked how many rooms my house had, and what it had cost. How many cars, dogs, horses, yachts I had. How much I earned in a year, how much I had been paid for *Rocks*.

How much did I give my wife to buy clothes with? Did I think a woman's place was in the home?

'In the heart,' I said flippantly, which pleased the women's mag girl who had asked, but was slightly sick-making to all the others.

Why didn't I go to live in a tax haven? I liked England. An expensive luxury? Very. And was I a millionaire? Perhaps some days, on paper, when share prices went up. If I was as rich as that, why did I work? To pay taxes, I said.

Clifford Wenkins had summoned up some caterers who brought coffee and cheese biscuits and bottles of Scotch. The Press poured the whisky into the coffee and sighed contentedly. I kept mine separate, but had great difficulty in explaining to the waiter that I did not like any liquor diluted in nine times as much water. In South Africa, I had already discovered, they tended to fill up the tumblers; and I supposed it made sense as a long drink in a hot climate, but while it was so cold it merely ruined good Scotch.

Clifford Wenkins eyed my small drink in its large glass.

'Let me get you some water.'

'I've got some. I prefer it like this . . .'

'Oh . . . really?'

He scuttled busily away and came back with an earn-estly bearded man trailing a hand microphone and a long lead. There was no sense of humour behind the beard, which made, I thought, for a fairly stodgy interview, but he assured me that what I had said was just right, just perfect for a five minute slot in his Saturday evening show. He took back the microphone which I had been holding, shook me earnestly by the hand, and disappeared into a large array of recording equipment in one corner.

After that I was supposed to do a second interview, this time for a woman's programme, but some technical hitches had developed in the gear.

I moved, in time, right round the room, sitting on the floor, on the arms of chairs, leaning on the window-sills, or just plain standing.

Loosened by the Scotch, they asked the other questions.

What did I think of South Africa? I liked it.

What were my opinions of their political scene? I hadn't any, I said. I had been in their country only one day. One couldn't form opinions in that time.

Most people arrived with them already formed, they observed. I said I didn't think that was sensible.

Well, what were my views on racial discrimination? I said without heat that I thought any form of discrimination was bound to give rise to some injustice. I said I thought it a pity that various people found it necessary to discriminate against women, Jews, Aborigines, American Indians and a friend of mine in Nairobi who couldn't get promotion in a job he excelled at because he was white.

I also said I couldn't answer any more of that sort of question, and could we please get off politics and civil rights unless they would like me to explain the differences between the economic theories of the Tory and Labour parties.

They laughed. No, they said. They wouldn't.

They reverted to films and asked questions I felt better able to answer.

Was it true I had started as a stunt man? Sort of, I said. I rode horses across everything from Robin Hood via Bosworth Field to the Charge of the Light Brigade. Until one day when I was doing a bit of solo stuff a director called me over, gave me some words to say, and told me I was in. Good clean romantic stuff, for which I apologized. It did happen sometimes like that though.

And then? Oh, then I got given a better part in his next film. And how old was I at the time? Twenty-two, just married, living on baked beans in a basement flat in Hammersmith, and still attending part-time speech and drama classes, as I had for three years.

I was standing more or less in the centre of the room when the door opened behind me. Clifford Wenkins turned his head to see who it was, frowned with puzzlement and went busily across to deal with the situation.

'I'm afraid you can't come in here,' he was saying bossily. 'This is a private room. Private reception. I'm sorry, but would you mind . . . I say, you can't . . . this is a private room . . . I say . . .'

I gathered Wenkins was losing. Not surprising, really.

Then I felt the clump on the shoulder and heard the familiar fruity voice.

'Link, dear boy. Do tell this . . . er . . . person, that we are old buddy buddies. He doesn't seem to want me to come in. Now, I ask you . . .'

I turned round. Stared in surprise. Said to Wenkins, 'Perhaps you would let him stay. I do know him. He's a cameraman.'

Conrad raised his eyebrows sharply. 'Director of Photography, dear boy. A cameraman indeed!'

'Sorry,' I said ironically. 'Have a Scotch?'

'Now that, dear boy, is more like it.'

Wenkins gave up the struggle and went off to get Conrad a drink. Conrad surveyed the relaxed atmosphere, the hovering smoke, the empty cups and half-empty glasses, and the gentle communicators chatting in seated groups.

'My God,' he said. 'My great God. I don't believe it. I didn't, in fact, believe it when they told me Edward Lincoln was giving a Press conference right here in Johannesburg at this very moment. I bet on it not being true. So they told me where. In that ritzy room at the top of the Randfontein, they said. Go and see for yourself. So I did.'

A laugh began rumbling somewhere down in his belly and erupted in a coughing guffaw.

'Shut up,' I said.

He spread his arms wide, embracing the room. 'They don't know, they just don't know what they're seeing, do they? They've just no idea.'

'Be quiet, Conrad, damn it,' I said.

He went on wheezing away in uncontainable chuckles. 'My dear boy. I didn't know you could do it. Off the set, that is. Talk about a lot of tame tigers eating out of your hand . . . Just wait until Evans hears.'

'He isn't likely to,' I said comfortably. 'Not from five thousand or so miles away.'

He shook with amusement. 'Oh no, dear boy. He's right here in Johannesburg. Practically in the next street.'

'He can't be!'

'We've been here since Sunday.' He choked off the last of his laughter and wiped his eyes with his thumb. 'Come and have some lunch, dear boy, and I'll tell you all about it.'

I looked at my watch. Twelve-thirty.

'In a while, then. I've still got one more bit of taping to do, when they get hold of a spare microphone.'

Roderick Hodge detached himself from a group by one of the windows and brought a decorative female over with him, and Clifford Wenkins dead-heated with Conrad's drink.

The girl, the would-be interviewer from the woman's radio programme, had the sort of face that would have been plain on a different personality: but she also had a bushy mop of curly brown hair, enormous yellow-rimmed sunglasses, and a stick-like figure clad in an orange and tan checked trouser suit. The spontaneous friendliness in her manner saved her from any impression of caricature. Conrad took in her colour temperature with an appreciative eye, while explaining he had been engaged on four films with me in the recent past.

Roderick's attention sharpened like an adjusted focus.

'What is he like to work with?' he demanded.

'That's not fair,' I said.

Neither Roderick nor Conrad paid any attention. Conrad looked at me judiciously, pursed his lips, lifted up a hand, and bent the fingers over one by one as he rolled his tongue lovingly around the words.

'Patient, powerful, punctual, professional, and puritanical.' And aside to me he stage-whispered, 'How's that?'

'Ham,' I said.

Roderick predictably pounced on the last one. 'Puritanical. How do you mean?'

Conrad was enjoying himself. 'All his leading ladies complain that he kisses them with art, not heart.'

I could see the headlines writing themselves in Roderick's head. His eye was bright.

'My sons don't like it,' I said.

'What?'

'When the elder one saw me in a film kissing someone

who wasn't his mother, he wouldn't speak to me for a week.'

They laughed.

But at the time it had been far from funny. Peter had also started wetting his bed again at five years old and had cried a lot, and a child psychiatrist had told us it was because he felt insecure: he felt his foundations were slipping away, because Daddy kissed other ladies, and quarrelled with Mummy at home. It had happened so soon after Libby's accident that we wondered whether he was also worrying about that: but we had never told him Libby had been ill because he had dropped her, and never intended to. One couldn't burden a child with that sort of knowledge, because a pointless, unnecessary feeling of guilt could have distorted the whole of his development.

'What did you do about that?' the girl asked sympathetically.

'Took him to some good clean horror films instead.'

'Oh, yeah,' Conrad said.

Clifford Wenkins came twittering back from another of his darting foraging expeditions. Sweat still lay in pearl-sized beads in the furrows of his forehead. How did he cope, I vaguely wondered, when summer came.

He thrust a stick microphone triumphantly into my hands. Its lead ran back to the corner where the radio apparatus stood. 'There we are ... er ... all fixed, I mean.' He looked in unnecessary confusion from me to the girl. 'There we are, Katya dear. Er . . . all ready, I think.'

I looked at Conrad. I said, 'I learned just one word of Afrikaans at the races yesterday, and you can do it while I tape this interview.'

Conrad said suspiciously, 'What word?'

'*Voetsek*,' I said conversationally.

They all split themselves politely. *Voetsek* meant bugger off.

Conrad's chuckles broke out again like a recurring infection, when they explained.

'If only Evan could see this . . .' he wheezed.

'Let's forget Evan,' I suggested.

Conrad put his hand on Roderick's arm and took him away, each of them enjoying a separate joke.

Katya's smallish eyes were laughing behind the enormous yellow specs. 'And to think they said that at the airport you were the chilliest of cold fish . . .'

I gave her a sideways smile. 'Maybe I was tired . . .' I eyed the notebook she clutched in one hand. 'What sort of things are you going to ask?'

'Oh, only the same as the others, I should think.' But there was a mischievous glint of teeth that boded no good.

'All set, Katya,' a man called from the row of electronic boxes and dials. 'Any time you say.'

'Right.' She looked down at the notebook and then up at me. I was about three feet away from her, holding my glass in one hand and the microphone in the other.

She considered this with her curly head on one side, then took a large step closer. Almost touching.

'That's better, I think. There will be too much background noise if either of us is too far from that microphone. It's an old one, by the looks of it. Oh, and maybe I'd better hold it. You look a bit awkward . . .' She took the microphone and called across the room. 'OK, Joe, switch on.'

Joe switched on.

Katya jerked appallingly from head to foot, arched backwards through the air and fell to the floor.

The murmuring peaceful faces turned, gasped, cried out, screwed themselves up in horror.

'Switch off,' I shouted urgently. 'Switch everything off. At once.'

Roderick took two strides and bent over Katya with outstretched hands to help her, and I pulled him back.

'Get Joe to switch that bloody microphone off first, or you will take the shock as well.'

The Joe in question ran over, looking ill.

'I have,' he said. 'It's off now.'

I thought that all, that any of them would know what to do, and do it. But they all just stood and knelt around looking at me, as if it were up to me to know, to do, to be the resourceful man in all those films who always took the lead, always . . .

Oh God, I thought.

Just look at them, I thought. And there was no time to waste. No time at all. She was no longer breathing.

I knelt down beside her and took her glasses off. Pulled open the neck of her shirt. Stretched her head back. Put my mouth on hers, and blew my breath into her lungs.

'Get a doctor,' Roderick. 'And an ambulance . . . Oh Christ . . . Hurry. Hurry . . .'

I breathed into her. Not too hard. Just with the force of breath. But over and over, heaving her chest up and down.

A lethal electric voltage stops the heart.

I tried to feel a pulse beating in her neck, but couldn't find one. Roderick interpreted my fingers and picked up her wrist, but it was no good there, either. His face was agonized. Katya was a great deal more, it seemed, than just a colleague.

Two thousand years passed like two more minutes. Roderick put his ear down on Katya's left breast. I went on breathing air into her, feeling as the seconds passed that it was no good, that she was dead. Her flesh was the colour of death, and very cold.

He heard the first thud before I felt it. I saw it in his face. Then there were two separate jolts in the blood vessel I had my fingers on under her jaw, and then some uneven, jerky little bumps, and then at last, unbelievably, slow, rhythmic, and strengthening, the life-giving ba-boom ba-boom ba-boom of a heart back in business.

Roderick's mouth tightened and twisted as he raised his head, and the cords in his neck stood out with the effort he was putting into not weeping. But the tears of relief ran for all that down his cheeks, and he tried to get rid of them with his fingers.

I pretended not to see, if that was what he wanted. But I knew, heaven forgive me, that one day I would put that face, that reaction, into a film. Whatever one learned, whatever one saw, and however private it was, in the end, if one were an actor, one used it.

She breathed in, convulsively, on her own, while I was still breathing in myself, through my nose. It felt extraordinary, as if she were sucking the air out of me.

I took my mouth away from hers, and stopped holding her jaws open with my hands. She went on breathing: a bit sketchily at first, but then quite regularly, in shallow bodyshaking, audible gasps.

'She ought to be warmer,' I said to Roderick. 'She needs blankets.'

He looked at me dazedly. 'Yes. Blankets.'

'I'll get some,' someone said, and the breath-held quietness in the room erupted with sudden bustle. Frozen shock turned to worried shock, and that to relieved shock, and from that to revival via the whisky bottle.

I saw Clifford Wenkins looking down at Katya's still unconscious form. His face was grey and looked like putty oozing, as the sweat had not had time to dry. For once, however, he had been reduced to speechlessness.

Conrad, too, seemed temporarily to have run out of 'dear boys'. But I guessed sharply that the blankness in his face as he watched the proceedings was not the result of shock. He was at his business, as I had been at mine, seeing an electrocution in terms of camera angles, atmospheric shadows, impact-making colours. And at what point, I wondered, did making use of other people's agonies become a spiritual sin.

Someone reappeared with some blankets, and with shaking hands Roderick wrapped Katya up in them, and put a cushion under her head.

I said to him, 'Don't expect too much when she wakes up. She'll be confused, I think.'

He nodded. Colour was coming back to her cheeks. She seemed securely alive. The time of fiercest anxiety was over.

He looked suddenly up at me, then down at her, then up at me again. The first thought that was not raw emotion was taking root.

As if it were a sudden discovery, he slowly said, 'You're Edward Lincoln.'

For him too the dilemma of conscience arose: whether or not to make professional copy out of the near-death of his girlfriend.

I looked round the room, and so did he. There had been a noticeable thinning of the ranks. I met Roderick's eyes and knew what he was thinking: the Press had made for the telephones, and he was the only one there from the *Rand Daily Star*.

He looked down again at the girl. 'She'll be all right, now, won't she?' he said.

I made an inconclusive gesture with my hands and

didn't directly answer. I didn't know whether or not she would be all right. I thought her heart had probably not been stopped for much over three minutes, so with a bit of luck her brain would not be irreparably damaged. But my knowledge was only the sketchy remains of a long-past first-aid course.

The journalist in Roderick won the day. He stood up abruptly and said, 'Do me a favour . . .? Don't let them take her to hospital or anywhere before I get back.'

'I'll do my best,' I said; and he made a highly rapid exit.

Joe, the radio equipment man, was coiling up the lead of the faulty microphone, having disconnected it gingerly from its power socket. He looked at it dubiously and said, 'It's such an old one I didn't know we had it. It was just there, in the box . . . I wish to God I hadn't decided to use it. It just seemed quicker than waiting any longer for the replacement from the studio. I'll make sure it'll do no more damage, anyway. I'll dismantle it and throw it away.'

Conrad returned to my side and stood looking down at Katya, who began showing signs of returning consciousness. Her eyelids fluttered. She moved under the blankets.

Conrad said, 'You do realize, dear boy, that until very shortly before the accident you were holding that microphone yourself.'

'Yes,' I said neutrally. 'I do.'

'And,' said Conrad, 'just how many people in this

room showed the slightest sign of knowing that the only hope for the electrocuted is artificial respiration, instantly applied?'

I looked at him straightly.

'Did you know?'

He sighed. 'You are so cynical, dear boy. But no, I didn't.'

CHAPTER SIX

Danilo arrived at the Iguana Rock at four o'clock with a hired Triumph, a scarlet open-necked shirt and a sun-tanned grin.

I had been back there less than an hour myself, Conrad and I having dawdled over a beer and sandwich lunch in an unobtrusive bar. Katya had gone to hospital, with Roderick in frantic tow, and the other journalists were currently stubbing their fingernails on their type-writers. Clifford Wenkins had twittered off at some unmarked point in the proceedings, and when Conrad and I left we saw him, too, engaged in earnest conver-sation on the telephone. Reporting to Worldic, no doubt. I stifled a despairing sigh. Not a butterfly's chance in a blizzard that anyone would ignore the whole thing as uninteresting.

Danilo chatted in his carefree way, navigating us round the elevated Sir de Villiers Graaf ring road, that God's gift to the city's inhabitants which took the through traffic out of their way, over their heads.

'I can't imagine what Johannesburg was like before

they built this highway,' Danilo commented. 'They still have a big traffic problem downtown, and as for parking . . . there's more cars parked along the streets down there than one-armed bandits in Nevada . . .'

'You've been here quite a time, then?'

'Hell, no,' he grinned. 'Only a few days. But I've been here before, once, and anyway it sure only takes twenty minutes of searching around to teach you that all the car parks are permanently full and that you can never park within a quarter-mile of where you want to be.'

He drove expertly and coolly on what was to him the wrong side of the road.

'Greville lives down near Turffontein,' he said. 'We drop down off this elevated part soon now . . . did that sign say Eloff Street Extension?'

'It did,' I confirmed.

'Great.' He took the turn and we left the South African M1 and presently passed some football fields and a skating rink.

'They call this "Wembley",' Danilo said. 'And over there is a lake called Wemmer Pan for boating. And say, they have a water organ there which shoots coloured fountains up into the air in time to the music.'

'Have you been there?'

'No . . . Greville told me, I guess. He also says it's a great place for fishing out rotting corpses and headless torsos.'

'Nice,' I said.

He grinned.

Before we reached Turffontein he turned off down a side road which presently became hard impacted earth covered with a layer of dust.

'They've had no rain here for four–five months,' Danilo said. 'Everything's sure looking dry.'

The grass was certainly brownish, but that was what I expected. I was surprised to learn from Danilo that in a month's time, when the rain came and the days were warmer, the whole area would be lush, colourful, and green.

'It's sure sad you won't be here to see the jacarandas,' Danilo said. 'They'll flower all over, after you've gone.'

'You've seen them before?'

He hesitated. 'Well no, not exactly. Last time I was here, they weren't flowering. It's just that Greville says.'

'I see,' I said.

'Here it is. This is Greville's place, right in here.' He pointed, then turned in between some severe-looking brick pillars and drove up a gravel drive into a stable which looked at if it had been transplanted straight from England.

Arknold himself was already out in the yard talking to a black African whom he introduced as his head boy, Barty. Arknold's head lad looked as tough as himself: a solid strong-looking man of about thirty, with a short thick neck and unsmiling cold eyes. He was the first black African I had seen, I thought in mild surprise, whose natural expression had not been good-natured.

There was nothing in his manner, however, but

civility, and he nodded to Danilo's greeting with the ordinary acknowledgement of people who meet each other fairly often.

Arknold said that everything was ready, and we started looking round the boxes without more ado. The horses were all like those I had seen on the track; up on their toes, with slightly less bone all round than those at home.

There was nothing at all to distinguish Nerissa's horses from their stable-mates. They looked as well, had legs as firm, eyes as bright; and they were not all stabled in one block, but were scattered among the rest. Colts in one quadrangle, fillies in another. Everything as it should be, as it normally would be in England.

The lads – the boys – were all young and all black. Like lads the world over they were possessively proud of the horses they cared for, though alongside this pride there emerged a second, quite definite, pattern of behaviour.

They responded to me with smiles, to Arknold with respect, and to Barty with unmistakable fear.

I had no knowledge of what sort of tribal hold he had over them, and I never did find out, but in their wary eyes and their shrinking away at his approach, one could see he held them in a bondage far severer than any British head lad could have imposed.

I thought back to the iron hand my father had once wielded. The lads had jumped to what he said, the apprentices had scurried, and indeed I had wasted no time, but I could not remember that anyone had held him in actual physical fear.

I looked at Barty and faintly shivered. I wouldn't have liked to work under him, any more than Arknold's lads did.

'This is Tables Turned,' Arknold was saying, approaching the box door of a dark chestnut colt. 'One of Mrs Cavesey's. Running at Germiston on Saturday.'

'I thought I might go to Germiston,' I said.

'Great,' Danilo said with enthusiasm.

Arknold nodded more moderately, and said he would arrange for me to pick up free entrance tickets at the gate.

We went into the box and stood in the usual sort of appreciative pause, looking Tables Turned over from head to foot while Arknold noted how he was looking compared with the day before and I thought of something not too uncomplimentary to say about him.

'Good neck,' I said. 'Good strong shoulders.' And a bit rat-like about the head, I thought to myself.

Arknold shrugged heavily. 'I took him down to Natal for the winter season, along with all the others. Had nearly the whole string down there for getting on for three months, like we do every year. We keep them at Summerveld, do you see?'

'Where is Summerveld?' I asked.

'More like what is Summerveld,' he said. 'It's a large area with stabling for about eight hundred horses, at Shongweni, near Durban. We book a block of stables there for the season. They have everything in the area one could need – practice track, restaurants, hostels for the boys, everything. And the school for jockeys and apprentices is there, as well.'

'But you didn't do much good, this year?' I said sympathetically.

'We won a few races with the others, but Mrs Cavesey's string . . . Well, to be frank, there are so many of hers that I can't afford to have them all go wrong. Does my reputation no good, do you see?'

I did see. I also thought he spoke with less passion than he might have done.

'This Tables Turned,' he said, slapping the horse's rump, 'on his breeding and his early form he looked a pretty good prospect for the Hollis Memorial Plate in June . . . that's one of the top two-year-old races . . . and he ran just like you saw Chink do at Newmarket. Blew up five hundred metres from home and finished exhausted, though I'd have sworn he was as fit as any of them.'

He nodded to the boy holding the horse's head, turned on his heel, and strode out of the box. Further down the line we reached another of Nerissa's, who evoked an even deeper display of disgust.

'Now this colt, Medic, he should have been a proper world-beater. I thought once that he'd win the Natal Free Handicap in July, but in the end I never sent him to Clairwood at all. His four races before that were too shameful.'

I had a strong feeling that his anger was half genuine. It puzzled me. He certainly did seem to care that the horses had all failed, yet I was still sure that he not only knew why they had but had engineered it himself.

With Barty in attendance, pointing out omissions with a stabbing black forefinger to every intimidated stable boy, we finished inspecting every one of the string, and afterwards went across to the house for a drink.

'All of Mrs Cavesey's lot are now counted as three-year-olds, of course,' Arknold said. 'The date for the age-change out here is August 1st, not January 1st as with you.'

'Yes,' I said.

'There isn't much good racing here on Rand tracks during August. Nothing much to interest you, I dare say.'

'I find it all extremely interesting,' I said truthfully. 'Will you go on running Mrs Cavesey's string as three-year-olds?'

'As long as she cares to go on paying their training fees,' he said gloomily.

'And if she decides to sell?'

'She'd get very little for them now.'

'If she sold them, would you buy any of them?' I asked.

He didn't answer immediately as he was showing us the way into his office, a square room full of papers, form books, filing cabinets and hard upright chairs. Arknold's guests were not, it seemed, to be made so comfortable that they outstayed their limited welcome.

692

I repeated my question unwisely, and received the full glare of the Arknold displeasure.

'Look, Mister,' he said fiercely. 'I don't like what you're suggesting. You are saying that maybe I lose races so I can buy the horses cheap, then win races when I have them myself, and then sell them well for stud. That's what you're saying, Mister.'

'I didn't say anything of the sort,' I protested mildly.

'It's what you were thinking.'

'Well,' I agreed. 'It was a possibility. Looking at it from outside, objectively, wouldn't that have occurred to you, too?'

He still glowered, but the antagonism slowly sub-sided. I wished I could decide whether he had been angry because I had insulted him, or because I had come too near the truth.

Danilo, who had been tagging along all the way making sunny comments to no one in particular, tried to smooth his ruffled friend.

'Aw, c'mon Greville, he meant no harm.'

Arknold gave me a sour look.

'Hey, c'mon. Aunt Nerissa probably told him to poke around for reasons, if he got the chance. You can't blame her, when she's pouring all that money into bad horses, now can you, Greville?'

Arknold made a fair pretence at being pacified and offered us a drink. Danilo smiled hugely in relief and said it wouldn't do, it wouldn't do at all, for us to quarrel.

I sipped my drink and looked at the two of them.

Glossy young golden boy. Square surly middle-aged man. They both drank, and watched me over the rims of the glasses.

I couldn't see an inch into either of their souls.

Back at the Iguana Rock there was a hand-delivered letter waiting for me. I read it upstairs in my room, standing by the window which looked out over the gardens, the tennis courts, and the great African out-doors. The light had begun fading and would soon go quickly, but the positive handwriting was still easy to see.

Dear Mr Lincoln,

I have received a cable from Nerissa Cavesey asking me to invite you to dinner. My wife and I would be pleased to entertain you during your visit, if you would care to accept.

Nerissa is the sister of my late brother's wife, Portia, and has become close to us through her visits to our country. I explain this, as Mr Clifford Wenkins of Worldic Cinemas, who very reluctantly informed me of your whereabouts, was most insist-ent that you would not welcome any private invitations.

Yours sincerely,
Quentin van Huren.

Behind the stiffly polite sentences, one could feel the irritation with which he had written that note. It was not only I, it seemed, who would do things slightly against their will, for Nerissa's sake: and Clifford Wenkins, with his fussing misjudgement of his responsibilities, had clearly not improved the situation.

I went over to the telephone beside the bed and put a call through to the number printed alongside the address on the writing-paper.

The call was answered by a black voice who said she would see if Mr van Huren was home.

Mr van Huren decided he was.

'I called to thank you for your letter,' I said. 'And to say that I would very much like to accept your invitation to dine with you, during my stay.' Two, I reckoned, could be ultra polite.

His voice was as firm as his handwriting, and equally reserved.

'Good.' He didn't sound overjoyed, however. 'It is always a pleasure to please Nerissa.'

'Yes,' I said.

There was a pause. The conversation could hardly be said to be rocketing along at a scintillating rate.

I said helpfully, 'I shall be here until a week next Wednesday.'

'I see. Yes. However, I shall be away from home all next week, and we are already engaged this Saturday and Sunday . . .'

'Then please don't worry,' I said.

He cleared his throat. 'I suppose,' he suggested doubtfully, 'that you would not be free tomorrow? Or, indeed, this evening? My house is not far from the Iguana Rock . . . but of course I expect you are fully engaged.'

Tomorrow morning, I thought, all the newspapers would be flourishing a paragraph or two about Roderick Hodge's girlfriend. By tomorrow night, Mrs van Huren, if she felt like it, could fill her house with the sort of party I didn't like to go to. And tomorrow night I had agreed to have dinner with Conrad, though I could change that if I had to.

I said, 'If it is not too short notice, tonight would be fine.'

'Very well, then. Shall we say eight o'clock? I'll send my car to fetch you.'

I put down the receiver half regretting that I had said I would go, as his pleasure in my acceptance was about as intense as a rice-pudding. However, the alternatives seemed to be the same as the night before: either dine in the Iguana Rock restaurant with the sideways glances reaching me from the other tables, or upstairs alone in my room, wishing I was home with Charlie.

The house to which the van Hurens' car took me was big, old, and spelled money from the marble doorstep onwards. The hall was large, with the ceiling soaring away into invisibility, and round all four sides there was a graceful colonnade of pillars and arches: it looked like a small, splendid Italian piazza, with a roof somewhere over the top.

SMOKESCREEN

In the hall, from a door under the colonnade on the far side, came a man and a woman.

'I am Quentin van Huren,' he said. 'And this is my wife Vivi.'

'How do you do?' I said politely, and shook their hands.

There was a small hiatus.

'Yes ... well,' he said, making a gesture which was very nearly a shrug. 'Come along in.'

I followed them into the room they had come from. In the clearer light there, Quentin van Huren was instantly identifiable as a serious man of substance, since about him clung that unmistakable aura of know-how, experience and ability that constitutes true authority. As solidity and professionalism were qualities I felt at home with, I was immediately prepared to like him more than it seemed probable he would like me.

His wife Vivi was not the same: elegant-looking, but not in the same league intellectually.

She said, 'Do sit down, Mr Lincoln. We are so pleased you could come. Nerissa is such a very dear friend . . .'

She had cool eyes and a highly practised social manner. There was less warmth in her voice than in her words.

'Whisky?' van Huren asked, and I said 'Thank you,' and got the tumbler full of water with the tablespoon of Scotch.

'I'm afraid I haven't seen any of your films,' van

Huren said, without sounding in the least sorry about it, and his wife added, 'We seldom go to the cinema.'

'Very wise,' I said without inflection, and neither of them knew quite how to take it.

I found it easier on the whole to deal with people intent on taking me down a peg rather than with the sycophantically over-flattering. Towards the snubbers I felt no obligation.

I sat down on the gold-brocaded sofa which she had indicated, and sipped my enervated drink.

'Has Nerissa told you she is . . . ill?' I asked.

They both sat without haste. Van Huren shifted a small cushion out of his way, twisting in his armchair to see what he was doing, and answered over his shoulder.

'She wrote a little while ago. She said she had something wrong with her glands.'

'She's dying,' I said flatly, and got from them their first genuine response. They stopped thinking about me. Thought about Nerissa. About themselves. The shock and regret in their faces were real.

Van Huren still held the cushion in his hand.

'Are you sure?' he said.

I nodded. 'She told me herself. A month or two, she says, is all she has.'

'Oh no,' Vivi said, her grief showing through the social gloss like a thistle among orchids.

'I can't believe it,' van Huren exclaimed. 'She is always so full of life. So gay. So vital.'

I thought of Nerissa as I had left her: vitality gone and life itself draining away.

'She is worried about her racehorses,' I said. 'The ones Portia left her.'

Neither of them was ready to think about racehorses. Van Huren shook his head, finished putting the cushion comfortably in his chair, and stared into space. He was a well-built man, at a guess in his fifties, with hair going neatly grey in distinguished wings above his ears. Seen in profile his nose was strongly rounded outwards from the bridge, but stopped straight and short with no impression of a hook. He had a firm, full-lipped, well-defined mouth, hands with square well-manicured nails, and a dark grey suit over which someone had taken a lot of trouble.

The door from the hall opened suddenly and a boy and a girl, quite remarkably alike, came in. He, about twenty, had the slightly sullen air of one whose feelings of rebellion had not carried him as far as actually leaving his palatial home. She, about fifteen, had the uncomplic-ated directness of one to whom the idea of rebellion had not yet occurred.

'Oh sorry,' she said. 'Didn't know we had anyone for dinner.' She came across the room in her jeans and a pale yellow tee-shirt, with her brother behind her dressed very much the same.

Van Huren said, 'This is my son Jonathan, and my daughter Sally . . .'

I stood up to shake hands with the girl, which seemed to amuse her.

'I say,' she said. 'Did anyone ever tell you you look like Edward Lincoln?'

'Yes,' I said. 'I am.'

'You are what?'

'Edward Lincoln.'

'Oh yeah.' She took a closer look. 'Oh golly. Good heavens. So you are.' Then doubtfully, afraid I was making a fool of her. 'Are you really?'

Her father said, 'Mr Lincoln is a friend of Mrs Cavesey . . .'

'Aunt Nerissa! Oh yes. She told us once that she knew you well . . . She's such a darling, isn't she?'

'She is,' I agreed, sitting down again.

Jonathan looked at me steadily with a cold and unimpressed eye.

'I never go to see your sort of film,' he stated.

I smiled mildly and made no answer: it was typical of the putting-down brand of remark made to me with varying degrees of aggression almost every week of my life. Experience had long ago shown that the only unprovocative reply was silence.

'Well, I do,' Sally said. 'I've seen quite a few of them. Was it really you riding that horse in *Spy Across Country*, like the posters said?'

I nodded, 'Mm.'

She looked at me consideringly. 'Wouldn't you have found it easier in a hackamore?'

I laughed involuntarily. 'Well, no. I know the script said the horse had a very light mouth, but the one they actually gave me to ride had a hard one.'

'Sally is a great little horsewoman,' her mother said unnecessarily. 'She won the big pony class at the Rand Easter show.'

'On Rojedda Reef,' Sally added.

The name meant nothing to me. But the others clearly thought it would. They looked at me expectantly, and in the end it was Jonathan who said with superiority, 'It's the name of our gold mine.'

'Really? I didn't know you had a gold mine.' I half deliberately said it with the same inflection that father and son had said they didn't see my films, and Quentin van Huren heard it. He turned his head quite sharply towards me, and I could feel the internal smile coming out of my eyes.

'Yes,' he said thoughtfully, holding my gaze. 'I see.' His lips twitched. 'Would you care to go down one? To see what goes on?'

From the surprised expressions on the rest of his family, I gathered that what he had offered was more or less the equivalent of my suggesting a Press conference.

'I'd like it enormously,' I assured him. 'I really would.'

'I'm flying down to Welkom on Monday morning,' he said. 'That's the town where Rojedda is . . . I'll be there the whole week, but if you care to come down with me Monday, you can fly back again the same evening.'

I said that would be great.

701

By the end of dinner the van Huren–Lincoln *entente* had progressed to the point where three of the family decided to go to Germiston that Saturday to watch Nerissa's horses run. Jonathan said he had more important things to do.

'Like what?' Sally demanded.

Jonathan didn't really know.

CHAPTER SEVEN

Friday turned out to be a meagre day for world news, which left a lot too much space for the perils of Katya. Seldom had the Press been invited in advance to such a spectacle, and in most papers it seemed to have made the front page.

One of them first unkindly suggested that it had all been a publicity stunt which had gone wrong, and then denied it most unconvincingly in the following paragraph.

I wondered, reading it, how many people would believe just that. I wondered, remembering that mischievous smile, whether Katya could possibly even have set it up herself. She and Roderick, between them.

But she wouldn't have risked her life. Not unless she hadn't realized she was risking it.

I picked up the *Rand Daily Star*, to see what they had made of Roderick's information, and found that he had written the piece himself. 'By our own *Rand Daily Star* eye-witness, Roderick Hodge' it announced at the top. Considering his emotional involvement it was not

703

too highly coloured, but it was he, more than any of the others, who stressed, as Conrad had done, that if Katya had not taken the microphone away from me, it would have been I who got the shock.

I wondered how much Roderick wished I had done. For one thing, it would have made a better story.

With a twisting smile I read on to the end. Katya, he reported finally, was being detained in hospital overnight, her condition described as 'comfortable'.

I shoved the papers aside, and while I showered and shaved came to two conclusions. One was that what I had done was not particularly remarkable and certainly not worth the coverage, and the other was that after this I was going to have even more trouble explaining to Nerissa why all I could bring her were guesses, not proof.

Down at the reception desk I asked if they could get me a packed lunch and hire me a horse for the day out in some decent riding country. Certainly, they said, and waved a few magic wands: by mid-morning I was twenty-five miles north of Johannesburg setting out along a dirt road in brilliant sunshine on a pensioned-off race-horse who had seen better days. I took a deep contented breath of the sweet smell of Africa and padded along with a great feeling of freedom. The people who owned the horse had gently insisted on sending their head boy along with me so that I shouldn't get lost, but as he spoke little English and I no Bantu, I found him a most peaceful companion. George was small, rode well, and had a great line in banana-shaped smiles.

We passed a cross-roads where there was a large stall, all by itself, loaded with bright orange fruit and festooned with pineapples, with one man beaming beside them.

'*Naartjies*,' George said, pointing.

I made signs that I didn't understand. One thing about being an actor, it occasionally came in useful.

'*Naartjies*,' George repeated, dismounting from his horse and leading it towards the stall. I grasped the fact that George wanted to buy, so I called to him and fished out a five-rand note. George smiled, negotiated rapidly, and returned with a huge string bag of *naartjies*, two ripe pineapples, and most of the money.

In easy undemanding companionship we rode further, dismounted in some shade, ate a pineapple each, and cold chicken from the Iguana Rock, and drank some refreshing unsweet apple juice from tins George had been given to bring along. The *naartjies* turned out to be like large lumpy tangerines with green patches on the skin: they also tasted like tangerine, but better.

George ate his lunch thirty feet away from me. I beckoned to him to come closer, but he wouldn't.

In the afternoon we trotted and cantered a long way over tough scrubby brown dried grass, and finally, walking to cool the horses, found ourselves approaching the home stables from the opposite direction to the way we set out.

They asked ten rand for the hire of the horse, though the day I had had was worth a thousand, and I gave

George five rand for himself, which his employers whispered was too much. George with a last dazzling smile handed me the bag of *naartjies* and they all gave me friendly waves when I left. If only life were all so natural, so undemanding, so unfettered.

Five miles down the road I reflected that if it were, I would be bored to death.

Conrad was before me at the Iguana.

He met me as I came into the hall and surveyed me from head to foot, dust, sweat, *naartjies* and all.

'What on earth have you been doing, dear boy?'

'Riding.'

'What a pity I haven't an Arriflex with me,' he exclaimed. 'What a shot . . . you standing there looking like a gypsy with your back to the light . . . and those oranges . . . have to work it into our next film together, can't waste a shot like that . . .'

'You're early,' I remarked.

'Might as well wait here as anywhere else.'

'Come upstairs, then, while I change.'

He came up to my room and with unfailing instinct chose the most comfortable chair.

'Have a *naartjie*,' I said.

'I'd rather have a Martini, dear boy.'

'Order one, then.'

He rang for his drink and it came while I was in the shower. I towelled dry and went back into the bed-

706

room in underpants to find him equipped also with a Churchill-sized cigar, wreathed in smoke and smelling of London clubs and plutocracy. He was looking through the pile of newspapers which still lay tidily on the table, but in the end left them undisturbed.

'I've seen all those,' he said. 'How do you like being a real hero, for a change?'

'Don't be nutty. What's so heroic about first aid?'

He grinned. Changed the subject.

'What in hell's name made you come out here for a premiere after all those years of refusing to show your face off the screen?'

'I came to see some horses,' I said, and explained about Nerissa.

'Oh, well, then, dear boy, that does make more sense, I agree. And have you found out what's wrong?'

I shrugged. 'Not really. Don't see how I can.' I fished out a clean shirt and buttoned it on. 'I'm going to Germiston races tomorrow, and I'll keep my eyes open again, but I doubt if anyone could ever prove anything against Greville Arknold.' I put on some socks and dark blue trousers, and some slip-on shoes. 'What are you and Evan doing here, anyway?'

'Film making. What else?'

'What film?'

'Some goddam awful story about elephants that Evan took it into his head to do. It was all set up before he got roped in to finish *Man in a Car*, and since he chose to ponce around in Spain for all that time, we were late getting out here. Should be down in the Kruger Game Park by now.'

I brushed my hair.

'Who's playing the lead?'

'Drix Goddart.'

I glanced at Conrad over my shoulder. He smiled sardonically.

'Wax in Evan's hands, dear boy. Laps up direction like a well patted puppy.'

'Nice for you all.'

'He's so neurotic that if someone doesn't tell him every five minutes that he's brilliant, he thinks everyone hates him.'

'Is he here with you?'

'No, thank God. He was supposed to be, but now he comes out with all the rest of the team after Evan and I have sorted out which locations we want to use.'

I put down the brushes and fastened my watch round my wrist. Keys, change, handkerchief into trouser pockets.

'Did you see the rushes of the desert scenes while you were in England?' Conrad asked.

'No,' I said. 'Evan didn't invite me.'

'Just like him.' He took a long swallow and rolled the Martini round his teeth. He squinted at the long ash on the end of his mini-torpedo. He said, 'They were good.'

'So they damn well ought to be. We did them enough times.'

He smiled without looking at me. 'You won't like the finished film.'

After a pause, as he didn't explain, I said, 'Why not?'

'There's something in it besides and beyond acting.' He paused again, considering his words. 'Even to a jaundiced eye like mine, dear boy, the quality of suffering is shattering.'

I didn't say anything. He swivelled his eyes in my direction.

'Usually you do not reveal much of yourself, do you? Well, this time, dear boy, this time . . .'

I compressed my lips. I knew what I'd done. I'd known while I did it. I had just hoped that no one would be perceptive enough to notice.

'Will the critics see what you saw?' I asked.

He smiled lop-sidedly. 'Bound to, aren't they? The best ones, anyway.'

I stared despondently at the carpet. The trouble with interpreting scenes too well, with taking an emotion and making the audience feel it sharply, was that it meant stripping oneself naked in public. Nothing as simple as naked skin, but letting the whole world peer into one's mind, one's beliefs, one's experience.

To be able to reproduce a feeling so that others could recognize it, and perhaps understand it for the first time, one had to have some idea of what it felt like in reality. To show that one knew meant revealing what one had felt. Revealing oneself too nakedly did not come easily to a private man, and if one did not reveal oneself, one never became a great actor.

I was not a great actor. I was competent and popular, but unless I whole-heartedly took the step into frightening personal exposure, I would never do anything great. There was always for me, in acting beyond a certain limit, an element of mental distress. But I had thought, when I risked doing it in the car, that my own self would be merged indiscernibly with the trials the fictional character was enduring.

I had done it because of Evan: to spite him, more than to please him. There was a point beyond which no director could claim credit for an actor's performance, and I had gone a long way beyond that point.

'What are you thinking?' Conrad demanded.

'I was deciding to stick exclusively in future to unreal entertaining escapades, as in the past.'

'You're a coward, dear boy.'

'Yes.'

He tapped the ash off his cigar.

'No one is going to be satisfied, if you do.'

'Of course they are.'

'Uhuh.' He shook his head. 'No one will settle for paste after they see they could have the real thing.'

'Stop drinking Martinis,' I said. 'They give you rotten ideas.'

I walked across the room, picked up my jacket, put it on, and stowed wallet and diary inside it.

'Let's go down to the bar,' I said.

He levered himself obediently out of the chair.

'You can't run away from yourself for ever, dear boy.'

'I'm not the man you think I am.'

'Oh yes,' Conrad said. 'Dear boy, you are.'

At Germiston races the next day I found waiting for me at the gate not only the free entrance tickets promised by Greville Arknold, but also a racecourse official with a duplicate set and instructions to take me up to lunch with the Chairman of the Race Club.

I meekly followed where he led, and was presently shown into a large dining-room where about a hundred people were already eating at long tables. The whole van Huren family, including a sulky Jonathan, occupied chairs near the end of the table closer to the door, and when he saw me come in, van Huren himself rose to his feet.

'Mr Klugvoigt, this is Edward Lincoln,' he said to the man sitting at the end of the table: and to me added, 'Mr Klugvoigt is the Chairman.'

Klugvoigt stood up, shook hands, indicated the empty chair on his left, and we all sat down.

Vivi van Huren in a sweeping green hat sat opposite me, on the Chairman's right, with her husband beside her. Sally van Huren was on my left, with her brother beyond. They all seemed to know Klugvoigt well, and as a personality he had much in common with van Huren:

same air of wealth and substance, same self-confidence, same bulk of body and acuity of mind.

Once past the preliminaries and the politeness (how did I like south Africa: nowhere so comfortable as the Iguana Rock: how long was I staying) the conversation veered naturally back to the chief matter in hand.

Horses.

The van Hurens owned a four-year-old which had finished third in the Dunlop Gold Cup a month earlier, but they were giving it a breather during these less important months. Klugvoigt owned two three-year-olds running that afternoon with nothing much expected.

I steered the conversation round to Nerissa's horses without much difficulty, and from there to Greville Arknold, asking, but not pointedly, how he was in general regarded, both as man and trainer.

Neither van Huren nor Klugvoigt were of the kind to come straight out with what they thought. It was Jonathan who leant forward and let out the jet of truth.

'He's a rude bloody bastard with hands as heavy as a gold brick.'

'I have to advise Nerissa, when I get home,' I commented.

'Aunt Portia always said he had a way with horses,' Sally objected, in defence.

'Yeah. Backwards,' said Jonathan.

Van Huren gave him a flickering glance in which humour was by no means lacking, but he changed the subject immediately with the expertise of one thoroughly awake to the risk of slander.

'Your Clifford Wenkins, Link, telephoned to me yesterday afternoon to offer us all some tickets to your premiere.' He looked amused. I gratefully accepted that he had loosened with me to the point of dropping the meticulous 'Mr' and thought that in an hour or two I might get around to Quentin.

'Apparently he had had second thoughts about his abruptness to me when I asked for your address.'

'Probably been doing some belated homework,' agreed Klugvoigt, who seemed to know all about it.

'It's only a . . . an adventure film,' I said. 'You might not enjoy it.'

He gave me a dry sardonic smile. 'You won't accuse me again of condemning what I haven't seen.'

I smiled back. I considerably liked Nerissa's sister's husband's brother.

We finished the excellent lunch and wandered out for the first race. Horses were already being mounted, and Vivi and Sally hurried off to upset the odds with a couple of rand.

'Your friend Wenkins said he would be here today,' van Huren remarked.

'Oh dear.'

He chuckled.

Arknold, in the parade ring, was throwing his magenta-shirted jockey up into the saddle.

'How heavy is a gold brick?' I asked.

Van Huren followed my gaze. 'Seventy-two pounds, usually. You can't lift them as easily, though, as seventy-two pounds of jockey.'

Danilo was standing by the rails, watching. He turned as the mounted horses walked away, caught sight of us, and came straight across.

'Hi, Link. I've been looking out for you. How's about a beer?'

I said, 'Quentin,' (not two hours: ten minutes) 'this is Danilo Cavesey, Nerissa's nephew. And Danilo, this is Quentin van Huren, whose sister-in-law, Portia van Huren, was Nerissa's sister.'

'Gee,' Danilo said. His eyes widened and stayed wide, without blinking. He was more than ordinarily surprised.

'Good heavens,' van Huren exclaimed. 'I didn't even know she had a nephew.'

'I kinda dropped out of her life when I was about six, I guess,' Danilo said. 'I only saw her again this summer, when I was over in England from the States.'

Van Huren said he had only twice met Nerissa's husband, and never his brother, Danilo's father. Danilo said he had never met Portia. The two of them sorted out the family ramifications to their own content and seemed to meet in understanding in a very short time.

'Well, what do you know?' Danilo said, evidently pleased to the roots. 'Say, isn't that just too much?'

When Vivi and Sally and Jonathan rejoined us after the race they chattered about it like birds, waving their arms about and lifting their voices in little whoops.

'He's a sort of cousin,' said Sally positively. 'Isn't it the greatest fun?'

Even Jonathan seemed to brighten up at the idea of receiving the sunshine kid into the family, and the two of them presently bore him away on their own. I saw him looking back over his shoulder with a glance for me that was a lot older than anything Jonathan or Sally could produce.

'What a nice boy,' Vivi said.

'Nerissa is very fond of him,' I agreed.

'We must ask him over, while he is here, don't you think, Quentin? Oh look, do you see who's down there ... Janet Frankenloots ... haven't seen her for ages. Oh, do excuse me, Link ...' The great hat swooped off to meet the long-lost friend.

Van Huren was too depressingly right about Clifford Wenkins being at the races. To say that the Distribution Manager approached as directly as Danilo had done would be inaccurate: he made a crabwise deprecating semicircle, tripping over his feet, and ended damply by my side.

'Er ... Link, good to see you ... er, would you be Mr van Huren? Pleased ... er ... to meet you, sir.'

He shook hands with van Huren, who from long social practice managed not to wipe his palm on his trousers afterwards.

'Now. Er ... Link. I've tried to reach you a couple of times, but you never seem, er ... I mean ... I haven't

called you when you are ... er ... in. So I thought ...
well, I mean, er ... I would be certain to see you here.'

I waited without much patience. He pulled a batch of
papers hastily out of an inside pocket.

'Now, we want . . . that is to say, Worldic have
arranged ... er ... since you did the press interviews, I
mean ... they want you to go to ... let's see ... there's a
beauty competition to judge next Wednesday for Miss
Jo'burg ... and er ... guest of honour at the Ladies'
Kinema Luncheon Club on Thursday ... and on Friday
a fund-raising charity reception given by ... er ... our
sponsors for the premiere ... er, that is Bow-Miouw
Pet-food, of course ... and er ... well ... Saturday's ...
the official opening of er . . . the Modern Homes'
Exhibition ... all good publicity ... er ...'

'No,' I said. And for hell's sake don't lose your temper
here, I told myself severely.

'Er,' Wenkins said, seeing no danger signals. 'We ...
er ... that is, Worldic, do think ... I mean ... that you
really ought to cooperate ...'

'Oh they do.' I slowed my breathing deliberately.
'Why do you think I won't let Worldic pay my
expenses? Why do you think I pay for everything
myself?'

He was extremely unhappy. Worldic must have been
putting on the pressure from one side, and now I am
resisting him from the other. The beads sprang out on
his forehead.

'Yes, but ...' He swallowed. 'Well ... I expect ... I

mean . . . the various organizations might be prepared to offer . . . er . . . I mean . . . well, *fees*.'

I counted five. Squeezed my eyes shut and open. Said, when I was sure it would come out moderately, 'Mr Wenkins, you can tell Worldic that I do not wish to accept any of those invitations. In fact, I will go only to the premiere itself and a simple reception before or after, as I said.'

'But . . . We have told everybody that you will.'

'You know that my agent particularly asked you, right at the beginning, not to fix anything at all.'

'Yes, but Worldic say . . . I mean . . .'

Stuff Worldic, I thought violently. I said, 'I'm not going to those things.'

'But . . . you can't . . . I mean . . . *disappoint* them all . . . not now . . . they will not go to your films, if you don't turn up when . . . er . . . we've . . . er . . . well . . . promised you will.'

'You will have to tell them that you committed me without asking me first.'

'Worldic won't like it . . .'

'They won't like it because it will hurt their own takings, if it hurts anything at all. But it's their own fault. If they thought they could make me go to those functions by a species of blackmail, they were wrong.'

Clifford Wenkins was looking at me anxiously and van Huren with some curiosity, and I knew that despite my best intentions the anger was showing through.

I took pity on Clifford Wenkins and a grip on myself.

'Tell Worldic I will not be in Johannesburg at all next week. Tell them that if they had had the common sense to check with me first, I could have told them I am committed elsewhere, until the premiere.'

He swallowed again and looked even unhappier.

'They said I must persuade you . . .'

'I'm sorry.'

'They might even fire me . . .'

'Even for you, Mr Wenkins, I can't do it. I won't be here.'

He gave me a spanked-spaniel look which I didn't find endearing, and when I said no more he turned disgustedly away and walked off, stuffing the papers roughly into the side pocket of his jacket.

Van Huren turned his handsome head and gave me an assessing look.

'Why did you refuse him?' he asked. No blame in his voice; simply interest.

I took a deep breath: got the rueful smile out, and stifled the irritation which Clifford Wenkins had raised like an allergic rash.

'I never do those things . . . beauty contests and lunches and opening things.'

'Yes. But why not?'

'I haven't the stamina.'

'You're big enough,' he said.

I smiled and shook my head. It would have sounded pretentious to tell him that so-called 'personal appearances' left me feeling invaded, battered, and devoured, and that complimentary introductory speeches gave me nothing in return. The only compliment I truly appreciated was the money plonked down at the box-office.

'Where are you off to, next week, then?' he asked.

'Africa is huge,' I said, and he laughed.

We wandered back to look at the next batch of hopefuls in the parade ring, and identified number eight as Nerissa's filly, Lebona.

'She looks perfectly all right,' van Huren commented.

'She will start all right,' I agreed. 'And run well for three-quarters of the way. Then she'll tire suddenly within a few strides and drop right out, and when she comes back her sides will be heaving and she'll look exhausted.'

He was startled. 'You sound as if you know all about it.'

'Only guessing. I saw Chink run like that at Newmarket on Wednesday.'

'But you think they are all running to the same pattern?'

'The form book confirms it.'

'What will you tell Nerissa, then?'

I shrugged. 'I don't know . . . Probably to change her trainer.'

In due course we returned to the stands and watched Lebona run as expected. Van Huren seeming in no haste to jettison me for more stimulating company, and I well content to have him as a buffer state, the two of us, passing the cluster of tables and chairs under sun umbrellas, decided to sit down there and order refreshers.

For the first day since I had arrived, the sunshine had grown hot. No breeze stirred the fringes round the flowered umbrellas, and ladies in all directions were shedding their coats.

Van Huren, however, sighed when I commented on the good weather.

'I like winter best,' he said. 'When it's cold, dry, and sunny. The summers are wet, and far too hot, even up here on the highveld.'

'One thinks of South Africa as always being hot.'

'It is, of course. Once you get down near to sea level, it can be scorching even as early as this.'

The shadows of two men fell across the table, and we both looked up.

Two men I knew. Conrad: and Evan Pentelow.

I made introductions, and they pulled up chairs and joined us; Conrad his usual flamboyant self, scattering dear boys with abandon, and Evan, hair as unruly as ever, and eyes as hot.

Evan weighed straight in. 'You won't now refuse to turn up at the premiere of my *Man in a Car*, I hope.'

'You sound very proprietary,' I said mildly. 'It isn't altogether yours.'

'My name will come first in the credits,' he asserted aggressively.

'Before mine?'

Posters of Evan's films were apt to have Evan Pentelow in large letters at the top, followed by the name of the film, followed, in the last third of the space, by the actors' names all squashed closely together. Piracy, it was, or little short.

Evan glared, and I guessed he had checked my contract for the film, and found, as I had done, that in the matter of billing my agent had made no mistakes.

'Before the other director,' he said grudgingly.

I supposed that was fair. Although he had directed less than a quarter, the shape of the finished film would be his idea.

Van Huren followed the sparring with amusement and attention.

'So billing does matter as much as they say.'

'It depends,' I smiled, 'on who is sticking knives into whose back.'

Evan had no sense of humour and was not amused. He began instead to talk about the film he was going to make next.

'It's an allegory . . . every human scene is balanced by a similar one involving elephants. They were supposed to be the good guys of the action, originally, but I've been learning a thing or two about elephants. Did you know they are more dangerous to man than any other animal in Africa? Did you know that nothing preys on them except ivory hunters, and as ivory hunting is banned in the Kruger Park, the elephants are in the middle of a population explosion? They are increasing by a thousand a year, which means that in ten years there will be no room for any other animals, and probably no trees in the park, as the elephants uproot them by the hundred.'

Evan, as usual on any subject which took his attention, was dogmatic and intense.

'And do you know,' he went on, 'that elephants don't like Volkswagens? Those small ones, I mean. Elephants seldom attack cars ordinarily, but they seem to make a bee-line for Volkswagens.'

Van Huren gave a disbelieving smile which naturally stirred Evan to further passion.

'It's true! I might even incorporate it in the film.'

'Should be interesting,' Conrad said with more than a touch of dryness. 'Leaving a car around as bait at least makes a change from goats and tigers.'

Evan glanced at him sharply, but nodded. 'We go down to the park on Wednesday.'

Van Huren turned to me with a look of regret.

'What a pity you can't go down there too, Link, next week. You want somewhere to go, and you'd have liked it there. The game reserves are about all that's left of the old natural Africa, and the Kruger is big and open and still pretty wild. But I know the accommodation there is always booked up months ahead.'

I didn't think Evan would have wanted me in the least, but to my surprise he slowly said, 'Well, as it happens, we made reservations for Drix Goddart to be down there with us, but now he's not coming for a week or two. We haven't cancelled . . . there will be an empty bed, if you want to come.'

I looked at Conrad in amazement but found no clue in his raised eyebrows and sardonic mouth.

If it hadn't been for Evan himself I would have leapt at it; but I supposed that even he was a great deal preferable to Clifford Wenkins's programme. And if I didn't go to the Kruger, which very much appealed to me, where else?

'I'd like to,' I said. 'And thanks.'

CHAPTER EIGHT

Danilo fetched up at the sun-shade flanked by his two van Huren satellites.

Sally waited for no introductions to Conrad and Evan. She looked to see that she was not actually interrupting anyone in mid-sentence, and then spoke directly to her father.

'We told Danilo you were taking Link down the gold mine on Monday, and he wants to know if he could go too.'

Danilo looked slightly embarrassed to have his request put so baldly, but after only a fraction's hesitation van Huren said, 'Why, of course, Danilo, if you would like to.'

'I sure would,' he said earnestly.

'Gold mine?' said Evan intently, pouncing on the words.

'The family business,' explained van Huren, and scattered introductions all round.

'There could be great background material . . . a gold mine . . . something I could use one day.' He looked expectantly at van Huren who was thus landed unfairly with the choice of being coerced or ungracious. He took it in his stride.

'By all means join us on Monday, if you would care to.'

Evan gave him no chance to retract and included Conrad in the deal.

When they and the three young ones had all gone off to place their bets, I apologized to van Huren that his generosity should have been stretched.

He shook his head. 'It will be all right. We seldom take large parties of visitors down the mine as it slows or stops production too much, but we can manage four of you without a break in work, if you are all sensible, as I am sure you will be.'

By the end of the afternoon the number had grown to five, as Roderick Hodge also turned up at Germiston, and having learned of the expedition begged van Huren privately to be allowed to tag along with a view to a feature article in the *Rand Daily Star*.

I would have thought that gold mines were a stale topic in Johannesburg, but Roderick had his way.

I found him unexpectedly at my elbow while I was watching Tables Turned amble round the parade ring looking the prize colt he was not. Danilo and all the van Hurens had gone to tea with the Chairman, a meal I preferred to do without, and Conrad and Evan were away in the distance being accosted by the ever perspiring Clifford.

Roderick touched me on the arm, and said tentatively, 'Link?'

I turned. His fortyish face had grown new lines in the last few days and looked much too old for the length of his trendy hair and the boyish cut of his clothes.

'How is Katya?' I asked.

'She's fine. Remarkable, really.'

I said I was glad, and then asked if he often went to the races.

'No . . . actually I came to see you. I tried to get you at the Iguana Rock but they said you were at the races . . .'

'Did they indeed,' I murmured.

'Er . . .' he explained. 'I have what you might call a *source* there. Keeps me informed, you see.'

I saw. All over the world there was a grey little army which tipped off the Press and got tipped in return: hotel porters, railway porters, hospital porters, and anyone within earshot of VIP lounges at airports.

'I live this side of the city, so I thought I might just as well drift along.'

'A nice day,' I said.

He looked up at the sky as if it would have been all one to him if it had been snowing.

'I suppose so . . . Look, I got a call this morning from Joe . . . that's the chap who was setting up the radio equipment at Randfontein House.'

'I remember,' I said.

'He said he had taken that microphone to pieces, and

there was nothing wrong with it. The outer wire of the coaxial cable was of course connected to the metal casing, though . . .'

'Ah,' I interrupted. 'And what exactly is a coaxial cable?'

'Don't you know? It's an electric cable made of two wires, but one wire goes up the centre like a core, and the other wire is circular, outside it. Television aerial cables are coaxial . . . you can see that by the ends, where you plug them into the sets.'

'Oh yes,' I agreed. 'I see.'

'Joe says he found the earth wire and the live wire had been fastened to the wrong terminals in the power plug of the recorder he was using for Katya. He says people are warned over and over again about the dangers of doing that, but they still do it. The current would go straight through the mike's casing, and earth itself through whoever was holding it.'

I thought. 'Wouldn't the whole recorder had been live too?'

He blinked. 'Yes. Joe says that inside it must have been. But no one would have got a shock from it. The casing of the recorder was plastic, the knobs were plastic, and Joe himself was wearing rubber-soled shoes, which he says he always does anyway, as a precaution.'

'But he must have used that recorder before,' I protested.

'He says not. He says he plugged it in because it was just standing there when something went wrong with his own. He didn't know whose it was, and no one seems to have claimed it since.'

Arknold gave his jockey a leg up on to Tables Turned and the horses began to move out for the race.

I said, 'It was all very bad luck.'

'Joe thinks so,' he agreed. There was, however, a shade of doubt in his voice, and I looked at him enquiringly. 'Well . . . it's an appalling thing to say, but Joe wondered whether it could possibly have been a publicity stunt that went too far. He says that Clifford Wenkins was fussing round the electronic equipment after your first broadcast, and that you yourself set up the conference, and you did get the most fantastic Press coverage for saving Katya . . .'

'I agree it's an appalling thing to say,' I said cheerfully. 'Consider me appalled. Consider also that I have already wondered whether it was a publicity stunt set up by you and Katya . . . which went too far.'

He stared. Then relaxed. Then ruefully smiled.

'All right,' he said. 'Neither of us fixed it. How about our Clifford?'

'You know him better than I do,' I said. 'But although he seems to have sold his soul to Worldic Cinemas, he doesn't strike me as having the nerve or the ingenuity to fix it all up.'

'You fluster him,' Roderick observed. 'He isn't always as futile-seeming as he's been since you arrived.'

Further along the rails from us stood Danilo, watching Nerissa's colt with a smile on his frank and bonny face. I thought that if he had known he was so soon to inherit them, he would have been anxious instead.

Arknold joined him, and together they walked on to the stands to watch. Roderick and I tailed along after. We all watched Tables Turned set off at a great rate, run out of puff two furlongs from home, and finish a spent force.

Arknold, muttering under his breath and looking like thunder, bumped into me as he made his way down the stand steps to hold a post-mortem with the jockey.

He focused on me and said abruptly, 'It's too much, Mister. It's too much. That's a bloody good colt and he should have won by a mile in that company.' He shut his mouth like a trap, brushed past me, and thrust his way down through the crowd.

'Whatever's all that about?' Roderick asked casually; so casually that I remembered the *Rand Daily Star*, and didn't tell him.

'No idea,' I said, putting on a bit of puzzle: but Roderick's sceptical expression said that he similarly was remembering where I worked.

We walked down from the stands. I considered ways and means, and decided Klugvoigt was the best bet for what I wanted. So I drifted Roderick gently to where Conrad and Evan were discussing adjourning to the bar, inserted him into their notice, and left as he began telling Conrad the theories of Joe and the coaxial cable.

The Chairman was in his private box surrounded by

ladies in decorative hats. He saw me hovering alone, beckoned to me to come up the adjacent stairs, and when I reached his side, pressed into my hand some drowned whisky in a warmish glass.

'How are you doing?' he asked. 'Winning, I hope.'

'Not losing, anyway.' I smiled.

'What do you fancy in the next?'

'I'd have to see them in the parade ring first.'

'Wise fellow,' he agreed.

I admired the facilities. 'The stands look new,' I commented.

'Not long built,' he agreed. 'Very much needed, of course.'

'And the weighing room . . . from the outside it looks so comfortable.'

'Oh, it is, my dear chap.' A thought struck him. 'Would you care to see round inside it?'

'How very kind of you,' I said warmly and made ready-to-go-at-once movements so that he shouldn't forget. After a moment or two we parked our unfinished drinks and strolled easily across to the large square administrative block which housed the weighing and changing rooms on the ground floor and the racecourse offices upstairs.

The whole thing was modern and comfortable, a long way from all too many English equivalents. There was a large room furnished with easy-chairs where owners and trainers could sit in comfort to plan their coups and dissect their flops, but Klugvoigt whisked me past it into the inner recesses.

The jockeys themselves shared in the bonanza, being supplied with man-sized wire lockers for their clothes (instead of a peg), a sauna bath (as well as showers) and upholstered daybeds to rest on (instead of a hard narrow wooden bench).

The man I had hoped to see was lying on one of the black leather-covered beds supporting himself on one elbow. He was known to me via the number boards as K. L. Fahrden. He was Greville Arknold's jockey.

I told Klugvoigt I would be interested to speak to him, and he said sure, go ahead, he would wait for me in the reception room by the door, as there was someone there he too wanted to speak with.

Fahrden had the usual sharp fine bones with the usual lack of fatty tissue between them and the skin. His wary, narrow-eyed manner changed a shade for the better when Klugvoigt told him my name, but underwent a relapse when I said I was a friend of Mrs Cavesey.

'You can't blame me for her horses running so stinking,' he said defensively.

'I don't,' I said patiently. 'I only wanted to ask you how they felt to you personally, so that I could tell Mrs Cavesey what you said.'

'Oh. Oh, well, then.' He considered, and came across. 'They give you a good feel, see, at the start. Full of running, and revelling in it. Then you go pick 'em up, see, and there's bloody nothing there. Put on the pressure, see, and they blow up instant like.'

'You must have given them a lot of thought,' I said. 'What do you think is wrong with them?'

He gave me a sideways look. 'Search me,' he said.

'You must have a theory,' I urged.

'Only the same as anyone would,' he agreed reluctantly. 'And I'm not saying more than that.'

'Mm . . . Well, what do you think of Mr Arknold's head lad?'

'Barty? That great brute. Can't say as I've ever thought much about him. Wouldn't want to meet him alone on a dark night, if that's what you mean.'

It wasn't entirely what I meant, but I let it go. I asked him instead how he got on with Danilo.

'A real nice guy, that,' he said, with the first sign of friendliness. 'Always takes a great interest in Arknold's horses, of course, seeing as how so many of them are his aunt's.'

'Did you meet him when he was over here before?' I asked.

'Oh sure. He stayed in the hotel down in Summerveld, for a couple of weeks. A great guy. Always good for a laugh. He said he'd just been staying with his aunt, and she was a great girl. He was the only cheerful thing around, when the horses started running badly.'

'When was that?' I asked with sympathy in my voice.

'Oh, way back in June sometime. Since then there's

been every investigation you could think of, into why they flop. Dope tests, vets, the lot.'

'Is Arknold a good man to ride for?' I asked.

He closed up at once. 'More than my job's worth to say different.'

I fielded Klugvoigt from the reception room, thanked him, and walked back with him towards the parade ring. Someone button-holed him on the way, so I wandered by myself right across the course to the simple stand of plain wooden steps on the far side. From there one had a comprehensive view of the whole lay-out: the long sweep of stands, the small patch of sun umbrellas, the block of private boxes. Behind them all, the parade ring and the weighing room.

And round and about, mingling, chatting, exchanging information and sipping at cooling glasses, went Danilo and Arknold, Conrad and Evan, Roderick and Clifford Wenkins, and Quentin, Vivi, Jonathan and Sally van Huren.

I booked a telephone call to Charlie when I got back to the Iguana Rock that evening, and it came through punctually the next morning, Sunday, at ten o'clock.

We could hear each other as clearly as if we had been six miles apart instead of six thousand. She said she was glad I had called and glad that I wasn't electrocuted: yes, she said, it had been in all the papers at home yesterday, and one or two disgustedly hinted that it had all been a put-up job.

'It wasn't,' I said. 'I'll tell you all about it when I get home. How are the kids?'

'Oh, fine. Chris says he's going to be an astronaut, and Libby has managed to say "pool" when she wants to go in the water.'

'That's great,' I said, meaning Libby's advance, and Charlie said yes, it was great, it really was.

'I do miss you,' I said lightly, and she answered with equal lack of intensity, 'It seems a lot longer than four days since you went away.'

'I'll be back straight after the premiere,' I said. 'Before that I'm taking a look round a gold mine and then going to the Kruger National Park for a few days.'

'Lucky sod.'

'After the kids have gone back to school, we'll have a holiday somewhere, just by ourselves,' I said.

'I'll hold you to it.'

'You can choose, so start planning.'

'OK,' she said it casually, but sounded pleased.

'Look . . . I really rang about Nerissa's horses.'

'Have you found out what's wrong with them?'

'I don't know,' I said. 'But I have had a fairly cataclysmic idea. I can't be sure I'm right, though, until, or in fact unless, you can do something for me in England.'

'Shoot,' she said economically.

'I want you to take a look at Nerissa's will.'

'Wow.' She drew in a sharp breath. 'How on earth do I do that?'

'Ask her. I don't know how you'll manage it, but if she's had fun drawing it up, she might not mind talking about it.'

'Well . . . what exactly do you want me to look for if she lets me see it?'

'I want to know particularly if besides the horses she has left the residue of her estate to Danilo.'

'All right,' she said doubtfully. 'Is it very important?'

'Yes and no.' I half laughed. 'Young Danilo is out here in South Africa at this moment.'

'Is he?' she exclaimed. 'Nerissa didn't tell us that.'

'Nerissa doesn't know,' I said. I described the golden Danilo to her, and also Arknold, and explained how the horses all lost to the same pattern.

'Sounds like the trainer nobbling them,' she commented.

'Yes. I thought so too, at first. But now . . . well, I think it's the Californian kid, our Danilo.'

'But it can't be,' she objected. 'Whatever could he have to gain?'

'Death duties,' I said.

After a pause Charlie said doubtfully, 'You can't mean it.'

'I do mean it. It's a theory, anyway. But I can't begin to prove it.'

'I don't really see . . .'

'Imagine,' I said, 'that when Danilo went to see

Nerissa in the early summer, their first reunion after all those years, she told him she had Hodgkin's disease. He had only to look it up in a medical directory . . . he would find out it is always fatal.'

'Oh dear,' she sighed. 'Go on.'

'Nerissa liked him very much,' I said. 'Well . . . he's an attractive boy in many ways. Supposing that, after she'd decided to, she told Danilo she was leaving him her horses, and some money as well.'

'It's an awful lot of supposing.'

'Yes,' I agreed. 'Would you ask Nerissa? Ask her if she told Danilo what illness she had, and also if she told him what she was leaving him.'

'Darling, she'd be terribly distressed, at this stage, to find she was wrong about him.' Charlie herself sounded upset. 'She is so very pleased to have him to leave things to.'

'Just get her chatting on the subject, if you can, and ask her casually. I agree that it's important not to distress her. It might actually be better to let Danilo get away with it. In fact, I've been thinking about that for most of the night. He has been defrauding her of the prize money she might have won. How much would she mind?'

'She might even laugh. Like you did just now. She might even think it was a pretty bright idea.'

'Yes . . . Of course he has also been defrauding the South African betting public, but I suppose it's up to the racing authorities here to deal with it, if they catch him.'

'What makes you think it is Danilo?'

'It's so insubstantial,' I said with frustration. 'Mostly a matter of chance remarks and impressions, and terribly few facts. Well . . . for one thing, Danilo was around the horses when they started doing badly. Their jockey told me Danilo was in Africa then, in June, for a fortnight, which must have been just after he had stayed with Nerissa, because he talked about having seen her. After that he presumably went back to the States for a while, but the horses went on losing, so obviously he was not doing the actual stopping himself. It's difficult to see how he could ever have the opportunity of doing it himself, anyway, but he seems to have an understanding with Arknold's head lad: and I'll admit that all I have to go on *there*, is the way they look at each other. Danilo never guards his face, by the way. He guards his tongue, but not his face. So suppose it is Barty, the head boy, who is arranging the actual fixing, with suitable rewards from Danilo.'

'Well . . . if you are right . . . how?'

'There are only two completely undetectable ways which can go on safely for a long time . . . over-exercising, which loses the race on the gallops at home (though in that case it is always the trainer who's guilty, and people notice and talk) . . . and the way I think Barty must be using, the plain old simple bucket of water.'

Charlie said, 'Keep a horse thirsty, maybe even put lashings of salt in its feed, and then give it a bucket or two of water before the race?'

'Absolutely. The poor things can't last the distance with three of four gallons sloshing around in their stomachs. And as for Barty . . . even if he were not always around to supply the water at the right time, he has all the other lads intimidated to such an extent that they'd probably cut off their own ears if he told them to.'

'But,' she objected, 'if the head lad has been doing this for weeks and weeks surely the trainer would have cottoned on?'

'I think he has,' I agreed. 'I don't think he likes it, but he's letting it pass. He said it was "too much" when one of Nerissa's best colts got beaten out of sight yesterday in a poor class race. And then he himself gave me a version of what might be going on, and what may happen in the future. He accused me of implying that he was losing with the horses so that Nerissa would sell them: he would then buy them cheap, start winning, and sell them at a vast profit for stud. I had only vaguely been thinking along those lines, but he crystallized it as though the thought were by no means new to him. It was that, really, which set me wondering about Danilo. That, and the way he was smiling while he watched one of the horses go out to race. That smile was all wrong. Anyway . . . if he can reduce the value of the horses to nearly nil by Nerissa's death, there will be a great deal less duty to pay on them than if they were all winning. The difference would run into many thousands, considering there are eleven horses. That would be a profit well worth the outlay on a couple of trips to South Africa and payola for the head lad. I think they are going to change the system, but as the tax laws stand at present he would have to be in line for the residue of the estate, for there to be any point in his doing it.'

'Unscramble my brains,' Charlie said.

I laughed. 'Well. Estate duty will be paid on everything Nerissa owns. Then the separate bequests will be handed out. Then what is left will be the residue. Even though the horses are in South Africa, estate duty on them will be levied in England, because Nerissa lives there. So if the estate has to pay out all those thousands in death duties on the horses, there will be that many thousands less in the residue for Danilo to inherit.'

'Gotcha,' she said. 'And wow again.'

'Then, after they are safely his, he stops the watering lark, lets them win, sells them or puts them to stud, and collects some more lolly.'

'Oh, neat. Very neat.'

'Pretty simple, too.'

'I say,' she said. 'Isn't there anything we could try along the same lines? All that mountain of surtax we pay . . . and then when one of us dies we lose another terrific chunk of what we've paid tax on once already.'

I smiled. 'Can't think of anything which fluctuates in value so easily as a horse.'

'Let's buy some more, then.'

'And of course you have to know, pretty well to a month, exactly when you are going to die.'

'Oh damn it,' Charlie said laughing. 'Life is a lot of little green apples and pains in the neck.'

'I wonder if "a pain in the neck" originated from the axe.'

'The axeman cometh,' she said. 'Or for axe, read tax.'

'I'll bring you back a nugget or two from the gold mine,' I promised.

'Oh thanks.'

'And I'll telephone again on ... say ... Thursday evening. I'll be down in the Kruger Park by then. Would Thursday be OK for you?'

'Yes,' she said soberly, the fun vanishing like mist. 'I'll go over to Nerissa's before then, and see what I can find out.'

CHAPTER NINE

You can't keep a good Dakota down.

There were two of them waiting at the small Rand Airport near Germiston racecourse, sitting on their tail wheels and pointing their dolphin snouts hopefully to the sky.

We onloaded one of them at eight on Monday morning, along with several other passengers and a sizeable amount of freight. Day and time were unkind to Roderick, making it clearer than ever that letting go of a semblance of youth was long overdue. The mature man, I reflected, was in danger of wasting altogether the period when he could look most impressive: if Roderick were not careful he would slip straight from ageing youth to obvious old age, a mistake more often found in show business than journalism.

He was wearing a brown long-sleeved suede jacket with fringes hanging from every possible edge. Under that, an open-necked shirt in an orange-tan colour, trousers which were cut to prove masculinity, and the latest thing in desert boots.

741

Van Huren, at the other end of the scale in a dark city suit, arrived last, took control easily, and shunted us all aboard. The Dakota trip took an hour, and landed one hundred and sixty miles south, at an isolated mining town which had Welkom on the mat and on practically everything else.

The van Huren mine was on the far side from the airport, and a small bus had come to fetch us. The town was neat, modern, geometrical, with straight bright rows of little square houses and acres of glass-walled super-markets. A town of hygienic packaging, with its life blood deep underground.

Our destination looked at first sight to be a collection of huge whitish grey tips, one with its railway track climbing to the top. Closer acquaintance revealed the wheel-in-scaffolding at the top of the shaft, masses of administration buildings and miners' hostels, and dozens of decorative date palms. The short frondy trees, their sunlit leaf-branches chattering gently in the light breeze, did a fair job at beating the starkness, like gift-wrapping on a shovel.

Van Huren apologized with a smile for not being able to go down the mine with us himself: he had meetings all morning which could not be switched.

'But we'll meet for lunch,' he promised, 'and for that drink which you will all need!'

The guide someone a couple of rungs down the hier-archy had detailed to show us round was a grumpy young Afrikaaner who announced that he was Pieter

Losenwoldt and a mining engineer, and more or less explicitly added that his present task was a nuisance, an interruption of his work, and beneath his dignity.

He showed us into a changing room where we were to sink all differences in white overalls, heavy boots, and high-domed helmets.

'Don't take anything of your own down the mine except your underpants and a handkerchief,' he said dogmatically. 'No cameras.' He glowered at the equipment Conrad had lugged along. 'Camera flashes are not safe. And no matches. No lighters. When I say nothing, I mean nothing.'

'How about wallets?' Danilo demanded, antagonized and showing it.

Losenwoldt inspected him, saw a better looking, richer, more obviously likeable person than himself, and reacted with an even worse display of chips on shoulder.

'Leave everything,' he said impatiently. 'The room will be locked. Everything will be quite safe until you get back.'

He went away while we changed, and came back in similar togs.

'Ready? Right. Now, we are going 4,000 feet down. The lift descends at 2,800 feet a minute. It will be hot in places underground. Anyone who feels claustrophobic or ill in any way is to ask to return to the surface straight away. Understand?'

He got five nods and no affection.

He peered suddenly at me, speculating, then

dismissed the thought with pursed lips and a shake of the head. No one enlightened him.

'Your light packs are on the table. Please put them on.'

The light packs consisted of a flat power pack which one wore slung over the lumbar region, and a light which clipped on to the front of the helmet. A lead led from one to the other. The power packs fastened round one's waist with webbing, and were noticeably heavy.

Much like the seven dwarfs we tramped forth to the mine. The cage we went down in had half-sides only, so that the realities of rock burrowing hit at once. No comfort. A lot of noise. The nasty thought of all that space below one's booted feet.

It presumably took less than two minutes to complete the trip, but, as I was jammed tight between Evan, whose hot eyes looked for once apprehensive, and a six-foot-four twenty-stone miner who had joined with several cronies at the top, I couldn't exactly check it by stop-watch.

We landed with a clang at the bottom and disembarked. Another contingent were waiting to go up, and as soon as we were out, they loaded and operated the system of buzzers which got them clanking on their way.

'Get into the trucks,' said Losenwoldt bossily. 'They hold twelve people in each.'

Conrad surveyed the two trucks, which looked like wire cages on wheels with accommodation for one large dog if he curled himself up, and said sideways to me: 'Sardines have struck for less.'

I laughed. But the trucks did hold twelve; just. The last man in had to sit in the hole that did duty as doorway, and trust to what he could find to hang on to that he didn't fall out. Evan was last in. He hung on to Losenwoldt's overalls. Losenwoldt didn't like it.

Loaded to the gunnels, the trucks trundled off along the tunnel which stretched straight ahead for as far as one could see. The walls were painted white to about four feet: then there was a two-inch-deep bright red line, then above that the natural grey rock.

Conrad asked Losenwoldt why the red line was there: he had to shout to be heard, and he had to shout twice, as Losenwoldt was in no hurry to answer.

Finally he crossly shouted back. 'It is a guide to the tunnellers. When the tunnel is painted like this, they can see that they are making it straight and level. The red line is an eye-line.'

Conversation lapsed. The trucks covered about two miles at a fast trot and stopped abruptly at nowhere in particular. It was suddenly possible to hear oneself speak again, and Losenwoldt said, 'We get out here, and walk.'

Everyone unsqueezed themselves and climbed out. The miners strode purposefully away down the tunnel, but there was, it seemed, a set pattern for instructing visitors. Losenwoldt said ungraciously (but at least he said it), 'Along the roof of the tunnel you can see the cables from which we have the electric lights.' The lights were spaced overhead at regular intervals so that the whole tunnel was evenly lit. 'Beside it there is a live electric rail.' He pointed. 'That provides power for the trucks which take the rock along to the surface. The rock goes up in a faster lift, at more than 3,000 feet a minute. That big round pipe up there carries air. The mine is ventilated by blowing compressed air into it at many points.'

We all looked at him like kids round a teacher, but he had come to the end of that bit of official spiel, so he turned his back on us and trudged away down the tunnel.

We followed.

We met a large party of black Africans walking the other way. They were dressed as we were except that they were wearing sports jackets on top of their overalls.

Roderick asked, 'Why the jackets?'

Losenwoldt said, 'It is hot down here. The body gets accustomed. Without a jacket, it feels cold on reaching the surface. You can catch chills.'

Evan nodded wisely. We went on walking.

Eventually we came to a wider space where a second tunnel branched off to the right. Another party of Africans was collecting there, putting on jackets and being checked against a list.

'They have finished their shift,' Losenwoldt said, in his clipped way, hating us. 'They are being checked to make sure none of them is still underground when blasting takes place.'

'Blasting, dear boy?' said Conrad vaguely.

The expert eyed him with disfavour. 'The rock has to be blasted. One cannot remove it with pickaxes.'

'But I thought this was a gold mine, dear boy. Surely one does not need blasting to remove gold? Surely one digs out gravel and sifts the gold from it.'

Losenwoldt looked at him with near contempt. 'In California and Alaska, and in some other places, this may be so. In South Africa the gold is not visible. It is in minute particles in rock. One has to blast out the gold-bearing rock, take it to the surface, and put it through many processes, to remove the gold. In this mine, one has to take three tons of rock to the surface to obtain one ounce of pure gold.'

I think we were all struck dumb. Danilo's mouth actually dropped open.

'In some mines here in the Odendaalsrus gold field,' Losenwoldt went on, seeming not to notice the stunned reaction, 'it is necessary to remove only one and a half tons to get one ounce. These mines are of course the richest. Some need more than this one: three and a half or four tons.'

Roderick looked around him. 'And all the gold has been taken from here? And from where we came?'

His turn for the look of pity-contempt.

'This tunnel is not made through gold-bearing rock. This tunnel is just to enable us to get to the gold-bearing rock, which is in this part of the mine. It can only be reached at more than 4,000 feet underground.'

'Good God,' Conrad said, and spoke for us all.

Losenwoldt plodded grudgingly on with his lecture, but his audience were riveted.

'The reef . . . that is to say, the gold-bearing rock . . . is only a thin layer. It slopes underground from the north, being deepest beyond Welkom, further south. It extends for about eight miles from east to west, and about fourteen miles from north to south, but its limits are irregular. It is nowhere more than three feet in depth, and in this mine it is on average thirteen inches.'

He collected a lot of truly astonished glances, but only Danilo had a question.

'I suppose it must be worth it,' he said doubtfully. 'All this work and equipment, just to get so little gold.'

'It must be worth it or we would not be here,' said Losenwoldt squelchingly, which I at least interpreted as ignorance of the profit and loss figures of the business. But it must be worth it, I reflected, or van Huren would not live in a sub-palace.

No one else said anything. Seldom had cheerful casual conversation been more actively discouraged. Even Evan's natural inclination to put himself in charge of everything was being severely inhibited; and in fact, after looking apprehensive in the lift he now seemed the most oppressed of us all at the thought of millions of tons of rocks pressing down directly above our heads.

'Right,' said Losenwoldt with heavy satisfaction at having reduced the ranks to pulped silence. 'Now, switch on your helmet lights. There are no electric lights further along there.' He pointed up the branch tunnel. 'We will go to see the tunnelling in progress.'

He strode off without checking to see that we all followed, but we did, though Evan gave a backward glance in the direction of the shaft which would have warned a more careful guide not to take too much for granted.

The tunnel ran straight for a while and then curved to the right. As we approached the corner we could hear a constantly increasing roaring noise, and round on the new tack it increased noticeably.

'What's that noise?' Evan asked in a voice still the safe side of active anxiety.

Losenwoldt said over his shoulder, 'Partly the air-conditioning, partly the drilling,' and kept on going. The spaced electric light bulbs came to an end. The lights on our helmets picked the way.

Suddenly, far ahead, we could discern a separate glimmer of light beyond the beams we were ourselves throwing. Closer contact divided the glimmer into three individual helmet lights pointing in the same direction as ours: but these lit only solid rock. We were coming to the end of the tunnel.

The walls at this point were no longer painted a comforting white with a red line, but became the uniform dark grey of the basic rock, which somehow emphasized the fanaticism of burrowing so deep in the earth's undisturbed crust, in search of invisible yellow dust.

The air pipe stopped abruptly, the compressed air

roaring out from its open mouth. Beyond that the noise of the drilling took over, as aggressive to the eardrums as six fortissimo discotheques.

There were three miners standing on a wooden platform, drilling a hole into the rock up near the eight-foot-high roof. Our lights shone on the sweat on their dark skins and reflected on the vests and thin trousers they wore in place of everyone else's thick white overalls.

The racket came from a compressor standing on the ground, as much as from the drill itself. We watched for a while. Evan tried to ask something, but it would have taken a lip reader to get anywhere.

Finally Losenwoldt, with a tight mouth and tired eye-lids, jerked his head for us to go back. We followed him, glad about the lessening load on our ears. Walking last, I turned round where the air pipe ended, switched off my helmet light for a moment, and looked back. Three men on their scaffolding, intent on their task, enveloped in noise, and lit only by the glow-worms on their heads. When I had turned and gone, they would be alone with the primaeval darkness closing in behind them. I was left with a fanciful impression of a busy team of devils moleing along towards Inferno.

Once back in the wider section Losenwoldt continued our instruction.

'They were drilling holes about six feet deep, with tungsten drills. That,' he pointed, 'is a pile of drills.'

We looked where he pointed. The horizontal stack of six-foot rods by the tunnel wall had looked more like a heap of unused piping before: but they were solid metal rods about two inches in diameter with a blade of tungsten shining at the end of each.

'The rods have to be taken to the surface every day, to be sharpened.'

We nodded like wise owls.

'Those three men have nearly finished drilling for today. They have drilled many holes in the face of the tunnel. Each hole will receive its charge of explosive, and after the blasting the broken rock will be removed. Then the drillers return and start the process again.'

'How much tunnel can you make in one day?' Roderick asked.

'Eight feet a shift.'

Evan leant against the rock wall and passed a hand over a forehead that Clifford Wenkins could not have bettered.

'Don't you ever use pit-props?' he said.

Losenwoldt answered the face of the question and didn't see the fear behind it.

'Of course not. We are tunnelling not through earth, but through bedrock. There is no danger of the tunnel collapsing inwards. Occasionally, loosened slabs of rock fall from the roof or the wall. This usually happens in areas recently blasted. Where we see such loosened rocks, we pull them down, if we can, so that there is no danger of them falling on anyone later.'

Evan failed to look comforted. He dug out his handkerchief and mopped up.

'What sort of explosive do you use,' Danilo asked, 'for blasting?'

Losenwoldt still didn't like him, and didn't answer. Roderick, who was also interested, repeated the same question.

Losenwoldt ostentatiously stifled a sigh and replied in more staccato sentences than ever.

'It is Dynagel. It is a black powder. It is kept in locked red boxes fastened to the tunnel wall.'

He pointed to one of them a little further on. I had walked past two or three of them, padlocks and all, without wondering what they were for.

Danilo, with sarcasm, said to Roderick, 'Ask him what happens when they blast,' and Roderick did.

Losenwoldt shrugged. 'What would you expect? But no one sees the blasting. Everyone is out of the mine before the charges are detonated. No one returns down the mine for four hours after blasting.'

'Why not, dear boy?' drawled Conrad.

'Dust,' Losenwoldt said succinctly.

'When do we get to see this gold rock . . . this reef?' asked Danilo.

'Now.' Losenwoldt pointed along the continuation of the main tunnel. 'Further down there it will be very hot. There is a stretch with no air conditioning. Beyond that there is air again. Leave your helmet lights on, you will need them. Take care where you walk. The floor of the tunnel is rough in places.'

He finished with a snap and as before set off with his back to us.

Again we followed.

I said to Evan, 'Are you OK?' which irritated him into straightening his spine and flashing the eyes and saying of course he damn well was, did I think he was a fool.

'No,' I said.

'Right then.' He strode purposefully past me to get nearer to the pearls spat from Losenwoldt's lips and I again brought up the rear.

The heat further on was intense but dry, so that although one felt it, it produced no feeling of sweat. The tunnel at this point grew rough, with uneven walls, no painted lines, no lights, and a broken-up floor: it also sloped gradually downhill. We trudged on, boots crunching on the gritty surface.

The further we went, the more activity we came across. Men in white overalls were everywhere, busy, carrying equipment, with their helmet lights shining on other people's concentrated faces. The peak of each helmet tended to throw a dark band of shadow across every man's eyes, and once or twice I had to touch Roderick, who was in front of me, so that he would turn and reassure me that I was still following the right man.

At the end of the hot stretch it felt like stepping straight into the Arctic. Losenwoldt stopped there and consulted briefly with two other young miners he found talking to each other.

'We will split up here,' he said finally. 'You two with

me.' He pointed to Roderick and Evan. 'You two with Mr Anders.' He assigned Conrad and Danilo to a larger version of himself. 'You,' he pointed at me, 'with Mr Yates.'

Yates, younger than the others, appeared unhelpfully subservient to them, and spoke with a slight speech impediment in the order of a cleft palate. He gave me a twitchy smile and said he hoped I wouldn't mind, he wasn't used to showing people round, it wasn't usually his job.

'It's kind of you to do so,' I said soothingly.

The others were moving off in their little groups and were soon lost in the general crowd of white overalls.

'Come along then.'

We continued down the tunnel. I asked my new guide what the gradient was.

'About one in twenty,' he said. But after that he lapsed into silence, and I reckoned if I wanted to know any more I would have to ask. Yates did not know the conducted tour script like Losenwoldt, who in retrospect did not seem too bad.

Holes appeared from time to time in the left-hand wall, with apparently a big emptiness behind them.

'I thought this tunnel was through solid rock,' I observed. 'So what are those holes?'

'Oh ... we are now in the reef. The reef has been removed from much of that portion behind that wall. In a minute I'll be able to show you better.'

'Does the reef slope at one in twenty, then?' I asked.

He thought it a surprising question. 'Of course,' he said.

'That tunnel which is still being drilled, back there, where is that going?'

'To reach another area of reef.'

Yes. Silly question. The reef spread laterally for miles. Quite. Removing the reef must be rather like chipping a thin slice of ham out of a thick bread sandwich.

'What happens when all the reef is removed?' I asked. 'There must be enormous areas with nothing holding up the layers of rock above.'

He answered willingly enough. 'We do not remove all supports. For instance, the wall of the tunnel is thick, despite the holes, which are for blasting and ventilation purposes. It will hold the roof up in all this area. Eventually, of course, when this tunnel is worked out and disused, the layers will gradually close together. I believe that most of Johannesburg sank about three feet, as the layers below it closed together, after all the reef was out.'

'Not recently?' I said, surprised.

'Oh, no. Long ago. The Rand gold fields are shallower and mining began there first.'

People were carrying tungsten rods up the tunnel and others were passing us down it.

'We are getting ready to blast,' Yates said without being asked. 'All the drilling is finished and the engineers are setting the charges.'

'We haven't very long, then,' I said.

'Probably not.'

'I'd like to see how they actually work the reef.'

'Oh . . . yes. Just down here a bit further, then. I will take you to the nearest part. There are others further down.'

We came to a larger than usual hole in the wall. It stretched from the floor to about five feet up, but one could not walk straight through it, as it sloped sharply upwards inside.

He said, 'You will have to mind your head. It is very shallow in here.'

'OK,' I said.

He gestured to me to crawl in ahead of him, which I did. The space was about three feet high but extended out of sight in two directions. A good deal of ham had already gone from this part of the sandwich.

Instead of a firm rock floor, we were now scrambling over a bed of sharp-edged chips of rock, which rattled away as one tried to climb up over them. I went some way into the flat cavern and then waited for Yates. He was close behind, looking across to our right where several men lower down were working along a curving thirty-foot stretch of the far wall.

'They are making final checks on the explosive charges,' he said. 'Soon everyone will begin to leave.'

'This loose stuff we are lying on,' I said. 'Is this the reef?'

'Oh . . . no, not exactly. These are just chips of rock. See, the reef used to lie about midway up the stope.'

'What is the stope?'

'Sorry . . . the stope is what we are now in. The place we take the reef from.'

'Well . . . down there, in the part which is not blasted yet, how do you tell which is the reef?'

The whole thing looked the same to me. Dark grey from top to bottom. Dark grey uneven roof curving down in dark grey uneven walls, merging into dark grey shingle floor.

'I'll get you a piece,' he said obligingly, and crawled crabwise on his stomach over to where his colleagues were working. It was barely possible to sit up in the stope. Just about possible to rise to hands and knees, if one kept one's head down. I supported myself on one elbow and watched him borrow a small hand pick and lever a sliver of rock out of the far wall.

He scrambled back.

'There you are . . . This is a piece of reef.'

We focused both our lights on it. A two-inch-long grey sharp-edged lump with darker grey slightly light-reflecting spots and streaks on its surface.

'What are those dark spots?' I said.

'That's the ore,' he said. 'The paler part is just ordinary rock. The more of those dark bits there are in the reef, the better the yield of gold per ton of rock.'

'Then is this dark stuff . . . gold?' I asked dubiously.

'It has gold in it,' he nodded. 'Actually it is made up of four elements: gold, silver, uranium and chrome. When the reef is milled and treated, they are separated out. There is more gold than silver or uranium.'

'Can I keep this piece?' I asked.

'Certainly.' He cleared his throat. 'I am sorry, but they have a job for me to do down there. Could you possibly find your own way back up the tunnel? You cannot get lost.'

'That's all right,' I said. 'You go on, I don't want to interfere with your job.'

'Thank you,' he said, and scrambled away in haste to please the people who really mattered to him.

I stayed where I was, for a while, watching the engineers and peering into the interminable dug-out space uphill. The light of my helmet couldn't reach its limits: it stretched away into impenetrable blackness.

The workers below me were thinning out, returning to the tunnel to make their way back towards the shaft. I put the tiny piece of reef in my pocket, took a last look round, and began to inch my way back to the hole where I had come in. I turned round to go into the tunnel feet first, but as I started to shuffle backwards I heard someone begin to climb into the stope behind me, the light from his helmet flashing on my overalls. I stopped, to let him go by. He made a little forward progress and I glanced briefly over my shoulder to see who it was. I could see only the peak of his helmet, and shadow beneath.

Then my own helmet tipped off forward and a large chunk of old Africa clobbered me forcefully on the back of the head.

Stunned, it seemed to me that consciousness ebbed

away slowly: I fell dizzily down endless mine shafts with flashing dots before my eyes.

I had blacked out completely long before I had hit the bottom.

CHAPTER TEN

Blackness.

Nothing.

I opened my eyes. Couldn't see. Put my hand to my face to feel if my eyelids were open.

They were.

Thought was entirely disconnected. I didn't know where I was, or why I was there, or why I couldn't see. Time seemed suspended. I couldn't decide whether I was asleep or not, and for a while I couldn't remember my own name.

Drifted away again. Came back. Snapped suddenly into consciousness. Knew I was awake. Knew I was me.

Still couldn't see.

I moved; tried to sit up. Discovered I was lying on my side. When I moved, I heard the crunching noise and felt the sharp rock chips shifting against my pressure.

In the stope.

Cautiously I put up a hand. The rock ceiling was a couple of feet above my head.

No helmet on my head. A tender lump on the back of it and a thumping pain inside it.

Bloody hell, I thought. I must have bashed my head. I'm in the stope. I can't see because there isn't any light. Everyone has left the mine. And the blasting charges will go off at any minute.

For a paralysing age I couldn't think beyond the fact that I was going to be blown to bits before I had even finished realizing it. After that I thought it might have been better if I'd been blown to bits before I woke up. At least I wouldn't now be awake worrying. After that, and not before time, I began wondering what to do.

Light, first.

I felt around to my back, found the lead from the power pack and gently pulled it. The other end scraped towards me over the choppy shingle, but when I picked up the torch I knew I wasn't going to get any light. The glass and the bulb were both smashed.

The light unit had come off the bracket on the helmet. I felt around with an outstretched hand, but couldn't find the helmet.

Must get out, I thought urgently, and in the same split second wondered . . . which way was out.

I made myself stay still. The last thing I remembered was agreeing with Yates that I could find my own way back. I must have been stupid enough to try to raise my head too high. Must literally have hit the roof. I couldn't remember doing it. The only thing that seemed clear was that I had smashed my helmet light when I fell, and that no one had seen me lying there in the dark.

Bloody fool, I cursed myself. Clumsy bloody fool, getting into this mess.

Gingerly, with one arm outstretched, I shifted myself a foot forward. My fingers found nothing to touch except stone chips.

I had to know which way I was going. Otherwise, I thought, I may be crawling away from safety, not towards it. I had to find the hole in the tunnel.

I picked up a handful of the flinty pebbles and began throwing them methodically round in a circle, starting on my right. It was an erratic process, as some hit the roof and some the ground, but enough went far enough before they fell to assure me that there was a small space all around me in front.

I rolled over on to my back and the power pack dug into me. I unfastened the webbing and pulled it off. Then I threw another lot of stones in arc round my legs.

The wall of the tunnel was there. A lot of the stones hit it.

My heart by then was thudding so much it was deafening me. Shut up, shut up, I said to myself. Don't be so bloody scared, it isn't of any practical use.

I threw more stones, this time not to find the wall, but the hole in it. I found it almost at once. Threw more stones to make sure: but there it had to be, just to the left of where my feet were pointing, because all the stones that went over there were falling further away, and clattering after they landed. They weren't round enough to roll, but heavy enough to continue downhill when they fell. Downhill ... on the steep little slope from the stope into the tunnel.

More stones. I moved my feet, then my whole body, until the hole was straight in front over my toes. Then on my elbows and my bottom, keeping my head well back, I shuffled forwards.

More stones. Hole still there.

More shuffling. Another check.

It couldn't have been more than ten feet. Felt like ten miles.

I tentatively swept my arms around in the air. Could feel the roof, nothing else.

Went forward another two or three feet. Felt around with my arms. Touched solid rock. Ahead, to the right.

Another foot forward. Felt my feet turn abruptly downwards, bending my knees. Put both my hands out sideways and forwards and felt rock on both sides. Half-way out of the hole ... and gingerly, lying flat, I inched forward until my feet scrunched on the tunnel floor. Even then I bent my knees and continued slithering without raising my head, all too aware of the hard sharpness of the rock above the vulnerability of my unhelmeted skull.

I ended on my knees in the tunnel, gasping and feeling as frightened as ever.

Think.

The holes had been in the left-hand wall, as we came

down. Once in the tunnel, Yates had said, I couldn't get
lost.

OK. Turn right. Straight forward. Dead simple.

I stood up carefully, and with the hole at my back,
turned left. Put my hand on the rough rock wall. Took a
step forward.

The scrunch of my boot on the rock floor made me
realize for the first time how quiet it was. Before, I had
had both the stones and my own heart to fill my ears.
Now, there was nothing. The silence was as absolute as
the darkness.

I didn't waste time brooding about it. Scrunched
ahead as fast as I dared, step by careful step. No
sound . . . that meant that the air-conditioning had been
switched off . . . which hardly mattered, there was a
mineful still to breathe . . . even if it was hot.

My hand lost the wall suddenly, and my heart set up a
fresh chorus. Taking a grip on my breath I took a step
backwards. Right hand back on wall. OK. Breathe out.
Now, kneel down, grope along floor, keep in contact
with wall on right . . . navigate past another of the holes
which led through to the stope.

Holes which would let the blast out of the stope, when
the charges exploded.

Blast travelled far when confined in a long narrow
space. Blast was a killing force, as deadly as flying rocks.

Oh God, I thought. Oh hell's bloody bells. What did
one think about if one were probably going to die at any
minute?

I thought about getting as far back up the mine as quickly as I could. I thought about not losing contact with the right-hand wall when I passed the holes in it, because if I did I might turn round in the darkness and find the other wall instead, and go straight back towards the explosion. I didn't think about anything else at all. Not even about Charlie.

I went on. The air became hotter and hotter. The stretch that had been hot coming down was now an assault on the nerve endings.

Struggling on, I couldn't tell how fast I was going. Very slowly, I imagined. Like in a nightmare, trying to flee from a terror at one's heels, and not being able to run.

I got back in the end to the wider space, and the explosion still hadn't happened. Another explosion was due to take place down the branch tunnel also . . . but the bend in the tunnel should disperse some of the blast.

Beginning at last to let hope creep in, and keeping my hand on the right-hand wall literally for dear life, I trudged slowly on. Two miles to go, maybe, to the bottom of the shaft . . . but every step taking me nearer to safety.

Those lethal pockets of dynagel never did explode; or not while I was down the mine.

One minute I was taking another step into darkness. The next, I was blinded by light.

I shut my eyes, wincing against the brightness, and I

stopped walking and leaned against the wall instead. When I opened my eyes again, the electric lights were blazing in all their glory, and the tunnel looked as solid, safe, and reassuringly painted, as it had done on the way in.

Weakened by relief, I shifted off the wall and went on again, with knees that were suddenly trembling, and a head that was back to aching like a hang-over.

There was a background hum now again in the mine, and from far away up the tunnel a separate noise detached itself and grew louder: the rattle of the wire cage trucks making the outward journey. Eventually it stopped and then there was the sound of several boots, and then finally, round a shallow curve, came four men in white overalls.

Hurrying.

They spotted me, and began to run. Slowed and stopped just before they reached me, with relief that I was mobile showing on their faces. Losenwoldt was one of them: I didn't know the others.

'Mr Lincoln . . . are you all right?' one of them asked anxiously.

'Sure,' I said. It didn't sound right. I said it again. 'Sure.' Much better.

'How did you get left behind?' Losenwoldt said reprovingly, shifting all possible blame from himself. Not that I would have allotted him any: he was just forestalling it.

I said, 'I'm sorry to have been such a nuisance . . . I

think I must have hit my head and knocked myself out, but I can't actually remember how . . .' I wrinkled my forehead. 'So damned stupid of me.'

One of them said, 'Where were you, exactly?'

'In the stope,' I said.

'Good grief . . . You probably lifted your head too sharply . . . or maybe a piece of rock fell from the roof and caught you.'

'Yes,' I said.

Another of them said, 'If you were unconscious in the stope, however did you get back here?'

I told them about the stones. They didn't say anything. Just looked at each other.

One of them walked round my back and after a moment said, 'There's some blood on your hair and down your neck, but it looks dry . . . I don't think you're still bleeding.' He came round to my side. 'Do you feel all right to walk to the trucks? We brought a stretcher . . . just in case.'

I smiled. 'Guess I can walk.'

We walked. I asked, 'How did you discover I was down here?'

One of them said ruefully, 'Our system of checking everyone is out of the mine before blasting is supposed to be infallible. And so it is, as far as the miners are concerned. But visitors . . . you see, we don't often have small groups of unofficial visitors, like today. Mr van Huren seldom invites anyone, and no one else is allowed to. Nearly all the visitors we have here are official tourist groups, of about twenty people, and the mine more or less stops while we show them round, but we only do that every six weeks or so. We don't usually blast at all, on those days. Today, though, one of your party felt ill and went back before the others, and I think everyone took it for granted that you had gone with him. Tim Yates said when he last saw you, you were just about to return up the tunnel.'

'Yes . . .' I agreed. 'I remember that.'

'The other three visitors went up together, and the checkers accounted for every miner, so we assumed everyone was out, and were all set to detonate . . .'

A tall thin man took up the story. 'Then one of the men who counts the numbers going up and down in the lift said that one more had gone down than had come up. The shift checkers said it was impossible, each group had been checked out by name. The lift man said he was sure. Well . . . that only left the visitors. So we checked them. The three in the changing room said you hadn't changed yet, your clothes were still there, so you must be in the first-aid room with one called Conrad, who had not felt well.'

'Conrad,' I exclaimed. I had thought they meant Evan. 'What was wrong with him?'

'I think they said he had an attack of asthma. Anyway, we went and asked him, and he said you hadn't come up with him.'

'Oh,' I said blankly. Certainly, if I had been with him I

would have gone up, but I hadn't seen him at all after we had separated at the beginning of the reef.

We came to the trucks and climbed in. A lot of space with only five people instead of twelve.

'The one who was ill,' Losenwoldt stated virtuously, 'the stout one with the droopy moustache, he was not with me. If he had been, of course I would have escorted him back to the trucks, and of course I would have known you were not with him.'

'Of course,' I said dryly.

We clattered back along the tunnel to the bottom of the shaft, and from there, after the exchange of signal buzzes, rose in the cage through three-quarters of a mile of rock up to the sunlight. Its brilliance was momentarily painful, and it was also cold enough to start me shivering.

'Jacket,' exclaimed one of my escorts. 'We took down a blanket . . . should have put it round you.' He hurried off into a small building by the shaft and came back with a much used tweed sports coat, which he held for me to put on.

There was an anxious-looking reception committee hovering around: Evan, Roderick, Danilo, and van Huren himself.

'My dear fellow,' he said, peering at me as if to reassure himself that I was real. 'What can I say?'

'For heaven's sake,' I said, 'it was my own fault and I'm terribly sorry to have caused all this fuss . . .' Van Huren looked relieved and smiled, and so did Evan, Roderick and Danilo. I turned back to the three strangers who had come down for me: Losenwoldt had already gone. 'Thank you,' I said. 'Thank you very much.'

They all grinned. 'We want payment,' one said.

I must have looked bewildered. I was wondering what was right. How much.

'Your autograph,' one of them explained.

'Oh . . .' I laughed. 'OK.'

One of them produced a notebook, and I wrote a thank-you to each of them, on three separate pages. And cheap at the price, I thought.

The mine's doctor swabbed stone dust from the cut on my head, said it wasn't deep, nothing serious, didn't need stitching, didn't need a plaster, even, unless I wanted one . . .

'I don't,' I said.

'Good, good. Swallow these, then. In case you develop a headache.'

I swallowed obediently. Collected Conrad, now breathing normally again, from a rest room next door, and followed directions to the bar and dining-room for lunch. On the way, we swopped operations, so to speak. Neither of us felt much pleased with himself.

The five of us sat at a table with Quentin van Huren, plus two other senior executives whose names I never learned. My narrow escape was chewed over by every-one all over again, and I said with feeling to Roderick that I would be much obliged if he would keep my embarrassment out of his inky columns.

He grinned. 'Yeah . . . Much better copy if you'd been blown up. Not much news value in a checker doing his job properly.'

'Thank God for that,' I said.

Conrad looked at me sideways. 'There must be a jinx on you in South Africa, dear boy. That's the second time you've been close to extinction within a week.'

I shook my head. 'No jinx. Just the opposite. I've survived twice. Look at it that way.'

'Only seven lives left,' Conrad said.

The talk worked back to gold. I suspected that in Welkom it always did, like Newmarket and horses.

'Say, how do you get it out of the rock?' Danilo demanded. 'You can't even see it.'

Van Huren smiled indulgently. 'Danilo, it is simple. You crush the rock in mills until it is powdered. You add cyanide of potassium, which holds the gold particles in solution. You add zinc, to which the gold particles stick. You then wash out the acid. You then separate the zinc from the gold again, using aqua regia, and finally you retrieve the gold.'

'Oh, simple,' Conrad agreed. 'Dear boy.'

Van Huren warmed to him, and smiled with pleasure. 'That is not exactly all. One still has to refine the gold . . . to remove impurities by melting it to white heat in giant crucibles, and pouring it out into bricks. The residue flows away, and you are left with the pure gold.'

Danilo did a rapid calculation. 'You'll have gotten around three thousand five hundred tons of reef out of the mine, for one little old brick.'

'That's so,' agreed van Huren, smiling. 'Give or take a ton or two.'

'How much do you bring out in a week?' Danilo asked.

'Just over forty thousand metric tons.'

Danilo's eyes flickered as he did the mental arithmetic. 'That means ... er ... about eleven and a half gold bricks every week.'

'Do you want a job in the accounting department, Danilo?' asked van Huren, much amused.

But Danilo hadn't finished. 'Each brick weighs 71 lbs, right? So that makes ... let's see ... around 800 lbs of gold a week. Say, what's the price of gold per ounce? Gee, this is sure the right business to be in. What a gas!' He was deeply stimulated, as he had been by the whole trip, with a strong inner excitement shining out of his eyes. An attraction towards money-making, and the calculations needed to work out estate-duty dodging, seemed to me to be all of a piece.

Van Huren, still smiling, said, 'You're forgetting the wages, the maintenance, and the shareholders. There are only a few grains of dust left after they've all taken their cut.'

Danilo's curving mouth showed he didn't believe it.

Roderick shot an orange cuff out of the brown suede sleeve to reveal half a ton of tiger's eye doing duty as a cufflink.

'Don't you own the mine altogether, then, Quentin?' he asked.

The executive and van Huren himself both smiled indulgently at Roderick for his naïvety.

'No,' van Huren said. 'My family own the land and the mineral rights. Technically, I suppose, we do own the gold. But it takes an enormous amount of capital, many millions of rands, to sink a shaft and build all the surface plant needed. About twenty-five years ago my brother and I floated a company to raise capital to start drilling, so the company has hundreds of private shareholders.'

'That mine doesn't look twenty-five years old,' I objected amiably.

Van Huren shifted his smiling eyes in my direction and went on explaining.

'The part you saw this morning is the newest tunnel, and the deepest. There are other tunnels at higher levels ... in past years we have taken out all the up-slope areas of the reef.'

'And there's still a lot left?'

Van Huren's smile had the ease of one who would never be short of a thousand. 'It will see Jonathan out,' he said.

Evan chose to find the mechanics and economics less interesting than the purpose, and waved his arms about as he pinned every gaze down in turn with the fierce eyes and declaimed with his usual intensity.

'What is gold for, though? This is what we should be asking. What everyone should be asking. What is the *point*? Everyone goes to so much trouble to get it, and pays so much for it, and it has no real *use*.'

'Gold-plated lunar bugs,' I murmured.

Evan glared at me. 'Everyone digs it out of the ground here and puts it back underground at Fort Knox, where it never sees daylight again ... Don't you see ... the whole thing is *artificial*? Why should the whole world's wealth be based on a yellow metal which has no *use*?'

'Good for filling teeth,' I said conversationally.

'And for pure radio contacts in transistor units,' Roderick added, joining the game.

Van Huren listened and watched as if he found the entertainment a nice change for a Monday. I stopped baiting Evan, though, because after seeing the mine I half held his views.

I travelled back to Johannesburg in the Dakota that evening sitting next to Roderick and feeling a trifle worn. A hot afternoon spent walking round the surface buildings of a mine, watching gold being poured from a crucible, seeing (and hearing) the ore being crushed, and visiting one of the miners' hostels, had done no good at all to a throbbing head. Half a dozen times I had almost dropped out, but, especially with Roderick's ready typewriter in the background, I hadn't wanted to make a fuss.

The visit to the hostel had been best: lunch was being cooked for the next surface shift off work, and we tasted it in the kitchen. Vast vats of thick broth with a splendid flavour, vegetables I couldn't identify and hadn't the energy to ask about, and thick wads of cream-coloured mealie bread, a sort of fatless version of pastry.

From there we went next door into the hostel's bar, where the first of the returning shift were settling down to the serious business of drinking what looked like half-gallon plastic tubs of milky cocoa.

'That's Bantu beer,' said our afternoon guide, who had proved as sweet as Losenwoldt was sour.

We drank some. It had a pleasant dry flavour but tasted nothing like beer.

'Is it alcoholic, dear boy?' Conrad asked.

The dear boy said it was, but weak. Considering that we saw one man dispatch his whole tubful in two great draughts, the weakness was just as well.

Our guide beckoned to one of the men sitting at a table with his colleagues, and he got to his feet and came over. He was tall and not young, and he had a wide white grin which I found infectious.

The guide said, 'This is Piano Nyembezi. He is the checker who insisted we had left someone down the mine.'

'Was it you?' I asked with interest.

'*Yebo*,' he said, which I later learned meant yes in

Zulu. ('No' turned out to consist of a click, a glottal stop, and an 'aa' sound. As far as a European was concerned, it was impossible to say no in a hurry.)

'Well, Piano,' I said. 'Thank you very much.' I put out my hand and he shook it, an event which drew large smiles from his friends, an indrawn breath from our guide, a shake of the head from Roderick and no reaction whatsoever from Evan, Conrad or Danilo.

There was a certain amount of scuffling in the background, and then one of the others brought forward a well-thumbed copy of a film magazine.

'It is Piano's paper,' the newcomer said, and thrust it into his hands. Nyembezi looked embarrassed, but showed me what it was. Full page, and as boring-looking as usual.

Wrinkling my nose I took the magazine from him and wrote across the bottom of my picture, 'I owe my life to Piano Nyembezi', and signed my name.

'He'll keep that for ever,' the guide said.

Until tomorrow, perhaps, I thought.

The Dakota droned on. The evening sun fell heavily across my eyelids as we banked round on to a new course, and I gingerly lifted my head off the seat-back to put it down the other way. The cut on my head, though not deep, was sore.

For some reason the small movement triggered off a

few sleepy nerve cells, and in a quiet fashion I remembered that there had been someone with me in the stope.

I remembered I had been turning round to leave feet first, and had stopped to let someone else in. I remembered that I hadn't seen his face: didn't know who he was.

If he had been there when I bashed my head, why on earth hadn't he helped me?

Such was my fuzzy state of mind that it took me a whole minute more to move on to the conclusion that he hadn't helped me because he'd applied the rock himself.

I opened my eyes with a jolt. Roderick's face was turned towards mine. I opened my mouth to tell him. Then I shut it again, firmly. I did not in the least want to tell the *Rand Daily Star*.

CHAPTER ELEVEN

I used a lot of the time I could more profitably have spent sleeping that night in coming to terms with the thought that someone might have tried to kill me.

Didn't know who. Couldn't guess why. And still was not certain whether my memory was complete: perhaps the other man in the stope had gone away again, and I had forgotten it.

Also, even if I had been 100 per cent certain, I didn't know what I should do about it.

Telephone van Huren? Start an investigation? But there had been so many people down the mine, all dressed alike, and half in darkness. Any investigation was going to produce more talk and doubt than results, and 'Lincoln complains of attempted murder' were gossip-column snippets I could do without.

Twice within a week, Conrad had said, 'Close to extinction.'

It didn't make sense. It was only in films that the chaps I played got threatened and attacked, and made miraculous escapes.

Yet if I did nothing about it, what then? If someone really had been trying to kill me, there was nothing to stop him trying again. How could I possibly protect myself every minute of every day . . . especially against unforeseen things like microphones and rocks in gold mines?

If . . . and I wasn't altogether convinced . . . two murder attempts had been made, they had both been arranged to look like accidents. So it was of little use taking future precautions against things like poison and bullets and knives-in-the-back down dark alleys. One would have to beware instead of cars with no brakes, deadly insects in one's shoes, and disintegrating balconies.

I shied away for a long time from thinking about *who*, for it had to be someone who had been down in the mine.

A miner who didn't like my films taking steps to avoid sitting through any others? He wouldn't have to kill me: could simply vote with his feet.

Someone smouldering from ungovernable professional jealousy? The only person I knew of who regularly swore undying hatred was Drix Goddart, but he was not yet in South Africa, let alone 4,000 feet under Welkom.

None of the people working the mine had known I was going to be there, and before the incident, none of them had used my name.

That left . . . Oh hell, I thought. Well . . . it left

Evan ... and Conrad ... and Danilo ... and Roderick. And also van Huren, who owned a lot of souls and could have things done by proxy.

As for *why* ... Evan's professional resentment was surely not obsessive enough, and Danilo didn't know my guess of what he was up to with the horses; and in any case, even if he did, he wouldn't try to cover up such a minor crime with murder. More likely to confess and laugh, I would have thought, and meet a warning-off with a what-the-hell shrug.

Motives for Conrad, Roderick and van Huren took even less cogitation. I couldn't rake up a decent one between them.

They had all (except Conrad who had been in the surgery) looked relieved when I stepped safely out of the mine ... could they possibly have looked relieved just because I said I couldn't remember how I got knocked out?

It all seemed so improbable. I couldn't imagine any of them plotting away in murky labyrinths of villainy. It didn't make sense. I must, I concluded, be imagining things. I had been involved in too much fiction, and I had begun to project it on to reality.

I sighed. Realized that my head had stopped aching and that the unsettled feeling of concussion was subsiding, and presently, imperceptibly, went to sleep.

In the morning the night thoughts seemed even more preposterous. It was Conrad who had suggested a con-

nection between the mike and the mine; and Conrad
had got it wrong.

Roderick telephoned at breakfast time. Would I care to
have dinner at his flat, with Katya, just the three of us
and no fuss: and when I hesitated for a few seconds over
replying, he added quickly that it would all be strictly off
the record, anything I said would not be taken down and
used against me.

'OK,' I agreed, with a smile in my voice and reservations in my mind. 'Where do I find you?'

He told me the address, and said, 'That chauffeur of
yours will know where to find it.'

'Oh. Yes,' I agreed.

I put the receiver down slowly: but there was no
reason why he shouldn't know about the hired car-and-
driver, and there was of course his source at the Iguana.
Roderick had all along known where I was going, what I
was doing, and how often I brushed my teeth.

Almost before I had taken my hand off it, the telephone rang again.

Clifford Wenkins. Could he, er, that was to say, would
it be convenient for him to come to the club that morning
to discuss, er, details, for the, er, premiere?

Er yes, I said.

After that, Conrad rang. Was I going to travel down
to the Kruger Park with him and Evan?

'How long are you staying there?' I asked.

'About ten days, I should think.'

'No, then. I'll have to come back by next Tuesday, at the latest. I'll drive down separately. It will be better anyway to have two cars, with you and Evan concentrating on locations.'

'Yeah,' he said, sounding relieved: hadn't wanted to spend a week at close quarters keeping Evan and me off each other's throats, I imagined.

They would come around for a drink before lunch, he said. Evan, it appeared, was bursting with inspirations for his new film. (When was he not?)

After that, Arknold.

'Look, Mister Lincoln. About Mrs Cavesey's horses . . . Look . . .' He petered heavily out.

After waiting in vain for him to start up again I said, 'I'll be here all morning, if you'd care to come over.'

Three heavy breaths. Then he said, 'Perhaps. Might be as well. Yes. All right. About eleven, then, after I've watched the horses work.'

'See you,' I said.

Hot sunshine, blue sky.

I went downstairs and drank my coffee out on the terrace, and read the newspaper. Close columns filled with local issues, all assuming a background of common knowledge which I didn't have. Reading them was like going into a film halfway through.

A man had been murdered in Johannesburg: found two days ago, with a wire twisted round his neck.

With a shiver I put down the paper. No one was trying to murder me. I had decided it was nonsense. Another man's death had no business to be raising hairs on my skin. The trouble was, no one had told my subconscious that we were all through with red alerts.

'Morning,' said a fresh young voice in my ear. 'What are you doing?'

'Watching the flowers grow.'

She sat down opposite me, grinning all over her fifteen-year-old face.

'I've come to play tennis.'

She wore a short white dress, white socks, white shoes, and carried two racquets in zipped waterproof covers. Her dark shoulder-length hair was held back by a green head-band, and the van Huren wealth spoke as eloquently as ever in her natural confidence and poise.

'Coffee?' I suggested.

'Rather have orange juice.'

I ordered it.

'Didn't you just love the gold mine?' she demanded.

'I just did,' I agreed, imitating Danilo's accent, as she had done his turn of phrase.

She wrinkled her nose, amused. 'You never miss a damn thing, do you? Dad says you have an intuitive mind, whatever the hell that is.'

'It means I jump to conclusions,' I said.

She shook her head dubiously. 'Uhuh. He seemed to think it was good.'

The orange juice came and she drank some, clinking the ice. She had long dark eyelashes and more cream than peaches. I stifled as always the inner lurch of regret that young girls like Sally gave me: my own daughter might grow up as pretty, but the zest and the flash would be missing.

She put down the glass and her eyes searched the hotel buildings behind me.

'Have you seen Danilo anywhere?' she said. 'The swine said he'd be here at ten, and it's a quarter after already.'

'He was busy doing sums all yesterday,' I said gravely. 'I expect they wore him out.'

'What sums?' she said suspiciously.

I told her.

She laughed. 'He can't help doing sums, then, I shouldn't think. All Saturday at the races, he was doing it. A living computer, I called him.' She took another orange sip. 'I say, did you know he's a terrific gambler? He had ten rand on one of those horses. *Ten rand!*'

I thought van Huren had made a sensible job of her, if a ten-rand bet still seemed excessive.

'Mind you,' she added, 'The horse won. I went with him to collect the winnings. Twenty-five rand, would you believe it? He says he often wins. He was all sort of gay and laughing about it.'

'Everyone loses in the end,' I said.

'Oh, don't be such a downpour,' she exploded. 'Just like Dad.'

Her eyes suddenly opened wider, and she transferred her attention to somewhere behind me.

Danilo joined us. White shorts, sturdy sunburned legs, light blue windcheater hanging open.

'Hi,' he said happily, including us both.

'Hi,' echoed Sally, looking smitten.

She left me and the half-finished orange juice without a backward glance, and went off with the bright boy as girls have been going off since Eve. But this girl's father had a gold mine; and Danilo had done his sums.

Arknold came, and the reception desk directed him to the garden. He shook hands, sat down, huffed and puffed, and agreed to a beer. Away in the distance Danilo and Sally belted the ball sporadically over the net and laughed a lot in between.

Arknold followed my gaze, recognized Danilo, and consolidated his indecision in a heavy frown.

'I didn't know Danilo would be here,' he said.

'He can't hear you.'

'No ... but ... Look, Mister ... Do you mind if we go indoors?'

'If you like,' I agreed; so we transferred to the lounge, where he was again too apprehensive to come to the boil, and finally up to my room. One could still see the tennis courts; but the tennis courts couldn't see us.

He sat, like Conrad, in the larger of the two armchairs, seeing himself as a dominant character. The slab-like features made no provision for subtle nuances of feeling to show in changing muscle tensions round eyes, mouth or jaw line, so that I found it as nearly impossible as always to guess what he was thinking. The overall impression was of aggression and worry having a ding-dong: the result, apparent indecision about whether to attack or placate.

'Look,' he said in the end. 'What are you going to tell Mrs Cavesey when you get back to England?'

I considered. 'I haven't decided.'

He thrust his face forward like a bulldog. 'Don't you go telling her to change her trainer.'

'Why precisely not?'

'There's nothing wrong with the way I train them.'

'They look well,' I agreed. 'And they run stinking. Most owners would have sent them to someone else long ago.'

'It's not my fault they don't win,' he asserted heavily. 'You tell her that. That's what I came to say. You tell her it's not my fault.'

'You would lose their training fees, if they went,' I said. 'And you would lose face, perhaps. But you would gain freedom from the fear of being prosecuted for fraud.'

'See here, Mister,' he began angrily, but I interrupted him.

'Alternatively, you could sack your head boy, Barty.'

Whatever he had been going to say remained unsaid. His trap-like mouth dropped open.

'Should you decide to sack Barty,' I said conversationally, 'I could advise Mrs Cavesey to leave the horses where they are.'

He shut his mouth. There was a long pause while most of the aggression oozed away and a tired sort of defeatism took its place.

'I can't do that,' he said sullenly, not denying the need for it.

'Because of a threat that you will be warned off?' I suggested. 'Or because of the profit to come?'

'Look, Mister . . .'

'See that Barty leaves before I go home,' I said pleasantly.

He stood heavily up, and gave me a hard stare which got him nowhere very much. Breathing loudly through his nose, he was inarticulate; and I couldn't guess from his expression whether what hung fire on his tongue was a stream of invective, a defence in mitigation, or even a plea for help.

He checked through the window that his buddy Danilo was still on the courts, then turned away abruptly and departed from my room without another word: a man on a three-pronged toasting fork if ever I saw one.

*

I returned to the terrace: found Clifford Wenkins walking indecisively about peering at strangers behind their newspapers.

'Mr Wenkins,' I called.

He looked up, nodded nervously, and scuttled around tables and chairs to reach me.

'Good morning ... er ... Link,' he began and half-held out one hand, too far away for me to shake it. I sketched an equally noncommittal welcome. His best friend must have been telling him, I thought.

We sat at one of the small tables in the shade of a yellow and white sun awning, and he agreed that ... er ... yes ... a beer would be fine. He pulled another untidy wad of papers out of an inner pocket. Consulting them seemed to give him strength.

'Er ... Worldic have decided ... er ... they think it would be best, I mean, to hold the reception before ... er ... the film, you see.'

I saw. They were afraid I would vanish during the showing, if they arranged things the other way round.

'Here ... er ... is a list of people ... er ... invited by Worldic ... and here ... somewhere here ... ah, yes, here is the Press list and ... er ... a list of people who have bought tickets to the reception . . . We limited the ... er ... numbers, but we have ... er ... had ... I mean ... it may be ... perhaps ... just a bit of a *crush*, if you see what I mean.'

He sweated. Mopped up with a neatly folded white square. Waited, apparently, for me to burn. But what could I say? I'd arranged it myself; and I supposed I was grateful that people actually wanted to come.

'Er . . . if that's all right . . . I mean . . . well . . . there are still some tickets left . . . er . . . for the premiere itself, you see . . . er . . . some at twenty rand . . .'

'Twenty rand?' I said. 'Surely that's too much?'

'It's for charity,' he said quickly. 'Charity.'

'What charity?'

'Oh . . . er . . . let's see . . . I've got it here somewhere . . .' But he couldn't find it. 'Anyway . . . for charity . . . so Worldic want you to . . . I mean, because there are still some tickets, you see, to . . . er . . . well, some sort of publicity stunt . . .'

'No,' I said.

He looked unhappy. 'I told them . . . but they said . . . er . . . well . . .' He faded away like a pop song, and didn't say that Worldic's attitude to actors had made the KGB seem paternal.

'Where is the reception to be?' I asked.

'Oh . . . er . . . opposite the Wideworld Cinema, in the Klipspringer Heights Hotel. I . . . er . . . I think you will like it . . . I mean . . . it is one of the best . . . er . . . hotels in Johannesburg.'

'Fine,' I said. 'I'll be back here by, say, six o'clock next Tuesday evening. You could ring me here for final arrangements.'

'Oh yes . . . er,' he said, 'but . . . er . . . Worldic said they would like . . . er . . . to know where you are staying . . . er . . . in the Kruger Park.'

'I don't know,' I said.

'Well, er . . . could you find out?' He looked unhappy. 'Worldic said . . . er . . . on no account . . . should I not find out . . .'

'Oh. Very well,' I said. 'I'll let you know.'

'Thank you,' he gasped. 'Now . . . er . . . well . . . I mean . . . er . . .' He was working himself into a worse lather than ever over what he was trying to say next. My mind had framed one large *No* before the thought of Worldic on his tail had goaded him to get it out.

'We . . . well, that is to say . . . Worldic . . . have fixed a . . . er . . . photographic . . . session for you . . . I mean . . . well, this afternoon, in fact.'

'What photographic session?' I asked ominously.

He had another mop. 'Just . . . well . . . photographs.'

He had a terrible time explaining, and a worse time when I got it straight, that what Worldic wanted were some pictures of me reclining in bathing trunks under a sun umbrella beside a bosomy model in a bikini.

'You just run along and tell Worldic that their promotion ideas are fifty years out of date, if they think cheese-cake will sell twenty-rand seats.'

He sweated.

'And furthermore you can tell Worldic that one more damn fool suggestion and I'll never again turn up at anything they handle.'

'But . . .' he stuttered. 'You see . . . after those pics in the newspapers . . . of you giving Katya the kiss of life . . . after that . . . see . . . we were flooded . . . simply flooded . . . with enquiries . . . and all the cheaper seats went in a flash . . . and the reception tickets, too . . . all went . . .'

'But that,' I said slowly and positively, 'was not a publicity stunt.'

'Oh no.' He gulped. 'Oh no. Of course not. Oh no. Oh no . . .' He rocked to his feet, knocking his chair over. The beads were running down his forehead and his eyes looked wild. He was on the point, the very point of panic flight, when Danilo and Sally came breezily back from the courts.

'Hullo, Mr Wenkins,' Sally said in her adolescent unperceptive way. 'I say, you look almost as hot and sweaty as we do.'

Wenkins gave her a glazed, mesmerized look and fumbled around with his handkerchief. Danilo looked at him piercingly and thoughtfully and made no remark at all.

'Well . . . I'll . . . er, tell them . . . but they won't . . . like it.'

'You tell them,' I agreed. 'No stunts.'

'No stunts,' he echoed weakly; but I doubted whether he would ever have the nerve to pass on the message.

Sally watched his backview weave unsteadily into the club, as she sprawled exhaustedly in her garden chair.

'I say, he does get himself into a fuss, don't you think? Were you bullying the poor lamb, Link?'

'He's a sheep, not a lamb.'

'A silly sheep,' Danilo said vaguely, as if his thoughts were somewhere else.

'Could I have some orange juice?' Sally said.

Evan and Conrad arrived before the waiter, and the drinks order expanded. Evan was at his most insistent, waving his arms about and laying down the law to Conrad in the usual dominating I-am-the-director-and-the-rest-of-you-are-scum manner. Conrad looked half patient, half irritated: lighting cameramen were out-ranked by directors, but they didn't have to like it.

'Symbolism,' Evan was saying fiercely. 'Symbolism is what the film is all about. And post office towers are the new phallic symbol of national strength. Every virile country has to have its revolving restaurant . . .'

'It might be just because every country has one, that the one in Johannesburg is not news,' Conrad murmured, in a tone a little too carefully unargumentative.

'The tower is *in*,' stated Evan with finality.

'Even if you can't find an elephant that shape,' I said, nodding.

Conrad choked and Evan glared.

Sally said, 'What is a phallic symbol?' And Danilo told her kindly to look it up in the dictionary.

I asked Evan where exactly we would be staying in the Kruger Park, so that I could be found if necessary.

'Don't expect me to help,' he said unhelpfully. 'The production department made the bookings months ago.

Several different camps, starting in the south and working north, I believe.'

Conrad added casually, 'We do have a list, back at the hotel . . . I could copy it out for you, dear boy.'

'It isn't important,' I said. 'It was only Worldic who wanted it.'

'Not important!' Evans exclaimed. 'If Worldic wants it, of course they must have it.' Evan had no reservations towards companies that might screen his masterpieces. 'Conrad can copy the list and send it to them direct.'

I looked at Conrad in amusement. 'To Clifford Wenkins, then,' I suggested. 'It was he who asked.'

Conrad nodded shortly. Copying the list from friendliness was one thing and on Evan's orders another: I knew exactly how he felt.

'I don't suppose you are intending to bring the chauffeur Worldic gave you,' Evan said bossily to me. 'There won't be any rooms for him.'

I shook my head. 'No,' I said mildly. 'I'm hiring a car to drive myself.'

'All right, then.'

Even on a fine Tuesday morning with a healthy gin half-drunk and no pressure on him at all, he still flourished the hot eyes like lances and curled his fingers so that the tendons showed tight. The unruly curly hair sprang out vigorously like Medusa's snakes, and the very air around him seemed to quiver from his energy output.

Sally thought him fascinating. 'You'll love it in the

793

game park,' she told him earnestly. 'The animals are so sweet.'

Evan only knew how to deal with girls that young if he could bully them in front of a camera: and the idea that animals could be sweet instead of symbolic seemed to nonplus him.

'Er . . .' he said uncertainly, and sounded exactly like Wenkins.

Conrad cheered up perceptibly: smoothed his moustache and looked on Sally benignly. She gave him an uncomplicated smile and turned to Danilo.

'You'd love it too,' she said. 'Next time you come to South Africa, we must take you down there.'

Danilo could scarcely wait. Conrad asked him how much longer he was staying this time, and Danilo said a week or so, he guessed, and Sally insisted anxiously that he was staying until after Link's premiere, surely he remembered he was going to the reception with the van Hurens. Danilo remembered: he sure was.

He grinned at her. She blossomed. I hoped that the sun kid dealt in compassion alongside the mathematics.

Evan and Conrad stayed for lunch, endlessly discussing the locations they had picked throughout the city. They were, it appeared, going to incorporate a lot of *cinéma vérité*, with Conrad humping around a hand-held Arriflex to film life as it was lived. By the end of the cheese, the whole film, symbolism, elephants, and all, seemed to me doomed to be a crashing bore.

Conrad's interest was principally technical. Mine was non-existent. Evan's, as usual, inexhaustible.

'So we'll take the Arriflex with us, of course,' he was telling Conrad. 'We may see unrepeatable shots ... it would be stupid not to be equipped.'

Conrad agreed. They also discussed sound-recording equipment and decided to take that too. The production department had fixed up for a park ranger to show them round in a Land Rover, so there would be room to use everything comfortably.

Anything which they could not cram into their hired station wagon for the journey down, they said, could go in my car, couldn't it? It could. I agreed to drive to their hotel first thing in the morning to embark the surplus.

When they had gone I paid off the car and chauffeur Worldic had arranged, and hired a modest self-drive saloon instead. A man from the hiring company brought it to the Iguana, showed me the gear system, said it was a new car only just run-in and that I should have no trouble with it, and departed with the chauffeur.

I went for a practice drive, got lost, bought a map, and found my way back. The car was short on power uphill, but very stable on corners; a car for Sunday afternoons, airing Grandma in a hat.

CHAPTER TWELVE

The map and the car took me to Roderick's flat just as it was getting dark.

I tested the brakes before I set off, the car having stood alone in the car park for hours. Nothing wrong with them, of course. I sneered inwardly at myself for being so silly.

Roderick's flat was on the sixth floor.

It had a balcony.

Roderick invited me out first thing to look at the view.

'It looks marvellous at this time of night,' he said, 'with the lights springing up in every direction. In the daytime there are too many factories and roads and mining tips, unless of course you find the sinews of trade stimulating . . . and soon it will be too dark to see the shape of things in the dusk . . .'

I hovered, despite myself, on the threshold.

'Come on,' he said. 'Are you afraid of heights?'

'No.'

I stepped out there, and the view lived up to his commercial. The balcony faced south, with the kite-shaped Southern Cross flying on its side in the sky straight ahead; and orange lights stretching like a chain away towards Durban down the motorway.

Roderick was not leaning on the pierced ironwork which edged the balcony. With part of my mind shivering and the rest telling me not to be such an ass, I kept my weight nearer the building than his: I felt guilty of mistrust and yet couldn't trust, and saw that suspicion was a wrecker.

We went in. Of course, we went in. Safely. I could feel muscles relax in my jaw and abdomen that I hadn't known were tense. Silly fool, I thought: and tried to shut out the fact that for both mike and mine, Roderick had been there.

His flat was small but predictably full of impact. A black sack chair flopped on a pale olive carpet: khaki-coloured walls sprouted huge brass lamp brackets between large canvases of ultra simple abstracts in brash challenging colours: a low glass-topped table stood before an imitation tiger-skin sofa of stark square construction; and an Andy Warholish imitation can of beer stood waist-high in one corner. Desperately trendy, the whole thing; giving like its incumbent, the impression that way out was where it was all at, man, and if you weren't out there as far as you could go you might as well be dead. It seemed a foregone conclusion that he smoked pot.

Naturally, he had expensive stereo. The music he chose was less underground than could be got in

London, but the mix of anarchy and self-pity came across strongly in the nasal voices. I wondered whether it was just part of the image, or whether he sincerely enjoyed it.

'Drink?' he offered, and I said Yes, please.

Campari and soda, bitter-sweet pink stuff. He took it for granted I would like it.

'Katya won't be long. She had some recording session or other.'

'Is she all right now?'

'Sure,' he said. 'A hundred per cent.' He underplayed the relief, but I remembered his tormented tears: real emotions still lived down there under the with-it front.

He was wearing another pair of pasted-on trousers, and a blue ruffled close-fitting shirt with lacing instead of buttons. As casual clothes, they were as deliberate as signposts: the rugged male in his sexual finery. I supposed my own clothes too made a statement, as indeed everyone's did, always.

Katya's statement was as clear as a trumpet, and said, 'look at me'.

She arrived like a gust of bright and breezy show-biz, wearing an eye-stunning yellow catsuit which flared widely from the knees in black-edged ruffles. She looked like a flamenco dancer split up the middle, and she topped up the impression with a high tortoise-shell man-tilla comb pegged like a tiara into her mop of hair.

Stretching out her arms she advanced on me with life positively spurting from every pore, as if instead of harming her the input of electric current had doubled her vitality.

'Link, darling, how marvellous,' she said extravagantly. And she had brought someone with her.

The barriers in my mind rose immediately like a hedge and prickled away all evening. Roderick and Katya had planted a bombshell to lead me astray, and were betraying their intention through the heightened mischief in Katya's manner. I didn't like the game, but I was an old hand at it, and nowadays I never lost. I sighed regretfully for the quiet no-fuss dinner which Roderick had promised. Too much ever to hope for, I supposed.

The girl was ravishing, with cloudy dark hair and enormous slightly myopic-looking eyes. She wore a soft floaty garment, floor-length and green, which swirled and lay against her as she moved, outlining now a hip, now a breast, and all parts in quite clearly good shape.

Roderick was watching my reactions sideways, while pretending to pour out more Camparis.

'This is Melanie,' Katya said as if inventing Venus from the waves; and there was perhaps a touch of the Botticellis in the graceful neck.

Christened Mabel, no doubt, I said to myself uncharitably, and greeted her with a lukewarm smile and a conventional handshake. Melanie was not a girl to be put off by a cool reception. She gave me a gentle flutter of lengthy lashes, a sweet curve of soft pink lips, and a smouldering promise in the smoky eyes. I thought: She's done this sort of thing before, and she is as aware of her power as I am when I act.

Melanie just happened to sit beside me on the tiger-skin sofa, stretching out languorously so that the green material revealed the whole slender shape. Just happened to have no lighter of her own, so that I had to help her with Roderick's orange globe table model. Just happened to have to cup my hand in both of her own to guide the flame to the end of her cigarette. Just happened to steady herself with a hand on my arm as she leant forward to flick off ash.

Katya gaily sparkled and Roderick filled my glass with gin when he thought I wasn't looking, and I began to wonder where he had hidden the tape-recorder. If this little lot was to be off the record, I was the plumber's mate.

Dinner was laid with candles on a square black table in a mustard-painted dining alcove. The food was great and the talk provocative, but mostly the three of them tossed the ball among themselves while I replied when essential with murmurs and smiles, which couldn't be picked on as quotes.

Melanie's scent was as subtle as Joy, and Roderick had laced my wine with brandy. He watched and spoke and attended to me with friendly eyes, and waited for me to deliver myself up. Go stuff the *Rand Daily Star*, I thought: my friend Roderick is a bastard and my tongue is my own.

Something of my awareness must have shown in my

eyes, for a thoughtful look suddenly crossed his forehead and he changed his tack in two sentences from sexual innuendo to meaningful social comment.

He said, 'What do you think of apartheid, now that you've been here a week?'

'What do you?' I replied. 'Tell me about it. You three who live here . . . you tell *me*.'

Roderick shook his head and Katya said it was what visitors thought that mattered, and only Melanie, who was playing different rules, came across with the goods.

'Apartheid,' she said earnestly, 'is necessary.'

Roderick made a negative movement, and I asked, 'In what way?'

'It means living separately,' she said. 'It doesn't mean that one race is better than the other, just that they are different, and should remain so. All the world seems to think that white South Africans hate the blacks and try to repress them, but it is not true. We care for them . . . and the phrase, "black is beautiful" was thought up by white Africans to give black Africans a sense of being important as individuals.'

I was intensely surprised, but Roderick reluctantly nodded. 'That's true. The Black Power Movement have adopted it as their own, but they didn't invent it. You might say, I suppose, that the phrase has achieved everything it was intended to, and a bit more besides.'

'To read foreign papers,' said Melanie indignantly, warming to her subject, 'you would think the blacks are a lot of illiterate cheap labour. And it isn't true.

Schooling is compulsory for both races, and factories pay the rate for the job, regardless of skin colour. And that,' she added, 'was negotiated by the white trade unionists.'

I liked her a lot better since she'd forgotten the sexpot role. The dark eyes held fire as well as smoke, and it was a change to hear someone passionately defending her country.

'Tell me more,' I said flippantly.

'Oh . . .' She looked confused for a moment, then took a fresh hold on enthusiasm, like a horse getting its second wind. 'Black people have everything the same as white people. Everything that they want to have. Only a minority have big houses because the majority don't like them: they like to live out of doors, and only go into shelters to sleep. But they have cars and businesses and holidays and hospitals and hotels and cinemas . . . everything like that.'

The white people on the whole had more money, I thought; and undoubtedly more freedom of action. I opened my mouth to make some innocuous remark about the many entrance doors marked 'non-whites' and 'whites only', but Melanie jumped right in to forestall any adverse comment, which was not in the least what Roderick wanted. He frowned at her. She was too busy to notice.

'I know what you're going to say,' she said inaccurately. 'You're going to talk about injustice. Everyone from England always does. Well, certainly, of course, there are injustices. There are in every country in the world, including yours. Injustices make the headlines. Justice is not news. People come here purposely seeking for injustice, and of course they find it. But they never report on the good things, they just shut their eyes and pretend there aren't any.'

I looked at her thoughtfully. There was truth in what she said.

'Every time a country like England attacks our way of life,' she said, 'they do more harm than good. You can feel the people here close their ranks and harden their attitude. It is stupid. It slows down the progress our country is gradually making towards partnership between the races. The old rigid type of apartheid is dying out, you know . . . and in five or ten years' time it will only be the militants and extremists on both sides who take it seriously. They shout and thump, and the foreign press listens and pays attention, like they always do to crackpots, and they don't see, or at any rate they never mention, the slow quiet change for the better which is going on here.'

I wondered how she would feel about it if she were black: even if things were changing, there was still no overall equality of opportunity. Blacks could be teachers, doctors, lawyers, priests. They couldn't be jockeys. Unfair, unfair.

Roderick, waiting in vain for me to jump in with both feet, was driven again to a direct question.

'What are your views, Link?'

I smiled at him.

'I belong to a profession,' I said, 'which never discriminates against blacks or Jews or women or Catholics or Protestants or bug-eyed monsters, but only against non-members of Equity.'

Melanie looked blank about Equity but she had a word to say about Jews.

'Whatever white South Africans may be accused of,' she contended, 'we have never sent six million blacks to the gas chamber.'

Which was rather like saying, I thought frivolously, that one might have measles, but had never infected anyone with whooping cough.

Roderick gave up angling for a quotable political commitment and tried to bounce Melanie back into sultry seduction. Her own instincts were telling her she would get further with me if she laid off the sex, because the doubt showed clearly in her manner as she attempted to do as he wanted. But evidently it was important to them both that she should persevere, and she refused to be discouraged by my lack of answering spark. She smiled a meek feminine smile to deprecate every opinion she had uttered, and bashfully lowered the thick black lashes.

Katya and Roderick exchanged eye-signals as blinding as lighthouses on a dark night, and Katya said she was going to make coffee. Roderick said he would help: and why didn't Melanie and Link move over to the sofa, it was more comfortable than sitting round the table.

Melanie smiled shyly. I admired the achievement: she was as shy underneath as a sergeant-major. She draped herself beautifully over the sofa with the green material swirling closely across the perfect bosom which rose and fell gently with every breath. She noted the direction of my eyes and smiled with pussy-cat satisfaction.

Premature, dearest Melanie, premature, I thought.

Roderick carried in a tray of coffee cups and Katya went out on to the balcony. When she came in, she shook her head. Roderick poured out the coffee and Katya handed it round: the suppressed inner excitement, absent during dinner, was fizzing away again in the corners of her smile.

I looked at my watch. A quarter past ten.

I said, 'I must be going soon. Early start tomorrow morning, I'm afraid.'

Katya said quickly, 'Oh no, you can't go yet, Link,' and Roderick handed me a bulbous glass with enough brandy to sink a battleship. I took a sip but made it look like a swallow, and reflected that if I'd drunk everything he'd given me I would have been in no state to drive away.

Melanie kicked off her golden slippers and flexed her toes. On them she wore pearly pink nail varnish and nothing else: and with a quick flash of bare ankle and calf she managed to plant the idea in my mind that under the green shift there were no other clothes.

The coffee was as good as the dinner: Katya was more expert a cook than conspirator. Within twenty minutes she again strolled out on to the balcony, and this time, when she came back, the message as a nod.

I looked at all three of them, wondering. Roderick with his old-young face, Katya yellow-frilly and irresponsible, Melanie conscientiously weaving her web. They had laid some sort of trap. The only thing was . . . what?

Twenty to eleven. I finished my coffee, stood up, and said, 'I really must go now . . .'

This time there was no resistance. They all three uncurled themselves to their feet.

'Thank you,' I said, 'for a great evening.'

They smiled.

'Marvellous food,' I said to Katya.

She smiled.

'Splendid drinks,' I said to Roderick.

He smiled.

'Superb company,' I said to Melanie.

She smiled.

Not a really genuine smile among them. They had watchful, expectant eyes. My mouth, for all the available liquid, felt dry.

We moved towards the lobby, which was an extension of the sitting-room.

Melanie said, 'Time I was going too . . . Roderick, would you order me a taxi?'

'Sure, love,' he said easily, and then, as if the thought was just striking, 'but you go the same way as Link . . . I'm sure he would give you a lift.'

They all looked at me, smiling.

'Of course,' I said. What else. What else could I say?

The smiles went on and on.

Melanie scooped up a tiny wrap from beside the front door, and Roderick and Katya saw us down the hall and into the lift, and were still waving farewell as the doors closed between us. The lift sank. One of those automatic lifts which stopped at every floor one had pre-selected. I pressed G for ground, and at G for ground it stopped.

Politely I let Melanie out first. Then I said, 'I say . . . terribly sorry . . . I've left my signet ring on the wash basin in Roderick's bathroom. I'll just dash back for it. You wait there, I won't be a second.'

The doors were closing before she could demur. I pressed the buttons for floors 2 and 6. Got out at 2. Watched the pointer begin to slide towards Roderick's floor at 6, and skipped quickly through the doors of the service stairs at the back of the hall.

The unadorned concrete and ironwork steps wound down round a small steep well and let me out into an area full of stacked laundry baskets, central-heating boilers, and rows of garbage cans. Out in the narrow street behind the covered yard I turned left, skirted the whole of the next door block at a fast pace, and finally, more slowly, inconspicuously walked in the shadows back towards Roderick's.

I stopped in a doorway a hundred yards away, and watched.

There were four men in the street, waiting. Two

opposite the front entrance of Roderick's apartment block. Two others patiently standing near my hired car. All of them carried objects which gleamed in the street lamps, and whose shapes I knew all too well.

Melanie came out of the apartment block and hurried across the road to talk to two of the men. The green dress clung to her body and appeared diaphanous to the point of transparency in the quality of light in the street. She and the men conferred agitatedly, and there was a great deal of shaking of heads.

All three of them suddenly looked up, and I followed the direction of their gaze. Roderick and Katya were standing out on the balcony, calling down. I was too far away to hear the exact words, but the gist was entirely guessable. The quarry had got away, and none of them was pleased.

Melanie and the two men turned and walked in my direction, but only as far as the other two beside my car. They all five went into a huddle which could produce no happiness, and in the end Melanie walked back alone and disappeared into the flats.

I sighed wryly. Roderick was no murderer. He was a newspaperman. The four men had come armed with cameras. Not knives. Not guns.

Not my life they were after; just my picture.

Just my picture outside a block of flats at night alone with a beautiful girl in a totally revealing dress.

I looked thoughtfully at the four men beside my car,

decided the odds were against it, turned on my heel, and quietly walked away.

Back at the Iguana Rock (by taxi), I telephoned Roderick.

He sounded subdued.

I said, 'Damn your bloody eyes.'

'Yes.'

'Have you got this telephone bugged?'

A pause. Then on a sigh again he said, 'Yes.'

'Too late for honesty, my friend.'

'Link . . .'

'Forget it,' I said. 'Just tell me why.'

'My paper . . .'

'No,' I said. 'Newspapers don't get up to such tricks. That was a spot of private enterprise.'

A longer pause.

'I guess I owe it to you,' he said slowly. 'We did it for Clifford Wenkins. The little runt is scared silly by Worldic, and he begged us, in return for favours he has done us from time to time, to set you up for him. He said Worldic would sack him if he couldn't persuade you to do a girly session to sell their twenty-rand seats, and he had asked you, and you had absolutely refused. Melanie is our top model girl, and he got her to help in a good cause.'

'That Wenkins,' I said bitterly, 'would sell his soul for publicity stunts.'

809

'I'm sorry, Link . . .'

'Not as sorry as he will be,' I said ominously.

'I promised him I wouldn't tell you . . .'

'Stuff both of you,' I said violently, and rattled the receiver into its cradle.

CHAPTER THIRTEEN

The next morning, the Iguana management having kindly sent someone with the keys to fetch my hired car from outside Roderick's flat, I packed what little I would need for the Kruger Park, and chuntered round to Evan and Conrad's hotel.

The loading of their station wagon was in process of being directed by Evan as if it were the key scene in a prestige production, and performed by Conrad at his most eccentric. Boxes, bags, and black zipped equipment littered the ground for a radius of ten yards.

'Dear boy,' Conrad said as I approached, 'for God's sake get some ice.'

'Ice?' I echoed vaguely.

'Ice.' He pointed to a yellow plastic box about two feet by one. 'In there. For the film.'

'What about beer?'

He gave me a sorrowful, withering glance. 'Beer in the red one, dear boy.'

The red thermal box had had priority; had already been clipped tight shut and lifted on to the car. Smiling,

I went into the hotel on the errand and returned with a large plastic bagful. Conrad laid the ice-pack in the yellow box and carefully stacked his raw stock on top. The yellow box joined the red one and Evan said that at this rate we wouldn't reach the Kruger by nightfall.

At eleven the station wagon was full to the gunnels but the ground was still littered with that extraordinary collection of wires, boxes, tripods and clips which seemed to accompany cameramen everywhere.

Evan waved his arms as if by magic wand and the whole lot would leap into order. Conrad pulled his moustache dubiously. I opened the boot of my saloon, shovelled the whole lot in unceremoniously, and told him he could sort it all out when we arrived.

After that we adjourned for thirst quenchers, and finally got the wheels on the road at noon. We drove east by north for several hours and descended from the high Johannesburg plateau down to a few hundred feet above sea level. The air grew noticeably warmer on every long downhill stretch, which gave rise to three or four more stops for sustenance. Conrad's cubic capacity rivalled the Bantus'.

By five we arrived at the Numbi gate, the nearest way into the park. The Kruger itself stretched a further two hundred miles north and fifty east with nothing to keep the animals in except their own wish to stay. The Numbi gate consisted of a simple swinging barrier guarded by two khaki-uniformed black Africans and a small office. Evan produced passes for two cars and reservations for staying in the camps, and with grins and salutes the passes were stamped and the gates swung open.

Brilliant scarlet and magenta bougainvillaea just inside proved misleading: the park itself was tinder dry and thorny brown after months of sun and no rain. The narrow road stretched ahead into a baked wilderness where the only man-made thing in sight was the tarmac itself.

'Zebras,' shouted Evan, winding down his window and screaming out of it.

I followed his pointing finger, and saw the dusty herd of them standing patiently under bare-branched trees, slowly swinging their tails and merging uncannily into the striped shade.

Conrad had a map, which was just as well. We were headed for the nearest camp, Pretoriuskop, but roads wound and cross-crossed as we approached it, unmade-up dry earth roads leading off at tangents to vast areas inhabited believably by lion, rhinoceros, buffalo and crocodile.

And, of course, elephant.

The camp turned out to be an area of several dozen acres, enclosed by a stout wire fence, and containing nothing so camplike as tents. Rather like Butlins gone native, I thought: clusters of round, brick-walled, thatched-roofed cabins like pink-coloured drums with wide-brimmed hats on.

'*Rondavels*,' Evan said in his best dogmatic manner, waving a hand at them. He checked in at the big reception office and drove off to search for the huts with the right numbers. There were three of them: one each. Inside, two beds, a table, two chairs, fitted cupboard, shower room, and air-conditioning. Every mod con in the middle of the jungle.

Evan banged on my door and said come out, we were going for a drive. The camp locked its gates for the night at six thirty, he said, which gave us forty minutes to go and look at baboons.

'It will take too long to unpack the station wagon,' he said. 'So we will all go in your car.'

I drove and they gazed steadfastly out of the windows. There were some distant baboons scratching themselves in the evening sunlight on a rocky hill, and a herd of impala munching away at almost leafless bushes, but not an elephant in sight.

'We'd better go back before we get lost,' I said, but even then we only whizzed through the gates seconds before closing time.

'What happens if you're late?' I asked.

'You have to spend the night outside,' Evan said positively. 'Once the gate is closed, it's closed.'

Evan, as usual, seemed to be drawing information out of air, though he gave the game away later by producing an information booklet he had been given in reception. The booklet also said not to wind down windows and scream 'zebra' out of them, as the animals didn't like it. Wild animals, it appeared, thought cars were harmless and left them alone, but were liable to bite any bits of humans sticking out.

Conrad had had to unpack the whole station wagon to unload the red beer box, which was likely to reverse his priorities. We sat round a table outside the huts, cooling our throats in the warm air and watching the dark creep closer between the *rondavels*. Even with Evan there it was peaceful enough to unjangle the screwiest nerves . . . and lull the wariest mind into a sense of security.

Thursday, the following day, we set off at daybreak and breakfasted at the next camp, Skukuza, where we were to stay that night.

Skukuza was larger and boasted executive-status *rondavels*, which Evan's production company had naturally latched on to. They had also engaged the full-time attendance of a park ranger for the day, which would have been splendid had he not been an Afrikaner with incomplete English. He was big, slow-moving, quiet and unemotional, the complete antithesis of Evan's fiery zeal for allegory.

Evan shot questions and had to wait through silences for his answers: no doubt Haagner was merely translating the one into Afrikaans in his head, formulating the other and translating that into English, but the delay irritated Evan from the start. Haagner treated Evan with detachment and refused to be hurried, which gave

Conrad the (decently concealed) satisfaction of an underdog seeing his master slip on a banana skin.

We set off in Haagner's Range Rover, accompanied by the Arriflex, a tape recorder, half a dozen smaller cameras, and the red thermal box loaded with a mixed cargo of film, beer, fruit, and sandwiches in plastic bags. Evan had brought sketch pads, maps and notebooks, and six times remarked that the company should have equipped him with a secretary. Conrad murmured that we should be glad that we weren't equipped with Drix Goddart, but from the sour look Evan slid me he didn't necessarily agree.

'*Olifant*,' Haagner said, pointing, having been three times told of the aim of the expedition.

He stopped the van. 'There, in the valley.'

We looked. A lot of trees, a patch of green, a winding river.

'There, man,' he said.

Eventually our untrained eyes saw them: three dark hunched shapes made small by distance, flapping a lazy ear behind a bush.

'Not near enough,' Evan said disgustedly. 'We must get nearer.'

'Not here,' said Haagner. 'They are across the river. The Sabie river. *Sabie* is Bantu word: it means Fear.'

I looked at him suspiciously but he was not provoking Evan in any way; simply imparting information. The slow peaceful-looking water wound through the valley and looked as unfearful as the Thames.

Evan had no eyes for the various antelope-like species Haagner pointed out, nor for the blue jays or turkey buzzards or vervet monkeys or wildebeest, and particularly not for the herds of gentle impala. Only the implicitly violent took his attention: the vulture, the hyena, the wart-hog, the possibility of lion and the scarcity of cheetah.

And, of course, *olifants*. Evan adopted the Afrikaans word as his own and rolled it round his tongue as if he alone had invented it. *Olifant* droppings on the road (fresh, said Haagner) excited him almost to orgasm. He insisted on us stopping there and reversing for a better view, and on Conrad sticking the Arriflex lens out of the window and exposing about fifty feet of film from different angles and with several focal lengths.

Haagner, patiently positioning the van for every shot, watched these antics and clearly thought Evan unhinged, and I laughed internally until my throat ached. Had the obliging elephant returned Evan would no doubt have directed him to defecate again for Scene 1, Take 2. He would have seen nothing odd in it.

Evan left the heap reluctantly and was working out how to symbolize it in an utterly meaningful way. Conrad said he could do with a beer, but Haagner pointed ahead and said 'Onder-Sabie', which turned out to be another rest camp like the others.

'*Olifant* in Saliji river,' said Haagner coming back from a chat with some colleagues. 'If we go now, you see them perhaps.'

Evan swept us away from the shady table and our half-empty glasses and scurried forth again into the increasing noonday heat. All around us, more sensible mortals were fanning themselves and contemplating siesta, but *olifants*, with Evan, came before sense.

The Range Rover was as hot as an oven.

'It is hot, today,' Haagner said. 'Hotter tomorrow. Summer is coming. Soon we will have the rain, and all the park will be green.'

Evan, alarmed, said, 'No, no. The park must be burned up, just like this. Inhospitable land, bare, hungry, predatory, aggressive and cruel. Certainly not soft and lush.'

Haagner understood less than a tenth. After a long pause he merely repeated the bad news: 'In one month, after the rains start, the park will be all green. Then, much water. Now, not much. All small rivers are dry. We find *olifant* near bigger rivers. In Saliji.'

He drove several miles and stopped beside a large wooden sun shelter built high at the end of a valley. Below, the Saliji river stretched away straight ahead, and the *olifants* had done Evan proud. A large family of them were playing in the water, squirting each other through their trunks and taking care of their kids.

As it was an official picnic place especially built in an area of cleared ground, we were all allowed out of the car. I stretched myself thankfully and dug into the red box for a spot of irrigation. Conrad had a camera in one hand and a beer in the other, and Evan brandished his enthusiasm over us all like a whip.

Haagner and I sat in ninety degrees in the shade at one of the small scattered tables and ate some of the packed sandwiches. He had warned Evan not to go too far from the shelter while filming as it presented an open invitation to a hungry lion, but Evan naturally believed that he would not meet one: and he didn't. He took Conrad plus Arriflex fifty yards downhill into the bush for some closer shots, and Haagner called him urgently to come back, telling me his job would be lost if Evan were.

Conrad soon climbed up again, mopping drops from his brow which were not all heat, and reported that 'something' was grunting down there behind some rocks.

'There are twelve hundred lion in the park,' Haagner said. 'When hungry, they kill. Lions alone kill thirty thousand animals in the park every year.'

'God,' said Conrad, visibly losing interest in Evan's whole project.

Eventually Evan returned unscathed, but Haagner regarded him with disfavour.

'More *olifant* in the north,' he said. 'For *olifant*, you go north.' Out of his district, his tone said.

Evan nodded briskly and set his mind at rest.

'Tomorrow. We set off northwards tomorrow, and tomorrow night we stay in a camp called Satara.'

Reassured, Haagner drove us slowly back towards

Skukuza, conscientiously pointing out animals all the way.

'Could you cross the park on a horse?' I asked.

He shook his head decisively. 'Very dangerous. More dangerous than walking, and walking is not safe.' He looked directly at Evan. 'If your car break down, wait for next car, and ask people to tell rangers at the next camp. Do not leave your car. Do not walk in the park. Especially do not walk in the park at night. Stay in car all night.'

Evan listened to the lecture with every symptom of ignoring it. He pointed instead to one of the several unmetalled side roads we had passed with 'no entry' signs on them, and asked where they led.

'Some go to the many Bantu ranger stations,' said Haagner after the pause for translation. 'Some to water holes. Some are fire breaks. They are roads for rangers. Not roads for visitors. Do not go down those roads.' He looked at Evan, clearly seeing that Evan would not necessarily obey. 'It is not allowed.'

'Why not?'

'The park is 8,000 square miles ... visitors can get lost.'

'We have a map,' Evan argued.

'The service roads,' Haagner said stolidly, 'are not on the maps.'

Evan ate a packet of sandwiches mutinously and rolled down the window to throw out the plastic bag.

'Do not do that,' Haagner said sharply enough to stop him.

'Why not?'

'The animals eat them, and choke. No litter must be thrown. It kills the animals.'

'Oh very well,' said Evan ungraciously, and handed me the screwed-up bag to return to the red box. The box was clipped shut and tidy, so I shoved it in my pocket. Evan polished off the job of being a nuisance by throwing out instead the half-eaten crust of his cheese-and-tomato.

'Do not feed the animals,' said Haagner automatically.

'Why not?' Evan, belligerent, putting on an RSPCA face.

'It is unwise to teach animals that cars contain food.'

That silenced him flat. Conrad twitched an eyebrow at me and I arranged my face into as near impassiveness as one can get while falling about inside.

Owing to an *olifant* waving its ears as us within cricket-ball distance we did not get back to Skukuza before the gates shut. Evan, oblivious to the fast-setting sun, saw allegories all over the place and had Conrad wasting film by the mile, taking shots through glass. He had wanted Conrad to set up a tripod in the road to get steadier than hand-held pictures, but even he was slightly damped by the frantic quality in Haagner's voice as he told him not to.

'*Olifant* is the most dangerous of all the animals,' he

said earnestly, and Conrad equally earnestly assured him that for nothing on earth would he, Conrad, leave the safety of the Range Rover. Haagner wouldn't even have the window open and wanted to drive away at once. It appeared that when *olifants* waved their ears like that they were expressing annoyance, and since they weighed seven tons and could charge at 25 m.p.h., it didn't do to hang about.

Evan didn't believe that any animal would have the gall to attack such important humans as E. Pentelow, director, and E. Lincoln, actor. He persuaded Conrad to get clicking, and Haagner sat there with the engine running and his foot on the clutch. When the elephant finally took one step in our direction we were off down the road with a jolt that threw Conrad, camera and all, to the floor.

I helped him up, while Evan complained about it to Haagner. The ranger, nearing the end of his patience, stopped the car with an equal jerk and hauled on the hand brake.

'Very well,' he said. 'We wait.'

The elephant came out on to the road, a hundred yards behind us. The big ears were flapping like flags.

Conrad looked back. 'Do drive on, dear boy,' he said with anxiety in his voice.

Haagner folded his lips. The elephant decided to follow us. He was also accelerating to a trot.

It took more seconds than I cared before Evans cracked. He was saying 'For God's sake, where is the

Arriflex?' to Conrad, when it seemed at last to dawn on him that there might be some real danger.

'Drive away,' he said to Haagner urgently. 'Can't you see that that animal is charging?'

And it had tusks, I observed.

Haagner too decided that enough was enough. He had the hand brake off and the gears in mesh in one slick movement, and the elephant got a trunkful of dust.

'What about the next car coming along?' I asked. 'They'll meet it head on.'

Haagner shook his head. 'No cars will come this way any more today. It is too late. They will all be near the camps now. And that *olifant*, he will go straight away into the bush. He will not stay on the road.'

Conrad looked at his watch. 'How long will it take us to get back to Skukuza?'

'With no more stops,' Haagner said with bite, 'about half an hour.'

'But it is six fifteen already!' Conrad said.

Haagner made a noncommittal movement of his head and didn't answer. Evan appeared subdued into silence and a look of peaceful satisfaction awoke on the Afrikaner's face. For the whole of the rest of the way it stayed there, first in the quick dust, then in the reflected glow of the headlights. Before we reached Skukuza he swung the Range Rover down one of the no entry side roads, a detour which brought us after a mile or two suddenly and unexpectedly into a village of modern

823

bungalows with tiny little flower gardens and street lighting.

We stared in amazement. A suburb, no less, set down greenly in the brown dry veldt.

'This is the ranger village,' Haagner said. 'My house is over there, the third down that road. All the whites who work in the camp, and the white rangers, we live here. The Bantu rangers and workers also have villages in the park.'

'But the lions,' I said. 'Are the villages safe, isolated like this?'

He smiled. 'It is not isolated.' The Range Rover came to the end of the houses, crossed about fifty unlit yards of road and sped straight into the back regions of Skukuza camp. 'But also, no, it is not entirely safe. One must not walk far from the houses at night. Lions do not normally come near the gardens . . . and we have fences round them . . . but a young Bantu was taken by a lion one night on that short piece of road between our village and the camp. I knew him well. He had been told never to walk . . . it was truly sad.'

'Are people often . . . taken . . . by lions?' I asked, as he pulled up by our *rondavels*, and we unloaded ourselves, the cameras, and the red box.

'No. Sometimes. Not often. People who work in the park; never visitors. It is safe in cars.' He gave Evan one last meaningful stare. 'Do not leave your car. To do so is not safe.'

*

Before dinner in the camp restaurant I put a call through to England. Two hours' delay, they said, but by nine o'clock I was talking to Charlie.

Everything was fine, she said, the children were little hooligans, and she had been to see Nerissa.

'I spent the whole day with her yesterday . . . Most of the time we just sat, because she felt awfully tired, but she didn't seem to want me to go. I asked her the things you wanted . . . not all at once, but spread over . . .'

'What did she say?'

'Well . . . You were right about some things. She did tell Danilo she had Hodgkin's disease. She said she didn't know herself that it was fatal when she told him, but she doesn't think he took much notice, because all he said was that he thought only young people got it.'

If he knew that, I thought, he knew a lot more.

'Apparently he stayed with her for about ten days, and they became firm friends. That was how she described it. So she told him, before he went back to America, that she would be leaving him the horses as a personal gift, and also, as he was all the family she had, all the rest of her money after other bequests had been met.'

'Lucky old Danilo.'

'Yes . . . Well, he came to see her again, a few weeks ago, late July or early August. While you were in Spain, anyway. She knew by then that she was dying, but she didn't mention it to Danilo. She did show him her will, though, as he seemed interested in it. She said he was so

825

sweet when he had read it, and hoped not to be inheriting for twenty years.'

'Little hypocrite.'

'I don't know,' said Charlie doubtfully, 'because although you were right about so much, there is a distinct fly in the wood pile.'

'What's that?'

'It can't be Danilo who is making the horses lose. It simply cannot.'

'It must be,' I said. 'And why not?'

'Because when Nerissa told him she was worried about the way they were running, and wished she could find out what was wrong, it was Danilo himself who came up with the idea of sending *you*.'

'It can't have been,' I exclaimed.

'It definitely was,' Charlie said. 'She was positive about it. It was Danilo's own suggestion.'

'Blast,' I said.

'He wouldn't have suggested she send someone to investigate, if he'd been nobbling them himself.'

'No . . . I suppose not.'

'You sound depressed,' she said.

'I haven't any other answers for Nerissa.'

'Don't worry. You weren't anyway going to tell her her nephew was up to no good.'

'That's true,' I agreed.

'And it wasn't difficult for Danilo to read her will. She leaves it lying around all the time on that marquetry table in the corner of the sitting-room. She showed it to me immediately, as soon as I mentioned it, because it interests her a lot. And I saw what keepsakes she is leaving us, if you're interested.'

'What are they?' I asked idly, thinking about Danilo.

'She's leaving you her holding in something called Rojedda, and she's leaving me a diamond pendant and some earrings. She showed them to me ... they are absolutely beautiful and I told her they were far too much, but she made me try them on so she would see how I looked. She seemed to be so pleased ... so happy ... isn't she incredible? I can hardly bear ... oh ... oh dear ...'

'Don't cry, darling,' I said.

There were some swallowing noises.

'I ... can't ... help it. She is already much worse than when we saw her before, and she's very uncomfortable. One of her swollen glands is pressing on things in her chest.'

'We'll go and see her as soon as I get back.'

'Yes.' She sniffed away the tears. 'God, I do miss you.'

'Me too,' I said. 'Only one more week. I'll be home a week today, and we'll take the kids down to Cornwall.'

After the call I went outside and walked slowly past our *rondavels* and out on to the rough grassy area beyond. The African night was very quiet. No roar of traffic from any distant city, just the faint steady hum of the generator supplying Skukuza with electricity, and the energetic music of cicadas.

Nerissa had given me my answers.

I saw what they meant, and I didn't want to believe it.

A gamble. No more, no less.

With my life as the stake.

I went back to the telephone and made one more call. Van Huren's manservant said he would see, and Quentin came on the line. I said I knew it was an odd thing to ask, and I would explain why when next I saw him, but could he possibly tell me what size Nerissa's holding in Rojedda was likely to be.

'The same as my own,' he said without hesitation. 'She has my brother's holding, passed to her by Portia.'

I thanked him numbly.

'See you at the premiere,' he said. 'We are looking forward to it very much.'

For hours, I couldn't go to sleep. Yet where could I be safer than inside a guarded camp, with Evan and Conrad snoring their heads off in the huts next door?

But when I woke up, I was no longer in bed.

I was in the car I had hired in Johannesburg.

The car was surrounded by early daylight in the Kruger National Park. Trees, scrub, and dry grass. Not a *rondavel* in sight.

Remnants of an ether smell blurred my senses, but one fact was sharp and self-evident.

One of my arms lay through the steering wheel, and my wrists were locked together in a pair of handcuffs.

CHAPTER FOURTEEN

This had to be some ghastly practical joke. Evan, being malicious.

This had to be Clifford Wenkins thinking up some frightful publicity stunt.

This had to be anything but real.

But I knew, deep down in some deathly cold core, that this time there was no girl called Jill coming to set me free.

This time the dying was there to be done. Staring me in the face. Straining already across my shoulders and down my arms.

Danilo was playing for his gold mine.

I felt sick and ill. Whatever anaesthetic had been used on me had been given crudely. Probably far too much for the purpose. Not that that was likely to worry anyone but me.

For an age I could think no further. The dizziness kept coming back in clammy pea-green waves. My physical wretchedness blocked any other thought; took up all my attention. Bouts of semi-consciousness brought me each time to a fresh awakening, to renewed awareness of my plight, to malaise and misery.

The first objective observation which pierced the fog was that I had gone to bed wearing shorts, and now had clothes on. The trousers I had worn the day before, and the shirt. Also, upon investigation, socks and slip-on shoes.

The next discovery, which had been knocking at the door of consciousness for some time but had been shut out as unwelcome, was that the car's seat belts were fastened. Across my chest and over my lap, just as in the Special.

They weren't tightly fastened, but I couldn't reach the clip.

I tried. The first of many tries at many things. The first of many frustrations.

I tried to slide my hands out of the handcuffs: but, as before, they were the regulation British police model, designed precisely not to let people slide their hands out. My bones, as before, were too big.

I tried with all my strength to break the steering wheel, but although this one looked flimsy compared with the one in the Special, I still couldn't do it.

I could move a shade more than in the film. The straps were not so tight and there was more room round my legs. Apart from that, there was little in it.

For the first of many times I wondered how long it would be before anyone set out to look for me.

Evan and Conrad, when they found me missing,

would surely start a search. Haagner, surely, would alert every ranger in the park. Someone would come along very soon. Of course they would. And set me free.

The day began to warm up, the sun in a cloudless sky shining brightly through the window on my right. The car was therefore facing north . . . and I groaned at the thought, because in the southern hemisphere the sun shone at midday from the north, and I should have its heat and light full in the face.

Perhaps someone would come before midday.

Perhaps.

The worst of the sickness passed in an hour or two, though the tides of unease ebbed and flowed for much longer. Gradually, however, I began to think again, and to lose the feeling that even if death were already perched on my elbow I was too bilious to care.

Clear thought number one was that Danilo had locked me in this car so that I should die and he would inherit Nerissa's half share in the van Huren gold mine.

Nerissa was leaving her Rojedda holding to me in her will, and Danilo, having read the will, knew.

Danilo was to inherit the residue. Should I die before Nerissa, the Rojedda bequest would be void, and the holding would become part of his residue. Should I live, he stood to lose not only a share of the mine, but hundreds of thousands of pounds besides.

As the law stood then, and would still stand when Nerissa died, estate duty on everything she possessed would be paid out of the residue. Danilo personally stood to lose every penny of the estate duty paid on the inheritance which Nerissa was leaving to me.

If only, I thought uselessly, she had told me what she was doing: I could have explained why she shouldn't. Perhaps she hadn't realized how immensely valuable the Rojedda holding was: she had only recently received it from her sister. Perhaps she hadn't understood how estate duty worked. Certainly, in view of the enjoyment she had found in her long-lost nephew, she had not intended me to prosper out of all proportion at Danilo's expense.

Any accountant would have told her, but wills were usually drawn up by solicitors, not accountants, and solicitors didn't give financial advice.

Danilo, with his mathematical mind, had read the will and seen the barbs in it, as I would have done. Danilo must have begun plotting my death from that very moment.

He had only had to tell me what she had written. But how could he know that? If he himself in reversed positions would have stuck two fingers up in my face, perhaps he thought that I, that anyone, would do that too.

Nerissa, I thought. Dear, dear Nerissa. Meaning good to everyone, and happily leaving them presents, and landing me in consequence in the most unholy bloody mess.

Danilo the gambler. Danilo the bright lad who knew that Hodgkin's disease was fatal. Danilo the little schemer who started by lowering the value of a string of racehorses to pay less estate duty on them, and who, when he found that the real stakes were much higher, had the nerve to move at once into the senior league.

I remembered his fascination down the mine, his questions about quantities at lunch, and his tennis game with Sally. He was after the whole works, not just half. Inherit one half and marry the other. No matter that she was only fifteen: in two more years it would be a highly suitable alliance.

Danilo . . .

I tugged uselessly, in sudden shaking fury, at the obstinate steering wheel. Such cruelty was impossible. How could he . . . how could anyone . . . lock a man in a car and leave him to die of heat and thirst and exhaustion? It only happened in films . . . in one film . . . in *Man in a Car*.

Don't get out of the car, Haagner had said. It is not safe to get out of the car. And a right bloody laugh that was. If I could get out of this car I would take my chance with the lions.

All that screaming and shouting I had done in the film. I remembered it coldly. The agony of spirit I had imagined and acted. The disintegration of a soul, a process I had dissected into a series of pictures to be presented one by one until the progression led inexorably to the empty shell of a man too far gone to recover his mind, even if his body were saved.

The man in the Special had been a fictional character. The man had been shown as reacting to every situation throughout the story with impulsive emotion, which was why his weeping fits *in extremis* had been valid. But I was not like the man: in many respects, diametrically opposite. I saw the present problem in mainly practical terms, and intended to go on doing so.

Someone, sometime, would find me. I would just have to try, in any way I could, to be alive – and sane – when they did so.

The sun rose high and the car grew hot; but this was only a secondary discomfort.

My bladder was full to bursting.

I could stretch my hands round the wheel to reach and undo the fly zip fastener, which I did. But I couldn't move far on the seat and even if I managed to open the door with my elbow, there would be no chance of clearing the car. Although there was no sense in it, I postponed the inevitable moment until continence was nearer a pain than a nuisance. But reluctance had its limits. When in the end I had to let go, a lot went as far as the floor, but a lot of it didn't, and I could feel the wetness soaking into my trousers from crutch to knee.

Sitting in a puddle made me extremely angry. Quite unreasonably, forcing me to mess myself seemed a more callous act than putting me in the car in the first place. In the film, we had glossed over this problem as being secondary to the mental state. We had been wrong. It was part of it.

The net result on me was to make me more resolved than ever not to be defeated. It made me mean and revengeful.

It made me hate Danilo.

The morning wore on. The heat became a trial and I got tired of sitting still. I had, however, I told myself, spent three weeks in Spain in precisely this position. There, in fact, it had been much hotter. I wilfully ignored the thought that in Spain we had knocked off for lunch.

Lunchtime was pretty near, by my watch. Well . . . maybe someone would come . . .

And how would they get there, I wondered. Ahead of me there was no road, just small trees, dry grass and scrubby undergrowth. To each side, just the same. But the car must have been driven there, not dropped by a passing eagle . . . Twisting my neck and consulting the reflection in the mirror, I saw that the road, such as it was, lay directly at my back. It was an earth road showing no sign of upkeep and all too many of desertion, and it petered out completely twenty yards or so from where I sat. My car had been driven straight off the end of it into the bush.

In less than a month it would rain: the trees and the grass would grow thick and green, and the road turn to mud. No one would find the car, if it were still there when the rains came.

If I . . . were still there when the rains came.

I shook myself. That way led straight towards the mental state of the man in the film, and of course I had decided to steer clear of it.

Of course.

Perhaps they would send a helicopter . . .

It was a grey car; nondescript. But surely any car would show up, from the air. There was a small aerodrome near Skukuza, I'd seen it marked on the map. Surely Evan would send a helicopter . . .

But where to? I was facing north, off the end of an abandoned track, I could be anywhere.

Maybe if I did after all make a noise, someone would hear . . . All those people driving along miles away in their safe little cars with the engines droning and the windows securely shut.

The car's horn . . . Useless. It was one of those cars which had to have the ignition on before the horn would sound.

In the ignition . . . no keys.

Lunchtime came and went. I could have done with a nice cold beer.

A heavy swishing in the bush behind me sent my head twisting hopefully in its direction. Someone had come . . . Well, hadn't I known they would?

No human voices, though, exclaimed over me, bringing freedom. My visitor, in fact, had no voice at all, as he was a giraffe.

The great fawn sky-scraper with paler patches rolled rhythmically past the car and began pulling at the sparse leaves scattering the top of the tree straight ahead. He was so close that his bulk shut out the sun, giving me a welcome oasis of shade. Huge and graceful, he stayed for a while, munching peacefully and pausing now and then to bend his great horned head towards the car, peering at it from eyes fringed by outrageously long lashes. The most seductive lady would be reduced to despair by a giraffe's eyelashes.

I found myself talking to him aloud. 'Just buzz off over to Skukuza, will you, and get our friend Haagner to come here in his Range Rover at the bloody double.'

The sound of my voice startled me, because in it I heard my own conviction. I might hope that Evan or Conrad or Haagner or the merest passing stranger would soon find me, but I didn't believe it. Unconsciously, because of the film, I was already geared to a long wait.

But what I did believe was that in the end someone would come. The peasant would ride by on his donkey, and see the car, and rescue the man. That was the only tolerable ending. The one I had to cling to, and work for.

For in the end, people would search.

If I didn't turn up at the premiere, there would be questions and checks, and finally a search.

The premiere was next Wednesday.

Today, I supposed, was Friday.

People could live only six or seven days without water.

I stared sombrely at the giraffe. He batted the fantastic eyelashes, shook his head gently as if in sorrow, and ambled elegantly away.

By Wednesday night I would have spent six whole days without water. No one would find me as soon as the Thursday.

Friday or Saturday, perhaps, if they were clever.

It couldn't be done.

It had to be.

When the giraffe took away with him his patch of shade I realized how fierce the sun had grown. If I did nothing about it, I thought, I would have me a nasty case of sunburn.

The parts of me most relentlessly in the sun were oddly enough my hands. As in most hot-country cars, the top third of the windscreen was tinted green against glare, and if I rolled my head back I could get my face out of the direct rays; but they fell unimpeded on to my lap. I solved the worst of that by unbuttoning my shirt cuffs and tucking my hands in the opposite sleeves, like a muff.

After that I debated the wisdom of taking my shoes and socks off, and of opening a window to let in some fresh and cooler air. I could get my feet, one at a time, up to my hands to get my socks off. I could also swivel enough in my seat to wind the left-hand window handle with my toes.

It wasn't the thought of invasion by animals that stopped me doing it at once, but the niggling subject of humidity.

The only water available to me for the whole of the time I sat there would be what was contained at that moment in my own body. With every movement and every breath I was depleting the stock, releasing water into the air about me in the form of invisible water vapour. If I kept the windows shut, the water vapour would mostly stay inside the car. If I opened them, it would instantly be lost.

The outside air, after all those rainless months, was as dry as Prohibition. It seemed to me that though I couldn't stop my body losing a lot of moisture, I could to some extent re-use it. It would take longer, in damper air, for my skin to crack in dehydration. Re-breathing water vapour would go some small way to postponing the time when the mucous linings of nose and throat would dry raw.

So what with one thing and another, I didn't open the window.

Like a man with an obsession I turned back again and again to the hope–despair see-saw of rescue, one minute convinced that Evan and Conrad would have sent out sorties the moment they found me gone, the next that they would simply have cursed my rudeness and set off by themselves towards the north, where Evan would become so engrossed with *olifant* that E. Lincoln would fade from his mind like yesterday's news.

No one else would miss me. Everyone back in Johannesburg – the van Hurens, Roderick, Clifford Wenkins – knew I had gone down to the game reserve for the rest of the week. None of them would expect to hear from me. None of them would expect me back before Tuesday.

The only hope I had lay in Evan and Conrad . . . and the peasant passing by with his donkey.

At some point during the long afternoon I thought of seeing if I still had in my trouser pockets the things I had had there the day before. I hadn't emptied the pockets when I undressed, I had just laid my clothes on the second bed.

Investigation showed that my wallet was still buttoned into my rear pocket, because I could feel its shape if I pushed back against the seat. But money, in these circumstances, was useless.

By twisting, lifting myself an inch off the seat, and tugging, I managed to get my right-hand pocket round to centre front, and, carefully exploring, brought forth a total prize of a packet of Iguana Rock book matches, with four matches left, a blue rubber band, and a three-inch stub of pencil with no point.

I put all these carefully back where they came from, and reversed the tugging until I could reach into the left-hand pocket.

Two things only in there. A handkerchief . . . and the forgotten screwed-up plastic bag from Evan's sandwiches.

'Don't throw plastic bags out of car windows,' Haagner had said. 'They can kill the animals.'

And save the lives of men.

Precious, precious plastic bag.

Never cross a desert without one.

I knew how to get half a cup of water every twenty-four hours from a sheet of plastic in a hot climate, but it couldn't be done by someone strapped into a sitting position inside a car. It needed a hole dug in the ground, a small weight, and something to catch the water in.

All the same, the principle was there, if I could make it work.

Condensation.

The hole in the ground method worked during the night. In the heat of the day one dug a hole, making it about eighteen inches deep, and in diameter slightly smaller than the available piece of plastic. One placed a cup in the hole, in the centre. One spread the sheet of plastic over the hole, and sealed it down round the edges with the dug-out earth or sand. And finally one placed a small stone or some coins on the centre of the plastic, weighing it down at a spot directly over the cup.

After that, one waited.

Cooled by the night, the water vapour in the hot air trapped in the hole condensed into visible water droplets, which formed on the cold unporous plastic, trickled downhill to the weighted point, and dripped from there into the cup.

A plastic bagful of hot air should produce a teaspoonful of water by dawn.

It wasn't much.

After a while I pulled one hand towards me as far as it would go, and leaned forward hard against the seat belt, and found I could reach far enough to blow into the bag if I held its gathered neck loosely with an O of forefinger and thumb.

For probably half an hour I breathed in through my nose, and out through my mouth, into the plastic bag. At the end of that time there were hundreds of small water droplets sticking to the inside of the bag . . . the water vapour out of my lungs, trapped there instead of escaping into the air.

I turned the bag inside out and licked it. It was wet. When I'd sucked off as much as I could, I laid the cool damp surface against my face, and perhaps because of the paltriness of what I had achieved, felt the first deep stab of desolation.

I fished out the blue rubber band again, and while the sunlit air was still hot, filled the bag with it, twisting the neck tight and fastening it with the band to one side of the steering wheel. It hung there like a fool's balloon, bobbing lightly away if I touched it.

I had been thirsty all day, but not unbearably.

After dark some hovering internal rumbles identified themselves as hunger. Again, not unbearably.

The bladder problem reappeared and was again a disaster. But time, I supposed, would lessen the difficulty: no input, less output.

Hope had to be filed under 'pending', after dark. Twelve hours to be lived before one could climb on to the will-they-won't-they treadmill again. I found them long, lonely, and dreadful.

The cramps which I had so imaginatively constructed for the film began to afflict my own body in earnest, once the heat of the day drained away and let my muscles grow stiff.

At first I warmed up by another dozen wrenching

attempts to break the steering wheel off the control column, the net result of which was considerable wear and tear on me, and none on the car. After that I tried to plan a sensible series of isometric exercises which would keep everything warm and working, but I only got about half of them done.

Against all the odds, I went to sleep.

The nightmare was still there when I woke up.

I was shivering with cold, creakingly stiff, and perceptibly hungrier.

I had nothing to eat but four matches, a handkerchief, and a blunt pencil.

After a small amount of thought I dug out the pencil, and chewed that. Not exactly for the food value, but to bare the lead. With that pencil, I decided, I could bring Danilo down.

Before dawn the realization crept slowly in that Danilo could not have abandoned me in the car without help. He would have needed someone to drive him away when he had finished locking me in. He wouldn't have walked through the game reserve, not only because of the danger from animals, but because a man on foot would have been as conspicuous as gallantry.

So someone had helped him.

Who?

Arknold . . .

He had shut his eyes to Danilo's fraud, when he had discovered it: had kept silent, because by not arranging better security he had put his licence at risk. But would he step down into murder to save himself a suspension?

No. He wouldn't.

Barty, for money?

I didn't know.

One . . . any . . . of the van Hurens, for any reason at all?

No.

Roderick, for news? Or Katya, or Melanie?

No.

Clifford Wenkins, for publicity?

If it was him, I was safe, because he wouldn't leave me there much longer. He wouldn't dare. Worldic, for a start, wouldn't want the merchandise turning up in a damaged state. I wished I believed it was Wenkins, but I didn't.

Evan? Conrad?

I couldn't face it.

They had both been there. On the spot. Sleeping next door. Handy for breaking in in the night and smothering me with ether.

One of them could have done it while the other slept. But which? And why?

If it were either Evan or Conrad I was going to die, because only they could save me.

The dawn came up on this bleakest of thoughts and showed me that my theories on water vapour were correct. I could see nothing of the Kruger National Park, because all the windows were fogged and beaded with condensation.

I could reach the glass beside me, and I licked it. It felt great. The dryness of my tongue and throat became instantly less aggravating, though I could still have done with a pint of draught.

I looked through the licked patch. Same old wilderness. Same old no one there.

My spoonful of water had formed all right inside the now cold plastic bag. Carefully I loosened its neck in the rubber band and squeezed the shrunken air out, to prevent it expanding again when the day grew hot, and reabsorbing the precious liquid. I wouldn't drink it until later, I decided. Until things got worse.

*

With all the precious humidity clinging to the inside of the windows, it was safe to embark on a change of air. I took off my sock and turned the handle with my toes, and opened the left-hand window a scant inch. Couldn't risk not being able to shut it again: but when the sun came up I got it shut without much trouble. When the growing heat cleared the windows by re-evaporating the water, at least I had such comfort as there was in knowing it was all still inside the car, doing its best.

The pencil I had chewed in the night (and stowed for safe storage under my watch strap) was showing signs of usefulness. One more session with the incisors, and it had enough bare lead at the tip to write with.

The only thing to write on that I had in my pockets was the inside of the book of matches, which was room enough for 'Danilo did it', but not for my whole purpose. There were maps and car documents, however, in the glove compartment in front of the passenger seat, and after a long struggle, tying my toes in knots and using up a great deal too much precious energy, I collected into my hands a large brown envelope, and a book of maps with nice blank end papers.

There was a lot to write.

CHAPTER FIFTEEN

Danilo had suggested to Nerissa that I go to South Africa because there, far from home, he could take or make any opportunity that offered to bring me to an accidental-looking death. He had lured me to the killing ground with a bait he knew I would take – a near-dying request from a woman I liked and was grateful to.

A death which was clearly a murder would have left him too dangerously exposed as a suspect. An obvious accident would be less suspiciously investigated . . . like a live microphone.

Danilo hadn't been there, in Randfontein House.

Roderick had been there, and Clifford Wenkins, and Conrad. And fifty others besides. If Danilo had provided the live mike, someone at the Press interview must have steered it into my hands. Luck alone had taken it out again.

Down the mine, at the suddenly opportune moment . . . bash.

Except for the steadfastness of a checker called Nyembezi, that attempt would have come off.

849

This wouldn't look like a natural accident, though. The handcuffs couldn't be called accidental.

Perhaps Danilo intended to come back, after I was dead, and take them away. Perhaps people would believe then that I had lost my way in the park and had died in the car rather than risk walking.

But the time span was tight. He couldn't wait a week to make sure I was dead before coming back, because by then everyone would be searching for me, and someone might have reached me before he did.

I sighed dispiritedly.

None of it made any sense.

The day proved an inferno compared with the one before. Much worse even than Spain. The scorching fury of the heat stunned me to the point where thought became impossible, and cramps wracked my shoulders, arms and stomach.

I tucked my hands into my sleeves and rolled my head back out of the direct rays and just sat there enduring it, because there was nothing else to do.

So much for my pathetic little attempts at water management. The brutal sun was shrivelling me minute by minute, and I knew that a week was wildly optimistic. In this heat, a day or two would be enough.

My throat burned with thirst and saliva was a thing of the past.

A gallon of water in the car's radiator ... as out of reach as a mirage.

When I couldn't swallow without wincing or breathe without feeling the intaken air cut like a knife, I untied the plastic bag and poured the contents into my mouth. I made the divine H_2O last as long as possible; rolled it round my teeth and gums, and under my tongue. There was hardly enough left to swallow, and when it was gone I felt wretched. There was nothing, now, between me and nightfall.

I turned the bag inside out and sucked it, and held it against my mouth until the heat had dried it entirely, and then I filled it again with hot air, and with trembling fingers fumbled it back into the rubber band on the steering wheel.

I remembered that the boot of the car still held, as far as I knew, a lot of oddments of Conrad's equipment. Surely he would need it, would come looking for that, if not for me.

Evan, I thought, for God's sake come and find me.

But Evan had gone north in the park which stretched two hundred miles to the boundary on the great grey-green greasy Limpopo river. Evan was searching there for his Elephant's Child.

And I ... I was sitting in a car, dying for a gold mine I didn't want.

*

851

Night came, and hunger.

People paid to be starved in health farms, and people went on hunger strikes to protest about this or that, so what was so special about hunger?'

Nothing. It was just a pain.

The night was cool, was blessed. In the morning, when I had licked as much of the window as I could reach, I went on with the writing. I wrote everything I could think of which would help an investigation into my death.

The heat started up before I had finished. I wrote 'give my love to Charlie', and signed my name, because I wasn't certain that by that evening I would be able to write any more. Then I slid the written papers under my left thigh so that they wouldn't slip out of reach on the floor, and tucked the little pencil under my watch strap, and collapsed the air out of the plastic bag to keep the next teaspoonful safe, and wondered how long, how long I would last.

By midday I didn't want to last.

I held out until then for my sip of water, but when it was gone I would have been happy to die. After the bag had dried against my face it took a very long time, and a great effort of will, for me to balloon it out and fix it again to the steering wheel. Tomorrow, I thought, the thimbleful would form again, but I would be past drinking it.

We had been wrong in the film, I thought. We had focused on the mental state of the man too much, to the neglect of the physical. We hadn't known about legs like lead and ankles swollen to giant puffballs. I had long ago shed my socks, and would have had as much chance of forcing my shoes on again as of flying.

We hadn't known the abdomen would become agonizingly distended with gas or that the seat belts would strain across it like hawsers. We hadn't guessed that the eyes would feel like sand paper when the lachrymal glands dried up. We had underestimated what dehydration did to the throat.

The overwhelming heat battered all emotions into numbness. There was nothing anywhere but pain, and no prospect that it would stop.

Except, of course, in death.

In the late afternoon an elephant came and uprooted the tree the giraffe had browsed from.

That should be allegorical enough for Evan, I thought confusedly. Elephants were the indestructible destroyers of the wilderness.

But Evan was miles away.

Evan, I thought, Evan . . . Oh God, Evan . . . come . . . and find me.

The elephant ate a few succulent leaves off the tree and went away and left it with its roots in the air, dying for lack of water.

Before dark I did write a few more sentences. My hands trembled continually, and folded into tight cramps, and were in the end too weak to hold the pencil.

It fell down on the floor and rolled beneath my seat. I couldn't see it, or pick it up with my swollen toes.

Weeping would have been a waste of water.

Night came again and time began to blur.

I couldn't remember how long I had been there, or how long it was until Wednesday.

Wednesday was as far away as Charlie, and I wouldn't see either of them. I had a vision of the pool in the garden with the kids splashing in it, and it was the car that seemed unreal, not the pool.

Tremors shook my limbs for hours on end.

The night was cold. Muscles stiffened. Teeth chattered. Stomach shrieked to be fed.

In the morning, the condensation on the windows was so heavy that water trickled in rivulets down the glass. I could only, as ever, reach the small area near my head. I licked it weakly. It wasn't enough.

I hadn't the energy any more to open the window for a change of air: but cars were never entirely airtight, and it wouldn't be asphyxiation which saw me off.

The inevitable sun came back in an innocent rosy dawn, gentle prelude to the terrifying day ahead.

I no longer believed that anyone would come.

All that remained was to suffer into unconsciousness, because after that there would be peace. Even delirium would be a sort of peace, because the worst torment was to be aware, to understand. I would welcome a clouded mind, when it came. That, for me, would be the real death. The only one that mattered. I wouldn't know or care when my heart finally stopped.

Heat bullied into the car like a battering ram.

I burned.

I burned.

CHAPTER SIXTEEN

They did come.

When the sun was high, Evan and Conrad came in the station wagon. Evan stampeding about in a frenzy of energy, waving his arms about, with his hair sticking out crazily and his eyes too hot for comfort. Conrad, puffing slightly under the droopy moustache, mopping his forehead with a handkerchief.

They simply walked up to the car and opened the door. Then they stood still. And stared.

I thought they were unreal; the onset of delusion. I stared back, waiting for them to vanish.

Then Evan said, 'Where the hell have you been? We've been searching the whole bloody park for you since yesterday morning.'

I didn't answer him. I couldn't.

Conrad was saying, 'My God, my God, dear boy, my God . . .' as if the needle had stuck.

Evan went back to the station wagon, drove it across the grass, and parked it alongside the car I was in. Then he scrambled into the back and unclipped the red ice box.

'Will beer do?' he shouted. 'We didn't bring any water.'

Beer would do.

He poured it from a can into a plastic cup and held it to my mouth. It was cold; alive; incredible. I only drank half, because it hurt to swallow.

Conrad opened the left-hand door and sat on the seat beside me.

'We haven't a key for the handcuffs,' he said apologetically.

A laugh twitched somewhere inside me, the first for a long time.

'Phew,' Evan said, 'You do stink.'

They saw I couldn't talk. Evan poured more beer into the cup and held it for me, and Conrad got out of the car and rummaged about in the boot. He came back with four short lengths of strong wire and a roll of insulating tape, and with these he proceeded to set me free.

He stuck the four wires into the barrel of the handcuff lock, bound the protruding ends tightly together to give a handle for leverage, and began to turn. The makeshift key did a grand job. With a lot of swearing and a couple of fresh starts when the wires slipped out, Conrad got the ratchet on my right wrist opened.

And who cared about the other? It could wait.

They unclipped the seat belts and tried to help me out of the car, but I had been sitting in the same restricted position for over eighty hours, and like concrete my body seemed to have set in the mould.

Evan said doubtfully, 'I think one of us should go and find a doctor.'

I shook my head decidedly. There were things I wanted to tell them before the outside world broke in. I felt jerkily under my thigh for the papers I had written, and made writing motions with my hands. Conrad silently produced the gold ballpoint he always carried, and I shakily wrote on an unused corner of brown envelope, '*If you do not tell anyone you have found me, we can catch the man who put me here.*' And as an afterthought, I added, '*I want to do that.*'

They read the uneven words and stood wondering, almost literally scratching their heads.

I wrote a bit more. '*Please put something over the windscreen.*'

That at least made sense to them. Conrad draped the front of the car with a heavy groundsheet which effectively brought the temperature down by ten degrees.

Evan saw the plastic bag hanging from the steering wheel and pulled it off its rubber band.

'What the hell is this?' he said.

I pointed to the still undrunk mouthful of water lurking in one corner. Evan understood, and looked completely appalled.

He took the written pages out of my hand, and read them. I drank some more beer, holding the cup with trembly fingers but feeling life flowing back through all the dying channels with every difficult swallow.

He read right to the end and handed the pages to Conrad. He stared at me with stunned speechlessness. An unaccustomed state for Evan. After a long time he said slowly, 'Did you really think Conrad or I had helped to leave you here?'

I shook my head.

'And you can cross off poor old Clifford Wenkins, too, because he's dead. They fished him out of the Wemmer Pan on Saturday afternoon. He went boating, and drowned.'

The news took a while to percolate. I thought, no more stuttering, no more damp palms, no more nervous little man . . . poor little nervous man . . .

I lifted Conrad's golden pen, and Evan gave me one of his ubiquitous notebooks to write on.

'*I'd like to lie down. In the station wagon?*'

'Sure,' he said, seeming to be glad of an excuse for activity. 'We'll make you a bed.'

He hopped into the estate car again and hauled all their equipment to one side. In the cleared space he constructed a mattress from the back seats of both cars, and made a thick pillow out of coats and sweaters.

'The Ritz,' he said, 'is at your service.'

I tried a smile and caught sight of it in the driving mirror.

Ghastly. I had a four-day beard and sunken pinkish eyes and looked as grey and red as a sunburned ghost.

With more gentleness than I would have thought either of them had in their natures, they helped me out of the car and carried more than supported me over to the station wagon. Bent double, creaking in every muscle, and feeling that my lumbar vertebrae were breaking, I completed the journey, and once lying on the makeshift bed began the luxuriously painful process of straightening myself out. Evan took the groundsheet off my car and spread it over the roof of the station wagon, as much to shut out the heat as for shade.

I wrote again. '*Stay here, Evan*', because I thought they might start my car with a jump lead, and drive off for help. He looked doubtful, so I added with a fair amount of desperation, '*Please don't leave me.*'

'Christ,' he said, when he read that. 'Christ, mate, we won't leave you.' He was clearly emotionally upset, which surprised me. He didn't even like me, and in the Special had heaped on the discomfort without mercy.

I drank some more beer, mouthful by separate mouthful. My throat still beat a raging case of tonsillitis out of sight, but the lubrication was slowly taking effect. I could move my tongue better, and it was beginning to feel less like a swollen lump of liver.

Evan and Conrad sat in the front seats of the estate car and began discussing where to go. They had no accommodation reserved at Skukuza, which it appeared was still the nearest camp, and it was two hours' drive to the beds booked at Satara.

Satara and the beds won, which seemed good enough for me.

Evan said, 'We might as well get going, then. It's too bloody hot here. I've had enough of it. We'll find a patch of decent shade along the road, and stop for lunch. It's after two, already, and I'm hungry.'

That was a lot more like the Evan I knew and detested. With an inward smile, I had another go with the pen.

'*Remember how to get back here.*'

'Someone else can fetch the car,' said Evan impatiently. 'Later.'

I shook my head. '*We must come back.*'

'Why?'

'*To catch Danilo Cavesey.*'

They looked from the pad to my face. Then Evan merely said, 'How?'

I wrote down how. They read it. The air of excited intensity reawoke in Evan, and rapid professional calculations furrowed Conrad's forehead, for what I was asking them to do was much to their liking. Then a separate, secondary thought struck both of them, and they looked at me doubtfully.

'You can't mean it, dear boy,' Conrad said.

I nodded.

'What about the person who helped him?' Evan asked. 'What are you going to do about him?'

'*He's dead, now.*'

'Dead?' He looked incredulous. 'You don't mean . . . Clifford Wenkins?'

I nodded. I was tired. I wrote '*Tell you when I can talk.*'

They agreed to that. They shut the doors of my car, climbed into the front seats of the station wagon, turned it, and set off along the dirt road which had for so long for me been just a reflection in a three-by-six inch looking glass.

Conrad drove, and Evan made a map. They seemed to have found me by the merest chance, as I had been a mile up a side branch of an equally unkempt road leading to a now dry water hole. The water hole road joined into another, which led finally back to the roads used by visitors. Evan said he could find the way straight back to my car: it was easy. They had searched, he added, every side road they could find between Skukuza and Numbi, and that had been yesterday. Today, they had tried the dry sparse land to the south of the Sabie river, and they had found me on the fifth no-entry they had explored.

After five or six miles we came to a small group of trees throwing some dappled shade: Conrad at once pulled in and stopped the car, and Evan without more ado started burrowing into the red box. They had brought more sandwiches, more fruit, more beer.

I thought I would postpone sandwiches and fruit. Beer was doing wonders. I drank some more.

The other two munched away as if the whole picnic were routine. They opened the windows wide, reckoning that any sensible animal would be sleeping in this heat, not looking out for unwary humans.

No cars passed. Every sensible human, too, was busy at siesta in the air-conditioned camps. Evan, of course, was impervious to heat, and Conrad had to lump it.

I wrote again, '*What made you start looking for me?*'

Evan spoke round bits of ham sandwich. 'We kept wanting the things of Conrad's which were in your car. It became most annoying not to have them. So yesterday morning we telephoned the Iguana to tell you how selfish you had been to take them away with you.'

'They said you weren't there,' Conrad said. 'They said they understood you were going to the Kruger Park for several days.'

'We couldn't understand it,' Evan nodded. 'In view of your note.'

'What note?' I tried automatically to say the words, but my throat still wouldn't have it. I wrote them instead.

'The note you left,' Evan said impatiently. 'Saying you had gone back to Johannesburg.'

'*I left no note.*'

He stopped chewing and sat with his mouth full as if in suspended animation. Then he took up chewing again, and said, 'No. That's right. You couldn't have.'

'We thought you had, anyway,' Conrad said. 'It was just a piece of paper, written in capital letters, saying, "*Gone back to Johannesburg. Link.*" Bloody rude and ungrateful, dear boy, we thought of it. Packing all your gear and buzzing off at the crack of dawn without even bothering to say good-bye.'

'*Sorry.*'

Conrad laughed. 'After that we tried to reach Clifford Wenkins, because we thought he might know where you were, but all we got at his number was some hysterical woman saying he'd been drowned in the Wemmer Pan.'

'We tried one or two other people,' Evan went on. 'The van Hurens, and so on.'

'*Danilo?*' I wrote.

'No.' Evan shook his head. 'Didn't think of him. Wouldn't know where he's staying, for a start.' He ate a mouthful, reflecting. 'We thought it a bit unhelpful of you to go off without letting anyone know where you could be found, and then we thought perhaps you'd been damn bloody careless and got lost in the park, and never got back to Johannesburg at all. So after a bit of argy-bargy we persuaded the reception office at Satara to check what time you went out of the Numbi gate on Friday morning, and the gate keeper said that according to their records you hadn't gone out at all.'

'We telephoned Haagner, dear boy,' Conrad said, 'and explained the situation, but he didn't seem to be much worried. He said people often talked their way out of Numbi without papers, even though one was supposed to produce receipts to show one had paid for staying in camps. Mr Lincoln would only have to say, Haagner said, that Evan and Conrad were still in the park, and had paid for him. The Numbi men would check with Skukuza, and then let Mr Lincoln go. He also said you couldn't be lost in the park. You were too sensible, he said, and only fools got lost. People who drove miles down no-entry roads and then had their cars break down.'

And that, I presumed, was what they thought had happened. But I wouldn't grumble.

They opened cans of beer and gulped. I went on sipping.

'We had sure enough paid for you at Skukuza,' Evan said accusingly. 'Including the window you broke.'

I only had to pick up the pen.

'My God,' Evan said, before I got it to the paper. 'Danilo Cavesey broke the window . . . to get into your *rondavel*.'

I supposed so. He had got past the locked door without waking me.

'You're a fairly valuable property, dear boy,' Conrad said, finishing the saga. 'So we decided we ought perhaps to spend a day or so looking for you.'

'We saw a splendid herd of elephants yesterday afternoon,' said Evan, pointing out that the delay to their original plans had not been an entire waste. 'And we might see some more today,' he said.

They helped me into the *rondavel* in Satara and I asked them to turn the air-conditioning off, as to me the hut felt cold. If I got cold again I would get stiff again, which would only add to my aches . . . I lay on one of the beds with three blankets over me and felt lousy.

Conrad fetched a glass of water and he and Evan stood around looking helpless.

Evan said, 'Let's take your stinking clothes off. You'd embarrass a pig, as you are.'

I shook my head.

'If we bring you some water, would you like to wash?'

No, again.

Evan wrinkled his nose. 'Well, you won't mind if neither of us sleeps in here with you?'

I shook my head. My smell was offensive to myself as well, now that I'd breathed so much clean fresh air.

Conrad went off to the camp shop to find something I could swallow and presently came back with a pint of milk and a tin of chicken soup. The only opener they had was the beer can opener, but they got the soup out into a jug in the end. There was nothing to heat the soup with, so they tipped in half the milk and stirred it around until it was runny. Then they poured out a glassful, and, grateful for their clumsy care, I drank it bit by bit.

'Now,' said Evan briskly, satisfied that they had done the best possible for me, 'let's get on with planning the trap.'

This time, when I tried, some semblance of speech came out.

'Danilo is staying at the Vaal Majestic,' I said.

'What did you say?' Evan demanded. 'Thank God you can talk again, but I couldn't understand a word of it.'

I wrote it down.

'Oh. Right.'

I said, 'Telephone in the morning, and tell him . . .' It was a croak, rough and cracked.

'Look,' Evan interrupted. 'We'll get along quicker if you write it.'

I nodded. Much easier on my throat, if he preferred it that way.

'At breakfast time, tell Danilo you are trying to find out where I am, because I have Conrad's equipment in my car. Tell him I also have Conrad's gold pencil in my pocket, and he especially wants it back. Tell him I also have one of your notebooks, and you need your notes. Tell him you are worried because I had some theory that someone I knew had been trying to kill me.'

Evan read, and looked dubious. 'Are you sure that will bring him?'

I wrote: *'Would you risk my being able to write down that theory, if you knew I had pencil and paper within reach?'*

He considered. He said, 'No. I wouldn't.'

'I did do it.'

'So you did.'

Conrad sat heavily down in the armchair, nodding.

'What next, dear boy?'

I wrote: '*This evening, telephone Quentin van Huren. Tell him where and in what state you found me. Say I wrote some notes. Read them to him. Tell him about the trap for Danilo. Ask him to tell the police. With his authority, he can arrange it properly.*'

'Sure. Sure.' Evan, with undaunted wiry energy, collected up my writings from the car and his notebook with all our plans, and strode off at once to the telephone in the main buildings.

Conrad stayed behind and lit a cigar, no doubt to fend off evil odours.

'It was Evan who insisted on looking for you, dear boy,' he said. 'Absolutely fanatical, he was. You know how he never lets up when he gets an idea. We went up every unlikely track . . . bloody silly, I thought . . . until we found you.'

'Who,' I said slowly, trying to speak clearly, 'told Danilo about the film . . . *Man in the Car*?'

He shrugged a little uncomfortably. 'Maybe I did. At Germiston. They were all asking about your latest work . . . the van Hurens, Clifford Wenkins, Danilo . . . everybody.'

It didn't matter. Wenkins could have got hold of the film's plot easily enough, through Worldic.

'Dear boy,' Conrad said thoughtfully. 'The make-up is all wrong in the film.' He puffed the cigar. 'Mind you,' he said, 'what you actually look like would be pretty poor box-office.'

'Thanks.'

He smiled. 'Have some more soup?'

Evan was gone a long time and came back looking earnest and intense.

'He wants me to ring back later. He was pretty incoherent when I'd finished.' Evan raised his eyebrows, surprised that anyone should need time to assimilate so many unwelcome facts. 'He said he would think over what ought to be done. And oh yes, he said to ask you why you now thought it was Clifford Wenkins who helped Danilo.'

I said, 'Clifford Wenkins would have helped . . .'

'Write it down,' said Evan impatiently. 'You sound like a crow with laryngitis.'

I wrote: '*Clifford Wenkins would do anything for publicity stunts. He would exchange recording gear and microphones, for instance. I do not believe he thought anyone would be killed, but if I got an electric shock at a Press conference, it would put my name and the purpose of my visit in the papers. I believe Danilo put it all into his head, and gave him the live equipment. Wenkins was terrified when Katya was so badly shocked and afterwards I saw him telephoning, looking very worried. I thought he was calling Worldic, but he might have been telling Danilo that the stunt had gone wrong.*'

'It went better, dear boy, from Worldic's point of view,' Conrad commented.

'*Worldic drove Clifford Wenkins unmercifully to arrange publicity stunts . . . so if Danilo suggested to him that they should kidnap me and lock me in a car, just like in my new film, he would have been foolish enough to agree.*

'*When I'd been in the car for three days, I did not think it could be Wenkins who'd been helping Danilo because I knew Wenkins would not leave me there very long. But once Wenkins was dead, no one but Danilo knew where I was. He had only to leave me there . . .*

'*After my body was discovered, people would work out that it had been a publicity stunt planned by Wenkins and myself, which went wrong because he drowned and could not set in motion the necessary search.*

'*I expect it was in Wenkins's car that he and Danilo drove into the park, so that the Numbi gate office would have it on record that he had been there.*'

Evan practically tore the notebook out of my hands, as he had been striding around with impatience while I wrote. He read to the end and handed the notebook to Conrad.

'Do you realize,' he demanded, 'that you are practically accusing Danilo of killing Clifford Wenkins, so that you shouldn't be found?'

I nodded.

'I think he did,' I croaked. 'For a gold mine.'

*

They left me with water and soup to hand and went off to dinner in the restaurant. When they came back, Evan had telephoned again to van Huren.

'He'd grasped everything a bit better,' Evan allowed condescendingly. 'I read him what you wrote about Wenkins, and he said he thought you could be right. He said he was upset about Danilo, because he had liked him, but he would do as you asked. He said that he himself would come down here . . . he's flying down to the Skukuza airstrip first thing in the morning. The police will be properly genned up. Conrad and I will meet them and van Huren at Skukuza, and go on from there, if it looks likely that Danilo has taken the bait.'

We were going to call Danilo in the morning. Even if he, too, flew down as fast as possible, everyone should be in position before he came.

The night was paradise compared with its predecessors, but still far short of heaven. In the morning I felt a good deal stronger; there were no more cramps and the fire in my throat would no longer frighten Celsius. I got myself to the bathroom looking as bent as old Adam the gardener, but I got there; and I ate the banana which Conrad brought me for breakfast.

Evan had gone to telephone Danilo, Conrad said, and Evan came later with a satisfied smile.

'He was there,' he said. 'And I'd say there was no doubt he swallowed it. He sounded pretty worried . . .

sharp voice, that sort of thing. He asked why I was so sure about the gold pencil. Can you believe it? I said Conrad had lent it to you Thursday evening and I'd seen you put it in your pocket. Then, Friday morning, you went off to Johannesburg without giving it back.'

CHAPTER SEVENTEEN

The hardest thing I ever did was to get back into that car.

We reached it at half past ten, and Evan and Conrad busily rigged up various bits and pieces, including a warning buzzer which would tell me when Danilo was approaching.

Half an hour later, when they had finished, the day was stoking up to another roaster. I drank the whole of the bottle of water we had brought from Satara and ate another banana.

Evan danced up and down. 'Come on. Come on. We haven't got all day. We've got to hurry to Skukuza to meet van Huren.'

I left the station wagon, hobbled across to the car, sat in the front seat, and fastened the seat belts.

The dying aches flared up at once.

Conrad approached with the handcuffs, and my throat closed. I couldn't look at him, couldn't look at Evan ... at anything. Couldn't do it ... all my nerves and muscles revolted.

Couldn't.

Conrad, watching me, said practically, 'You haven't got to, Link. It's your own idea, dear boy. He will come, whether you are here or not.'

'Don't try and dissuade him,' Evan said crossly. 'Not now we've gone to all this trouble. And as Link pointed out himself, if he isn't in the car when Danilo comes, nothing will be conclusive.'

Conrad still hesitated. My fault.

'Get on with it,' Evan said.

I put my arm through the steering wheel. It was trembling.

Conrad clicked the handcuffs shut first on one wrist and then the other, and I shuddered from head to foot.

'Dear boy . . .' Conrad said doubtfully.

'Come on,' Evan urged.

I didn't say anything. I thought that whatever I might start to say, it would come out as a screaming plea that they wouldn't leave me. Leave me, however, they must.

Evan shut the car door brusquely, and jerked his head for Conrad to follow him into the estate car. Conrad went with his head turned backwards, looking to see if I were calling him.

They climbed into the front seat, reversed, turned, drove away. The silence of the tinder-dry park settled around me.

I wished I had never suggested this plan. The car seemed hotter than ever, the heat more intolerable.

Within an hour, and in spite of the quantities of water I had drunk that morning, fierce thirst returned.

Cramps began again in my legs. My spine protested. My shoulders pulled with strain.

I cursed myself.

Supposing he took all day, I thought. Supposing he didn't fly down, but drove. Eight o'clock, when Evan telephoned him. At least five hours' drive to Numbi, another hour and a half to reach me . . . He might not come until three or four . . . which meant five hours in the car . . .

I tucked my hands into my shirt sleeves and rolled my head back out of the sun.

There was no water vapour, no plastic bag, to keep my mind occupied. The pencil-written sheets lay on my knees, with Conrad's gold pencil, companion to his pen, clipping them together. There was no leaping from hope to despair and back again, which was certainly a blessed relief, but unexpectedly left too much time free for pure feeling.

Every minute dragged.

The premiere, I thought, was due to be held the following night. I wondered who would be arranging everything, with poor Clifford Wenkins in his watery grave. I wondered if I would get to the Klipspringer Heights Hotel on time. In another twenty-four hours, shaved, bathed, rested, watered and fed, perhaps I might just make it. All those people paying twenty rand for a seat . . . unfair not to turn up, if I could . . .

Time crawled. I looked at my watch. It wasn't trying.

One o'clock came. One o'clock went.

Conrad had fixed a radio transmitter with a button for me to press if I simply could not stand any more. But if I pressed it, the whole of today's effort would be wasted. If I pressed it, the cohorts would rush to my rescue, but Danilo would see the activity, and would never come near.

I wished Conrad hadn't insisted on that button. Evan said it was necessary, so that he and van Huren and the police would know for certain that Danilo had come, if they should by some mischance miss him on the road.

One buzz was to mean that Danilo had come.

Two buzzes that he had left again.

A series of short buzzes would bring them instantly at any time to set me free.

I would wait another ten minutes before I gave up, I thought.

Then another ten.

Then another.

Ten minutes was always possible.

Conrad's warning buzzer sounded like a wasp in my ear and jerked me into action.

*

Danilo drove up beside me and stopped where the station wagon had been.

I pressed the buttons taped within reach on the steering column.

I put all the actor's art I had into looking not far from death: and didn't have to elaborate all that much on what I knew of the real thing. A couple of vultures had conveniently flapped and spiralled down, and now perched on a nearby tree like brooding anarchists awaiting the revolution. I eyed them sourly, but Danilo was reassured.

He opened the door and through slit eyes I saw him draw back when the unmitigated heat-stoked stench met his nostrils. It had been worth not washing, not changing my clothes. There was nothing about me to show I hadn't sat in that spot continuously since he had left me there, and a great deal to prove I had.

He looked at my lolling head, my flaccid hands, my bare swollen feet. He showed no remorse whatever. The sun blazed on the bright blond head, giving him a halo. The clean-featured all-American boy, as shiny, cold and ruthless as ice.

He bent down and practically snatched the papers off my lap. Unclipped the pencil and threw it on the back seat of the car. Read what I had written, right to the end.

'So you did guess . . . you did write . . .' he said. 'Clever Ed Lincoln, too clever by half. Too bad no one will ever read this . . .' He peered down into my half shut eyes to make sure I could hear him, could see him. Then

877

he took out a cigarette lighter, flicked the flint, and set the corners of the papers into the flame.

I shook feebly in my seat, in mute protest. It pleased him.

He smiled.

He turned the papers, burning them all up, and then ground the ashes into just more dust in the dusty grass.

'There,' he said cheerfully.

I made a small croak. He paid attention.

I said, 'Let . . . me . . . go.'

'Not a chance.' He put his hand in his pocket and brought out a bunch of keys. 'Keys to the car.' He held them up, jingling. 'Key to the handcuffs.' He waved it in front of my eyes.

'Please . . .' I said.

'You're worth too much to me dead, pal. Sorry and all that. But there it is.'

He put the keys in his pocket, shut the door on me, and without another glance, drove heartlessly away.

Poor Nerissa, I thought. I hoped she would die before she found out about Danilo; but life was not always kind.

In time, four cars rolled back into the reflection in the driving mirror, and stopped in a cluster round my car.

Evan and Conrad's estate wagon. A chauffeur-driven car with van Huren. Two police cars; the first containing, I later discovered, their photographer and their surgeon; the second, three senior police officers . . . and Danilo Cavesey.

They all stood up outside the cars; a meal and a half for any passing pride of lion. Wild animals, however, kept decently out of sight. Danilo outdid them all for savagery.

Conrad bustled over and pulled open the door.

'You all right, dear boy?' he said anxiously.

I nodded.

Danilo was saying loudly and virtuously, 'I told you, I'd just found him, and I was driving away to get help.'

'Oh yeah,' Conrad muttered, digging out his bits of wire.

'He has the key of the handcuffs in his pocket,' I said.

'You don't mean it, dear boy?' He saw I did mean it. He went over and told the police, and after a short scuffle they found the key. Also the car keys. And now, perhaps Mr Cavesey would explain why he was driving away, when he had in his pocket the means of freeing Mr Lincoln?

Mr Cavesey glowered and declined. He had been going for help, he said.

Evan, enjoying himself immensely, walked over to the tree the elephant had uprooted, and from its withering foliage disentangled the Arriflex on its tripod.

'Everything you did here, we filmed,' he told Danilo. 'Link had a cable to the car. He started the camera when you arrived.'

Conrad fished his best tape-recorder out from under the car and unhitched the sensitive microphone from just inside the door frame.

'Everything you said here,' he echoed, with equal satisfaction, 'we recorded. Link switched on the recorder, when you came.'

The police produced a pair of handcuffs of their own, and put them on Danilo, who had gone blue-white under the sun-tan.

Quentin van Huren walked over to the car and looked down at me. Conrad had forgotten the small detail of bringing back the key to free me. I still sat, locked and helpless, where I had begun.

'For God's sake . . .' van Huren looked appalled.

I smiled lop-sidedly and shook my head. 'For gold's sake,' I said.

His mouth moved, but no words came out.

Gold, greed and gilded boys . . . a thoroughly bad mixture.

Evan was strutting around looking important, intense, and satisfied, as if he had stage-managed and directed the entire performance. But he saw that I was still tethered, and for once some twitch of compassion reached him. He went to fetch the handcuff key and brought it over.

He stood beside van Huren for a second, staring down at me as if seeing something new. For the first time ever he smiled with a hint of friendship.

'Cut,' he said. 'No re-takes, today.'

DICK FRANCIS

Bonecrack

£5.99

'Excitement and sheer readability'
Daily Telegraph

It started with mistaken identity and a threat to life. And
rapidly became a day-to-day nightmare with little glimmer
of escape.

For Neil Griffon, temporarily in charge of his father's
racing stables, blackmail is now a terrible reality. A reality
not only threatening valuable horses but testing his nerves
to the limit.
   And proving how brittle bones can be . . .

'A classic entry with a fine turn of speed'
Evening Standard

DICK FRANCIS

In the Frame

£5.99

'A writer of champion class'
The Times

Charles Todd makes a living as a painter of horses. Someone
else is making a lot more, forging paintings by masters such as
Stubbs and Munnings. And selling them to people like Charles'
cousin and his wife. People who usually end up dead.

When Charles arrives in Australia, he's not there for the surf at
Bondi beach. He's right on the trail of the ruthless fraudsters, to
whom violence and corruption are part of normal business
practice. And he's right in the frame for murder . . .

'When the gloves are off it's very gritty indeed'
Daily Telegraph

DICK FRANCIS

To the Hilt

£6.99

'Another one for the winner's enclosure'
The Times

Alexander Kinloch found solitude and a steady income painting in a bothy on a remote Scottish mountain. Until the morning the strangers arrived to rough him up, and Alexander was dragged reluctantly back into the real and violent world he thought he had left behind.

Millions of pounds are missing from his stepfather's business. A valuable racehorse is under threat. Then comes the first ugly death and the end of all Alexander's doubts. For the honour of the Kinlochs he will face the strangers . . . committed up to the hilt . . .

'The book is a cracker . . . the former champion jockey is still taking the jumps with consumate grace'
Sunday Telegraph

'Fast-moving, readable and beautifully constructed . . . a cracking yarn'
Country Life

DICK FRANCIS

Rat Race

£6.99

'Impossible to stop reading'
Daily Telegraph

Matt Shore was an experienced pilot. He'd done it all. From big jets to flying in supplies to war zones. So when he gets a job ferrying high class punters around England's racecourses he might be forgiven for expecting the quiet life. But then his plane explodes in a massive fireball. He could have been in it. Some quiet life.

Instead he's landed in the middle of a nightmare world where there is big money at stake. Very big money.
From then on he finds himself hurtling down a tortuous trail where people are not all they appear, and all around him is sudden bloody death . . .

'A thriller that really thrills'
Daily Mail

DICK FRANCIS

Come to Grief

£6.99

'This is Francis writing at his best'
Evening Standard

Sid Halley, the ex-champion jockey turned investigator who appears in *Odds Against* and *Whip Hand*, is back. In *Come to Grief* he faces new dangers, new deeply demanding decisions.

Sid Halley has uncovered an obnoxious crime committed by a friend whom he – and everyone else – has held in deep affection. On the morning set for the opening of the friend's trial, at which Sid is due to be called as a witness, other people's miseries explode and send him spinning into days of hard rational detection and heart-searching torment.

Troubled, courageous and unwilling to admit defeat, for Sid Halley it is business as usual.

Winner of the Edgar Allen Poe award for
best crime novel of the year.

'Dick Francis is firmly in the saddle and
leaving the opposition standing . . .'
Sunday Telegraph

DICK FRANCIS

Wild Horses

£6.99

'A marvellous storyteller and an immaculate craftsman'
Daily Mail

Movie director Thomas Lyon came to Newmarket to rake
the ashes of an old Jockey Club scandal for a new Holly-
wood film. Too late, he found himself listening to a
blacksmith's dying confession. Found himself watching as
the past came violently back to life.

Capturing the shockwaves over one woman's macabre
death nearly thirty years before is drama. But a frenzied
knife attack on the set of *Unstable Times* is definitely
attempted murder. Who stood to gain from the threats?
Between truth and shadowy fiction, Thomas Lyon already
knew too much.

Following the real story could mean the difference
between life and death. His own . . .

'Still the best bet for a winning read'
Mail on Sunday

DICK FRANCIS

Flying Finish

£6.99

'Extremely exciting . . . lots of action'
Sunday Times

Lord Henry Grey was an amateur jockey and pilot. But
when he decided to abandon his desk-bound job for an
active career in the bloodstock market, he found there
was more to couriering valuable horses around the world
than he'd ever suspected . . .

Meeting Gabriella in Italy is the first, most pleasurable
surprise. But a colleague's disappearance on the next
Milan trip gives him a nasty jolt: for two of his predecessors have already gone absent without leave.
  Thousands of feet up, in the hands of a sadistic killer, it
seems that Grey has discovered the truth too late . . .

'With this book, Dick Francis takes his place at
the head of the field as one of the most intelligent
thriller writers in the business'
Sunday Express

All Pan Books are available at your local bookshop or newsagent, or can be ordered direct from the publisher. Indicate the number of copies required and fill in the form below.

Send to: Macmillan General Books C.S.
             Book Service By Post
             PO Box 29, Douglas I-O-M
             IM99 1BQ

or phone: 01624 675137, quoting title, author and credit card number.

or fax: 01624 670923, quoting title, author, and credit card number.

or Internet: http://www.bookpost.co.uk

Please enclose a remittance* to the value of the cover price plus 75 pence per book for post and packing. Overseas customers please allow £1.00 per copy for post and packing.

*Payment may be made in sterling by UK personal cheque, Eurocheque, postal order, sterling draft or international money order, made payable to Book Service By Post.

Alternatively by Access/Visa/MasterCard

Card No.   ☐☐☐☐☐☐☐☐☐☐☐☐☐☐☐☐☐☐

Expiry Date ☐☐☐☐☐☐☐☐☐☐☐☐☐☐☐☐☐☐

Signature   _____

Applicable only in the UK and BFPO addresses.

While every effort is made to keep prices low, it is sometimes necessary to increase prices at short notice. Pan Books reserve the right to show on covers and charge new retail prices which may differ from those advertised in the text or elsewhere.

NAME AND ADDRESS IN BLOCK CAPITAL LETTERS PLEASE

Name _____

Address _____

_____

_____

_____

8/95

Please allow 28 days for delivery.
Please tick box if you do not wish to receive any additional information. ☐